DAW Books Presents
The Finest in Imaginative Fiction by
TAD WILLIAMS

TAILCHASER'S SONG

THE WAR OF THE FLOWERS

SHADOWMARCH
Volume 1

MEMORY, SORROW AND THORN
THE DRAGONBONE CHAIR
STONE OF FAREWELL
TO GREEN ANGEL TOWER

OTHERLAND
CITY OF GOLDEN SHADOW
RIVER OF BLUE FIRE
MOUNTAIN OF BLACK GLASS
SEA OF SILVER LIGHT

Shadowmarch

Volume One

Tad Williams

Shadowmarch

Volume One

DAW BOOKS, INC.

DONALD A. WOLLHEIM, FOUNDER

375 Hudson Street, New York, NY 10014

ELIZABETH R. WOLLHEIM
SHEILA E. GILBERT
PUBLISHERS

http://www.dawbooks.com

First printing, November 2004
1   2   3   4   5   6   7   8   9

DAW TRADEMARK REGISTERED
U.S. PAT. OFF. AND FOREIGN COUNTRIES
—MARCA REGISTRADA
HECHO EN U.S.A.

PRINTED IN THE U.S.A.

This book is dedicated to my children, Connor Williams and Devon Beale, who as I write this are still small but extremely powerful. They amaze me every day.

Someday, when they are grown and their mother and I have ambled on to the Fields Beyond, I hope the two of them will be warmed by the knowledge of how fiercely we loved them, and a tiny bit embarrassed by how wickedly they took advantage of it, charming, funny little buggers that they are.

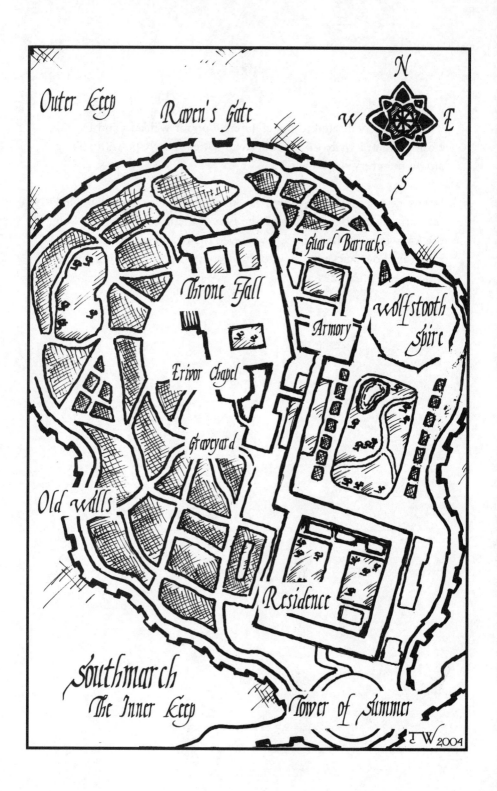

Outer Keep

Raven's Gate

N
W   E
S

Guard Barracks

Throne Hall

Wolfstooth
Spire

Armory

Erivor Chapel

Graveyard

Old walls

Residence

Southmarch
The Inner Keep

Tower of Summer

TW 2004

No book is written without help, and few authors need as much help as I do, so . . . on with the parade of gratitude!

Many thanks, as always, to my fabulous wife, Deborah Beale, for her unfailing support and brilliant help and discerning reader's eye, and to my most excellent agent Matt Bialer, for having my back when the quibbles are flying.

Thanks also to our talented assistant, Dena Chavez, who keeps Deborah and I as close to sane as we are ever likely to get, in part by immense organizational skill, in part by preventing my beloved children from helping me too much when I really need to finish something.

My overseas editors, Tim Holman in the UK and Dr. Ulrike Killer in Germany, have been big supporters of my work and give me a great deal of confidence with all the projects I undertake. They have my overwhelming gratitude, too.

And of course all my friends at DAW Books—who also (conveniently!) happen to be my American publishers—including Debra Euler, Marsha Jones, Peter Stampfel, Betsy Wollheim, and Sheila Gilbert, cannot escape much vigorous thank-ification. Betsy and Sheila have been my editors and partners-in-crime since I started on this wild book-writing endeavor twenty years ago, and the more years that pass, the more I come to realize what a great gift that has been and how lucky I am. Thanks, guys. We've had fun, huh?

Last but not least, I must also mention that this particular book owes a huge debt of gratitude and inspiration to all the mad, wonderful folk on the Shadowmarch.com bulletin board, a repository of wisdom, support, silliness, and recipes for rhubarb like no other. Thanks for Shadowmarch (the online project) are especially due to Josh Milligan and the incomparable Matt Dusek, the latter still helming the site as Tech Wizard in Residence. I hope many of you new readers will come and join us—I spend a lot of time kibitzing on the board there, and I'd enjoying meeting you.

Causeway to Mainland Southmarch

Brenn's Bay

W N

S E

Basilisk Gate

Trigonate Temple

Market Square

Outwall

Harbor

West Lagoon

(Skimmer's Lagoon)

North Lagoon

Tower
of Spring

Tower of Winter

Funderling Town Gate

New Walls

Observatory

Inner Keep

Tower of Summer

Tower of Autumn

East Lagoon

Southmarch
The Outer Keep

Brenn's Bay

TW 2004

Author's Note

For those who wish to feel securely grounded in the Who, What, and Where of things, there are several maps and, at the end of the book, indexes of characters and places and other important materials.

The maps have been compiled from an exhaustive array of traveler's tales, nearly illegible old documents, transcripts of oracular utterances, and the murmurings of dying hermits, not to mention the contents of an ancient box of land-office records discovered at a Syannese flea market. A similarly arcane and wearying process was responsible for the creation of the indexes. Use them well, remembering that many have died, or at least seriously damaged their vision and scholarly reputations, to make these aids available to you, the reader.

Contents

PART THREE: FIRE

A Brief History of Eion,
With special Attention paid to Rise of the
March Kingdoms of the North
Summarized by Finn Teodoros, scholar,
from Clemon's **The History of Our Continent of**
Eion and its Nations,
at the request of his lordship Avin Brone,
Count of Landsend, Lord Constable of Southmarch
Presented this Thirteenthth day of Enneamene,
in the year 1316 of the Holy Trigon

FOR ALMOST A THOUSAND YEARS before our Trigonate Era, history was written only in the ancient kingdoms of Xand, the southern continent that was the world's first seat of civilization. The Xandians knew little about their northern neighbor, our continent of Eion, because most of its interior was hidden by impassable mountains and dense forests. The southerners traded only with a few pale-skinned savages who dwelled along the coasts, and knew little or nothing about the mysterious Twilight People, called "Qar" by the scholarly, who lived in many places across Eion, but were and are most numerous in the far north of our continent.

As generations passed and Xandian trade with Eion increased, Hierosol, the chief of the new trading port towns on the Eionian coast, grew as well, until it had become by far the most populous city of the northern lands. By about two centuries before the advent of the blessed Trigon, it had grown to rival in size and sophistication many of the decadent capitals of the southern continent.

Hierosol in its early years was a city of many gods and many competing priesthoods, and matters of doctrinal dispute and godly rivalry were often settled by slander and arson and bloody riots in the streets. At last, the followers of three of the most powerful deities—Perin, lord of the sky, Erivor of the waters, and Kernios, master of the black earth—made a compact. This *trigon,* the coalition of the three gods and their followers, quickly lifted itself above all the other priesthoods and their temples in power. Its leader took the name Trigonarch, and he and his successors became the mightiest religious figures in all of Eion.

With rich trade flooding through its ports, its army and navy growing in power, and religious authority now consolidated in the hands of the Trigonate, Hierosol became not just the dominant power in Eion, but eventually, as the empires of the southern continent Xand spiraled down into decadence, of all the known world. Hierosoline supremacy lasted for almost six hundred years before the empire collapsed at last of its own weight, falling before waves of raiders from the Kracian peninsula and the southern continent.

Younger kingdoms in Eion's heartland rose from Hierosol's imperial ashes. Syan outstripped the others, and in the ninth century seized the Trigonate itself, moving the Trigonarchy and all its great church from Hierosol to Tessis, where they still remain. Syan became the seat of fashion and learning for all Eion, and is still by most measures the leading power of our continent today, but its neighbors have long since shrugged off the mantle of the Syannese Empire.

Since a time before history, the men of Eion have shared their lands with the strange, pagan Qar, who were known variously as the Twilight People, the Quiet People, or most often "the fairy folk." Although stories tell of a vast Qar settlement in the far north of Eion, a dark and ancient city of dire report, the Qar at first lived in many places throughout the land, although never in such concentrations as men, and mostly in rural, untraveled areas. As men spread across Eion, many of the Qar retreated to the hills and mountains and deep forests, although in some places they remained, and even lived in peace with men. There was little trust, though, and for most of the first millennium after the Trigon the unspoken truce between the two peoples was largely due to the small numbers of the Twilight folk and their isolation from men.

As the year 1000 approached, the Great Death came, a terrible plague that appeared first in the southern seaports and spread across the land, causing great woe. It killed in days, and few who were exposed to it survived. Farmers deserted their fields. Parents abandoned their children. Healers would not attend the dying, and even the priests of Kernios would not help perform ceremonies for the dead. Entire villages were left empty except for corpses. By the end of the first year it was said that a quarter of the people in the southern cities of Eion had succumbed, and when the plague returned with the warm weather the following spring, and even more died, many folk believed the end of the world had come. The Trigon and its priests declared that the plague was punishment for the irreligiousness of mankind, but most men at first blamed foreigners and especially southerners for poisoning the wells. Soon, though, an even more obvious culprit was suggested—the Qar. In many places the mysterious Twilight People were already considered to be evil spirits, so the idea that the plague was caused by their malice spread quickly through the frightened populace.

The fairy folk were slaughtered wherever they were found, whole tribes captured and destroyed. The fury spread across Eion, spearheaded by makeshift armies of men calling themselves "Purifiers," dedicated to eradicating the Qar, although it is doubtful they killed more fairies than they did their own kind, since many villages of men already devastated by the Great Death were burned to the ground by Purifiers as a lesson to those who might resist what they considered their sacred mission.

The remaining Twilight folk fled north, but turned to make a stand at a Qar settlement called Coldgray Moor, less than a day's walk from where I sit writing this in present-day Southmarch. ("Coldgray," although an accurate description for the site of the battle, was apparently a misunderstanding of *Qul Girah,* which Clemon suggests means "place of growing" in the fairy tongue, although his sources for this are unknown to me.) The battle was terrible, but the Qar were defeated, in large part due to the arrival of an army led by Anglin, lord of the island nation of Connord, who was distantly connected by blood to the Syannese royal family. The Twilight People were driven out of the lands of men completely, back into the desolate, thickly forested lands of the north.

Like thousands of other less famous mortals, Karal, the king of Syan, was killed in the battle at Coldgray Moor, but his son, who would reign as Lander III, and would later be known as "Lander the Good" and "Lander Elfbane," granted the March Country to Anglin and his descendants to be their fief, so that they could be the wardens of humanity's borders against the Qar. Anglin of Connord was the first March King.

After Coldgray Moor, the north experienced a century of relative peace, although troops of mercenary soldiers known as the Gray Companies, who had risen during the dreadful times following the Great Death and the collapse of the Syannese Empire, remained a powerful danger. These lawless knights sold themselves to various despots to fight their neighbors, or chose an easier enemy, kidnapping nobles for ransom and robbing and murdering the peasantry.

Anglin's descendants had divided the March Country up into four March Kingdoms—Northmarch, Southmarch, Eastmarch, and Westmarch, although Southmarch was the chief of them—and these, governed by Anglin's family and its clan of noble relations, ruled the northern lands in general harmony. Then, in the Trigonate year 1103, an army of Twilight People swept down out of the north without warning. Anglin's descendants fought bitterly, but they were pushed out of most of their lands and forced to fall back to their southernmost borders. Only the support of the small countries along that border (known as "the Nine") allowed the March folk to hold off the Qar while waiting for help from the great kingdoms of the south—help which was painfully slow in coming. It is said that in the midst of this terrible struggle a sense of true northern solidarity—as well as a certain distrust of the southern kingdoms—was created for the first time.

Only a fierce winter that first year allowed the humans to hold the Qar in place in the March Country. In the spring, armies arrived at last from Syan and Jellon and the city-states of Krace. Although men far outnumbered the Twilight folk, the battle against the Qar raged off and on across the north for long years. When the March Kingdoms and their allies at last defeated the invaders in 1107 and tried to pursue the Qar back into their own lands to eliminate the threat once and for all, the retreating fairy folk created a barrier that, although it did not keep men out, confused and bewitched all who passed it. After several companies of armed men disappeared, with only a few maddened survivors returning, the mortal allies gave up and declared the misty boundary they named the Shadowline to be the new border of the lands of men.

Southmarch Castle was reconsecrated by the Trigonarch himself—the Qar had used it as their fortress during the war—but the Shadowline cut across the March Kingdoms, and all of Northmarch and much of Eastmarch and Westmarch were lost behind it. But although their northern fiefs and castles were gone, Anglin's line survived in his great--grandnephew, Kellick Eddon, whose bravery in the fight against the fairy folk was already legendary. When the border nations known as the Nine banded together and gave their loyalty to the new king at Southmarch (in part for protection from the rapacious Gray Companies, who were growing strong again in the chaos following the war against the Twilight People), the March King once more became the greatest power in the north of Eion.

In Our Present Day
Containing the opinions of Finn Teodoros, Himself,
and no Responsibility to the late Master Clemon of Anverrin

In this Year of the Trigon 1316, three hundred years after Coldgray Moor and two centuries since the loss of the northern marchlands and the establishment of the Shadowline, the north has changed little. The shadowboundary has remained constant, and effectively marks the outer edge of the known world—even ships that wander off course in northern waters seldom return.

Syan has almost entirely lost its hold over its former empire, and is now merely the strongest of several large kingdoms in the heartland of Eion, but there are other threats. The might of the Autarch, the god-king of Xis on the southern continent, is growing. For the first time in almost a thousand years, Xandians are exerting power across the northern continent. Many of the countries on the southernmost coast of Eion have already begun to pay the Autarch tribute, or are ruled by his puppets.

The House of Eddon in all its honor still rules in Southmarch, and our March Kingdom is the only true power in the north—Brenland and Settland, as is commonly known, are small, rustic, inward-looking nations—but the March King's descendants and their loyal servants have begun to wonder how much farther the Autarch's arm might reach into Eion and what woe that might mean for us, as witness the unfortunate events that have befallen our beloved monarch, King Olin. We can only pray that he will be brought back safe to us.

This is my history, prepared at your request, my lord. I hope it pleases you.

(signed,) Finn Teodoros

Scholar and Loyal Subject of His Majesty, Olin Eddon

Prelude

COME AWAY, dreamer, come away. Soon you will witness things that only sleepers and sorcerers can see. Climb onto the wind and let it bear you—yes, it is a swift and frightening steed, but there are leagues and leagues to journey and the night is short.

Flying higher than the birds, you pass swiftly over the dry lands of the southern continent of Xand, above the Autarch's startlingly huge temple-palace stretching mile upon mile along the stone canals of his great city of Xis. You do not pause—it is not mortal kings you spy upon today, not even the most powerful of them all. Instead you fly across the ocean to the northern continent of Eion, over timeless Hierosol, once the center of the world but now the plaything of bandits and warlords, but you do not linger here either. You hurry on, winging over principalities that already owe their fealty to the Autarch's conquering legions and others who as yet do not, but soon will.

Beyond the cloud-scraping mountains that fence the southern part of Eion from the rest, across the trackless forests north of the mountains, you reach the green country of the Free Kingdoms and stoop low over field and fell, speeding across the thriving heartlands of powerful Syan (which was once more powerful still), over broad farmlands and well-traveled roads, past ancient family seats of crumbling stone, and on to the marches that border the gray country beyond the Shadowline, the northernmost lands in which humans still live.

On the very doorstep of those lost and inhuman northern lands, in the country of Southmarch, a tall old castle stands gazing out over a wide bay, a fortress isolated and protected by water, dignified and secretive as a queen who has outlived her royal husband. She is crowned with magnificent towers, and the patchwork roofs of the lower buildings are her skirt. A slender causeway that joins the castle to the mainland, stretches out like a bridal train spreading out to make the rest of her city, which lies in the folds of the hills and along the mainland edge of the bay. This ancient stronghold is a place of mortal men now, but it has an air of something else, of something that has come to know these mortals and even deigns to shelter them, but does not entirely love them. Still, there is more than a little beauty in this stark place that many call Shadowmarch, in its proud, wind-tattered flags and its streets splashed by down-stabbing sunlight. But although this hilly fortress is the last bright and welcoming thing you will see before entering the land of silence and fog, and although what you are shortly to experience will have dire consequence here, your journey will not stop at Southmarch—not yet. Today you are called elsewhere.

You seek this castle's mirror-twin, far in the haunted north, the great fortress of the immortal Qar.

And now, as suddenly as stepping across a threshold, you cross into their twilight lands. Although the afternoon sun still illumines Southmarch Castle, only a short ride back across the Shadowline, all that dwells on this side of that invisible wall is in perpetual quiet evening. The meadows are deep and dark, the grass shiny with dew. Couched on the wind, you observe that the roads below you gleam pale as eel's flesh and seem to form subtle patterns, as though some god had written a secret journal upon the face of the misty earth. You fly on over high, storm-haloed mountains and across forests vast as nations. Bright eyes gleam from the dark places beneath the trees, and voices whisper in the empty dells.

And now at last you see your destination, standing high and pure and proud beside a wild, dark, inland sea. If there was something otherworldly about Southmarch Castle, there is very little that is worldly at all about this other: a million, million stones in a thousand shades of darkness have been piled high, onyx on jasper, obsidian on slate, and although there is a fine symmetry to these towers, it is a type of symmetry that would make ordinary mortals sick at the stomach.

You descend now, dismounting from the wind at last so that you may hurry through the mazy and often narrow halls, but keep to the widest and most brightly lit passages: it is not good to wander carelessly in Qul-na-Qar, this eldest of buildings (whose stones some say were quarried so many aeons ago that the oceans of the young earth were still warm) and in any case, you have little time to spare.

The shadow-dwelling Qar have a saying which signifies, in rough translation: "Even the Book of Regret starts with a single word." It means that even the most important matters have a unique and simple beginning, although sometimes it cannot be described until long afterward—a first stroke, a seed, a nearly silent intake of breath before a song is sung. That is why you are hurrying now: the sequence of events that in days ahead will shake not just Southmarch but the entire world to its roots is commencing here and now, and you shall be witness.

In the deeps of Qul-na-Qar there is a hall. In truth there are many halls in Qul-na-Qar, as many as there are twigs on an ancient, leafless tree—even on an entire bone-dead orchard of such trees—but even those who have only seen Qul-na-Qar during the unsettled sleep of a bad night would know what hall this is. It is your destination. Come along. The time is growing short.

The great hall is an hour's walk from end to end, or at least it appears that way. It is lit by many torches, as well as by other less familiar lights that shimmer like fireflies beneath dark rafters carved in the likeness of holly bough and blackthorn branch. Mirrors line both long walls, each oval powdered so thick with dust that it seems odd the sparkling lights and the torches can be seen even in dull reflection, odder still that other, darker shapes can also be glimpsed moving in the murky glass. Those shapes are present even when the hall is empty.

The hall is not empty now, but full of figures both beautiful and terrible. Were you to speed back across the Shadowline in this very instant to one of the great markets of the southern harbor kingdoms, and there saw humanity in all its shapes and sizes and colors drawn together from all over the wide world, still you would marvel at their sameness after having seen the Qar, the Twilight People, gathered here in their high, dark hall. Some are as stunningly fair as young gods, tall and shapely as the most graceful kings and queens of men. Some are small as mice. Others are figures from mortal nightmares, claw-fingered, serpent-eyed, covered with feathers or scales or oily fur. They fill the hall from one end to the other, ranked according to intricate primordial hierarchies, a thousand different forms sharing only a keen dislike of humankind and, for this moment, a vast silence.

At the head of the long, mirror-hung room two figures sit on tall stone chairs. Both have the semblance of humanity, but with an unearthly twist that means not even a drunken blind man could actually mistake them for mortals. Both are still, but one is so motionless that it is hard to believe she is not a statue carved from pale marble, as stony as the chair on which she sits. Her eyes are open, but they are empty as the painted eyes of a doll, as though her spirit has flown far from her seemingly youthful, white-robed figure and cannot find its way back. Her hands lie in her lap like dead birds. She has not moved in years. Only the tiniest stirring, her breast rising and falling at achingly separated intervals beneath her robe, tells that she breathes.

The one who sits beside her is taller by two hands' breadth than most mortals, and that is the most human thing about him. His pale face, which was once startlingly fair, has aged over the centuries into something hard and sharp as the peak of a windswept crag. He has about him still a kind of terrible beauty, as dangerously beguiling as the grandeur of a storm rushing across the sea. His eyes, you feel sure would be clear and deep as night sky, would seem infinitely, coldly wise, but they are hidden behind a rag knotted at the back of his head, most of it hidden in his long moon-silver hair.

He is Ynnir the Blind King, and the blindness is not all his own. Few mortal eyes have seen him, and no living mortal man or woman has gazed on him outside of dreams.

The lord of the Twilight People raises his hand. The hall was already silent, but now the stillness becomes something deeper. Ynnir whispers, but every thing in that room hears him.

"Bring the child."

Four hooded, manlike shapes carry a litter out of the shadows behind the twin thrones and place it at the king's feet. On it lies curled what seems to be a mortal manchild, his fine, straw-colored hair pressed into damp ringlets around his sleeping face. The king leans over, for all the world as though he is looking at the child despite his blindness, memorizing his features. He reaches into his own gray garments, sumptuous once, but now weirdly threadbare and almost as dusty as the hall's mirrors, and lifts out a small bag on a length of black cord, the sort of simple object in which a mortal might carry a charm or healing simple. Ynnir's long fingers carefully lower the cord over the boy's head, then tuck the bag under the coarse shirt and against the child's narrow chest. The king is singing all the while, his voice a drowsy murmur. Only the last words are loud enough to hear.

"*. . . By star and stone, the act is done,*
Not stone nor star the act shall mar."

Ynnir pauses for a long moment before he speaks again, with a hesitation that might almost be mortal, but when he speaks, his words are clear and sure. "Take him." The four figures raise the litter. "Let no one see you in the sunlight lands. Ride swiftly, there and back."

The hooded leader bows his head once, then they are gone with their sleeping burden. The king turns for a moment toward the pale woman beside him, almost as if he expected her to break her long silence, but she does not move and she most certainly does not speak. He turns to the rest of those watching, to the avid eyes and the thousand restless shapes—and to you, too, dreamer. Nothing that Fate has already woven is invisible to Ynnir.

"It begins," he says. Now the stillness of the hall is broken. A rising murmur fills the mirrored room, a wash of voices that grows until it echoes in the dark, thorn-carved rafters. As the din of singing and shouting spills out through the endless halls of Qul-na-Qar, it is hard to say whether the terrible noise is a chant of triumph or mourning.

The blind king nods slowly. "Now, at last, it begins."

Remember this, dreamer, when you see what is to follow. As the blind king said, this is a beginning. What he did not say, but which is nonetheless true, is that what begins here is the ending of the world.

PART ONE
BLOOD

"As the woodsman who sets snares cannot always know what he may catch," *the great god Kernios said to the wise man, "so, too, the scholar may find* *that his questions have brought him unforeseen and dangerous answers."*

—from A Compendium of Things That Are Known,
The Book of the Trigon

1
A Wyvern Hunt

THE NARROWING WAY:

Under stone there is earth
Under earth there are stars; under stars, shadow
Under shadow are all the things that are known

—from *The Bonefall Oracles,*
out of the Qar's *Book of Regret*

THE BELLING OF THE HOUNDS was already growing faint in the hollows behind them when he finally pulled up. His horse was restive, anxious to return to the hunt, but Barrick Eddon yanked hard on the reins to keep the mare dancing in place. His always-pale face seemed almost translucent with weariness, his eyes fever-bright. "Go on," he told his sister. "You can still catch them."

Briony shook her head. "I'm not leaving you by yourself. Rest if you need to, then we'll go on together."

He scowled as only a boy of fifteen years can scowl, the expression of a scholar among idiots, a noble among mud-footed peasants. "I don't need to rest, strawhead. I just don't want the bother."

"You are a dreadful liar," she told her brother gently. Twins, they were bound to each other in ways as close as lovers' ways.

"And no one can kill a dragon with a spear, anyway. How did the men at the Shadowline outpost let it past?"

"Perhaps it crossed over at night and they didn't see it. It isn't a dragon, anyway, it's a wyvern—much smaller. Shaso says you can kill one with just a good clop on the head."

"What do either you or Shaso know about wyverns?" Barrick demanded. "They don't come trotting across the hills every day. They're not bloody cows."

Briony thought it a bad sign that he was rubbing his crippled arm without even trying to hide it from her. He looked more bloodless than usual, blue under the eyes, his flesh so thin he sometimes looked almost hollow. She feared he had been walking in his sleep again and the thought made her shudder. She had lived in Southmarch Castle all her life, but still did not like passing through any of its mazy, echoing halls after dark.

She forced a smile. "No they're not cows, silly, but the master of the hunt asked Chaven before we set out, remember? And Shaso says we had one in Grandfather Ustin's day—it killed three sheep at a steading in Landsend."

"Three whole sheep! Heavens, what a monster!"

The crying of the hounds rose in pitch, and now both horses began to take fretful little steps. Someone winded a horn, the moan almost smothered by the intervening trees.

"They've seen something." She felt a sudden pang. "Oh, mercy of Zoria! What if that thing hurts the dogs?"

Barrick shook his head in disgust, then brushed a damp curl of dark red hair out of his eyes. "The dogs?"

But Briony was truly frightened for them—she had raised two of the hounds, Rack and Dado, from puppyhood, and in some ways they were more real to this king's daughter than most people. "Oh, come, Barrick, please! I'll ride slowly, but I won't leave you here."

His mocking smile vanished. "Even with only one hand on the reins, I can outride you any hour."

"Then do it!" she laughed, spurring down the slope. She was doing her best to poke him out of his fury, but she knew that cold blank mask too well: only time and perhaps the excitement of the chase would breathe life back into it.

Briony looked back up the hillside and was relieved to see that Barrick was following, a thin shadow atop the gray horse, dressed as though he were in mourning. But her twin dressed that way every day.

Oh, please, Barrick, sweet angry Barrick, don't fall in love with Death. Her own extravagant thought surprised her—poetical sentiment usually made

Briony Eddon feel like she had an itch she couldn't scratch—and as she turned back in distraction she nearly ran down a small figure scrambling out of her way through the long grass. Her heart thumping in her breast, she brought Snow to a halt and jumped down, certain she had almost killed some crofter's child.

"Are you hurt?"

It was a very small man with graying hair who stood up from the yellowing grass, his head no higher than the belly-strap of her saddle—a Funderling of middle age, with short but well-muscled legs and arms. He doffed his shapeless felt hat and made a little bow. "Quite well, my lady. Kind of you to ask."

"I didn't see you . . ."

"Not many do, Mistress." He smiled. "And I should also . . ."

Barrick rattled past with hardly a look at his sister or her almost-victim. Despite his best efforts he was favoring the arm and his seat was dangerously bad. Briony scrambled back onto Snow, making a muddle of her riding skirt.

"Forgive me," she said to the little man, then bent low over Snow's neck and spurred after her brother.

The Funderling helped his wife to her feet. "I was going to introduce you to the princess."

"Don't be daft." She brushed burrs out of her thick skirt. "We're just lucky that horse of hers didn't crush us into pudding."

"Still, it might be your only chance to meet one of the royal family." He shook his head in mock-sadness. "Our last opportunity to better ourselves, Opal."

She squinted, refusing to smile. "Better for us would mean enough coppers to buy new boots for you, Chert, and a nice winter shawl for me. Then we could go to meetings without looking like beggars' children."

"It's been a long time since we've looked like children of any sort, my old darling." He plucked another burr out of her gray-streaked hair.

"And it will be a longer time yet until I have my new shawl if we don't get on with ourselves." But she was the one who lingered, looking almost wistfully along the trampled track through the long grass. "Was that really the princess? Where do you suppose they were going in such a hurry?"

"Following the hunt. Didn't you hear the horns? *Ta-ra, ta-ra!* The gentry are out chasing some poor creature across the hills today. In the bad old days, it might have been one of us!"

She sniffed, recovering herself. "I don't pay heed to any of that, and if you're wise, neither will you. Don't meddle with the big folk without need and don't draw their attention, as my father always said. No good will come of it. Now let's get on with our work, old man. I don't want to be wandering around near the edge of Shadowline when darkness comes."

Chert Blue Quartz shook his head, serious again. "Nor do I, my love."

The harriers and sight hounds seemed reluctant to enter the stand of trees, although their hesitation did not make them any quieter. The clamor was atrocious, but even the keenest of the hunters seemed content to wait a short distance up the hill until the dogs had driven their quarry out into the open.

The lure of the hunt for most had little to do with the quarry anyway, even so unusual a prize as this. At least two dozen lords and ladies and many times that number of their servitors swarmed along the hillside, the gentlefolk laughing and talking and admiring (or pretending to admire) each others' horses and clothes, with soldiers and servants plodding along behind or driving oxcarts stacked high with food and drink and tableware and even the folded pavilions in which the company had earlier taken their morning meal. Many of the squires led spare horses, since it was not unusual during a particularly exciting hunt for one of the mounts to collapse with a broken leg or burst heart. None of the hunters would stand for missing the kill and having to ride home on a wagon just because of a dead horse. Among the churls and higher servants strode men-at-arms carrying pikes or halberds, grooms, houndsmen in mud-stained, tattered clothes, a few priests—those of lesser status had to walk, like the soldiers—and even Puzzle, the king's bony old jester, who was playing a rather unconvincing hunting air on his lute as he struggled to remain seated on a saddled donkey. In fact, the quiet hills below the Shadowline now contained what was more or less an entire village on the move.

Briony, who always liked to get out of the stony reaches of the castle, where the towers sometimes seemed to blot out the sun for most of the day, had especially enjoyed the momentary escape from this great mass of humanity and the quiet that came with it. She couldn't help wondering what a hunt must be like with the huge royal courts of Syan or Jellon—she had heard they sometimes lasted for weeks! But she did not have long to think about it.

Shaso dan-Heza rode out from the crowd to meet Barrick and Briony as they came down the crest. The master of arms was the only member of the gentry who actually seemed dressed to kill something, wearing not the finery most nobles donned for the hunt but his old black leather cuirass that was only a few shades darker than his skin. His huge war bow bumped at his saddle, bent and strung as though he expected attack at any moment. To Briony, the master of arms and her sullen brother Barrick looked like a pair of storm clouds drifting toward each other and she braced herself for the thunder. It was not long in coming.

"Where have you two been?" Shaso demanded. "Why did you leave your guards behind?"

Briony hastened to take the blame. "We did not mean to be away so long. We were just talking, and Snow was hobbling a little . . ."

The old Tuani warrior ignored her, fixing his hard gaze on Barrick. Shaso seemed angrier than he should have been, as though the twins had done more than simply wander away from the press of humanity for a short while. Surely he could not think they were in danger here, only a few miles from the castle in the country the Eddon family had ruled for generations? "I saw you turn from the hunt and ride off without a word to anyone, boy," he said. "What were you thinking?"

Barrick shrugged, but there were spots of color high on his cheeks. "Don't call me 'boy.' And what affair is it of yours?"

The old man flinched and his hand curled. For a frightening moment Briony thought he might actually hit Barrick. He had dealt the boy many clouts over the years, but always in the course of instruction, the legitimate blows of combat; to strike one of the royal family in public would be something else entirely. Shaso was not well-liked—many of the nobles openly maintained that it was not fitting for a dark-skinned southerner, a former prisoner of war as well, to hold such high estate in Southmarch, that the security of the kingdom should be in the hands of a foreigner. No one doubted Shaso's skill or bravery—even once he had been disarmed in the Battle of Hierosol, in which he and young King Olin had met as enemies, it had taken a half dozen men to capture the Tuani warrior, and he had still managed to break free long enough to knock Olin from his horse with the blow of a hammering fist. But instead of punishing the prisoner, the twins' father had admired the southerner's courage, and after Shaso had been taken back to Southmarch and had survived nearly ten years of unransomed captivity, he had continued to grow in Olin's estimation until at last he was set free except for a bond of honor to the Eddon family and given a position of responsibility. In the more than two decades since the Battle of Hierosol, Shaso dan-Heza had upheld his duties with honor, great skill, and an almost tiresome rigor, eclipsing all the other nobles so thoroughly—and earning resentment for that even more strongly than for the color of his skin—that he had advanced at last to the lofty position of master of arms, the king's minister of war for all the March Kingdoms. The ex-prisoner had been untouchable as long as the twins' father sat on the throne, but now Briony wondered whether Shaso's titles, or even Shaso himself, would survive this bleak time of King Olin's absence.

As if a similar thought passed through his head as well, Shaso lowered his hand. "You are a prince of Southmarch," he told Barrick, brusque but quiet. "When you risk your life without need, it is not me you are harming."

Her twin stared back defiantly, but the old man's words cooled some of the heat of his anger. Briony knew Barrick would not apologize, but there would not be a fight either.

The excited barking of the dogs had risen in pitch. The twins' older brother Kendrick was beckoning them down to where he was engaged in conversation with Gailon Tolly, the young Duke of Summerfield. Briony rode down the hill toward them with Barrick just behind her. Shaso gave them a few paces start before following.

Gailon of Summerfield—only half a dozen years senior to Barrick and Briony, but with an uncomfortable formality that she knew masked his dislike of some of her family's broader eccentricities—removed his green velvet hat and bowed to them. "Princess Briony, Prince Barrick. We were concerned for your well-being, cousins."

She doubted that was entirely true. Barring the Eddons themselves, the Tollys were the closest family in the line of succession and they were known to have ambitions. Gailon had proved himself capable of at least the appearance of honorable subservience, but she doubted the same could be said for his younger brothers, Caradon and the disturbing Hendon. Briony could only be grateful the rest of the Tollys seemed to prefer lording it over their massive estate down in Summerfield to playing at loyal underlings here in Southmarch, and left that task to their brother the duke.

Briony's brother Kendrick seemed in a surprisingly good mood considering the burdens of regency on his young shoulders during his father's absence. Unlike King Olin, Kendrick was capable of forgetting his troubles long enough to enjoy a hunt or a pageant. Already his jacket of Sessian finecloth was unbuttoned, his golden hair in a careless tangle. "So there you are," he called. "Gailon is right—we were worried about you two. It's especially not like Briony to miss the excitement." He glanced at Barrick's funereal garb and widened his eyes. "Has the Procession of Penance come early this year?"

"Oh, yes, I should apologize for my clothes," Barrick growled. "How terribly tasteless of me to dress this way, as though our father were being held prisoner somewhere. But wait—our father *is* a prisoner. Fancy that."

Kendrick winced and looked inquiringly at Briony, who made a face that said, *He's having one of his difficult days.* The prince regent turned to his younger brother and asked, "Would you rather go back?"

"No!" Barrick shook his head violently, but then managed to summon an unconvincing smile. "No. Everyone worries about me too much. I don't mean to be rude, truly. My arm just hurts a bit. Sometimes."

"He is a brave youth," said Duke Gailon without even the tiniest hint of mockery, but it still made Briony bristle like one of her beloved dogs. Last year Gailon had offered to marry her. He was handsome enough in a long-chinned way, and his family's holdings in Summerfield were second only to Southmarch itself in size, but she was glad that her father had been in no hurry to find her a husband. She had a feeling that Gailon Tolly would not be as tolerant to his wife as King Olin was to his daughter—that if she were his, he would make certain Briony did not go riding to the hunt in a split skirt, straddling her horse like a man.

The dogs were yapping even more shrilly now, and a stir ran through the hunting party gathered on the hill. Briony turned to see a movement in the trees of the dell below them, a flash of red and gold like autumn leaves carried on a swift stream. Then something burst out of the undergrowth and into the open, a large serpentine shape that was fully visible for the space of five or six heartbeats before it found high grass and vanished again. The dogs were already swarming after it in a frenzy.

"Gods!" said Briony in sudden fear, and several around her made the three-fingered sign of the Trigon against their breasts. "That thing is huge!" She turned accusingly to Shaso. "I thought you said you could kill one of them with no more than a good clop on the head."

Even the master of arms looked startled. "The other one . . . it was smaller."

Kendrick shook his head. "That thing is ten cubits long or I'm a Skimmer." He shouted, "Bring up the boar spears!" to one of the beaters, then spurred down the hill with Gailon of Summerfield racing beside him and the other nobles hurrying to find their places close to the young prince regent.

"But . . . !" Briony fell silent. She had no idea what she'd meant to say—why else were they here if not to hunt and kill a wyvern?—but she suddenly felt certain that Kendrick would be in danger if he got too close. *Since when are you an oracle or a witching-woman?* she asked herself, but the worry was strangely potent, the crystallization of something that had been troubling her all day like a shadow at the corner of her eye. The strangeness of the gods was in the air today, that feeling of being surrounded by the unseen. Perhaps it was not Barrick who was seeking Death—perhaps rather the grim deity, the Earth Father, was hunting them all.

She shook her head to throw off the swift chill of fear. *Silly thoughts, Briony. Evil thoughts.* It must have been Barrick's sorrowing talk of their own imprisoned father that had done it. Surely there was no harm in a day like this, late in Dekamene, the tenth month, but lit by such a bold sun it still seemed high summer—how could the gods object? The whole hunt was riding in Kendrick's wake now, the horses thundering down the hill after the hounds, the beaters and servants bounding along behind, shouting excitedly, and she suddenly wanted to be out in front with Kendrick and the other nobles, running ahead of all shadows and worries.

I won't hang back like a girl this time, she thought. *Like a proper lady. I want to see a wyvern.*

And what if I'm the one who kills it? Well, why not?

In any case, her brothers both needed looking after. "Come on, Barrick," she called. "No time to mope. If we don't go now, we'll miss it all."

"The girl, the princess—her name's Briony, isn't it?" Opal asked after they had been hiking again for a good part of an hour.

Chert hid a smile. "Are we talking about the big folk? I thought we weren't supposed to meddle with that sort."

"Don't mock. I don't like it here. Even though the sun's overhead, it seems dark. And the grass is so wet! It makes me feel all fluttery."

"Sorry, my dear. I don't like it much here either, but along the edge is where the interesting things are. Almost every time it draws back a little there's something new. Do you remember that Edri's Egg crystal, the one big as a fist? I found it just sitting in the grass, like something washed up on a beach."

"This whole place—it's not natural."

"Of course it's not natural. Nothing about the Shadowline is natural. That's why the Qar left it behind when they retreated from the big folk armies, not just as a boundary between their lands and ours, but as a . . . a warning, I suppose you'd call it. *Keep out.* But you said you wanted to come today, and here you are." He looked up to the line of mist running along the grassy hills, denser in the hollows, but still thick as eiderdown along the hilltops. "We've almost reached it."

"So you say," she grunted wearily.

Chert felt a pang of shame at how he teased her, his good old wife. She could be tart, but so could an apple, and none the less wholesome for it. "Yes, by the way, since you asked. The girl's name's Briony."

"And that other one, dressed in black. That's the other brother?"

"I think so, but I've never seem him so close. They're not much for public show, that family. The old king, Ustin—those children's grandfather—he was a great one for festivals and parades, do you remember? Scarcely a holy day went by . . ."

Opal did not seem interested in historical reminiscence. "He seemed sad, that boy."

"Well, his father's being held for a ransom the kingdom can't afford and the boy's got himself a gammy arm. Reasons enough, perhaps."

"What happened to him?"

Chert waved his hand as though he were not the type to pass along idle gossip, but it was only for show, of course. "I've heard it said a horse fell on him. But Old Pyrite claims that his father threw him down the stairs."

"King Olin? He would never do such a thing!"

Chert almost smiled again at her indignant tone: for one who claimed not to care about the doings of big folk, his wife had some definite opinions about them. "It seems far-fetched," he admitted. "And the gods know that Old Pyrite will say almost anything when he's had enough moss-brew . . ." He stopped, frowning. It was always hard to tell, here along the

edge where distances were tricky at the best of times, but there was definitely something wrong.

"What is it?"

"It's . . . it's moved." They were only a few dozen paces away from the
boundary now—quite as close as he wanted to get. He stared, first at the
ground, then at a familiar stand of white oak trees now half smothered by
mist and faint as wandering spirits. For the first time he could remember,
the unnatural murk had actually advanced past their trunks. The hairs on
the back of Chert's neck rose. "It has *moved!*"

"But it's always moving. You said so."

"Slipping back from the edge a wee bit, then coming up to it again, like
the tide," he whispered. "Like something breathing in and out. That is why
we find things here, when the line has drifted back toward the shadowlands." He could feel a heaviness to the air unusual even for this haunted
place, a heightened watchfulness: it made him feel reluctant even to speak.
"But from the moment two centuries ago when the Twilight People first
conjured it up, it's never moved any closer to us, Opal. Until now."

"What do you mean?"

"It's come *forward*." He didn't want to believe it but he had spent as much
time in these hills as anyone. "Like floodwaters coming over the banks. At
least a dozen paces ahead of where I've ever seen it."

"Is that all?"

"Is that all? Woman, the Twilight People made that line to keep men out
of the shadowlands. No one crosses it and returns, not that I've ever heard
of. And before today, it hasn't moved an inch closer to the castle in two
hundred years!" He was breathless, dizzy with it. "I have to tell someone."

"You? Why should you be the one to get tangled up with this, old man?
Aren't there big-folk guards that watch the Shadowline?"

He waved his hands in exasperation. "Yes, and you saw them when we
went past their post-house, although they didn't see us, or didn't care. They
might as well be guarding the moon! They pay no heed to anything, and
the task is given to the youngest and greenest of the soldiers. Nothing has
changed on this foggy border in so long they don't even believe anything
could change." He shook his head, suddenly troubled by a low noise at the
edge of his hearing, a tremble of air. Distant thunder? "I can barely believe
it myself, and I have walked these hills for years." The dim rumbling was
growing louder and Chert finally realized it wasn't thunder. "Fissure and
fracture!" he swore. "Those are horses coming toward us!"

"The hunt?" she asked. The damp hillside and close-leaning trees seemed capable of hiding anything. "You said the hunt was out today."

"It's not coming from that direction—and they would never come so far this direction, so near to . . ." His heart stumbled in his chest. "Gods of raw earth—it's coming from the shadowlands!"

He grabbed his wife's hand and yanked her stumbling along the hill away from the misty boundary, short legs digging, feet slipping on the wet grass as they scrambled for the shelter of the trees. The noise of hooves seemed impossibly loud now, as though it were right on top of the staggering Funderlings.

Chert and Opal reached the trees and threw themselves down into the scratching underbrush. Chert grabbed his wife close and peered out at the hillside as four riders erupted from the mist and reined in their stamping white mounts. The animals, tall and lean and not quite like any horses Chert had ever seen, blinked as though unused to even such occluded sunlight. He could not see the faces of the riders, who wore hooded cloaks that at first seemed dark gray or even black, but which had the flickering sheen of an oily puddle, yet they too seemed startled by the brightness of this new place. A tongue of mist curled about the horses' feet, as though their shadowy land would not entirely let them go.

One of the riders slowly turned toward the trees where the two Funderlings lay hidden, a glint of eyes in the depths of the shadowed hood the only indication it was not empty. For a long moment the rider only stared, or perhaps listened, and although Chert's every fiber told him to leap to his feet and run, he lay as still as he could, clutching Opal so tightly that he could feel her silently struggling to break his painful grip.

At last the hooded figure turned away. One of its fellows lifted something from the back of its saddle and dropped it to the ground. The riders lingered for a moment longer, staring across the valley at the distant towers of Southmarch Castle. Then, without a sound, they wheeled and rode their ghostwhite horses back into the ragged wall of mist.

Chert still waited a dozen frightened heartbeats before he let go of his wife.

"You've crushed my innards, you old fool," she moaned, climbing up onto hands and knees. "Who was it? I couldn't see."

"I . . . I don't know." It had happened so quickly that it almost seemed a dream. He got up, feeling the ache of their clumsy, panicked flight begin to throb in all his joints. "They just rode out, then turned around and rode back . . ." He stopped, staring at the dark bundle the riders had dropped. It was moving.

"Chert, where are you going?"

He didn't intend to touch it, of course—no Funderling was such a fool, to snatch up something that even those beyond the Shadowline did not want. As he moved closer, he could not help noticing that the large sack was making small, frightened noises.

"There's something in it," he called to Opal.

"There's something in lots of things," she said, coming grimly after him. "But not much between your ears. Leave it alone and come away, you. No good can come of it."

"It's . . . it's alive." A thought had come into his head. It was a goblin, or some other magical creature banished from the lands beyond. Goblins were wish-granters, that was what the old tales said. And if he freed it, would it not give those wishes to him? A new shawl . . . ? Opal could have a queen's closet full of clothes if she wished. Or the goblin might lead him to a vein of firegold and the masters of the Funderling guilds would soon be coming to Chert's house with caps in hands, begging his assistance. Even his own so-proud brother . . .

The sack thrashed and tipped over. Something inside it snarled.

Of course, he thought, *there could be a reason they took it across the Shadowline and tossed it away like bones on a midden. It could be something extremely unpleasant.*

An even stranger sound came from the sack.

"Oh, Chert." His wife's voice was now quite different. "There's a child in there! Listen—it's crying!"

He still did not move. Everyone knew there were sprites and bogles even on this side of the Shadowline that could mimic the voices of loved ones in order to lure travelers off the path to certain doom. Why expect better of something that actually came from inside the twilight country?

"Aren't you going to do anything?"

"Do what? Any kind of demon could be in there, woman."

"That's no demon, that's a child—and if you're too frightened to let it out, Chert of the Blue Quartz, I will."

He knew that tone all too well. He muttered a prayer to the gods of deep places, then advanced on the sack as though it were a coiled viper, stepping carefully so that in its thrashing it would not roll against him and, perhaps, bite. The sack was held shut with a knot of some gray rope. He touched it carefully and found the cord slippery as polished soapstone.

"Hurry up, old man!"

He glared at her, then began cautiously to unpick the knot, wishing he had brought something with him sharper than his old knife, dulled by digging out stones. Despite the cool, foggy air, sweat had beaded on his forehead by the time he was able to tease the knot apart. The sack had lain still and silent for some time. He wondered, half hoping it was so, whether the thing inside might have suffocated.

"What's in there?" his wife called, but before he had time to explain that he hadn't even opened the cursed thing, something shot out of the heavy sack like a stone from the mouth of a culverin and knocked him onto his back.

Chert tried to shout, but the thing had his neck gripped in clammy hands and was trying to bite his chest through his thick jerkin. He was so busy fighting for his life that he couldn't even make out the shape of his attacker until a third body entered the fray and dragged the clutching, strangling monstrosity off him and they all tumbled into a pile.

"Are you . . . hurt . . . ?" Opal gasped.

"Where is that thing?" Chert rolled over into a sitting position. The sack's contents were crouching a short distance away, staring at him with squinting blue eyes. It was a slender-limbed boy, a child of perhaps five or six years, sweaty and disheveled, with deathly pale skin and hair that was almost white, as though he had been inside the sack for years.

Opal sat up. "A child! I told you." She looked at the boy for a moment. "One of the big folk, poor thing."

"Poor thing, indeed!" Chert gently touched the scraped places on his neck and cheeks. "The little beast tried to murder me."

"Oh, be still. You startled him, that's all." She held out her hand toward the boy. "Come here—I won't hurt you. What's your name, child?" When the boy did not reply, she fumbled in the wide pockets of her dress and withdrew a heel of brown bread. "Are you hungry?"

From the fierce glint in his eye, the boy was clearly very interested, but he still did not move toward her. Opal leaned forward and set the bread on the grass. He looked at it and her, then snatched the bread up, sniffed it, and crammed it into his mouth, scarcely bothering to chew before swallowing. Finished, the boy looked at Opal with fierce expectancy. She laughed in a worried way and felt in her pocket until she located a few pieces of dried fruit, which she also set on the grass. They disappeared even faster than the bread.

"What's your name?" she asked the boy. "Where are you from?"

Searching his teeth with his tongue for any fragments of food that might have escaped him, he only looked at her.

"Dumb, it seems," said Chert. "Or at least he doesn't speak our . . ."

"Where is this?" the boy asked.

"Where . . . what do you mean?" said Chert, startled.

"Where is this . . . ?" The boy swept his arm in a circle, taking in the trees, the grassy hillside, the fogbound forest. "This . . . place. Where are we?" He sounded older than his age somehow, but younger, too, as though speaking were a new thing to him.

"We are on the edge of Southmarch—called Shadowmarch by some, because of this Shadowline." Chert gestured toward the misty boundary, then swung himself around to point in the opposite direction. "The castle is over there."

"Shadow . . . line?" The boy squinted. "Castle?"

"He needs more food." Opal's words had the sound of an inarguable decision rendered. "And sleep. You can see he's nearly falling over."

"Which means what?" But Chert already saw the shape of it and did not like it much at all.

"Which means we take him home, of course." Opal stood, brushing the loose grass from her dress. "We feed him."

"But . . . but he must belong to someone! To one of the big-folk families!"

"And they tied him in a sack and left him here?" Opal laughed scornfully. "Then they are likely not pining for his return."

"But he came . . . he came from . . ." Chert looked at the boy, who was sucking his fingers and examining the landscape. He lowered his voice. "He came from the *other side.*"

"He's here now," Opal said. "Look at him. Do you really think he's some unnatural thing? He's a little boy who wandered into the twilight and was tossed out again. Surely we, of all people, should know better than to believe everything that has to do with the Shadowline is wicked. Does this mean you plan to throw back the gems you've found here, too? No, he probably comes from some other place along the boundary—somewhere leagues and leagues away! Should we leave him here to starve?" She patted her thigh, then beckoned. "Come along with us, child. We'll take you home and feed you properly."

Before Chert could make further objection Opal set off, stumping back along the hillside toward the distant castle, the hem of her old dress trailing in the wet grass. The boy paused only to glance at Chert—a look the little man first thought was threatening, then decided might be as much fear as bravado—before following after her.

"No good will come of it," Chert said, but quietly, already resigned through long experiece to whatever complex doom the gods had planned for him. In any case, better some angry gods than an angry Opal. He didn't have to share a small house with the gods, who had their own vast and hidden places. He sighed and fell into step behind his wife and the boy.

The wyvern had been brought to bay in another copse of trees, a dense circle of rowans carpeted with bracken. Even through the milling ring of hounds, wild with excitement but still cautious enough to keep their distance, perhaps put off by the unusual smell or strange slithering movements of their quarry, Briony could see the length of the thing as it moved restlessly from one side of the copse to the other, its bright scales glimmering in the shadows like a brushfire.

"Cowardly beasts, dogs," said Barrick. "They are fifty to one but still hold back."

"They are not cowards!" Briony resisted the urge to push him off his horse. He was looking even more drawn and pale, and had tucked his left arm inside his cloak as though to protect it from chill, though the afternoon air was still sun-warmed. "The scent is strange to them!"

Barrick frowned. "There are too many things coming across the Shadowline these days. Just back in the spring there were those birds with the iron beaks that killed a shepherd at Landsend. And the dead giant in Daler's Troth . . ."

The thing in the copse reared up, hissing loudly. The hounds started away, whining and yipping, and several of the beaters shouted in terror and scuttled back from the ring of trees. Briony could still see only a little of the beast as it slipped in and out through the gray rowan trunks and the tangled undergrowth. It seemed to have a head narrow as a sea horse's, and as it hissed again she glimpsed a mouth full of spiny teeth.

It almost seems frightened, she thought, but that did not make sense. It was a monster, an unnatural thing: there could be nothing in its dark mind but malevolence.

"Enough!" cried Kendrick, who was holding his frightened horse steady near the edge of the copse. "Bring me my spear!"

His squire ran to him, face wan with dread, looking determinedly at anything except the hissing shape only a few paces away. The young man, one of Tyne Aldritch's sons, was in such terrified haste to hand over the spear and escape that he almost let the long, gold-chased shaft with its crosshaft and its heavy iron head fall to the ground as the prince reached for it. Kendrick caught it, then kicked out at the retreating youth in irritation.

Others of the hunting party were calling for spears as well. With the kill so close, the two dozen immaculately coiffed and dressed noblewomen who had accompanied the hunt, most riding decorously on sidesaddles, a few even carried in litters—their awkward progress had slowed everyone else quite a bit, to Briony's disgust—took the opportunity to withdraw to a nearby hillock where they could watch the end from a safe distance. Briony saw that Rose and Moina, her two principal ladies-in-waiting, had spread a blanket for her between them on the hillside and were looking at her expectantly. Rose Trelling was one of Lord Constable Brone's nieces, Moina Hartsbrook the daughter of a Helmingsea nobleman. Both were good-hearted girls, which made them Briony's favorites out of what she thought of as a mediocre stable of court women, but she sometimes found them just as silly and hidebound as their older relatives, scandalized by the slightest variation from formal etiquette or tradition. Old Puzzle the jester was sitting with them, restringing his lute, biding his time until he could see what food the ladies might have in their hamper.

The idea of withdrawing to the safety of the hill and watching the rest of the hunt while her ladies-in-waiting gossiped about people's jewelry and clothes was too painful. Briony scowled and waved at one of the beaters as he staggered past with several of the heavy spears in his arms. "Give me one of those."

"What are you doing?" Barrick himself could not easily handle the long spears with only one arm, and had not bothered to call for one. "You can't go near that creature. Kendrick won't let you."

"Kendrick has quite enough to think about. Oh, gods curse it." She scowled. Gailon of Summerfield had seen and was spurring toward them.

"My lady! Princess!" He leaned out as if to take the spear from her, and only realized at the last moment that he would be overstepping. "You will hurt yourself."

She managed to control her voice, but barely. "I do know which end points outward, Duke Gailon."

"But this is not fitting for a lady . . . and especially with such a fearsome beast . . . !"

"Then you must make sure and kill it first," she said, a bit more gently but no more sweetly. "Because if it reaches me, it will get no farther."

Barrick groaned, then called the bearer back and took a spear for himself, clutching it awkwardly under one arm while still holding the reins.

"And what are you doing?" she demanded.

"If you're going to be a fool, strawhead, someone has to protect you."

Gailon Tolly looked at them both, then shook his head and rode off toward Kendrick and the hounds.

"I don't think he's very happy with us," Briony said cheerfully. From somewhere back along the hillside she heard the master of arms shout her name, then her brother's. "And Shaso won't be either. Let's go."

They spurred forward. The dogs, surrounded now by a ring of men with spears, were beginning to find their courage again. Several of the lymers darted into the copse to snap at the swift-moving, reddish shape. Briony saw the long neck move, quick as a whipcrack, and one of the dogs yelped in terror as it was caught in the long jaws.

"Oh, hurry!" she said, miserable but also strangely excited. Again she could feel the presence of invisible things swirling like winter clouds. She said a prayer to Zoria.

The dogs began to swarm into the copse in numbers, a flood of low shapes swirling in the dappled light beneath the trees, barking in frightened excitement. There were more squeals of pain, but then a strange, creaking bellow from the wyvern as one of the dogs got its teeth into a sensitive spot. The barking suddenly rose fiercely in pitch as the beast fought its way through the pack, trying to escape the confinement of the trees. It crushed at least one of the hounds under its clawed feet and gutted several others, shaking one victim so hard that blood flew everywhere like red rain. Then it burst out of the leaves and moving shadows into the clear afternoon sunlight, and for the first time Briony could see it whole.

It was mostly serpentine body, a great tube of muscle covered with glimmering red and gold and brown scales, with a single pair of sturdy legs a third of the way down its length. A sort of ruff of bone and skin had flared out behind the narrow head, stretching even wider now as the thing rose up on those legs, head swaying higher than a man's as it struck toward

Kendrick and the two other nobles closest to it. It had come on them too quickly for the men to dismount and use their long boar spears properly. Kendrick waited until the strike had missed, then dug at the creature's face with his spear. The wyvern hissed and sideslipped the blow, but as it did so one of the other men—Briony thought it might be Tyne, the hunting-mad Earl of Blueshore—drove his spearhead into the thing's ribs just behind its shoulders. The wyvern contorted its neck to snap at the shaft. Kendrick seized the opportunity to drive his own spear into the creature's throat, then spurred his horse forward so that he could use its force to pin the wyvern against the ground. The spear slid in through a sluice of red-black blood until the crosshaft that was meant to keep a boar from forcing its way up the shaft stopped it. Kendrick's horse reared in alarm at the thing's agonized, furious hiss, but the prince stood in his stirrups and leaned his weight on the spear, determined to keep the thing staked to the earth.

The dogs swarmed forward again; the other members of the hunt began to close in too, all anxious to be in at the kill. But the wyvern was not beaten.

In a sudden, explosive movement the thing coiled itself around the spear, stretching its neck a surprising distance to bite at Kendrick's gloved hand. The prince's horse reared again and he almost lost his grip on the spear entirely. The monster's tail lashed out and wrapped around the horse's legs. The black gelding nickered in terror. For a brief moment they were all tangled together like some fantastical scene from one of the ancient tapestries in the castle's throne room, everything so strange that Briony could not quite believe it was truly happening. Then the wyvern tightened itself around the legs of Kendrick's horse, crushing bones in a drumroll of frighteningly loud cracks, and the prince and his mount collapsed downward into a maul of red-gold coils.

As Barrick and Briony stared in horror from twenty paces away, Summerfield and Blueshore both began to jab wildly at the agitated monster and its prey. Other nobles hurried forward, shouting in fear for the prince regent's life. The crush of eager dogs, the writhing loops of the injured wyvern's long body, and the thrashing of the mortally injured horse made it impossible to see what was happening on the ground. Briony was light-headed and sick.

Then something came up suddenly out of the long grass, speeding toward her like the figurehead of a Vuttish longboat cutting the water—the wyvern, making a desperate lunge at escape, still dragging Kendrick's spear in its neck. It darted first to one side, then to the other, hemmed in by terrified horses and jabbing spears, then plunged through an opening in the ring of hunters, straight at Briony and Barrick.

A heartbeat later it rose before them, its black eye glittering, head swaying like an adder's as it measured them. As if in a dream, Briony lifted her spear. The thing hissed and reared higher. She tried to track the moving head, to keep the point firmly between it and her, but its looping motions were quick and fluidly deceptive. A moment later Barrick's spear slipped from his clumsy, one-handed grasp and banged sideways into Briony's arm, knocking her weapon out of her hands.

The wyvern's narrow jaws spread wide, dripping with bloody froth. The head lunged toward her, then suddenly snapped to one side as though yanked by a string.

The monster's strike had come so close that when she undressed that night Briony found the thing's caustic spittle had burned holes in her deerhide jerkin: it looked as though someone had held the garment over the flames of a dozen tiny candles.

The wyvern lay on the ground, an arrow jutting from its eye, little shudders rippling down its long neck as it died. Briony stared at it, then turned to see Shaso riding toward them, his war bow still in his hand. He looked down at the dead beast before lifting his angry stare to the royal twins.

"Foolish, arrogant children," he said. "Had I been as careless as you, you would both be dead."

2

A Stone in the Sea

WEEPING TOWER:

Three turning, four standing
Five hammerblows in the deep places
The fox hides her children

—from *The Bonefall Oracles*

THIS WAS ONE OF Vansen's favorite spots, high on the old wall just beneath the rough, dark stone of Wolfstooth Spire, and also one of the most satisfying things about his given task: he had good reason to be up here in the stiff breeze that flew across Brenn's Bay, with nearly all of Southmarch, castle and town, arranged beneath him in the autumn sun like objects on a lady's table. Was it shameful that he enjoyed it so?

When he was a child in the dales, Ferras Vansen and the boys from the next croft had liked to play King on the Hill, each trying to hold a singular place at the top of some hummock of soil and stone they had chosen for their battleground, but even in those instants when the others had gone tumbling down to the bottom and Ferras had stood by himself, master of the high place, still the foothills had loomed over them all, and beyond those hills the northern mountains themselves, achingly high, as if to remind young Ferras even in triumph of his true place in life. When he had grown older, he had learned to love those heights, at least those he could reach; at times he had purposely let the sheep wander off, trading one of his father's sometimes violent punishments for the pleasure of following the straying herd into the high places. Until his manhood, he knew no greater pleasure than a stretch of afternoon when he could clamber up to one of the crests and look out over the folds of hillock and valley that lay before him like a bunched blanket—deep, dark places and airy prominences that no one else in his family had ever seen, although they lay less than a mile from the family croft.

Vansen sometimes wondered if this hunger for height and solitude the gods had put in him might not be stronger now than ever, especially with the much greater number of people around him in Southmarch, swarms of them filling the castle and town like bees in a hive. Did any of them, noble or peddler, soldier or serf, ever look up as he did and wonder at the loftiness of Wolfstooth Spire, a black scepter-shape that loomed over even the castle's other towers as the distant snowcapped mountains had dominated the hills of his boyhood country? Did any of the other guardsmen marvel at the sheer size of the place as they walked the walls, these two great uneven rings of stone that crowned Midlan's Mount? Was he the only one secretly thrilled by the liveliness of the place, the people and animals streaming in and out through the gates from sunup until sundown, and by its grandeur, the antique splendor of the king's hall and the massive residence whose roofs seemed to have as many chimneys as a forest had trees? If not, Ferras Vansen couldn't understand it: how could you spend every day beneath the splendid season-towers, each of the four a different shape and color, and not stop to stare at them?

Perhaps, Vansen considered, it was different if you were born in the midst of such things. Perhaps. He had come here half a dozen years ago and still could not begin to grow used to the size and liveliness of the place. People had told him that Southmarch was as nothing compared to Tessis in Syan or the sprawling, ancient city-state of Hierosol with its two-score gates, but here were riches to spare for a young man from dark, lonely Daler's Troth, where earth and sky were both oppressively wet most of the time and in winter the sun seemed scarcely to top the hills.

As if summoned by chill memory, the wind changed, bringing needles of cold air from the ocean that pierced even Vansen's mail shirt and surcoat. He pulled his heavy watch-cloak more tightly around him, forced himself to move. He had work to do. Just because the royal family and, it seemed, half the nobles in the March Kingdoms were across the water hunting in the northern hills did not mean he could afford to spend the afternoon lost in useless thought.

That was his curse, after all, or at least so his mother had once told him: *"You dream too much, child. Our kind, we make our way with strong backs and closed mouths."* Strange, because the tales she had told to him and his sisters in the long evenings, as the single small fire burned down, had always been about clever young men defeating cruel giants or witches and winning the king's daughter. But in the light of day she had instructed her children, *"You will make the gods angry if you ask for too much."*

His Vuttish father had been more understanding, at least sometimes. "Remember, I had to come far to find you," he liked to tell Vansen's mother. "Far from those cold, windy rocks in the middle of the sea to this fine place. Sometimes a man must reach out for more."

The younger Ferras hadn't completely agreed with the old man, certainly not about the place itself—their croft in the hills' dank green shadows, where water seemed to drip from the trees more than half the year, was to him a place to be escaped instead of a destination—but it was nice to hear his father, a onetime sailor who by habit or blood was a man of very few words, talk of something other than a chore young Ferras had forgotten to do.

And now it seemed Vansen had at last proved his mother wrong, for he had come to the city with nothing, and yet here he was, captain of the Southmarch royal guard, with the north's greatest stronghold spread before him and the safety of its ruling family his responsibility. Anyone would be proud of such an achievement, even men born to a much higher station.

But in his heart Ferras Vansen knew his mother had been right. He still dreamed too much, and—what was worse and far more shameful—he dreamed of the wrong things.

"He's like a hawk, that one," a soldier at the residence guardhouse said quietly to his companion as Vansen walked away, but not so quietly that Vansen didn't hear. "You don't ever want to rest for a moment because he'll just drop down on you, sudden-like." Vansen hadn't even punished them when he found them with their armor off, playing dice, but he had made his anger bitingly clear.

Vansen turned back. The two guardsmen looked up, guilty and resentful. "Next time it might be Lord Brone instead of me, and you might be on your way to the stronghold in chains. Think about that, my lads." There was no whispering this time when he went out.

"They can like you or they can fear you," his old captain Donal Murroy had

always said, and even in his last years Murroy had not hesitated to use his knobby knuckles or the flat of his hand to reinforce that fear in a soldier who was insolent or just too slow in his obedience. Vansen had hoped when he was promoted to Murroy's place that he could substitute respect for fear, but after nearly a year he was beginning to think the old Connordman had been right. Most of the guards were too young to have known anything except peace. They found it hard to believe that a day might come when stealing a nap on duty or wandering away from their posts might have fatal consequences for themselves or the people they protected.

Sometimes it was hard for Vansen himself to believe it. There were days here on the edge of the world, in a little kingdom bounded by misty, ill-omened mountains in the north and the ocean almost everywhere else, where it seemed like nothing would ever change but the wind and weather, and those would only be the familiar small changes—from wet to slightly less wet and then back to wet again, from swirling breeze to stiff gale—that so wearied the inhabitants of this small stone in the shallows of the sea.

Southmarch Castle was ringed by three walls: the huge, smooth outwall of gray-white southern granite that circled the mount and whose foundations in many places were actually beneath the waters of Brenn's Bay, a skirt of fitted stone which, along with the bay itself, made the little sometimes-island into what had been for centuries a fortress that could resist any siege; the New Wall, as it was called (though no one could remember a time before it had existed), that surrounded the royal keep and touched all the cardinal towers except the one named for summer; and the Old Wall that bounded the inmost heart of the keep, and within whose protective shadow lay the throne hall and the royal residence. These two edifices were as riddled with hallways and chambers as anthills, so old and vast and beset by centuries of intermittent neglect that they both contained rooms and passages that had not been entered or even remembered for years.

The smaller buildings that surrounded them made the lower castle just as intricate a maze as the residence and throne hall, jumble of temples and shops, stables and houses, from the high-timbered mansions of the nobility nestled inside the Old Wall to the stacked hovels of those of less lofty station, piled so leaningly high that they turned the narrow streets between them into shadowy arbors of dark wood and plaster. Most of the buildings of Southmarch had been connected over the years by a ramshackle aggregation of covered walkways and tunnels to protect the denizens from the wet northern weather and the often ruthless winds, so that sometimes all the castle's disparate structures, built over generations, seemed to have fused together like the contents of one of the tide pools in the rocks at the ocean edge of Brenn's Bay, where stone and plants and shells grew together into one semiliving—and no longer separable—mass.

Still, there was sun here, Ferras Vansen told himself, far more of it in a year than he had seen in his entire youth in the Dales, not to mention fresh winds off the sea. That made it all bearable, and more than bearable: there were times when just being in the place filled him with joy.

By the time the afternoon had begun to fade, Vansen had walked most of the uneven circle of the Old Wall, stopping at each guard post, even those that consisted of nothing more than a lonely soldier with a pike standing before a locked door or gate and trying not to doze. Drunk on sea air and some rare time to pursue his own thoughts without the distractions of command, Vansen briefly considered a course around the much lengthier New Wall, but a look at the harbor and the sails of the newly arrived carrack from Hierosol reminded him that he could not afford the time. There would be a hundred tasks before the end of the day; the visitors must be safely lodged, guarded, and watched, and Avin Brone, the lord constable, would expect Vansen to take charge of the task himself. The ship had four masts—a good-sized vessel, which meant that the envoy might have come with a sizable bodyguard. Vansen cursed quietly. More than one day's pleasurable solitude was going to be sacrificed to this ship and its passengers. He would have to keep his men and the southerners apart as much as possible. With King Olin a captive of Hierosol's Ludis Drakava, there was much bad blood between the Hierosolines and the Southmarch folk.

When he came out of the small guard tower by the West Green, he was distracted from his planning by the sight of someone else on the walls, a cloaked and hooded figure that seemed slight enough to be a woman or a young boy. For an illogical moment he wondered if it could be her, the one he dared not think of too often. Had fate somehow brought her here alone to this place where they could not help but speak? The thought of all the things he might say to her, careful, respectful, sincere, passed through his mind in a heartbeat before he realized that it could not be her, that she was still out with the others hunting in the hills.

As though this swirl of confused thoughts made a sound as audible and frightening as a swarm of hornets, the hooded figure suddenly seemed to notice him; it immediately stepped down from the wall into the stairwell and disappeared from his sight. By the time Vansen reached the stairs he could not discern that particular dark, hooded cloak in the throng of people in the narrow streets below the wall.

So I am not the only one who likes the view from high places, he thought. He felt a pang; it took him a moment to realize, to his surprise, that it was loneliness.

"You're too much inside yourself, Vansen," old Murroy had once told him. "You think more than you talk, but that's little use when the others can see so plainly what you're thinkin'. They know that you think well of yourself, and often not so well of them. The older men in particular, Laybrick and Southstead, don't like it."

"I do not like men who . . . who take advantage," Vansen had answered, trying to explain what was in his heart but not quite having the words. "I do not like men who take what the gods give and pretend it's their due."

Hearing that, Murroy's leathery old face had creased in one of his infrequent smiles. "Then you must not like most men."

Ferras Vansen had wondered ever since whether his captain's words were true. He liked Captain Murroy himself slightly more than he feared him, or at least he liked the man's brutal evenhandedness, his unwillingness to complain, his occasional flashes of sour humor. Donal Murroy was staying that way to the end: even as the wasting sickness stole his life, he offered no complaint against fate or the gods, saying only that he wished he had known what was going to happen so he could have given his wife's lying, bragging younger brother a thrashing while he still had the strength. "As it is, I'll have to leave it to the next man whose hospitality or good sense he offends. I hope it's someone who has the time to beat him within a hair of his useless life."

Vansen marveled at how the older man could laugh despite the racking cough and the blood on his lips and stubbled chin, how his shadowed, deep-sunken eyes were still as bright and heartlessly fierce as a hunting bird's.

"You'll follow me as guard captain, Vansen," said the dying man. "I've told Brone. Himself has no powerful objections, though he thinks you a bit young. The great man's right, of course, but I wouldn't trust that ass Dyer with the bung from an empty cask and all the older men are too fat and lazy. No, it's you, Vansen. Go ahead and muck things up if you want to. They'll just come and put flowers on my grave and miss me." Another laugh, another spray of red-tinged spittle.

"Thank you, sir."

"Don't bother, lad. If you do it right, you'll spend all your life working at it with no more payment than a little land to build a house and p'raps a spot in a proper graveyard at the end of it instead of the potter's field." He wiped his chin with a gnarled hand. *"Which reminds me—don't let them forget there's a place set aside for me in the guards' cemetery. I don't want to end up out in the western hills somewhere, but I don't want Mickael Southstead pissing on my grave, either, so you keep an eye on me after I'm gone."*

He hadn't cried when the captain died, but he sometimes felt as if he wanted to when he thought about him now. The captain's manner of going had been much like that of Ferras' own father, now that he thought on it. He hadn't cried for Pedar Vansen either, and hadn't been to his father's grave in the old temple yard at Little Stell for years, but that wasn't really so surprising: Vansen's sisters, what was left of the crofter's family, were all in Southmarch-town now, settled with husbands and children of their own. Daler's Troth was several days' ride away in the hills to the west. His life was here now, in this dizzyingly large and crowded citadel.

He made his way around to the western tower of the Raven's Gate. The men in the guardhouse there had a well-stoked fire and he stopped to warm his hands before going to see what Lord Brone wanted done about the southerners. The easy chatter had fallen off when he had come in, as usual, and all the men were standing around in awkward silence except for Collum Dyer, the officer in charge, closest thing to a friend Ferras Vansen had. He dreaded the day he would have to draw that line Murroy had talked of so often, and discipline Dyer for something—whatever Dyer felt about Vansen was certainly not fear, and did not quite seem like respect either—because he was certain that would be the day that their friendship, slight as it was, would end.

"Been out wandering the walls, Captain?" Dyer asked him. Vansen was grateful that Dyer at least named him by his rank in front of the men. That was a small nod of respect, wasn't it? "Any sign of invading forces?"

Vansen let himself smile. "No, and Perin be thanked for that, today and every day. But there is a Hierosoline ship in the harbor and there will be fighting men on board, so let us not take things too lightly, either."

He left them and made his way down the stairs to the sloping road that led up to the Great Hall. The lord constable had his work chambers in the maze of corridors behind the throne room, and at this time of the day Vansen felt certain he would be there. As he walked up the road toward the vast carved facade, where the guards were already straightening at their young captain's approach, he looked up at the high hall nestled in the midst of the Mount's towers like a gem on a royal crown and felt a clutch of worry that something might change, that some error of his own or the whim of feckless gods might take all this away from him.

I am a fortunate man, he told himself. *Heaven has smiled on me, far beyond what I have earned, and I have everything I could want—or nearly so. I must accept these great riches and not ask more, not anger the gods with my greed.*

I am a fortunate man and I cannot, even in the foolishness of my secret heart, ever forget that.

3
Proper Blue Quartz

THE BIRD WHO IS A RIDDLE:

*Beak of silver, bones of cold iron
Wings of setting sun
Claws that catch only emptiness*

—from *The Bonefall Oracles*

THE BOY FROM BEHIND the Shadowline stopped to stare at the castle's jutting towers. The three of them were on the lower reaches of the hill road now, which wound down through rolling farmlands to the edge of the city on the shoreline. The heights of Midlan's Mount were still distant across the causeway, Wolfstooth Spire looming above all like a dark claw scratching the belly of the sky.

"What is that place?" the child asked, almost in a whisper.

"Southmarch Castle," Chert told him. "At least the part with the towers out on that rock in the middle of the bay—the bit on this side is the rest of the town. Yes, Southmarch . . . some call it Shadowmarch, did I already say that? On account of it's so close to the . . ." He remembered where the boy came from and trailed off. "Or you can call it 'The Beacon of the Marches,' if you like poetry."

The boy shook his head, but whether because he didn't like poetry or for some other reason wasn't clear. "Big."

"Hurry up, you two." Opal had marched ahead.

"She's right—we have a long walk yet."

The boy still hesitated. Chert laid his hand on the boy's arm. The child seemed strangely reluctant, as though the distant towers themselves were something menacing, but at last he allowed himself to be urged forward. "There's nothing to be afraid of, lad," Chert told him. "Not as long as you're with us. But don't wander off."

The boy shook his head again.

As they made their way down from the hilly farmlands into the mainland town, they found wide Market Road lined with people, almost entirely big folk. For a moment Chert wondered why so many people had come out of their houses and shops to stare curiously at two Funderlings and a ragged, white-haired boy, then realized that the royal family's hunting party must have passed just ahead of them. The crowd was beginning to disperse now, the hawkers desperately reducing the prices of their chestnuts and fried breads, fighting over the few remaining customers. He heard murmurs about the size of something the hunters had caught and paraded past, and other descriptions—scales? Teeth?—that made little sense unless they had been hunting something other than deer. The people seemed a little dispirited, even unhappy. Chert hoped the princess and her sullen brother were safe—he had thought she had kind eyes. But if something had happened to them, he reasoned, surely folk would be talking about it.

It took the best part of the fading afternoon to make their way through the city to the shore, but they arrived at the near end of the causeway with a little time to spare before the rising tide would turn Midlan's Mount back into an island.

The causeway between the shore and the castle on the Mount was little more than a broad road of piled stones, most of which would vanish under the high tide, but the place where it met the docks outside the castle gate had been built up by generations of fishermen and peddlers until what hung over the water there was nearly a small town in itself, a sort of permanent fairground on the wind-lashed doorstep of Midlan's Mount. As the Funderling, his wife, and their new guest trudged across the piers and wooden platforms filled with flimsy, close-leaning buildings whose floors stood only a few cubits above the reach of high tide, dodging wagons and heavily laden foot-peddlers hurrying to cross back over the causeway before nightfall, Chert looked out through a crack between two rickety shops, across the mouth of Brenn's Bay to the ocean. Despite the last of the bright afternoon sun there were clouds spread thick and dark along the horizon, and Chert suddenly remembered the shocking thing that the arrival of the riders and the mysterious boy had driven from his mind.

The Shadowline! Someone must be told that it's moved. He would have liked to think that the king's family up in the castle already knew, that they had taken all the facts into careful consideration and decided that it meant nothing, that all was still well, but he couldn't quite make himself believe it.

Someone must be told. The thought of going up to the castle himself was daunting, although he had been inside the keep several times as part of Funderling work gangs, and had even led a few, working directly with Lord Nynor, the castellan—or with his factor, in any case. But to go by himself, as though he were a man of importance . . .

But if the big folk do not know, someone must tell them. And perhaps there will even be some reward in it—enough to buy Opal that new shawl, if nothing else. Or at least to pay for what this young creature will eat when Opal gets him home.

He regarded the boy for a moment, horrified by the sudden realization that Opal might very well intend to keep him. A childless woman, he thought, was as unpredictable as a loose seam in a bed of sandstone.

Hold now, one thing at a time. Chert watched the clouds hurrying across the ocean, their black expanse making the mighty towers suddenly seem fragile, delicate as pastry. Someone needed to tell the king's people about the Shadowline, there was no arguing it. *If I go to the Guild, there will be days of argument, then Cinnabar or puffed-up Young Pyrite will be appointed messenger and I will get no reward.*

Nor will you get the punishment if you're wrong, he reminded himself.

For some reason he again saw before his mind's eye the young princess and her brother, Briony's frightened gaze when she thought she had run him down, the prince's face as troubled and impersonal as the sky out beyond the Mount, and he felt a sudden warmth that almost, if it had not been so ridiculous, felt like loyalty.

They need to know, he decided, and suddenly the idea of what might be coming closer behind that line of moving darkness pushed anything so abstract as the good graces of the royal family from his mind. There was another way to pass the news, and he would use it. *Everyone needs to know.*

Although his horse was dead, left behind for three servants to bury on the hillside where the wyvern had died, Prince Kendrick himself had suffered little more than bruises and a few burns from the creature's venomous froth. Of all the company he was the only one who seemed in good cheer as they made their way back toward the castle, the huge corpse of the wyvern coiled on an open wagon for the amazement of the populace. Market Road was crowded with people, hundreds and hundreds waiting to see the prince regent and his hunting party. Hawkers, tumblers, musicians, and pickpockets had turned out too, hoping to earn a few small coins out of the spontaneous street fair, but Briony thought most of the people seemed glum and worried. Not much money was changing hands, and those nearest the road watched the nobles go by with hungry eyes, saying little, although a few called out cheers and blessings to the royal family, especially on behalf of the absent King Olin. Kendrick had been splashed in blood from head to foot; even after he had washed and then rubbed himself with rags and soothing leaves, much of him was still stained a deep red. Despite the itch where the wyvern's spittle burned him, he made it a point to wave and smile to the citizens crowded in the shadows of the tall houses along the Market Road, showing them that the blood was not his own.

Briony felt as though she, too, were covered with some painful substance she could not shake off. Her twin Barrick was so miserable about his clumsy failure even to raise his spear properly that he had not spoken a word to her or anyone else on the ride home. Earl Tyne and others were whispering among themselves, no doubt unhappy that the foreigner Shaso had stolen their sport by killing the wyvern with an arrow. Tyne Aldritch was one of that school of nobles who believed that archery was a practice fit only for peasants and poachers, an activity whose primary result was to steal the glory from mounted knights in war. Only because the master of arms might have saved the lives of the young prince and princess was the hunters' unhappiness muttered instead of proclaimed aloud.

And more than a dozen of the dogs, including sweet Dado, a brachet who in her first months of life had slept in Briony's bed, lay cold and still on the leafy hillside beside Kendrick's horse, waiting to be buried in the same pit.

I wish we'd never come. She looked up to the pall of clouds in the northeastern sky. It was as though some foreboding thing hung over the whole day, a crow's wing, an owl's shadow. She would go home and light a candle at Zoria's altar, ask the virgin goddess to send the Eddons her healing grace. *I wish they'd just gone out and killed that creature with arrows in the first place. Then Dado would be alive. Then Barrick wouldn't be trying so hard not to cry that his face has turned to stone.*

"Why the grim look, little sister?" Kendrick demanded. "It is a beautiful day and summer has not entirely left us yet." He laughed. "Look at the clothes I have ruined! My best riding jacket. Merolanna will skin me."

Briony managed a tiny smile. It was true—she could already hear what their great-aunt would have to say, and not just about the jacket. Merolanna had a tongue that everyone in the castle, except perhaps Shaso, feared, and Briony would have given odds that the old Tuani only hid his terror better than others did. "I just . . . I don't know." She looked around to make sure that her black-clad twin was still a few dozen paces behind them. "I fear for Barrick," she said quietly. "He is so angry of late. Today has only made it worse."

Kendrick scratched his scalp, smearing himself anew with drying blood. "He needs toughening, little sister. People lose hands, legs, but they continue with their lives, thanking the gods they have not suffered worse. It does no good for him to be always brooding over his injuries. And he spends too much time with Shaso—the stiffest neck and coldest heart in all the marchlands."

Briony shook her head. Kendrick had never understood Barrick, although that had not kept him from loving his younger brother. And he didn't understand Shaso very well either, although the old man was indeed stiff and stubborn. "It's more than that . . ."

She was interrupted by Gailon Tolly riding back down the road toward them, followed by his personal retinue, the Summerfield boar on their green-and-gold livery brighter than the dull sky. "Highness! A ship has come in from the south!"

Briony's chest tightened. "Oh, Kendrick, do you think it's something about Father?"

The Duke of Summerfield looked at her tolerantly, as though she might have been his own young and slightly sheltered sister. "It is a carrack—the *Podensis* out of Hierosol," he told the prince regent, "and it is said there is an envoy on board sent from Ludis with news of King Olin."

Without realizing it, Briony had reached out and grabbed at Kendrick's red-smeared arm. Her horse bumped flanks with her brother's mount. "Pray all heaven, he is not hurt, is he?" she asked Gailon, unable to keep the terror from her voice. The cold shadow she had felt all day seemed to draw closer. "The king is well?"

Summerfield nodded. "I am told the man says your father continues unharmed, and that he brings a letter from him, among other things."

"Oh, the gods are good," Briony murmured.

Kendrick frowned. "But why has Ludis sent this envoy? That bandit who calls himself Protector of Hierosol can't think we have found all the ransom for the king yet. A hundred thousand gold dolphins! It will take us at least the rest of the year to raise it—we have dragged every last copper out of the temples and merchant houses, and the peasants are already groaning under the new taxes."

"Peasants always groan, my lord," said Gailon. "They are as lazy as old donkeys—they must be whipped to work."

"Perhaps the envoy from Hierosol saw all these nobles in their fine clothes, out hunting," Barrick suggested sourly. None of them had noticed him riding closer. "Perhaps he has decided that if we can afford such expensive amusements, we must have found the money."

The Duke of Summerfield looked at Barrick with incomprehension. Kendrick rolled his eyes, but otherwise ignored his younger brother's gibe, saying, "It must be something important that brings him. Nobody sails all the way from Hierosol to carry a letter from a prisoner, even a royal prisoner."

The duke shrugged. "The envoy asks for an audience tomorrow." He looked around and spotted Shaso riding some distance back, but lowered his voice anyway. "And another thing. He is as black as a crow."

"What has Shaso's skin to do with anything?" Kendrick demanded, irritated.

"No, the envoy, Highness. The envoy from Hierosol."

Kendrick frowned. "That is a strange thing."

"The whole of it is strange," said Gailon of Summerfield. "Or so I hear."

If the nameless boy had seemed disturbed by his first glimpse of the castle, he appeared positively terrified by the Basilisk Gate in the castle's massive outwall. Chert, who had been in and out of it so many times he had lost count, allowed himself to see it now with a stranger's eyes. The granite facing four times a man's height—and many more times Chert's own small stature—was carved in the likeness of a glowering reptilian creature whose twining coils surmounted the top of the gate and looped down on either side. The monster's head jutted out above the vast oak-and-iron doors, its staring eyes and toothy mouth dressed with thin slabs of gemstone and ivory, its scales edged with gold. In the Funderling guilds, if not among the big folk, it was common knowledge that the gate had been here far longer than the human inhabitants.

"That monster is not alive," he told the child gently. "Not even real. It is only chiseled stone."

The boy looked at him, and Chert thought that something in his expression seemed deeper and stranger than mere terror.

"I . . . I do not like to see it," he said.

"Then close your eyes while we walk through, otherwise we will not be able to reach our house. That is where the food is."

The boy squinted up at the lowering worm for a moment through his pale lashes, then shut his eyes tight.

"Come on, you two!" Opal called. "It will be dark soon."

Chert led the boy under the gate. Guards in high-crested helmets and black tabards watched curiously, unused to the sight of a human child being led by Funderlings. But if these tall men wearing the Eddons' silver wolf-and-stars emblem were concerned by the oddity, they were not concerned enough to lift their halberds and move out of the last warm rays of the sun.

The princess and her party had already reached their destination. As the Funderlings and their new ward reached arcade-fenced Market Square in front of the great Trigon temple, Chert could see all the way to the new wall at the base of the central hill, where the lights of the inner keep were as numerous as fireflies on a midsummer evening. The keep's Raven's Gate was open and dozens of servants with torches had come out from the residence to meet the returning hunters, to take the horses and equipment and guide the nobles to hot meals and warm beds.

"Who rules here?" asked the boy.

It seemed an odd sort of question, and now it was Chert who hesitated. "In this country? Do you mean in name? Or in truth?"

The boy frowned—the meaning was chopped too fine for him. "Who rules in that big house?"

It still seemed a strange thing for a child to ask, but Chert had experienced far stranger today. "King Olin, but he is not here. He is a prisoner in the south." Almost half a year had passed since Olin had left on his journey to urge the small kingdoms and principalities across the heartland of Eion to make federation against Xis. He had hoped to unite them against the growing menace of the Autarch, the god-king who was reaching out from his empire on the southern continent of Xand to snap up territories along the lower coast of Eion like a spider snaring flies, but instead Olin had been delivered by the treachery of his rival Hesper, King of Jellon, into the hands of the Protector of Hierosol, an adventurer named Ludis Drakava who was now master of that ancient city. But Chert scarcely understood all the details himself. It was far too much to try to explain to a small, hungry child. "The king's oldest son Kendrick is the prince regent. That means he is the ruler while his father is gone. The king has two younger children, too—a son and daughter."

A gleam came to the boy's eyes, a light behind a curtain. "Merolanna?"

"Merolanna?" Chert stared as if the child had slapped him. "You have heard of the duchess? You must be from somewhere near here. Where are you from, child? Can you remember now?"

But the small white-haired boy only looked back at him silently.

"Yes, there is a Merolanna, but she is the king's aunt. Kendrick's younger brother and sister are named Barrick and Briony. Oh, and the king's wife is carrying another child as well." Chert reflexively made the sign of the Stone Bed, a Funderling charm for good luck in childbirth.

The strange gleam in the boy's eyes faded.

"He's heard of Duchess Merolanna," Chert told Opal. "He must be from these parts."

She rolled her eyes. "He'll probably remember a lot more when he gets a meal and some sleep. Or were you planning to stand in the street all night talking to him of things you know nothing about?"

Chert snorted but waved the boy forward.

More people were streaming out of the castle than were going in, mostly inhabitants of the mainland part of the city whose work brought them onto the Mount and who were now returning home at the end of the day. Chert and Opal had a hard time forcing their way against a tide of much larger people. Opal led them out of Market Square and through echoing covered walkways into the quieter, somewhat gloomy back streets behind the south waterway, called Skimmer's Lagoon, and its docks, one of two large moorings inside the castle's outwall. The Skimmers had carved the wooden dock pilings into weird shapes, animals and people bent and stretched until they were almost unrecognizable. The colorful paint was dulled by the dying light, but Chert thought the carved pilings still seemed as strange as ever, like trapped foreign gods staring out across the water, trying to get a glimpse of some lost homeland. The still shapes even seemed to mourn out loud: as boats full of half-naked Skimmer fishermen unloaded the day's catch on several of the smaller docks, the air of the lagoon was full of their groaning (and to Chert's ear, almost completely tuneless) songs.

"Aren't those people cold?" the boy asked. With the sun now behind the hills, chill winds were beginning to run across the waterway, sending white-tipped wavelets against the pillars.

"They're Skimmers," Chert told him. "They don't get cold."

"Why not?"

Chert shrugged. "The same reason a Funderling can pick something up off the ground faster than you big folk can. We're small. Skimmers have thick skins. The gods just wanted it that way."

"They look strange."

"They are strange, I suppose. They keep to themselves. Some of them, it's said, never step farther onto dry land than the end of a loading dock. Webbed feet like a duck, too—well, a bit between the toes. But there are even odder folk around here, some claim, although you can't always tell it to look at them." He smiled. "Don't they have such things where you come from?"

The boy only looked at him, his expression distant and troubled.

They were quickly out of the back alleys of Skimmer's Lagoon and into the equally close-leaning neighborhoods of the big folk who worked on or along the water. The light was failing quickly now and although there were torches at the crossings and even a few important people being led by lantern-bearers, most of the muddy streets were lit only by the candlelight and firelight that leaked from soon-to-be-shuttered windows. The big folk were happy to build their ramshackle buildings one on top of the other, ladders and scaffolding thick as hedgehog bristles, so that they almost choked off the narrow streets entirely. The stench was dreadful.

Still, this whole place has good bones, Chert could not help thinking, *strong and healthy stone, the living rock of the Mount. It would be a pleasure to scrape away all this ugly wood. We Funderlings would have this place looking as it should in a trice. Looking as it once did . . .*

He pushed away the odd thought—where would all these big folk go, for one thing?

Chert and Opal led the boy down the narrow, sloping length of Stone-cutter's Way and through an arched gate at the base of the New Wall, leading him out from beneath the evening sky and into the stony depths of Funderling Town.

This time Chert was not surprised when the boy stopped to stare in awe:

even those big folk who did not particularly trust or like the small folk agreed that the great ceiling over Funderling Town was a marvel. Stretching a hundred cubits above the small people's town square and continuing above all the lamplit streets, the ceiling was a primordial forest carved in every perfect detail out of the dark bedrock of the Mount. At the outer edges of Funderling Town, closest to the surface, spaces had even been cut between the branches so that true sky shone through, or so that when night fell (as it was falling even now), the first evening stars could be seen sparkling through the gaps in the stone. Each twig, each leaf had been carved with exquisite care, centuries of painstaking work in all, one of the chief marvels of the northern world. Birds feathered in mother-of-pearl and crystal seemed as though they might burst into song at any moment. Vines of green malachite twined up the pillar-trunks, and on some low branches there were even gem-glazed fruits hanging from stems of improbably slender stone.

The boy whispered something that Chert could not quite hear. "It is wonderful, yes," the little man said. "But you can look all you want tomorrow. Let us catch up with Opal, otherwise she will teach you how a tongue can be sharper than any chisel."

They followed his wife down the narrow but graceful streets, each house carved back into the stone, the plain facades giving little indication of the splendid interiors that lay behind them, the careful, loving labor of generations. At each turning or crossing oil lamps glowed on the walls inside bubbles of stone thin as blisters on overworked hands. None of the lights were bright, but they were so numerous that all night long the ways of Funderling Town seemed to tremble on the cusp of dawn.

Although Chert himself was a man of some influence, their house at the end of Wedge Road was modest, only four rooms all told, its walls but shallowly decorated. Chert had a moment of shame remembering the Blue Quartz family manor and its wonderful great room covered with deeply incised scenes of Funderling history. Opal, for all her occasional spikiness of tongue, had never made him feel bad that the two of them should live in such a modest dwelling while her sisters-in-law were queening it in a fine house. He wished he could give her what she deserved, but Chert could no more have stayed in the place, subservient to his brother Nodule—or "Magister Blue Quartz," as he now styled himself—than he could have jumped to the moon. And since his brother had three strong sons, there was no longer even a question of Chert inheriting it should his brother die first.

"I am happy here, you old fool," Opal said quietly as they stepped through the door. She had seen him staring at the house and had guessed his thoughts. "At least I will be if you go and clear your tools off the table so we may eat like decent people."

"Come, boy, and help me with the job," he told the little stranger, making his voice loud and jovial to cover the fierce, sudden love he felt for his wife. "Opal is like a rockfall—if you disregard her first quiet rumblings, you will regret it later on."

He watched the boy wipe dust from the pitted table with a damp cloth, moving it around more than actually cleaning it. "Do you remember your name yet?" he asked.

The boy shook his head.

"Well, we must call you something—Pebble?" He shouted to Opal, who was stirring a pot of soup over the fire, "Shall we call him Pebble?" It was a common name for fourth or fifth boys, when dynastic claims were not so important and parental interest was waning.

"Don't be foolish. He shall have a proper Blue Quartz family name," she called back. "We will call him Flint. That will be one in the eye for your brother."

Chert could not help smiling, although he was not entirely happy about the idea of naming the child as though they were adopting him as their heir. But the thought of how his self-important brother would feel on learning that Chert and Opal had brought in one of the big folk's children and given him miserly old Uncle Flint's name was indeed more than a little pleasing.

"Flint, then," he said, ruffling the boy's fair hair. "For as long as you stay with us, anyway."

Waves lapped at the pilings. A few seabirds bickered sleepily. A plaintive, twisting melody floated up from one of the sleeping-barges, a chorus of high voices singing an old song of moonlight on open sea, but otherwise Skimmer's Lagoon was quiet.

Far away, the sentries on the wall called out the midnight watch and their voices echoed thinly across the water.

Even as the sound faded, a light gleamed at the end of one of the docks. It burned for a moment, then went dark, then burned again. It was a shuttered lantern; its beam pointed out across the dark width of the lagoon. No one within the castle or on the walls seemed to mark it.

But the light did not go entirely unobserved. A small, black-painted skiff slid silently and almost invisibly across the misty lagoon and stopped at the end of the dock. The lantern-bearer, outline obscured by a heavy hooded cloak, crouched and whispered in a language seldom spoken in Southmarch, or indeed anywhere in the north. The shadowy boatman answered just as quietly in the same language, then handed something up to the one who had been waiting for almost an hour on the cold pier—a small object that disappeared immediately into the pockets of the dark cloak.

Without another word, the boatman turned his little craft and vanished back into the fogs that blanketed the dark lagoon.

The figure on the dock extinguished the lantern and turned back toward the castle, moving carefully from shadow to shadow as though it carried something extremely precious or extremely dangerous.

4
A Surprising Proposal

THE LAMP:

The flame is her fingers
The leaping is her eye as the rain is the cricket's song
All can be foretold

—from *The Bonefall Oracles*

PUZZLE LOOKED SADLY at the dove that he had just produced from his sleeve. Its head was cocked at a very unnatural angle; in fact, it seemed to be dead.

"My apologies, Highness." A frown creased the jester's gaunt face like a crumpled kerchief. A few people were laughing nastily near the back of the throne room. One of the noblewomen made a small and somewhat overwrought noise of grief for the luckless dove. "The trick worked most wonderfully when I was practicing earlier. Perhaps I need to find a bird of hardier constitution . . ."

Barrick rolled his eyes and snorted, but his older brother was more of a diplomat. Puzzle was an old favorite of their father's. "An accident, good Puzzle. Doubtless you will solve it with further study."

"And a few dozen more dead birds," whispered Barrick. His sister frowned.

"But I still owe Your Highness the day's debt of entertainment." The old man tucked the dove carefully into the breast of his checkered outfit.

"Well, we know what he's having for supper," Barrick told Briony, who shushed him.

"I will find some other pleasantries to amuse you," Puzzle continued, with only a brief wounded look at the whispering twins. "Or perhaps one of my other renowned antics? I have not juggled flaming brands for you for some time—not since the unfortunate accident with the Syannese tapestry. I have reduced the number of torches, so the trick is much safer now . . ."

"No need," Kendrick said gently. "No need. You have entertained us long enough—now the business of the court waits."

Puzzle nodded his head sadly, then bowed and backed away from the throne toward the rear of the room, putting one long leg behind the other as though doing something he had been forced to practice even more carefully than the dove trick. Barrick could not help noticing how much the old man looked like a grasshopper in motley. The assembled courtiers laughed and whispered behind their hands.

We're all fools here. His dark mood, alleviated a little by watching Puzzle's fumbling, came sweeping back. *Most of us are just better at it than he is.* Even at the best of times he found it difficult to sit on the hard chairs. Despite the open windows high above, the throne room was thick with the smell of incense and dust and other people—too many other people. He turned to watch his brother, conferring with Steffans Nynor the lord castellan, making a joke that set Summerfield and the other nobles laughing and made old Nynor blush and stammer. *Look at Kendrick, pretending like he's Father. But even Father was pretending—he hated all this.* In fact, King Olin had never liked either priggish Gailon of Summerfield or his loud, well-fed father, the old duke.

Maybe Father wanted *to be taken prisoner, just to get away from it all.* . . .

The bizarre thought did not have time to form properly, because Briony elbowed him in the ribs.

"Stop it!" he snarled. His sister was always trying to make him smile, to force him to enjoy himself. Why couldn't she see the trouble they were in—not just the family, but all of Southmarch? Could he really be the only one in the kingdom who understood how wretched things were?

"Kendrick wants us," she said.

Barrick allowed himself to be pulled toward his elder brother's chair—not the true throne, the Wolf's Chair, which had been covered with velvet cloth when Olin left and not used since, but the second-best chair that previously stood at the head of the great dining table. The twins gently elbowed their way past a few courtiers anxious to snatch this moment with the prince regent. Barrick's arm was throbbing. He wished he were out on the hillside again, riding by himself, far from these people. He hated them all, loathed everyone in the castle ... except, he had to admit, his sister and brother ... and perhaps Chaven. ...

"Lord Nynor tells me that the envoy from Hierosol will not be with us until almost the noon hour," Kendrick announced as they approached.

"He said he was unwell after his voyage." The ancient castellan looked worried, as always; the tip of his beard was chewed short—a truly disgusting habit, in Barrick's opinion. "But one of the servants told me that he saw this envoy talking to Shaso earlier this morning. Arguing, if the lazy fellow is to be trusted, which he is not to be, necessarily."

"That sounds ominous, Highness," suggested the Duke of Summerfield.

Kendrick sighed. "They are both, from appearance, anyway, from the same southern lands," he said patiently. "Shaso sees few of his own kind here in the cold north. They might have much to talk about."

"And argue about, Highness?" Summerfield asked.

"The man is a servant of our father's captor," Kendrick pointed out. "That's reason enough for Shaso to argue with the man, is it not?" He turned to the twins. "I know how little you both care for standing around, so you may go and I'll send for you when this fellow from Hierosol finally graces us with his attendance." He spoke lightly, but Barrick could see that he was not very happy with the envoy's tardiness. His older brother, Barrick thought, was beginning to develop a monarchical impatience.

"Ah, Highness, I almost forgot." Nynor snapped his fingers and one of his servants scuttled forward with a leather bag. "He gave me the letters he bears from your father and the so-called Lord Protector."

"Father's letter?" Briony clapped her hands. "Read it to us!"

Kendrick had already broken the seal, the Eddon wolf and crescent of stars in deep red wax, and was squinting at the words. He shook his head. "Later, Briony."

"But Kendrick ... !" There was real anguish in her voice.

"Enough." Her older brother looked distracted, but his voice said there would be no arguing. Barrick could feel the strain in Briony's abrupt silence.

"What's all that rumpus?" asked Gailon Tolly a moment later, looking around. Something was happening at the other end of the throne room, a stir among the courtiers.

"Look," Briony whispered to her twin. "It's Anissa's maid."

It was indeed, and Barrick's sister was not the only one whispering. Now that the twins' stepmother was close to giving birth, she seldom left her suite of rooms in the Tower of Spring. Selia, her maid, had become Queen Anissa's envoy to the rest of the great castle, her ears and eyes. And as eyes went, even Barrick had to admit they were a most impressive pair.

"See her flounce." Briony did not hide her disgust. "She walks like she's got a rash on her backside and she wants to scratch it on something."

"*Please,* Briony," said the prince regent, but although the Duke of Summerfield looked dismayed by her rude remark, Kendrick was mostly amused. Still, he had been distracted from the letter and was watching the maid's approach as carefully as anyone else.

Selia was young but well-rounded. She wore her black hair piled high in the manner of the women of Devonis, the land of her and her mistress' birth, but although she kept her long-lashed eyes downcast, there was little of the shy peasant girl about her. Barrick watched her walk with a kind of painful greed, but the maid, when she looked up, seemed to see only his brother, the prince regent.

Of course, Barrick thought. *Why should she be any different than the rest of them . . . ?*

"If it please you, Highness." She had been only a season in the marches, and still spoke with a thick Devonisian accent. "My mistress, your stepmother, sends her fond regarding and asks leave for talking to the royal physician."

"Is she unwell again?" Kendrick truly was a kind man: although none of them much liked their father's second wife, even Barrick believed his brother's concern was genuine.

"Some discomforting, Highness, yes."

"Of course, we will have the physician attend our stepmother at once. Will you carry the message to him yourself?"

Selia colored prettily. "I do not know this place so well yet."

Briony made a noise of irritation, but Barrick spoke up. "I'll take her, Kendrick."

"Oh, that's too much trouble for the poor girl," Briony said loudly, "going all the way across to Chaven's rooms. Let her go back to assist our suffering stepmother. Barrick and I will go."

He looked at his twin in fury, and for a moment regretted putting her on the list of people he did not despise. "I can do it myself."

"Go, the both of you, and argue somewhere else." Kendrick waved his hand. "Let me read these letters. Tell Chaven to see to our stepmother at once. You are both excused attendance until the noon hour."

Listen to him, Barrick thought. *He really does think he's king.*

Even accompanying the lovely Selia could not redeem Barrick's mood, but he still took care to make sure that his bad arm, wrapped in the folds of his cloak, was on her opposite side as they went out of the throne room into the light of a gray autumn morning. As they descended the steps into the shadowed depths of Temple Square, four palace guards who had been finishing a morning meal hurried to fall in behind them, still chewing. Barrick caught the girl's eye for a moment and she smiled shyly at him. He almost turned to make sure she was not looking over his shoulder at someone else.

"Thank you, Prince Barrick. You are very kind."

"Yes," answered his twin. "He is."

"And Princess Briony, of course." The girl smiled a little more carefully, but if she was startled by the growl in Briony's voice she did not show it. "Both of you, so very kind."

When they had passed through the Raven's Gate and acknowledged the salutes of the guards there, Selia paused. "I go from here to the queen. You are certain I do not go with you?"

"Yes," said Barrick's sister. "We are certain."

The girl made another courtesy and started off toward the Tower of Spring in the keep's outer wall. Barrick watched her walk.

"Ow!" he said. "Don't push."

"Your eyes are going to fall out of your head." Briony hurried her stride and turned into the long street that wound along the wall of the keep. The people who saw the twins moved respectfully out of their way, but it was a crowded, busy road full of wagons and loud arguments, and many scarcely noticed them, or did their best to make it appear that way. King Olin's court had never been as formal as his father's, and the people of the castle were used to his children walking around the keep without fanfare, accompanied only by a few guards.

"You're rude," Barrick told his sister. "You act like a commoner."

"Speaking of common," Briony replied, "all you men are alike. Any girl who bats her eyes and swings her hips when she walks into the room turns you all into drooling bears."

"Some girls *like* to have men look at them." Barrick's anger had congealed into a cold unhappiness. What did it matter? What woman would fall in love with him, anyway, with all his problems, his ruined arm and all his . . . strangeness? He would find a wife, of course, even one who would pretend to revere him—he was a prince, after all—but it would be a polite lie.

I will never know, he thought. *Not as long as I am of this family. I will never know what anyone truly thinks of me, what they think of the crippled prince. Because who would ever dare to mock the king's son to his face?*

"Some girls like to have men look at them, you say? How would you know?" Briony had turned her face from him now, which meant she was truly angry. "Some men are just horrid, the way they stare."

"You think that about all of them." Barrick knew he should stop, but he felt distant and miserable. "You hate all men. Father said he couldn't imagine finding someone you would agree to marry who would also agree to put up with your hardheadedness and your mannish tricks."

There was a sharp intake of breath, then a deathly silence. Now she was not speaking to him either. Barrick felt a pang, but told himself it was Briony who interfered first. It was also true, everyone talked about it. His sister kept the other women of the court at arm's length and the men even farther. Still, when she did not speak for half a hundred more steps, he began to worry. They were too close, the pair of them, and although both were fierce by nature, wounding the other was like wounding themselves. Their word-combats almost always moved to swift bloodletting, then an embrace before the wounds had even stopped seeping.

"I'm sorry," he said, although it didn't sound much like an apology. "Why should you care what Summerfield and Blueshore and those other fools think, anyway? They are useless, all of them, liars and bullies. I wish that war with the Autarch really would come and they would all be burned away like a field of grass."

"That's a terrible thing to say!" Briony snapped, but there was color in her cheeks again instead of the dreadful, shocked paleness of a moment before.

"So? I don't care about any of them," he said. "But I shouldn't have told you what Father said. He meant it as a joke."

"It is no joke to me." Briony was still angry, but he could tell that the worst of the fight was over. "Oh, Barrick," she said abruptly, "you will meet hordes of women who want to make eyes at you. You're a prince—even a bastard child from you would be a prize. You don't know how some girls are, how they think, what they'll do . . ."

He was surprised by the frightened sincerity in her voice. So she was trying to protect him from voracious women! He was pained but almost amused. *She doesn't seem to have noticed that the fairer sex are having no trouble resisting me so far.*

They had reached the bottom of the small hill on which Chaven's observatory-tower was set, its base nestled just inside the New Wall, its top looming above everything else in the castle except the four cardinal towers and the master of all, Wolfstooth Spire. As they climbed the spiral of steps, they put distance between themselves and the heavily armored guards.

"Hoy!" Barrick called down to the laboring soldiers. "You sluggards! What if there were murderers waiting for us at the top of the hill?"

"Don't be cruel," said Briony, but she was stifling a giggle.

Chaven—he probably had a second name, something full of Ulosian *as* and *os*, but the twins had never been told it and had never asked—was standing in a pool of light beneath the great observatory roof, which was open to the sky, although the clouds above were dark and a few solitary drops of rain spattered the stone floors. His assistant, a tall, sullen young man, stood waiting by a complicated apparatus of ropes and wooden cranks. The physician was kneeling over a large wooden case lined with velvet that appeared to contain a row of serving plates of different sizes. At the sound of their footsteps Chaven looked up.

He was small and round, with large, capable hands. The twins often joked about the unpredictability of the gods' gifts, since tall, rawboned Puzzle, with his gloomily absorbed manner, would have made a much better royal astrologer and physician, and the cheerful, mercurial, dexterous Chaven seemed perfectly formed to be a court jester.

But, of course, Chaven was also very, very clever—when he could be bothered.

"Yes?" he said impatiently, glancing in their direction. The physician had lived in the marchlands so long he had scarcely a trace of accent. "Do you seek someone?"

The twins had been through this before. "It's us, Chaven," Briony announced.

A smile lit his face. "Your Highnesses! Apologies—I am much absorbed with something I have just received, tools that will help me examine a star or a mote of dust with equal facility." He carefully lifted one of the plates, which proved to be made of solid glass, transparent as water. "Say what you wish about the unpleasantness of its governor, there are none in all the rest of Eion who can make a lens like the grinders of Hierosol." His mobile face darkened. "I am sorry—that was thoughtless, with your father a prisoner there."

Briony crouched down beside the case and reached a tentative hand toward one of the circles of glass, which gleamed in an angled beam of sunlight. "We have received something from this ship as well, a letter from our father, but Kendrick has not let us read it yet."

"Please, my lady!" Chaven said quickly, loudly. "Do not touch those! Even the smallest flaw can spoil their utility. . . ."

Briony snatched her hand back and caught it on the clasp of the wooden case. She grunted and lifted her finger. A drop of red grew on it, dribbled down toward her palm.

"Terrible! I am sorry. It is my fault for startling you." Chaven fussed in the pockets of his capacious robe, producing a handful of black cubes, then a curved glass pipe, a fistful of feathers, and at last a kerchief that looked as if it had been used to polish old brass.

Briony thanked him, then unobtrusively pocketed the dirty square of cloth and sucked the blood from her finger instead.

"So you have received no news yet?" the physician asked.

"The envoy is not to see Kendrick until noon." Barrick felt angry again, out of sorts. The sight of blood on his sister's hand troubled him. "Meanwhile, we are running an errand. Our stepmother wishes to see you."

"Ah." Chaven looked around as though wondering where his kerchief had got to, then shut the lenses back in their case. "I will go to her now, of course. Will you come with me? I wish to hear about the wyvern hunt. Your brother has promised me the carcass for examination and dissection, but I have not received it yet, although I hear troubling rumors he has already given the best parts of it away as trophies." He was already bustling toward the door, and called back over his shoulder, "Shut the roof, Toby. I have changed my mind—I think it will be too cloudy tonight for observation, in any case."

With a look of pure, weary despair, the young man began turning the huge crank. Slowly, inch by inch, with a noise like the death groan of some mythological beast, the great ceiling slid closed.

Outside, the twins' four heavily armored guards had reached the observatory door and had just stopped to catch their breath when the trio appeared and hurried past them down the stairs, bound for the Tower of Spring.

★   ★   ★

A girl no more than six years old opened the door to Anissa's chambers in the tower, made a courtesy, then stepped out of the way. The room was surprisingly bright. Dozens of candles burned in front of a flower-strewn shrine to Madi Surazem, goddess of childbirth, and in each corner of the room new sheaves of wheat stood in pots to encourage the blessing of fruitful Erilo. A half dozen silent ladies-in-waiting lurked around the great bed like cockindrills floating in one of the moats of Xis. An older woman with the sourly practical appearance of a midwife or hedge-witch took one look at Barrick and said, "He can't come in here. This is a place for women."

Before the prince could do more than bristle, his stepmother pulled aside the bed's curtains and peered out. Her hair was down, and she wore a voluminous white nightdress. "Who is it? Is it the doctor? Of course he can come to me."

"But it is the young prince as well, my lady," the old woman explained.

"Barrick?" She pronounced it *Bah-reek*. "Why are you such a fool, woman? I am respectably dressed. I am not giving birth today." She let out a sigh and collapsed back out of sight.

By the time Chaven and the twins had crossed the open floor to the bed, the curtains were open again, tied up by the maid Selia, who gave Barrick a quick smile, then caught sight of Briony and changed it to a respectful nod for both of them. Anissa reclined, propped upright on many pillows. Two tiny growling dogs tugged at a piece of cloth between her slippered feet. She was not wearing her usual pale face paint, and so looked almost ruddy with health. Barrick, who unlike Briony had not even tried to like his stepmother, was certain they had been summoned on a pointless errand whose real purpose was only to relieve Anissa's boredom.

"Children," she said to them, fanning herself. "It is kind of you to come. I am so ill, I see no one these days." Barrick could feel Briony's tiny flinch at being called a child by this woman. In fact, seeing her with her dark hair loose, and without her usual paint, he was surprised by how young their stepmother looked. She was only five or six years older than Kendrick, after all. She was pretty, too, in a fussy sort of way, although Barrick thought her nose a little too long for true beauty.

She does not compare to her maid, he thought, sneaking a glance, but Selia was looking solicitously at her mistress.

"You are feeling poorly, my queen?" asked Chaven.

"Pains in my stomach. Oh, I cannot tell you." Although she was small-boned and still slender even this close to giving birth, Anissa had a certain knack for dominating a room. Briony sometimes called her the Loud Mouse.

"And have you been faithfully taking the elixir I have made up for you?"

She waved her hand. "That? It binds up my insides. Can I say this, or is it impolite? My bowels have not moved for days."

Barrick had heard enough of the secrets of the sickbed for one day. He bowed to his stepmother, then backed toward the door and waited there. Anissa held his twin for a moment with impatient questions about the lack of news from the Hierosoline envoy and complaints that she had not been given Olin's letter before Kendrick, then Briony at last made a courtesy and edged away to join him. Together they watched Chaven kindly and quickly examine the queen, asking questions in such a normal tone of voice that it almost escaped Barrick's notice that the little round doctor was folding back her eyelid or sniffing her breath while doing so. The other women in the room had gone back to their stitching and conversation, excepting the old midwife, who watched the physician's activities with a certain territorial jealousy, and the maid Selia, who held Anissa's hand and listened as though everything her mistress said was pure wisdom.

"Your Highnesses, Briony, Barrick?" Despite the fact that he had one hand down the back of the queen's nightdress, Chaven had managed to take the small clock he wore on a chain out of the pocket of his robe. He held it up for them to see. "Noon is fast approaching. Which reminds me—have I told you of my plan to mount a large pendulum clock on the front of the Trigon temple, so that all can know the true time? For some reason, the hierarch is against the idea. . . ."

The twins listened politely for a moment to Chaven's grandiose and rather baffling plan, then made excuses to their stepmother before hurrying out of the Tower of Spring: they had a long way to go back across the keep. Their guards, who had been gossiping with the queen's warders, wearily pushed themselves away from the tower wall and trotted after them.

The crowd that was gathered in the huge Hall of the March Kings—only the Eddon family called it "the throne room," perhaps because the castle was their home as well as their seat of power—looked a much more serious group than the morning's disorganized rout. Briony again felt a clutch of worry. The castle almost appeared to be on war-footing: half a pentecount of guardsmen stood around the great room, not slouching and talking quietly among themselves like the twins' bodyguards, but rigidly erect and silent. Avin Brone, Count of Landsend, was one of the many nobles who had appeared for the audience. Brone was Southmarch Castle's lord constable and thus one of the most powerful men in the March Kingdoms. Decades earlier, he had made what turned out to be the shrewd choice of giving his unstinting support to the then child-heir Olin Eddon after the sudden death of Olin's brother, Prince Lorick, as King Ustin their father had been on his own deathbed, his heart failing. For a while, civil war had seemed likely as various powerful families had put themselves forward as the best protectors of the underage heir, but Brone had made some kind of bargain with the Tollys of Summerfield, Eddon relations and the chief claimants to a greater role in the governance of Southmarch, and then, with Steffans Nynor and a few others, Brone had managed to keep the child Olin on the throne by himself until he was old enough to rule without question. The twins' father had never forgotten that crucial loyalty, and titles and land and high responsibilities had fallen Brone's way thereafter. Whether the Count of Landsend's loyalty had been completely pure, or driven by the fact that he would have lost all chance for power under a Tolly protectorate was beside the point: everyone knew he was shrewd, always thinking beyond the present moment. Even now, in the midst of conversation with the court ladies or gentlemen, his eye was roving across the throne room to his guard troops, looking for sagging shoulders, bent knees, or a mouth moving in whispered conversation with a comrade.

Gailon Tolly, Duke of Summerfield, was in the Great Hall as well, along with most of the rest of the King's Council—Nynor the castellan, last of Brone's original allies; the twins' first cousin Rorick, Earl of Daler's Troth; Tyne Aldritch, Blueshore's earl; and a dozen other nobles, all wearing their best clothes.

Watching them, Briony felt a flame of indignation. *This ambassador comes from the man who has kidnapped my father. What are we doing, dressing up for him as though he were some honored visitor?* But when she whispered this thought to Barrick, he only shrugged.

"As you well know, it is for display. See, here is our power gathered!" he said sourly. "Like letting the roosters strut before the cockfight."

She looked at her brother's all-black garb and bit back a remark. *And they say we women are consumed with our appearances!* It was hard to imagine a lady of the court wearing the equivalent of the outrageous codpieces sported by

Earl Rorick and others of the male gentry—massive protrusions spangled with gems and intricate stitching. Trying to imagine what the women's equivalent might be threatened to set her laughing out loud, but it was not a pleasant feeling. The fear that had been gnawing at her all morning, as if the gods were tightening their grip on her and her home, made her feel that such a laugh, once started, would not stop—that she might end by having to be carried from the room, laughing and weeping together.

She looked around the massive hall, lit mostly by candles even at midday. The dark tapestries on every wall, figured with scenes of dead times and dead Eddon ancestors, made her feel close and hot, as though they were heavy blankets draped over her. Beyond the high windows she saw only the gray limestone prominence of the Tower of Winter with a blessed chink of cool sky on either side. Why, she wondered, in a castle surrounded by the water was there nowhere in that great hall that a person could look out on the sea? Briony felt suddenly out of breath. *Gods, why can't it all start?*

As if the heavenly powers had taken pity on her, a murmur rose from the crowd near the doorway as a small company of armored men in tabards decorated with what looked from this distance to be Hierosol's golden snail shell took up stations on either side of the entrance.

When the dark-skinned figure came through the door, Briony had a moment of bewilderment, wondering, *Why is everyone making such a fuss for Shaso?* Then she remembered what Summerfield had said. As the envoy came closer to the dais and Kendrick's makeshift throne, which he had set in front of his father's grander seat, she could see that this man was much younger than Southmarch's master of arms. The stranger was handsome, too, or Briony thought he was, but she found herself suddenly uncertain of how to judge one so different. His skin was darker than Shaso's, his tightly curled hair longer and tied behind his head, and he was tall and thin where the master of arms was stocky. He moved with a compact, self-assured grace, and the cut of his black hose and slashed gray doublet was as stylish as that of any Syannese court favorite. The knights of Hierosol who followed him seemed like clanking, pale-skinned puppets by comparison.

At the last moment, when it seemed to the entire room as though the envoy meant to do the unthinkable and walk up onto the very dais where the prince regent sat, the slender man stopped. One of the snail-shell knights stepped forward, cleared his throat.

"May it please Your Highness, I present Lord Dawet dan-Faar, envoy of Ludis Drakava, Lord Protector of Hierosol and all the Kracian Territories."

"Ludis may be Protector of Hierosol," Kendrick said slowly, "but he is also master of forced hospitality—of which my father is a recipient."

Dawet nodded once, smiled. His voice was like a big cat rumbling when it had no need yet to roar. "Yes, the Lord Protector is a famous host. Very few of his guests leave Hierosol unchanged."

There was a stir of resentment in the crowd at this. The envoy Dawet started to say something else, then stopped, his attention drawn to the great doors where Shaso stood in his leather armor, his face set in an expressionless mask. "Ah," Dawet said, "I had hoped to see my old teacher at least once more. Greetings, Mordiya Shaso."

The crowd whispered again. Briony looked at Barrick, but he was just as confused as she was. What could the dark man's words mean?

"You have business," Kendrick told him impatiently. "When you are finished, we will all have time to talk, even to remake old friendships, if friendships they are. Since I have not said so yet, let it be known to all that Lord Dawet is under the protection of the March King's Seal, and while he is engaged on his peaceful mission here none may harm or threaten him." His face was grim. He had done only what civility required. "Now, sir, speak."

Kendrick had not smiled, but Dawet did, examining the glowering faces around him with a look of quiet contentment, as though everything he could have wished was assembled in this one chamber. His gaze passed across Briony, then stopped and returned to her. His smile widened and she fought against a shiver. Had she not known who he was, she might have found it intriguing, even pleasing, but now it was like the touch of the dark wing she had imagined the day before, the shadow that was hovering over them all.

The envoy's long silence, his unashamed assessment, made her feel she stood naked in the center of the room. "What of our father?" she said out loud, her voice rough when she wished it could be calm and assured. "Is he well? I hope, for your master's sake, he is in good health."

"Briony!" Barrick was embarrassed—ashamed, perhaps, that she should speak out this way. But she was not one to be gawked at like a horse for sale. She was a king's daughter.

Dawet gave a little bow. "My lady. Yes, your father is well, and in fact I have brought a letter from him to his family. Perhaps the prince regent has not shown it to you yet . . . ?"

"Get on with it." Kendrick sounded oddly defensive. Something was going on, Briony knew, but she could not make out what it was.

"If he has read it, Prince Kendrick will perhaps have some inkling of what brings me here. There is, of course, the matter of the ransom."

"We were given a year," protested Gailon Tolly angrily. Kendrick did not look at him, although the duke, too, had spoken out of turn.

"Yes, but my master, Ludis, has decided to offer you another proposition, one to your advantage. Whatever you may think of him, the Lord Protector of Hierosol is a wise, farsighted man. He understands that we all have a common enemy, and thus should be seeking ways to draw our two countries together as twin bulwarks against the threat of the greedy lord of Xis, rather than squabbling over reparations."

"Reparations?" Kendrick said, struggling to keep his voice level. "Call it what it is, sir. Ransom. Ransom for an innocent man—a king!—kidnapped while he was trying to do just what you claim to want, which is organize a league against the Autarch."

Dawet gave a sinuous shrug. "Words can separate us or bring us together, so I will not quibble with you. There are more important issues, and I am here to present you with the Lord Protector's new and generous offer."

Kendrick nodded. "Continue." The prince regent's face was as empty as Shaso's, who was still watching from the far end of the throne room.

"The Lord Protector will reduce the ransom to twenty thousand gold dolphins—a fifth of what was asked and what you agreed to. In return, he asks only something that will cost you little, and will be of benefit to you as well as to us."

The courtiers were murmuring now, trying to make sense of what was going on. Some of the nobles, especially those whose peasantry had grown restive under the taxes for the king's ransom, even had hope on their faces. By contrast, Kendrick looked ashy.

"Damn you, speak your piece," he said at last—a croak.

Lord Dawet displayed an expression of carefully constructed surprise. *He looks like a warrior,* Briony thought, *but he plays the scene like a mummer. He is enjoying this.* But her older brother was not, and seeing him so pale and unhappy set her heart beating swiftly: Kendrick looked like a man trapped in an evil dream. "Very well," Dawet said. "In return for reducing the ransom for King Olin's return, Ludis Drakava, Lord Protector of Hierosol, will accept Briony te Meriel te Krisanthe M'Connord Eddon of Southmarch in marriage." The envoy spread his big, graceful hands. "In less high-flown terms, that would be your Princess Briony."

Suddenly, *she* was the one who was tumbling into nightmare. Faces turned toward her like a field of meadowsweet following the sun, pale faces, startled faces, calculating faces. She heard Barrick gasp beside her, felt his good hand clutch at her arm, but she was already pulling away. Her ears were roaring, the whispers of the assembled court now as loud as thunder.

"No!" she shouted. "Never!" She turned to Kendrick, suddenly understanding his chilled, miserable mask. "I will never do it!"

"It is not your turn to speak, Briony," he rasped. Something moved behind his eyes—despair? Anger? Surrender? "And this is not the place to discuss this matter."

"She can't!" Barrick shouted. The courtiers were talking loudly now, surprised and titillated. Some echoed Briony's own refusal, but not many. "I won't let you!"

"You are not the prince regent," Kendrick declared. "Father is gone. Until he comes back, I am your father. Both of you."

He meant to do it. Briony was certain. He was going to sell her to the bandit prince, the cruel mercenary Ludis, to reduce the ransom and keep the nobles happy. The ceiling of the great throne room and its tiled pictures of the gods seemed to swirl and drop down upon her in a cloud of dizzying colors. She turned and staggered through the murmuring, leering crowd, ignoring Barrick's worried cries and Kendrick's shouts, then slapped away Shaso's restraining hand and shoved her way out the great doors, already weeping so hard that the sky and the castle stones ran together and blurred.

5
Songs of the Moon and Stars

THE LOUD VOICE:

In a snail shell house
Beneath a root, where the sapphire lies
The clouds lean close, listening

—from *The Bonefall Oracles*

YOUNG FLINT DIDN'T seem very taken with the turnip porridge, even though it was sweetened with honey. *Well,* Chert thought, *perhaps it's a mistake to expect one of the big folk to feel the same way about root vegetables as we do.* Since Opal had gone off to the vent of warm subterranean air behind Old Quarry Square to dry the clothes she had washed, he took pity on the lad and removed the bowl.

"You don't need to finish," he said. "We're going out, you and I."

The boy looked at him, neither interested nor disinterested. "Where?"

"The castle—the inner keep."

A strange expression flitted across the child's face but he only rose easily from the low stool and trotted out the door before Chert had gathered up his own things. Although he had only come down Wedge Road for the first time the night before, the boy turned unhesitatingly to the left. Chert was impressed with his memory. "You'd be right if we were going up, lad, but we're not. We're taking Funderling roads." The boy looked at him questioningly. "Going through the tunnels. It's faster for the way we're going. Besides, last night I wanted to show you a bit of what was aboveground—now you get to see a bit more of what's down here."

They strolled down to the bottom of Wedge Road, then along Beetle Way to Ore Street, which was wide and busy, full of carts and teams of diggers and cutters on their way to various tasks, many leaving on long journeys to distant cities that would keep them away for half a year or more, since the work of the Funderlings of Southmarch was held in high regard nearly everywhere in Eion. There was much to watch in the orderly spoked wheel of streets at the center of Funderling Town, peddlers bringing produce down from the markets in the city above, honers and polishers crying their trades, and tribes of children on their way to guild schools, and Flint was wide-eyed. The day-lanterns were lit everywhere, and in a few places raw autumn sunlight streamed down through holes in the great roof, turning the streets golden, although all in all the day outside looked mostly dark.

Chert saw many folk he knew, and most called out greetings. A few saluted young Flint as well, even by name, although others looked at the boy with suspicion or barely-masked dislike. At first, Chert was astonished that anyone knew the boy's new name, but then realized Opal had been talking with the other women. News traveled fast in the close confines of Funderling Town.

"Most times we'd turn here," he said, gesturing at the place near the Gravelers Meeting Hall where the ordered ring of roads began to become a little less ordered and Ore Street forked into two thoroughfares, one level, one slanting downward, "but the way we're going all the tunnels aren't finished yet, so we're making a stop at the Salt Pool first. When we get there you have to be quiet and you can't cut up."

The boy was busy looking at the chiseled facades of the houses, each one portraying a complicated web of family history (not all of the histories strictly true) and did not ask what the Salt Pool might be. They walked for a quarter of an hour down Lower Ore Street until they reached the rough, largely undecorated rock that marked the edge of town. Chert led the boy past men and a few women idling by the roadside—most waiting by the entrances to the Pool in hopes of catching a day's work somewhere—and through a surprisingly modest door set in a wall of raw stone, into the glowing cavern.

The Pool itself was a sort of lake beneath the ground; it filled the greater part of the immense natural cave. It was salt water, an arm of the ocean that reached all the way into the stone on which the castle stood, and was the reason that even in the dimmest recesses of their hidden town the Funderlings always knew when the tides were high or low. The rim of the lake was rough, the stones sharp and spiky, and the dozens of other Funderlings who were already there moved carefully. It would have been the work of a few weeks at the most to make the cavern and its rocky shore as orderly as the middle of town, but even the most improvement-mad of Chert's people had never seriously considered it. The Salt Pool was one of the centers of earliest Funderling legend—one of their oldest stories told how the god the big folk called Kernios, who the Funderlings in their own secret language named "Lord of the Hot Wet Stone," created their race right there on the Salt Pool's shores in the Days of Cooling.

Chert did not explain any of this to the boy. He was not certain how long the child would stay with them and the Funderlings were cautious with outsiders; it was far too early even to consider teaching him any of the Mysteries.

The boy scrambled across the uneven, rocky floor like a spider, and he was already waiting, watchful features turned yellow-green by the light from the pool, when Chert reached the shore. Chert had only just taken off his pack and set it down by the boy's feet when a tiny, crooked-legged figure appeared from a jumble of large stones, wiping its beard as it swallowed the last bite of something.

"Is that you, Chert? My eyes are tired today." The little man who stood before them only reached Chert's waist. The boy stared down at the newcomer with unhidden surprise.

"It is me, indeed, Boulder." Now the boy looked at Chert, as surprised by the name as by the stranger's size. "And this is Flint. He's staying with us." He shrugged. "That was Opal's idea."

The little fellow peered up at the boy and laughed. "I suppose there's a tale there. Are you in too much of a hurry to tell it to me today?"

"Afraid so, but I'll owe it to you."

"Two, then?"

"Yes, thank you." He took a copper chip out of his pocket and gave it to the tiny man, who put it in the pouch of his wet breeches.

"Back in three drips," said Boulder, then scampered back down the rocky beach toward the water, almost as nimble as the boy despite his bent legs and his many years.

Chert saw Flint staring after him. "That's the first thing you have to learn about our folk, boy. We're not dwarfs. We are meant to be this size. There are big folk who are small—not children like you, but just small—and those are dwarfs. And there are Funderlings who are small compared to *their* fellows, too, and Boulder is one of those."

"Boulder . . . ?"

"His parents named him that, hoping it would make him grow. Some tweak him about it, but seldom more than once. He is a good man but he has a sharp tongue."

"Where did he go?"

"He is diving. There's a kind of stone that grows in the Salt Pool, a stone that is made by a little animal, like a snail makes a shell for itself, called *coral*. The coral that grows in the Salt Pool makes its own light . . ."

Before he could finish explaining, Boulder was standing before them, holding a chunk of the glowing stuff in each hand; even though it was starting to darken after having been taken from the water, the light was still so bright that Chert could see the veins in the little man's fingers. "These have just kindled," he said with satisfaction. "They should last you all day, maybe even longer."

"We won't need them such a time, but my thanks." Chert took out two pieces of hollow horn from his pack, both polished to glassy thinness, and dropped a piece of coral into each, then filled them with a bit of salt water from Boulder's bucket to wake the light and keep the little animals inside the coral alive. Submerged in the water, the stony clumps began to glow again.

"Don't you want reflecting bowls?" asked Boulder.

Chert shook his head. "We won't be working, only traveling. I just want us to be able to see each other." He capped both hollow horns with bone plugs, then took a fitted leather hood out of his bag, tied it onto Flint's head, and put one of the glowing cups of seawater and coral into the little harness on the front of the hood above the boy's eyes. He did the same for himself, then they bade Boulder farewell and made their way back across the cavern of the Salt Pool. The boy moved in erratic circles, watching the light from his brow cast odd shadows as he scrambled from stone to stone.

Although the road had been braced and paved, it was so far out along the network of tunnels that it had no name yet. The boy, only named himself the night before, did not seem to mind.

"Where are we?"

"Now? Even with the gate to Funderling Town, more or less, but it's a good way back over there. We're passing away from it and along the line of the inner keep wall. I think the last new road we crossed, Greenstone or whatever they're calling it now, climbs back up and lets out quite close to the gate."

"Then we're going past . . . past . . ." The boy thought for a moment. "Past the bottom of the tower with the golden feather on top of it."

Chert stopped, surprised. The boy had not only remembered a small detail on the tower's roof from the previous afternoon's walk, but had calculated the distances and directions, too. "How can you know that?"

Little Flint shrugged, the keen intelligence suddenly hidden behind the gray eyes again like a deer moving from a patch of sunlight into shadow.

Chert shook his head. "You're right, though, we're passing underneath the Tower of Spring—although not right under it. Once we come up out of the deepest parts of Funderling Town, we don't go directly under the inner keep. None of the high Funderling roads do. It's . . . forbidden."

The boy sucked on his lip, thinking again. "By the king?"

Chert was certainly not going to delve straight into the deep end of the Mysteries, but something in him did not want to lie to the child. "Yes, certainly, the king is part of it. They do not want us to tunnel under the heart of the castle in case the outer keep, and Funderling Town, should be overrun in a siege."

"But there's another reason." It was not a question but a disconcertingly calm assertion.

Chert could only shrug. "There is seldom only one reason for anything in this world."

He led the boy upward through a series of increasingly haphazard diggings. Their ultimate destination was inside the inner keep, and the fact that they could actually reach it from the tunnels of Funderling Town was a secret that only Chert of all his people knew—or at least he believed that was the case. His own knowledge was the result of a favor done long ago, and although it was conceivable someone could use this route as a way of going under the wall of the inner keep and attacking the castle itself, he couldn't imagine anyone not of Funderling blood and upbringing finding their way through the maze of half-finished tunnels and raw scrapes.

But what about the boy? he thought suddenly. *He's already shown he has a fine memory.* But surely even those clever, hooded eyes could not remember every twist and turn, the dozens of switchbacks, the crossings honeycombed with dozens of false trails that would lead anyone but Chert down endless empty passages and, if they were lucky enough not to be lost in the maze forever, eventually funnel them back into the main roads of Funderling Town.

Still, could he really risk the secret route with this child, of whom he knew so little?

He stared at the boy laboring along beside him in the sickly coral-light, putting one foot in front of the other without a word of complaint. Despite the child's weird origins Chert could sense nothing bad in him, and it was hard to believe anyone could choose one so young as a spy, not to mention plan with such skill that the one person who knew these tunnels would wind up taking the child into his home. It was all too far-fetched. Besides, he reminded himself, if he changed his mind now, he would not only have wasted much of the day, he would have to present himself at the Raven's Gate and try to talk his way past the guards and into the inner keep that way. He didn't think they were likely to let him in, even if he told them who he was going to see. And if he told them the substance of his errand, it would be all over the castle by nightfall, causing fear and wild stories. No, he would have to go forward and trust his own good sense, his luck.

It was only as they turned down the last passage and into the final tunnel that he remembered that "Chert's luck"—at least within his own Blue Quartz family—was another way of saying "no luck at all."

The boy stared at the door. It was a rather surprising thing to find at the end of half a league of tunnels that were little more than hasty burrows, the kind of crude excavations that Funderling children got up to before they were old enough to be apprenticed to one of the guilds. But this door was a beautiful thing, if such could be said of a mere door, hewn of dark hardwoods that gleamed in the light of the coral stones, its hinges of heavy iron overlaid with filigree patterns in bronze. All that trouble, and for whom? Chert knew of no one else beside himself who ever used it, and this was only his third time in ten years.

It didn't even have a latch or a handle, at least on the outside.

Chert reached up and pulled at a braided cord that hung through a hole in the door. It was a heavy pull, and whatever bell it rang was much too far away to hear, so Chert pulled it again just to make certain. They had what seemed a long wait—Chert was just about to tug the cord a third time—before the door swung inward.

"Ah, is it Master Blue Quartz?" The round man's eyebrows rose. "And a friend, I see."

"Sorry to trouble you, sir." Chert was suddenly uncomfortable—why had he thought it would be a good idea to bring the boy with him? Surely he could simply have described him. "This boy is . . . well, he's staying with us. And he's . . . he's part of what I wanted to talk to you about. Something important." He was uncomfortable now, not because Chaven's expression was unkind, but because he had forgotten how sharp the physician's eyes were—like the boy's but with nothing hidden, a fierce, fierce cleverness that was always watching.

"Well, then we must step inside where we can talk comfortably. I am sorry to have kept you waiting, but I had to send away the lad who works for me before I came. I do not share the secret of these tunnels lightly." Chaven smiled, but Chert wondered if what the physician was politely not saying was, *Even if some others do.*

He led them down a series of empty corridors, damp and windowless because they were below the ground-floor chambers, passages set directly into the rocky hill beneath the observatory.

"I told you the truth," Chert whispered to the boy. "About not digging under the inner keep, that is. You see, we've just crossed under its walls, but not until we were inside this man's house, as it were. Our end of the tunnel stops outside the keep."

The boy looked at him as though the Funderling had claimed he could juggle fish while whistling, and even Chert was not sure why he felt compelled to point out this distinction. What loyalty could the boy have to the royal family? Or to Chert himself, for that matter, except for the kindness of a bed and a few meals?

Chaven led them up several flights of stairs until they reached a small, carpeted room. Jars and wooden chests were stacked along the walls and on shelves, as though the room was as much a pantry as a retiring room. The small windows were covered with tapestries whose night-sky colors were livened by winking gems in the shapes of constellations.

The physician was more fit than he appeared: of the three of them, Chert alone was winded by the climb. "Can I offer you something to eat or drink?" asked Chaven. "It might take me a moment to fetch. I've sent Toby off on an errand and I'd just as soon not tell any of the servants there's a guest here who didn't come in through any of the doors—at least any of the doors they know about . . ."

Chert waved away the offer. "I would love to drink with you in a civilized way, sir, but I think I had better get right to the seam, as it were. Is the boy all right, looking around?"

Flint was moving slowly around the room, observing but not handling the various articles standing against the wall, mostly lidded vessels of glass and polished brass.

"I think so," Chaven said, "but perhaps I should withold my judgment until you tell me what exactly brings you here—and him with you."

Chert described what he had seen the day before in the hills north of the castle. The physician listened, asking few questions, and when the little man had finished, he didn't speak for a long time. Flint was done examining the room and now sat on the floor, looking up at the tapestries and their twining patterns of stars.

"I am not surprised," Chaven said at last. "I had . . . heard things. Seen things. But it is still fearful news."

"What does it mean?"

The physician shook his head. "I can't say. But the Shadowline is something whose art seems far beyond ours, and whose mystery we have never solved. Scarcely anyone who passes it returns, and those who have done so are no longer in their right minds. Our only solace has been that it has not moved in centuries—but now it is moving again. I have to think that it will keep moving unless something stops it, and what would that be?" He rose, rubbing his hands together.

"Keep moving . . . ?"

"Yes, I fear that now it has started the Shadowline will keep moving until it has swept across Southmarch—perhaps all of Eion. Until the land is plunged back into shadow and Old Night." The physician frowned at his hands, then turned back to Flint. His voice was matter-of-fact but his eyes belied it. "Now I suppose I had better have a look at the boy."

Moina and Rose and her other ladies, despite all their kind words and questions, could not stop Briony's furious weeping. She was angry with herself for acting so wildly, so childishly, but she felt lost beyond help or even hope. It was as though she had fallen down a deep hole and was now beyond the reach of anyone.

Barrick pounded at the chamber door, demanding that she speak to him.

He sounded angry and frightened, but although it felt as if she were casting off a part of her own body, she let Rose send him away. He was a man—what did he know of how she felt? No one would dream of selling *him* to the highest bidder like a market pig.

Eighty thousand dolphins discounted for my sake, she thought bitterly. A great deal of gold—most of a king's ransom, in fact. *I should be proud to command such a high price.* She threw a pillow against the wall and knocked over an oil lamp. The ladies squealed as they rushed to stamp out the flames, but Briony did not care if the entire castle burned to the ground.

"What goes on here?"

Treacherous Rose had opened the door, but it was not Barrick who had come in, only Briony's great-aunt, the Dowager Duchess Merolanna, sniffing. Her eyes widened as she saw Moina smothering the last of the flames and she turned on Briony. "What are you doing, child, trying to kill us all?"

Briony wanted to say yes, she was, but another fit of weeping overcame her. As the other ladies tried to fan the smoke out the open door, Merolanna came to the bed and sat her substantial but carefully groomed self down on it, then put her arms around the princess.

"I have heard," she said, patting Briony's back. "Do not be so afraid—your brother may refuse. And even if he doesn't, it isn't the worst thing in the world. When I first came here to wed your father's uncle, years and years and years ago, I was as frightened as you are."

"But Ludis is a m–monster!" Briony struggled to stop sobbing. "A murderer! The bandit who kidnapped our father! I would rather marry . . . marry anyone—even old Puzzle—before allowing someone like that . . ." It was no use. She was weeping again.

"Now, child," Merolanna said, but clearly could think of nothing else to say.

Her great-aunt had gone, and Briony's ladies-in-waiting kept their distance, as though their mistress had some illness which might spread—and indeed she did, Briony thought, because unhappiness was ambitious.

A messenger had just arrived at the door, the third in an hour. She had returned no message to her older brother, and hadn't been able to think of anything sufficiently cutting to send back to Gailon, Duke of Summerfield.

"This one comes from Sister Utta, my lady," Moina said. "She sends to ask why you have not visited her today, and if you are well."

"She must be the only one in the castle who doesn't know," said Rose, almost laughing that anyone could be so remote from the day's events. A look at Briony's tearstained face and the lord constable's niece quickly sobered. "We'll tell her you can't come . . ."

Briony sat up. She had forgotten her tutor entirely, but suddenly wanted nothing more than to see the Vuttish woman's calm face, hear her measured voice. "No. I will go to her."

"But, Princess . . ."

"I will go!" As she struggled into a wrap, the ladies-in-waiting hurried to pull on their own shoes and cloaks. "Stay here. I am going by myself." The feared darkness having enfolded her now, she felt no need to waste her strength on niceties. "I have guards. Don't you think that's enough to keep me from running away?"

Rose and Moina stared at her in hurt surprise, but Briony was already striding out the door.

Utta was one of the Sisters of Zoria, priestesses of the virgin goddess of learning. Zoria once had been the most powerful of goddesses, some said, mistress of a thousand temples and an equal of even her divine father Perin, but now her followers had been reduced to advising the Trigon on petty domestic policy and teaching highborn girl-children how to read, write, and—although it was not deemed strictly necessary in most noble families—to think.

Utta herself was almost as old as Duchess Merolanna, but where Briony's great-aunt was a royal barge, elaborately painted and decorated, the Vuttish woman was spare as a fast sailing ship, tall and thin, with gray hair cropped almost to her scalp. She was sewing when Briony arrived, and her pale blue eyes opened wide when the girl immediately burst into tears, but although her questions were sympathetic and she listened carefully to the answers, the priestess of Zoria was not the type to put her arms around even her most important pupil.

When Briony had finished the story, Utta nodded her head slowly. "As you say, our lot is hard. In this life we women are handed from one man to another, and can only hope that the one we come to at last will be a kind steward of our liberties."

"But no man owns you." Briony had recovered herself a little. Something strong about Utta, the unassuming strength of an old tree on a windy mountainside, always calmed her. "You do what you want, without a husband or a master."

Sister Utta smiled sadly. "I do not think you would wish to give up all I have given up to become so, Princess. And how can you say I have no master? Should your father—or now your brother—decide to send me away or even kill me, I would be trudging down Market Road within an hour or hanging from one of the mileposts."

"It's not fair! And I won't do it."

Utta nodded again, as if she was truly considering what Briony said. "When it comes to it, no woman can be turned against her own soul unless she wills it. But perhaps it is too early for you to be worrying. You do not know yet what your brother will say."

"Oh, but I do." The words tasted bitter in her mouth. "The council—in fact, almost all the nobles—have been complaining for months about the price of Father's ransom, and they have also been telling Kendrick that I should be married off to some rich southern princeling to help pay for it. Then when he resists them, they whisper behind their hands that he is not old enough yet to rule the March Kingdoms. Here is a chance for him to stop their moaning in an instant. I'd do it, if I were him."

"But you are not Kendrick, and you have not yet heard his decision." Now Utta did an unusual thing, leaned over and for a moment took Briony's hand. "However, I will not say your worries are baseless. What I hear of Ludis Drakava is not encouraging."

"I won't do it! I won't. It is all so unfair—the clothes they always want me to wear, the things they want me to say and do . . . and now this! I hate being a woman. It's a curse." Briony looked up suddenly. "I could become a priestess, like you! If I became a Sister of Zoria, my maidenhood would be sacred, wouldn't it?"

"And permanent." Utta could not quite muster a smile this time. "I am not certain you could join the sisterhood against your brother's wishes, anyway. But is it not too early to be thinking of such things?"

Briony had a sudden recollection of the envoy Dawet dan-Faar, of eyes proud and leopard-fierce. He did not seem the type to stand around for weeks waiting for a defeated enemy to agree to the terms of surrender. "I don't think I have much time—until tomorrow, perhaps. Oh, Sister, what will I do?"

"Talk to your brother, the prince regent. Tell him how you feel. I believe he is a good man, like your father. If there seems no other way . . . well, perhaps there is advice I might give you then, even assistance." For a moment, Utta's long, strong face looked troubled. "But not yet." She sat up straight.

"We have an hour left before the evening meal, Princess. Shall we spend it usefully? Learning may perhaps keep your mind off your sorrows, at least for a little while."

"I suppose." Briony had cried so much she felt boneless. The room was quite dark, with only one candle lit. Most of the light in the spare apartment came from the window, a descending beam that ended in a bright oblong climbing steadily higher on the wall as the sun dropped toward its evening harbor. Earlier she had felt sure the worst had happened, but now she thought she could feel the shadowy wings still beating above her, as if there was some threat as yet undiscovered.

"Teach me something, then," she said heavily. "What else do I have left?"

"You have learning, yes," Utta told her. "But you also have prayers. You must not forget your prayers, child. And you have Zoria's protection, if you deserve it. There are worse things to cling to."

Finished examining the boy, Chaven reached into his pockets and produced a disk of glass pent in a brass handle. Flint took it from him and looked through it, first staring up at the flickering lamp, then moving it close to the wall so he could examine the grain of stone in the spaces between the tapestries.

Maybe he'll make a Funderling yet, thought Chert.

The boy turned to him, smiling, one eye goggling hugely behind the glass. Chert laughed despite himself. At the moment, Flint seemed to be no more than he appeared, a child of five or six summers.

Chaven thought so, too. "I find nothing unusual about him," the physician said quietly as they watched the boy playing with the enlarging-glass. "No extra fingers, toes, or mysterious marks. His breath is sweet—for a child who seems to have eaten spiced turnips today, that is—and his eyes are clear. Everything about him seems ordinary. This all proves nothing, but unless some other mysterious trait shows itself, I must for the moment assume he is what your wife guessed him to be, some mortal child who wandered beyond the Shadowline and, instead of wandering back again as some do, met the riders you saw and was carried out instead." Chaven frowned. "You say he has little memory of who he is. If that is all he has lost, he is a lucky one. As I said before, those who have wandered across and returned before now have had the whole of their wits clouded if not ruined."

"Lucky. Yes, it seems that way." Chert should have been relieved, especially since the child would be sharing their house for at least the present, but he could not rid himself of a nagging feeling that there was something more to be discovered. "But why, if the Shadowline is moving, would the . . . the Quiet Folk oh-so-kindly carry a mortal child across the line? It seems more likely they would slit his throat like a rabbit and leave him in the foggy forest somewhere."

Chaven shrugged. "I have no answer, my friend. Even when they were slaughtering mortals long ago at Coldgray Moor, the Twilight People did things that no one could understand. In the last months of the war, one company of soldiers from Fael moving camp by midnight stumbled onto a fairy-feast, but instead of slaughtering them—they were far outnumbered—the Qar only fed them and led them into drunken revels. Some of the soldiers even claimed they mated with fairy women that night."

"The . . . Qar?"

"Their old name." Chaven waved his hand. "I have spent much of my life studying them but I still know little more than when I began. They can be unexpectedly kind to mortals, even generous, but do not doubt that if the Shadowline sweeps across us, it will bring with it a dark, dark evil."

Chert shuddered. "I have spent too much time on its borders to doubt that for a moment." He watched the boy for a moment. "Will you tell the prince regent and his family that the line has moved?"

"I expect I will have to. But first I must think on all this, so that I can go to them with some proposal. Otherwise, decisions will be made in fear and ignorance, and those seldom lead to happy result." Chaven rose from his stool and patted his bunched robe until it hung straight again. "Now I must get back to my work, not least of which will be thinking about the news you've brought me."

As Chert led Flint to the door, the boy turned back. "Where is the owl?" he asked Chaven.

The physician stiffened for a moment, then smiled. "What do you mean, lad? There is no owl here, nor ever has been one, as far as I know."

"There was," Flint said stubbornly. "A white one."

Chaven shook his head kindly as he held the door, but Chert thought he looked a little discomposed.

After checking to make sure none of his servants were in sight, the physician let Chert and the boy out through the observatory-tower's front

door. For reasons he did not quite know himself, Chert had decided to go
back aboveground, out through the Raven's Gate. The guard would have
changed at midday and there should be no reason for those on duty now
to doubt that their predecessors questioned Chert closely before letting
him and his young charge into the inner keep.

"What did you mean about the owl?" Chert asked as they made their
way down the steps.

"What owl?"

"You asked that man where the owl was, the owl that had been in his
room."

Flint shrugged. His legs were longer than Chert's and he did not need
to look down at the steps, so he was watching the afternoon sky. "I don't
know." He frowned, staring at something above him. The morning's clouds
had passed. Chert could see nothing but a faint sliver of moon, white as a
seashell, hanging in the blue sky. "He had stars on his walls."

Chert recalled the tapestries covered with jeweled constellations. "He
did, yes."

"The Leaf, the Singers, the White Root—I know a song about them."
He pondered, his frown deepening. "No, I can't remember it."

"The Leaf . . . ?" Chert was puzzled. "The White Root? What are you
talking about?"

"The stars—don't you know their names?" Flint had reached the cob-
blestones at the base of the steps and was walking faster, so that Chert, still
moving carefully down the tall steps, could barely make out what he said.
"There's the Honeycomb and the Waterfall . . . but I can't remember the
rest." He stopped and turned. His face beneath the shock of almost white
hair was full of sad confusion, so that he looked like a little old man. "I can't
remember."

Chert caught up to him, out of breath and troubled. "I've never heard
those names before. The Honeycomb? Where did you learn that, boy?"

Flint was walking again. "I used to know a song about the stars. I know
one about the moon, too." He hummed a snatch of melody that Chert
could barely make out, but whose mournful sweetness made the hairs lift
on the back of his neck. "I can't remember the words," Flint said. "But they
tell about how the moon came down to find the arrows he had shot at the
stars . . ."

"But the moon's a woman—isn't that what all you big folk believe?" A
moment of sour amusement at his own words—the boy was but Chert's

own height, even a little shorter—did not puncture his confusion. "Mesiya, the moon-goddess?"

Flint laughed with a child's pure enjoyment at the foolishness of adults. "No, he's the sun's little brother. Everyone knows that."

He skipped ahead, enjoying the excitement of a street full of people and interesting sights, so that Chert had to hurry to catch up with him again, certain that something had just happened—something important—but he could not for the life of him imagine what it might have been.

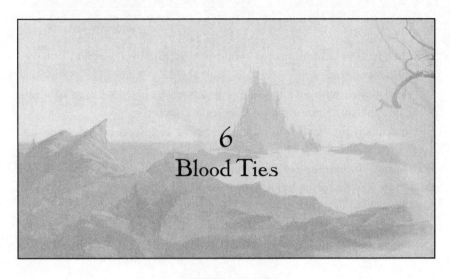

6
Blood Ties

A HIDDEN PLACE:

Walls of straw, walls of hair
Each room can hold three breaths
Each breath an hour

—from *The Bonefall Oracles*

SHE DID NOT MAKE her dwelling in the ancient, labyrinthine
city of Qul-na-Qar, although she had long claim to a place of honor
there, by her blood and by her deeds—and by deeds of blood as well.
Instead, she made her home on a high ridgetop in the mountains called
Reheq-s'Lai, which meant Wanderwind, or something close to it. Her
house, although large enough to cover most of the ridge, was a plain thing
from most angles, as was the lady herself. Only when the sunlight was in
the right quarter, and a watcher's face turned just so, could crystal and sky-
stone be seen gleaming among the dark wall stones. In one way at least her
house was like great Qul-na-Qar: it extended deep into the rocky ridge,
with many rooms below the light of day and a profusion of tunnels extending beyond them like the roots of an old, old tree. Above the ground
the windows were always shuttered, or seemed that way. Her servants were
silent and she seldom had visitors.

Some of the younger Qar, who had heard of her madness for privacy,
but of course had never seen her, called her Lady Porcupine. Others who
knew her better could not help shuddering at the accidental truth of the

name—they had seen how in moments of fury a nimbus of prickly shadow bloomed about her, a shroud of phantom thorns.

Her granted name was Yasammez, but few knew it. Her true name was known to only two or three living beings.

The lady's high house was called *Shehen,* which meant "Weeping." Because it was a s'a-Qar word, it meant other things, too—it carried the intimation of an unexpected ending, and a suggestion of the scent of the plant that in the sunlight lands was called myrtle—but more than anything else, it meant "Weeping."

It was said that Yasammez had only laughed twice in all her long life, the first time when, as a child, she first saw a battlefield and smelled the blood and the smoke from the fires. The second time had been when she had first been exiled, sent away from Qul-na-Qar for crimes or deeds of arrogance long since forgotten by most of the living. "You cannot hide me, or hide from me," she is said to have told her accusers, "because you cannot find me. I was lost when I first drew breath." Yasammez was made for war and death, all agreed, as a sword is made, a thing whose true beauty can only be seen when it brings destruction.

It was also said that she would laugh for the third time only when the last mortal died, or when she herself took her final breath.

None of the stories said anything about the sound of her laughter, except that it was terrible.

Yasammez stood in her garden of low, dark plants and tall gray rocks shaped like the shadows of terrified dreamers, and looked out over her steep lands. The wind was as fierce as ever, wrapping her cloak tightly around her, blowing her hair loose from the bone pins that held it, but was still not strong enough to disperse the mist lurking in the ravines that gouged the hillside below like claw-scratches. Still, it blew loudly enough that even if any of her pale servants had been standing beside her they would not have been able to hear the melody Lady Yasammez was singing to herself, nor would they even have believed their mistress might do such a thing. They certainly would not have known the song, which had been old before the mountain on which she stood had risen from the earth.

A voice began to speak in her ear and the ancient music stopped. She did not turn because she knew the voice came from no one in the stark garden or high house. Secretive, angry, and solitary as she was, Yasammez still knew this voice almost better than she knew her own. It was the only voice that ever called her by her true name.

It called that name again now.

"*I hear, O my heart,*" said Lady Porcupine, speaking without words. "*I must know.*"

"*It has already begun,*" the mistress of the ridgetop house replied, but it stabbed her to hear such disquiet in the thoughts of her beloved, her great ruler, the single star in her dark, cold sky. After all, this was the time for wills to become stony, for hearts to grow thorns. "*All has been put into motion. As you wished. As you commanded.*"

"*There is no turning back, then.*"

It almost seemed a question, but Yasammez knew it could not be. "*No turning back,*" she agreed.

"*So, then. In the full raveling of time we will see what new pages will be written in the Book.*"

"*We shall.*" She yearned to say more, to ask why this sudden concern that almost seemed like weakness in the one who was not just her ruler but her teacher as well, but the words did not come; she could not form the question even in the silence of shared thought. Words had never been friends to Yasammez; in this, they were like almost everything else beneath the moon or sun.

"*Farewell, then. We will speak again soon, when your great task reaches fulfillment. You have my gratitude.*"

Then Lady Porcupine was alone again with the wind and her thoughts, her strange, bitter thoughts, in the garden of the house called Weeping.

The longer, heavier sword skimmed off Barrick's falchion and crashed down against the small buckler on his left arm. A lightning flash of pain leaped through his shoulder. He cried out, sagged to one knee, and only just managed to throw his blade up in time to deflect the second blow. He climbed to his feet and stood, gasping for breath. The air was full of sawdust. He could barely hold even his own slender sword upright.

"Stop." He stepped back, letting the falchion sag, but instead of lowering his own longer sword, Shaso suddenly lunged forward, the point of his blade jabbing down at Barrick's ankles. Caught by surprise, the prince hesitated for an instant before jumping to avoid the thrust. It was a mistake. As the prince landed awkwardly, the old man had already turned his sword around so he clutched the blade in his gauntlets. He thumped Barrick hard in the chest with the sword's pommel, forcing out the rest of the boy's air. Gasping, Barrick took one step backward and collapsed. For a moment black clouds closed in. When he could see again, Shaso was standing over him.

"Curse you!" Barrick wheezed. He kicked out at Shaso's leg, but the old man stepped neatly away. "Didn't you hear? I said stop!"

"Because your arm was tired? Because you did not sleep well last night? Is that what you will do in battle? Cry mercy because you fight only with one hand and it has wearied?" Shaso made a noise of disgust and turned his back on the young prince. It was all Barrick could do not to scramble to his feet at this display of contempt and skull the old Tuani with the padded falchion.

But it was not just his remaining shreds of civility and honor that stopped him, nor his exhaustion; even in his rage, Barrick doubted he would actually land the blow.

He got up slowly instead and pulled off the buckler and gauntlets so he could rub his arm. Although his left hand was curled into something like a bird's claw and his forearm was thin as a child's, after countless painful hours lifting the iron-headed weights called *poises* Barrick had strengthened the sinews of his upper arm and shoulder enough that he could use the buckler effectively. But—and he hated to admit it, and certainly would not do so aloud—Shaso was right: he still was not strong enough, not even in the good arm which had to wield his only blade, since even a dagger was too much for his crippled fingers.

As he pulled on the loose deerskin glove he wore to hide his twisted hand, Barrick was still furious. "Does it make you feel strong, beating a man who can only fight one-armed?"

The armorers, who today had the comparatively quiet task of cutting new leather straps at the huge bench along the room's south wall, looked up, but only for a moment—they were used to such things. Barrick had no doubt they all thought him a spoiled child. He flushed and slammed down his gauntlets.

Shaso, who was unstitching his padded practice-vest, curled his lip. "By the hundred tits of the Great Mother, boy, I am not beating you. I am teaching you."

They had been out of balance all day. Even as a way to spend the tedious, stretching hours until his brother convened the council, this had been a mistake. Briony might have made it something civil, even enjoyable, but Briony was not there.

Barrick lowered himself to the ground and began removing his leg pads. He stared at Shaso's back, irritated by the old man's graceful, unhurried movements. Who was he, to be so calm when everything was falling apart? Barrick wanted to sting the master of arms somehow.

"Why did he call you 'teacher'?"

Shaso's fingers slowed, but he did not turn. "What?"

"You know. The envoy from Hierosol—that man Dawet. Why did he call you 'teacher?' And he called you something else—'Mor-ja.' What does that mean?"

Shaso shrugged off the vest. His linen undershirt was soaked with sweat, so that every muscle on his broad, brown back was apparent. Barrick had seen this so many times, and even in the midst of anger, he felt something like love for the old Tuani—a love for the known and familiar, however unsatisfying.

What if Briony really leaves? he thought suddenly. *What if Kendrick really sends her to Hierosol to marry Ludis? I will never see her again.* His outrage that a bandit should demand his sister in marriage, and that his brother should even consider it, suddenly chilled into a simpler and far more devastating thought—Southmarch Castle empty of Briony.

"I have been asked to answer that for the council," Shaso said slowly. "You will hear what I say there, Prince Barrick. I do not want to speak of it twice." He dropped the vest to the floor and walked away from it. Barrick could not help staring. Shaso was usually not only meticulous in the care of his weapons and equipment, but sharp-tongued to any who were not—Barrick most definitely included. The master of arms set the long sword in the rack without oiling it or even taking off the padding, took his shirt from a hook, and walked out of the armory without another word.

Barrick sat, as short of breath as if Shaso had struck him again in the stomach. He had long felt that among all the heedless folk in Southmarch, he was the only one who understood how truly bad things had become, who saw the deceptions and cruelties others missed or deliberately ignored, who sensed the growing danger to his family and their kingdom. Now that proof was blossoming before him, he wished he could make it all go away—that he could turn and run headlong back into his own childhood.

After supper Chert's belly was full, but his head was still unsettled. Opal was fussing happily over Flint, measuring the boy with a knotted string while he squirmed. She had used the few copper chips she had put aside for a new cooking pot to buy some cloth, since she planned to make a shirt for the child.

"Don't look at me that way," she told her husband. "I wasn't the one who took him out and let him rip and dirty this one so badly."

Chert shook his head. It was not paying for the boy's new shirt that concerned him.

The bell for the front door rang, a couple of short tugs on the cord. Opal handed the boy her measuring string and went to answer it. Chert heard her say, "Oh, my—come in, please."

Her eyebrows were up when she returned trailed by Cinnabar, a handsome, big-boned Funderling, the leader of the important Quicksilver family.

Chert rose. "Magister, you do me an honor. Will you sit down?"

Cinnabar nodded, grunting as he seated himself. Although he was younger than Chert by some dozen years, his muscled bulk was already turning to fat. His mind was still lean, though; Chert respected the man's wits.

"Can we offer you something, Magister?" Opal asked. "Beer? Some blueroot tea?" She was both excited and worried, trying to catch her husband's eye, but he would not be distracted.

"Tea will do me well, Mistress, thank you."

Flint had gone stock-still on the floor beside Opal's stool, watching the newcomer like a cat spying an unfamiliar dog. Chert knew he should wait until the tea was served, but his curiosity was strong. "Your family is well?"

Cinnabar snorted. "Greedy as blindshrews, but that's nothing new. It strikes me you've had an addition yourself."

"His name is Flint." Chert felt sure this was the point of the visit. "He's one of the big folk."

"Yes, I can see that. And of course I've heard much about him already—it's all over town."

"Is there a problem that he stays with us? He has no memory of his real name or parents."

Opal bustled into the room with a tray, the best teapot, and three cups. Her smile was a little too bright as she poured for the magister first. Chert could see that she was frightened.

Fissure and fracture, is she so attached to the boy already?

Cinnabar blew on the cup nestled in his big hands. "As long as he breaks none of the laws of Funderling Town, you could guest a badger for all it matters to me." He turned his keen eyes on Opal. "But people do talk, and they are slow to welcome change. Still, I suppose it is too late to reveal this secret more delicately."

"It is no secret!" said Opal, a little sharply.

"Obviously." Cinnabar sighed. "It is your affair. That's not why I'm here tonight."

Now Chert was puzzled. He watched Cinnabar snuffle at his tea. The man was not only head of his own family, but was one of the most powerful men in the Guild of Stonecutters. Chert could only be patient.

"That is good, Mistress," Cinnabar said at last. "My own lady, she will boil the same roots over and over until it is like drinking rainwater." He looked from her expectant, worried face to Chert's and smiled. It cracked his broad, heavy-jawed face into little wrinkles, like a hammerblow on slate. "Ah, I am tormenting you, but do not mean to. There's nothing ill in this visit, that's a promise. I need your help, Chert."

"You do?"

"Aye. You know we're cutting in the bedrock of the inner keep? Tricky work. The king's family wants to expand the burial vaults and stitch together various of their buildings with tunnels."

"I've heard, of course. That's old Hornblende in charge, isn't it? He's a good man."

"Was in charge. He's quit. Says it's because of his back, but I have my doubts, though he is of an age." Cinnabar nodded slowly. "That's why I need your help, Chert."

He shook his head, confused. "What . . . ?"

"I want you to chief the job. It's a careful matter, as you know—digging under the castle. I don't need to say more, do I? I hear the men are skittish, which may have something to do with Hornblende's wanting nothing more of it."

Chert was stunned. At least a dozen other Funderlings had the experience to take Hornblende's place, all more senior or more important than he was, including one of his own brothers. "Why me?"

"Because you have sense. Because I need someone I can trust as chief over this task. You've worked with the big folk before and made out well." He flicked a glance at Opal, who had finished her tea and was again measuring the child, although Chert knew she was listening to every word. "We can speak more of it later, if you tell me you will do it."

How could he say no? "Of course, Magister. It's an honor."

"Good. Very good." Cinnabar rose, not without a small noise of effort. "Here, give me your hand on it. Come to me tomorrow and I'll give you the plans and your list of men. Oh, and thanking you for your hospitality, Mistress Opal."

Her smile was genuine now. "Our pleasure, Magister."

He did not leave, but took a step forward and stood over Flint. "What do you say, boy?" he asked, mock-stern. "Do you like stone?"

The child regarded him carefully. "Which kind?"

Cinnabar laughed. "Well questioned! Ah, Master Chert, perhaps he has the making of a Funderling at that, if he grows not too big for the tunnels." He was still chuckling as Chert let him out.

"Such wonderful news!" Opal's eyes were shining. "Your family will regret their snubs now."

"Perhaps." Chert was glad, of course, but he knew old Hornblende for a levelheaded fellow. Was there a reason he had given up such a prestigious post? Could there be something of a poisoned offering about it? Chert was not used to kindnesses from the town leaders, although he had no reason to mistrust Cinnabar, who was reputed for fair-dealing.

"Little Flint has brought us good luck," Opal purred. "He will have a shirt, and I will have that winter shawl and . . . and you, my husband, you must have a handsome new pair of boots. You cannot go walking through the big folk's castle in those miserable old things."

"Let's not spend silver we haven't seen yet," he said, but mildly. He might have been a little uncertain about this surprising good fortune, but it was good to see Opal so happy.

"And you would have left the boy there," she said, almost giddy. "Left our luck sitting in the grass!"

"Luck's a strange thing," Chert reminded her, "and as they say, there is much digging before the entire vein is uncovered." He sat down to finish his tea.

Kendrick had convened the council in the castle's Chapel of Erivor, dedicated to the sea god who had always been the Eddon family's special protector. The main chamber was dominated by the statue of the god in green soapstone trimmed with bright metal, with golden kelp coiling in Erivor's hair and beard and his great golden spear held high to calm the waters so Anglin's ancestors could cross the sea from Connord. Generations of Eddons had been named and married at the low stone altar beneath the statue, and many had lain in state there, too, after they had died: the echoes that drifted back from the chapel's high, tiled ceiling sometimes seemed to be voices from other times.

Barrick had enough difficulty with unwanted voices as it was: he didn't like the chapel much.

Today a ring of chairs had been set up on the floor just beneath the steps that led to the low stone altar. "It is the only chamber in this castle where we can close the door and find any privacy," Kendrick explained to the nobles. "Anything important said in the throne room or the Oak Chamber will be spread across Southmarch before the speaker has finished."

Barrick moved uncomfortably in the hard, high-backed chair. He had been chewing willow bark since supper but his crippled arm still ached miserably from Shaso's blows. He darted a sour look at the master of arms. Shaso's face was a mask, his eyes fixed on the frescoes that, with so many lamps lit, gleamed daytime-bright, as though the birth and triumph of Erivor was the most interesting thing he had ever seen. Barrick had not attended many of these councils: he and Briony had only been invited since their father's departure, and this was his first without her, which added to his discomfort. He could not shake off the feeling that a part of him was gone, as though he had woken up to find he had only one leg.

Gailon of Summerfield was talking quietly into the prince regent's left ear. Sisel, Hierarch of Southmarch, had been given the position of honor on Kendrick's other hand. The hierarch, a slender, active man of sixty winters or so, was the leading priest of the marchlands, and although in some things he was forced to act as the hand of the Trigonarch in distant Syan, he was also the first northerner to hold the position, and thus unusually loyal to the Eddons. The Trigonarchy had been unhappy that Barrick's father Olin had chosen to elevate one of the local priests over their own candidate, but neither Syan nor the Trigon itself wielded as much power in the north as they once had.

Ranged around the table were many of the other leading nobles of the realm, Blueshore's Tyne, Lord Nynor the castellan, the bearlike lord constable, Avin Brone, and Barrick's dandified cousin Rorick Longarren, who was Earl of Daler's Troth (strangely matched with those dour, plainspoken folk, Barrick always felt) as well as a half dozen more nobles, some clearly sleepy after the midday meal, others indifferently hiding their irritation at giving up a day of hunting or hawking. That sort would not even have been present were it not for their interest in seeing some relief from the royal levy, Barrick felt sure. The fact that his sister was the bargaining chip bothered them not at all.

He would gladly have seen them all skewered on Erivor's golden fish spear.

Shaso alone seemed suitably grave. He had taken a place at the table's far end, with a space between himself and the nearest nobles on either side: Barrick thought he looked a bit like a prisoner brought to judgment.

"Your argument should be made to all," Kendrick loudly told Gailon, who was still whispering to him. At this signal, the other nobles turned their attention to the head of the table.

Duke Gailon paused. A bit of a flush crept up his neck and onto his handsome face. Other than Barrick and the prince regent, he was the youngest man at the gathering. "I simply said that I think we would be making a mistake to so easily give the princess to Ludis Drakava," he began. "We all want nothing more than to have our King Olin back, but even if Ludis honors the bargain and delivers him without treachery, what then? Olin, may the gods long preserve him, will grow old one day and die. Much can happen before that day, and only the unsleeping Fates know all, but one thing is certain—when our liege is gone, Ludis and his heirs will have a perpetual claim on the throne of the March Kings."

And his claim will be a better one than yours, Barrick thought, *which is your real objection.* Still, he was heartened to discover he had an ally, even one he cared for as little as he did Gailon Tolly. He supposed he should be grateful Gailon was the oldest of the Tolly sons. He might be an ambitious prig, but he looked noble as Silas when set beside his brothers, shiftless Caradon and mad Hendon.

"Easy enough for you to say, Summerfield," growled Tyne Aldritch, "with all your share of the ransom gathered already. What of the rest of us? We would be fools not to take up Ludis' bargain."

"Fools?" Barrick straightened. "We are fools if we don't sell my sister?"

"Enough," said Kendrick heavily. "We will come back to this question later. First there are more pressing matters. Can Ludis and his envoy even be trusted? Obviously, if we were to agree to this offering . . . and I speak only of possibilities, Barrick, so please keep still . . . we could not allow my sister to leave our protection until the king was released and safe."

Barrick squirmed, almost breathless with fury—he would never have believed that Kendrick could talk so carelessly about giving his own sister to a bandit—but the prince regent had spoken with another purpose.

"In fact," Kendrick continued, "we know little about Ludis, except by reputation, and less of his envoy. Shaso, perhaps you can make us wiser about this man Dawet dan-Faar, since you seem to know him."

His question settled on the master of arms as softly as a silken noose. Shaso stirred. "Yes," he said heavily. "I know him. We are . . . related."

This set the table muttering. "Then you should not be seated in this council, sir," said Earl Rorick loudly. The royal cousin was dressed in the very latest fashion, the slashes in his deep purple doublet a blazing yellow. He turned to the prince regent, bright and self-assured as a courting bird. "This is shameful. How many councils have we held, speaking, though we knew it not, for the benefit not only of the marchlands but Hierosol as well?"

At last, Shaso seemed to pay attention. Like an old lion woken from sleep, he blinked and leaned forward. One hand had fallen to his side, close to the hilt of his dagger. "Stay. Are you calling me a traitor, my lord?"

Rorick's return look was haughty, but the earl's cheeks had gone pale. "You never told us you were this man's relative."

"Why should I?" Shaso stared at him for a moment, then sagged back, his energy spent. "He was of no importance to any of you before he arrived here. I myself did not know he had taken service with Ludis until the day he arrived. Last I had heard of him, he led his own free company, robbing and burning across Krace and the south."

"What else do you know of him?" Kendrick asked, not particularly kindly. "He called you a name—'Mordiya'?"

"It means 'uncle,' or sometimes 'father-in-law.' He was mocking me." Shaso closed his eyes for a moment. "Dawet is the fourth son of the old king of Tuan. When he was young I taught him and his brothers, just as I have taught the children of this family. He was in many ways the best of them, but in more ways the worst—swift and strong and clever, but with the heart of a desert jackal, looking only for what would advantage himself. When I was captured by your father in the battle for Hierosol, I thought that I would never see him or any of the rest of my family again."

"So how does this Dawet come to be serving Ludis Drakava?"

"I do not know, as I said, Ke . . . Highness. I heard that Dawet had been exiled from Tuan because of . . . because of a crime he had committed." Shaso's face had gone hard and blank. "His bad ways had continued and worsened, and at last he despoiled a young woman of good family and even his father would no longer protect him. Exiled, he crossed the ocean from Xand to Eion, then joined a mercenary company and rose to lead it. He did not fight for his father or Tuan when our country was conquered by the Autarch. Nor did I, for that matter, since I had already been brought here."

"A complicated story," said Hierarch Sisel. "Your pardon, but you ask us to take much on faith, Lord Shaso. How is it that you heard of his doings after your exile here?"

Shaso looked at him but said nothing.

"See," Rorick proclaimed. "He hides something."

"These are foul times," Kendrick said, "that we should all be so mistrustful. But the hierarch's question is a fair one. How do you come to know of what happened to him after you left Tuan?"

Shaso's expression became even more lifeless. "Ten years ago, I had a letter from my wife, the gods rest her. It was the last she sent me before she died."

"And she used this letter to tell you about one of what must have been many students?"

The master of arms placed his dark hands flat on his knees, then looked down at them carefully, as though he had never seen such unusual things as hands before. "The girl he ruined was my youngest daughter. Afterward, in her grief, she went to the temple and became a priestess of the Great Mother. When she sickened and died two years later, my wife wrote to tell me. My wife thought it was a shattered heart that had taken Hanede—that our daughter had died from shame, not just fever. She also told me something of Dawet, full of despair that such a man should live and prosper when our daughter was dead."

Silence reigned for long moments in the small chapel.

"I . . . I am grieved to hear it, Shaso," Kendrick said at last. "And doubly grieved that I have forced you to think of it again."

"I have thought of nothing else since I first heard the name of Hierosol's envoy," the old man said. Barrick had seen Shaso do this before—go away to somewhere deep inside himself, like the master of a besieged castle.

"Were Dawet dan-Faar not under the March King's seal, one of the two of us would already be dead."

Kendrick had clearly been caught by surprise, and just as clearly had not enjoyed it. "This . . . this speaks badly of the envoy, of course. Does it also mean his offer is not to be trusted?"

Hierarch Sisel cleared his throat. "I, for one, think the offer is honest, although the messenger be not. Like many bandit-lords, Ludis Drakava is desperate to make himself a true monarch—already he has petitioned the Trigon to recognize him as Hierosol's king. It would be to his advantage to link himself to one of the existing noble houses as well. Syan and Jellon will not do it—even with the mountains between, Hierosol is too close to them, and they deem Ludis too ambitious. Thus, I suspect, his mind has turned to Southmarch." He frowned, considering. "It could even be he planned this all along, and is the reason he took King Olin."

"He wanted the ransom to begin to pinch before he offered us this other bargain?" asked a baron from Marrinswalk, shaking his head. "Very crafty."

"All this talk of why and what happened does not change the facts," snapped Earl Tyne. "He has the king. We do not. He wants the king's daughter. Do we give her to him?"

"Do you agree with the hierarch, Shaso?" Kendrick looked at the master of arms keenly. He had never felt Briony's loyalty to the old Tuani, but he did not share Barrick's grudges either. "Is the offer to be trusted?"

"I think it genuine, yes," Shaso said at last. "But the Earl of Blueshore has reminded us of the true question here."

"And what do you think?" Kendrick prodded him.

"It is not for me to say." The old man's eyes were hooded. "She is not my sister. The king is not my father."

"The final decision will be mine, of course. But I wish to hear counsel first, and you were always one of my father's most trusted councillors."

Barrick could not help but notice that Kendrick had called Shaso his father's trusted councillor, not his own. The master of arms grew even more stony at this slight, but he spoke carefully. "I think it a bad idea."

"Again, one who does not suffer has an easy choice," said Tyne Aldritch. "You have no ransom to raise, no tithe of crops to deliver. What does it matter to you whether the rest of us are crippled by this?"

Shaso would not answer the Earl of Blueshore, but Gailon Tolly did. "Can none of you see any farther than the boundaries of your own smallholdings?" he demanded. "Do you think you alone suffer hardship? If we do not give the princess to Ludis, as I think we should not, we all must still share the burden of the greatest hardship—the king's absence!"

"What did our father say?" Barrick asked suddenly. The whole gathering had been like a bad dream, a confusion of voices and faces. He still could not believe his brother was giving the Lord Protector's suit any consideration at all. "You read his letter, Kendrick—he must have said something about this."

His brother nodded but did not meet his younger brother's eye. "Yes, but in few words, as though he did not take it seriously. He called it a foolish offer." Kendrick blinked, suddenly weary. "Does this help us to decide, Barrick? You know that Father would never allow himself to be bartered for anyone, even the lowest pig farmer. He has always put his ideals above all else." There was a note of bitterness, now. "And you know he dotes on Briony, and has since she was in swaddling clothes. You've complained of it often enough, Barrick."

"But he's right! She is our sister!"

"And we Eddons are the rulers of Southmarch. Even Father has always put those responsibilities above his own desires. Who do you think is more important to our people, our father or sister?"

"The people love Briony!"

"Yes, they do. Her absence would sadden them, but it would not make them fearful, as they have been since the king has been gone. A kingdom without its monarch is like a man without a heart. Better Father were dead, the gods preserve him and us, than simply gone!"

A shocked silence fell over the table at this near-treason, but Barrick knew that his brother was right. Although everyone had tried to pretend otherwise, the king's absence had been a kind of living death for the March Kingdoms, as unnatural as a year without sunshine. And now, for the first time, Barrick could see the strain beneath what he sometimes thought of as his brother's guileless features, the immense worry and exhaustion. Barrick could only wonder what other things Kendrick had been hiding from him.

The other nobles took up the argument. It quickly became apparent that Shaso and Gailon were in the minority, that Tyne and Rorick and even Lord Constable Avin Brone thought that since one day Briony would be married off for political gain anyway, her maidenhead might as well be bartered now for something as valuable as restoring King Olin. However, few beside Tyne were honest enough to admit that part of the plan's appeal was that it would spare them many golden dolphins as well.

Tempers frayed and the discussion became loud. At one point, Avin Brone threatened to knock in Ivar of Silverside's head, although both were arguing in favor of the same position. At last Kendrick demanded quiet.

"It is late and I have not made up my mind yet," the prince regent said. "I must think and then sleep on it tonight. My brother Barrick is right in one thing, especially—this is my sister, and I'll do nothing lightly that will so greatly affect her. Tomorrow I will announce my decision."

He stood; the others rose and bade him good night, although ill will was still in the air. Barrick was dissatisfied with many things, but he did not for a moment envy his older brother, who like a cattle herder's dog had to nip at the heels of these vexatious bulls to keep them moving together.

"I want to talk to you," he told Kendrick as his brother left the chapel. The prince regent's guards had already formed a silent wall behind him.

"Not tonight, Barrick. I know what you think. I still have much to do before I sleep."

"But . . . but, Kendrick, she's our sister! She is terrified—I went to her chambers and heard her sobbing . . . !"

"Enough!" the prince regent almost shouted. "By Perin's hammer, can't you leave me alone? Unless you have some magical solution to this problem, all I want from you tonight is silence." Despite his fury, Kendrick seemed on the verge of weeping himself. He waved his hand. "No more."

Stunned, Barrick could only stand and watch his older brother walk back toward his chambers. When Kendrick stumbled, one of the guards kindly reached out a hand to steady him.

"That's enough, Briony. I cannot tell you more—not yet. I still must think and talk on this entire matter. You are my sister and I love you, but I must be the ruler here while our father is gone. Go to bed."

Remembering Kendrick's words of only a few hours ago, thinking back on the whole terrible day, she lay sleepless in the dark—although, judging by the sounds, her ladies were not having the same problem: as always, pretty little Rose was snoring like an old dog. Briony had managed to drowse for a short while, but a terrible dream had awoken her, in which Ludis Drakava—who in truth she had never seen; all she knew about him was that he was near her father's age—had been an ancient thing of cobwebs, dust, and bones, pursuing her through a trackless gray forest. She had not been able to sleep since. She wondered if it was dreams of that sort which robbed Barrick of his sleep and health.

What hour is it? she wondered. She had not heard the temple's midnight bell yet, but surely it could not be far away. *I must be the only one in the castle still awake.*

In other times such a thought would have been more exciting than troubling, but now it was only testament to the terrible fate hanging over her like a headsman's ax.

Has Kendrick decided?

He had given away nothing of his thoughts when she had visited him in his chambers during the evening. She had wept, which made her angry with herself now. She had also begged him not to marry her to Ludis, then had apologized for her selfishness. *But he must know I want Father back as much as anyone does!*

Kendrick had been distant the whole time she was in his chamber, but had taken her hand when they parted and kissed her cheek, something he rarely did. In fact, the memory of that kiss now chilled her more than his preoccupation. She felt certain that he had been kissing her good-bye.

Pain was wearying. Perpetual fear became numbness. For a little while Briony's mind wandered and she imagined all the things, good and bad, that could happen. Somehow her father could escape and Ludis would have no claim on the Eddons. Or she could find that the Lord Protector was a slandered man, that truly he was handsome and kind. Or that he was worse than the tales, in which case she would have no choice but to kill him in his sleep, then kill herself. She lived so many lives in that hour, both grim and fanciful, that at last she slipped into a true dream without knowing it—a kinder one this time, the twins playing at hide-and-seek with Kendrick, children together once more—and slept through the midnight bell. But she did not sleep through the shriek that came just a short while later.

Briony sat upright in bed, half certain she had imagined it. Nearby young Rose squirmed in her sleep, lost in some nightmare of her own.

"The black man . . . !" the girl moaned.

Briony heard it again—a terrified wail, growing louder. Moina was awake now, too. Something banged hard on the chamber door and Briony almost fell out of her bed in fright.

"The Autarch!" Moina squealed, plucking at the charm she wore about her neck. "Come to kill us all in our beds . . . !"

"It is only one of the guards," Briony told the Helmingsea girl harshly, trying to convince herself as well. "Go and take off the bolt."

"No, Princess! They'll ravish us!"

Briony pulled her dagger from beneath her mattress, then wrapped the blanket around her and stumbled to the door, heart fluttering as she called out to learn who was on the other side. The voice was not one of the guards', but even more familiar: as the door opened, Briony's great-aunt Merolanna flapped into the room, her nightdress askew, her long gray hair down on her shoulders, crying, "Gods preserve us! Gods preserve us!"

"Why is everyone shouting?" Briony asked, fighting against growing dread. "Is it a fire?"

Merolanna stumbled to a halt, panting and peering shortsightedly. Her cheeks were wet with tears. "Briony, is that you? Is it? Oh, praise the gods, I thought they had taken you all."

The old woman's words ran through her like icy water. "All . . . ? What are you talking about?"

"Your brother—your poor brother . . ."

The chill threatened to stop her heart. She cried, "Barrick!" and shoved past Merolanna.

There were no guards outside, but the passage was full of disembodied sounds, wails and distant shouting, and as she emerged into the high-ceilinged Tribute Hall, she found it full of people drifting confusedly in the near-darkness, calling questions or babbling religious oaths, a few carrying candles or lamps, and all in their nightclothes. The vast hall, strange even in bright daylight with its weird statues and other objects brought back from foreign lands, like the stuffed head of the great-toothed oliphant that hung above the fireplace and was as ugly as any demon in the Book of the Trigon, now also seemed filled with pale ghosts. Steffans Nynor, wearing a ridiculous sleeping cap and with his beard tied up in a strange little bag, stood in the center of the room shouting orders, but no one was listening to him. The scene was all the more dreamlike because no one stopped Briony or even spoke to her as she ran past them. Everyone seemed to be going in the wrong direction.

She reached the hall outside Barrick's chamber but found it deserted, her brother's door closed. She had only a moment to wonder at this before something grabbed her arm. She let out a small, choked shriek, but when she saw whose wide-eyed face was beside her she grabbed at him and pulled him close. "Oh, oh, I thought you . . . Merolanna said . . ."

Barrick's red hair was disheveled from bed, wild as a gale-blown haystack. "I saw you go past." He seemed like one dragged from sleep yet still dreaming, his eyes wide but curiously empty. "Come. No, perhaps you shouldn't . . ."

"What? Her relief vanished as swiftly as it came. "Barrick, what in the name of all the gods is going on?"

He led her around the corner into the main hall of the residence. The corridor was full, and guards armed with halberds were pushing servants and others back from the door of Kendrick's chambers. She suddenly realized her misunderstanding.

"Merciful Zoria," she whispered.

Now she could see in the light of the torches that Barrick's face was not empty, but slack with horror, his lips trembling. He took her hand and pulled her through the crowd, which shrank back from them as though the twins might carry some plague. Several of the women were weeping, faces grotesque as festival masks.

The guards kneeling around the body glanced up at the twins' approach but for a moment did not seem to recognize them. Then Ferras Vansen, the captain of the royal guard, stood, his face full of dreadful pity, and yanked one of the crouching soldiers out of the way. The prince regent's room was full of terrible smells, slaughterhouse smells. They had turned Kendrick onto his back. His face gleamed red in the torchlight.

There was so much blood that for a fleeting instant she could tell herself it was someone else, that this horror had been visited on some stranger, but Barrick's groan destroyed the flimsy hope.

Her dagger fell from her hand and clinked onto the flags. Her knees sagged and she half fell, then crawled toward her older brother like a blind animal, tangling herself for a moment with one of the guards as he mumbled a prayer. Kendrick's face twitched. One blood-slicked hand opened and closed.

"He's *alive!*" Briony screamed. "Where is Chaven? Has someone sent for him?" She tried to lift Kendrick, but he was too wet, too heavy. Barrick pulled her back and she struck at her twin. "Let me go! He's alive!"

"He can't be." Barrick, too, was in some other world, his voice confused and distant. "Just look at him . . ."

Kendrick's mouth worked again and Briony almost climbed on top of him, so desperate was she to hear him speak, to know that he was still her brother, that life was in him. She searched for his wounds so she could stop them up, but the whole front of him was soaking wet, his shirt in tatters and the skin beneath it just as ragged.

"Don't," she said in his ear. "Hold on to me!" Her brother's eyes rolled; he was trying to find her. His mouth opened.

". . . *Isss* . . ." A sibilant whisper that only Briony could hear.

"Don't leave us, oh, dear dear Kendrick, don't." She kissed his bloody cheek. He let out a whimper of pain, then curled as slowly as a leaf on hot coals until he was lying on his side, bent double. He kicked, whimpered again, then the life was out of him.

Barrick still pulled at her, but he was weeping, too— *Everyone is crying,* Briony thought, *the whole world is crying.* Dimly, as though it were happening in another country, she could hear people shouting down the corridor.

"The prince is dead! The prince has been murdered!"

Guard Captain Vansen was trying to lift her away from Kendrick. She turned and slapped at him, then grabbed at the man's heavy tunic and tried to pull him down, so full of fury she could barely think.

"How did this happen?" she shrieked, her thoughts as red and slippery as her hands. "Where were you? *Where were his guards?* You are all traitors, murderers!"

For a moment Vansen held her at arm's length, then his face convulsed with grief and he released his grip. Briony scrambled to her feet, struck hard at his shoulders and face. Ferras Vansen did nothing more to defend himself than lower his head until Barrick pulled her off.

"Look!" her brother said, pointing. "Look there, Briony!"

Her eyes blurred with tears, she did not at first understand what she was seeing—two stained lumps of shadow on the floor beside the prince regent's bed. Then she saw the Eddon wolf on the slashed tunic of one of the figures and the pool of blood a shiny blackness beneath them both, and understood that Kendrick's guards, too, were dead.

7

Sisters of the Hive

DAYS:

*Each light between sunrise
And sunset
Is worth dying for at least once*

—from *The Bonefall Oracles*

THE SMOKY SCENT OF THE jasmine candles and the perpetual sleepy buzz of the Hive temple, the half-frightened, half-exalted breathing of the other girls, all the sounds and odors that surrounded her at the moment the world changed beyond all recognition would never again completely leave her mind. But how could it be otherwise? It would have been overwhelming enough just to meet the Living God on Earth, the Autarch Sulepis Bishakh am-Xis III, Elect of Nushash, the Golden One, Master of the Great Tent and the Falcon Throne, Lord of All Places and Happenings, a thousand, thousand praises to His name, but what happened to Qinnitan at this moment was beyond belief—and always would be.

Even a year later, when she would have to abandon a life of splendid leisure in the Palace of Seclusion and run in terror of death through the dark streets of Great Xis, every moment of this day would still be alive inside her . . . a day that had begun like many others, with her friend Duny poking her out of bed in the darkness before sunrise.

Duny had been so aflutter with excitement that morning she could barely keep her voice in a proper whisper. "Oh, get up, Qin-ya, get up! It's today! He's coming! To the Hive!"

The events of that day would lift Qinnitan up to heavenly heights, to honors not just undreamed-of, but so impossible as to be ludicrous even to imagine. Still, if she had known all of what was to come, she would have done anything to escape, as a jackal in a trap will gnaw through its own leg in its desperation for freedom.

They hurried down the corridor, two lines of girls with hair still damp from the water they had splashed on their faces and heads in the ritual cleansing, their robes sticking to their bodies, making a lively chill that would not last long in the rising heat of the day. Qinnitan's own black hair hung in lank, loose ringlets, the odd reddish streak hardly visible when it was wet. When she was a baby, the old women of Cat's Eye Street had called it a witch streak and made the pass-evil sign, but no sign of witchery or anything out of the ordinary at all had followed. Some of the other children had called her "Striped Cat," but other than that, by the time she was old enough to range the streets and alleys in the neighborhood of her parents' house, no one paid any more attention to it than they did to a mole on the nose or crossed eyes.

"But why is He coming here?" Qinnitan asked, still not quite awake.

"To find out what the bees think," Duny said. "Of course."

"Think about what?" The priestesses and the Hive Mistress often spoke about autarchs coming to seek the wisdom of the sacred bees, tiny oracles of the all-powerful fire god Nushash, but the names they cited were of the impossibly distant past—Xarpedon, Lepthis, rulers whom Qinnitan had only ever heard mentioned during the boasting of the Great Hive's caretakers. But now the real, living autarch, the god-on-earth himself, was coming to consult with the fire god's bees. It was hard to believe. Her father had been a priest in the temple of Nushash all his life but had never been favored with a visit from an actual autarch. Qinnitan had been a sworn acolyte priestess for scarcely more than a year. It almost didn't seem fair.

This autarch, Sulepis, was a fairly young god-on-earth still. He had only been on the Falcon Throne for a short time—Qinnitan could remember his father, the old autarch Parnad, dying (followed more violently by several of his other sons, who had been the current autarch's rivals) when she had first gone to serve the bees, the funereal hush that had lain so deeply on the Hive temple that she had been surprised later to discover things were not always that way. Perhaps the autarch's youthfulness explained why he was doing astounding things like visiting a smoke-filled apiary in one of the more obscure corners of Nushash's sprawling, ancient fire temple.

"Do you think He'll be handsome?" Duny asked in a strangled whisper, clearly shocked and thrilled by her own daring. Sulepis had spent most of his first months on the throne chastising some of the outer provinces who had thought, falsely and to their subsequent regret, that the new, young autarch might prove timid. Thus, he had not found time for the sort of processions or public events that made the common people feel as though they knew their ruler. Qinnitan could only shrug and shake her head. She couldn't think of the autarch in that way and it hurt her head even to try. It was like a worm trying to decide whether a mountain was the right color. She wasn't angry, though: she knew her friend was frightened, and who wouldn't be? They were going to meet the living god, a being as far above them as the stars, someone who could snuff all their lives more easily than Qinnitan could kill a fly.

For a brief moment—it was always too brief—the acolytes passed out of the narrow passageway into the high-windowed gallery that crossed from the living quarters to the temple complex. Twelve to fifteen steps at most, depending on how quickly the leading girl was marching, but it was the only chance Qinnitan had to see below her the magnificent city of Great Xis, a city in which she had once, if not exactly run free, at least lived at street level, among people that spoke in normal tones of voice. In the Hive scarcely anyone ever spoke above a whisper—although sometimes the whispers could be as intrusive as shouts.

"Do you think He'll speak? What do you think He'll sound like?"

"Quiet, Duny!"

Qinnitan had just a few moments each day to savor the world outside the temple, even if she only saw it at a distance, and she missed it very much. As always, she opened her eyes wide as they crossed the windowed gallery, trying to drink in every bit she could absorb, the blue sky bleached mostly gray with the smoke of a million fires, the pearl-white rooftops stretching far beyond sight like an endless beach covered with squared stones, interrupted here and there where the towers of the greatest families thrust up into the air. The towers' colorful stripes and gold ornaments made them look like the sleeves of splendid garments, as though each tower were a man's fist raised toward the heavens. But of course the rich men of the tower families had no complaints against the heavens: instead of clenched in a fist, their tower-hands should be spread wide, in case the gods should decide to throw down even more good fortune on people already choked with it.

Qinnitan often wondered what would have happened if her own family had been one of the ruling elite instead of only a middling merchant family, her father a landholder instead of a mere functionary in the administration of one of Nushash's larger temples. She supposed it could have been worse—he could have been a lackey of one of the other gods, fast losing power to the great fire god. "We are so lucky to have this for you," her parents had told her when she had been admitted as an acolyte of the Sisters of the Hive, although she herself had prayed—blasphemy, but there it was—that it would not happen. "Far richer families than ours would shed blood for such an honor. You will be serving in the autarch's own temple!"

The temple, of course, had proved to be a sprawl of connected buildings that seemed only slightly smaller than Great Xis itself, and Qinnitan one of so many hundreds of Hive Sister acolytes that it was doubtful even the priestess in charge of her living quarters knew more than a few of their names.

"I don't know what I'll do if He looks at me. If I faint, will He have me put to death?"

"Please, Duny. No, I'm sure people faint all the time. He's a god, after all."

"You say that so strangely, Qin. Are you feeling ill?"

Her momentary glimpse of freedom ended: the mighty city disappeared as they stepped out of the gallery and into the next corridor. One of Qinnitan's aunts had told her that Xis was so big that a bird could live its entire life while flying from one side of the city to the other, perching along the way to sleep, eat, and perhaps even start a family. Qinnitan was not certain that was true—her father had poured scorn on the notion—but it was certainly true that there was a world outside so much bigger than her own constrained circumstances, so much more vast than her march from living quarters to temple each morning and back again each evening, that she ached to be a bird, flaunting herself above a city that never ended.

Even fretful, chattering Duny at last fell silent as they passed into the great hypostyle hall, awed as they all were, every day, by the size of the stone pillars shaped like cedars that stretched up a dozen times the girls' height or more before disappearing into the inky shadows beneath the ceiling. When she had first come to the temple, Qinnitan had thought it strange that Nushash should live in such a dark place, but after a while she had come to see how right it was. Fire was never brighter than when it bloomed out of blackness, never more important than when it was the only light in a sunless place.

At the end of the great hall the eyes of Nushash were opening even now as the temple's oldest priest lit the great lanterns, moving more slowly than it seemed any human being could manage and yet still be alive, extending his long lighting-pole with the creeping pace of an insect that thinks it might be observed by a hungry bird. This priest was one of the only men Qinnitan and her fellow acolytes saw during the conduct of their daily duties. Despite the fact that he was Favored, and thus a reason far more compelling than mere age ensured he was no threat to a large congregation of virgins, Qinnitan thought the Hive Sisters must have picked him because he was old enough to be doubly safe. They certainly had not picked him for his skill and dispatch. He must have already been at his maddeningly slow work for hours this morning, she decided: more than half the lanterns had been kindled. Their flicker exposed the looping lines of the sacred writing on the wall behind them, the gold characters of the Hymn to the Fire God glinting red with reflected flame:

It is from You, O Great One, that all things good arise,
Mighty Nushash,
O bright-eyed, the foundation of heaven's hearth.
We ourselves arise from You and, like smoke, we live in the air for a short time
only, proceeding from Your warmth,
But we survive forever in the depth of the flame which is Your immortal heart . . .

Beyond the massive and ornately decorated archway lay the maze and inner sanctuary of Nushash himself, chief god of the world, the lord of fire whose wagon was the sun—a wagon bigger even than the autarch's earthly palace, Qinnitan's father had bragged, its wheels higher than the tallest tower. (Her father Cheshret was nothing if not proud of his employer.) Mighty Nushash crossed the sky each day in this great cart and then, despite all the snares that Argal the Dark One laid for him, despite the monsters that thronged his path, continued on through the night beyond the dark mountains, so he could bring the light of fire back to the sky each morning, thus allowing the earth and all who dwelled in it to live.

Somewhere beyond that archway glowered the great golden statue of Nushash himself, as well as all the endless corridors and chambers of his great temple, the chapels and the priests' living quarters and the storage rooms so filled with offerings that a vast part of his army of priests had no other task except to receive and catalog them. Beyond that archway lay the seat of the fire god's power on earth, and it formed—along with the autarch's palace—the axis of the entire spinning world. But of course, girls like Qinnitan were not allowed into *that* part of the temple, nor were any other women, not even the autarch's paramount wife or his venerated mother.

The procession of acolyte priestesses turned left down the smaller hall-way, hurrying on softly pattering feet toward the Temple of the Hive of the Fire God's Sacred Bees, to give it its full name. If the youngest Hive Sisters had not been waiting weeks for this day, it was at this moment that they would have first realized today was not to be like the others: the high priestess herself was waiting for them, along with her chief acolyte. Al-though she was not as venerated as the Oracle Mudry, High Priestess Rugan was the mistress of the Hive temple and thus one of the most pow-erful women in Xis. That being the case, she was a remarkably ordinary and even kindly woman, although she did not suffer foolish behavior well.

High Priestess Rugan clapped her hands and the girls all fell silent, gath-ered in a semicircle around her. "You all know what day this is," she said in her deep voice, "and who is coming." She touched her own ceremonial robe and hood, as if to be sure she had remembered to put them on. "I do not need to tell you the temple must be spotless."

Qinnitan suppressed a groan. They had been cleaning all week—how could it get any cleaner?

Rugan's face was appropriately stern. "You will give thanks as you work. You will praise Nushash and our great autarch for this honor. You will con-sider the monumental importance to all our lives of this visit. And most im-portantly, as you work, you will reflect on the sacred bees and their own ceaseless, uncomplaining toil."

"They are so beautiful," said the chief acolyte.

Qinnitan paused for a moment in her work to look at the great hives behind their clouds of smoky silk netting, vast cylinders of fired clay deco-rated with bands of copper and gold and warmed in winter by pots of boil-ing water set beneath the bulky ceremonial stands—one of the least enjoyable of the acolytes' jobs: Qinnitan had more than a few burns on her hands and wrists where a spill had scalded her. The fire god's bees lived in houses far more splendid than any but the most exalted and fortunate of men. As if they knew it, the bees were singing quietly, contentedly, a hum deep enough to make ears tickle and hair lift on the back of the neck. "Yes, Mistress Chryssa," said Qinnitan, meaning it. It was perhaps the thing she liked best about the Hive temple—the hives themselves, the bees, busy and serene. "They truly are."

"It is a wonderful day for us." The chief acolyte was herself still a young woman, pretty in a thin-faced way when one learned to look past the scar that ran from her eye to her cheek. The scar made her the subject of much giggling speculation in the acolytes' quarters. Qinnitan had never summoned the nerve to ask her how she had received it. "An entirely wonderful day. But for some reason, child, you do not seem entirely happy."

Qinnitan took a breath, suddenly shocked and frightened that her strange mood should show on her face. "Oh, no, Mistress. I am the luckiest girl in the world to be here, to be a Hive Sister."

The chief acolyte didn't look like she entirely believed her, but she nodded approvingly. "It's true, there are probably more girls who would happily take your place here than there are grains of sand on the beach, and you have had the even greater good fortune of having caught the eye of Eminence Rugan herself. Otherwise a girl of your . . . otherwise you might not have been selected out of so many other worthy candidates." Chryssa reached out and patted Qinnitan on the arm. "It was your clever tongue, you know, although you still need to learn when *not* to use it. I think Her Eminence has hopes you might be a chief acolyte yourself one day, which would be an even greater honor." She nodded a little, acknowledging her own hard work and good fortune. "Still, it is a high, lonely calling, and sometimes it can be difficult to leave behind your family and friends. I know it was for me, when I was young."

Before Qinnitan could seize this chance to ask the revered and mysterious Mistress Chryssa some questions about her childhood before the temple, the nets in front of the hives billowed a little in a sudden draft, although the weight of hundreds of bees clinging to them kept them from moving too much. The breeze carried something through the great room, a whisper of sudden fear and excitement that made both the chief acolyte and her young charges straighten and turn to the door where the High Priestess had suddenly appeared, her arms held up, her hands open in the air like flowers.

"Praises to the highest," breathed Chryssa, "He is here!"

Qinnitan got down on her knees beside the chief acolyte. A murmur of footsteps became louder, swishing and booming on the polished stone floors, as soldiers began to file in, each with a great curved sword on his belt and bearing on his shoulder a long, bell-mouthed tube of brightly polished figured steel—the Autarch's Leopards, they had to be, no one else was allowed to wear that black-and-gold armor. It was astonishing: she had never thought to see any men here in the Hive's great portico, let alone a hundred of them with muskets. This rarity was followed by several dozen robed priests of Nushash, then an even larger troop of soldiers, these carrying more conventional but still frightening weapons, long spears and swords. At last the shuffling of feet stopped. Qinnitan sneaked a look over at Mistress Chryssa, whose face was radiant with excitement and something even stronger—a sort of joy.

A vast litter appeared in the doorway, a thing of gold-painted wood and heavy curtains embroidered with the wide-winged falcon of the royal family. The brawny soldiers who held it set the litter down just to the side of the doorway and one of them leaped forward to pull back the curtains. Although none of the women in the temple chamber said a word, Qinnitan thought she could feel them, dozens of them, all drawing breath at the same time. A face appeared from the shadows in the depths of the litter, picked out by the lanterns.

Qinnitan swallowed, although for a moment it seemed impossible to do so. The autarch was a monster.

No, not quite a monster she saw at her second glance, but the youth in the litter was bent and gnarled as though by extreme age and his head was far too large for his spindly body. He blinked and looked absently from side to side like a sleepy man realizing he has opened the wrong door, then withdrew into the darkness of his curtained bower once more.

Even as Qinnitan gaped, the Leopard guards all lifted their guns off their shoulders, held them high, then slammed their feet against the floor with a deafening report—*boom, boom!* For a moment she thought the guns had all gone off, and some of the Hive Sisters let out shrieks of fear and dismay. As the echoes died, a half dozen more men in black-and-gold armor appeared in the doorway and then a figure almost as strange as the one in the litter followed them into the temple room.

He was tall, half a head above the biggest of the Leopards, but not as freakishly so as he first appeared: it was the length of his neck and the narrowness of his face that made him seem so unusual, and the spidery stretch of his fingers as he raised his hand. Beneath the high, dome-shaped crown his face, too, seemed like an ordinary face that had been pulled a bit beyond its appropriate shape—a long jaw and a curved, bony nose like a hawk's beak that matched oddly with his youth—smooth brown flesh stretched tight across the skull. He wore a small trimmed black beard and his eyes seemed unnaturally large and bright as he stared around the room. A few of the Nushash priests stepped forward and began chanting and swinging their censers, filling the air around the tall young man with smoke.

"Who is that?" Qinnitan whispered under cover of the priests' noise.

Chryssa was clearly shocked that she should dare to whisper, even when it was more or less safe to do so under the cover of the priests' voices. "The autarch, you fool girl!"

It certainly made more sense that the tall one was their ruler—he had an undeniable power to him. "But then who is that . . . who is the man in the litter?"

"The scotarch, of course—his heir. Now be silent."

Qinnitan felt stupid. Her father had once told her that the scotarch, the autarch's ceremonial heir, was sickly, but she had entirely forgotten, and had certainly never guessed him to be so obviously afflicted. Still, considering that the autarch's own life and rule hinged on the health and continued well-being of the scotarch, by ancient Xixian tradition, Qinnitan couldn't help wondering at the autarch's choice of such a frail reed.

It didn't matter, she reminded herself. These folk were as much above her—all the doings of the high house were as far above her—as the stars in the sky.

"Where is the mistress of this temple?" The autarch's voice was high-pitched but strong; it rang in the great room like a silvery bell.

Eminence Rugan came forward, head bowed, her usual brisk walk transformed almost into the slinking of a frightened beast. That, more than the soldiers or priests or anything else, made Qinnitan understand that she was in the presence of matchless, terrifying power: Rugan bowed to no one else that Qinnitan had ever seen. "Your glory reflects on us all, O Master of the Great Tent," Rugan said, voice quavering a little. "The Hive welcomes you and the bees are gladsome in your presence. Mother Mudry is coming to offer you any wisdom the Sacred Bees of Nushash can grant. She begs your generous indulgence, Golden One. She is too old to wait here in the drafty outer temple without great discomfort."

The look that crossed the autarch's corvine features was almost a smirk. "She does me too much honor, does old Mudry. You see, I haven't come to consult the oracle. I want nothing from the bees."

Even cowed by the presence of a hundred armed soldiers, many Sisters of the Hive couldn't restrain a gasp of surprise—some of the noises even sounded suspiciously like disapproval. Come to the temple and not consult the sacred bees?

"I'm . . . I'm afraid I don't understand, O Golden One." Clearly confused, Eminence Rugan took a step back, then sank to one knee. "The high priest's messenger said you wished to come to the Hive because you were searching for something. . . ."

The autarch actually laughed. It had a strange edge to it, something that made Qinnitan's flesh prickle on her arms. The curtain of the scotarch's litter twitched as though the sick young man was peering out. "Yes, he did," the autarch said. "And I am. Come, Panhyssir, where are you?"

A bulky shape in dark robes with a long, narrow beard like a gray waterfall trundled out from behind the Leopard guards—Panhyssir, the high priest of Nushash, Qinnitan guessed, and thus another of the most powerful people in the entire continent of Xand. He looked as fat and unconcerned with trivial human things as one of the drones in the sacred hives. "Yes, Golden One?"

"You said that this was the place I would find the bride I sought."

Panhyssir didn't look anywhere near as worried as the Hive priestesses; he had already overseen the collection of hundreds of brides for the autarch, so perhaps this seemed a bit routine. "She is definitely here, Golden One. We know that."

"Ah, is she, now? Then I will find her myself." The autarch took a few steps, his eyes sweeping along the rows of kneeling, terrified Hive Sisters. Qinnitan had no better an idea of what was going on than any of her comrades, but she saw the autarch and his Leopards moving across the temple toward them and so she turned her face toward the floor and tried to stay as still as the paving stones.

"This is the one," said the autarch from somewhere nearby.

"Yes, that is the bride, Golden One," said Panhyssir. "The Master of the Great Tent cannot be fooled."

"Good. She will be brought to me this evening, along with her parents."

It was only when the guards' rough hands closed on her arms and lifted her to her feet that Qinnitan realized that this astounding, unbelievable thing had happened to no one but her.

8

The Hiding Place

MEADOW AND SKY:

Dew rises, rain falls
Between them is mist
Between them lies all that is

—from *The Bonefall Oracles*

IT HAD BEEN THE LONGEST hour of his life. The young woman he admired beyond any other, without a hope of his affection ever being returned, had just spat on him and blamed him for her brother's murder, and he was not at all certain she was wrong. Bleeding runnels showed where she had gouged his cheeks with her nails; the wounds burned, stinging with tears and sweat, both his own. But worst of all, his failure, the failure of every man sworn to protect the royal family, pressed on him like the walls of a lead coffin. King Olin had been gone for months, held prisoner in a far country. Now his son and heir was dead, butchered in his own bedchamber in the middle of Southmarch Castle.

If the world was indeed ending, thought Ferras Vansen, captain of the royal guard, then he hoped the end would come quickly. At least it would mean an end to this most horrible of nights.

Hierarch Sisel, shocked wide-eyed and murmuring to himself, had hurried from his guest chambers in the Tower of Summer, and was now struggling to remember the words to the death rite—he had not been an ordinary priest for a long time—as he leaned over Prince Kendrick's

bloodied corpse. The dead prince had been lifted onto the bed and unfolded from his death spasm; he lay now with eyes closed and arms at his
sides in a semblance of peaceful rest. A cloth stitched with gold had been
draped over his wounded body so that only the naked shoulders and face
were showing, but scarlet flowers of blood were already beginning to
bloom through the covering. Chaven the physician, as pale-faced and disturbed as Vansen had ever seen him, waited to examine the murdered
prince before the royal body was taken by the Maids of Kernios to be prepared for the funeral.

Wordless as survivors of a terrible battle, the twins had not left their dead
brother's side. Blood had dried on their nightclothes—Briony in particular
was so red-painted that a newcomer would be forgiven in mistaking her
for the prince's killer. She kneeled weeping on the floor by the bed, her
head resting on Kendrick's arm. *The prince must be uncomfortable,* Vansen
thought absently, then remembered as if in a dream that the prince was now
beyond all bodily discomfort.

Lord Constable Avin Brone, huge and deep-voiced and as much a part
of the Eddon family as anyone not of the blood could be, was perhaps the
only one who could even think of trying to move the princess from her
dead brother's side. "There are things to do, my lady," he rumbled. "It is not
meet that he should lie here untended. Come away and let the physician
and the death-maids do their work."

"I'm not leaving him." She would not even glance at Brone.

"Talk sense to her," the lord constable growled at her pale twin brother.
Barrick looked half his years, a frightened child, his hair still tousled from
bed. "Help me, Highness," Brone asked him more gently. "We will never
find what happened here, never discover the cruel hand that did this if we
cannot . . . if we must work with a mourning family watching us."

"The dark man . . . !" Briony lifted her head, a sudden feverish light in
her eyes. "My maid woke dreaming of a dark man. Where is that villain
Dawet? Did he do this? Did he kill . . . my . . . my . . . ?" Her mouth curled,
lost shape, then she was weeping again, a raw, heartbreaking sound. She
pressed her head against Kendrick's side.

"My lady, you must come," Brone told her, tugging his beard in anxious
frustration. "You will have a chance for a proper farewell to the prince, I
promise you."

"He's not a prince—he's my brother!"

"He was both, Highness."

"It's time to get up, Briony," Barrick said weakly, as if telling a lie he did not think anyone would believe.

Avin Brone looked to the guard captain for help. Vansen moved forward, hating what his duty made him do. Brone already had one of the girl's arms in his broad hands. Vansen took the other, but Briony resisted, glaring at him with such complete hatred that he let her pull away.

"Princess!" Brone hissed. "Your older brother is dead and you cannot change that. Look around you. Look there!"

"Leave me alone."

"No, gods curse this night, look out the door!"

Outside the prince regent's chamber dozens of pale faces hovered silently in the corridors, phantoms of lantern light, the castle's residents were crowded there, watching in disbelief and horror.

"You and your brother are the heads of the Eddon family now," Brone told her in a harsh whisper. "The people need to see you be strong. Your grief should wait until you are private. Can you not stand and be strong for your people?"

At first she seemed more likely to spit at him than speak, but after a long moment Briony shook her head, then wiped her cheeks and eyes with the back of her hand.

"You are right, Lord Constable," she said. "But I will not forgive you for it."

"I am not in my post to be either loved or forgiven, Mistress. Come, you are in mourning, but you are still a princess. Let us all get on with what we have to do here." He offered her his wide arm.

"No, thank you," she said. "Barrick?"

Her twin took an unsteady step toward her. "Are we . . . ?"

"We will go to the chapel." Briony Eddon's face was a mask now, hard and pale as fired white clay. "We will pray for Kendrick there. We will light candles. And if the lord constable and this supposed captain of the guard manage to find the one who killed our brother under their very noses, we will be composed to pass fitting sentence on him."

Taking her brother's arm, she stepped around Ferras Vansen without a look, as though he were a cow or sheep, something too stupid to clear the way of its own volition. As she passed, he could see that her eyes were brimming over again but that she held her head straight. The servants and others in the hall shrank back against the walls to let them pass. Some called out fearful questions, but Briony and her brother walked through them as though they were no more than trees, their voices only the rush of the wind.

"Eminence, will you go with them?" Avin Brone asked Hierarch Sisel when the twins had passed from earshot. "We need them out of the way so we may do our work, but my heart sinks for them and for the kingdom. Will you go and lead them in prayers, help them to find strength?"

Sisel nodded and followed the prince and princess. Vansen could not help being impressed at the way his master had dispatched the hierarch—a man of the gods who answered only to the Trigonarch himself in distant Syan—as though he were a lowly groom.

When they were all gone, Brone scowled and spat. Such disrespect in the prince's death chamber shocked Vansen, but the lord constable seemed caught up with other things. "At least the Raven's Gate is closed for the night," he growled. "But, tomorrow, word of this will move from house to house through the city like a fire, and will be carried to all the lands around, whether we like it or not. We cannot shut out questions or seal in the truth. The young prince and princess will need to show themselves soon or we will have great fear in the people."

There is a hole in the kingdom now, Ferras Vansen realized. *A terrible hole.* This might be the time when a strong man could step in and fill it. What if Avin Brone thought of himself as that sort of man?

He certainly looked the type. The lord constable was as tall as Vansen, who was not a small fellow, but Brone was almost twice as wide, with a huge bushy beard and shoulders as broad as his substantial belly. In his black cloak—which Ferras suspected he had simply thrown over his night things, then stuffed his feet into boots—the older man looked like a rock on which a ship might founder . . . or on which a great house might be built. And there were others in the kingdom who might also think themselves a good size to wear a crown.

As the physician Chaven busied himself with the prince's body, Avin Brone moved to stand over the two slain guardsmen. "This one is Gwatkin, yes? I do not recognize the other."

"Caddick—a new fellow." Ferras frowned. Just days earlier the men had been mocking Caddick Longlegs for never having kissed a girl. Now the youth was new in death as well. "There would have been two more here, but I thought I would rather keep an eye on the end of the keep where the foreigners are lodged." He swallowed an abrupt surge of bile. "There should have been two more to guard the prince . . ."

"And have you spoken to those guards yet? By the gods, man, what if they are all dead and the foreigners are now ranging the keep with bloody swords?"

"I have long since sent a messenger and had one back. One of my best men leads them—Dyer, you know him—and he swears the Hierosoline envoy and his company have not left their rooms."

"Ah." Brone nudged one of the guards' bodies with his boot toe. "Slashed. A bit fine for swordplay, looks like. But how could a troop of men attack and murder the prince without anyone knowing? And how could something smaller than a troop do such grim work?"

"I do not know how it could be a troop and go unnoticed, my lord. The corridors were not empty." Ferras stared at Gwatkin's wide-eyed face, the jaw hanging open as though death had been more a surprise than anything else. "But the servants did hear something earlier in the evening—arguing, some shouting, but muffled. They could make out no words and did not recognize the voices, but all agreed it did not sound like men fighting for their lives."

"Where are the prince's bodyservants? Where are his pages?"

"Sent away." Ferras could not help but smart a little under Brone's questioning. Did the lord constable think that because Guard Captain Vansen's father was a farmer, the son had no wit? That he hadn't thought to see to these things himself? "The prince himself sent them away. They thought it was because he wanted to be alone, either to think or perhaps to discuss his sister's fate privately with someone."

"Someone?"

"They do not know, Lord. He was alone when he sent them away. They ended by sleeping in the kitchen with the potboys. It was one of the pages, returning for a religious trinket of some sort, who found the dying prince and raised the alarm."

"I will speak to that one, then." Brone carefully lowered his heavy frame into a squat beside the murdered guardsmen. He pulled at the nearest man's jerkin. "He is wearing armor."

"Most of the blood on him comes from a slashed throat. That is what killed him."

"The other, too?"

"His throat was slashed and bleeding, but that wasn't what did for him, my lord. Look at his face."

Brone squinted at the second body. "What happened to his eye?"

"Something sharp went through it, my lord. And deep into his skull, too, from what I can see."

Avin Brone whistled in surprise and levered himself upright like a bear stumbling out of its cave in spring. "If we cannot find a troop of assassins, then have we but one killer? Our murderer must be a fine fighter, to kill two armored men. And Kendrick is not clumsy with a sword either." Startled by his own words, Brone made a pass-evil. "*Was* not. Did he have a chance to arm himself?"

"We have seen no sign of any weapon yet except the guards'." He thought for a moment. "Perhaps somehow the prince was attacked first. Perhaps he sent these guards out on some errand as he did his other servants, and they returned to find the murderer had already struck."

Brone turned to Chaven, who had removed the golden cloth and was probing at the body. The prince regent already looked like a tomb-statue, Ferras thought, cold and white as marble. "Can you guess what killed him?" the lord constable asked.

The royal physician looked up, his round face troubled. "Oh, yes. No, better to say, I can show you why he died. Come look."

Ferras and the lord constable moved to the bedside. Now it was Ferras who helplessly made the pass-evil—a fist around his thumb to keep Kernios the death god from noticing him. He had seen many score of violent deaths since his childhood, but he had not made the gesture for as long as he could remember.

The prince's bloodless pallor and yellow hair made him appear disquietingly like his younger sister—Ferras suddenly felt troubled to be looking on his helpless nakedness, although he had often seen Kendrick bathing in the river after a long, dusty hunt. The corpse's arms were covered with shallow slashes now cleaned of blood—wounds of defense. The blood had been wiped from his chest and stomach as well, but there was no way to prettify these larger wounds, half a dozen straight gashes livid along their edges and deeply, upsettingly red in their depths.

"Not a sword," said the lord constable after a moment. He was breathing a little harshly, as if the sight disturbed him more than he let show. "A knife?"

"Perhaps." Chaven frowned. "Perhaps a curved one—see how the cuts are wider on one end . . . ?"

"A curved knife?" Brone's bushy eyebrows slid up. He looked to Ferras, who felt his heart speed with surprise and fear.

"I know who has a knife like that," he said.

"We all do," said the lord constable.

Barrick's head felt hollow. The rustle of the blanket Briony wore wrapped around her nightdress, the slap of his own feet, the murmur of the people in the corridor, all rolled around his skull like the roar of the ocean in a seashell. He was finding it difficult to believe that what had just happened was real.

"Prince Barrick," someone called—one of the pages. "Is he really dead? Is our lord Kendrick really dead?"

Barrick did not dare speak. Only holding his teeth clenched together kept him from bursting into tears or worse.

Briony waved the onlookers back and they turned to beseech Hierarch Sisel for news instead, slowing his progress. At the end of the corridor the twins turned toward the Erivor Chapel, but then at the next turning Briony walked swiftly in the wrong direction.

"No, this way," Barrick said dully. His poor sister, lost in her own house.

She shook her head and continued down the corridor, then turned again.

"Where are we going?"

"Not to the chapel." Her voice sounded strangely light, as though nothing unusual had happened, but when she turned toward him a blasted emptiness was in her eyes, a look so unfamiliar that it terrified him. "They'll only find us there."

"What? What do you mean?"

His sister took his arm and pulled him down another corridor. Only when they reached the old pantry door did he understand. "We haven't been here for . . . for years."

She pulled a stub of candle from the shelf just inside, then turned back to light it from one of the wall sconces. When they pulled the door closed behind them the light on the shelves cast all the familiar shadows that Barrick had once known as well as the shape of his own knuckles.

"Why didn't we go to the temple?" he asked. He was half afraid to hear the answer. He had never seen his sister quite like this.

"Because they'll find us. Gailon, the hierarch, all that lot. And then they'll make us do things." Her face was pale but intent. "Don't you understand?"

"Understand what? Kendrick . . . Briony, they killed Kendrick! Someone killed Kendrick." He wagged his head, trying to make sense. "But who?"

His sister's eyes were bright with tears. "It doesn't matter! I mean, it does, but don't you see? Don't you see what's going to happen? They're going to make you prince regent, and they're going to send me to Hierosol to marry

Ludis Drakava. They'll be even more certain to do it now. They'll be terrified—they'll do anything to get Father back."

"They're not the only ones." Barrick could not keep up with Briony, who was thinking so quickly it seemed she had dived into a rushing river and left him on the bank, stuck in mud. Barrick couldn't think at all. It seemed the nightmares that plagued his sleep had stormed and conquered his waking life as well. Someone had to make things right again. He was astonished to hear himself say it, but at this moment it was true: "I want Father back, too. I want him back."

Briony started to say something, but her lip was quivering. She sat down on the dusty floor of the pantry and wrapped her arms around her knees. "Poor . . . K–Kendrick!" She fought back the tears. "He was so cold, Barrick. Even before he . . . before the end. He was shivering." She made a snuffling noise, pressed her face against her arms.

Barrick looked up at the pantry ceiling, which undulated like water in the flickering candlelight. He wished he and Briony were on a river together, floating away. "We used to hide from him here when we were little, remember? He used to get so angry when he couldn't find us. And it worked so many times!"

"Even after Aunt Merolanna told him, he'd always forget." She looked up with a crooked smile. "Up and down the halls. 'Barrick! Briony! I'll tell Father!' He would get so angry!"

For a long moment they fell silent, listening for a phantom echo.

"What are we going to do, then? I don't want to be the cursed prince regent." Barrick considered. "We can run away. If we're gone, they can't make me the prince regent and they can't give you to Ludis."

"But who will rule Southmarch?" Briony asked.

"Let Avin Brone do it. Or that prig Gailon. The gods know he wants to."

"All the more reason he shouldn't. Sister Utta says that people who want power are the first who should be mistrusted with it."

"But they're the only ones who want it." He crouched beside her. "I don't want to be prince regent. Besides, why shouldn't it be you, anyway? You're older."

Even in the very pit of misery, his sister could not help smiling. "You are such a wretched monster, Barrick. That's the first time you have ever admitted that. And it was only a matter of moments, anyway."

Barrick slumped down. He had no smile to give back. A poisonous weariness poured through his limbs, heart, and head like a gray smoke, fogging his thoughts. "I want to die, that's what I want. Go with Kendrick. Much easier than running away."

"Don't you dare say that!" Briony grabbed his arm and leaned forward until her face was only a handspan from his. "Don't you *dare* think about leaving me alone."

For a moment he almost told her—gave up the secret he had hidden so long, all those nights of fear and misery . . . But the habit of years could not be so easily broken, even now. "You're the one who will be leaving me," he said instead.

In the middle of the long, dark silence that followed, someone rapped lightly on the pantry door. The twins, startled, looked at each other, eyes wide in the candlelight. The door scraped open.

Their great-aunt, Duchess Merolanna, stepped in. "I knew you'd be here. You two. Of course you would be."

"They sent you after us," Briony said accusingly.

"They did—oh, they did. The whole castle is in terror, looking for you. How could you be such wicked children?" But Merolanna was not as angry as she sounded. In fact, she seemed like another sleepwalker. Her pale, wide face, devoid of paint, looked like something dragged out of its burrow and into the sunlight. "Don't you know the worst thing you could do is to vanish like this, after . . . after . . ."

A great choking gasp came out of Briony, who crawled to Merolanna and buried her face in the old woman's voluminous nightdress. "Oh, Auntie 'Lanna, they k–k–killed him! He's . . . he's gone!"

Merolanna reached down and stroked her back, although she was struggling to keep her balance against the girl's weight on her legs. "I know, dear . . . Yes, our poor, sweet little Kendrick . . ."

And then the horrible fact of it climbed up Barrick's backbone and into his head again, a ghastly, overwhelming thing that choked out all light and sense, and he clambered over to Merolanna and wrapped his arms around her waist, forcing her off balance again. She had no choice but to claw at the shelves and let herself fold to the floor of the pantry in a great slipping and bunching of cloth. She held them both with their heads together in her lap, their hair mingling like the waters of two rivers, red and gold, both of them weeping like small children.

Merolanna was crying again, too. "Oh, my poor ducks," she said, looking at nothing as tears ran down her wrinkled cheek. "Oh, my poor little chickens, yes. My poor, dear ones . . ."

Briony had dried her eyes before they reached Avin Brone and the others, and had even let Merolanna fuss her hair back into some kind of order, but she still felt like a prisoner dragged from a cell to face a high justice.

But although Hierarch Sisel (who Merolanna had told them had walked halfway around the castle looking for them) looked annoyed beneath his appropriately serious and mournful expression, Lord Brone did not tax Barrick and Briony for their waywardness.

"We have been waiting for you," he said as the twins approached, staying close to Merolanna for whatever protection she might afford them. "We have grim business still to do tonight, and you are the head of the Eddon family now."

"Which of us?" asked Barrick a little nastily. "You can't have two heads."

"Either of you," said Brone, surprised for a moment, as though he had not thought of this particular conundrum. "Both of you. But you must see what we do, that justice is done."

"What are you talking about?" demanded Briony. The man Vansen, the captain of the guards, was standing behind the lord constable. He had bloody scratches on his face, and for a moment she felt a twinge of shame, thinking of how she had attacked him. *But he is the one who is alive, and my brother is murdered,* she thought, and the feeling evaporated. He did not meet her eye, which made it easier to ignore him.

"I am talking about the knife that made the wounds on your brother and his guards, Princess." Brone turned at a clattering noise. A troop of guards entered the corridor and stopped at the end, waiting. "Tell them about it, Captain Vansen."

The man still could not look her in the face. "It was curved," he said quietly. "The physician Chaven saw that when he looked at . . . at the wounds. A curved dagger."

Brone waited for him to say more, then grunted with impatience and turned to the twins. "A Tuani dagger, Highnesses."

It took a moment for Briony to make out what he was saying, then the mocking, handsome face of the envoy came rushing into her mind. "That man Dawat . . . !" She would see him skinned. Burned alive.

"No," said Brone. "He did not leave his chambers all night. Nor did any of his entourage. We had guards watching them."

"Then . . . then what?" said Briony, but a moment later she began to understand.

"Shaso?" Barrick's voice was strange, tight, full of both fear and a kind of weird exhilaration. "Are you saying that *Shaso* killed our brother?"

"We do not know for certain," the lord constable said. "We must go and confront him. But he is a promoted peer of Southmarch, an honored friend of your father's. We need you two to be there."

As Brone led them down the hall toward the armory, the troop of guards fell in behind them, faces hard, eyes shadowed beneath their helmets. The hierarch and Merolanna did not accompany them, heading for the family chapel to pray instead.

What is going on? Briony wondered. *Has everything in the world turned upside down at once? Shaso?* It could not be true—someone must have stolen the old man's dagger. In fact, why must it have even been Shaso's dagger? She found it hard to disbelieve Chaven, but surely there were other explanations—there must be dozens of Tuani weapons available in the waterside markets. But when she whispered this to Barrick, he only shook his head. As if he had cried out all his brotherly feeling with his tears, he barely looked at her.

Merciful Zoria, will he turn into another Kendrick now? Will he send me to Ludis because it's best for the whole kingdom? Her skin was needled by a sudden chill.

Three guards waited in the armory outside the door of Shaso's chamber. "He has not left," said one of them, looking at empty air as he talked, clearly confused as to whether to speak directly to the lord constable or his captain, Vansen. "But we have heard strange noises. And the door is bolted."

"Break it down," said Brone, then turned to the twins. "Stand back, if you please, Highnesses."

A half dozen kicks from booted feet and the bolt splintered away from the inside. The door swung in. The guards stepped through with halberds extended, then quickly stepped back again. A dark shape appeared in the opening like a monstrous spirit summoned from the netherworld.

"Kill me then," it growled, but the voice was strangely liquid. For a moment Briony thought that Shaso had indeed been invested by some kind of demon, one which had not learned to use its usurped body properly, for the master of arms was swaying in the doorway, unable to stand upright. "I suppose I am . . . a traitor. So kill me. If you can."

"He's drunk," Barrick said slowly, as though this was the biggest surprise the night had produced.

"Take him," Avin Brone called. "But 'ware—he is dangerous."

Briony could not make herself believe it. "Don't hurt him! Alive! He must be taken alive!"

The guards moved forward, jabbing with the pike ends of their halberds, forcing the dark-skinned man out of the doorway and back into his chamber. Briony could see that the room was in disarray behind him, the bedclothes torn to pieces and scattered across the floor, the shrine in the corner knocked to flinders. *He is mad, then, or sick.* "Don't hurt him!" she shouted again.

"Will you condemn some of these guardsmen to death?" Avin Brone growled. "That old man is still one of the fiercest fighters alive!"

Briony shook her head. She could only watch with Barrick as the guards tried to subdue Shaso. Barrick was right, the man was reeling, clearly drunk or damaged in some way, but even without a weapon he was a formidable quarry.

Shaso did not remain weaponless for long. He snatched a halberd away from one of the guards and stunned the man with the butt, then crashed it against the helm of another who tried to take advantage of the opening. Already two of the guards were down. The room was too small for proper pike work. Shaso put his back against the far wall and stood there, chest heaving. Blood was smeared all over his arms and some on his face as well—old blood, dried until it was scarcely visible against his skin.

"Captain," Brone said, "bring me archers."

"No!" Briony tried to rush forward, but the lord constable seized her arm and held her despite all her struggles.

"Forgive me, my lady," he said through clenched teeth. "But I will not lose another Eddon tonight."

Suddenly someone else slipped past him—Barrick. Even as Avin Brone cursed, Briony's brother stopped just inside the doorway.

"Shaso!" he shouted. "Put that down!"

The old man lifted his head and shook it. "Is that you, boy?"

"What have you done?" The prince's voice trembled. "Gods curse you, what have you done?"

Shaso tipped his head quizzically for a moment, then smiled a bitter, horrible smile. "What I had to—what was right. Will you kill me for it? For the honor of the family? Now there is irony for you."

"Give yourself up," Barrick said.

"Let the guards take me, if they can." Even slurred with drink, his laugh was dreadful. "I do not care much if I live or not."

For a moment no one spoke. Briony was numb with despair. The dark wings of her ominous mood had not been black at all, it seemed, but blood-red; now they had spread over the whole of the house of Eddon.

"You owe your life to our father." Barrick's voice was tight with misery or fear or something else that Briony could not recognize. "You speak of honor—will you give away even that last vestige of it? Kill some of these innocent men instead of surrendering?"

Shaso goggled at him. For a moment he lost his balance where he leaned on the wall, but then the halberd came up again quickly. "You would do that to me, boy? Remind me of that?"

"I would. Father saved your life. You swore that you would obey him and all his heirs. We are his heirs. Put up your weapon and do the honorable thing, if you have not become a stranger to honor altogether. Be a man."

The master of arms looked at him, then at Briony. He barked a laugh that ended in a ragged tatter of breath. "You are crueler than your father ever was—than your brother, even." He threw the halberd clattering to the floor. A moment later he swayed again and this time crumpled and fell. The guards rushed forward and swarmed on him until it was clear he was not feigning, that he had fallen senseless from drink or exhaustion or something else.

The guards heaved him up from the floor, one on each leg and arm. It was not easy—Shaso was a large man. "To the stronghold with him," Brone commanded them. "Chain him well. When he wakes we will question him closely, but I cannot doubt we have found our murderer."

As he was carried past Briony, Shaso's eyes flicked open. He saw her and tried to say something but could only groan, then his eyes slid shut again. His breath smelled of drink.

"It can't be," she said. "I don't believe it."

Ferras Vansen, the captain of the guard, had found something on the floor beside Shaso's spare bed. He picked it up with a polishing cloth and brought it to the twins and the lord constable, bearing it gingerly, like a servant carrying a royal crown.

It was a curved Tuani dagger nearly as as long as a man's forearm—a dagger that all of them had seen before, scabbarded on Shaso's belt. The hilt was wrapped in figured leather. The sharp blade, always kept glitteringly polished, was smeared up and down with blood.

9
A Gleam of Pale Wings

MOUNTAIN SPIRIT'S BELT:

He is cloaked in mistletoe and the musk of bees
Lightning makes the trees grow
And makes the earth cry out

—from *The Bonefall Oracles*

"**T**OBY!" THE PHYSICIAN bellowed as he staggered through the door. He did not know whether to weep or scream or beat his head against the wall—he had been restraining his feelings too long. "Curse you, where are you hiding?"

The other two servants, his old manservant and his housekeeper (who had just barely managed to beat Chaven home, hurrying back from a gathering of worried citizens in the torchlit square between the West Green and the Raven's Gate) scuttled away down the corridors of Observatory House, grateful that their master's unhappiness had settled on someone other than themselves.

The young man appeared, wiping his hands on his smock. "Yes, Master?"

Chaven made a face at the black smears on Toby's clothing, but was surprised to find the young fellow at his tasks so early in the morning; it was usually hard to get him to work even when the sun was high in the sky. "Bring me something to drink. Wine—that Torvian muck is already open on my bedside table. By the gods, the world is falling apart."

The young man hesitated. Chaven could see fear behind the usual sullenness. "Is . . . will there . . . will there be war?"

Chaven shook his head. "War? What do you mean?"

"Mistress Jennikin and Harry, they say the older prince is dead, sir. Murdered. My da' told me once that when Olin's brother died there was almost a war."

The physician fought down the urge to berate this poor blunt tool. Everyone in the castle was terrified—he himself had not felt so desperate in all the years since fleeing Ulos. Why should the boy feel any differently? "Yes, Toby, the older prince is dead. But when Olin's brother Lorick died, the country was rich and unthreatened, and it was worth the time of any number of ambitious nobles to try to put themselves or some useful puppet on the Southmarch throne instead of a child heir. Now I suppose it will be young Barrick earns the regency, and no one will want the blame for what is about to happen here, so they will gratefully let him have the honor of keeping his father's chair warm."

"So there won't be a war?" Toby ignored Chaven's bleak sarcasm as though it were a foreign language. He could not meet his master's eye directly, and had his head down like a stubborn goat that would not be forced through a gate. "You are telling the truth, Master? You are certain?"

"I'm certain of nothing," Chaven said. "Nothing. Now go fetch me the wine and perhaps a bit of cheese and bread and dried fish, too, then let me think."

He let the hanging fall back across the window. It was still dark outside, although he could smell dawn on the breeze, which should have been reassuring but was not. The wine had done nothing to relieve the pressure in his skull, the fear that he was watching the first moments of a collapse that might soon begin to spread so quickly there would be no stopping it. He had been in the middle of such a frenzy before, although not in Southmarch: he never wanted to experience it again. And of all the people who had been in the castle tonight dealing with the horror of the prince regent's death, Chaven alone knew of the movement of the Shadowline.

He had questions he wanted to ask before he slept—*needed* to ask. Unusual questions.

The idea had been preying on him since the first dreadful moment looking down on Kendrick's murdered body and had kept tugging at him since, far more powerful than the urge for wine he had just satisfied. He had tried to fight it down because there was more than a little shame in his hunger and he had promised himself not to indulge again so soon, but he reassured himself that it was clearly an exceptional night, a night for suspending his own rules. And (he also told himself) the things he might learn could save his life, perhaps even save the kingdom.

"Kloe?" he called quietly. He snapped his fingers and looked around. "Where are you, my mistress?"

She did not appear immediately, upset perhaps that after a rude and hurried excursion from their shared bed earlier he had been back in his house for an hour, but this was the first time he seemed to have thought of her.

"Kloe, I apologize. I have been discourteous."

Mollified, she appeared from behind a curtain and stretched. She was spotted like a pard, but all in shadow-tones of black and gray, with only a little white around her eyes. Chaven could not have said exactly why he found her beautiful but he did. He snapped his fingers again and she came to him, exactly slow enough to demonstrate whose need was greater. But when he scratched under her chin she forgot herself enough to purr.

"Come," he said, and gave the cat the last bit of dried fish before lifting her. "We have work to do."

It was a room that no living person in Southmarch Castle except Chaven had ever seen, a small dark compartment deep beneath the observatory, with a door that opened off the corridor where he had let in the Funderling Chert and his strange ward. On one wall a row of shelves began near the flagstone floor and stretched to the low ceiling, and every shelf contained a row of objects covered with dark cloths. With the door safely closed and bolted behind him, Chaven put down his candleholder and picked up a covered object too large to rest beside the others, which had been leaning propped against the wall. Kloe, after a brief sniff around the room, leaped up onto one of the upper shelves and curled into a ball, her eyes bright and watchful.

He took off the velvet cover very carefully, then unfolded the wooden wings so that the mirror could stand by itself. It was one of his largest: with the base on the floor, the top reached almost to the physician's waist.

Chaven lowered himself into a sitting position on the flags in front of the mirror and for a long time said nothing, staring deep into the glass. The candlelight made strange angles of things and cast long, swaying shadows: if something had actually been moving in the mirror's depths, it would have taken an observer a little while to be sure.

Chaven remained silent for a long, long time. At last, without turning from the glass, he said, "Kloe? Come here, now, Mistress. Come."

The cat stretched, then jumped down from the shelf and stepped delicately across the floor toward him. When she stopped, he reached out and tapped on the mirror.

"Do you see that? Look there, Kloe! A mouse!"

She brought her blunt gray-and-black face close to the glass, staring. Her ears twitched. Indeed, there was something moving in the dark corner of the room, but only in the room as it was reflected. Kloe hunched lower, tail kinking and unkinking as she watched the scurrying shadow in the depths of the mirror. Chaven stared at it, too, fixedly, as though he dared not close his eyes or even breathe. Oddly, the mirror seemed not to reflect either the cat or physician, but only the empty room behind them.

Without warning, Kloe lunged forward. For a moment it actually seemed that her paw passed through the reflecting surface, but she hissed in frustration as though she had struck only cold glass. Chaven abruptly picked her up, stroked her, and then unbolted the door and put her outside in the corridor.

"Wait for me."

Balked, but by what it was hard to say, Kloe let out a warble of irritation.

"You would not be happy in here," he told the cat as he closed the door. "And you would never have tasted that mouse anyway, I fear."

Now he sat before the mirror again. The candle was apparently burning low because the room swiftly grew darker. All that showed in the mirror were the reflected walls, except that the mirror-chamber contained a tiny bundle of darkness lying on the mirror-floor near the front of the glass.

Chaven sang a little in a very old language, was quiet for some time, then sang a little more. He sat and stared at the small dark shape. He waited.

When it came, it was like a sudden flame, an explosion of pale light. Despite his strong, schooled nerves, Chaven let out a quiet grunt of surprise. Feathers rippled and gleamed in the depths of the mirror as it clutched the dead mouse with a taloned foot, then bent to take the offering in its sharp beak. For a moment the tail hung like a thread, then the shadow-mouse was swallowed down and a huge white owl stared out of the glass with eyes like molten copper.

"I don't understand," said the boy Flint, scowling. "I like the tunnels. Why do we have to walk up here?"

Chert looked back to make sure the Funderling work crew were in an orderly line behind him. Dawn was just beginning to lighten the sky and turn the shadows silvery: if they had been big folk and unused to darkness, they would have been carrying torches. Chert's guildsmen were straggling a little, a few whispering avidly among themselves, but that was within the bounds of suitable respect. He turned back to the boy. "Because when we go to work in the keep, we always come in at the gate. Remember, there are no tunnels that lead into the inner keep from below." He gave the boy a significant look, praying silently to the Earth Elders that the child would not start prattling about the underground doorway into Chaven's observatory within the hearing of the other Funderlings.

Flint shook his head. "We could have gone a lot of the way underground. I *like* the tunnels!"

"I'm glad to hear it, because if you stay with us, you'll be spending a lot of your days in them. Now, hush—we're coming to the gate."

A young Trigon priest awaited them at the guard tower of the Raven's Gate. He was thick in the waist and looked as though he didn't deny himself much, but he did not treat Chert as though he were half-witted as well as half-heighted, which made everything much more pleasant.

"I am Andros, Lord Castellan Nynor's proxy," announced the priest. "And you are . . ." he consulted a leatherbound book, ". . . Hornblende?"

"No, he took ill. I'm Chert and I'll be chief of this job." He produced the Stonecutter's Guild's *astion,* a circle of crystal polished very thin (but startlingly durable) that he wore around his neck on a cord. "Here is my token."

"That is well, sir." The priest frowned in distraction. "I am here not to contest your authority, but to tell you that your orders have changed. Are you aware of what happened here only one night ago?"

"Of course. All of Funderling Town is in mourning already." Which was not entirely the truth, but certainly the news had shot from house to house over the last grim day like an echo, and most of the inhabitants of the underground city were shocked and frightened. "We wondered whether it was appropriate to come this morning as had been originally ordered, but since we had not heard otherwise . . ."

"Quite right. But instead of the work that was planned, we have a sadder and more pressing task for you. The family vault where we will lay Prince Kendrick has no more room. We knew of this, of course, but did not think we should need to enlarge it so soon, never expecting . . ." He broke off and dabbed at his nose with a sleeve. This man was genuinely mourning, Chert could see. *Well, he knew the prince, no doubt—perhaps spoke to him often.* Chert himself was feeling quite unsettled, and he had never seen the prince regent closer than a hundred yards. "We are happy to serve," he told Andros.

The priest smiled sadly. "Yes. Well, I have your instructions here, directly from Lord Nynor. The work must be swift, but remember this is the burial place for an Eddon prince. We will not have time to paint the new tomb properly, but we can at least make sure it is clean and well-measured."

"It will be the best work we can do."

The interior of the tomb cast a shadow on Chert's heart. He looked at little Flint, wide-eyed but unbothered by the heavy carvings, the stylized masks of wolves snarling out of deep shadows, the images of sleeping warriors and queens on top of the ancient stone caskets. The tomb walls were honeycombed with niches, and every niche held a sarcophagus. "Does this frighten you?"

The boy looked at him as though the question made no sense. He shook his head briskly.

I only wish I could say the same, thought Chert. Behind him the work gang was also quiet as they made their way through the mazy tomb. It was not the idea of mortal spirits that disturbed him, of ghosts—although in this dark, quiet place he was not quick to dismiss the thought—but of the ultimate futility of things. *Do what you will, you will come to this. Whether you sit lonely in your house and store up money, or sing loud in the guildhall, buying tankards of mossbrew for all your friends and relations, in the end you will find this—or it will find you . . .*

He paused beside one niche. On the coffin lid was carved a man in full armor, his helmet in the crook of his elbow, his sword hilt clasped upon his chest. His beard was wound with ribbons, each wrought in careful, almost loving detail.

"Here lies the king's father," he told Flint. "The old king, Ustin. He was a fierce man, but a scourge to the country's enemies and a fair-dealer to our people."

"He was a hard-hearted bastard," said one of the work gang quietly.

"Who said that?" Chert glared. "You, Pumice?"

"What if I did?" The young Funderling, not three years a guild member, returned his stare. "What did Ustin or any of his kind ever do for us?

We build their castles and forge their weapons so they can slaughter each other—and us, every few generations—and what do we get in return?"

"We have our own city . . ."

Pumice laughed. He was sharp-eyed, dark, and thin. Chert thought the youth had somehow got himself born into the wrong family. *He should have been a Blackglass, that one.* "Cows have their own fields. Do they get to keep their milk?"

"That's enough." Some of the others on the work gang were stirring, but Chert could not tell whether they were restless with Pumice's prating or in agreement with him. "We have work to do."

"Ah, yes. The poor, sad, dead prince. Did he ever step into Funderling Town, ever in his life?"

"You are speaking nonsense, Pumice. What has got into you?" He glanced at Flint, who was watching the exchange without expression.

"You ask me that? Just because I have never loved the big folk? If someone needs to explain, I think it's you, Chert. None of the rest of us have adopted one of *them* into our own household."

"Go out," Chert told the boy. "Go and play—there is a garden up above." A cemetery, in truth, but garden enough.

"But . . . !"

"Do not argue with me, boy. I need to talk to these men and you will only find it boring. Go out. But stay close to the entrance."

Flint clearly felt he would find the conversation anything but boring, but masked his feelings in that way he had and walked across the tomb and up the stairs. When he was gone, Chert turned back to Pumice and the rest of the work gang.

"Have any of you a complaint with my leadership? Because I will not lead men who grumble and whine, nor will I chief a job where I do not trust my workers. Pumice, you have had much to say. You do not like my feelings about our masters. That is your privilege, I suppose—you are free and a guildsman. Do you have aught else to say about me?"

The younger man seemed about to start again, but it was an older man, one of the Gypsum cousins, who spoke instead. "He doesn't talk for the rest of us, Chert. In fact, we've spent a bit too much time listening to him lately, truth be told." A few of the other men grunted agreement.

"Cowards, the lot of you," Pumice sneered. "Slaving away like you were in the Autarch's mines, working yourselves almost to death, then down on your knees to thank the big folks for the privilege."

A sour smile twisted Chert's mouth. "The day I see you working your-self almost to death, Pumice, will be a day when all the world has finally gone wheels-over-ore-cart." The rest of the men laughed and the moment of danger passed. A few rocks had tumbled free, but there had been no slide. Still, Chert was not happy that there had been such ill-feeling already on the first day.

Maybe old Hornblende just didn't want to work with Pumice. Reason enough to have a bad back, perhaps . . . Less than an hour past dawn and already his head hurt. "Right, you lot. Whatever some of you may think, these are sad times and this is an important chore. So let's get to work."

"I cannot sit through this," Barrick abruptly declared.

Briony felt ambushed that he should turn on her in front of Avin Brone and the other nobles. "What do you mean?" she whispered. Her voice seemed a sharp hiss like a snake; she could feel the councillors, all men, looking at her with disapproval. "Shaso has not confessed, Barrick. It is not a certain thing that he has killed Kendrick. After all these years, you owe the man something!"

Barrick waved his hand—dismissively, it seemed, and for a moment Briony felt a stab of anger sharp as any Tuani knife. Then she saw that Barrick's eyes were closed, his face even more pale than usual. "No. I do not . . . feel well," he said.

So terrible had this morning been, so topsy-turvy, that despite the clutch at her heart to see his waxy face—so frighteningly like Kendrick's blood-less, lifeless mask—she still felt a squeezing suspicion. Did Barrick want nothing to do with what was coming next, for some reason? Had Lord Constable Brone and the others been talking to him already?

Her brother staggered a little as he got up. One of the guards stepped forward to take his elbow. "Go on," Barrick told her. "Must lie down."

Another and even more horrifying thought: *What if he is not just ill—what if he has been poisoned?* What if someone had set on a track of killing all the Eddons? Horrified and frightened, she murmured a quick prayer to Zoria, then dutifully asked the Trigon's help as well. Who would do such a thing? Who could even conceive of such moon-madness?

Someone who wanted the throne . . . She looked at Gailon of Summerfield, but the duke looked quite normally concerned to see Barrick so sweaty and weak. "Get him straight to bed, and send for Chaven," she directed the man holding his arm. "No, let one of the pages fetch Chaven now, so that he can meet my brother in his chambers."

When Barrick had been helped from the room, Briony noted with some approval that her own mask was still in place—the public mask of imperturbability that her father had taught her to make of her features. She had despised Avin Brone for a heartless bully on the night of Kendrick's murder, but she was grateful to him for reminding her of her duty. She had a responsibility to the Eddon family as well as to her people: she would not give away the truth of her feelings so easily again. But, oh, it was hard to be stiff and stern when she was so frightened!

"My brother, Prince Barrick, will not be coming back," she said. "So there is no sense in making our guest wait longer. Send him in."

"But, Highness . . . !" began Duke Gailon.

"What, Summerfield, do you think I have no wit at all? That I am a marionette who can only speak when one of my brothers or my father is present to work my strings? I said bring him in." She turned away. *Zoria give me strength,* she prayed. *If you have ever loved me, love me now. Help me.*

The intensity with which the councillors whispered among themselves would in ordinary circumstances have made Briony very uneasy, but circumstances were not ordinary and they might never be so again. Gailon Tolly and Earl Tyne of Blueshore did not even try to hide their anger at her. These men had seldom had to take an order from any woman, even a princess.

I cannot afford to care what they think, and I cannot even be as forbearing with them as Father. In him, they think it an odd humor. In me, they will be certain to mark it as weakness . . .

The door opened and the dark man was led in by the royal guard. Guard Captain Ferras Vansen was again pointedly not looking at her—another man, she felt certain, who held her as worthless. Briony had not decided yet what she wanted to do with Vansen, but surely some example would have to be made. Could the reigning prince of the March Kingdoms be murdered in his bed and no more come of it than if an apple were stolen off a peddler's cart?

At her nod the guards stopped and allowed the man they had escorted to continue by himself to the foot of the dais and the twins' two chairs, which for the moment stood side by side in front of King Olin's throne.

"My deepest condolences," said Dawet dan-Faar, bowing. He had exchanged his finery of a few days before for restrained black. On him, it somehow looked exotically handsome. "Of course there is nothing I can say to ease your loss, my lady, but it is painful to see your family so bereft. I am certain that my lord Ludis would wish me to send his deep sympathies as well."

Briony scanned his face for some trace of mockery, the faintest gleam of dark amusement in his eye. For the first time she could see that he was not a young man, that he was perhaps only a decade younger than her own father, though his brown skin was unlined, his jaw firm as a youth's. Beyond that, she saw nothing untoward. If he was dissembling, he did it splendidly.

Still, that is his skill—it must be. Were he not a veteran dissembler and flatterer he would not be an envoy for ambitious Ludis. And there was also the story of Shaso's daughter, which Barrick had told her—another reason to despise this man. But there was no denying he was good to look upon.

"You are not entirely beyond suspicion yourself, Lord Dawet, but my guards say you and your party did not stray from your chambers . . ."

"It is gracious of them to speak what is only the honest truth." The attractive and completely untrustworthy smile that she remembered made its first appearance of the day, but only for an instant, then the seriousness of the matter chased it away again. "We slept, my lady."

"Perhaps. But murder must not always be committed by the hand of its principal." She was finding it easier and easier to keep her face hard, her gaze stern and unblinking. "Murder can be bought, just as easily as a pie in a pie shop."

Now his smile returned. He seemed genuinely amused. "And what would you know of buying things in pie shops, Princess?"

"Not much," she admitted. "Sadly, I know a bit more of murder, these days."

He nodded. "True. And a useful reminder that as much as I enjoy bandying words with you—and I do, my lady—there are more sad and serious matters before us. So rather than indulge myself with a great sham of indignation, Highness, let me instead ask you a question. What benefit would it be to me to kill your poor brother?"

She had to bite down hard on her lip to keep the sudden noise of misery from escaping. Only a very short time ago Kendrick had been alive. If only there were some way to reach back into the day before yesterday, like reaching into a house through a window instead of walking all the way around to the door—some way to change those horrible events or prevent them entirely. "What benefit?" she asked, rallying her thoughts. "I don't know." Her voice was less firm than she would have liked. Avin Brone and the others were watching closely—mistrustfully, it seemed to her. As if because the man was comely and well-spoken, she would be any the less careful and doubting! Her cheeks grew hot with resentment.

"Let us speak honestly, my lady. This is a terrible time and honesty may be the best friend to us all. My master, Ludis Drakava, holds your father hostage, whatever name we put on it. We await either a vast ransom in gold or a ransom worth even more—because you, lovely princess, will be part of it." His smile was gently mocking again. But was he making sport of her or something else? Perhaps even himself? "From Hierosol's vantage, all that your elder brother's death will do is muddy the waters and slow down the paying of that ransom. We have the king and have not harmed him—why should we murder the prince now? In fact, the only reason you even ask me is because I am a stranger in the castle . . . and not precisely a friend. But I regret the last. I do sincerely."

She could not let herself be distracted. He was too smooth, too quick—it must be how a mouse felt in front of a snake. But *this* mouse would not be so easily confused. "Because you are a stranger and no friend, yes. And because, as you may know, my brother seems to have been killed with a Tuani knife. Like the one on your belt."

Dawet looked down. "I would take it out to let you see that there is no blood upon it, Princess, but your guard captain tied it tightly in its sheath before I was brought to you."

Briony looked up to see that Ferras Vansen, who had ignored her earlier, was now staring at her fixedly. But upon catching her eye he colored and turned his gaze to the floor. *Is the man mad?*

"He would have preferred to take it away entirely," Dawet continued, "but among my people we do not take off our knives once we have reached the age of manhood. Unless we are in bed."

Now she was the one to flush. "You speak many words, my lord Dawet, but few to any point. Knives can be washed. Reputations are not so easily made clean and new."

His eyes widened. "Are we crossing blades again, Highness, testing each other's style of battle? No, I think I will not engage, for I see rather that you are one of those who trades blows only for a little while, then aims straight for the heart. What do you know of me, Princess? Or what do you think you know of me?"

"More than I care to remember. Shaso told us of what happened to his daughter."

And now something passed across the high-boned face that surprised her—not shame, or irritation at being caught out, but a real and indignant anger like the god Perin when he awoke on Mount Xandos to find his hammer stolen. "Ah, did he?"

"Yes. And that your cruelty drove her into a temple, and that she died there."

Now Dawet's anger turned into something even stranger—a sudden banking of the flame, not unlike the way Shaso often retreated behind his own stony features. Not surprising, perhaps—they were related, after all. "She died, yes. And he said that I am the one who drove her there?"

"Is it not true, sir?"

He let his long-lashed eyes close for a moment. When the lids sprang up again, his eyes fixed on hers. "There are many kinds of truth, my lady. One is that I ruined a girl of a noble house in my own land. Another might be that I loved her, and that the wound done to her reputation by the gossiping of witless women in the palace was greater than any harm I ever did her. And that when her father drove her out of their house, I would have taken her in, would have made her my own, but that she could not bear to have her father and mother cast her out of their lives forever. She hoped—foolishly, I thought—that someday they would take her back. So, instead, she went to the temple. Did she die there? Yes. Of a broken heart? Yes, perhaps. But who broke it?" He shook his head and for the first time looked around at the Southmarch nobles. With his gaze no longer on her, Briony realized she had been leaning forward in her chair. "Who broke it?" he said again, quietly, but with a force that suggested he was truly addressing the entire room. "That is a question that even the wisest folk might dispute."

She sat back, a bit uncertain. The nobles, especially the council members, watched her suspiciously. Nor could she entirely blame them this time: it seemed to her, and must have been very clear to them, that for some time there had been no one in the room but herself and the dark stranger.

"So . . . so you blame Shaso for his own daughter's death?"

He gave a kind of shrug. "Wise folk may toy with any contention, my lady, and truth seems sometimes entirely mutable. That is the age in which we live."

"Which is to say you will not answer that question outright, since you have so prettily painted the picture of it already without having to show yourself mean-spirited. But if you feel that way, I must suppose you would also believe he could be the murderer of my brother."

Dawet looked a little surprised. "Has he not confessed it? Someone told me that he had. I thought you prodded me about my innocence in your brother's death only to see whether because I was his countryman I was also his confederate. But I assure you, my lady, find any Tuani beyond infancy and he will tell you of Shaso's famous hatred of me." He frowned. "But if it is not proved that he did it—then, no. I would not think him a murderer."

"What?" Briony's voice was much louder than she would wish. Gailon of Summerfield looked at her disapprovingly. She felt a momentary urge to have the young duke clapped in leg irons or something—queens used to be able to do such things, so why not the princess regent? Despite his other faults, Dawet dan-Faar at least did not frown at her like an old servant just because she had raised her voice. "Do you jest?" she demanded. "You hate the man. It is clear in your every word and glance!"

The emissary shook his head. "I do not love him, and just as he thinks I have done him harm, I think he has done me as much or more. But my disregard does not make him a murderer. I cannot believe he would treacherously kill someone, especially not someone of your family."

"What do you mean?"

"All know that he owed your father a debt of honor. When my father fought against the last Autarch, Parnad the Unsleeping, Shaso did not return to help because he could not break his oath to your father. When his wife was ill, he also did not return, because he could not break that oath, nor did he return for her funeral. And so now I am asked whether I think he would kill Olin's son? Drunkenly and treacherously? There may be stiffer spines and more stubborn hearts that have come out of Xand than Shaso dan-Heza's—but I have not seen one."

What he said made her feel even more uncertain of things, and not just about Shaso's guilt. Was this man Dawet a clever monster, or was he misunderstood? People often thought Barrick unpleasant, even cruel, because they did not see the whole of him.

Barrick. A sudden twinge of alarm. *He is lying ill in bed. I should go to him.* In truth, the conversation had made her feel quite disturbed: she would not be unhappy to stop it. "I will consider your words, Lord Dawet. Now you may go."

He bowed once more. "Again, my condolences, Lady."

As he left, the councillors still watched her, but their faces were more shuttered than before. She suddenly realized that she had known most of them her entire life, these neighbors and family friends and even relatives, but did not trust a single one.

"Make yourself vulnerable to no one but your family," her father had once said. *"Because that makes a small enough company that you can watch them all carefully."* She had thought at the time he was joking.

But *I have little family left, anyway,* she thought. *Mother and Kendrick are dead. Father is gone and may never come back. All I have is Barrick.*

The room seemed full of hateful strangers. Suddenly, all she wanted was to see her twin. She stood up and walked out of the throne room without another word, so quickly that the guards had to scramble to catch up to her.

"It will not be easy," Chert told Opal as he finished his soup. "We don't have enough men to do a proper job, and the guild may not be able to get me more in time—the funeral is to be in five days. So for now we're just throwing rubble down into the very pits where we were going to be working before the prince died. It'll all have to be cleared out again afterward."

"Who could do such a terrible thing?" she said.

For a moment, with his mind full of the task, he could not understand what she meant. "Ah. Do you mean killing the prince?"

"Of course, you old fool. What else?" Her cross expression, mostly for effect, softened. "That family is under a curse. That's what people were saying in Quarry Square today. The king captured, the younger prince a cripple, now this. And I suppose the children's mother dying, too, though that was years ago . . ." She frowned. "But what about the new queen? If something happens to those poor twins, will her baby inherit the throne? Think of that . . . before it is even born."

"Fissure and fracture, woman, the twins are still alive—do you wish to bring something down on them? Never give the idle gods anything to think about." The idea of something happening to the girl Briony, who had spoken to him just as freely and kindly as though he were a friend or family member, made him fearful in a way that a whole day in the royal tomb had not accomplished. "Where is Flint?"

"In his bed. He was tired."

Chert got up and walked into the sleeping room where Flint's straw pallet now lay at the foot of their own bed. The boy hurriedly shoved something under the rolled shirt which he used to cushion his head.

"What's that? What have you got, lad?" An ordinary child would probably have denied everything, Chert thought as he bent down, but Flint only watched with a certain hooded intent as he reached under the shirt and his hand closed around a confusing combination of shapes.

Lifted out and held in the light of the lamp, he saw that they were two separate objects, a small black sack on a cord, which looked a bit familiar, and a lump of translucent, grayish-white stone.

"What is this?" he asked, holding up the sack. Whatever it held so snugly was hard and almost as heavy as stone. The top of the bag was sewed shut, but the threadwork on the rest of it was intricate and beautiful. "Where did you find this, boy?"

"He didn't," said Opal in the doorway. "He was wearing it when *we* found *him*. It's his, Chert."

"What's in it?"

"I don't know. It isn't ours to open, and he hasn't wanted to."

"But this could have . . . I don't know, perhaps something in it telling of his real parents. A piece of jewelry with his family name on it, perhaps." *Or a costly heirloom that might help pay for his room and board,* Chert could not help thinking.

"It is his," said Opal again, quietly. She knelt beside the boy and stroked his pale hair and Chert suddenly understood that she didn't necessarily want to find out the boy's true name, his parent's names. . . .

"Well," he began, looking at the sack, but now his attention was caught by the stone. What he had at first thought was only a sedimentary lump polished by rain or sea, or perhaps even just a weathered piece of pottery, was something much stranger. It *was* a stone, that seemed clear, but as he stared at it, he realized it was of a kind he had never seen before, nor could he even recognize where it fit in the Family of Stones and Metals. A Funderling not recognizing a stone's family was something like a dairy farmer stumbling across not just a new breed of cow, but one that could fly.

"Look at this," he said to Opal. "Can you make anything of it?"

"Cloudchip?" she suggested, naming an obscure kind of crystal. "Earth-ice?"

He shook his head. "No, it's neither of those. Flint, where did you find this stone, boy?"

"In the garden place. Outside where you were digging." The boy stuck out his hand. "Give them back."

Chert glanced from the boy to the bag on a cord, the mysterious, sewn-shut bag. He handed it back to Flint but hung onto the murky crystal. He and Opal would need to talk about this mysterious legacy, but there was no sense worrying about everything at once. "I'm going to take this stone," he told the child. "Not to keep, but because I've never seen anything like it and I want to see if someone can tell me what it is." He looked at the boy, who stared back expectantly. It took Chert a moment to understand why. "If I may, that is," he said. "You found it, after all."

The boy nodded, satisfied. As Chert and Opal went out, Flint rolled onto his back, staring at the ceiling as he squeezed the little leather bag between his fingers.

Opal returned to her clearing up, but Chert only sat, turning the crystal over and over in his hand. It seemed to have an artificial shape, that was the strange thing, a regularity—it appeared to have been chipped out of some larger piece, but there were no fracture-markings; in fact, the edges were quite rounded. And it was definitely, incontrovertibly, something he had not seen before. A dark spot seemed to move in its depths.

It troubled him, and the more he thought about it the more troubled he grew. It seemed like something that could only have come from behind the Shadowline, but if so, what was it doing deep inside Southmarch Castle? And was it coincidence that the boy found it in the cemetery, only a few hundred steps from the chambers where the prince regent was murdered? Or that the boy from beyond the Shadowline had been the one who found it?

He looked at Opal, who was contentedly darning a hole in the knee of Flint's breeches. He desperately wanted to ask her opinion, but knew he was going to spend a mostly sleepless night himself and was reluctant to rob her of what might be her last contented slumber for some time. Because a fear was growing inside him.

What was it that Chaven had said? *"Do not doubt that if the Shadowline sweeps across us, it will bring with it a dark, dark evil."*

Let Opal at least have this night, he decided. *Let her be happy this one night.*

"You're quiet, Chert. Are you feeling poorly?"

"All is well, my old darling," he said. "Never fear."

10
Halls of Fire

INVOCATION:

Here is the kingdom, here are its tears
Two sticks
Nothing is known about any day that is past

—from *The Bonefall Oracles*

IT WAS ALWAYS BAD IN the lands of sleep, but this was worse than the other nights, far worse. The long halls of Southmarch were again full of the shadow-men, the insubstantial but relentless figures who dripped and flowed like black blood, who oozed from the cracks between the stones and then took shape, faceless and whispering. But this night, everywhere they went, flames followed them, blazing up in the wake of their pursuit, until it seemed as though the very air would catch fire.

Everywhere he went more of them appeared, oozing up from beneath the flagstones, clotting as they slid or shuffled after him, solidifying into vague man-shapes. Eyeless, still they stared, and they called mouthlessly after him, noises of both threat and promise. They followed him, many still joined to their brethren in a near-solid mass, and fire came behind them, catching in the tapestries and licking upward toward the ancient ceiling as the faceless men followed his hopeless attempt at flight from room to room, through corridor after corridor.

They killed Kendrick! His heart seemed lopsided in his chest; his lungs burned. Room after room was wreathed in flame, but still the dark men swarmed after him.

They want to kill me, too—kill us all! The air was so hot it scorched his nostrils and crackled in his throat, as though the entire palace had become an oven. These phantoms of soot, shadow, and blood had killed his brother and now they would kill him, too, chase him like a wounded deer and hound him to his death through endless halls of flame. . . .

"Make him well!"

Chaven stood slowly. At his feet, the page who crouched beside Barrick's bed dabbed at the prince's brow with a wet cloth. "It is not so easy, Princess . . ."

"I don't care! My brother is burning up with fever!" Briony felt a balance inside her tipping dangerously. "He is in pain!"

Chaven shook his head. "With all respect, I think not so much, Highness. It is one of the boons of fever—it clouds much of the hurt of the illness and lets the mind float free of the body."

"Float free?" She struggled to control herself but her finger was trembling as she pointed at her writhing, moaning twin. "Look at him! Do you think he is free of anything?"

The other physician, Brother Okros, cleared his throat. "Actually, my lady, we have seen others afflicted this way, but in a few days many have been well again."

She turned on this small, diffident man who had come from Eastmarch Academy in the mainland town to consult with Chaven. Okros took a step back as though she might hit him, and for a moment she felt a hysterical sense of pleasure at his fear, at the power of her own anger. "Yes? Many? What does that mean? And how long have you all known about this fever-plague?"

"Since the ending of the last festival month, Highness." There was a slight squeak in his voice. Okros was a priest, but mostly in name only, a teacher of the sciences who had probably seldom set foot in a Trigon temple since his ordainment. "Your brother—your other brother—was informed by the academy when the first groups of sufferers began to come to us. But he . . ."

"Was killed? Yes." She took a deep breath, but it did not calm her. "Yes, that might explain why he hasn't given his time to this issue. Did you plan to wait until everyone else in my family was dead from one thing or another before mentioning this plague to me?"

"Please, Princess," said Chaven. "Briony. Please."

The use of her name caught her for a moment, made her look at the court physician. She couldn't quite read the expression on his round face, but it was clear he was trying to tell her something. *I am making a fool of myself, that is what.* She looked around at the servants and guards in Barrick's room and knew there were more castle folk outside, no doubt with their ears pressed to the door. She blinked against what felt like the beginning of tears. *I am frightening everyone.*

"It is not a plague, Highness," Okros said carefully. "Not yet. We have fever seasons like this almost every year. This is simply more severe than most."

"Just tell me what will happen to my brother."

"His elements are out of balance," Chaven explained. "He is full of fire, at least in a sense. I do not want to insult you with what may seem like old superstitions, but it is hard to explain illness without also explaining how the elements within us correspond to the elements without—in our earth and in our firmament." He rubbed his head wearily. "So I will only say that his blood is too heated because the elements are out of balance. Normally the elements of earth and water already inside him would serve to keep that balance, just as stones ring a blaze and water extinguishes it when necessary. But he is all fire and air at the moment, gusting and burning."

Gusting and burning. She looked down in horror at Barrick's dear face, so contorted now and so oblivious. *Oh, merciful Zoria, please don't take him from me. Don't leave me alone in this haunted place. Please.*

"Many have already survived this fever, Princess," said little Brother Okros. "We have had news of it from southern travelers in prior days. It has already been in Syan and Jellon for months."

"Perhaps it came in with the ship from Hierosol," Chaven suggested. He had tugged the page boy away and was examining Barrick again, smelling his breath. Briony's twin was a little quieter, but he still murmured worriedly in his sleep, his face sparkling with sweat.

"It doesn't matter," she said. It was the bleak and ruthless will of the gods, the dark wings she had felt spreading above them all. It was her every dire premonition coming true. "It doesn't matter where it came from. Just tell me this—how many die from it and how many live?"

"We hate to make pronouncements of that type, my lady . . ." began the academy physician.

Chaven frowned at him. "At least half have survived. Unless they were babies or old folk."

"Half?" She was on the verge of shrieking again. She closed her eyes and felt the world spinning around her. All had gone mad. All had gone completely mad. "And what is the treatment?"

"Open windows," Okros said promptly. "Dirt from the temple of Kernios beneath the head and foot of his bed. And wrap him in wet cloths—water from Erivor's temple basins would be particularly good, and we must make prayers to Erivor, of course, since he is your family's special patron. All this will serve to soothe the influence of fire and air."

"There are also herbs that might help." As Chaven rubbed at his forehead again, considering, Briony noticed for the first time that the court physician looked dreadful. His features were pale and sagging, and he carried circles dark as bruises beneath his eyes. "Willow bark. And tea made from elder flowers might also help bring down the fever . . ."

"We should bleed him as well," added Okros, glad to be talking about something meaningful. "A bit less blood will ease his suffering."

Briony nudged Chaven to one side, none too gently, and with an immense rustling of skirts sank down beside her brother. *These clothes keep me trussed like a troublesome horse,* she thought as she struggled to find a comfortable position. *Or a captured thief. It hurts even to bend.*

Her brother's eyes were mere slits, but his pupils darted about between the lids.

"Barrick? It's me, Briony. Oh, please, can't you hear me?" She touched his cheek then took his hand; despite its warmth, it was damp as something found in a rock pool. "I won't leave you."

"You *must* leave him, my lady," said a new voice. Briony looked up to see Avin Brone standing in the doorway, filling it with his bulk. "I beg your pardon, but the truth must be told. There is much to do. Tomorrow we bury the prince regent. Tomorrow someone must take up the scepter so that the people can see an Eddon still sits the throne. If Prince Barrick is too ill, then it must be you. And I have other news for you as well."

She felt a weird little thrill. *So the only person I can absolutely trust not to send me to Ludis,* she realized, *will be on that throne.* For a moment she had an image of all the things she might do, all the petty wrongs she could reverse.

Then she looked down at Barrick again and the idea of what she might accomplish seemed pointless.

"How many are sick with this?" she asked Chaven.

"How many have the fever now?" He looked at the physician from the academy. "A few hundred in the town, perhaps. Is that right, Okros? And a dozen or so in the castle. Three of the kitchen servants, I think. Your stepmother's maid and two of Barrick's own pages." He patted the head of the little boy who held the wet cloth. "Those are the ones I knew about when your brother began to sicken."

"Anissa's maid? But how is Anissa herself?"

"Your stepmother is well and so is the baby she carries."

"And none of those who came with that man Dawet have the fever?"

Chaven shook his head.

"Strange it should be brought on their ship and yet none of them should sicken."

"Yes, but fever is a strange thing," said this pale, battered-looking Chaven—a man who almost seemed a stranger to her. She found herself wondering for perhaps the first time ever in her life what he did when he was by himself, what life and thoughts he kept secret from others, as everyone did. "It can touch one and leave another standing just beside him unharmed."

"Like murder," she said.

Briony was almost the only one in the room who did not make the sign to ward away evil after she had spoken. Even Barrick groaned in his fevered sleep.

He had run until he was beyond the immediate reach of the faceless shapes, the whisperers, but he knew they were still somewhere behind him, flowing through the honeycombed rooms, sniffing for him like dogs. He was in a wing of the castle he didn't know, chamber after chamber of dusty, unfamiliar objects flung around without order or care. A broken orrery stood on a table, metal arms bent so that they protruded in all directions like the quills of some spiky creature. Carpets and tapestries were draped across each other, bunched and crumpled at the edges, even spread onto the timbered ceiling so that it was somehow difficult to tell which way was up, and they were beginning to curl with the rising heat.

He stopped. Someone—or something—was calling his name.

"Barrick! Where are you?"

He realized with a spasm of terror that it was not only the shadow-men who were looking for him, the men of smoke and blood, but something else as well. Something dark and tall and singular. Something that had been hunting him a long, long time.

His swift walk became a run. Moments later it became a wild, headlong dash. Still his own name floated to him like a lonely echo from one benighted mountaintop to another, or like the cry of some lost soul stranded upon the moon.

"Barrick? Come back!"

He was in a long corridor open on one side, he realized, sprinting through a gallery that dropped away next to him, a dizzying plunge to the stone flags just a misstep away. All the castle must be afire now—here the tapestries were burning at the bottom edges, flames beginning to lick their way up the stylized hunting scenes and representations of adventuring gods and ancient kings seated in glory.

"Barrick?"

He pulled up, heart speeding. The flames were climbing higher, the gallery filling with black smoke. He could feel a baking heat all down his right side that hurt his skin. He wanted to run, but something was moving in the smoke ahead of him, something stained red and orange by leaping firelight.

"I am angry. Very angry."

Barrick's heart felt as though it might crack his breastbone. The shape trudged out of the murk, smoke dripping down its length like water, fire curling in the dark beard.

"You shouldn't run from me, boy." His father's stare was dull and empty, cloudy as the eyes of a dead fish in a bucket. *"Shouldn't run. It makes me angry with you."*

For all her discontent with her clothing, Briony was glad for once that Moina and Rose had laced her so tightly, glad that her embroidered stomacher was stiff as armor. It seemed to be all that held her upright on her battered wooden chair—the chair that at least for this mad moment had become the throne of all the March Kingdoms.

Did anyone else feel the same as she did? Did everyone? Were all these castle folk in their ornate finery no more than confused souls hiding inside costumes, as the hard shells of snails protected the helpless, naked things that lived within them?

"He says *what?*" She was frightened again, even if she forced herself not to show it. She fought hard to keep her eyes on the lord constable, not to let her glance dart into the shadows in anxious search for the assassins and traitors who had seemed all around her in the terrible hour of Kendrick's death, but whose phantom presences had been mostly absent since Shaso's capture. "But we found the bloody knife—surely you have told him that. What does he claim?"

"He will not tell us anything else." Avin Brone looked almost as tired as Chaven had, his great body sagging. He would clearly have liked to sit down, but Briony did not call for a stool. "He simply says he did not kill your brother or his guards."

"Pay no attention to this nonsense, Briony." Gailon Tolly's anger seemed genuine, and for once it was not aimed at her. "Would an innocent man not tell everything he knew? Shaso is taken by shame, that is all. Though I am surprised it could happen with such a villain."

"But what if he is telling the truth, Duke Gailon?" Briony turned back to Brone. "Or what if he is not the only murderer? It still seems strange he should kill all three by himself."

"Not so strange, Highness," suggested the lord constable. "He is a deadly fighter, and they would not have been prepared—he would have caught them all unsuspecting. He likely stabbed the first guard and set on the second in a mere moment. Once the second guard was killed, he then attacked your unarmed brother."

Briony felt queasy. She couldn't bear to think too deeply about it—about Kendrick alone, helpless, holding up his arms, perhaps defending himself against a man he had known and trusted all his life. "And you still say there is no one else in the castle who could have done it, or even aided Shaso in the murder?"

"I have not said that, my lady. I've said that we cannot find any such person, despite our hardest labors, but it is not certain we ever could. Even at night, hundreds are quartered inside this keep. Captain Vansen and his guards have spoken to almost everyone, searched nearly every room, but there are ten hundred more that enter here during the hours of day who might have hidden, then escaped after the murder in the alarm and confusion."

"Vansen." She snorted, but then anger overcame her. "There are not ten hundred in the whole *world* who would want to kill my brother! But there are some, and I suspect I know many of them." The courtiers stirred nervously and their whispers became even quieter. Many fewer were in the throne room than usual: dozens were keeping to their rooms or houses in fear, both of assassins and the fever. "Ten hundred, Lord Brone—that is wordplay! Are you telling me that the simpleton boy who brings the turnips from the Marrinswalk wagons might be one of Kendrick's murderers? No, it is someone with something to gain."

Brone frowned and cleared his throat. "You do me . . . and yourself . . . a disservice, Highness. Of course, what you say is true. However, though we must suspect almost everyone, we must insult no one needlessly. Would you have me mew up every noble who might be thought to benefit from the prince regent's death? Is that your command?" He looked around the room and a sudden silence fell. The courtiers looked startled as geese caught in the open by a thunderstorm.

A part of her would indeed have liked to see all these idle, over-dressed, and overpainted folk made to answer for themselves, but Briony knew that was just rage and despair. One or two of them might well be guilty, might be part of a conspiracy with Shaso, but the rest would then be blameless and would rightly resent ill-treatment. The landowning nobility were not famous for their patience and humility. And if the Eddons did not have the support of the nobility, then the Eddons were nothing.

We've lost Father and Kendrick. I won't lose our throne as well.

"Of course I don't want that," she said, measuring her words. "Rough times make for rough jokes, Lord Avin, so I forgive you, but please do not instruct me. I may be green in years, but in my father's absence and my brother Barrick's illness, I *am* the throne of Southmarch."

Something flickered in Brone's eyes, but he bowed his head. "I stand fairly chastised, Highness."

Briony's strength was failing. She badly needed to lie down and sleep— she had not had more than a few unbroken hours of it for several nights. She wanted to see her twin well, and her other brother alive again. Most of all, she wanted her father back, someone who would hold her and protect her. She took a slow, deep breath. It did not matter what she wanted, of course: there would be no rest any time soon.

"No, Lord Brone, we all are chastised," she said. "The gods humble us all."

The face was twisted into something almost unrecognizable, but there was no question who it was. Barrick turned and ran. Smoke and flames swirled around him as though he had tumbled down one of the rooftop chimneys, or down a gash in the earth toward the regions of fire. His father came after, boots echoing on the flags, a fuming Kernios with beard ablaze and voice booming.

"*Come here, child! You are making me very angry!*"

The downward course of the stairs twisted in a great arc like the limbs of a wind-tortured tree, as blurry in the smoke as something seen beneath deep water, but it was his only escape and he did not hesitate. For a moment his feet were solid beneath him, but then a hand clawed at his back, snagged in his garments, tried to grapple him.

"*Stop . . . !*"

And then his feet were out from under him and he was tumbling down the steps beside the abyss, sliding, flung like a pebble, thumped and rattled down against hard stone until his breath was out of his body and his brains were out of his head. As he fell the voices of the whispering shadow-men became a shout, a roar, and all he could think was, *Not again!*

Oh, gods, not again . . . !

He woke, shivering and weeping. He did not know where he was or even who he was.

A round man with a somber, kindly face bent over him, but for an instant it was that other face that he saw again, that familiar face twisted into a hateful mask and bearded in flame, and he shrieked and struck out. In his weakness his hand barely twitched; the shriek was a stifled moan.

"Rest," the man said. Chaven. His name was Chaven. "You have a fever, but there are people caring for you."

Fever? he thought. *It is no fever.* The castle was on fire and they were under attack. Evil flowed inside the walls like poisoned blood in a dying man. *Briony!* He remembered her suddenly, and as if in imitation of their collateral birth, with her name his own came back as well. *She has to know—she must be told.* He strained again to make a noise, this time to speak. ". . . Briony . . ."

"She is well, Highness. Drink this." A beautiful coolness was poured into his throat, but he could not immediately remember how to swallow. When he had finished sputtering and coughing, and had taken a little more, Chaven's cool hand touched his forehead. "Now sleep, Highnness."

Barrick tried to shake his head. How could they not understand? He felt the darkness reach out to drag him down. He had to tell them about the shadow-men who swarmed the castle, about the fires. They had been hiding here for years, but now they had come out in full force. Perhaps the family's enemies were only a few chambers away by now! And he also had to tell Briony about Father—what if he came to her? What if she did not know, did not understand, and let him in?

The darkness was pulling, sucking at him, making him liquid.

"Tell Briony..." he managed, then slid beneath the surface of light once more, down into the burning depths.

Young Raemon Beck was finding it hard to think of anything but Helmingsea. They were still two days west of Southmarch and his home lay another two days' ride beyond that, but he had been away for a month and a half and it was hard not to think of his wife and his two small boys, hard to keep his eagnerness under control.

Easier when we were in Settland and still weeks away from home, he thought. *Easier when we had things to occupy us, bargaining, buying, selling. Now there is nothing left to do but ride and think....*

He looked ahead along the line of their small caravan, almost a score of high-laden mules and half that many horses pulling wagons, all under the hand of his cousin Dannet Beck, who in turn ruled this mercantile venture on behalf of his father, Raemon's uncle. Dannet had made a few mistakes over the past weeks, Raemon thought—like many untried men, he was quick to take resistance to his authority as a personal slight—but overall he had not done badly, and the mules and wagons were loaded down with miles of the finest dyed wool thread from Settland ready for the factories of the March Kingdoms. And Raemon himself would benefit from this venture, not merely by his own share, which, though tiny, would still bring him more money than he had ever had in his twenty-five years—enough to leave his parents' house, perhaps and build his own—but through greater responsibilities in the future, and someday perhaps a good-sized share in the family venture.

His improving fortunes aside, though, he mostly felt a breathless impatience to see Derla again and hold her close, to see his children and his own father and mother and to eat bread at his own table. Only a few days, but the wait seemed longer now than it did when the journey had only just begun.

We would go faster if we had not combined with that Settish prince's daughter and her party. The girl, scarcely fourteen, with eyes like a frightened fawn, was being sent to marry Rorick Longarren, Earl of Daler's Troth and a cousin of the Eddon family. From what Beck knew of Rorick, it seemed surprising that he would marry at all, let alone a girl of the remote and mountainous eastern lands, but royalty was royalty, it seemed, and any prince's daughter no mean prize.

Beck had nothing against the girl, and it was a reassurance even in these fairly peaceful times to have her dozen armored guards riding with the caravan, but she had been frequently ill; at least three times the groups had been forced to stop early for the day because of it, something that had driven homesick Raemon Beck almost to despair.

He looked back at the Settlanders, then ahead at the uneven procession of pack mules. One of the drovers saw him looking and waved, then pointed at the chinks between the trees and the cloudless autumn sky as if to say, "Look how lucky we are!" The first days of their return journey had been bitter with cold rain off the eastern mountains, so this was indeed a kindly change.

He waved back, but in truth he did not much like these forested hills. He remembered them from the outbound trip, how they seemed to loom and lower in the rain, and how they still did even under sunlit skies. Even on a fairly warm day such as this they bore their own thick mists along the summit and in the valleys between the slopes. In fact, a tongue of fog seemed to be stretching its way down along the hillside ahead of them even now, crawling through the trees and across the dark green grass toward the road.

Still, it is faster than going by sea, he thought. *All that way south, down through the straits and up the eastern coast just to get there—I would have been parted from Derla and the boys for half a year . . . !*

Someone shouted up ahead. Raemon Beck was startled to see that the tongue of fog had already covered the road at the front of the caravan. Beyond a score of paces he now could see little except dark tree shadows and the vague outline of men and of beasts of burden. He looked up. The sky had swiftly gone dark, as though the mist crept above the trees as well as below.

A storm . . . ?

The shouting was quite loud now, with a strange edge to it—he heard not just confusion or irritation in the men's voices, but real fear. The hairs rose on his neck and arms.

An attack? Bandits, taking advantage of the sudden fog? He looked for the armored men who escorted the prince's daughter, saw two of them thunder out of the mist and hurtle past him, and realized to his dismay that the fog was behind him now as well. They were all adrift in it like a boat on the ocean.

Even as he squinted into the mist, a shape leaped out and his horse reared in terror. Raemon Beck had only a moment to glimpse what had frightened his mount, but that moment was enough to make his heart stumble and almost stop with fright; it was a thing of tatters and cobwebs that flailed at him—pale, long-armed, and eyeless—with a mouth as ragged as a torn sack.

His horse reared again and then stumbled as its feet touched the earth. Beck had to cling for his life. Men were screaming all around him now—horses, too, dreadful shrieks unlike anything he had ever heard.

Shapes staggered in and out of the mist, men and other things, grappling, struggling. Some of the voices he had first thought were his companions he now could hear were calling or even singing in some unfamiliar language. More of the tattered things came twitching up out of the brush, but they made up only a small share of the bizarre shapes that danced and gibbered through the mist. Some of the attackers seemed only a little more substantial than the fog itself. Men and horses still screamed, but now the terrible sounds began to grow more faint, as though the mist were thickening into something heavy as stone, or as though Raemon himself had fallen into a hole that was now being filled in atop him.

A group of tiny, red-eyed shapes like malevolent bearded children leaped out of the grass and clawed at his stirrups. His horse kicked its way through them and bolted in shrilling panic. Branches lashed Raemon Beck's face, but then a heavier limb snatched him completely out of the saddle and flung him to the ground, knocking out his breath and his wits in one blow.

He woke feeling like a sack of broken eggs. For a heart-clutching moment he saw a face peering down at him from the fog that still swirled all around—a strangely beautiful face, but cold and lifeless as one of the godly statues on a Trigon temple. He held his breath as though he might that way escape the demon's attention, but it only stared at him. Its skin was pale, its eyes shiny as candleflame behind the thick glass of a temple window. He thought it was male, but truly it was hard to think of it as anything so simple and human. Then it was gone, simply vanished, and the fog swirled down around him and turned the world gray.

Raemon Beck squeezed his eyes shut and gasped for breath, waiting to die. When he had stayed unmoving long enough to become aware of his aching back and ribs, of the pounding of his head and the countless cuts and scratches on his skin, he opened his eyes once more. The fog was gone. He was in the shade of a deep dell, but he could see bits of blue sky above him through the leaves.

He sat up and looked around. The dell was empty.

Beck dragged himself to his feet, wincing but doing his best to remain silent, then crept back along the path of broken branches left by his horse's flight from the road. There was no sign of the horse. There was no noise from any animals or men. Beck braced himself for the terrible scene he knew he would find.

He reached the road. A horse—not his own, but one of the caravan's—stood there as if waiting for him. Its sides were heaving but it was otherwise unharmed, cropping grass by the roadside. As he walked toward it the horse startled a bit, then allowed itself to be stroked. After a moment it quieted and returned to grazing.

Other than this one animal, the road was empty. Of the dozens of men and horses and mules, the wool wagons, the armored soldiers, and the prince's daughter, not to mention whatever army of nightmares had attacked them, no sign remained. Even the fog had vanished.

Terror and disbelief squeezed him like a brutal hand. Raemon Beck felt his stomach convulse, then he brought up the remains of his morning meal. He wiped his mouth and clambered hurriedly into the horse's saddle, grunting at the pain in his ribs and back. His companions had disappeared so completely there was nowhere he could think of to begin a search, and in any case he did not want to search, did not want to spend another instant in this haunted spot. He only wanted to ride and ride until he reached a place where people lived.

He knew he could never come into these hills again. If that meant he must give up his place in the family venture and his wife and children must join him begging for coppers in the street, there was no help for it.

He kicked his heels against his new mount's ribs and started east, huddled low against the horse's neck and weeping.

It was early in the morning and she couldn't sleep—had not slept all night, despite immense weariness. Briony lay in her bed staring into the darkness, listening to the slumber sounds of Rose and Moina and three other young noblewomen who were staying in the castle on this night before Kendrick's funeral. How could *any* of them sleep, she wondered. Did they not know that everything was in danger—that the entire kingdom tottered?

If Shaso was the murderer and had acted alone, there could be no comprehensible reason for it, and so how could she trust anyone ever again? If somehow he had been suborned, or if someone else performed this terrible murder and painted him with the blame, then the Eddons had been purposefully struck to the heart by a terrible enemy, and struck as they slept in their own house. How could anyone ever sleep again?

Her heart had begun beating swiftly even before she realized what the new sound was: a quiet knock at the door of her chamber. There were guards outside, she knew. Even that careless fool Ferras Vansen would not leave her unguarded at a time like this. She pulled a cloak over her nightdress—the room and the stone floors were cold—and started toward the door.

But Kendrick had guards, she remembered, and her skin took a deeper chill. *He would have thought he was safe, too.*

"Princess?" The voice was quiet, but she recognized it. Now she was frightened for a completely different reason. She hurried forward, hesitated again for a moment.

"Chaven? It is you? Truly you?"

"It is."

"We are here, too, Highness." It was one of the guards. She recognized the gruff voice, although she couldn't remember the man's name. "You can open the door."

Still, such had been the terror of the last days that she had to force herself not to flinch when the door at last swung open. Chaven and the guards stood waiting in the pool of torchlight outside. The physician's face was serious and haggard with exhaustion, but the terrible look she expected to see was not there.

"Is it my brother?"

"It is, my lady, but do not fear. I come to say that I think his fever has broken. He will not quickly be himself again, but I strongly believe he will live and recover. He was asking for you."

"Merciful Zoria! Thank all the gods!" Briony fell to her knees and lowered her head in prayer. She should have been delirious with joy, but instead she was suddenly dizzy. This one terrible fear allayed, it was as though the rigor with which she had held herself up now ended in a moment. She tried to stand, but instead swayed and began to collapse. Chaven and one of the guards caught at her arms.

"We will survive," she whispered.

"Yes, Princess," he said, "but tonight you will go back to bed."

"But, Barrick . . . !" The room still spun around her.

"I will tell him that you will come with the first light. He is probably asleep now, anyway."

"Tell him I love him, Chaven."

"I will."

She allowed herself to be helped onto her own bed—for a moment she could not avoid thinking of poor Kendrick in the hands of the death-maids of Kernios at this very moment. But even this horror, or the walls that seemed slowly to revolve, could not keep exhaustion at bay.

"Tell Barrick . . ." she said, ". . . tell Barrick . . ." but that was all she could manage before weariness finally breached the stronghold and conquered her.

11

Bride of the God

THE BERRIES:

White as bones, red as blood
Red as coals, white as clay
Are none of them sweet?

—from *The Bonefall Oracles*

IF QINNITAN HAD THOUGHT the autarch's throne room would be a more intimate setting than the cavernous Temple of the Hive, she would have been very wrong: the majesty of the Golden One's entourage was even more overwhelming here, the white-and-black-tiled hall packed with hundreds of soldiers and servants and the representatives of dozens of noble families and of trade and bureaucratic interests, all joined together under the eyes of the watchful, wide-eyed gods painted on the ceiling. The autarch himself sat at the center of it all on the great Falcon Throne, an immense bird's head covered in topaz feathers, the eyes red jasper; Sulepis Bishakh am-Xis III himself was seated beneath the awning made by the upper part of the giant raptor's gaping golden beak. The autarch was surrounded by his legendary musketeers, the Leopards, and the Leopards were surrounded in turn by an almost equally famous troop of Perikalese mercenaries, the White Hounds. These Hounds were all second or third generation now, their forefathers originally captured by the current autarch's grandfather in a famous sea battle. Few of them could still speak the language of Perikal, but the master of much of the continent of Xand had more than enough pale-skinned women at his disposal to keep the present generation of Hounds as white as their forebears. They were strange-looking men, these northerners, even to Qinnitan's frightened, confused gaze, built more like the bears she had seen in pictures than like hounds, hairy and wide-bearded, broad of back and shoulder.

From behind the Perikalese mercenaries, one of the Leopard soldiers was staring at her—an important soldier, judging by the long black tail on his helmet. He had a frown like a gash, and his elaborate armor only emphasized his own broad shoulders. Terrified she had already done something wrong, Qinnitan dropped her eyes.

When she looked up again, the knot of courtiers was moving away from the Falcon Throne, shuffling backward with many bows and flutterings of hands, and she could see the autarch once more. The young god-on-earth leaned back and gazed up at the stretching beak above his head as if the room was empty but for himself, and briefly scratched his long nose. His gold finger-stalls glittered, tiny guardians of the safety of all creation: it was a truth as powerful as the blueness of the sky that the autarch must not accidentally touch something impure.

Qinnitan's mother was weeping again. Qinnitan was frightened, too, but she still couldn't understand such behavior. She bumped her mother's side with an elbow, a piece of impertinence that would have been unthinkable in most families. "Hush!" she whispered, which would have been thought even more inexplicable.

"We are so lucky!" her mother said, sniffling.

We? Even through the terror at being singled out, the overwhelming strangeness of it all, and even an unavoidable tingle of pride at having somehow caught the eye of the most powerful man in the world, Qinnitan knew one thing: she didn't want to marry the autarch. There was something about him that frightened her very much, and it was not simply his matchless power or the things she had heard about his cruel whims. There was something in his eyes, something she had never seen in another person, but might have seen once in the eyes of a horse that had bounced its rider off his saddle and then, when the man's foot caught in the stirrup, dragged him to his death through the crowded marketplace, smashing the rider's head against the cobbles for a hundred paces before a soldier brought the beast down with an arrow. As the horse lay gasping out its last bubbling red breaths, she had seen its eye rolling in the socket, the eye of something that was not seeing what was really there.

The autarch, although calm and apparently amused by what he observed around him, had such an eye. She did not—*did not*—want to be given to such a man, to go to his bed, to undress for him and be touched and entered by him, even if he truly was a god upon the earth. The very idea made her shudder as if she had a fever.

Not that she had any other choice. To refuse would be to die, and to see her father and mother and sisters and brothers die before her—and none of the deaths, she felt sure, would be swift.

"Where are the bee-girl's parents?" the autarch asked suddenly. The room fell silent at his voice. Someone let out a little nervous cough.

"They stand there, Golden One," said an older man wearing what looked like ceremonial armor made out of silver cloth, pointing a finger toward the place where Qinnitan's mother and father huddled facedown on the stone floor. Qinnitan suddenly realized she had not abased herself, and put her head down. She imagined the man in silver cloth must be Pinimmon Vash, the paramount minister.

"Bring them up," commanded the autarch in his strong, high voice. Someone coughed again. It sounded loud in the silence that followed the autarch's words and she was terribly glad it wasn't either of her parents.

"Do you give her up to be the bride of the god?" the minister asked her mother and father, who still cowered, unable to look up at the autarch. Even through her own misery, Qinnitan was ashamed of her father. Cheshret was a priest, able to stand before the altar of Nushash himself, so why should he be unable to face the autarch?

"Of course," her father said. "We are honored . . . so . . . we are . . ."

"Yes, you are." The autarch flicked his glittering finger at a wooden casket. "Give the money to them. Jeddin, send some of your men to help them carry it home." The Leopard soldier who had been staring at her earlier murmured a few words and two of the autarch's riflemen stepped forward and lifted the chest. It was clearly heavy.

"Ten horses worth of silver," the autarch said. "Generous payment for the honor of bringing your daughter into my house, is it not?"

The men with the money chest had already started back across the throne room. Qinnitan's parents scrambled awkwardly after it, trying to keep it in sight but not daring to turn their backs even slightly on the autarch.

"You are too kind, Master of the Great Tent," her father called, bowing and bowing. "You bring too much honor on our house." Qinnitan's mother was crying again. A moment later, they were gone.

"Now . . ." said the autarch, then somebody coughed again. The autarch's lean face writhed in annoyance. "Who is that? Bring him up here."

Three more Leopards sprang down from the dais and out into the room, their polished, decorated guns held high. The crowd shrank back from them. A moment later they returned to the dais, dragging a frail young man. The crowd drew even farther back, as though he might be carrying a fatal illness, which in fact he probably was, since he had drawn the angry attention of the god-on-earth.

"Do you hate me so much, that you must interrupt me with your braying?" the autarch demanded. The young man, who had fallen onto his knees when the Leopard soldiers let go of him, could only shake his head, weeping with terror. He was so terrified his face had turned the color of saffron. "Who are you?"

The youth was clearly too frightened to answer. At last the paramount minister cleared his throat. "He is an accounting scribe from my ministry of the Treasury. He is good with sums."

"So are a thousand merchants in Bird Snare Market. Can you tell me any reason I should not have him killed, Vash? He has wasted too much of my time already."

"Of course he has, Golden One," said the paramount minister with a gesture of infinite regret. "All I can offer in his favor is that I am told he is a hard worker and very well liked among the other scribes."

"Is that so?" The autarch stared up at the famous tiled ceiling for a moment, scratched his long nose with a long finger. He already seemed bored with the subject. "Very well, here is my sentence. Leopards, take him away. Beat him and break his bones with the iron bar. Then, if he is to survive, these so-called friends of his in the Treasury may take care of him, feed him, so on. We shall see how far their friendship truly extends."

The large crowd murmured approvingly at the wisdom of the autarch's sentence, even as Qinnitan suppressed a shriek of horrified fury. The young man was taken away, his feet dragging on the floor, leaving a wet track like a snail. He had fainted, but not before emptying his bladder. A trio of servitors scurried to wipe the flagstones clean again.

"As for you, girl," the autarch said, still angry, and Qinnitan's heart suddenly began to beat even more swiftly. Had he tired of her already? Was he going to have her killed? He had just bought her like a market chicken from her parents and no one would raise a finger to save her. "Stand before me."

Somehow she made her legs work just well enough to carry her up the steps and onto the dais. She was grateful to reach the spot before the Falcon Throne, grateful to be able to slump down onto her knees and not have to feel them quivering. She put her forehead against the cool stone and wished that time would stop, that she would never have to leave this spot and find out what else was in store for her. A powerful, sweet scent filled her nostrils, threatening to make her sneeze. She peered from half-opened lids. A group of priests had surrounded her like ants on a crumb of cake, blowing incense on her out of bronze bowls, perfuming her for the presence of the autarch.

"You are very lucky, little daughter," said Pinimmon Vash. "You are favored above almost all women on the earth. Do you know that?"

"Yes, Lord. Of course, Lord." She pushed her forehead harder against the stone, felt the area of cold spread on her skin. Her parents had sold her to the autarch without even a question as to what might become of her. She wondered if she could hit her head against the tiles hard enough to kill herself before someone stopped her. She didn't want to marry the lord of the world. Just looking at his long face and strange, birdlike eyes made her heart feel as though it would stop beating. This close, she almost thought she could sense the heat of his body coming off him, as though he were a metal statue that had sat all day in the sun. The idea of those thin-fingered hands touching her, the gold stalls scraping her skin as that face came down onto her own . . .

"Stand up." It was the autarch himself. She got to her feet, so wobbly that the paramount minister had to put his dry old hand under her elbow. The living god's pale, pale eyes moved over her body, up to her face, back down over her body. There was no lechery in it, nothing really human: it felt as though she hung on a butcher's hook.

"She's thin but not ugly," said the autarch. "She must go to the Seclusion, of course. Give her to old Cusy and tell her that this one must have special and very careful treatment. Panhyssir will tell her what is expected."

To her astonishment, Qinnitan found herself raising her eyes to meet the autarch's, heard herself say, "Lord, Master, I don't know why you've chosen me, but I will do my best to serve you."

"You will serve me well," he said with an odd, childlike laugh.

"May I ask one favor, Great Master?"

"You will address the Autarch Sulepis as 'Living God on Earth' or as 'Golden One,' " the paramount minister said sternly, even as the assembled throng murmured at her forwardness.

"Golden One, may I ask a favor?"

"You may ask."

"May I say good-bye to my sisters in the Hive, my friends? They were very kind to me."

He looked at her for a moment, then nodded. "Jeddin, send some of your Leopards to take her back for her farewells and to bring with her anything she needs from her old life. Then she will enter the Seclusion." His pallid eyes narrowed a little. "You do not seem happy with the honor I have given you, girl?"

"I am . . . overwhelmed, Golden One." Fear had gripped her now. She could barely make her voice loud enough for him to hear a few paces away; she knew that to the rest of those assembled in the vast room she would be unheard, not even a murmur. "Please believe that I do not have the words to describe my happiness."

The contingent of Leopards marched her through the long passages of the Orchard Palace, a labyrinth that she had only heard about but which, it seemed, would now be her home for the rest of her life. Thoughts swirled in her head like choking incense.

Why does he want me? He had scarcely even looked at me before today. "Not ugly," he said. That is what one says about an arranged marriage. But I bring nothing. My parents—nobodies! Why on earth should he choose me, even as one new wife among hundreds . . . ?

The Leopard band's captain, the muscular, serious-faced soldier called Jeddin, was watching her again. He seemed as if he had been doing it for more than a moment, but she had only just noticed. "Mistress, I apologize," he said, "but I cannot give you long for your farewells. We are expected at the Seclusion in a short time."

She nodded. He had fierce eyes, but his glint seemed decidedly more human than the animating force behind the autarch's bottomless stare.

When they came to the Hive, all the girls seemed somehow to have known Qinnitan was coming. *Perhaps the oracle predicted it,* she thought, sour and miserable. She was about to pass beyond the reach of even the golden bees and the thought frightened her. From the feminine deeps of the Hive to the female prison of the Seclusion. It did not seem like a good trade, however astonishing the honor of being chosen.

High Priestess Rugan bade her farewell with pride but little sentiment.

"You have brought great honor to us," she said, and kissed Qinnitan on each cheek before returning to her chambers and her accounts. Chief Acolyte

Chryssa, on the other hand, seemed genuinely sorry to see her go, although there was a powerful pride in her face as well. "No one has ever gone from the Hive into the Seclusion," she said, eyes glowing with the same light of religiosity that filled her when the bees spoke. Qinnitan could believe that Chryssa might be dreaming of how wonderful it would have been if she instead of Qinnitan had been chosen.

Qinnitan was doing the same.

"Do you really have to go?" Duny was crying, but she seemed almost as excited and pleased as Chryssa. "Why can't you live here until it happens?"

"Don't be foolish, Dunyaza," the chief acolyte told her. "Someone who is to be the autarch's wife cannot live in the Hive. What if someone . . . what if she . . . ?" Chryssa frowned. "It just would not be right. He is the Living God on Earth!"

When the chief acolyte had gone, Qinnitan had begun putting her few personal articles into a bag—the carved bone comb her mother had given her when she had first been called to the sacred bees, a necklace of polished stones from her brothers, a tiny metal mirror from her sisters, the festival dress she had never worn since becoming a Hive Sister. As she packed these things up, trying to answer Duny's excited questions as best she could—after all, how much could she tell when she had no idea what was to happen to her, why she had been chosen, or how she had been noticed?—she realized that from now on she was not going to be a person any more, at least for her Hive Sisters, but a Story.

I'm going to be Qinnitan, the girl the autarch noticed and plucked out of their midst. They're going to talk about me at night. They'll wonder if it ever might happen again, to one of them. They're going to think it's a wonderful, romantic tale, like Dasmet and the Girl With No Shadow.

"Don't forget about me," she said suddenly.

Duny stared at her in amazment. "Forget about you? Qin-ya, how could we ever . . . ?"

"No, I mean don't forget about the real Qinnitan. Don't make up silly stories about me." She stared at her friend, who for once was shocked into silence. "I'm scared, Duny."

"Getting married isn't so bad," her friend said. "My older sister told me . . ." She broke off, eyes wide. "I wonder if gods do it the same way people do . . . ?"

Qinnitan shook her head. Duny would never understand. "Do you think you could come visit me?"

"What? You mean . . . in the Seclusion?"

"Of course. It's only men who aren't allowed in. Please say you will."

"Qin, I'll . . . yes! Yes, I'll come, as soon as the Sisters will let me."

She threw her arms around Duny. Mistress Chryssa was standing in the doorway of the acolytes' hall, letting her know that the soldiers were growing impatient outside the temple. "Don't forget about me," Qinnitan whispered in her friend's ear. "Don't make me into some . . . princess."

Duny could only shake her head in confusion as Qinnitan took the sack with her pitiful array of possessions and followed the chief acolyte.

"One more thing," Chryssa said. "Mother Mudry wishes a word with you before you go."

"The . . . oracle? With me?" Mudry could hardly know Qinnitan at all. They had never been any nearer to each other than a dozen paces since Qinnitan had come to the Hive. Did even that august old woman desire to curry a little favor with the autarch? Qinnitan supposed she must. *But the nicest thing he said about me was that I wasn't ugly. Doesn't give me much power to get favors done, now does it?*

They walked through the darkest part of the Hive. The sleepy murmuring of the bees washed in through the air shafts high in the walls—there was nowhere in the Hive their song could not be heard. If the bees noticed the departure of one of the younger acolytes, it didn't seem to bother them.

The oracle's room smelled of lavender water and sandalwood incense. Oracle Mudry sat in her high-backed chair, her face lifted expectantly toward the door, blind eyes moving behind the lids. She reached out her hands. Qinnitan hesitated: they looked like claws.

"Is that the child? The girl?"

Qinnitan looked around but Chryssa had left her at the doorway to the inner chamber. "It's me, Mother Mudry," she said.

"Take my hands."

"It's very kind of you . . ."

"Hush!" She said it harshly, but without anger, a warning to a child not to touch a naked flame. Her cold hands closed on Qinnitan's fingers. "We have never sent one to the Seclusion before, but Rugan tells me she thought you . . . unusual." She shook her head. "Did you know that it was all ours, once, girl? Surigali was the Mistress of the Hive, and Nushash her cowering consort."

Qinnitan had no idea what this meant, and it had been a long and confusing day. She stood silent as Mudry squeezed her fingers. The old woman paused as if listening, face lifted to the ceiling, much as earlier that day the autarch had stared at nothing while deciding to have a man's bones shattered because he had coughed. The old woman's hands seemed to grow warmer, almost hot, and Qinnitan had to force herself not to pull away. The oracle's lined face seemed to grow slack, then the toothless mouth fell open in a gape of dismay.

"It is as I feared," Mother Mudry said, letting go of Qinnitan's hands. "It is bad. Very bad."

"What? What do you mean?" Did the oracle have some knowledge of her fate? Was she to be slain by her husband-to-be, as so many others had been slain?

"A bird will fly before the storm." Mudry spoke so quietly Qinnitan could barely hear her. "Yet it is hurt, and can scarcely keep wing. Still, that is all the hope that remains when the sleeper awakens. Still, the old blood is strong. Not much hope at all . . ." She swayed for a moment, then stopped, her face turned straight toward Qinnitan's. If she had been sighted, she might have stared. "I am tired, forgive me. There is little we can do and it is of no use to frighten you. You must remember who you are, girl, that is all."

Qinnitan had no idea if this was how the old woman usually behaved, but she knew the oracle was indeed frightening her, whether she wanted to or not. "What do you mean, remember? That I'm a Hive Sister?"

"Remember who you are. And when the cage is opened, you must fly. It will not be opened twice."

"But I don't understand . . . !"

Chryssa put her head in the door. "Is everything all right? Mother Mudry?"

The old woman nodded. She gave Qinnitan's hand one last leathery squeeze, then let go. "Remember. Remember."

It was all Qinnitan could do not to cry as the Chief Acolyte handed her back over to the soldiers and their captain, silently glowering Jeddin, so they could conduct the new bride-to-be away to the hidden fastness of the Seclusion.

12
Sleeping in Stone

ON THE LONG AFTERNOON:

What are these that have fallen?
They sparkle beside the trail like jewels, like tears
Are they stars?

—from *The Bonefall Oracles*

CHERT WATCHED MICA and Talc dressing the stone on the wall above the tomb. The Schists could be clannish, and since they were Hornblende's nephews, he had thought they might give trouble to their uncle's replacement, but instead they had been nothing but helpful. In fact, his whole crew had been exemplary—even Pumice was doing his work with a minimum of complaining: whatever they might not have liked about the original job, they had swallowed it for the sake of getting the prince regent's tomb ready. And a good thing, too. The only light where Chert stood were the torches in the stone wall sconces—four of the sconces new-carved—but he felt certain the morning sun must already be creeping above the eastern battlements, which meant only a few hours remained until the funeral.

It had not been easy, any of it, and Chert could only thank his Blue Quartz ancestors that it had been a comparatively small task, the construction of one new room, and that they were working mostly with limestone. Even so, in some cases they had been forced to cut corners—or *not* cut corners, to be more accurate: the new chamber was oddly shaped and still unfinished on the far end where a low tunnel opened into farther caverns, and they had dressed only the wall into which the prince regent's tomb had been cut. Lumps of hard flint still floated like islands in all the finished walls, and most of the carvings would have to be completed later as well. There had barely been time for Little Carbon to decorate the tomb itself and the wall just around it, but the craftsman had done a fine job despite the haste, turning a raw hole in the bones of the Mount into a sort of forest bower. The stone plinth on which the prince regent's coffin would lie seemed a bed of long, living grasses; the tree trunks and hanging leafy branches carved into the walls of the crypt had been crafted with such delicacy that they seemed to fall away into the distance, row upon row. Chert almost felt he could walk into the carving toward the heart of a living forest.

"It is splendid," he told Little Carbon, who was doing a last bit of finework on a group of flowers in the plinth. "No one will be able to say that the Funderlings have not done their part and more."

Little Carbon wiped dust from his sweaty face. He looked older than his true age—he was only a few years married, but already had the wizened features of a grandfather and white in his beard that did not come from limestone dust. "Sad job, though. You'd have thought this was to be my son's to do, or even my grandson's, not mine. He went too young, the poor prince. And who'd have believed that southerner fellow would have done it? After all these years, he seemed almost civilized."

Chert turned and called to the others to hurry with pulling down the scaffolding. Mica and Talc were on the ground now and nearly done, but the work gang still had to plaster the holes where the scaffold beams had been driven into the walls, and it needed to be done soon: Nynor the castellan had a dozen men and women waiting to fill the Eddon family crypt with flowers and candles.

Little Carbon squinted at a stone bloom, gave it a couple of last pokes with his chisel, then began working it with a polishing-stick. "Speaking of sons, where's that one of yours?"

Chert felt an odd mixture of pride and irritation to hear the boy referred to as his son. "Flint? I sent him out before you got here—he'll be playing upground. All his messing about was going to send me mad." Which was only part of the truth. The child had been acting so strangely that it had frightened him a little. In fact, Flint had been acting up so much that for a few moments Chert had feared it might be bad air leaking in through the cavern end of the tomb—*breath of the black deep* his people called it, and it had killed many a Funderling over the years—but none of the others had been affected. It had quickly become clear that the boy's behavior was odder than even a pocket of bad air could explain: he seemed both drawn to and afraid of the dark opening at the end of the tomb, grunting to himself as he peered into it like a much younger child—or even like an animal, Chert had thought fearfully—and singing snatches of unrecognizable songs. But when he had pulled the boy away, Flint had answered questions with no less reticence than usual, saying that the sound of the cavern beyond frightened him, whatever that meant, that he could hear voices and smell things.

"Things I don't understand," was all he would or could offer by way of explanation, *"that I don't want to understand,"* but when Chert had grabbed a chunk of glowing coral and got down on his knees to poke his head into the raw, unworked limestone cavern beyond, he had found nothing unusual.

With a pressing job and the memory of what Cinnabar had said about the men's restiveness fresh in his thoughts, Chert had made up his mind quickly. He didn't want the boy kicking up a fuss and putting the men off their work, so he had taken Flint up the stairs and told him to stay inside the boundaries of the cemetery, but under no circumstances to go out of sight of the top steps of the tomb. With Chert's men carrying limestone chips out of the mound in wheeled barrows all day, he had thought the boy could not get into too much trouble without being noticed.

Thinking about it now, as Little Carbon used a wet rag dipped in fine sand to scrape away a few last imperfections, Chert realized that he hadn't heard or seen anything of the boy in some time, although he would have expected him to have come back down by now looking for his midmorning meal. He called a few last suggestions to the men tugging apart the scaffolding, patted Little Carbon on the shoulder, then stumped off to see what the child was up to.

A few of Nynor's big folk were working in the outer chambers of the tomb, cleaning and preparing it for the burial procession, scrubbing soot off the walls where torches had burned, strewing rushes and neverfade blossoms on the floor. All these growing things filled the rock halls with a smell that reminded Chert of the days when he was courting Opal and took her upground to walk along the sea-meadows at Landsend. She had later told him that for a girl who had almost never been out of Funderling Town, it had been both exciting and frightening to stand looking down at the sea and that immensity of open sky. He remembered feeling an expansive pride—as though he had made it all for her.

But the scent of flowers and a few happy memories of his younger days could not change the nature of the place. In niche after niche lay the mortal remains of the Eddons who had ruled Southmarch, of lives that might once have been grand or insignificant, but were all the same now. *Still, when they were alive, someone cared for them,* he thought. Their bodies were brought to this place by weeping mourners just as others would bring the murdered prince this day, then they had been left to sleep in stone until the machineries of time wore them away to dry dust and knobs of bone.

It did not make Chert fearful, although the Funderlings themselves did not bury their dead, but neither could he ignore the presence of so many finished lives. Some of the grander caskets, made in stone or metal to outlast the ages, had an effigy not of the occupant as he or she looked in life, although there were many of those, but of the occupant in death, withering and decaying, a style of funerary art from three centuries earlier. During those years after the plague, it seemed that many of the dying wished to remind the living just how transitory their good luck would be.

Why all the mystery? Chert wondered. *These bodies of ours come out of the earth, come out of all we eat and drink and breathe, and they go back to earth in the end, whatever the gods may do with the spark that is inside us.* But he could not be as blithe as he wished, and even though there were big folk busily at work in the catacombs around him, still he hurried. Lately—even before the prince regent's death—all around him had begun to seem tinged with the chill breath of mortality, a hint of the endings of things.

For once a child of stone was glad to see the raw daylight, but the lift in his spirits did not last long. Flint was nowhere to be seen, and although Chert walked through all the graveyard and even into the gardens beyond, calling and calling, he could not find him.

Briony stood, naked and cold from the bath, looking down at her own pale limbs and hating the weakness of her womanhood.

If I were a man, she thought, *then Summerfield and Lord Brone and the others would not seize at my every word. They would not think me weak. Even if I had a withered arm like Barrick's, they would fear my anger. But because of the accident of my birth, of my sex, I am suspect.*

The room was chill and she was trembling. *Oh, Father, how could you leave us?* She closed her eyes and for a moment she became a child again, shivering while the nurses bustled around her, drying her small body with flannels, the great house full of familiar sounds. *Where does time go when it is used up?* she wondered. *Is it like the sound of voices that echo and echo in a long hallway, growing smaller and smaller until they're too faint to hear? Is there an echo somewhere of that time when we were all together—Kendrick alive, Father here, Barrick well?*

But even if there were, it would only be a dying echo, populated by ghosts.

She raised her arms. "Dress me," she told Moina and Rose.

The thought of her father, the sudden urge to see him, or at least to hear his voice, had reminded her of something: where was his letter, the one Dawet dan-Faar had brought from Hierosol? Perhaps it was with some of Kendrick's other effects—she had not had a chance to look through them all yet. But her father's letter was not like other papers: she not only needed to see it, she wanted to, desperately. She would look for it after the funeral. Kendrick's funeral.

The horror of what lay ahead made her knees weak, but she straightened, held herself firm. She would not show her ladies how fearful she was, how helpless and hopeless.

Rose and Moina were strangely quiet. Briony wondered if they were as overwhelmed as she was, or merely respecting her mood and the dread weight of the day. And what did it matter? Death made its own respect, one way or another.

They slipped on her chemise, working a little to pull it into place over her damp skin. The petticoat tied at the back with points; she was still barefoot and it pooled around her feet. Rose pulled the laces too tight as she tied the corset and Briony grunted but did not ask her to loosen it. She had learned that these formal clothes served a purpose: like a soldier's armor, they gave an outward semblance of strength even when the body inside was weak.

But I don't want to be weak! I want to be strong, like a man, for the family and for our people. But what did that mean? There were many kinds of strength, the bearlike power of someone like Avin Brone or the more subtle force Kendrick had possessed: her older brother had once thrown one of the bigger guards so hard in a wrestling match that the man had to be carried away. Thinking of him made her breath hitch. *He was so alive—he can't be gone. How can a single night change the world?*

But there were other kinds of strength, too, she thought as Moina and Rose helped her into the black silk dress stiff with black brocade and delicate silver-and-gold filigree. *Father almost never raises his voice, and I have never seen him strike a blow in anger, but only fools ever called him weak. And why are only men thought strong? Who has held this family together in the past days? Not me, may Zoria forgive me.* It had not been Barrick either, or even the lord constable. No, it had been Briony's great-aunt Merolanna, stern and set as the Mount itself, who had ordered life and made a little sense of death.

Rose and Moina were busy as bees around a dark flower, unbending and spreading the ruffled cuffs of Briony's dress, trimming a loose thread from the hem and then slipping on her shoes, one of them bracing her so she could lift her foot while the other guided the black slipper into place. For a moment she was filled with love for these girls. They, too, were being brave, she decided. Men's wars happened far away and they proved their courage in front of armies of other men. Women's wars were more subtle things and were witnessed mostly by others of their sex. Her ladies-in-waiting and all the other women in the castle were waging a battle against chaos, struggling to lend sense to a world that seemed to have lost it.

She did not like what the world had forced upon her, but today, Briony decided, she was still proud to be what she was.

When they had finished with her shoes, the ladies-in-waiting draped her in a cloak of heavy black velvet that her father had given her but which she had never worn. She sat on a high stool, or rather leaned, half standing, so that Rose could bring out her jewelry and Moina and one of the younger maids could begin to arrange her hair.

"Don't bother with all that," she told Moina, but gently. Her lady-in-waiting stopped, the curling iron already in her hands. "I will wear a head-dress—the one with silver stitching."

With as much ceremony as a mantis producing a shrine's sacred object, Rose set the jewel casket on a cushion and opened the lid. She pulled out the largest necklace, a heavy chain of gold with pendant ruby, a gift from Briony's father to the mother she had scarcely known.

"Not that," Briony said. "Not today. There—the hart and nothing else."

Rose lifted the slender silver necklace, confusion showing on her face. The leaping-deer pendant was a small and insignificant piece and seemed out of keeping with the heavy majesty of her other garments.

"Kendrick gave it to me. A birthday gift."

Rose's eyes filled as she draped it around her mistress' neck. Briony tried to wipe the girl's tears away, but the sleeves of her gown were too stiff, her cloak too massive. "Curse it, don't you dare start that. You'll have me going, too."

"Cry if you want to, my lady," Moina said, sniffling. "We haven't begun your face yet."

Briony laughed a little despite herself. The wretched sleeves would not let her wipe her own eyes either, so she could only sit helplessly until Rose brought a kerchief to blot her dry again.

Her hair pulled back and knotted at the back of her head, she sat as patiently as she could while the two ladies-in-waiting begin to daub things on her cheeks and eyelids. She hated face paint, but today was not an ordinary day. The people—her people—had already seen her cry. Today they had to see her strong and dry-eyed, her face a mask of composure. And it was a distraction for Rose and Moina, as well, this unusual liberty: they were laughing again as they brushed rouge onto her cheeks, despite their still-damp eyes.

When they had finished, they lowered the gabled headdress onto her head and fastened it with pins, then spread its black velvet fall onto her shoulders and down her back. Briony felt solid and unbending. "The guards will have to come and carry me—I swear I cannot move an inch. Bring me a glass."

Moina blew her nose while Rose hurried to find the looking glass. The other maids formed into a respectful half circle around her, whispering, impressed. Briony regarded herself, all in black from head to foot with only a glint of silver at her brow and breast.

"I look like Siveda the moon-maiden. Like the Goddess of Night."

"You look splendid, Your Highness," said Rose, suddenly all formality.

"I look like a ship under full sail. Big as the world." Briony sighed and her breath caught. "Oh, gods, come and help me get up. I have to bury my brother."

A boy was clinging high on the wall on the outside of the chapel building, but even in this time of fear, when murderous enemies might still be at large, no one in Southmarch Castle seemed to have noticed him. At the moment he was crouching in the corner of a vast window frame, the colored glass surrounding him like the background of a painting. Although the chapel was full of people, if anyone inside had taken note of the shadow at the bottom of the great window they had decided it was only grime or a drift of leaves.

A group of servants hurried up the path from the graveyard toward the doorway that led to the inner keep, still carrying the baskets they had brought down an hour before but with only a few petals now remaining in the bottoms; the rest had been scattered inside the tomb and along the winding path through the cemetery. The boy did not look down at them, and they were all far too intent on their just-finished tasks and their whispered conversations to look up.

Something above the boy's head caught his attention. A butterfly, a big one, all yellow and black, lit on the edge of the roof and sat there with its wings beating as slowly as a tranquil heart. It was late in the season for butterflies.

He found the edge of the window with his stubby, dirty fingers and pulled himself up until he was standing beside one edge of the leaded glass window. Anyone watching from the inside would now have seen the drift of leaves suddenly become a vertical column, but no sound came to him from behind the glass except the continuing low hum of a chorus singing the "Lay of Kernios," longest and most expansive of the funeral songs. A moment later the column was gone and the window was unshadowed again.

Flint pulled himself up onto one of the protruding carvings that decorated the outside wall of the chapel, then moved sideways like a spider to another before climbing up to a higher one. Within a matter of moments, even as a gate on the far side of the graveyard closed behind the basket-carrying servants and their voices fell away, he was onto the roof.

The chapel rooftop was a great angled field of slate with spiral chimneys protruding every few yards like trees. Moss and even living tufts of long grass poked up between the slate, and the autumn wind had piled great drifts of leaves against the chimneys like red-and-brown snow. Many other rooftops were visible from this spot, plateaus almost touching each other in jostling profusion, but most of the towered inner keep still stretched far above his head on all sides, the forest of chimneys rendered in giant size.

Flint seemed to care about none of these things. At first he only lay on his belly and stared at the place where the butterfly sat near the roof's summit, fanning its wings indolently. Then the boy began to crawl upward, digging his feet into the eruptions of moss and lifted slate, until he was within arm's reach of the creature. His hand stretched and the butterfly suddenly sensed him, tumbled over the edge, and was gone, but the boy did not stop. His fingers closed on something quite different and he plucked it out of the grass and brought it close to his face.

It was an arrow, small as a darning needle. He squinted. It was fletched with tiny crests of the same yellow and black as the butterfly's wings.

For long moments the boy lay silently, motionlessly, staring at the arrow. Someone watching might have thought he had fallen asleep with his eyes open, so complete was his stillness, but the watcher would have been wrong. He abruptly rolled and scrambled across the rooftop to the nearest chimney, fast as a striking snake, and thrust with his hand first at one spot, then another, grabbing after something that fled through the little forest of grass around the base of the bricks.

His hand closed and suddenly he was still again. He pulled back his fist, holding it close to his body as he sat down with the chimney against his back. When he opened his hand, the thing huddling there did not move until he poked it gently with his finger.

The little man who now rolled over and crouched in Flint's palm was not much taller than that finger. The man's skin seemed sooty-dark, although it was hard to say how much of that was truly skin and how much was dirt. His eyes were wide, little pinpricks of white in the shadow of the boy's hand. He tried to leap free, but Flint curled his fingers into a cage and the little man crouched again, defeated. He was clothed in rags and bits of gray pelt. He wore soft boots and had a coil of coarse thread looped over his shoulder, a quiver of arrows on his back.

Flint bent and picked something out of the grass. It was a bow, strung so fine that the cord could barely be seen. Flint looked at it for a moment, then set it on his palm beside the little man. The captive looked from the bow toward his captor, then picked it up. He passed the bow slowly from hand to hand with a kind of wonder, as though it had become something totally different since he touched it last. Flint stared at him, unsmiling, brow furrowed.

The little man gulped air. "Hurt me not, master, I beg 'ee," he fluted, something like hope in his eyes where before there had been only terror. "Tha hast me fair, skin to sky. Grant thy wish, I will. All know a Roof-topper will keep un's word."

Flint frowned, then set the little man down on the slate. The prisoner got to his feet, hesitated, took a few steps, then stopped again. Flint didn't move.

His little face screwed up in confusion, the tiny man at last turned away and began scrambling up the moss paths between the slates, heading for the roofcrest with his bow dangling in his hand. Every few steps he looked back over his shoulder, as though expecting his apparent freedom to prove only a cruel game, but by the time he reached the top, the boy still had not moved.

"Oh, th'art good, young master," the tiny man cried, his voice almost inaudible from a yard and a half away. "Beetledown and un's aftercomers will remember thee. That be promised!" He vanished over the roofcrest.

Flint sat against the chimney until the sun was high above him, until the dim moan of the chorus below had ended, then began his climb back down.

She was grateful for Rose standing beside her with the kerchief, and furious with herself for needing it. It was hard to believe how terrible a varnished wooden box could be. The funeral songs droned on and on, but she was grateful for that, too: it gave her a chance to compose herself.

It seemed shameful to carry Kendrick to the tomb in a borrowed coffin, but there had been no time to prepare a proper one. In fact, Nynor had assured her the Funderling craftsmen had done well simply to prepare the tomb. The true coffin with its carved effigy should not be hurried, he said—would she want an imperfect likeness of her brother to gaze out at eternity, as if he were forced to hide behind a crude mask? Kendrick could be moved into the stone coffin when it was finished.

Still, it seemed shameful.

Despite the presence of members of the household like Rose and Moina, a dry-eyed but somber Chaven, and even old Puzzle, hatless and dressed in black-and-gray motley, his hair smoothed across his head in thin strands, the royal family's bench at the front of the chapel was only half full. Briony's stepmother Anissa sat a short distance away beside Merolanna, arms folded protectively across her belly. Her face was hidden by a black veil, but she sobbed and snuffled loudly. *At least we found something that could get her out of bed,* was Briony's bitter thought. She had not seen much of the queen lately. It was as though Anissa had turned the Tower of Spring into a sort of fortress, covering all the windows with heavy cloths and surrounding herself with women as a besieged monarch might surround himself with soldiers. Briony had never entirely warmed to her stepmother, but for the first time she was truly beginning to dislike her. *Your husband is imprisoned, woman, and one of his children is murdered. Even with a baby in your belly, surely you have more duties now than just to hide in that nest of yours like a she-crow brooding on her eggs.*

The chorus finished at last and Hierarch Sisel, in his finest red-and-silver robes, stood and took his place in front of the coffin to begin the funeral oration. It was the sort of thing Sisel did best, showing why King Olin had chosen him to fill such an important post despite the objections of Sisel's own superiors back in Syan (who had thought him too lukewarm in his support of the policies of the current trigonarch) and he spoke the familiar words with apparent compassion and sincerity. As the soothing Hierosoline litany filled the Erivor Chapel, Briony could almost let herself believe she had found one of those echoes of the past, a remnant of the days she would whisper with her brothers during services, annoying Merolanna and frustrating the old mantis Father Timoid, who knew that the children's father would never let them be scolded for a crime Olin himself deemed so insignificant.

But I'm not a child now. There is nowhere for me to hide from this moment.

As Sisel began to speak the words of the epitaph, the nobles dutifully repeating the significant phrases, Briony was distracted by a fuss at her elbow. Moina was talking sharply but quietly with a young page.

"What does the fellow want?" Briony whispered.

"I come from your brother, Highness," the child told her.

Held tightly around the middle by her confining garments, Briony did her best to bend toward the boy; it made her breathless. "Barrick?" But of course it had to be Barrick. If her other brother had sent her a message, it would not be carried by a young boy with a dripping nose. "Is he well?"

"He is better. He sends to say that you should not go to the cr . . . the cr . . ." The boy was nervous and couldn't remember the word.

This little fellow is facing the Goddess of the Night, after all, she thought. *Are you happy now, Lord Brone? I am not a weeping girl anymore—I have become a thing to scare children.* "The crypt?"

"Yes, Highness." The boy nodded rapidly but still couldn't meet her eye. "He says you should not go down to the crypt until you see what he is sending to you."

"What he is sending?" Briony looked to Rose, staring in damp misery at the coffin on the altar. It was draped in a banner blazoned with the

Eddon wolf and stars, but it was no less dreadful for its proud covering. Behind her, Briony could hear the courtiers whispering loudly and she felt herself growing angry at their disrespect. "Why are these fools talking? Rose, did you hear what the boy said? What could Barrick be sending?"

"Myself."

She turned and her heart thumped painfully in her breast. With his long black cloak only imperfectly covering the white nightdress and his face even paler than usual, Barrick might have been Kendrick himself in his winding-sheet. Her twin stood in the aisle of the chapel with a royal guardsman at each elbow helping him to stand upright. Just getting here had clearly been an effort; his face was damp with sweat and his eyes did not quite meet hers.

Briony levered herself upright and pushed past Moina, grateful that she was in the front of the chapel and not wedged between two rows of benches like a caravel in a too-tight berth. She threw her arms around Barrick as well as she could manage with her heavy clothes and confining corset, then realized everyone in the chapel must be looking at them. She leaned back a little and kissed his cheek, which was still warm from fever or effort.

"But, you wonderful fool," she said quietly, "what are you doing here? You should be in bed!"

He had been stiff in her embrace; now he stepped back, shaking off the two guardsmen who were trying to help him. "What am I doing here?" he asked loudly. "I am a prince of the House of Eddon. Did you think you would bury our brother without me?"

Briony put her hand to her mouth, surprised by his tone but even more shocked by the look of cold anger on his face. Something in her own features seemed to touch him in a way her embrace and kiss had not: his expression softened and he sagged. One of the guardsmen took his elbow. "Oh, Briony, I am sorry. I have been so ill. It was so hard to get here, I had to stop and catch my breath every few steps, but I had to . . . for Kendrick. Pay no attention. My mind has been full of so many foolish things. . . ."

"Of course—oh, Barrick, of course. Sit down." She helped him down onto the bench beside her. Even seated, he did not let go of her hand, holding her fast in his damp, hot grip.

Hierarch Sisel, after waiting while the courtiers reseated themselves, and with only the smallest and most tasteful look of puzzlement, resumed the eulogy.

⋆   ⋆   ⋆

" 'Whether we are born in time of joy or time of woe, and whether we make of our lives a wonder to all eyes or a shame before Heaven, still the gods grant us only our allotted time,' so said the oracle Iaris in the days of the splendor of Hierosol, and he spoke truth. To no man is given anything certain but death, be he ever so exalted. But be he ever so low, still can his spirit be seated with the immortals in Heaven.

"To Kernios of the black, fruitful earth, we commend this our beloved Kendrick Eddon's mortal raiment. To Erivor of the waters, we give back the blood that ran in his veins. But to Perin of the skies, we offer up his spirit, that it may be carried to Heaven and the halls of the gods as a bird is carried on the winds until it reaches the safety of its own nest once more.

"May the blessings of the Three be upon him, this our brother. May the blessings of the Three be also upon those who must remain behind. The world will be a darker place for the light that was his and is now gone, but it will shine brightly in the halls of the gods and shall be a star in Heaven. . . .' "

As he finished, the hierarch sprinkled a handful of earth on the coffin, then a few drops of water from a ceremonial jar; lastly, he set a single white feather atop them. As the gathered nobles spoke the response to Sisel's words, four guardsman stepped forward and slid two long poles through the coffin's handles, rucking the embroidered head of the Eddon wolf on the covering cloth so that its snarl seemed to turn to a look of confusion, then lifted the coffin and carried it to the door of the chapel.

Briony, going slowly so Barrick would not fall behind, moved to her place behind the coffin. She reached out a hand and lifted the family banner so she could touch the polished wood. She wanted to say something, but could not make herself believe that the Kendrick she knew was in that box.

It would be too cruel if he was—putting him down under all that stone. He loved to ride, to run . . .

She was weeping again as the coffin was carried out of the chapel behind a ceremonial guard, with all the noble mourners falling into line behind the twins.

The other residents of the palace had been waiting beside the flower-strewn path, the servants and lesser nobility who were now getting their only chance to see the casket that held the prince's remains. Many were crying and moaning as though Kendrick's death had just happened, and Briony found herself both moved and yet somehow angered by the noise—quite out of control for a moment, so that she had to fight herself not to turn around and run back into the chapel. She turned to Barrick instead and saw that he hardly seemed to notice the crowd. He was staring at the ground with clench-jawed ferocity, using all his strength just to stay moving behind the coffin. It was too painful for Briony to watch him, almost frightening: he looked like he was still locked in a fever-dream, as though only his body had come back to join the living.

She turned away from her twin and, as her eyes swept the crowd, she glimpsed a small face watching intently from a spot on the wall, a fair-haired boy who had apparently climbed up to get a better vantage point. For a moment she was fearful for the child—he was treetop-high—but he seemed as unconcerned as a squirrel.

Barrick had caught up again, and now he whispered in her ear. "They are all around, you know."

For a moment she thought he was talking about small boys like the one clinging to the wall. "Who are?"

He put his finger to his lips. "Softly, softly. They do not think I know, but I do. And when I have taken up my birthright, I will make them pay for what they have done." He fell back a pace and let his gaze drop to the ground once more, his mouth set in a tight, pained smile.

Please let this end soon, she prayed. *Merciful Zoria, just let us put our brother into the ground and let this day end.*

When they reached the graveyard, the procession wound among the slanting shadows of ancient stones until it reached the mouth of the family crypt. Briony and Barrick, Anissa, Merolanna, and a few others followed the guardsmen and their burden down into the ground, leaving the rest of the nobles to stand on the grass at the door of the tomb, deserted and awkward.

The graveyard was full of big folk, all of them in mourning dress. Chert felt like he was lost in a thicket of black trees. There was no sign of the boy anywhere.

All he could do was wait. The funeral had almost ended. In a few moments the royal family would come back out and the crowd would disperse. Maybe then he could find some trace of where the child had gone.

Opal will never forgive me, he thought. *What could have happened to him?*

With all these people here, could he have stumbled upon his real family? Chert thought even Opal could live with that, if they only knew it for certain.

But it's not just Opal, he admitted to himself. *I'll miss the boy, too, mourn the loss of him. Fissure and fracture, listen to me! Talking like it was Flint being put away in the dark instead of the prince. He's just run off somewhere, is all. . . .*

A hand touched his back. He turned to find the boy standing beside him.

"You! Where have you been?" Heart racing with unexpected joy and relief, Chert surprised himself by grabbing the boy and pulling him close. It was like hugging an unwilling cat. Chert released him and looked him over. The child seemed quiet and full of something—secrets, perhaps, but that was nothing new. "Where have you been?" Chert asked again.

"I met one of the old people."

"Who is that? What do you mean?"

But Flint did not answer. Instead he stared past Chert at the place where the royal family had descended into the tomb. Chert turned to see that some of them had come out again: the funeral was over.

"You still haven't told me where you went, boy . . ."

"Why is that woman looking at me?"

Chert swiveled until he saw the stout old woman in black-and-gold brocade, part of the funeral party. He almost recognized her, wondered if she might be the murdered prince's great-aunt, Merolanna. She was indeed staring at the boy, but as Chert watched, she swayed a little as though she might faint. Flint quickly moved behind Chert, but he did not look fearful, only cautious. Chert turned back to see the old woman's maids steadying her, leading her back toward the inner keep, but even as she walked, the woman kept looking around as if for the boy, her face set in an odd mixture of terror and need, until the milling crowd hid her from Chert's view.

Before he could make any sense out of what he had seen, a ripple passed through the crowd, a quiet murmuring. He caught at the boy's sleeve to make sure he didn't vanish again. The young prince and princess were being helped up the stairs and out of the crypt. They both looked shaken, the prince in particular so pale and hollow-eyed that he might have been one of the tomb's denizens escaped for a moment back into the outside air.

Poor Eddon family, Chert thought as the twins floated past, surrounded by courtiers and servants but somehow terribly alone, as though they were only partly in the world the rest of the castle folk shared. It was hard to believe they were the same pair he had seen riding in the hills only a few days earlier.

The weight of the world, that's what they're carrying now, he thought. For the first time, he could truly feel the meaning of the old phrase, the grim solidity of dirt and cold stone. It made him shiver.

PART TWO
MOONLIGHT

This king, Klaon, beloved grandchild of the Father of Waters, was troubled by what the beggar had told him, and so he swore that all the children who bore the sign of infamy should be found and then destroyed. . . .

—from *A Compendium of Things That Are Known*
The Book of the Trigon

13
Vansen's Charge

HALL OF PURSUIT:

A strong man who does not sing
A singng man who does not turn
Even when the door closes

—from *The Bonefall Oracles*

I DON'T WANT TO HEAR any more." He was tired and his head hurt. He still felt deathly ill—felt as though he would never again be truly well. He wanted only to go back to what he had been doing, bouncing the hard leather ball against the floor that had already been pitted with age in his great-grandfather's day, thinking about nothing.

"Please, Barrick, I beg of you." Gailon Tolly, Duke of Summerfield, was doing his best to keep impatience from his voice. It amused Barrick, but it angered him too.

"*Prince* Barrick. I am prince regent, now. I am not your little cousin any longer and you cannot treat me that way."

Gailon bobbed his head. "Of course, Highness. Forgive my disrespect."

Barrick smiled. "Better. Well, then, tell it to me again."

"I have . . ." The duke regained his look of patience. "It is simply this. Your sister has seen the envoy from Ludis again this morning. The black man, Dawet."

"By herself? Behind closed doors?"

Gailon colored. "No, Highness. In the garden, with others present."

"Ah." Barrick bounced the ball again. It did trouble him, but he wouldn't show it and give Gailon the satisfaction. "So my sister, the princess regent, was talking in the garden to an envoy of the man who's holding our father prisoner."

"Yes, but . . ." Gailon scowled and turned to Avin Brone. "*Prince Barrick* does not want to understand me, Brone. You explain."

The mountainous lord constable shrugged, a motion that looked as if it might start an avalanche. "She appears to enjoy the man's company. She listens very closely to what he has to say."

"While you were ill, he had a long audience with her, Highness," said Gailon. "She ignored everyone else who was present."

Ignored, thought Barrick. Through all the disturbing images that had not entirely left his head, through weariness and the strands of fever that still draped him like cobwebs, it was a word whose meaning he understood immediately. "She is paying more attention to him than to you, is that what you mean, Gailon?"

"No . . . !"

"It seems to me that you are trying to drive a wedge between my sister and myself." Barrick flung the leather ball down against the floor. It hit on the edge of a flagstone and went bouncing across the room. Two young pages dove out of the way as one of the larger dogs scrambled after it, then chased it into a corner behind a chest and growled in excited frustration. "But my sister and myself are almost the same thing, Duke Gailon. That is what you must know."

"You wrong me, Highness." Gailon turned to Brone, but the big man was watching the dog rooting behind the chest, making it clear that he wanted no responsibility for the duke's little embassy. "We are in a terrible time. We need to be strong—all the houses of Southmarch must stand together, Eddons, Tollys, all of us. I know that. But neither should the common people begin to whisper of . . . dalliances between your sister and your father's kidnappers."

"You go too far." Barrick was angry, but it was a distant fury like lightning over far hills. "Leave this room now and I will forgive your clumsy tongue, Gailon, but be careful. If you say such things in front of my sister, you may find yourself fighting for honor, and she will not ask for a champion. She will fight you herself."

"By the gods, is this whole family mad?" the duke cried, but Brone already had Gailon Tolly's shoulders and was steering him toward the door, whispering words of calm in his ear. The lord constable gave Barrick an odd look as he urged Gailon out, something that could equally have been surprised approval or disdain imperfectly masked.

Barrick did not feel strong enough to try to make sense of it all. In the three days he had been out of bed, through the ghastly funeral and the equally drawn-out and exhausting ceremony in the castle's huge, incense-choked Trigonate temple that had conferred the regency on both Briony and himself, he had never felt entirely well. That terrible fever had swept through him like a wildfire through a forest glade. Fundamental things were gone, roots and branches, and they would take time to grow back. At the same time, the fever itself seemed to have left behind unfamiliar spores, seeds of new ideas which he could feel quickening inside him, waiting to hatch.

What will I become? he wondered, staring at his bent left hand. *I was already a monster. Already a target for scorn, haunted by those terrible dreams, by . . . by Father's legacy. Am I a target for treachery now as well?* These new thoughts would not go away, feelings of distrust that scratched away at him at all hours, sleeping and waking, like rats in the walls. He had prayed and prayed, but the gods did not seem to care enough to relieve his misery.

Should I be listening to Gailon more carefully about this? But Barrick did not trust his cousin at all. Everyone knew that Gailon was ambitious, although he was by no means the worst of his family: his brothers, sly Caradon and the dangerously reckless Hendon, made the Duke of Summerfield seem almost maiden-shy by comparison. In fact, Barrick did not trust any of the Southmarch nobles, not Brone, not Tyne Aldritch of Blueshore, not even the old castellan, Nynor, no matter how valuable a servant any of them had been to his father. He trusted nobody but his sister, and now Gailon's words had begun to eat away at that bond, too. Barrick stood up, so full of rage and unhappiness that even the dog shied away. His two pages waited, solemn-faced, watching him as small animals watch a larger one who might be hungry. He had shouted at them more than a few times since dragging himself out of his fever-bed, and had struck both of them at least once.

"I must dress now," he said, trying to keep his voice level.

The council was meeting in an hour. Perhaps he should ask Briony straight out what her business was with the dark man, the envoy. The memory of Dawet's lean brown face and superior smile sent a little shudder of unease up Barrick's spine. It was so much like something from the fever dreams, those shadowy, heartless creatures that pursued him. But waking life had also been nightmarish since then. It was all he could do to remind himself that he *was* awake, that the walls were solid, that eyes did not watch him from every corner.

I almost told Briony about Father, he realized. That was one thing he must never do. It could be the end of any happiness either of them would ever have together. "I am waiting, curse it!"

The pages had been lifting his dark, fur-trimmed gown out of the chest; now they hurried toward him, awkward beneath the weight, bearing the heavy thing like the body of a dead foe.

What did Briony want with that envoy? And more importantly, why hadn't she told him, her brother? He couldn't help remembering that she had seemed quite prepared to take the regency without him, to leave him alone in his bed of pain. . . .

No. He forced the thoughts away but they did not go far: like starving beggars rebuffed, they moved only out of immediate reach. *No, not Briony. If there is anyone I can trust, it is Briony.*

His knees were shaking as the two young pages stood on their toes to drape the gown across his shoulders. He did not need to see these boys' faces. He knew they were looking at each other. He knew they thought something was wrong with him.

Am I still fevered? he wondered. *Or is this the thing that Father spoke of? Is this the true beginning of it?*

For a moment he was back in the shadowed passages of his illness, looking down a great distance into red-shot darkness. He could see no way out.

Sister Utta's long face showed amusement, but concern as well, and she spoke carefully. "I think it is a very bold idea, Highness."

"But not a good one, is that what you're saying?" Briony fidgeted. So many things were moving inside her these days, a torrent of feeling and need and sometimes even . . . well, it felt like *strength,* the kind that she had been asked to hide over and over again. All of these competing forces yanked at her limbs and thoughts as though she were on puppet strings. "You think I am asking for trouble. You want me not to do it."

"You are the princess regent now," said Utta. "You will do as you see fit. But this is a disturbed time—the waters are roiled and muddy. Is it really the time for the mistress of the nation to wear what everyone will think of as a man's garments?"

"Is it the time?" Briony clapped her hands together in frustration. "If not now, when? Everything is changing. Only a week ago, Kendrick was about to send me to marry the Bandit of Hierosol. Now I rule in Southmarch."

"With your brother."

"With my brother, yes. My twin. We can do whatever we want to do, whatever we think is right."

"First," said Utta, "remember that Barrick is your twin, but he is not you."

"Are you saying he will be angry with me? For dressing as I want to, wearing sensible, sturdy clothes instead of the frills of an empty-headed creature who is meant only to be pleasing to the eye?"

"I am saying nothing except that your brother, too, has seen the world he knows turned upside down. And so have all the people of the country. It has not been just a few days of change, Princess Briony. A year ago at the autumn harvest your father was on the throne and the gods seemed happy. Now all has changed. Remember that! There is a dark, cold winter coming—there is already snow in the high hills. People will huddle around their fires and listen to the wind whistling in the thatch and wonder what is coming next. Their king is imprisoned. The king's heir is dead—murdered, and no one can say why. Do you think during those dark, cold nights they will be saying, 'Thanks to the gods that we have two children on the throne now who are not afraid to turn all the old ways upside down!' "

Briony stared at the Zorian Sister's beautiful, austere face. *What I would not give to look like her,* Briony thought. *Wise, so wise and calm—no one would doubt me then! Instead I look like a milkmaid most of the time, red-faced and sweaty.* "I came to you for advice, didn't I?" she said.

Utta made a graceful little shrug. "You came for your lesson."

"Thank you, Sister. I will think about what you've said."

They had scarcely gone back to reading Clemon's *The History of Eion and Its Nations* when someone knocked quietly at the door.

"Princess Briony?" called Rose Trelling from the corridor. "Highness? It is nearly time for you to see your council."

Briony got up and gave Utta a kiss on her cool cheek before going out to her waiting maids. There wasn't room for them to walk three abreast in the narrow passageway so Rose and Moina dropped behind her; Briony could hear the sides of their skirts brushing the walls.

Moina Hartsbrook cleared her throat. "That man . . . says he would be honored if he could find you in the garden again tomorrow."

Briony couldn't help but smile at the girl's disapproving tone. "By 'that man' you mean Lord Dawet?"

"Yes, Highness." They all walked on in silence for a while, but Briony could sense Moina trying to work up the courage to speak again. "Princess," she said at last, "forgive me, but why do you see him? He is an enemy of the kingdom."

"And so are many foreign envoys. Count Evander of Syan and the old wheezing fellow from Sessio who smells like horse dung—you don't think those are our friends, do you? Surely you remember that fat pig Angelos, the envoy from Jellon, who smiled at me every day and fawned over Kendrick, until we woke up one morning and found that his master King Hesper had sold Father to Hierosol. I would have killed Angelos myself if he hadn't already made the excuse of a hunting trip and slipped away back to Jellon. But until we catch them doing something wrong, we put up with them. That's called statecraft."

"But . . . but is that really why you talk to him?" Moina was being stubborn; she ignored Rose's elbow bumping her ribs. "Just for . . . statecraft?"

"Are you asking if I spend time with him because I find him handsome?"

Moina blushed and looked down. Briony's other attendant was also having trouble meeting her eyes. "I don't like him either," Rose confessed.

"I'm not planning to marry him, if that's what you're wondering."

"Highness!" Her ladies-in-waiting were shocked. "Of course not!"

"Yes, he is handsome. But he is almost my father's age, don't forget. I'm interested in what he has to say about the many places he has seen, the southern continent where he was born and its deserts, or old Hierosol with all its ruins. I have not had much chance to see other places, you know." Her maids looked at her with the expressions of young women who associated journeying in foreign lands with little beside hardship and possible ravishment. She knew they would never understand her longing to learn of things beyond this damp, dark old castle. "But I am even more interested in what Dawet has to say about Shaso, of course. Who, you may remember, is in chains because he seems to have killed my brother. Is it acceptable to the two of you, that I should try to understand the reasons why Prince Kendrick was murdered?"

Rose and Moina were both caught up in sputtering apologies, but Briony knew she had not been entirely honest: there was more to her feelings about Dawet than simply admiration for his wide experience, although she was not exactly sure what those feelings were. She was no mere girl, she told herself, to fawn over a lovesome face, but something about the man truly had caught her attention and she considered him more than she should, wondered what he thought both of her and her court.

He would have carried me off to Ludis without a second thought, she reminded herself. *That is the kind of man he is. If Kendrick had announced it a day earlier, I would be halfway to Hierosol by now, on my way to meet my new husband, the Lord Protector.*

It suddenly occurred to her that since she felt certain Kendrick had in the end decided to give her to Ludis for the greater good of Southmarch, the prince regent's death had occurred at the last possible moment to prevent that from happening. The idea was so obvious and so surprising that she stopped in the middle of the hallway and her two ladies bumped into her from behind. It took a moment before they were all sorted out and moving again, but now Briony wished she did not have to go to the council chamber. This strange new thought made everything look different, as a cloud passing in front of the sun turned a bright day into sudden twilight.

But who would be so anxious to stop Kendrick sending me away? And where would Shaso fit into such a conspiracy? Or had it been arranged not to keep Briony herself in Southmarch, but by someone who wished to take the throne? *But even if it was someone in the family with a blood-claim, someone like Gailon Tolly or Rorick, there are still two better claims ahead of any of them—Barrick's and mine. They would have to kill us, too.*

No, there are more than two claims ahead of both Gailon and Rorick, Briony remembered. *There are three. There is also the child in Anissa's belly.*

And, of course, that infant would be the heir to the throne if he or she was born brotherless and sisterless into the world.

Anissa? Briony suddenly did not want to think about such things anymore. She had never much cared for her stepmother, but surely no woman would murder an entire innocent family for the sake of an unborn child—a child who might not even live! Surely not. But it was disturbingly hard to clear away such suspicions once they had begun to take root. Wasn't Anissa's family in Devonis related in some way to King Hesper of Jellon, the one who sold Briony's father to Hierosol in the first place?

Gailon, Rorick Longarren, her father's wife—she could not think of any of them now without suspicion. *This is what murder does,* she realized. She had reached the door of the council chamber and now waited to be announced. Barrick was slouched in one of the two tall chairs at the head of the table, arms folded tightly across his chest as though he were cold, the face framed in the collar of black fur even more pale than usual. *It does not make one phantom only—it makes hundreds.*

Once these halls were full of people I knew, even though I might not have liked them all. Now the house is crowded with demons and ghosts.

Wait and I will call for you, the message from Avin Brone commanded. Even without the Eddon wolf and stars and Brone's own sigil both stamped in wax at the bottom, the lord constable's thick, black pen strokes would have been unmistakable.

Ferras Vansen waited in his dress cloak just inside the doorway to the council chamber between two of his guardsmen. Two more guards waited out in the hall with the man they would present to the councillors. The council room, known as the Oak Chamber for the massive wooden table at its center, was an old room that had once been the castle treasury in the dangerous days of the marauding Gray Companies, a large but windowless space with only two doors, nested in the maze of corridors behind the throne hall. The captain of the royal guard had never much liked the stark, stony room: it was the kind of place built for last stands, for the dreadful heroics of defeat and disaster.

The guard captain had been furious at first that Lord Brone should treat their news so offhandedly, ordering it held until the end of a long council session full of far more trivial matters, but as first one hour passed, then another, Vansen had come to believe he understood Brone's thinking. Many days had passed since Prince Kendrick's death—a killing still unexplained as far as most of the people of Southmarch were concerned, even if the murderer himself had been captured. The business of the land had been almost uniformly ignored since then, and many things had already waited in pressing need of answer before the prince regent died. If Vansen had been allowed to present his own news first, it was possible that none of this other business would have had its audience.

So he waited—but it was not easy.

He let his eye rove across the dozen noblemen who made up today's council, playing a game of anticipating an attack on the royal twins first by this one, then by that, and trying to decide how he would counter it. The nobles looked bored, Vansen thought. They didn't seem to realize that after the recent events boredom was a privilege, perhaps even a luxury no one could afford.

Ferras also thought young Prince Barrick still appeared very ill, although perhaps the boy was just careworn. Whatever the cause, Barrick was certainly not paying the closest attention to the business of the kingdom. As case after case came up before them—the rents on royal lands in need of attention, official embassies of grief and support from Talleno, Sessio, and Perikal to be heard, important property disputes that had come up from the assize courts or the temple courts needing a final decision—the young prince barely seemed to attend the speakers. In most cases he simply waited for Briony to speak, then nodded his head in agreement, all the while rubbing the crippled arm that he held in his lap like a pet dog. Only a question from Lord Nynor the castellan seemed to awaken the boy from his lethargy at last and kindle a light in his eye: Nynor wanted to know how much longer the Hierosoline envoy Dawet dan-Faar would be with them, since the household purse had made allotment for only a fortnight's stay. But although he was clearly interested, Barrick became, if anything, even more silent and unmoving as Briony answered the question. The princess said that they could not of course hurry a reply to the man who held her father's safety in his hands, especially at so troubled a time. She seemed almost as distracted as her brother. Ferras Vansen thought that Barrick did not seem to like her answer much, but the prince made no spoken objection and Nynor was left to go grumbling off to rearrange the household finances.

The princess and her brother dispatched several dozen such questions over the course of two hours. The gathered nobles of the council offered suggestions, and on some occasions dissenting opinions as well, but mostly they seemed to be watching the twins at their new task—watching them and judging them. Gailon of Summerfield made none of his usual objections, and in fact seemed to be as absorbed by his own thoughts as the prince and princess were by theirs. When the subject of the envoy Dawet came up, it seemed Gailon might say something, but the moment passed and the handsome duke resumed picking at the leg of the council table with a small ceremonial dagger, barely hiding what was obviously some great frustration, although Ferras Vansen had no idea what its cause might be. For the first time Vansen could see Summerfield's duke for what he really was, despite all his power and wealth: a man younger than Vansen himself, and one with less training in silence and patience as well.

It must have been hard for him with that drunken blowhard of a father. Nobody outside Summerfield Court missed old Duke Lindon very much, and Vansen couldn't help guessing that there probably weren't many people in his duchy who missed him either.

The afternoon wore on, bringing nothing more interesting than reports of a sharp increase in the number of strange creatures that seemed to be coming from across the Shadowline. Something with spines and teeth had badly injured some children near Redtree, and a man had been killed by a goat with black horns and no eyes, which the locals had promptly captured, killed, and burned, but most of the reports were of creatures that seemed harmless despite their strangeness, many of them crippled or dying, as though they had not been prepared for the world on this side of the unseen barrier.

At last even the novelty of these tales began to fade. Some of the council members began to ignore the proceedings and talk openly among themselves despite sharp looks from Brone. Vansen was intrigued to see that the lord constable seemed also to have taken up the role of first minister, a position unfilled since the old Duke of Summerfield's death a year earlier. He wondered if this was part of the reason for the young duke's disgruntlement.

So many things are out of joint since the king went away, he thought.

"And now, if it pleases you, Highnesses," Avin Brone announced after a long dispute over the construction of a new Trigonate temple had left most of the table yawning, "there is some important business we have saved until last."

Several of the nobles, slumped and weary, actually straightened up, their attention finally caught. Vansen was about to fetch the witness when Brone surprised him by turning his back on him and summoning in two people Vansen had never even seen, a round-eyed man and a young girl. The man was bald as a turtle, although otherwise he seemed of healthy middle years, and even the girl was odd to look upon: she seemed to have plucked out her eyebrows entirely, as in the style of a hundred years before, and her hairline began far up her forehead. She wore a skirt and shawl that mostly hid her form, but the man certainly had the bulging chest and long, muscled arms typical of his kind.

Skimmers! Hundreds of the water-loving folk lived within the castle walls, and even though they generally stuck to their own kind and places, Vansen had encountered them often. But seeing them in the highest council chamber did surprise him, especially because he had thought that his own news would be asked for next.

"Highnesses," Avin Brone declared, "this is the fisherman Turley Longfingers and his daughter. They have something they wish to tell you."

Barrick stirred. "What is this, the entertainment? Have we put old Puzzle out to graze at last and found some new talents?"

Briony gave her brother a look of irritation. "The prince is tired, but he's right about one thing—this is unusual, Lord Brone. It feels like a bit of mummery, saved till last."

"Not last, I am afraid," responded the lord constable. "There will be more. But forgive the surprise. I did not know whether they would come forth and tell this story until just before the council came to the table. I have been chasing down the rumor for days."

"Very well." Briony turned to the fisherman, who was squeezing an already shapeless hood or hat in the clawlike hands that must have given him his name. "He said your name is Turley?"

The man swallowed. Vansen wondered what could make one of the normally imperturbable Skimmers, folk who routinely swam with sharks and killed them with knives when it was needful, look so harrowed. "Turley, yes," he said in a thick voice. "It is that, my queen."

"I'm not a queen and my brother isn't a king. The real king is our father, and he still lives, thank all the gods." She looked at him closely. "I have heard that among yourselves you Skimmers don't use Connoric names."

Turley's eyes widened. They had very little white around the edges. "We do have our own talk, Majesty, that's true."

"Well, if you would prefer to use a name like that, you may."

He looked for a moment as though he might actually bolt the room, but at last shook his gleaming head. "Prefer not, Majesty. Close-held, our names and talk. But no harm done to tell you of our clan. Back-on-Sunset-Tide, we are called."

She smiled a little, but her brother beside her just looked aggrieved. "A very fine name. Now why has Lord Brone brought you before the council?"

"My daughter Ena's tale it is, truly, but she was frightened to speak before them as high as yourselves, so came I with her." The man stretched out his long arm and his daughter moved against him. In her odd way, with her small stature and huge, watchful eyes, Vansen thought the girl almost pretty, but he could not ignore that oddity entirely: the Skimmers carried their strangeness around with them like a cloak. He had never yet talked to one without being reminded several times by his eyes and ears and even his nose that it was a Skimmer he was speaking to and not an ordinary person.

"Very well, then," said Briony. "We are listening."

"On the night . . . What happened, it was on the night before the night of the killing," said Turley.

Briony sat a little straighter. It was so quiet in the room Vansen could hear her skirts rustling. "The killing?"

"Of the prince. The one that just was buried."

Barrick was not slouching anymore either. "Go on."

"My daughter here, she was . . . she was . . ." The hairless man looked flustered again, as though he had been pulled out of a shadowy, safe place and into bright light. "Out when she should not be. With a young man, one of the Hull-Scrapes-the-Sand folk, who should know better."

"And where is this young man?" asked Briony.

"Nursing some bruises." Turley Longfingers spoke with a certain dark satisfaction. "He'll not be taking young girls midnight paddling in our lagoon for a bit."

"Go on, then. Or perhaps now that your daughter has seen us and heard us, she will be able to tell the story herself. Ena?"

The girl jumped at the sound of her name, although she had been listening to every word. She blushed, and Vansen thought the dark mottling on neck and cheeks robbed her of the momentary beauty she had showed before. "Yes, Majesty," the girl said. "A boat I saw, Majesty."

"A boat?"

"With no lights. It slid past the place where I was swimming with . . . with my friend, it did. All cut-paddled."

"Cut-paddled?"

"Dipping paddle blade sideways-like." Turley demonstrated. "That's what we call the stroke when someone tries to be quiet."

"This was in the South Lagoon?" Barrick asked. "Where?"

"Near the shore at Hangskin Row," the girl replied. "Someone was waiting for it on the Old Tannery Dock. That's how we name it. The one closest to the tower what has all the banners on it. They had a light—him on the dock, I mean—but it was hooded. Up the boat went to it, still cut-paddled, and then they gave them something."

"They?" Briony leaned forward. The princess looked unusually calm, but Ferras Vansen thought he could see something else behind her pale features, a fear she was struggling to hide, and for a moment all the helpless affection he had for her came surging up inside him. He would do anything for Briony Eddon, he realized, anything to protect her, no matter what she thought of him.

A jest, Vansen? He needed no enemies to do it—he could mock himself. *Do anything? You already had the protecting of her elder brother and now he's dead.*

"The one in the boat," the Skimmer girl said, "gave something to the one on the dock. We couldn't see what it was or who they were. Then the boat went away again, out toward the front seawall."

"And even after the prince was murdered the next night, you did not come forward?" Briony asked, her face gone hard. "Even after the ruling lord of Southmarch was killed? Are you so used to seeing things like this on the lagoon?"

"Dark boats paddling silent, yes, sometimes," the girl told her, gaining courage as she went. "Our folk and the fishermen have feuds and people get into trouble, and . . . and other things happen. But I still thought it meant no good, that shuttered light. I feared saying anything, though, because . . . because of my Rafe."

"Your Rafe!" snorted her father. "He'll be no one's Rafe if I see him near our dockhouse again. Hands soft as skateskin, *and* he's a Hullscraper!"

"He's kind," said the girl quietly.

"I think that's enough." Avin Brone came forward. "Unless Your Highnesses have other questions . . . ?"

"They can go," Briony said. Both she and Barrick looked troubled. Meanwhile Ferras Vansen was working it through in his head and realizing that the tower the girl mentioned must be the Tower of Spring—and that the prince and princess must know that, too.

Queen Anissa's residence, he thought. *But there are other things on that side of the castle as well—the observatory, more than a few taverns, and at least one of our own guardhouses, not to mention the homes of hundreds of Skimmers and ordinary folk. It tells us nothing truly useful.* Still, there was something about the idea that tugged at him, so that for a moment he nearly forgot his own pressing errand here.

As Lord Brone's man-at-arms showed out the two Skimmer folk, the court physician Chaven slipped in past them to stand just inside the council chamber doorway, an unsettled look on his round face.

"Now we have one last piece of business," said Brone. "A minor thing only, so I think that after such a long piece of talking and listening we might send the extra guards and servants away and let them get on with preparing for the midday meal. Will you indulge me in this, Prince Barrick, Princess Briony?"

The twins gave their assent and within a few moments the chamber was empty of everyone except the councillors themselves, Vansen and his guards, and Chaven, who still lingered beside the far door like a schoolboy waiting for punishment.

"So?" Barrick sounded tired and childishly irritated; it was hard to believe he and Briony were the same age. "Obviously you want to thwart rumors, Lord Brone, so why wait until after the news of this mystery boat has been delivered? Right now half the people you sent out are hurrying to find someone to tell about this."

"Because that is what we want people talking about, Highness," said Brone. "It is true about the boat, but at this point it's also meaningless. It will not frighten people, just intrigue them. Best of all, it will mean that no one will be in a hurry to find out what we are saying here, now."

"They already know what we're going to be saying, though, don't they?" asked Briony. "We are going to discuss what that Skimmer girl saw and whether it means anything."

"Perhaps," said Brone. "But perhaps not. Forgive me for playing a deep game, my lord and lady, but I have another bit of news for you, one that would make for much more fearful rumors. Captain Vansen?"

The moment came upon him so suddenly, and with his head still so full of questions about the Skimmers and of thoughts about the princess herself that for a painfully extended moment Ferras Vansen just stood, not quite hearing. Then he suddenly realized the lord constable was staring at him, waiting, as was everyone else in the council. He leaped toward the door, certain he could hear the prince and princess snickering behind him, and stepped out into the passage to call for the other guards to bring in the young man.

"So you stand before us again, Vansen," Briony said when he returned to the chamber. "I hope you are not looking for an advancement of your position?"

He waited a few moments to make sure he had control of his voice, would not misspeak. If she hated him, he could not but believe he had earned it. "Your Highnesses, Lords, this man beside me is named Raemon

Beck. He has only reached Southmarch this morning. He has a tale you should hear."

When it was finished and the first rush of amazed questions had gusted itself out, silence fell over the chill, windowless room.

"What does it mean?" the princess asked at last. "Monsters? Elves? Ghosts? It seems an unbelievable tale." She stared at Raemon Beck, who was shivering as though he had just come in out of a snowstorm instead of a day bright with autumn sunshine. "What are we to do with such news?"

"It is foolishness," growled Tyne of Blueshore. Several of the other council members nodded vigorous agreement. "Bandits, yes—the roads to the west are not safe even in these days. But this man has been struck on the head and dreamed the rest. That or he seeks to make a name for himself."

"No!" cried Beck. Tears welled in his eyes. He hid his head in his hands, muffling his voice. "It happened—it is all true!"

"And bandits or boggarts, why did you alone survive?" demanded one of the barons.

Chaven stepped forward. "Your pardon, my lords, but I suspect that this man was merely the one chosen to bear the message."

"What message?" Small spots blazed on Prince Barrick's cheeks as though his fever had returned. He seemed almost as frightened as Raemon Beck. "That the world has gone mad?"

"I do not know what the message is," said Chaven. "But I think I know who is sending it. I have been told by one I know, one I trust . . . that the Shadowline has begun moving."

"Moving?" Avin Brone, who had already heard the young merchant's story, now for the first time looked truly startled. "How so?"

Chaven explained how a Funderling man searching for rare stones in the hills had found the line moved some yards closer to the castle—the first such movement in anyone's memory. "I had planned to tell you of this, Your Highnesses, but the tragic events that you know of kept me busy, and then I did not wish to burden you when you still had your brother to bury."

"That was days and days ago," Briony said angrily. "Why have you kept silent since then?"

Gailon Tolly saved the physician from having to answer immediately. "What is all this about?" the Duke of Summerfield demanded loudly. "Scholar, you and this Helmingsea lackwit spout nurse's tales as though you spoke of true places like Fael or Hierosol. The Shadowline? There is nothing beyond it but mist and wet lands too cold to farm and . . . and old stories."

"You are young, my lord," said Chaven gently. "But your father knew. And his father. And your grandfather several times over was one of the men who regained Southmarch and this castle from the hands of the Twilight People." The small man shrugged, but there was something terrible in the gesture, an entire language of resignation that did not hide the fear. "It could be that after all these years the Quiet Folk seek to have it back."

The councillors all seemed to begin shouting at once, no one listening to any other. Briony stood up and extended a trembling hand. "Silence! Chaven, you will attend my brother and me at once in the chapel, or somewhere else we can have privacy. You will tell us everything you know. But that is not enough. Dozens of our countrymen have been robbed and perhaps murdered on the Settland Road. We must find out everything we can, immediately, before all trace of the attackers is gone." She looked at her twin, who nodded, but his face showed his unhappiness. "We must go to the place where this occurred, with force. We must find the track of these creatures and follow it. If they can take men away from the road, they will have left some mark of their passage." She turned on Raemon Beck, who had sunk to a crouch as though his legs could no longer support him. "Do you swear you have told us the truth, man? Because if I find . . . if we find that you have made up this story, you will spend the rest of a short and unhappy life in chains."

The merchant could only shake his head. "It is all true!"

"Then we will send a troop of soldiers at once," she said. "To follow the trail wherever it leads. That at least we can do while we consider what this may mean, what . . . message we have been sent."

"Across the Shadowline?" Avin Brone appeared surprised by the idea. "You would send men across the Shadowline?"

"Not you," she said scornfully. "Have no fear."

The lord constable stood. "There is no need to insult me, Princess."

They were the only two standing. Their eyes met over the heads of the others.

"Again, you have showed me hasty, Lord Brone," Briony said after a moment's silence, each word crisp as the sound of a small bell being struck. "Despite the trickery you have used today to put on this little show, you do not deserve as much anger as I have shown. I apologize."

He made a stiff little bow. "Accepted, of course, Highness. With thanks, although you do me too much honor."

"*I* will go," said Gailon suddenly. He rose, too, his face flushed as though with drink. "I will lead a troop to the spot. I will find these bandits—and I wager my good name that they will prove to be no more than that! But whatever they are, I will bring back them or their corpses to answer for the crime."

Vansen saw Briony exchange a look with her brother that the captain of the royal guard could not interpret.

"No," said Barrick.

"What?" The duke turned on the prince in anger. Gailon Tolly seemed to have lost his usual composure. Vansen's muscles tensed as he watched. "You cannot go yourself, Barrick! You are sick, crippled! And your sister may think she is a man, but the gods know she is not! I demand the honor of leading this troop!"

"But that is just the issue, Cousin," said Briony, speaking with cold care. "It is not an honor. And whoever goes must go with an open heart, not with an intent to prove himself right."

"But . . . !"

She turned her back on him and her gaze swept down the row of nobles at the table, Tyne and Rorick and many others, before it lit on Ferras Vansen where he stood behind the crumpled, sobbing form of the merchant Raemon Beck. For a moment her gaze met his and Vansen thought he saw a little smile flicker across her lips. It was not a kind smile. "You, Captain. You have failed to prevent my brother's murder and you have failed to find a reason that explains why Lord Shaso, one of our family's most loyal retainers, should have performed that murder. Perhaps you will be able to fulfill this new charge more successfully."

He couldn't look at her any longer. Staring at his boots, he said, "Yes, Highness. I will accept the charge."

"No!" Gailon was out of his seat again, so angry that for a worrying moment Ferras thought the duke actually meant to attack the prince and princess. Vansen was not the only one—the nobles on either side of Gailon Tolly snatched at his arms but failed to hold him. Brone's hand dropped to the hilt of his sword, but the lord constable was almost as far away as the guard captain and much slower.

Gods! Ferras took a stumbling step forward. *Too late, still too late, I have failed again!* But Summerfield only turned and stalked away from the great table toward the far door of the council chamber. When he turned in the doorway, the young duke's face was composed again, almost frighteningly so.

"I see I am not needed here, either in this council or in this castle. With your permission, Prince Barrick, Princess Briony, I will return to my own lands where there may be something of use I can do." Gailon Tolly had asked their leave, but he did not wait to receive it before departing the chamber. His bootheels banged away down the corridor.

Briony turned to Vansen again, as though Gailon had never been in the room. "You will take as many men as you and the lord constable think fit to assemble, Captain. You will take this man, too . . ." she gestured at Beck, "and go to the place his caravan was attacked. From there, send back messengers to tell us what you find, and if you can pursue the robbers, pursue them."

Raemon Beck realized what was being said. "Don't send me back, Highness!" he shrieked, scrabbling across the floor toward the prince and princess. "The gods' mercy, not there! Put me in irons, as you promised, rather than send me to that place."

Barrick pulled his foot back when the man would have grabbed it.

"How else will we know that the spot is the correct one?" Princess Briony asked gently. "If every trace is gone, as you have said? Your fellows may be alive. Would you steal away even the slim chance of rescuing them?" She turned to the table full of slack-mouthed councillors, a row of bewildered masks like the chorus of some antique mummer's play. "The rest of you may go, but you are sworn to secrecy about this attack. He who speaks a word about it joins Shaso in the stronghold. Chaven, you and Lord Brone come with my brother and myself to the chapel. Rorick and Tyne, come to us in an hour, please. Captain Vansen, you will leave tomorrow at dawn."

After she was gone and the chamber was all but empty, Vansen and two of his guardsmen helped the weeping Raemon Beck up from the floor.

"The princess does not take well to begging," Ferras Vansen told the young merchant as they led him toward the door. The guard captain's own thoughts were slow and numbed as fish at the bottom of a frozen stream. "Her older brother was killed—did you know that? But we will do our best to take care of you. For now, let us find you some wine and a bed. That's the best any of us will get tonight . . . or for some time to come, I think."

14

Whitefire

STORM MUSIC:

This tale is told on the headlands
The great one comes up from the deeps
His eye is a shrouded pearl, his voice the ocean wind

—from *The Bonefall Oracles*

BARRICK'S FIRST THOUGHT WAS that the man looked like a chained beast, both frightening and pitiable, like the bear brought to the castle during the last Perinsday feast and made to dance in the throne room. All the courtiers had laughed—he had even laughed himself to see its clumsy antics and hear its snort of irritation, so like a man's, when its trainer flicked its bandy legs with a whip. Only Briony had been angry.

But she always worries more about animals than people. If I had been one of the dogs, she would never have left my side while I was ill.

His father had not laughed either, he suddenly remembered. For on that Perinsday they had all still been together, Olin here in Southmarch, Kendrick alive, everything as it should be. Now all had changed, and since the fever even his own thoughts had become strange and untrustworthy.

He forced himself to concentrate, staring at Shaso with what he hoped was the proper expression of a ruling prince to a traitorous vassal. Despite the ankle-chain half hidden by the straw on the floor of the stronghold, its far end socketed into the stone wall, the Tuani man looked less like a bear than a captured lion.

You could never make a lion dance on its chain.

"There should be guards," said Avin Brone. "It is not safe . . ."

"You are here with us," Briony replied sweetly. "You are a famous fighter, Lord Constable."

"So is Lord Shaso, with all respect."

"But he is chained and you are not. And he is not armed."

Shaso stirred. Barrick had always found it hard to think of him as anything but ageless, but now the man's years showed in his slack skin and gray-whiskered cheeks. He had been given clean clothes, but they were poor and threadbare. Except for the muscles that still rippled in his forearms and the back that had not yet learned to bend, this old man might have been a street beggar in Hierosol or one of the other southern cities. "I will not hurt you," he growled. "I am not fallen so low."

Barrick fought down a gust of anger. "Is that what you told our brother before you killed him?"

The prisoner stared. His dark face seemed lightened, as though a layer of fine dust had sifted down onto him from the surrounding stones, or as if his time in the sunless depths had leached out some of his color. "I did not kill your brother, Prince Barrick."

"Then *what happened?*" Briony took a step forward, stopping before Brone was compelled to grab at her arm. "I would like to believe you. What happened?"

"I have told Brone already. When I left Kendrick, he was alive."

"But your dagger was bloodied, Shaso. We found it in your room."

The old Tuani warrior shrugged. "It was not the prince's blood."

"Whose was it?" Briony took another step closer, which made even Barrick uncomfortable—she was within the compass of the old man's chain now, and all three of his visitors knew his cat-quickness. "Just tell me that."

Shaso looked at her for a moment, then his mouth curved in what might be called a smile, except that there was no jot of mirth in it, nothing of happiness at all. "My own. The blood is my own."

Barrick's rage flared up again. "He's telling a shadow-tale, Briony—I know you want to believe him, but don't let yourself be fooled! He was with Kendrick. Our brother and two other men were killed, and the wounds were curved like his dagger, which we found covered in blood. He cannot even tell a good lie."

Briony was silent for a moment. "Barrick's right," she said at last. "You ask us to believe much that seems unbelievable."

"I ask nothing. It does not matter to me." But even Shaso's own hands betrayed him, Barrick thought—they sat in his lap like harmless things, but the dark fingers were working, clenching and unclenching.

"It does not matter to you that my brother is dead?" Now Briony could not keep her own voice calm. "That Kendrick has been murdered? He was good to you, Shaso. We have all been good to you."

"Oh, yes, you have been good to me, you Eddons." He moved a little and the chain clinked. Avin Brone stepped up beside Briony. "Your father defeated me on the battlefield and spared my life. He is a good man. And then he brought me home like a dog he had found in the road and made me into his servant. A very good man."

"You are worse than a dog, you ungrateful creature!" shouted Barrick. This was a different Shaso, sullen and self-pitying, but still his tormentor, still the one who so many times had made him feel less than whole. "You have never been treated like a servant! He made you a lord! He gave you land, a house, a position of honor!"

"And in that way he was cruelest of all." The frighteningly empty smile returned, a pale gash in the dark face. "As my old life slid away from me like a boat drifting from the bank, he gave me a new life, rich in wealth and honor. I could not even hate him. And later on, it is true, I myself played the slave master—I sold my own freedom. But just because of the two of us I was the worse traitor, that does not mean I have forgiven him."

"He admits he is a traitor!" Barrick moved forward to tug at Briony's arm, but she resisted him. "Come! He admits he hates our family. We have heard enough." He didn't want to be in the shadowy stronghold any longer, separated from the sun and air by yards of stone, caught in this place that stank of misery. He suddenly feared that Shaso held secrets more terrible than any blade, more devastating even than murder. He wanted the old man to stop talking.

Briony waited a moment before she spoke. "I don't understand everything you say, but I do know that if you feel any loyalty to our family at all, even a tainted loyalty, then you must tell us the truth. If it is your blood, how did it get there?"

Shaso slowly lifted his arms. The crisscross slashes had mostly healed. "I cut myself."

"Why?"

He only shook his head.

"More likely he was wounded by the guards or Kendrick," Barrick pointed out. "While they defended their lives."

"Was there blood on their weapons?" his sister asked. "I cannot remember." All this talk of blood had made Briony go quite pale. The Barrick of half a year ago, he knew, would have said something to distract her, to make it easier to discuss these dreadful things, but now he was hollowed, his insides burned black.

"Your brother had no weapon," answered Avin Brone, "which makes his killing even more cowardly. The guards were covered all over with blood from their own wounds, so it was impossible to tell if their blades had been bloodied before they died."

"You still have explained nothing," Briony told the old man. "If you want us to believe that, tell us why you cut yourself. What did you and Kendrick speak of, that led to such a strange thing?"

The master of arms shook his head. "That is between me and him. It will die with me."

"Those may not be idle words, Lord Shaso," said Avin Brone. "As you know, we have not kept the headsman as well employed in King Olin's day as in his father's, but his blade is still sharp."

The master of arms turned his red-rimmed eyes first on Barrick, then Briony. "If you want my head, then take it. I am tired of living."

"The gods damn your stubbornness!" Briony cried. "Would you rather die than tell us what happened? What obscure point of honor have you caught on, Shaso? If there is something that will save your life, then for the sake of all the gods, tell me!"

"I have told you the truth—I did not murder your brother. I would not have harmed him even if he had put his own blade to my throat, because I swore to protect your father and his household."

"Wouldn't have harmed him?" Barrick was feeling tired and sick again—even his anger had become only a distant storm. "Strange words— you have knocked me down and beaten me often enough. My bruises haven't healed from the last time."

"That was not to harm you, Prince Barrick." The old man's words had a sharp, cold edge. "That was an attempt to make you a man."

Now Barrick was the one who stepped toward the master of arms, hand upraised. Shaso did not move, but even before Avin Brone reached him, Barrick had stopped. He had remembered the courtiers who pelted the dancing bear with cherry-stones and crusts of bread, and how he had laughed to see the chained creature snapping at the missiles in annoyance.

"If you are the murderer of our brother," he said, "as I think you are, then you will receive your punishment soon enough. Lord Brone is right— Southmarch still has a headsman."

Shaso flapped his hand dismissively. His chin sank to his chest as though he was too weary to keep his head up any longer.

"That is your last word?" Briony asked. "That you did not harm Kendrick, that the blood on your knife was your own, but you won't tell us how it happened?"

The old man did not look up. "That is my last word."

As he followed Briony out the door, Barrick wondered if such a mad story could possibly be true. But if it was, then truth itself was not trustworthy, for there was no other explanation for Kendrick's death, no one else suspected but Shaso. Take that away and all was shadow, as treacherous and inconstant as the worst of his own fever-dreams.

He must be the murderer, Barrick told himself. If not, reason itself tottered.

Ferras Vansen studied the line of men as though they were suddenly discovered family—as, in a way, they were. They would be living together for weeks or months, traveling into the wild places, and even family did not breed any greater closeness than a company of soldiers—or in some cases, any greater contempt. They were only half a pentecount all together—any greater number would have excited too much attention—and their little troop was dwarfed not only by Wolfstooth Spire looming just above them, but by the empty expanses of the barracks' reviewing yard. Vansen had chosen to take seven mounted men including himself, and a dozen-and-a-half foot soldiers, a pair of them new recruits who were little more than farmboys, to watch after the donkey-cart. In order to make things easier for his lieutenant Jem Tallow, who would command the castle guard in his absence and needed able, levelheaded men, Vansen had deliberately chosen his troop so that more than half were young and inexperienced. There were fewer than ten of these men that Vansen really trusted in a fight: he hoped it would be enough.

Raemon Beck had been given a horse and a sword, both of which he handled like what he was, a merchant's nephew. Vansen had considered armoring the young man as well, but his own experiences in the bandit campaign of three years earlier had taught him that one unused to heavy gear would eventually make things hard for the others, even on horseback. He would keep the youth nearby, with himself and old hand Collum Dyer watching over him; that would be the young man's best armor.

"Don't look so grim," he told Beck. "Your caravan was caught unaware, and only the gods know the quality of the fighting men who were with you. Now you're with half a pentecount of hardy Southmarch Guard, many of them blooded in Krace and against the last of the Gray Companies. They won't run from shadows."

"Then they are fools." Beck was pale and his mouth trembled a little when he spoke, but he had gained composure since his audience with the prince and princess. "They have not seen these shadows. They have not seen the devils that live in them."

Vansen shrugged. He was not himself entirely happy about their mission; he had spoken largely to cheer the young merchant. Ferras Vansen was a child of Daler's Troth, and had grown up only a short distance from the haunted ruins of old Westmarch—on days the south wind blew back the mists, the broken shell of its keep could sometimes be seen from the highest hilltops. He and his people knew better than to speak contemptuously, as the Duke of Summerfield had, about the Shadowline and what lay beyond that cloudy border. But like the rest of his people, a fierce and generally standoffish community of hillside farmers and herders, he was also keenly aware that his family's land was a holding that had been only a few generations in the hands of mortals. The dale folk had long had a sense that there were forces waiting beyond the Shadowline to take back those lands, as well as an equally fierce and stubborn determination not to let that happen.

A messenger from Lord Brone trotted into the reviewing yard. Vansen called the troop to order. The horses stamped restlessly, waiting, and the donkey cropped dry grass from between the cobbles. The morning was already far advanced, but there was nothing to do but wait. Already the long shadow cast by Wolfstooth Spire was beginning to shrink back into itself.

She came at last, a slender shape in mourning black accompanied by two female attendants and the great bulk of the lord constable who, if he was not becoming the king, did seem to be changing into something like the father of the prince and princess, assuming a kind of ceremonial precedence over all the business of the Eddon family despite the comparative lowliness of his title. He was rich, though, with vast holdings of lands, and able enough that he had risen higher in the royal family's favor than any of their closer kinsmen. Vansen wondered if it could be this rather than anything else that had sent young Gailon of Summerfield home to his family's dukedom—the knowledge that Lord Brone had sealed off the avenues of approach to the royal twins, leaving Gailon with a superior claim by right of blood, but inferior access.

Ferras Vansen couldn't keep his mind for long on such bloodless matters as the princess approached. The past weeks had not been kind to her—she had not painted her face since the funeral and he could see by the blue shadows beneath her eyes that she had not slept well. Still, despite this, despite the cold look she turned upon him, he could not imagine another face that would make him feel as he so helplessly did.

Perhaps it really is as the ancients say, he thought. Perhaps a heart was indeed like a piece of dry birchwood, and could only take fire and burn brightly once—that any fire that came after would be only an ember, smaller and cooler. *Just my treacherous luck I should burn for her, for one I can never have, honorably or dishonorably, and who hates me in any case.*

"Captain Vansen," she said in a dry, firm voice, "my brother is resting, but he sends his wish that the gods speed your mission." Vansen was a little surprised to see that there was an expression other than contempt on her face, the first time since Kendrick Eddon's death that anything else had lit her features when looking at him. The problem was that he could not read the look, which might only have been weariness and disinterest. "I see you have your men ready."

"Yes, Highness. Your pardon, but are you certain you wish us to ride out so plainly in the middle of the day? Everyone will whisper of it."

"Everyone is already whispering. How many people did that man there, Beck, speak to before he was brought to the castle? Do you think there is anyone in Wharfside or the Three Gods who hasn't heard his story by now? You and your men will ride out down Market Road, across the causeway, and straight through Southmarch Town. Everybody will know that the Eddons are not so crippled by grief and fear that they ignore plundered caravans and kidnapped noblewomen." She looked to Brone, who nodded his approval. "And this is not only for show, Vansen. We are not taking it lightly, my brother and I. So I trust you will take advantage of any trustworthy travelers on the road to send word back to us of your progress."

"Yes, Your Highness. The monks of the university have a post service that travels back and forth on the Settland Road every fortnight, and it is a long time yet before the winter will stop them. I will keep you and Lord Brone informed, but I honestly hope I will not be gone so long."

"You will return only when you have answers to give us," she declared; sudden fury was like a whipcrack in her voice.

"Of course, Your Highness." He was stung, but in that moment he saw not just her anger, but something deeper and stranger in her expression, as though a frightened prisoner looked out from behind her face. *She is afraid!* It filled him with ridiculous thoughts, with the wild urge to kiss her hand, to declare his painful love for her. Thwarted in its natural direction and forced to find other escape, like steam hissing from beneath a pot lid, the sudden flicker of madness dropped him to his knees.

"I will not fail you again, Princess Briony," he declared. "I will do what you have sent me to do or I will die trying."

Even with his head down, he could sense the stir of surprise going through the other guardsmen, could hear Avin Brone's sucked-in breath.

"Get up, Vansen." Her voice sounded strange. When he was on his feet again, he saw that the anger was back in her eyes, along with a glitter that might have been tears. "I have had enough death, enough oaths, enough men's talk about honor and debts—I have swallowed them all until I am ready to scream.

"You may think I blame you for my brother's death. I do in part, and not only you, but I am not so foolish as to think some other guard captain would have saved him. You may think I have given you this charge because I want to punish you. There may be a little truth to that, but I also know you for a man who has done other things well, and who has the trust of his soldiers. I am told that you are levelheaded, too." She took a step forward until only the broad sweep of her skirts separated them. Vansen couldn't help holding his breath. "If you die without solving this mystery, you accomplish nothing. If you live, even if you have failed your charge, you still may do some good for this land at another time."

She paused, and for a teetering moment it seemed to Vansen that she might say absolutely anything at all.

"But if the safety of any of my family is ever again on your shoulders," she finally suggested, with a smile that would be cruel were it not so weary, "then you do indeed have my permission to die trying, Captain Vansen."

She turned to his men and called to them, "May all the gods protect you. May Perin himself make your road smooth and straight." A moment later she was walking back across the courtyard with Brone and the two ladies-in-waiting hurrying to catch up.

"Not quite a court favorite, Captain, are we?" asked Collum Dyer, and laughed.

"Mount up." Ferras Vansen did not understand what had just happened, but there were many miles ahead of them, days of riding, and he would have plenty of time to think about it.

The one known as The Scourge of the Shivering Plain rode down out of Shehen on her great black horse, letting the animal pick its way along the narrow hill paths with scarcely a tug on the rein, although in places the drop was so great that it was hard even to see the birds flying below her. Yasammez had no need for haste. Her thoughts were traveling before her, winged messengers faster than any bird, swifter even than the wind.

She descended from the heights and turned toward the oldest lands and the greatest city of all, which stood on the shores of the black ocean just outside the great northern circle of frost and ice. There were Qar folk that lived even in the northernmost lands beyond Qul-na-Qar, strange ones who walked in that permanent darkness and made songs with their fingers and their chill skin, but they had lived apart for so long that most of them had little to do with the rest of their race anymore. They scarcely even thought about the lost southern lands, for they had never lived there, and thus of all the Twilight People they had suffered the least at the hands of the mortal enemy. The cold ones would not serve Lady Porcupine: she would have to muster her armies from Qul-na-Qar and the lands that lay south of it, all the way down to the thrice-blessed fence that the mortals called Shadowline, and that the Qar themselves called *A'sish-Yarrit Sa*, which meant "Storm of Silence," or, with a slightly different intonation of voice or gesture of the hand, "White Thoughts."

The northerners might not care about the mortal thieves, but those who lived below their icy lands did. As Yasammez rode, they came up from the cavern towns of Qirush-a-Ghat, "Firstdeeps," and out from the forest villages in the great dark woods to see her pilgrimage. The starlight dancers paused and grew silent on the hilltops as she passed. Those who did not know her—for it had been long since Yasammez had last left her house at Shehen—knew only that one of the great powers was passing, terrible and beautiful as a comet, and although they feared and respected such might, they did not cheer her, but watched in troubled silence. Those of the Qar who did recognize her of old were fiercely divided, because they all knew that where Lady Porcupine went, she was blown on winds of war and blood. Some returned to their families or villages to tell them that bad weather was coming, that it was time to put away stores of what was needful and strengthen the walls and gates. Others followed her in a quiet but growing crowd, their numbers swelling behind her like a bride's train. All of these knew that the bridegroom to whom she went was Death, and that her husband and master would not be careful of whom he took, but they followed her anyway. Centuries of anger and fear pushed them together, clenched them like a fist.

Yasammez was the blade which that fist had raised in the past. Now it would be raised again.

Her arrival threw Qul-na-Qar into confusion. By the time she rode through the great leaning gates at the head of a silent flock of Qar, the ancient citadel had already broken into camps of fanatical supporters and equally fanatical opponents, and a party larger than those two put together whose only shared philosophy was resistance to both extremes, a willingness to wait and see the shape that time took. But none of this was obvious, and to the casual eye—if there had been such a thing in this place—the great capital would have seemed to move in its usual deceptively calm way, its immemorial ordered disorder.

The servitors of Yasammez who waited for her within Qul-na-Qar, almost all of whom had been born into that service since the last time she had visited the city, had scurried to air out her chambers on the sprawling castle's eastern side, heaving up the shutters for the first time in decades and opening the windows. The chill marine winds and the ocean's ceaseless noise, like the breathing of a vast animal, filled the rooms as they rushed to make things ready for their mistress. This was a day that all knew would someday form a chapter of its own in the *Book of Regret*.

But as she made her way through the Hall of the Gate, passing beneath its living sculptures without an upward glance, Yasammez was surrounded not only by her own minions but by all the dark city's excitement-seekers as well—those bright-eyed ones who dabbled in the showier magicks, others who passed their time refining the arts of war and the arts of courtship until they were scarcely distinguishable from each other, all the planners of secret campaigns and delvers of forgotten mysteries. She was surrounded by believers, too, those who had yearned for a voice to echo forcefully their own talk of catastrophe, to satisfy their yearnings for an all-smothering doom. All came singing and calling out questions, some in languages that even Yasammez herself did not speak. She paid none of them any attention, and passed instead from the Hall of the Gate to the Hall of Black Trees, then on through many more, the Hall of Silver Bones, the Hall of Weeping Children, the Hall of Gems and Dust. She stopped outside the Mirror Hall but did not go in, even though the blind king and silent queen waited behind the doors, aware of her coming since before she even left her high house.

Instead she told the servitor who guarded the entrance—a Child of the Emerald Fire who showed the faint glow of its kind even through its robe and mask—"Outside the gate there are thousands of our race who have followed me here from the countryside. See that they are well-treated. Soon I will speak to them."

The masked figure did not reply, but bowed. Yasammez turned away from the Mirror Hall—it was not yet time to seal the Pact of the Glass, although that time would come before she left Qul-na-Qar again—and made her way to her old chambers overlooking the sea and the dark twilight sky. The crowd that had gathered inside the great castle and followed her through the halls like ants through a rotting tree were left to stand, to wait, to stare at each other in glee or shame or madness, and eventually to disperse.

It did not matter. There would be a time for all of them, Yasammez knew.

She had donned her plate armor, forged in Greatdeeps in the days before the Book, cured for centuries in an ice mountain without a name. The black spikes covered it like the quills of her namesake, a dark bristling that was obscured but not hidden by her cloak, which seemed almost as insubstantial as a thundercloud. Her head was bare: she had set her featureless helmet on the table beside her, as though, like a favored pet, she wished it to watch the proceedings.

Seven other figures sat at the round table in Lady Porcupine's chamber. It was dark in the room, only a single candle burning, its flame a-tremble before the open windows, but Yasammez and her allies did not need to see each other.

Some of what they said was spoken, some passed only in shared thought.

"Eats-the-Moon, what of the Changing tribe?"

"Many are with us. I smell anger. I smell readiness. Ours were often the first of the People to meet the stone apes, back in the world before defeat, and the first to

suffer as well. Not all are fighters, but those who are not shall be ears and eyes for the rest, swift fliers, silent crawlers."

"Many? What number is that?"

A growl. *"Many. More than I can count."*

"And Greenjay? What of the Tricksters?"

"Cautious but willing to listen, as you would expect. Our tribe always likes to determine which side will win, and then join that side at an opportune time—not too late, but most definitely not too early."

"Your honesty is commendable."

"Can a frog be taught to fly? I tell you only what is true."

"There will be no winner in this fight, even if we triumph. This is only a moment in the great defeat. But the mortals will suffer, and our own suffering will become less. What the stone apes inherit when we are gone will no longer taste sweet to them—will never taste sweet again. Make no mistake, the time has come for your Tricksters—and all the others, too—to decide the manner of their passing—not as individuals, but as families of the People."

"But why, Lady? Why must we allow defeat? Still we are strong, and the old ways are strong. It is only our resolve that has been weak."

"I have not yet come to you, Stone of the Unwilling. Soon I will ask you what the Guard of Elementals thinks . . ."

"Ask me now."

A pause. *"Speak."*

"They think as I think. That we can retreat no farther, and that we can no longer live with exile and defeat. We must push them from our lands. We must put fire to all their houses and sickness in all their beds. We must shake down their temples and bury their cruel iron in the ground where it can become something clean again. We must bring on the Old Night."

"I have heard you. But no matter what they wish, will your tribe follow where I lead, whatever path I may choose? Because only one can lead in this thing."

"Can you lead, my lady? What of the Pact?"

"The Pact of the Glass will come to naught, an empty promise. But the old rules cannot be ignored, so I have agreed. It has been signed. Only an hour ago, I put my blood on it."

"You signed the Pact? Then have they given you the Seal of War?"

For answer she lifted her helmet from the table. In the dark room the thing that had been hidden beneath it gleamed like molten stone. She lifted the red gem on its heavy black chain and put it on, let the stone fall with a dull clank onto her breast. *"Here it is."*

For a moment only the sound of the ocean was heard, the waves pounding against the rocks.

"The Guard of Elementals will follow you, Lady Yassamez."

The others spoke, one by one, telling her of their tribes, of their readiness or unreadiness, but all agreed—there were enough to muster. There were enough to cross the line and make war.

"Then I have one more thing to show you." Yasammez reached beneath her great cloak. Buckles clicked. A moment later she lifted her scabbard and dropped it on the table, then wrapped her hand around the hilt of the sword and pulled it out. From point to pommel it was as white as packed snow, as licked bone. The candle flame, taxed by one too many chill breezes, shuddered and died. The only light in the room now was the subtle blindworm glow of the sword itself.

"I have taken Whitefire from its sheath." The voice of Yasammez, the People's Fire of Vengeance, was matter-of-fact, whether aloud or in winged thought. Her words had weight because of who she was and what she said. *"It will not be sheathed once more until I am dead or until what was taken from us is ours and the queen lives again."*

Briony found him outside, to her surprise and annoyance, wandering in the quiet and somewhat gloomy west garden of the residence. Except he was not wandering: he was staring up at the roofline where the chimneys clustered like mushrooms that had sprouted after rain.

"I . . . Did you see that?" Barrick rubbed his eyes.

"See what?"

"I thought I saw . . ." He shook his head. "I thought I saw a boy on the roof. Is it the fever? I saw many things when I had the fever . . ."

She squinted, shook her head. "Nobody would be up so high, certainly not a child. Why aren't you in bed? I came to see you and they told me you had refused to stay in your chamber."

"Why? Because I wanted to see the sun. But it's almost gone. I feel like a corpse, lying in that dark room." His face had closed again, the moment's vulnerability replaced by something harsher. "It's not like you need me, in any case."

Briony was shocked. "What do you mean? Merciful Zoria, Barrick, not need you? You're all I have left! Gailon has just left the castle—left Southmarch entirely. He will be back in Summerfield in days, full of discontent, telling anyone who will listen about it—and many people will listen to the Duke of Summerfield."

Her brother shrugged. "So what can we do? Unless Gailon's talking treason, we can't stop him saying what he wants. In fact, it wouldn't be easy to do even if he *were* talking treason. Summerfield Court has walls almost as thick as Southmarch and the Tollys keep a small army there."

"It's too early to worry about things like that, and if the gods are kind or Gailon has a shred of honor, we may not have to. But we have problems enough, Barrick, so no more of this nonsense, please. I need you to be well. Better a few days bored and restless in bed now than you being ill all through the winter months. Let Chaven tend you."

"No more of *what* nonsense?" He shot her another of his suspicious glances. "Are you certain you don't just want me out of the way so you can do something foolish? Pardon Shaso, perhaps?"

Her heart felt like a lump of lead. How could her twin, her beloved other half, think such things? Had the fever really changed him so much? "No! No, Barrick, I would never do such a thing without your approval."

He was staring at her almost as if she were a stranger. "Please, now is not the time for you and I to argue. We're all that's left of the family!"

"There's still Merolanna. And the Loud Mouse."

Briony grimaced. "That's a strange thing, now you mention it. I have never seen Aunt Merolanna so distracted—perhaps over Kendrick, but it seems odd. She was strong as stone before the funeral, but has been grieving like a madwoman since, hardly leaving her chambers. I've been to see her twice and she's barely spoken to me, as though she can't wait for me to leave. In fact, it seems that all the family we have left is at loose ends. Oh, and here's another surprise—since you mentioned her, I should tell you that our stepmother has asked us to dine with her tomorrow night."

"What's that about?"

"I don't know. But let's be openhearted and believe she wishes to be closer to her stepchildren now that Kendrick is gone."

Barrick's snort made his feelings clear.

"Another thing. Have you seen the letter Father wrote? The one Kendrick received from Hierosol the day before . . . before . . ."

Barrick shook his head. He looked annoyed—no, it was something more. He almost looked frightened. Why? "No. What does it say?"

"That's just it—I don't know where it's gone. I can't find it."

"I don't have it!" he said sharply, then waved his hand in weak apology. "I'm sorry—I suppose I really am tired. I don't know anything about it."

"But it's important we find it!" She looked at him, saw that it was no good pressing; he was exhausted. "Whatever the case, never forget, you *are* needed, Barrick. I need you. Desperately. Now go to bed. Rest, and let me do what needs to be done tomorrow, then I'll tell you about it when we go to dine with Anissa."

He looked at her, then looked around the garden. The sun had sunk behind the residence's western wing and the roofs were rapidly becoming dark silhouettes; an entire army of fever-children could have been hiding there now.

"Very well. I will stay in my bed for tomorrow," he said. "But no longer."

"Good. Now, I'll walk back with you."

"You see, I don't like sleeping," he told her as they made their way down the path. Almost without her noticing it, he had taken her hand, as he had done when they were both children. "I don't like sleeping at all. I have such very bad dreams—all of our family being cursed, haunted . . ."

"But that's all they are, Barrick, dear Barrick. Just dreams. Fever dreams." But his words had started a chill in her, even as the first evening breezes swirled through the garden and made the leaves of the hedges and ornamental trees scrape and rustle.

"I dream that darkness is coming down just like a storm," he said, almost whispering. "Oh, Briony, in my dreams I see the end of the world."

15
The Seclusion

THE BROTHER'S MAIDEN DAUGHTER:

She vanishes when we are all upright
Appears when we lay ourselves down
Look! Her crown is of gold and heather-blossom

—from *The Bonefall Oracles*

HE SECLUSION, Qinnitan quickly discovered, was not a building, or even a group of buildings, but something vastly larger, a walled city within the autarch's immense palace, sandstone brick buildings set in carefully husbanded grounds, most with shrines and scented gardens at their centers, all connected by hundreds of covered walkways that provided much-needed shade, so that one of the Seclusion's residents could travel from one side to the other, a journey that might take the best part of an hour, without ever feeling the direct touch of the harsh Xandian sun on her skin. It truly was a city all by itself, home not just to the autarch's hundreds of wives, but to the army of people necessary to care for them, thousands of maids, cooks, gardeners, and petty bureaucrats, and not a single one of them a man.

None were men in the conventional sense, but there were certainly many hundreds of people within the Seclusion's great high walls who had been born with at least the basic elements of masculinity, but who simply had not, for one reason or another, managed to hang onto all of them.

The Seclusion took up a sizable section of the autarch's gigantic Orchard

Palace, just as the palace itself took up a large portion of Great Xis, Mother of Cities. In truth, the Seclusion's share was proportionately larger than other sections of the ancient and monstrous sprawl of buildings formally known as Palace of the Flowering Spring Orchard, because those who lived and worked in other parts of the great palace could share gardens and dining halls and kitchens, but the Seclusion must be kept separate and protected, and so each function had to be carefully reproduced within its walls and staffed only with women or Favored.

If the Seclusion was a small city, the Favored were its priests and governors. Because of the famous sacrifice of Habbili, son of Nushash, Xis had always been a kingdom in which the castrated were held in some esteem— it was almost as established a route to the corridors of power as the priesthood. In fact, the Favored ruled not just the Seclusion, but many of the bureaucracies of the Orchard Palace, so that the more daring soldiers of the autarch's army sometimes sourly joked—in private, of course—that real men weren't wanted in most of the palace, and would only be welcomed in the one place they were absolutely barred, the Seclusion. The actual truth was that many ordinary men who still wore their stones held positions of influence throughout the autarch's court, like Pinimmon Vash, the paramount minister. The Favored as a group were some of the autarch's mightiest subordinates, but they were by no means all-powerful. They had to struggle, as did everyone else in the Orchard Palace, for every fleck of attention from the God-King Sulepis, from whom all power and glory radiated like the sun's light. But in the metaphorical darkness of the Seclusion, that country of women in which women held no nominal power—although the more important of the autarch's wives were powers unto themselves— the Favored ruled virtually without rivals.

The Favored of the Seclusion, perhaps in deference to a tradition no one could now remember (or perhaps for other, less exalted reasons) considered themselves women, not tremendously different from those over whom they watched, and made the traditional attributes of womanhood their own, although exaggerated into parody: they were almost all extremely excitable, romantic, vengeful, fickle. And of course the wives and their born-female servants had their own complicated webs of influence and intrigue as well. Altogether, walking into the Seclusion was like entering a magical cave out of a story, a place strung with invisible strands and snares, full of beautiful things guarded by deadly traps.

Qinnitan's own role in the place was confusing from the first, and within days of entering she had begun to long for the certainty of her old life, for her uncomplicated role as one of the youngest and thus lowest of the low among the Hive Sisters. All the autarch's wives and wives-to-be—and it was hard to tell sometimes what the difference in status meant, since he so seldom visited any of them—were of infinitely greater importance than any of the Seclusion's servants, and yet the hundredth wife, let alone new-minted Qinnitan who was something closer to the thousandth, had to wait weeks for even the briefest appointment to see Cusy, the immensely fat chief of the Seclusion's Favored—the Eunuch Queen, as she was sometimes laughingly called in the Orchard Palace. But nobody in the Seclusion would ever have laughed at old Cusy to her face. Of all the denizens of that place, only Arimone, the autarch's paramount wife—a flinty, beautiful young woman known as the Evening Star, who was the autarch's cousin and had been the wife of the last older brother Sulepis had murdered to clear his path to the throne—would have stood up to Cusy without a great deal of consideration. Since Arimone lived almost as removed from the Seclusion as the autarch himself (she had her own little palace and grounds nestled at one end of the vast compound like the inmost chamber of a nautilus, and no one, not even the other high-ranking wives, came there without an invitation) there was nobody to challenge the Eunuch Queen's authority.

Qinnitan had the fantastic luck—or so it seemed at the time—to be taken under the wing of Luian, one of Cusy's deputies, a motherly Favored (at least in size and demeanor, since she was not particularly old) who took an unexpected interest in the new wife and within days of Qinnitan's arrival invited her to come to her chambers and drink tea.

Qinnitan was treated to the promised tea, along with powdered Sania figs and several kinds of sweet breads, in a tented, cushion-strewn room in Luian's chambers. The meal was accompanied by a gale of gossip and other useful information about the Seclusion, but it was only at the end of the meal that Luian explained why her eye had lit on Qinnitan.

"You don't recognize me, do you?" she said as Qinnitan bent to kiss her hand in farewell. Qinnitan had been caught by the fact of Luian's large hands, one of the few things now that betrayed her beginnings as a man, and so she did not for a moment understand the question.

"Recognize you?" Qinnitan said when the import finally sank in.

"Yes, darling girl. You don't think I lavish my time on every little queen that comes through the door of the Seclusion, do you?" Luian patted her chest as if the idea gave her breathing problems; her jewelry rattled. "My goodness, we have had two already this month from Krace, which is practically the moon. I was shocked to hear they even spoke a human language. No, my sweetness, I asked for you because we grew up in the same neighborhood."

"Behind Cat's Eye Street?"

"Yes, my darling! I remember you when you could barely walk, but I see you don't remember me."

Qinnitan shook her head. "I . . . I must admit I don't, Favored Luian."

"Just Luian, dear, please. But of course I was different then. Big and clumsy, studying to be a priest. You see, that's what I thought I would be until I was Favored, and then I lost my taste for it. I even went to your father once for advice. I used to walk up and down the alleys between Cat's Eye and Feather Cape Row, reciting the four hundred Nushash prayers, or trying to . . ."

Qinnitan let go of Luian's hand and stood up. "Oh! Dudon! You're Dudon! I remember you!"

The Favored waved her fingers languidly. "Sssshh, that name! That was years ago. I hate that name these days—ungainly, unhappy creature. I am much more beautiful now, am I not?" She smiled as if to mock herself, but there was something other than self-mockery involved in the question. Qinnitan looked at the person before her—it was a little harder to think of Luian as female now, after the recollection of her former self—discreetly examined the broad features, the thick makeup, the large hands covered in rings, and said, "You are very beautiful now, of course."

"Of course." Luian laughed, pleased. "Yes, and you have learned your first lesson. *Everyone* in the Seclusion is beautiful, wives and Favored. Even if one of us should hold a knife to your throat and demand to be told she is looking poorly that day, just a little peaked around the eyes, perhaps, skin just a little less rosy than it should be, you will say only that you have never seen her more beautiful." For a moment Luian's kohl-rimmed eyes grew hard and shrewd. "Do you understand?"

"But I meant it sincerely."

"And that is the second lesson—say everything sincerely. Goodness, you *are* a clever girl. It is too bad that I will have so little to do with your training."

"Why is that, Luian?"

"Because for some reason the Golden One has ordered that you must be schooled by Panhyssir's priests. But I will keep a close eye on you and you will come to take tea with me often, if you would like."

"Oh, yes, Luian." Qinnitan wasn't quite certain what she'd done to rate such attention, but she wasn't going to turn her back on it. Having a link to one of the Favored, especially an important one like Luian, could make a world of difference in one's accommodations, in the skill and tact of one's assigned servants, in any number of things up to and including the continuing favor of the autarch himself. "Yes, I would like that very much." She paused in the doorway. "But how did you know who I was? I mean, I would have been not much more than a baby when you left our old neighborhood—how could you recognize me?"

Luian smiled, settling back in her cushions. "I didn't. My cousin did."

"Cousin?"

"The chief of the Leopards. The very, *very* handsome Jeddin." Favored Luian sighed in a way that suggested she had complicated feelings about this handsome cousin. "He recognized you."

Suddenly Qinnitan, too, remembered the solemn-faced warrior. "He . . . *recognized* me?"

"And you did not recognize him either, I see. Not surprising, I suppose. He has changed almost as much as I have. Would you remember if I called him Jin instead of Jeddin? Little Jin?"

Qinnitan put her hand to her mouth. "Jin? I remember him—a bit older than me. He used to chase after my brother and his friends. But he was so small!"

Luian chuckled deep in her throat. "He grew. Oh, my, he certainly did."

"And he recognized me?"

"He thought he did, but he was not certain until he saw your parents. By the way, please write and tell your mother that she will be invited to visit you when the time is right, and to stop pestering us with pleading messages."

Qinnitan was embarrassed. "I will, Favored Lu . . . I mean I will, Luian. I promise." She was still stunned by the idea that the slab-muscled Leopard captain could possibly be Little Jin, a perpetually wet-nosed boy whom her brothers had more than once smacked in the face and sent home crying. Jin—Jeddin—looked now as though he could break any of Qinnitan's brothers in half with one hand. "I've kept you too long, Luian," she said out loud. "Thank you so much for your kindness."

"You are quite welcome, my darling. We Cat's Eye girls must stick together, after all."

"The gardens are beautiful!" said Duny. "And the flowers smell so lovely. Oh, Qinnitan, you live in such a beautiful place!"

Qinnitan drew her friend away from the climbing roses and toward a bench at the middle of the courtyard. Queen Sodan's Garden was the largest in the Seclusion and its hedges were low, which was why she'd chosen it.

"I live in a very dangerous place," she told Duny quietly when they sat down on the bench. "I've been here two months and this is the first conversation I've had where I won't have to worry whether the person I'm talking to might decide to have me poisoned if I say the wrong thing."

Duny's mouth fell open. "No!"

Qinnitan laughed in spite of herself. "Yes, oh, yes. My dearest Dunyaza, you just don't know. The meanness of the older Sisters back at the Hive, the way they'd get after the younger ones or the pretty ones—that was *nothing*. Here if you're too pretty, they don't just push you down in the hallways or put dirt in your soup. If someone is jealous of you and you don't have a powerful protector, you'll end up dead. Five people have died since I've been here. They always say they fell ill, but everyone knows better."

Duny looked at her sternly. "You're teasing me, Qin-ya. I can't believe all that. These women have been chosen by the autarch himself! *He* wouldn't allow anything to happen to them, praise to his name."

"*He* scarcely ever comes, and there are hundreds of us, anyway. I doubt he remembers more than a few. Most of the brides are chosen for political alliances—you know, important families in other countries—but some of them are like me. Nobody knows why we've been chosen."

"We know why! Because he fell in love with you."

Qinnitan snorted. "I thought I asked you not to make up stories about me, Duny. Fell in love with me? He scarcely noticed me, even when he was making the arrangements with my parents, such as they were." She made a sour face. "Not that they could have said no, I suppose, but they sold me."

"To the autarch! That is not being sold, that is a great honor!" Duny's face suddenly froze. "Won't you be in trouble for saying such things?" she whispered.

"Now you know why I brought you out here, where there are no walls or high hedges for spies to hide behind." Qinnitan felt as though she had aged ten years since leaving the Hive, felt very much the older sister now. "Do you see that gardener over there, over by that pavilion?"

"Him in the baggy clothes?"

"Yes, but not a him, and the gods save you if you ever said that in front of her. That's Tanyssa, one of the Favored. Most of them go by women's names here. Anyway, it's her job to watch me, although I don't know who's given the job to her. Everywhere I go, there she is—for a gardener, she seems to travel from one part of the Seclusion to another very freely. She was in the baths yesterday morning, pretending to have some errand with the young Favored boy who heats the water." Qinnitan looked at the well-muscled gardener with distaste as Tanyssa pretended to examine the leaves of a monkeyfruit tree. "They say she killed that young Akarisian princess who died last month. Threw her out of a window, but of course they say she fell."

"But, Qin, that's terrible!"

She shrugged. "It's how things are here. I have some friends, too—not friends like you and I are friends, of course, although I may make some of those too someday. The kind of friends you have to have if you want to stay alive, if you don't want to fall over dead after drinking your tea some evening."

Duny looked at her without saying anything for a long time—a long time for Duny, anyway. "You seem different, Qinnitan. You seem hard, like one of those traveler girls that dance in Sun's Progress Square."

Qinnitan's laugh was a little harsh, but something about Duny's innocence made her angry. It was the fact that Duny could still afford to be innocent, more than anything else. "Well, I probably am. Everyone talks nicely here—oh, they do talk nicely. And other than the occasional hissing catfight, everything is quite peaceful and comfortable. Do you like my dress?" She lifted her arm and let the pleated sleeve fall, graceful and translucent as a dragonfly's wing.

"It's lovely."

"Yes, it is. As I said, everything is quite peaceful and comfortable . . . on the surface. But underneath, it is a pit full of scorpions."

"Don't talk like that, Qin. You're scaring me." Duny took her hand. "You are a queen! That must be wonderful, even if the people here are tiresome. What is the autarch like? Have you . . . did you . . . ?" She colored.

Qinnitan could not resist rolling her eyes—after all, it was a self-indulgence she could not allow herself most of the time. "Duny! Don't you listen? I already told you the autarch almost never comes here. When he wants to see one of his wives, he has her brought to his palace. Well, I suppose this is *all* his palace, but you know what I mean. He has never spoken to me since he bought me from my parents, let alone made love to me! So, yes, since you are wondering, I am still a virgin. As you may remember from listening to the older girls, in most cases a deflowerment requires the man and the woman to be in the same room."

"Qin-ya, you shouldn't talk like that!" Duny said, but whether because she was embarrassed or because she did not want to suffer further damage to her flowery illusions wasn't clear. After a moment, she asked, "But if he didn't fall in love with you, and you're not a princess of somewhere—you're not, are you?—then . . . then why did he marry you?"

"First off, he hasn't married me yet," Qinnitan told her. "At least I don't think so. I've had some religious instruction from the priests—some very strange rituals—so maybe that's why, to prepare me for the marriage ceremony. Some of the women here went through ceremonies, but some others were . . .well, just taken. But as to why he chose me . . . well, Duny, I don't know. And nobody else in this poisonous place seems to know quite why either."

"I have such a nice treat for you, darling," Luian announced when Qinnitan arrived, a little breathless, in the Favored's chambers. "We must primp and prepare, both of us. We don't have much time." She snapped her fingers and her pair of silent Tuani slave women came into the room like shadows.

"But . . . but, Luian. Thank you. What are we . . ."

"We are going to the palace, my sweet. Out of the Seclusion, yes! Someone very special wants to see you."

For a moment Qinnitan found it hard to breathe. "The . . . the autarch?"

"Oh, no!" Luian threw up her hands and laughed. The Tuani girl with the curling iron, who had come within an eyelash of burning her mistress on the arm, paled a little. "Oh, no, if it was the autarch himself they'd be preparing you for days. No, we are going to see my cousin."

It took a moment for Qinnitan to understand. "Jeddin? Of the Leopards?"

"Yes, my dearest, we are invited to see handsome Jeddin. He wishes to speak with you, to hear stories of the old neighborhood. I am going along as chaperone, lucky girl that I am. I do so admire that young man."

"But . . . am I allowed to meet with any men at all?"

A look of annoyance creased Luian's powdered forehead. "He is not any man, he is chief of the Leopards, chosen by our autarch himself, praise to his name. Besides, I will be with you, child, I told you. If that is not respectable, what is?" But the Favored's eyes darted briefly to the Tuani slave beside her, and Qinnitan could not help wondering if it was truly all as obvious and ordinary as Luian made it out to be.

When they were both ready, Favored Luian, rigged like a festival ship in a fringed-and-beaded robe, and Qinnitan in a less ostentatious and properly virginal white robe with a hood, different only in quality from something she might have worn in a Hive procession, they set out. Despite her misgivings, Qinnitan could not help being excited: it was the first time in three months she had been outside of the Seclusion's walls, even if it was only to another part of the great Orchard Palace. Other than Duny, and Qinnitan's mother, (who had spent most of her visit weeping over their family's good fortune) this would be her first chance to see anyone from outside. And, needless to say, Jeddin would be the first natural man she had seen since he and his soldiers had brought her here, to this invincible prison of beautiful blossoms, splashing fountains, and cool stone arcades.

The Favored who guarded the Seclusion's outer gate did not dress a bit like women. They were the largest people Qinnitan had ever seen, a half dozen hulking creatures with ceremonial swords whose flat, curved blades were almost wide enough to use as tea trays. They engaged in a long whispered discussion among themselves before Luian, Qinnitan, and the two silent Tuani servants were at last allowed to pass out of the Seclusion and into the greater palace, but only with one of the guards bringing up the rear of the small procession like an enormous dog guiding a herd of sheep. The little company continued on for a good portion of an hour, through lush but empty gardens and unused corridors and courtyards so opulent that they seemed to have been prepared for some royal princeling who had not yet moved into them.

At last they reached a small but prettily decorated courtyard that rang with the sounds of a fountain. At one edge of court, where the tiles gave way to a pocket garden with paths of pale sand, a muscular, sun-browned young man sat on mounds of cushions beneath a striped awning big enough for a dozen guests. As if he were the groom to Qinnitan's bride, he, too, wore a robe of flowing white. He stood as they approached, hesitated a moment between Qinnitan and Luian, between nominal rank and actual power, and then lowered himself to one knee before the girl.

"Mistress. So kind of you to come." He rose and turned to Luian. "Respected cousin, you do me honor."

Luian produced a fan from her sleeve and snapped it open with a clack like an eagle taking wing. "Always a pleasure, Captain."

Jeddin beckoned his visitors to join him beneath the awning, then sent his servant to fetch refreshments. After an appropriate time of small talk with Luian about her health and the health of various important residents of the Seclusion, he turned to Qinnitan.

"Luian says you remember me now."

She blushed, since many of her chief memories were of him being humiliated by older boys. It was even harder to reconcile that with the present now that she saw him again. The Leopard captain's muscles moved under his dark skin like those of a real leopard she had once seen in a cage in the Sun's Progress marketplace, the most fearsome animal she had ever encountered. For all its strength, though, despite its dreadful teeth and claws, that leopard had seemed sad to her and not altogether present, as though it saw not the crowds of people around it but the shadow-splashed woodlands where it had once roamed—saw those places, but knew it could not reach them.

Oddly, she thought she saw something of this in Jeddin's eyes as well, but knew she must simply be romanticizing, muddling this handsome young man with the trapped beast. "Yes. Yes, Captain, I do remember you. You knew my brothers."

"I did." Like an eminent man asked to recall the pivotal moments of his career, Jeddin began to reminisce at length about the days in Cat's Eye Street, describing the adventures of a group of young scapegraces—of whom, he felt compelled to admit, he had not been the least mischievous. To hear him speak, he had been one among equals, and none of the miseries she recalled on his behalf had ever truly happened. It was strange, as though he had lived his childhood on the other side of an ornamental screen from the rest of them, making up his own mind what things meant, seeing only what he wished to see. Several times Qinnitan had to bite her tongue when the urge to correct him became strong. There was something about Jeddin, the way he talked, that made her feel as though telling him now that even a small part of his memory was faulty would be no different than the way her brothers had sometimes pushed him from behind as he ran, making him go so much faster than his legs could carry him that he stumbled and fell.

The refreshments came, and as the servants poured tea and piled sweetmeats on plates, Qinnitan watched Luian watching Jeddin, which the Favored

did with the sort of avidity she usually reserved for things like the rosewa-
ter jelly being spooned into her bowl. It seemed unusual, not that Luian
should find Jeddin attractive—he was more than that, his body as hard and
wonderfully defined as a statue, his face befittingly serious and noble of cast,
with nose straight and strong and eyes a surprisingly bright green under the
heavy brows—but that someone like Luian, who in all other ways seemed
to have settled into a kind of premature, matronly old age, and who, after
all, had given up her original organs years ago, should still have such feelings at all.

"Well," Luian said abruptly, ending a silence. "To think that after so many
years we of the old neighborhood should have a reunion here!"

The captain's emerald eyes now turned to Qinnitan. "You must be very
happy, Mistress. Of all of us, well as we have done, you have risen highest. A wife of the Golden One himself." He dropped his gaze. "An un-
matched honor."

"Yes, of course." *Although I might as well be married to a hassock or a sandal
for all that comes of it,* she almost said, but didn't. Jeddin had the look of a religious man, and obviously he must be devout at least where the autarch
himself was concerned. "I am blessed by his notice."

"And he is blessed by . . ." He paused and to her amazement appeared to
blush.

"And he, our autarch, is blessed by all the heavens, and especially by his
heavenly father Nushash," said Luian abruptly and loudly.

"Yes, of course. All praise to the Golden One," said Jeddin. Qinnitan
echoed the blessing, but could not help feeling something important had
just happened and she had missed it.

"We should go now, Cousin." Luian waved for the Tuani girls to help her
to her feet, which they did, fighting the Favored's great weight like nomads
trying to put up a tent in a high wind. "Thank you for the refreshments
and the courtesy of your company." There was a new tone in Luian's voice,
faintly cold.

Jeddin scrambled to his feet. "Of course, respected cousin. You grace us
with your presence." He bowed to her, then to his other guest. He did it
with some grace, but that didn't surprise Qinnitan; she imagined that even
for a soldier, bowing well must be almost as important in the autarch's court
as handling a sword or a gun. "I wish you could stay longer."

"Propriety forbids it," said Luian shortly, setting sail for the door with her servants and Qinnitan fluttering in her wake like gulls. The huge Favored guard fell in behind them in the corridor, mute and sleepy-eyed.

"Did I do something wrong, Luian?" Qinnitan asked after they had walked for some distance in silence and were nearing the gate to the Seclusion. Luian only waved her hand, whether because of discretion or irritation was hard to say.

When they had left the immense guard behind and were back within the walls, Luian leaned toward her and said, in a harsh whisper that might or might not have been too quiet for the Tuani servants to hear, "You must be careful. And Jeddin must not be a fool."

"What do you mean? Why are you angry with me?"

Luian frowned. The paint on her lips had begun to smear a little into her face powder, and for the first time she appeared grotesque to Qinnitan and even a little frightening. "I'm not angry with you, although I will remind you that you are no longer a low-caste girl in the alleys behind Feather Cape Row. You have been given great honors, but you live in a dangerous world."

"I don't understand."

"Oh? You couldn't see what I could see as clearly as my own hand at the end of my arm? That man is in love with you."

Even in her astonishment, Qinnitan could not help thinking that the anguish on Luian's face seemed less like that of a guardian unheeded than a lover scorned.

16

The Grand and Worthy Nose

FLOATING ON THE POOL:

The rope, the knot, the tail, the road
Here is the place between the mountains
Where the sky freezes

—from *The Bonefall Oracles*

OLLUM DYER HAD BEEN cheerful all through the day's ride, full of mocking remarks and droll assessments of life in Southmarch, and had managed to coax a few weak smiles out of the merchant Raemon Beck, but even Collum was grimly silent as they reached the crossroad. Dyer came from near the Brennish borderlands in the east and had never seen the old Northmarch Road. Ferras Vansen had passed this crossroad many times, but still found it a disturbing place.

"Gods," said Collum. "It's huge—you could drive three team-wagons abreast on it."

"It is not that much wider than the Settland Road," said Ferras, feeling a need to defend the more mundane thoroughfare that had so entranced him in his youth, which had led him to Southmarch and his current life.

"But look, Captain," said one of the foot soldiers, pointing along the last clear stretch of the huge and disturbingly empty Northmarch Road before it vanished into the mist. "The ground drops away there on either side, but the road stays high."

"They built it that way," Vansen told them. "Because north of here it gets even wetter in the wintertime months. They built the roadbed up with stones and logs to keep it above the muck. They did things right back then. In the old days wagons and riders were going back and forth between Northmarch and Southmarch every day, and also the Westmarch Road joined it just on the other side of those hills." He pointed, but the hills could only be seen in his memory; the mists were so thick today that someone might have draped a huge white quilt across the forested lands. It was strange to think of so much life here once, merchants, princes with their retinues, travelers of all sorts in what was now such a desolate place.

A thought flitted across his mind, quick and startling as a bat. *Perin's Hammer, what if we have to ride into the mist? What if we must pursue the caravan across the Shadowline into that . . . nothingness?* In his life he had heard half a dozen people claim to have come back from the far side of that boundary, but he had not believed any of them. The one man of his village that everyone knew for certain had crossed the Shadowline and returned had never claimed anything. In fact, he had never spoken at all after his return, but had haunted the fringes of the village like a scavenging dog until the winter killed him. As a child, Ferras had seen that man's constant expression of astonished horror—a look that suggested whatever had happened to him across the Shadowline was happening to him still and would continue happening every moment of every day. Although no one had said anything but what was correct and pious, everyone in the village had been relieved when the mad old man had died.

Collum's question yanked him back to the here and now. "How far does the road lead?"

Ferras shook his head. "Northmarch Castle was about four or five days' ride from here, I think. So the old gaffers in my village said, although it was at least a century before their time when anyone could still go there. And its lands and towns extended a good way farther north, I think."

Collum Dyer clicked his tongue against his teeth. "Mesiya's teats! And just think—now it's all empty."

Vansen stared at the wide road cutting across the hummocky land to where the fogs swallowed it. "So you think. So we hope. But I don't want to consider it just now, to speak the plain truth. I don't like this place."

Collum turned and nodded toward Raemon Beck, sitting on his horse at the far side of the troop of guards, staring resolutely southward with a face pale as a fish's belly. "Neither does he."

*   *   *

Ferras Vansen felt a tug of yearning as they rode along the Settland Road past the towns and villages of Daler's Troth—Little Stell, Candlerstown, and Dale House, the seat of Earl Rorick Longarren, who would have wed the young woman stolen from Raemon Beck's caravan. Vansen had not returned to his hilly home since he was still a raw young soldier, and it was hard not to think about how some of the men in Creedy's Inn at Greater Stell would sit up to see him at the head of an entire troop, undertaking a mission at the direct order of the princess regent.

Yes, a mission that's little better than a banishment, he reminded himself.

But he was not much moved by the idea of preening in any case. His mother's death a year before had left little to tie him to this land of his childhood. His sisters and their husbands had followed him to Southmarch Town. The folk here that he remembered would scarcely remember him, and in any case, what was the enjoyment of trying to make them feel worse about their hardscrabble lives? It was only the children of the really wealthy farmers, the ones who had mocked him for his shabbiness, for his Vuttish father's strange way of speaking, that he would have wished to humiliate, and if they had inherited their fathers' holdings they were undoubtedly richer than any mere guard captain, even the guard captain to the royal family.

There truly is nothing here for me now, he realized, with some surprise. *Only my parents' graves, and those are a half day's ride off the road.*

A light rain had begun to fall; it took him a moment to pick Raemon Beck from the crowd of hooded riders. Vansen guided his horse over to the young merchant's side.

"You have a wife and some young ones at home, I think you said."

Beck nodded. His face was grim, but it was the grimness of a child who was one harsh word away from tears.

"What are their names?"

The young merchant looked at him with suspicion. Not all of Collum Dyer's rough jokes had been kind, and clearly he wondered whether Vansen was going to make sport of him, too. "Derla. My wife's name is Derla. And I have two boys." He took a deep breath, let it out in an unsteady hiss. "Little Raemon, he's the eldest. And Finton, he's still . . . still in swaddling . . ." Beck turned away.

"I envy you."

"Envy? I have not seen them in almost two months! And now . . ."

"And now you must wait weeks longer. I know. But we have sent them word that you are well, that you are doing the crown's business . . ."

Beck's laugh had a ragged edge. "Weeks . . . ? You're a fool, Captain. You didn't see what I saw. They're going to take you all, and me with you. I will never see my family again."

"Perhaps. Perhaps the gods mean our end. They have their own plans, their own ways." Ferras shrugged. "I would fear it more if I had more to lose, perhaps. I honestly hope you come safe to your family again, Beck. I will do my best to see that it happens."

The young merchant stared at his horse's neck. Beck had a good face, Vansen thought, with strong nose and clear eyes, but not much of a chin. He wondered what the man's wife looked like. *Depends on Beck's prospects with the family venture,* he decided: a man could become surprisingly taller and handsomer merely by the addition of wealthy relatives.

"Do you . . . are you married?" Beck asked him suddenly.

"To the royal guard!" shouted Collum Dyer from a few yards away. "And it is a warm coupling—the guard gives us all a swiving every payday!"

Ferras grunted, amused. "No, not married," he said. "Nor likely to be. One thing Dyer says is true—I am married to the guard." There had been a few over the years he had almost thought possible, especially a merchant's daughter he had met in the marketplace. They had liked each other, and had met and spoken several times, but she had already been pledged and so was duly married to a Marrinswalk furrier's son with lucrative Brennish connections. Other than that, his dalliances had reached too low or too high, the taverner's daughter at an inn called the Quiller's Mint, friendly but twice widowed and five years his senior, and when he had first joined the guard, a woman of the minor nobility whose husband ignored her.

Too high . . . ? he thought. *No, that was not too high—not compared to the madness that is in my heart these days.* The image of Princess Briony's face as she sent him away came to him, the strangeness of it, as though she did not entirely hate him after all. *A year now I have felt it, this terrible, hopeless ache. There is nothing higher that I could aspire to, or more foolish. How could I marry someone else, except for companionship? But how could I settle for any woman when I would think only of her?*

Well, he thought, *perhaps her wish will come true. Perhaps this journey will provide me with a chance to die honorably and everyone will be satisfied.*

No, not everyone would be satisfied, he realized. What Ferras Vansen really wanted was to live honorably, even happily. And to marry a princess, although that would not happen in this world or any other he could imagine.

He was meeting her near Merolanna's chambers, in the back hallway of the main residence, known as the Wolf Hall for the faded tapestry of the family crest that took up a large portion of its south wall. It had too many stars and a mysterious crescent moon hung above the wolf's snarling head, showing it to be a remnant of some earlier generation of Eddons. How long it had hung there no one could remember or even guess.

Like Briony, he had promised Merolanna he would come alone—no guards, no pages. She had been forced to speak sharply to Rose and Moina to get them to let her be, of course. Clearly her ladies feared she had an assignation with Dawet, but their resistance upset her just enough that she did not bother to tell them otherwise.

She watched her brother saunter up the corridor through the slanting colums of autumn light that filtered down from the windows, uneven light that made the passage seem as though it were under water and which turned the bucket and mop left inexplicably in the middle of the floor and the small offering-shrine to Zoria on the broad table into dully glimmering things that might have spilled from the belly of a sunken ship. For a moment, as Briony noted by the way her twin held his arm close to his body that it was hurting him, they might have been children again, escaped from their tutors for a morning to play scapegrace around the great castle.

But something was different, she saw. He seemed better—he no longer moved like a dying man, draggled and slow—but instead of becoming again the disdainful, unhappy Barrick Eddon she knew nearly as well as herself, he had a bounce in his step that seemed equally foreign, and his eyes as he neared her seemed to burn with a mischievous vigor.

"So someone in our family finally agrees to speak to us." Barrick did not stop to give her a kiss, did not stop at all, but swept past, still talking swiftly, leading her toward Merolanna's door as though he had been waiting for Briony, not the other way around. "After our stepmother, I begin to think they fear taking the plague from me."

"Anissa said she did not feel well herself. She is pregnant, after all."

"And it came on an hour before we were to dine with her? Perhaps that is all it is. Perhaps."

"You are jumping at shadows."

He turned to look at her, and again she wondered if the fever had truly left him. Why otherwise this eye bright as a bird's, this strange air, as though at any moment he might fly into pieces? "Shadows? A strange word to use." He paused and seemed to find himself a little. "All I'm saying is, why won't our stepmother talk to us?"

"We will give her a few more days. Then we will make it a command."

Barrick arched an eyebrow. "Can we do that?"

"We'll find out." She reached out and knocked on Merolanna's door. Eilis, the duchess' little serving maid, opened it and stood for a long moment stock-still and blinking like a mouse caught on a tabletop. At last she made a courtesy, found her voice. "She's lying down, Highnesses. She wants me to bring you to her."

Inside, several older women and a few young ones sat doing needlework. They rose and made their own courtesies to the prince and princess. Briony said a few words to each. Barrick nodded his head, but smiled only at those who were young and pretty. He was bouncingly impatient, as though he already wished he had not come.

Merolanna sat up in bed as the serving maid drew the curtain. "Eilis? Bid the other ladies go, please. You, too. I want to be alone with Barrick and Briony." Their great-aunt did not look ill, Briony thought with some relief, but she did look old and tired. These days Briony was not used to seeing Merolanna without face paint, so it was hard to know for certain whether the changes were real or just the ordinary punishments of time left unhidden, but there was no mistaking the swollen eyes. The duchess had been crying.

"There," the old woman said when the room was clear. "I cannot abide being listened to." There was an unusual violence in her voice. She fanned herself. "Some things are not for others to know."

"How are you, Auntie? We've been worried about you."

She manufactured a smile for Briony. "As well as can be expected, dear one. It's kind of you to ask." She turned to Barrick. "And you, boy? How are you feeling?"

Barrick's smile was almost a smirk. "The grip of old Kernios is a bit more slippery than everyone thinks, it seems."

Merolanna went quite pale. She brought her hand to her breast as though to keep her heart inside it. "Don't say such things! Merciful Zoria, Barrick, don't tempt the gods. Not now, when they have done us so much mischief already."

Briony was irritated with her brother, not least because it did seem foolish to make such a boast, but she was also puzzled by Merolanna's reaction,
her frightened eyes and trembling hands. All through the time before
Kendrick's funeral their great-aunt had been the strongest pillar of the family and the household. Was it just that her strength had run out?

"I'll say it again, Auntie." Briony reached out and took her hand. "We
have been worried about you. Are you ill?"

A sad smile. "Not in the sense you mean, dear. No, not like our poor
Barrick has been."

"I'm well now, Auntie."

"I can see that." But she looked at him as though she did not entirely
believe it. "No, I have just . . . had a turn, I suppose. A bad moment. But it
frightened me, and made me think I've not done right. I've spent time, a
great deal of time lately, talking to the Hierarch Sisel about it, you know.
He's a very kind man, really. A good listener."

"But not to Father Timoid?" It seemed odd—usually Merolanna and
the Eddon family priest were a conspiracy of two.

"He's a terrible gossip."

"That's never bothered you before."

Merolanna gave her a flat look, almost as though she spoke to a stranger.
"I've never had to worry about it before."

Barrick laughed suddenly, harshly. "What, Auntie? Have you begun a
love affair with someone? Or are you plotting to take the crown yourself?"

"Barrick!" Briony almost slapped him. "What a terrible thing to say!"

Merolanna looked at him and shook her head, but to Briony's eyes the
old woman still seemed oddly detached. "A few weeks ago, I would have
been after you with a stick, boy. How can you talk like that to me, who
raised you almost like a mother?"

"It was a jest!" He folded his arms and leaned against the bedpost, his
face a resentful mask. "A jest."

"What is it, then?" Briony asked. "Something is happening here, Auntie.
What is it?"

Merolanna fanned herself. "I'm going mad, that's all."

"What are you talking about? You're not going mad." But Briony saw
Barrick lean forward, his sullenness gone. "Auntie?" she asked.

"Fetch me a cup of wine. That pitcher, there. And not too much water."
When she had the cup in her hand, Merolanna sipped it, then sat up
straighter. "Come, sit on the bed, both of you. I cannot bear to have you

standing there, looking down on me." She patted the bed, almost begging. "Please. There. Now listen. And please don't ask me any questions, not until I finish. Because if you do, I will start crying and then I'll never stop."

It was finally Godsday, with Lastday to follow; Chert welcomed the days of rest. His bones ached and he had a hot throb in his back that would not go away. He was glad to bid the tennight good-bye for other reasons, too. The prince's funeral that began it, with its weight of hard work and terrible sadness, had taken much out of him, and the boy's disappearance that day had frightened him badly.

What is he? Chert wondered. *Not just his strangeness, but what is he to us? Is he a son? Will someone, his true parents, come and take him away from us?* He looked at Opal, who was sniffing at a row of pots she had set up on the far side of the table. *My old woman will be stabbed in the heart if the boy leaves us.*

As will I, he realized suddenly. The child had brought life to the house, a life that Chert had never realized was missing until now.

"I don't think this bilberry jam is much good," Opal said, "although it cost me three chips. Here, try it."

Chert scowled. "What am I, a dog? 'Here, this has gone off, you try it'?"

Opal scowled back. She was better at it than he was. "Old fool—I didn't say it had gone off, I said I don't think it's much good. I'm asking your opinion. You're certainly quick enough to give it most other times."

"Very well, pass it here." He reached out and took the pot, dipped a piece of bread into it, lifted it to his nose. It smelled like nothing more or less than bilberry jam, but it raised a strange thought: if the old stories were true, and there were Funderlings before ever there were big folk, then who grew the vegetables up in the sunlight? Who grew the fruits? *Did the Lord of the Hot Wet Stone create us to eat moles and cave crickets with never a bit of fruit, let alone bilberry jam?* But if not, where would such things have come from? Did the Funderlings of old have farms under the sun? It seemed strange to think of such a thing, but stranger still to think of a world with no . . .

"Jam, old man. What do you think of the jam?"

Chert shook his head. "What?"

"I take it back—you don't have the wits to be a fool, old man. You don't pay enough heed. The jam!"

"Oh. It tastes like jam, no more, no less." He looked around. "Where is the boy?"

"Playing out in front, not that you'd notice if he'd gone off to drown in the Salt Pool."

"Don't be cross, Opal. I'm tired. It was an uncomfortable piece of work, that tomb."

She took the pot of jam. "I'm sorry, old fellow. You do work hard."

"Give us a kiss, then, and let's not quarrel."

Opal had gone off to visit her friend Agate, wife of one of Chert's cousins, and after checking to make sure the boy Flint was still erecting his compli- cated miniature fortifications of damp earth and bits of stone outside the front door, Chert poured himself a mug of mossbrew and pulled out the mysterious stone Flint had found. A week or so had not made it any more familiar: the cloudy, unusually rounded crystal still matched nothing he had seen or even heard of. Chaven was traveling for a few days, visiting the out- lying towns with a colleague to check the spread of the disease that had al- most killed Prince Barrick, and now Chert was wishing he had spoken with the physician about it before he left. The stone troubled him, although except for the fact that it seemed like something that might have come from behind the Shadowline he couldn't say why. He had half a dozen other Shadowline stones right here in the house, after all—those which no one had wanted to buy, but which Chert had found too interesting to dis- card—and had not given any of them a second thought. But this . . .

I could take it to the Guild, he thought. But he felt strangely certain they would not recognize it either—maybe old High Feldspar would have, a man who had known more stonework and stone-lore than the rest of Fun- derling Town put together, but Feldspar's ashes had been returned to the earth three years ago and Chert did not think there were many in the Guild now who knew more than he did himself. Certainly not about Shadowline stones . . .

"When are you going to the talking and singing place?" a voice said be- hind him, making Chert jump and slosh his mug. Flint stood in the door- way, hands so dirty it looked like he was wearing dark gloves. As if he had been caught doing something wrong, Chert dumped the weird stone back into his purse and pulled the string.

"Talking and singing place?" He remembered the boy's reaction his first day in the tomb. "Oh. I'm not going to work today, lad, but if you don't like going there other days, you can stay home with Opal instead. She'd love to . . ."

"I want you to go there. Go now."

Chert shook his head. "This is a day of rest, lad. Everyone gets their days of rest each tennight, and this is one of mine."

"But I have to go there." The child was not angry or upset, merely fixed as a hard-driven wedge. "I want to go to where you work."

Flint could not or would not explain his sudden interest, but neither would he be talked out of it. Chert suddenly wondered if it had something to do with the stone—after all, the boy had claimed he found it out in the temple-yard, near the tomb. "But I can't work today," Chert explained. "It's Godsday—none of the other men will come. And in any case, clattering away with picks and cold chisels would be offensive to the others having their rest." *Both above and below ground,* he could not help thinking. He had become a bit leery of working in the tomb, although he still thought of himself as unmoved by big-folk superstition. Still, he would not be sad when the job was finished and he could move on to other tasks in other places.

"Then will you just come with me?" Flint said. "Will you take me there?"

Chert could not help being astonished. The child was ordinarily well-behaved, if a bit strange, but this was the most he had talked in days, and the only time Chert could remember that he had ever asked for anything, let alone asking this way, with the doggedness of an army laying siege.

"You want me to take you to the tomb?"

The boy shook his head. "To the temple-yard. That's what it's called, isn't it? Well, near there." He frowned, trying to think of something. "Just come." He held out his hand.

Feeling as though he had entered his own front door and found himself in someone else's house, Chert rose and followed the boy into the street.

"We won't go through the Funderling roads," the boy said matter-of-factly. "I don't want to go near the talking, singing place."

"If you're talking about the Eddon family vault, there aren't any tunnels from here that go there, or even close to it."

Flint gave him a look that seemed almost pitying. "It doesn't matter. We'll go up on top of the ground."

"Boy, don't you understand that my back aches and my feet ache and I just want to sit down?" Chert had barely kept up with the child, who seemed able to walk only for a moment or two before breaking into a sprint, then circling back like a dog anxious to be after the quarry. Chert's only chance to catch his breath had been at the Raven's Gate. The guards there were now used to the Funderling man with the adopted big-folk son, but they still found the situation amusing. This one time, Chert was grateful that they made him and the boy wait to pass through while they thought of clever things to say.

Finally, as the two of them walked through the winding ways of the inner keep, heading toward the temple-yard and the family vaults, he grabbed at the boy's shirt to hold him back—he had already had one experience of how fast the child could disappear.

"Where are we going?"

"Up there." Flint pointed to the roof of one of the residences. "They're waiting for me."

"Waiting for you? Who?" It took a moment to sink in. "Hold a bit—up there? On the roof? I'm not climbing that thing, boy, and neither are you. We have no business up there."

"They're waiting for me." Flint was entirely reasonable and very firm.

"Who?"

"The Old People."

"No, no, and definitely no. I don't know why you think . . ." Chert did not get a chance to finish his sentence. He had made the mistake of letting go of Flint's collar and the boy now bolted off across the temple-yard. "Come back!" Chert cried. It was one of the more useless things he had ever said.

"I've never taken the strap to a child . . ." Chert growled, then had to close his mouth as stone-dust and mortar and bits of dried moss pattered down on him from his own handhold. *You've never had a child to take a strap to,* he told himself sourly. His backache was worse than ever, and now his arms and legs felt as though he'd spent the entire morning wielding one of the heavy picks, something he hadn't done since his youth. *And you'll never take a strap to anyone if you fall and break all your bones, so give attention to what you're doing.* Still, he was furious and more than a little startled. He had not known a child could look you in the face like that, then disobey you. Flint had been a child with his own mind and his own secret thoughts since he had come to stay with them, but he had never been troublesome like this.

Chert looked down and wished he hadn't. It was years since he had been a scaffold man, and there was in any case something different about looking down at the distant ground when the rock ceiling of Funderling Town curved soothingly above your head. Climbing the outside of a building beneath the naked sky, even this wall with its relatively easy handholds, was altogether different and quite dizzying.

Shuddering, he lifted his gaze and looked around, certain that at this very moment a guard had noticed the intruder climbing the residence wall and was nocking an arrow, preparing to spit him like a squirrel. He had seen no one, but how long could that last?

"I've never taken the strap to a child, but this time . . ."

When he reached the top at last, it was all he could do to pull himself onto the tiled roof, gasping for air, arms and legs trembling. When he could at last drag himself up into a crouch and look around, he saw Flint only a short distance away, seated just below the crest of the roof with his back against one of the large chimney pots, waiting calmly and expectantly—but not for his adopted father, it appeared, since he was not even looking at him. Chert wiped the sweat from his face and began to clamber cautiously up the mossy slope toward the boy, cursing with every breath. *Heights.* He did not like heights. He didn't really think he liked children either. So what in the name of the Earth Elders was he doing on the roof of Southmarch Castle, chasing this mad boy?

His legs were shaking so badly by the time he reached the chimney that he had to cling to the bricks while he stretched and worked out the cramps. Flint looked at him with the same sober stare he employed in all other places and situations.

"I am angry, boy," Chert growled. He looked around to see if anyone could see them from an upper window, but the boy had picked a spot where the low roof was blocked by taller parts of the residence, windowless walls that turned this section into a kind of tiled canyon, protected from the view of any of the near towers. In fact, even the top of mighty Wolfstooth Spire was barely visible above them, blocked by the overhang of a nearby roof. But Chert still had a strong urge to whisper. "Did you hear me? I said I'm angry . . . !"

Flint turned to him and laid his finger across his lips. "Sssshhh."

Just before Chert lost his mind entirely, he was distracted by a flicker of movement along the crest of the roof. As he stared in utter astonishment, a figure appeared there. For the first moments he thought the tiny man-shape must be someone standing on the uppermost point of some distant tower, a tower which itself was blocked from his view by the roof on which he and the boy were sitting—what else could explain such a sight? But as the figure began clambering down the roof toward them, moving with surprising grace and speed along the moss-furred spaces between tiles, Chert could no longer pretend the newcomer was anything but a finger-high man. He sucked in air with a strangled wheeze and the little fellow stopped.

"That's Chert." Flint explained to the tiny man. "He came with me. I live in his house."

The minuscule fellow began to descend again, faster now, almost swinging from one handhold to another, until he reached Flint. He stood by the boy and peered past him at Chert with—as far as Chert could read in a face the size of a button—a measure of suspicion.

"And tha say un be good, so will I believe 'ee." The tiny fellow's voice was high as the fluting of a songbird, but Chert could make out every word.

"A Rooftopper . . ." Chert breathed. It was amazingly strange to see an old story standing in front of you, living and breathing and no bigger than a cricket. He had thought the Rooftoppers, if not entirely invented by generations of Funderling mothers and grannies, to be at least so distantly lost in history as to be the same thing. "Fissure and fracture, boy! Where did you find him?"

"Find me?" The little creature stepped toward him, fists cocked on his hips. "What, Beetledown the Bowman but a child's toy, found and dropped again? Bested me in fair fight, un did."

Chert shook his head in confusion, but Beetledown didn't seem to care. Instead, he turned and produced a tiny silver object from the inside of his jerkin and put it to his lips. If it made a noise, it was too quiet or high-reaching for Chert's old ears, but a moment later an entire crowd of diminutive shapes appeared over the crest of the roof, moving so quickly and silently that for a moment it seemed a small carpet was sliding down the tiles toward them.

There were at least two or three dozen Rooftoppers in the gathering or delegation or whatever it was. Those in the front were mounted on gray mice and carried long spears. Their plate armor looked to be made from nutshells and they wore the painted skulls of birds as helmets; as they pulled up their velvet-furred mounts, they regarded Chert balefully through the eyeholes above the long beaks.

The rest of the group followed on foot, but in their own way they were just as impressive. Although their clothes were almost uniformly of dark colors, and made of fabric too heavy and stiff to drape like the clothes of Funderling and big folk, they had clearly spent much time on these garments—the outfits were intricate in design, and both the men and the women moved with the gravity of people wearing their finest raiment.

All this, he thought, still sunk in the haze of astonishment, *to meet Flint?*

But even as the tiny men and women stopped in a respectful semicircle behind the mouse-riders, it became clear that the day's surprises were not over. The fellow who called himself Beetledown again raised his silver pipe and blew. A moment later an even more bizarre spectacle appeared on the roofline—a fat little man just slightly bigger than Chert's thumb, riding on the back of a hopping thrush. As the bird made its awkward way down the roof toward the rest of the gathering, Chert saw that the creature's wings were held fast against its body by the straps of the tall, boxlike covered saddle on its back. The fat man below the awning pulled aggressively on the reins, trying to direct the bird's track down the tiles, but it seemed to make little difference: the bird went only where it wanted to go.

I'll try to remember that if someone offers me a ride on a thrush someday, Chert thought, and was less amused by his own joke than he was impressed he could even conceive of one under the circumstances. The whole thing was like a dream.

When the thrush had finally lurched to a halt behind the mice, its rider was dangling halfway out of the saddle, but waved away two of the mouse-riders when they started forward to help him. He righted himself, then clambered down out of the covered seat with surprising nimbleness for his bulk. His climb was hampered a little by his clothes—he wore a fur-collared robe and a shiny chain on his breast. When he reached the tiles, he accepted deep bows from the other Rooftoppers as though they were his due, then stared squintingly at Chert and Flint as he stepped closer to them—but not so close as to advance more than a pace or two beyond the protective line of mouse-riders.

"Is he the king?" Chert asked, but Flint did not reply. The Rooftoppers themselves were watching the tiny fat man with wide-eyed attention as he leaned his entire head forward and . . . sniffed.

He straightened up, frowning, and then sniffed again, a great intake of air so powerful that Chert could hear it as a thin whistle. The fat man's frown became a scowl, and he said something in a quick high-pitched voice that Chert couldn't understand at all, but the other Rooftoppers all gasped and shrank back a few steps, looking up in fear at Chert and Flint as though they had suddenly sprouted fangs and claws.

"What did he say?" asked Chert, caught up in the drama.

Beetledown stepped forward, his face pale but resolute. He bowed. "Sorry, I be, but the Grand and Worthy Nose speaks the tongue of giants not so well as we men of the Gutter-Scouts." He shook his head gravely. "Even more sorry, I be, but he says tha canst not meet the queen today, because one of tha twain smells very, very wicked indeed."

"It was long ago—so long ago," Merolanna told them. "When I first came here from Fael to wed your great-uncle Daman. You do not remember him, of course—he died long before you two were born."

"His picture is in the long hall," said Briony. "He looks . . . very serious."

"I told you, dear, you may not interrupt. This is difficult enough. But, yes, that is how he looked. He was a serious man, an honorable man, but not . . . not a kind man. At least, not kind as your father is, or as Daman's brother the old king was when he was in his cups or otherwise in good cheer." She sighed. "Don't take what I say wrongly, children. Your great-uncle was not cruel, and in my way, I came to love him. But that first year, taken from my own family and brought to a country where I scarcely spoke the language, married to a man almost twice my age, I was very sad and frightened and lonely. Then Daman went to war."

Barrick was finding himself hard-pressed to sit still. He was full of ideas, full of vigor today. He wanted to do things, to make up for the time lost during his illness, not sit here all day listening to his great-aunt's stories. Merolanna's earlier talk of madness had caught his attention—almost it had seemed that she was about to confess the same night-visitations that had plagued him, but instead she seemed to be wandering into a story of events so ancient as to have taken place in an entirely different world. He wanted to get up off the bed, perhaps even to leave, but he saw Briony stiffen from the corner of his eye and decided to stay quiet. Everything had been so difficult of late: he couldn't bear the idea of having to fight with his stubborn sister.

"It was a small thing, just short of war, actually," Merolanna was explaining. "One of the sea barons of Perikal—a dreadful man, I cannot remember his name now—was harrying the shipping on the western coast, and

Ustin sent his brother to the assistance of the King of Settland. Daman went away and I was even more lonely than I had been, day after day by myself in this unfamiliar, cloudy place, all these dark stones, under all these frowning old pictures.

"There is no excuse, as I said to Hierarch Sisel, but . . . but after some months I found myself keeping company with one of the young men of the court. He was the only one who bothered to visit me, the only one who treated me as anything other than an outsider too clumsy with her new language to speak wittily, too removed from the center of court life to have any interesting gossip to share. He alone seemed to admire me for who I was. I fell in love with him." The old woman sat up a little straighter, but her eyes were fixed on the ceiling. She had stopped moving the fan. "More than that. I gave myself to him. I betrayed my husband."

It took Barrick a moment to understand what she was saying, then he was astonished and disgusted. It was one thing to understand that older people at one time must have felt the lusts of the body, another to be told about it and then be forced to imagine it. But before he could say anything, Briony's hand tightened hard on his arm.

"You were alone in a strange place, Auntie," his sister said gently. "And it was a long time ago." But Briony looked shocked, too, Barrick thought.

"No, that is just the thing," Merolanna said. "It would seem that way to you—that to someone my age it must be so far back that it can scarcely be remembered. But one day you will see, dear, you will see. It seems like it was yesterday." She looked at Barrick, then Briony, and there was something in her face that overcame Barrick's dislike of what she was saying, something lost and sad and defiant. "More than that. It seems like today."

"I don't understand," Briony said. "What was the man's name, Auntie? Your . . . lover."

"It doesn't matter. He is even longer dead than Daman. All gone, all of them." Merolanna shook her head. "And in any case, by the time Daman came back from the fighting in the west, it was all over. Except my shame. And the child."

"The child . . . ?"

"Yes. You do not think I would be so lucky, do you? To have my one transgression end so easily, so . . . harmlessly?" Merolanna laughed a little, dabbed at her eyes. "No, there was a child, and although when I found out I thought I might pass it off as my husband's since he was expected home soon, he was delayed by storms and squabbling among the victorious captains and did not return for almost a year. The Sisters of Zoria helped me, bless them. They saved me—took me into their temple at Helmingsea for the final months while all in the castle thought I had returned to my family in Fael to wait for my husband's return. Yes, well you may look, dear. Deception upon deception. Did you ever think your great-aunt was such a wicked woman?" She laughed again. Barrick thought it sounded like something broken and rasping. "And then . . . then my baby came."

Merolanna took a moment to regain her breath and her composure. "I could not keep him, of course. The Zorian sisters found a woman who would have him to raise, and in return I brought the woman back to Southmarch with me, to live on a farm in the hills outside the city. She is dead now, too, but for years I quietly sold some of my husband's gifts every year to pay for her living there. Even after the child was taken."

"Taken?" Barrick became interested again. "Taken by who?"

"I've never known." The old lady dabbed at her eyes. "I used to visit him, sometimes, the little boy. Oh, he was bonny, fair as fair could be! But I could not go there often—too many would notice, and some would have become curious. My husband was the king's brother, after all. So when the woman told me he had been stolen, I didn't really believe her at first—I thought her somewhat simpleminded greed had at last turned into something worse, that she had hidden the child and was going to threaten to tell my husband if I did not pay her more, but I saw quickly that she was truly heartbroken. She was a poor woman, and of course she blamed it on the Twilight People—'The fairies took him!' that's what she said. Just a little less than two years old, he was." The duchess stopped to blow her nose. "Gods, look at me! Fifty years ago and it could have been yesterday!"

"But after all those years, why does it pain you so much now, Auntie?" asked Briony. "It is terrible and sad, but why have you taken to your bed like this?"

"Such pain never really goes away, dear. But there is a reason my heart is so sore. Merciful Zoria, it is because I saw him. At Kendrick's funeral. I saw my child."

For a moment Barrick could only look at Briony. He felt queasy and strange. Nothing made sense anymore, and the duchess' confession was just another crumbling of what was ordinary and safe. "A shadow," he said, and wondered again what Merolanna's dreams were like. "The castle is full of them these days."

"Do you mean you saw your child grown? Maybe you did, Auntie. No one ever told you he was dead . . ."

"No, Briony, I saw him as a child. But not even the child he was when I saw him last. He had grown. But only a little. Only . . . a few years . . ." And she was weeping again.

Barrick grunted and looked to his sister again for help making sense of this, but she had clambered across the bed to put her arms around the old woman.

"But, Auntie," Briony began.

"No." Merolanna was fighting to keep the tears from overwhelming her. "No, I may be old—I may even be mad—but I am not foolish. What I saw, ghost or figment or waking nightmare, it was my own child. It was my boy—my child. The child I gave away!"

"Oh, Auntie." Suddenly, to Barrick's immense discomfort, Briony was crying too. He could think of nothing to do except to get up and pour Merolanna another cup of wine and then stand beside the bed holding it, waiting for the storm of tears to pass.

17
Black Flowers

THE SKULL:

Whistling, this one is whistling
A song of wind and growing things
A poem of warm stones in the ashes

—from *The Bonefall Oracles*

THE GRAND AND WORTHY NOSE, larger and fatter than his fellow Rooftoppers but still no taller than Chert's finger, had spoken: these strangers smelled of wickedness. There was to be no meeting with the queen. Chert didn't know whether to be relieved or disappointed—in fact, he didn't know much of anything. When he had risen this morning, the idea that he might end up on the roof of the castle with a crowd of people smaller than field mice had not even occurred to him.

Most of the Rooftoppers had backed away in fear from their two large visitors after the Nose's pronouncement. The boy Flint looked on, his thoughts and feelings well hidden as always. Only the tiny man named Beetledown seemed to be actively thinking, his little forehead pinched into wrinkles.

"A moment, masters, I beg 'ee," Beetledown said suddenly, then skittered across the sloping roof with surprising quickness to the Grand and Worthy Nose and said something to that plump dignitary in their own tongue, a thin, rapid piping. The Nose replied. Beetledown spoke again. The assembly of courtiers all listened raptly, making little noises of wonder like the cheeping of baby sparrows.

Beetledown and the Nose trilled back and forth at each other until Chert began to wonder again if he had lost his mind, if this entire spectacle might be happening only in his own head. He reached out to the roof tiles and stroked the fired clay between his fingers, poked at the damp moss between them. All real enough. He wondered what Opal would make of these creatures. Would she put them all in a basket, bring them tenderly home to hand-feed them with crumbs of bread? Or would she chase them off with a broom?

Ah, my good old woman—what madness have we gotten ourselves into with this stray boy?

At last, Beetledown turned and trotted down the roof toward them. "I beg grace of 'ee once more, masters. The Grand and Worthy Nose says tha can meet our queen, but only if we can put bowmen on shoulders of each of tha twain. 'Twas my idea, and I be sorrowed for its ungraciousness." He did indeed look ashamed, crushing his little cap in his hands as he spoke.

"What?" Chert looked to Flint, then back to Beetledown. "Are you actually saying you want to put little men with bows and arrows on our shoulders? What, so they can shoot us in the eyes if we do something they do not like?"

" 'Tis all that the Grand and Worthy Nose will agree," said Beetledown. "My word did be bond enough for the young one, but you, sir, be a stranger to even me."

"But you heard him. You heard him say that he lives with me—that I am his . . . stepfather, I suppose." Despite his anger, Chert couldn't help being a bit amused to find himself arguing with this absurd manikin as though with any ordinary man. Then he had a sudden, grim thought: was this how the big folk felt about him—that even treating him like a real person was an act of kindness on their part? He was ashamed. A Funderling, of all folk, ought to know better than to judge another person by his size. "Is that all they wish to do? Ride our shoulders and prevent us from doing wrong?" He realized he was as much worried for Flint as himself. *Fissure and fracture, I am truly becoming a father, will it or not.* "What if one of us coughs? Stumbles? I am not anxious to get an arrow in my eye, even a small one, over a misstep or a sudden chill on my chest."

The fat Rooftopper offered something else in his shrill voice.

"The Grand and Worthy Nose says we could bind 'ee, hands and feet," explained Beetledown. To his credit, he sounded a little dubious. " 'Twould take some time, but then no one would fear wrongdoing."

"Not likely," said Chert angrily. "Let someone tie my hands and feet, up here on a high, slippery roof? No, not likely." He saw that Flint was watching him; the boy was expressionless but Chert couldn't help feeling rebuked, as though he had pushed himself in where he was not wanted and was now spoiling it for everyone.

Well, perhaps I wasn't wanted. But should I have simply let the boy climb the roof without a word, without trying to follow him? What sort of guardian would I be? Still, it seemed it was up to him to make things right.

"Very well," he said at last. "Your archers may perch on me like squirrels on a branch, for all I care. I will move slowly, and so will the boy—do you hear me, Flint? Slowly. But tell your men that if one of them pinks me or the child without reason, then they will meet an angry giant for certain." Despite his irritation and fear, he was startled to realize that to these folk he was just that—a huge and fearsome giant. Chert the Giant. Chert the Ogre.

I could scoop them up by the handful and eat them if I wished, just like Brambinag Stoneboots out of the old stories. He did not, of course, share these thoughts with the Rooftoppers, but sat as still as he could while two of the mice, each bearing a rider, begin to climb his sleeves. The scratchy little claws tickled and he was tempted simply to lift the bowmen and their mounts into place, but he could imagine such a gesture being taken wrongly. The faces of the little men were frightened but determined within their bird-skull helmets, and he had no doubt their tiny arrows and pikes were sharp.

"What is this in aid of, by the way?" he asked when the guards were in place on his shoulders. "Lad, you have not told me why you are here, how you met these folk, anything. What does this all mean?"

The boy shrugged. "They want me to meet the queen."

"You? Why you?"

Flint shrugged again.

It is like trying to chip granite with a piece of soggy bread, Chert thought. The boy, as usual, was as talkative as a root.

He was distracted by a murmur in the crowd of tiny people, the courtiers all so carefully dressed in their rude homespun, ornamented with what looked like bits of butterfly wing and flecks of crystal and metal and feathers so small they might have come from the breasts of hummingbirds. They were all turning toward the roofcrest in anticipation. Even Chert found himself holding his breath.

Like the Grand and Worthy Nose, she came riding a bird, but this one was either more successfully trained or the restraints were hidden: the snow-white dove had no band around its wings. The tiny shape atop it did not teeter in a boxy covered saddle like the Nose, but rode directly between the dove's wings with her legs curled beneath her and the reins little more than a sparkling cobweb in her hands. Her gown was brown and gray, rich with ornament, and her hair was dark red.

The dove stopped. All the courtiers and guards had gone down on their knees, including those on the shoulders of Flint and Chert, although Chert could feel the needle-fine point of one of the soldiers' pikes resting against his neck—perhaps as a precaution. Even the Grand and Worthy Nose had prostrated himself.

Beetledown was the first to raise his head. "Her Exquisite and Unforgotten Majesty, Queen Upsteeplebat," he announced.

From what Chert could make out, the queen was not so much pretty as handsome, with a fine, strong-boned face and eyes that looked up to him without any discernible fear. Chert found himself bowing his head. "Your Majesty," he said, and for a moment there was no incongruity. "I am Chert of the Blue Quartz family. This is my . . . my ward, Flint."

"The child we know of already." She spoke slowly, but her Marchlands speech, although a bit musty in its sound, was far clearer than Beetledown's. "We give you both welcome."

The Nose laboriously lifted himself from his abasement and came forward, chattering something.

"Our adviser says there is a wicked scent about you," the queen reported. "I smell it not, but he has always been a trusted help to our person. He is the sixth generation of those who are First to the Cheese—his nostrils are of true breeding. But we also can see no wickedness in you or the boy, although we think there are other stories in the child, stories untold. Are we right, Chert of Blue Quartz? Is wickedness absent in truth?"

"As far as I know, Your Majesty. I did not even know your people still existed until an hour ago. I certainly bear you no ill will." Chert was realizing that the size of a queen meant little. This one impressed him and he wanted to please her. Wouldn't that make Opal spit if she knew!

"Fairly spoken." Queen Upsteeplebat waved; two of her soldiers sprang forward to help her down from the dove's back. She looked up briefly at the windowless stone walls all around. "This is a place well-chosen for a meeting—although it is long since we or our predecessors have used it for a gathering of this sort. You will forgive us, Chert of Blue Quartz, but we are unused to the manner of speaking with giants, although we have practiced the old ways to be ready for just such a day, unlikely as we thought its arrival."

"You speak our tongue very well, Majesty." Chert snatched a look at Flint. The boy was watching, but he seemed to think this no more interesting than any other conversation between adults. Why had they invited Flint in the first place? What did they hope to get from him?

The queen smiled and nodded. "Though our folk live in your shadows, and make our lives often beneath your tables and in your cupboards, generations have passed since we have spoken, one to the other. But times now demand it, we believe."

"I'm a bit confused, Majesty. Times demand what?"

"That your folk and ours should speak again. Because we of the high places are frightened, and not just for ourselves. That which we had thought asleep—we had in our royal keeping too much knowledge to think it dead—is now awakening. That which we so happily fled long ago now reaches out again . . . but it is not only the *Sni'sni'snik-soonah* who must fear it." The rapid click seemed a sound that only a squirrel or a mockingbird should be able to make.

"Not only who?"

"My people. Rooftoppers, in your tongue." The queen nodded her head. "So you must help us decide what is to be done. The boy finding Beetledown—we think we sense the Hand of the Sky in it. Certainly it has been a stretchingly long time since any of the giants has seen us against our will. We cannot help thinking that perhaps it truly is time for us to make common cause with your kind. Perhaps you will not listen to us and we must flee again, although fleeing will do us little good, I fear, but perhaps you will listen. That alone will not save us, but it would be a start."

Chert shook his head. "I don't understand any of this, I'm afraid. But I'm trying. Because the boy caught one of your people, you Rooftoppers want to make common cause with the big folk? Why?"

"Because although we have lived hidden in your shadows for long years, Old Night is a shadow that will cover all, and none of us will find our way out again." The royal mask seemed to slip a little; for the first time, Chert could see the fear she had hidden. "It is coming, Chert of Blue Quartz. We would have guessed in any case, but the truth has been directly spoken to us by the Lord of the Peak." Watching her speak so gravely, so carefully, Chert did not doubt that she was an able ruler. Despite her size, he could not help finding her very admirable. "The storm that we have feared since before my grandmother's grandmother's day is coming," said Queen Upsteeplebat. "It will be here soon."

"May the gods protect us," murmured Raemon Beck, but the young man didn't sound as though he believed that they would. Ferras Vansen stared in silence at the valley spread before them. It disturbed him, too, but it took a moment for him to understand why it seemed so particularly frightening. Then he remembered the old woman's house and what he had found there. He had been only eight or nine years old that day, already nearing a man's height but thin as a bowstave. He had thought himself very brave, of course.

Ferras' mother was concerned about the widow who lived on the next farm, perhaps because with her own husband so short of breath these days and barely able to get out of bed she had been anticipating her own upcoming widowhood. She at least had children, though; the old neighbor had none. Now they had not seen her for several days and her goats were wandering across the green but summer-dry hills. Fearing the old woman might have become too ill to take care of herself, his mother sent Ferras, her eldest, across the dale to look in on her with a jug of milk and a small loaf.

He recognized something in the silence of the place while he was still yards away, but without quite understanding what he sensed. The little wooden house was a familiar place—Ferras had been there several times with his sisters, bringing the old woman a baked festival sweet or some flowers from his mother. The old woman had never had much to say, but she always seemed happy to see the children and would always press some gift on them in return, although what she had to spare was seldom anything more than a shiny wooden bead from a necklace that had lost its string or a bit of dried fruit from one of the stubby trees in her dooryard. But now some new element was present and young Ferras felt the hairs on his arms and neck rise and tingle.

The wind was in the other direction or he would have smelled the body a long time before he reached the threshold. It was high summer, and as he pushed open the ill-fitting door the stench leaped out and clawed at his nose and eyes, sending him stumbling back, gagging and wiping away tears. Still holding the jug, generations of crofter thrift preventing him from spilling a drop of milk no matter the circumstances, Ferras paused a few steps from the house, uncertain what to do. He had smelled death before: he knew well enough now why they had not seen the old woman lately. Still, with the first shock lessened, he felt a powerful tug, a wondering, a needing to know.

He pinched his nose and stepped into the doorway. A little daylight spilled past him through the door, but the hut had only one window and it was shuttered, so it took him a moment to see anything but darkness.

She was dead, but she was alive.

No, not alive, not truly, but the thing that lay in the center of the rush-strewn dirt floor—facedown, he realized after staring for long moments, as though she had tried to crawl toward the doorway—was rippling with movement. Flies, beetles, and count-less other crawling things he could not identify covered her entirely, a person-shaped mass of glinting, wriggling life; other than a few wisps of white hair, there was scarcely anything to see of the old woman's body. It was horrifying, and yet in a way weirdly exciting as well; although he was ever after ashamed of the feeling, the memory would stay with him forever. All that life feeding off one death.

In the dim light, the old woman seemed to be dressed in glittering black armor, something like the "caparison of light" he had heard the priest speak of on festival day, the raiment in which dead heroes would be dressed when they went to meet the gods . . .

"What is it, Captain? Are you ill? What's happened?"

Vansen shook his head, unable to answer Collum Dyer's question.

It had been a strange day already, full of weird discoveries. The patches of bright-blooming meadow flowers they had found along the roadside had been strange enough, months out of season, bending nearly sideways in brisk autumn winds they were never meant to suffer. Then there had been the deserted village a few miles back where Vansen and the others had left the road to water the horses—a very small village, admittedly, the kind that sometimes emptied when a plague struck the livestock or the only well ran dry, but it had clearly been recently occupied. Ferras Vansen had stood in the midst of those empty houses holding a carved wooden toy he had found, a charmingly well-made horse that no child would willingly leave behind, growing increasingly certain that something disturbing was at work all across this quiet land. Now, as he stared out at the scene before them, there was no longer any doubt in his mind that the village and the unsea-sonal flowers were something more than happenstance.

Unlike the village, the valley before them was very much alive, but in a way more like the dead widow woman than Vansen would have liked. Its colors were . . . wrong. It was hard to say why at first—the trees had brown trunks and green leaves, the grass was yellowed but not beyond what seemed natural for this time of the year, before the heavy rains came—but there was definitely something amiss, some mischief of light that at first glance he had thought a freak of the low clouds. It was a cold, gray day, but he felt sure that alone could not make the valley's colors seem so bruised, so . . . oily.

As the company tramped down into the valley itself, Vansen could see that although the trees and meadowed hillsides did indeed seem to have taken on an unnatural hue, much of the strangeness was because of a single kind of plant, a brambly creeper that seemed to be choking out the other vegetation, which had made its way almost everywhere along the valley, even down to the edge of the broad Settland Road. Its leaves were so dark as to be almost black, but the color was nowhere near that simple: on close inspection he saw shades of purple and deep blue and even deeper slate gray, colors that almost seemed to move; the leaves gleamed like grape-skin after a rain and the coiling vines seemed quietly fearsome, like sleeping snakes. A chill breeze ruffled the plants, but he almost fancied they were moving more than the soft wind should warrant, that they had a tremor of independent life like the horrid carpet of insects in the crofter-woman's house

The vines also had thorns, nasty spikes half the length of his finger, but the strangest thing of all were the flowers, big velvety cabbage-shaped blossoms as night-dark as the robe of a priest of Kernios. The valley seemed to be choking in black roses.

"What is all this?" Dyer asked again from a tight throat. "Never seen anything like."

"Nor have I. Beck, do you recognize this?"

The face of the merchant's nephew was quite pale, but also oddly resigned, as though he were seeing something in the waking world that had long come to him in evil dreams. Still, he shook his head. "No. When we . . . where they came . . . there was nothing out of the ordinary. Only the mist I told you of, the long reach of mist."

"There's a house up there in the hill," Vansen said. "A cottage. Should we go look to see if someone's there?"

"Those vines are all over it." Collum Dyer had not made many jokes today; he sounded like it might be a while until he made any more. "There's no one left inside. That other village had emptied without any cause we could see, so who would stay around and wait for this mucky stuff to crawl over them? No point looking—they're gone."

That had been his thought, too. Ferras Vansen was secretly relieved. He had not been anxious to wade toward a deserted house through these vines that sighed and rippled in the wind.

"You're right," he told his lieutenant. "We ride on, then, since we will not make camp here, I think."

Dyer nodded. He, too, was happy to keep traveling. Raemon Beck had his eyes closed and seemed to be praying. They passed through the valley without speaking, looking to all sides as though riding through wild, foreign lands instead of following the familiar road to Settland. The hills leaned close and the huge flowers bounced gently beneath the wind's unseeable fingers, leaves rubbing, so that it almost seemed like Vansen and his men were surrounded by whispering watchers.

To the relief of Ferras Vansen and the rest of the company, the tangle of black vines did not extend beyond the valley, although the woods beside the hilly road remained unusually quiet.

What could happen to scare even the birds away? Vansen wondered. *The same things that took the caravan? Or am I only making worries? Perhaps whatever plague emptied that village has scattered the animals and birds, too. Wild things know much we have forgotten.*

The lowering skies and his own mood had made an ordinary hill-road look almost otherworldly. He couldn't help wondering what this land had been like before settlers. *The Twilight People—if the stories are true, they were here for long, long centuries before our ancestors arrived. What did they do here? What did they think when they first saw us, the rude tribes that would have come across the water or up from the south? Did they fear us?*

Of course, he realized, the shadow folk would have been right to fear the new creatures. Because those creatures would soon take their land from them.

All this place belonged to them once. It was a thought that had first come to him in childhood, on a day when through inattention he found himself a long way from home as the light began to fail in the fastness of the hills. There had been a stillness to the dales both frightening and magical, a change in the light, as though the sky itself had taken a breath and was holding it for a short while before blowing out the candle of the sun, and the dark world of a hundred fireside stories had risen up in his mind like smoke. *All this was theirs—the other people. The Old Ones.*

And what if now they want it back? he thought. The court physician had said the Shadowline was moving. What if this was more than the matter of a single plundered caravan? What if the Twilight People, like an eldest son returned from the wars to find his young brothers spoiling his inheritance, had decided to take all these lands back?

And, if so, what of us? Pushed out . . . or simply destroyed?

Two of Vansen's men found her while they were out picking up deadfall for the evening's campfire. It was a tribute to the mood they were all in that although she was young and might even have been passing pretty under the dirt, there were few rough jests. They held her arms as they brought her to him, although she did not seem interested in escaping. No fear showed in her dark-eyed face, only blankness alternating with moments of confusion and what almost seemed like flashes of secretive amusement.

"Wandering," one of her captors told Vansen. "Just looking up at the sky and the trees."

"She's talking nonsense," the other man said. "Do you think she's taken an injury? Or is it the fever?" He suddenly looked nervous, let go of the girl and stared at his hands as though some sign of plague might be seen there like a stain. There had been rumors about the sickness that had made its way into Southmarch, the fever that attacked Prince Barrick, though it spared his life, but which also killed several old people and more than one small child in the town.

"Leave her with me." Vansen led the girl in the ragged peasant smock a little way back from the fire, but not so far that the men wouldn't be able to see him. He wasn't so much worried about what they might think of his motives as he was concerned with what they were all feeling, the sensation of being lost in a strange place instead of camping beside a familiar road in the March Kingdoms on the northern edge of Silverside.

The girl looked like she had been living out-of-doors for some time. Her matted hair and the grime on her face and hands made it hard to tell how old she was: she could have been anything from a child just reaching womanhood to someone almost his own age.

"What is your name?"

She gave him a calculating look from behind the tangle of her hair, like a merchant who had been offered a ridiculously low price but suspected that bargaining might produce something better. "Puffkin," she said at last.

"Puffkin!" He let out a startled laugh. "What kind of name is that?"

"A good name for a cat, sir," she told him. "And she was always good, until the weather changed, my Puffkin." She had the local accent, not that different from what Vansen grew up with. "Best mouser in the kingdom, till the weather changed. Sweet as soup."

Vansen shook his head. "But what is your name?"

The girl's hands were in her lap, tugging at loose threads in her wool smock. "I used to be frightened of the thunder," she murmured. "When I was a little one . . ."

"Are you hungry?"

She was shaking now, suddenly, as though beset by fever. "But why are their eyes so bright?" She moaned a little. "They sing of friendship but they have eyes like fire!"

It was no use talking to her. He wrapped his cloak around her shoulders, then went to the fire, dipped up soup with his horn cup, and brought it back. She held it carefully and seemed to enjoy the warmth, but did not appear to understand what to do with it. Vansen took it from her hands and held it to her mouth, giving her little sips until she at last took it herself.

It was good to be able to do a small kindness, he realized as he watched her swallowing. She held out the cup for more and he smiled and went to get some. It was good to be able to take care of someone. For the first time in a disturbing day, and although all the mysteries were growing deeper rather than otherwise, he was almost content.

The clouds had passed, moving east. Another armada of them waited above the ocean, ready to sweep in, but for the moment much of Southmarch Castle's inner keep was in thin, bright sunlight. Barrick found a spot where there was no shade at all. Soaking up warmth, he felt like a lizard who had just crawled out of a dark, damp crevice. The sunlight was glorious, and for the first time in days a stranger would have realized that the keep's great towers, newly washed by rain, were all different colors, from the old soot-colored stones of Wolfstooth Spire to the green-copper roof of the Tower of Spring, Autumn's white-and-red tiles, Summer's hammered-gold ornamentation, Winter's gray stone and black wrought iron. They might have been part of some titanic bouquet.

Briony was still indoors, finishing up her day's lessons with Sister Utta. Barrick could not quite understand what more there was to learn when you were already a regent of the land—it was not as though, like a chandler's apprentice or a squire, you could aspire to bettering yourself, could you? Except for continued training in combat and tactics of war, he had finished his own formal education and couldn't imagine why he might need more. He could read and write (if not quite as fluently as Briony). He could ride and hawk and hunt as well as his mangled arm allowed, and identify the heraldic emblems of at least a hundred different families— which, as old Steffans Nynor, the castellan, had once told him, was very important in a war so that one could decide who would be the best opponent to capture for ransom. He knew a great deal about his own family, starting with Anglin the Great, a reasonable amount of the history of the March Kingdoms, a few things about the rest of the nations of Eion, and enough of the tales of the Trigon and the other gods that he could make sense of the things Father Timoid said, when he bothered to pay attention.

He didn't know everything, of course: watching Briony preside over the law courts, full of opinions and concerns about things that seemed to him to matter very little, made him feel almost an outsider. His sister sometimes stopped the day's proceedings for as much as an hour to argue with the various clerks over a fine point of fairness that she deemed important, leaving dozens of petitioners pushed back to the next day's docket and grumbling. "Better justice delayed than denied," was her defense of this foolishness.

He wondered if half a year ago he would have been the same—not with law, of course, which he had always found boring in the extreme, but in ferreting out the truth behind the attack on the caravan, or even trying to make certain of Shaso's guilt. In the early days of Kendrick's regency Barrick had entertained ideas about what he would do if he were in his brother's place, all the things he would do better. Now he was in his brother's place, but most days, after another night of haunted sleep, he could scarcely find the resolve to walk out into the courtyard and sit in the sun.

It was the dreams, of course, and the weight of his awful secrets, that held him back—not to mention the fever that had nearly killed him. Surely anyone could understand that? He had almost died, but sometimes it seemed that no one would have minded much if he had. *Even Briony . . .*

No, he told himself. *That's a wicked voice. That's not true.* And that was another problem: somehow the fever had not entirely gone. He had walked in his sleep and suffered with bad dreams as long as he could remember, even before the night that had changed everything for the worse. Once or twice in his childhood he had even been found outside the residence in the morning, shivering and confused. But now almost every single night his ragged sleep was alive with creeping things, with shadowy hands and bright eyes, and even when he was awake, they didn't entirely leave him. And the dreams seemed to get into his head and speak to him as well, telling him things that he usually did not believe, and certainly did not want to believe—that everyone around him was false, that they were whispering behind his back, that the castle was full of enemies in disguise who had slowly usurped those he knew and were only waiting until their numbers were so great as to be undefeatable before . . . before . . .

Before doing what? He sat up, suddenly quivering in every muscle. *Perhaps it's all real!* Despite the unbroken sunlight, the stone warming beneath his thighs so that he could feel its pleasant heat through his woolen hose, he had to fold his arms across his chest until the trembling passed. It was the residue of his illness, of course, nothing more, and so were the strange thoughts, the voices that plagued him. Briony was still Briony, his beloved, inseparable other half, and the people and things around him were unchanged. It was only the fever. He was certain of that. Nearly certain.

Distracted by such thoughts, he nevertheless recognized the young woman by her walk before anything else. Although her figure, displayed in a sea-green dress, was still desperately alluring, she seemed to have lost weight. Her face was thinner than he remembered, but the swaying of her hips was unchanged.

He stood as she reached the center of the courtyard where she noticed him for the first time, blinked, stopped for a moment. "Prince Barrick?" She put her hand to her mouth when she realized she had not made a courtesy and quickly remedied the omission.

"Hello, Selia." His stepmother's maid was an awkward distance away, several yards: too far for an ordinary conversation. He wished she would come toward him. Perhaps she was afraid to approach, to intrude on his private thoughts. "Please, come join me for a moment. The sun is lovely today, isn't it?" There, he thought with some satisfaction. Surely the famous bard Gregor of Syan himself could not have spoken more delicately to a lady.

"If Your Highness is certain . . ." She approached slowly, like a deer ready to leap at any noise. The new thinness of her face made her eyes seem even larger, and he could see that under the powder they were shadowed. For the first time, Barrick remembered what Chaven said about her.

"You have been ill. You had what I had."

She looked at him. "I had fever, yes? But certain that Your Highness was more ill than me."

He waved his hand in the manner of true nobility: comparisons were unworthy. He was pleased with this gesture, too, and the girl also seemed impressed. "How are you feeling now?"

She glanced down at her hands. "Still a little . . . strange, I think. Like the world is not quite being as it should. Yes? Do you understand me?"

"I do." Although the nearness of her had narrowed his attention very strongly—he felt that he could see every tiny hair against her neck where they spilled free from the headdress, that he could count each shining dark strand in an instant without even trying—he also felt a little strange, as though he had been too long in the sun. He looked up, suddenly certain that someone was watching from one of the rooftops, as improbable as that seemed, but he saw nothing out of the ordinary.

"Oh! Are you knowing you are well again, Prince Barrick?"

He nodded, took a deep breath. "Yes, I suppose so. Sometimes I feel like that, too. Like the world is not quite what it should be."

Her face was solemn. "It is frightening to have this feeling, yes? For me, anyway. Your stepmother thinks I am not listening to her, but it is only that sometimes I am . . . made confused."

"You will feel better," he said, on absolutely no authority but the wish to say something reassuring to a pretty young woman. "How old are you, Selia?"

"Seventeen years, I have."

Barrick frowned a little. He wished he were older—surely a girl who might be as much as two years his senior was only interested in him because he was the prince. On the other hand, she did seem content at the moment: anyone might come to the prince regent's command, but she did not seem in a hurry to leave. Experimentally, he took her hand. She didn't resist. The skin was surprisingly cool. "Are you sure you are well enough to be out of bed?" he asked. "You have a chill."

"Oh, yes, but sometimes I am warm, very warm," she said with a little laugh. "Sometimes I cannot even keep the blankets on me even when the night is cold, and my clothes are too hot when I sleep and I must take them off." This gave Barrick a picture to think about that promised to make concentration even more difficult. "Your stepmother, she scolds with me very much for badly sleeping." She looked down and her wide eyes grew wider. "Prince Barrick, you are holding my hand."

He let go, guiltily sure that she had put up with it only because of his high station. He had always loathed men who use their power to compel women's surrender, had watched with disapproval as Gailon Tolly and other nobles, and even his own brother, took advantage of serving girls. He remembered now with some pain that only a few months earlier he had started a shouting argument with Kendrick about the treatment of one such, a pretty little lady's maid named Grenna who Barrick had admired in silence for months. Kendrick had honestly not been able to understand his younger brother's anger, had pointed out that unlike some men, he never compelled any woman to do anything by force or threat, that the girl herself had been a willing partner and had accepted several expensive gifts before the dalliance played itself out. Kendrick had also suggested that his younger brother was becoming a prig before his time and that he would do better to concentrate on his own affairs rather than comment on those of his elders.

But you must treat them like birds, had been Barrick's only confused thought, then and now. *You must let them fly or they are not truly yours.* But no one had ever been his, so what right did he have to think he knew?

Meanwhile, even though he had let go of her hand, Selia had still not taken the opportunity to escape.

"I did not say that holding me was a bad thing . . ." A smile curled her lips, but she was interrupted by the appearance of someone else at the edge of the courtyard.

"Barrick? Are you out here?"

He had never been less happy to see his sister. Briony, however, was already walking along the cobbled path toward the place where he and Selia were sitting, shading her eyes with her hand. Something was odd about her garb, but he was so frustrated with the mere fact of her arrival that he did not at first understand what it was.

She hesitated as she neared them. "Oh, I'm sorry, Barrick. I didn't know you were speaking to someone. Selia, isn't it? Anissa's maid?"

Selia stood and made a courtesy. "Yes, Highness."

"And how is our stepmother? We were disappointed not to be able to dine with her."

"She had disappointment, too, my lady. But she was not feeling well because of the baby that is coming."

"Well, give her our best and say we look forward to another invitation, that we miss her."

Barrick had finally realized what was odd: Briony was wearing a riding skirt, split down the middle and far too informal for court functions. "Why are you dressed like that?" he asked her. "Are you going out for a ride?" He devoutly hoped it was true and that she was going right this moment.

"No, but it's too difficult to explain now. I need to speak with you."

"I should leave," said Selia quickly. She cast a shy glance toward Barrick. "I have already left my lady's errand too long and she will be wondering where I am."

Barrick wanted to say something but the rout had already been effected; he had been forced into surrender without a blow struck. Selia made another courtesy. "Thank you for your kindly conversation, Prince Barrick. I am happy to see that you are more well now, too." She moved off, perhaps still not her former self, but with that fine and life-enhancing sway to her walk that Barrick could only watch with immense regret.

She wasn't angry I held her hand, he thought. *Or just putting up with it. At least I don't think so . . .*

"If you can drag your eyes away from her backside for a moment," Briony said, "you and I have things to talk about."

"Like what?" he almost shouted.

"Temper, lad." Her grin flickered a little, then her face grew more serious. "Oh, Barrick, I'm sorry. I didn't interrupt on purpose."

"I find that hard to believe."

"See here, I may not approve of a little baggage like that, but I've said my piece once already. I love you, you're my dear, dearest brother and friend, but I'm not going to follow you around trying to make certain you only do what I want."

He snorted. "Strange, because that's how it worked out." For a moment he felt real anger. "And she's not a little baggage! She's not. You don't even know her."

Briony's eyes widened. "Fair enough. But I know you and I know what a turtle you are."

"Turtle?"

"Yes, with your hard shell on the outside. But the reason a turtle has a shell is because he is defenseless on the inside. I fear that someone will get inside your shell—someone I don't trust to do right by you. That's all."

He was oddly touched by her concern but also infuriated. His twin sister thought he was helpless, that he had no defenses. It was as good as calling him simple—or worse, weak. "Just you keep out of my shell, too, Briony. It's mine, after all." It came out a bit more harshly than he intended, but he was angry enough to leave it that way.

She stared. It seemed she might say more about this, perhaps apologize again, but the moment passed. "In any case," she said briskly, "we have other things to talk about. And I've come to you about one of them. Father's letter."

"We have another letter?" As always, it filled him with both happiness and fear. *What will I be like when he returns?* A chill passed through him. *And what if he doesn't return? What then? All alone . . .*

"No, not another letter—the last one."

It took him a moment to understand. "You mean the one that came with that envoy from Hierosol, the Tuani fellow. Your . . . friend."

She didn't rise to the unpleasant tone. "Yes, that letter. Where is it?"

"What do you mean?"

"Where is it, Barrick? I haven't read it—have you? I didn't think so. Nor has Brone, or Nynor, or anyone else as far as I've heard. The only person who actually saw it was Kendrick. And now it's gone."

"It must be among some of the other things he had in his chamber. Or in his secretary, that one with the Erivor carvings on it. Or Nynor has it in with the accounts and doesn't know it." His mood darkened. "That, or someone is lying to us."

"It's not among Kendrick's things. I've been looking. There are a lot of other matters we've got to deal with that are waiting there, but no letter from Father."

"But what else could have happened to it?"

Briony shook her head fiercely; for a moment he saw the warrior queen she could someday be and was sad to think he might not be around to see it; love, pride, and anger mixed in him, swirled like the clouds blowing in overhead. "Stolen—by his murderer, perhaps," she said. "Maybe there was something written there that someone didn't want us to see. In fact, I'm certain of it."

Barrick felt a wave of dread. Suddenly the darkening courtyard seemed an exposed place, a dangerous place, and he knew why lizards were so quick to slither back into the cracks at any sound—but he realized an instant later that his father's secret, his own secret, would not be the kind of thing that King Olin would commit to a letter, even a letter to his eldest son. Still, just the brief thought had been terribly disturbing.

"So what do we do?" he asked. The day had gone sour.

"We find that letter. We must."

She came to him in the middle of the night, climbed under the heavy cloak and pressed herself against him. For a moment he took it as part of his dream and pulled her close, calling her by a name he knew he should not utter even half-asleep, but then he felt her trembling and smelled the smoke and damp in her clothes and he was awake.

"What are you doing?" Vansen tried to sit up, but she clung. "Girl, what do you think you're doing?"

She pushed her head against his chest. "Cold," she moaned. "Hold me."

The fire was nothing but embers now. A few of the horses moved restlessly on their tethers, but none of the other men were stirring. The girl slid her hard, thin little body against him, desperate for comfort, and for a moment his loneliness and fear made the temptation great. But Vansen remembered the frightened-child look, the terror that he had seen peering out of her eyes like a wounded animal driven into a thicket. He pulled free and sat up, then wrapped the cloak around her and tugged her close, using the heavy wool to help pinion her arms. After all, he could only take so much of her blind, needy rubbing before his resolve would crumble like walls made of sand. "You are safe," he told her. "Don't fear. You are safe. We are soldiers of the king."

"Father?" Her voice was hoarse and confused.

"I am not your father. My name is Ferras Vansen. We found you wandering in the forest—do you remember?"

There were tears on her cheeks; he could feel them as she rubbed her face against his neck. "Where is he? Where is my father? And where is Collum?"

For a moment he thought she was talking about Collum Dyer, but it was a common enough name in the March Kingdoms—he supposed it might be a brother or sweetheart. "I don't know. What is your name? Do you remember how you came to be walking in the forest?"

"Quiet! They will hear you. At night, when the moon is high, you can only whisper."

"Who? Who will hear me?"

"Willow, the sheep are gone. That's what he said. I ran out and the moonlight was so bright, so bright! Like eyes."

"Willow? Is that your name?"

She burrowed in against his chest, struggling beneath the confining cloak to get as close to him as possible. Her neediness was so startling and pitiable that his few lingering thoughts of lovemaking drained away. She was like a puppy or kitten standing beside its dead mother, nosing at a body gone cold.

What happened to her father, then? And this Collum? "How did you come to be in the forest, Willow? That is your name, isn't it? How did you come to be in the forest?"

Her blind groping slowed, but more from the exhaustion of fighting against the folds of the heavy cloak, he thought, than from diminishing fear. "But I didn't," she said slowly, and lifted her face. In the moonlight the darks of her eyes seemed shrunken, mere pinpoints with white all around. "Don't you know? The forest came to me. It . . . swallowed me."

Ferras Vansen had seen such a look before and it stabbed at him like a knife. The old madman back in the village where he had grown up so long ago had worn a stare like that—the old man who had crossed the Shadowline and returned . . .

But we are still miles and miles from where the caravan was taken, he realized. The nodding black flowers, the deserted village . . . *By the gods, it is spreading fast.*

18
One Guest Less

Day is over, shadows in the nest
Where have the children gone?
All are running, scattering

—from *The Bonefall Oracles*

THE MAD MUDDLE OF LIFE, Chert thought, was enough to make a person want to lie down on the ground, close his eyes, and become a blindworm. Surely blindworms didn't have to put up with nonsense like this?

"Mica! Fissure and fracture! have you nothing better to do with your time and mine than argue?"

Hornblende's nephew looked around for his brother. Both of them could be difficult by themselves, but they were much less willing to put up a fight when they were on their own. "It's not right, Chert, putting tunnels here. It's too deep, too close to the Mysteries. If it collapses through to the next level, they'll be right on top of where they shouldn't be!"

"It is not your place to decide. The king's people want this tunnel system made bigger and that's what we're going to do. Cinnabar and the other chiefs of the Guild have approved the plans."

Mica scowled. "They haven't been here. Most of them haven't worked raw stone in years, and it's been even longer since any of them have been here." He brightened as his brother approached. "Tell him."

"Tell me what?" Chert took a deep breath. It had been a strange last few days since the bizarre miniature pageant on the castle roof; his head was so full of confusing thoughts and questions he could scarcely keep his mind on his work. That was the problem, of course—Hornblende's nephews and the rest of the men needed his full supervision. Funderlings always had a difficult time working so close to the royal family's residence and graves—superstition and resentment were never far away—but this growing proximity to the Funderlings' own sacred places was even more of a problem. He couldn't afford to be attending to his work with only half his usual attention.

"That we want to go before the Guild Council," said Mica's brother Talc. He was the older and more levelheaded of the two. "We want to be heard."

"Heard, that's what you young people always want—to be heard! And what is it you want to be heard about? That you're feeling mistreated. That you have to work too hard. That what you're given to do isn't fair or kind or . . . or something." Chert took another long breath. "Do you think your uncle or I ever got to ask so many questions? We took the work we were given to do and were grateful for it." Because his own apprenticeship had been in the last days of the Gray Companies, Chert remembered but did not say—because the big folk were frightened in those years and there had not been much work even for skilled Funderling craftsmen. Hundreds, perhaps thousands, had left their ancestral home under Southmarch in search of labor and had never returned, settling in spots all over the middle and south of Eion where the big folk had previously had to do their own stonework. But during Chert's own lifetime things had changed: even small cities now built great temples and underground baths, not to mention countless funeral vaults for rich merchants and clerics, and most of the Southmarch Funderlings found themselves in demand right here at home in the March Kingdoms.

Talc shook his head. He was stubborn, but he was also smart—the worst kind of shirker, Chert thought. Or was he a shirker at all? Chert suddenly felt empty and tired, like a rock face with the seam of valuable stone chiseled out of it. *Maybe they feel some of the same things I do. What did the tiny queen say? "Because we of the high places are frightened, and not just for ourselves." I am frightened myself, but it is because of things I have seen, felt . . .*

He did his best to clear his head of all the jibber-jabber. "Very well. I shall ask the Guild to grant you a hearing, if you will get on and finish this day's work. There is shoring and bracing to do in the new tunnels, if you are not too frightened to work alongside your fellows there."

Hornblende's nephews were still grumbling as they walked away, but there was a jauntiness to their step that suggested they secretly felt they had won a victory. It made Chert feel tired all over again.

Thank the Old Ones that Chaven has come back. I will go see him when the men stop to eat. This time, though, I will go in by the front door.

As he made his way through the twisting byways of the inner keep, ignoring the people who felt that it was acceptable to stare at a Funderling simply because he was a Funderling, Chert was grateful that the boy Flint was spending the day with Opal at the market. She had accepted Chert's astonishing report of meeting the Rooftoppers with a complacency that was almost more dumbfounding than the Rooftoppers themselves.

"Of course there are more things under the stones and stars than we will ever know," she had told her husband. *"The boy is a burning spark—you can just see it! He'll do wonderful things in this world. And I always believed there truly were Rooftoppers, anyway."*

He wondered now if it had been some kind of intentional ignorance. His wife was a clever woman—surely she couldn't think this was the ordinary way of life. Was she afraid of what these many new things portended—Flint himself, the Shadowline, this news of fabled creatures hiding in the roofs who talked of coming disaster—and so she covered it all in a blanket of the familiar?

Chert realized he had shared very little of his own fear with Opal. A part of him wanted to continue that way, protecting her, which felt like his rightful duty. Another part realized that such a duty could become very lonely.

It was not the young man Toby who opened the door at the Observatory House but the physician's old, long-whiskered manservant, Harry. He seemed flustered, even nervous, and for a moment Chert feared that Harry's master might be ill.

"I'll tell him you're here," the old man said, leaving Chert to wait in the front hall. A shrine to Zoria with lit candles was set there, which struck Chert as odd—surely if the court physician were going to have a shrine to the gods of the big people, shouldn't it be a Trigonate altar? Or perhaps to Kupilas, the god of healing? Then again, he had never been able to make much sense out of the big folk and their baskets full of gods.

Harry came back, his expression still unsettled, and beckoned Chert down the corridor toward the chambers in which Chaven conducted his experiments. Perhaps that explained the manservant's behavior; his master was doing something that he thought was dangerous.

To his surprise, Chert found when he stepped into the dark room with its long, high table piled with books and unfamiliar equipment—measuring devices, lenses, things for grinding and mixing substances, bottles and jars, and candles on seemingly every one of the very few empty surfaces—that Chaven was not alone.

I have seen this young fellow before . . . he thought for a puzzled moment.

The red-haired youth looked up as the door closed behind Chert. "It's a Funderling!"

Chaven turned, and smiled at Chert. "You say that as though it were a surprise, Highness. Yet I imagine you have noticed that everyone in this room is aware that my friend Chert is a Funderling."

The boy frowned. He was dressed from head to foot in black—shoes, hose, doublet, even his soft hat. Chert knew who he was now, and tried to keep the astonishment off his face as the boy complained, "You are mocking me, Chaven."

"A little, Highness." He turned to Chert. "This is one of our regents, Prince Barrick. Prince Barrick, this is my friend Chert of the Blue Quartz family, a very good man. He has recently done your family the helpful deed in a sad time of hurrying the construction of your brother's tomb."

Barrick flinched a little, but to his credit, smiled at the new arrival. "That was kindly done."

Chert did not quite know what to do. He made a bow as best he could. "It was the least we could offer, Highness. Your brother was well-loved among my people." *Most of my people,* he amended silently. *Well, a decent proportion.*

"And what brings you to see me today, good Chert?" asked Chaven. He seemed in an expansive mood—strangely so for someone who had been out viewing the sick and the dying.

How can I talk about the things I have seen in front of the prince regent? Chert wondered. He could not help contemplating the urge to hide anything unusual from those with more power. There was also an opposing impulse that was nearly as strong, the desire to pass any strange situation on to someone else. *I am more the type who wishes to know what I am doing first,* Chert decided. *And certainly I am not going to blurt out this mishmash of fears and suspicions and old-tales-come-to-life in front of one of the royal family.*

"I wished only to hear of your journeying," he said out loud, then realized he did not want to wait days more before sharing his concerns with the physician. "And perhaps talk a little more of that matter we discussed last time . . ."

Prince Barrick rose from the stool on which he had been perched off-balance and almost tipping over, Chert realized, like any ordinary young man. "I will not keep you, then," he told the physician. The prince spoke lightly, but Chert thought he heard disappointment and something else in the boy's words—anger? Worry? "But I would speak to you again. Tomorrow, perhaps?"

"Of course, Highness, I am at your service always. In the meantime, perhaps a glass of fortified wine before bed would help a bit. And please remember what I said. Things always look different when night is on the world. Let me escort you to the door."

Barrick rolled his eyes. "My guards are in the kitchen bothering your housekeeper and her daughter. Since Kendrick was killed, I cannot go anywhere without bumping elbows with men in armor. It was all I could do to convince them I did not want them in the room with me here." He waved his good hand. "I will find my own way out. Perhaps I can sneak past the kitchen and have an hour to myself before they know I'm gone."

"Don't do that, Highness!" Chaven's voice was hearty, even cheerful, but there was an edge to it. "People are frightened. If you disappear, even for a short time, some of those guardsmen will suffer."

Barrick scowled, then laughed a little. "I suppose you're right. I'll go and give them some warning before I run for it." He nodded in a distracted way toward Chert as he left.

"The Rooftoppers, eh?" Chaven took off the spectacles perched on his nose and wiped them on the cuff of his robe—a robe surprisingly stained considering he had worn it while receiving royalty—then put them back on and gave Chert a shrewd look. "It is very unusual news, this, but I confess that there are many you could tell it to who would be more surprised than me."

"You already knew?"

"No—or at least I have never seen them, let alone met their queen in such an unusual audience. But I have encountered . . . signs over the years that suggested to me that the Rooftoppers might be more than fable."

"But what does it mean? All this talk of shadows and the coming storm? Is it because the Shadowline is moving? There is talk back home in Quarry

Square that something came across the Shadowline in the hills to the west and took an entire caravan."

"For once, the talk is right," said Chaven, and quickly told his guest the merchant Raemon Beck's story. "Even now the prince and princess have sent a company of soldiers to the place it happened."

Chert shook his head. "I cannot believe it—I am more than ever certain that the old tales are coming to life. It is a curse to live in such times."

"Perhaps. But out of great fear and danger, heroism and beauty can come, too."

"I am not your man for heroes," said Chert. "Give me a soft seam and a hot meal at the end of the day."

Chaven smiled. "I am not so fond of heroism myself," he said, "but there is a part of me—my curiosity, I suppose—that dislikes too much comfort. It is, I think, the despoiler of learning, or at least of true understanding."

Chert suppressed a shudder. "Whatever sort of lessons the Rooftoppers spoke of—Old Night! That has a terrible sound. And the Lord of the Peak who warned them, some Rooftopper god, no doubt. In any case, those are the sort of lessons I would rather avoid."

"The Lord of the Peak?" Chaven's demeanor seemed to grow a little cool. "Is that what they said?"

"Y–yes—didn't I tell you? I must have forgot. They said the truth of all this was spoken to them by the Lord of the Peak."

Chaven stared at him for a moment as from a distance, and Chert feared he had offended somehow against their old but constrained friendship. "Well, I expect you are right," the physician said at last. "It is some god of theirs." He moved suddenly, rubbed his hands together. "It is good of you to bring this all to me. Your pardon, but you have given me much that is new to think on, and I have more than the royal family's physical bodies in my care."

"It . . . it was strange to see Prince Barrick. He is so young!"

"He and his sister are both growing older quickly. These are harsh times. Now I hope you will pardon me, good Chert—I have much to do."

With the distinct feeling that he was being hurried out, Chert had almost reached the door when he remembered: "Oh! And I have something else for you." He fumbled in the pocket of his jerkin, withdrew the unusual stone. "The child Flint, the one you met—he found this near the Eddon family graveyard. I have lived with and worked with stone as man and boy, but I have never seen anything like it. I thought perhaps you could tell me what it is." A sudden thought: "It did not occur to me, but it was with me when I met the Rooftoppers. Their little Nose-man said he could smell evil. I thought perhaps it was the scent of the shadowlands still on Flint . . . but perhaps it was this."

Chaven took it, gave it a quick glance. He did not seem impressed. "Perhaps," he said. "Or perhaps it was all part of the incomprehensible politick of the Rooftoppers—they are an old race about which we know little in these days. In any case, I will examine it carefully, good Chert." He gave it another look, then slipped it into one of the sleeves of his robe. "And now, good morning. We will talk longer when I am not just come back from the countryside."

Chert hesitated again. Chaven had never before made him feel unwelcome. He wanted to probe the unfamiliar situation like a sore tooth. "And your journey went well?"

"As well as could be hoped. The fever that struck the prince has come to many houses, but I do not think it was what I once feared—something that comes from beyond the Shadowline." He stood patiently by the door.

"Thank you for your time," the Funderling told him. "Farewell, and I hope I will see you again soon."

"I shall look forward to it," Chaven said as he closed the door firmly behind him.

The sky was high and clear today, but cold air stabbed down from the north and Briony was glad of her warm boots. Not everyone seemed to approve of her manlike choice of clothing: woolen hose and a tunic that had once been Barrick's; Avin Brone took one look at her and snorted, but then hurried into the day's business as if he did not trust himself to comment on her apparel. Instead, he complained about the fact that her brother apparently could not be bothered to attend.

"The prince's time and reasons are his own," Briony said, but secretly she was not displeased. She had reasons to hurry, and although she did her best to attend to the matters to be settled, the taxes to be assessed, the countless stories whose only desired audience was her royal self, she was distracted and paid only intermittent attention.

Finished, she stopped and went to a meal of cold chicken and bread in her own chambers. She would rather have had something warmer on such a day, but she had an assignation to keep . . .

What a way to think of it! She was amused and a little ashamed. *It is business— the crown's business, and overdue.* But she couldn't completely convince even herself.

Rose and Moina were in a frenzy of disapproval of her behavior today, both her immodest, masculine garb and her choice of meetings. Although they were neither of them forward enough to say much, it quickly became clear that the young noblewomen had been intriguing between themselves and would not be sent away without a fuss. After Briony's heated words were met with fierce resistance—but couched in the terms of purest obedience to their mistress' commands, of course—she gave up and allowed them to accompany her. *It is just as well,* she told herself. *It is perfectly innocent, after all, and now there will be no whispering gossip.* But she couldn't help being just the smallest bit resentful. Mistress of all the northern lands—well, alongside her brother—and she could not have a meeting without being surrounded by watchful eyes, as though she were a child in danger of hurting herself.

He was waiting in the spice garden. Because of the argument with her two ladies, he had waited longer than she would have liked. She couldn't help wondering whether chill weather like this felt more cruel to someone brought up in hot southern lands, but if Dawet dan-Faar was suffering, he was too subtle to show it.

"I had planned we would walk here," she said, "but it is so fearfully cold. Let us go across the way into Queen Lily's Cabinet instead."

The envoy smiled and bowed. Perhaps he was indeed glad to go somewhere warmer. "But you seem to have dressed for the weather," he commented, looking her up and down.

Briony was disgusted to find herself blushing.

The cabinet room was modest in size, just a place where Anglin's granddaughter had liked to sit and sew and enjoy the smells of the spice garden. At first all of Briony's guards seemed determined to join her in the cozy little paneled room, but this was too much; she sent all but two out again. This pair took up positions near the door where they could watch Rose and Moina doing needlework, then all four of them settled down to keep a close if covert eye on their mistress.

"I trust I find you well, Lord Dawet?" she asked when they had both been served with mulled wine.

"As well as can be expected, Highness." He sipped. "I confess that days like this, when the wind bites, I miss Hierosol."

"As well you might. It is very unwanted, this cold weather, but the season finally seems to have changed. We had been having unusually warm days for Dekamene, after all."

He seemed about to say something, then pursed his mouth. "And is it truly the weather that causes you to be dressed this way, Highness?" He indicated the thick hose and the long tunic—one of Barrick's that he never wore—that she had so carefully altered to fit her own slimmer waist and wider hips.

"I sense you do not approve, Lord Dawet."

"With respect, Highness, I do not. It seems to be a sin against nature to dress a woman, especially one as young and fair as yourself, in this coarse manner."

"Coarse? This is a prince's tunic, a prince's doublet—here, see the gold fretwork? Surely it is not coarse."

He frowned. It was a much greater pleasure than she would have guessed to see him discomfited—like watching a supercilious cat take a clumsy fall. "They are men's clothes, Princess Briony, however rich the fabric and workmanship. They make coarse what is naturally fine."

"So the mere fact of what I wear can make me less than fine, less than noble? I fear that leaves me very little room in which to maneuver, Lord Dawet, if I am already so close to coarseness that a mere doublet can carry me to it."

He smiled, but it was a surprisingly angry expression. "You seek to make sport of me, Highness. And you may. But you seemed to ask whether I approved, and I would be honest with you. I do not."

"If I were your sister, then, would you forbid me to dress this way?"

"If you were my sister or any other woman whose honor was given into my keeping, yes, I would certainly forbid you." His dark gaze suddenly touched hers, angry and somehow demanding. It was startling, as though she had been playing with what she thought was a harmless pet that had suddenly shown it could bite.

"Well, in point of fact, Lord Dawet, that is why I asked you to attend me."

"So it is not 'we' and 'us,' Highness?"

She felt her cheeks warming again. "We? Us? You overreach yourself, Lord Dawet."

He bowed his head, but she glimpsed the tiniest hint of a smile—the old one, the self-satisfied one. "I have been unclear, Highness. I apologize. I simply meant that you did not say 'we,' so I wondered if this was *not* then an audience with you and your royal brother, as I had been given to understand. I take it that instead you wish to speak more . . . informally?"

"No." Damn the man! "No, that is not what I meant, although of course I act today as co-regent and with my brother's approval. You make me regret speaking to you in a friendly way, Lord Dawet."

"May the Three Highest bring ruin on my house if I intended any such thing, Princess—if I intended anything other than respect and affection. I simply wished to know what sort of meeting we are having."

She sipped at her wine, taking a moment to recover her confidence. "As I said, your remark about me being a woman in your care was to the point. Only a few weeks gone, I might have *been* just such a forlorn creature, sent with you to marry your lord, like . . . like a bit of tribute. Do not forget, Lord Dawet, you come here as the ambassador of our enemy."

"You have greater enemies than my master Ludis, Highness. And I fear you also have friends who are even less trustworthy than me. But forgive me—I have interrupted you. Again, I am unforgivably rude."

He had flustered her again, but the anger gave her something to grip, a certain leverage. "It is finally time for the crown of Southmarch and the March Kingdoms to return an answer to your master, the Protector of Hierosol, and his offer of marriage. While my older brother was regent, there might have been a different answer, but now, as you may guess, the answer is no. We will ransom my father with money, not my maidenhood. If Ludis wishes to beggar the northern kingdoms, then he will find that when the Autarch comes to his front door, Hierosol will get no assistance from the north. Rather, though we hate the Autarch and would not ordinarily wish to see him gain even a handful of Eion's soil, we will rejoice at the defeat of Ludis Drakava." She paused, slowing her breath, making her voice firm. "But if he sees another way—if King Olin might be released for something less than this exorbitant amount of gold, for instance—then Ludis might discover he has allies here that will stand him well in days ahead."

Dawet raised an eyebrow. "Is that the message you wish me to give him, Princess Briony?"

"It is."

He nodded his head slowly. "And do I take this to mean that I am no longer a prisoner? That my escort and I are free to go back to Hierosol?"

"Do you doubt my word?"

"No, Highness. But sometimes things happen beyond the echo of a prince's voice."

"Avin Brone, the lord constable, knows my wishes . . . our wishes. He will return your men's arms. Your ship is prepared already, I think."

"Your castellan was kind enough to arrange that no harm should come to it, and that I could keep on it a small crew to see that things stayed in order." Dawet grinned. "I confess that although I will in many ways regret leaving, it is good to know I will have my freedom again, even though you will be one guest the less."

"Guest, indeed. Whatever you believe, Lord Dawet, I do not think you can say we treated you much like a prisoner."

"Oh, a valued prisoner, at the worst," he said. "But that is small solace to one who has spent years of his life living on horseback, never sleeping in the same place twice." He stirred. "Do I have leave to go and begin the preparations?"

"Of course. You will want to sail before the weather turns for good." She was oddly disappointed, but knew this was happening as it must. He and his Hierosoline company were a distraction in the castle; they attracted rumor and hostility as honey drew flies. Yes, he was a very distracting presence, this Dawet dan-Faar. Now that Brone had convinced her and Barrick beyond doubt that there was no way the envoy or his company could have been materially involved in her brother's murder, it made no sense to keep them and feed them through the long winter.

He bowed, took a few steps backward, then stopped. "May I speak frankly, Highness? Princess Briony?"

"Of course."

He glanced at the guards and her ladies-in-waiting, then came back and sat on the bench beside her. This close, he smelled of leather and some sweet hair oil. Briony saw Rose and Moina exchange a look. "I will take you at your word, Mistress, and hope you have played me fairly," he said quietly. "Listen carefully to me, please.

"I am glad you did not accept the suit of my lord Ludis. I think you would not have found life at his court very enjoyable—mostly, I suspect my master's interests and amusements would not have been to your taste. But I hope someday you can see the southlands, Princess, and perhaps even Xand . . . or at least those parts of it not choking under the Autarch's control. There are beauties you cannot imagine, green seas and high mountains red as a maiden's blush, and broad jungles full of animals you can scarcely imagine. And the deserts—you will remember I told you something of the silent, stark deserts. You may become a great queen someday, but you have seen little of the world, and that seems to me a shame."

Briony was stung. "I have been to Settland and Brenland and . . . and Fael." She had been only a child of five when her father took her to visit Merolanna's relatives—she remembered little except a great black horse given to her father by Fael's lord as a present, and of standing on a balcony above the sea watching otters at play in the water below.

Dawet smirked—there was nothing else to call it. "Forgive me if I do not count Settland and Brenland among the gods' greatest triumphs, my lady." Abruptly the smile dropped away. "And my wish for you to see more of the world is in part an idle and selfish wish . . . because I wish I could be the one to show these things to you." He lifted a long, brown hand. "Please, say nothing. You told me I could speak honestly. And there is more I would tell you." His voice dropped all the way to a whisper. "You are in danger, my lady, and it is closer to you than you think. I cannot believe that Shaso is the one who killed your brother, but I cannot prove he did not either. However I *can* tell you, and tell you from knowledge, that one who is much closer to you than me means you ill. Murderously ill." He held her gaze for a long moment; Briony felt lost, as though she were in an evil falling dream. "Trust no one."

"Why would you say such a thing?" she whispered harshly when she had found her voice again. "Why should I believe that you, the servant of Ludis Drakava, are not merely trying to stir unhappiness between me and those I trust?"

The smile returned one last time, with an odd twist to it. "Ah, the life I have led means I deserve that many times over. Still, I do not ask you to act on my words, Princess Briony, only to consider them—to remember them. It could be that the day will come when we can sit together once more and you can tell me whether I wished you ill this day . . . or well." He stood, donning his guise of easiness again like a cloak. "I hope you will be more suitably dressed, of course." He took her hand in a most ostentatious manner, brushed his lips upon it. Everyone else in the room was staring openly. "I thank you and your brother for your generous hospitality, Princess, and I grieve for your loss. I will give your message to my master in Hierosol."

He bowed and left the cabinet.

"I am quite sick of watching the two of you murmur," Briony growled at her ladies-in-waiting. She didn't quite know what she was feeling, but it was not pleasant. "Go away. I want to be by myself for a while. I want to think."

By day the dark-haired girl Willow came back to herself a little, although in some ways she seemed so childish that Ferras Vansen wondered if her problems were solely caused by having crossed the Shadowline—perhaps, he thought, she had already been a bit simpleminded. Whatever the case, under the small bit of sun that leaked through the clouds she became the most cheerful of the generally silent company, riding in front of Vansen and chattering about her family and neighbors like a small child being taken to the market fair.

" . . . She is so little, but she is the most stubborn of the lot. She will push the other goats away from the food—even the biggest of her brothers!"

Collum Dyer listened to her babble with a sour expression on his face. "Better you than me, Captain."

Ferras shrugged. "I am happy she is talking. Perhaps after a while she will say something that we will thank Perin Cloudwalker we learned."

"Perhaps. But, as I said, better you than me."

In truth, Ferras Vansen was almost glad of the distraction. The land through which they passed was less obviously strange than the previous two days' stretch of road, deserted and a bit gloomy but otherwise about what he would have expected as they neared the halfway point of the journey, and thus not particularly interesting. With the largest cities of Settland and the March Kingdoms several days' ride away in either direction, these lands had emptied in the years since the second war with the Twilight People, leaving only crofters and woodsmen of various sorts and the occasional farmer. The few small cities like Candlerstown and Faneshill had grown up south of the Settland Road, well away from the Shadowline. (These towns were also too far out of the way to be worth visiting this trip, a fact much mourned by Dyer and the rest of Vansen's men.) Winters were also milder closer to the water to the east or west: few felt the need to live out here in such dramatic solitude. The Settland Road passed through low hills and scrub that were even more undistinguished than the lands where Ferras had spent his childhood.

They could see the line again now, just a few miles away to the north, or at least they could see the breakfront of mist that marked it. It was wearying to ride hour after hour with it hovering so close, hard not to think of it as a malevolent thing watching them and waiting for an opportunity to do harm, but Ferras was much happier knowing where it was, able to see that there was still a crisp delineation between his side and the other.

Willow had moved from goats to the topic of her father and swine, and was explaining what her sire had to say about letting the hogs scavenge for mast—for the "oak corns" as she called them. Vansen, who had spent most of the last ten years of his life trying to forget about raising hogs and sheep, leaned over and asked her, "And what of Collum? Your brother?"

Either his guess was correct or she was madder than he supposed. "He would rather pick rushes than follow the pigs. He is a quiet one, our Collum. Only ten winters. Such dreams he has!"

"And where is he now?" He was trying to discover if there was any sense or meaning behind some of the things she had said.

Her look turned sad, even frightened, and he was almost sorry he'd asked. "In the middle of the night, he went. The moon called him, he said. I tried to go, too—he is just a little one!—but our father, he grabbed me and would not let me through the door." As if the subject caused her pain, she began talking again about cutting the rushes for rush candles, another activity Vansen knew only too well.

It would not have taken much calling by the moon or anything else to make me run away, Vansen thought. *But somehow I do not think this girl's brother has gone to the city to make his fortune.*

Late afternoon, with the sun falling fast, Vansen decided to make camp. The road had led them through the low, sparsely covered hills all day, but they were about to pass through a patch of forested ground. The stand of trees before them was not a place he wanted to wander in the growing dark.

"Look!" shouted one of the men. "A deer—a buck!"

"We'll have fresh meat," another cried.

Ferras Vansen looked up to see the creature standing just inside the shadows at the edge of the trees, half a hundred steps away. It was large and healthy, with an impressive spread of antler, but seemed otherwise quite ordinary. Still, something about the way it looked at them, even as a few of the men were nocking arrows, made him uneasy.

"Don't shoot," he said. One of the soldiers raised his bow and aimed. "Don't!" At Vansen's shout, even though it had been looking straight at them, the stag for the first time seemed to understand its peril. It turned and with two long leaps vanished into the cover of the trees.

"I could have had him," snarled the bowman, the old campaigner Southstead whose grumbling ways had been the reason Vansen brought him instead of leaving him home to gossip and spread dissatisfaction among the rest of the guardsmen.

"We do not know what is natural here and what is not." Ferras was careful to keep anger out of his voice. "You saw the flowers. You have seen the empty houses. We have enough to eat in our packs and saddlebags to keep us alive. Kill nothing that does not threaten you—do you all hear me?"

"What," demanded Southstead, "do you think it might be another girl, magicked into a deer?" He turned to the other guards with a loud, angry laugh. "He's already got one—that's just greedy, that is."

Vansen realized that the man was frightened by this journey through lands grown strange. *As are we all,* he told himself, *but that makes such talk all the more dangerous.* "If you think you know better than me how to lead this company, Mickael Southstead, then say so to me, not to them."

Southstead's smile faltered. He licked his lips. "I meant only a jest, sir."

"Well, then. Let us leave it at that and make camp. Jests will be more welcome over a fire."

When the flames were rising and the girl Willow was warming her hands, Collum Dyer made his way to Vansen's side. "You'll have to keep an eye on our Micka, Captain," he said quietly. "Too many years of too much wine has curdled his heart and brains, but I had not thought him so far gone as to mock his captain. He never would have dared it in Murroy's day."

"He'll still do well enough if there's something to do." Vansen frowned. "Raemon Beck, come here."

The young merchant, who had spent most of the journey like a man caught in a nightmare from which he couldn't awaken, slowly made his way toward Vansen and Dyer.

"Are you an honorable man, Beck?"

He looked at Ferras Vansen in surprise. "Why, yes, I am."

"Yes, *Captain,*" grunted Dyer.

Vansen raised his hand: it didn't matter. "Good. Then I want you to be the girl's companion. She will ride with you. Trying to get sense from her is like sifting a thousandweight of chaff for every grain of wheat, anyway, and you may recognize better than I can if she says something useful."

"Me?"

"Because you are the only one here who has been through something like what I believe she has seen and heard and felt." Ferras looked over to where the men were gathering more deadfall for the fire. "Also, to be frank, it is better if the men are angry with you than angry with me."

Beck did not look too pleased at this, but Collum Dyer was standing right beside him, cleaning his dirty fingernails with a very long dagger, so he only scowled and said, "But I am a married man!"

"Then treat her as you would want your wife treated if she were found wandering ill and confused beside the road. And if she says anything that you think might be useful, anything at all, tell me at once."

"Useful how?"

Vansen sighed. "In keeping us alive, for one thing."

He and Dyer watched as a chastened Beck walked back to the fire and sat himself down beside the near-child Willow.

"Do you think we're in such danger, Captain?" asked Dyer. "Truly? Because of a few flowers and a daft girl?"

"Perhaps not. But I'd rather come home with everyone safe and be laughed at for being too cautious—wouldn't you?"

The night passed without incident, and by midmorning the road had led them so deep into the trees that they could no longer see the dreary hills or the looming Shadowline. At first that seemed a blessing, but as the day wore on and the sun, glimpsed only for brief moments through chinks in the canopy, passed the peak of the sky and began to slide into the west, Vansen found himself wondering whether they would have to spend the night surrounded by forest, which was not a comfortable thought. As they took their midday meal of roadbread and cheese, he called Raemon Beck to his side again.

"There is nothing to tell," Beck said sullenly. "I have never heard so much prattling about pigs and goats in my entire life. If we were to come upon her father's farm now, I think I might put a torch to it myself."

"That is not what I wished to ask you. These woods—when you were riding through them, how long did it take you? On the way out toward Settland, I mean." He tried a kind smile. "I doubt you were paying much notice to such things on your ride back."

Beck's look was almost amused, but it didn't hide his misery. "We went through no forest like this on the way out."

"What do you mean? You traveled on the Settland Road, did you not?"

The merchant's nephew looked pale, weary. "Don't you understand, Captain? Everything has changed. Everything. I remember scarcely half these places from my journey."

"What nonsense is that? It was only a week or two ago. You must have passed through this wood. A road is not a river—it doesn't flood its banks and find a new channel."

Beck only shrugged. "Then I must have forgotten this wood, Captain Vansen."

The afternoon wore on. The cleared space where the road passed through the trees was quiet and gloomy, but there were signs of life—a few deer, squirrels, a pair of silvery foxes that passed through a clearing beside them like midday moonlight before vanishing into a thicket, and a raven that for a while seemed to keep pace with them, fluttering from branch to branch, cocking its head to examine them with bright yellow eyes. Then, one of the men on foot who could no longer stand the raven's persistence and silence chased it away with a stone. Vansen did not have the heart to scold him.

At last, as the sharp shadows of leaves and branches on the road began to blur into a more general murkiness, he decided that they could not go on any longer in the hope of outlasting the forest. It would be dark within an hour. He bade the company stop and set camp at the edge of the trees, beside the road.

He was kneeling in front of the first gathering of kindling, trying to strike a light from his recalcitrant flint, when one of the youngest guardsmen came racing toward them along the edge of the forest.

"Captain! Captain!" he shouted. "There is someone on the road ahead."

Vansen stood. "Armed? Could you tell? How many?"

The young soldier shook his head, wide-eyed. "Just one—an old man, I think. And he was walking away from us. I saw him! He had a staff and wore a cloak with the hood up."

Vansen was struck by the young man's almost feverish excitement. "A local woodsman, no doubt."

"He . . . he seemed strange to me."

Ferras Vansen looked around. Work setting up camp had stopped and all were now watching him. He could feel their curiosity and discomfort. "Well, then, we'll have a look. You come with me. Dyer? You, too. Perhaps we can all shelter somewhere a bit more comfortable tonight, if this old fellow lives nearby."

The pair climbed onto their horses and followed the young guard along the road, past the point where it turned and took them out of sight of the camp. There was indeed a small, dark figure hurrying along ahead of them. Although the shape was bent, Vansen thought that if he was an old man, he must be a very spry old man.

They left the young foot soldier and spurred ahead, thinking to catch up to the cloaked shape in a matter of moments, but it was growing dark quickly and somehow even though the road curved again only a little, they could not find him.

"He's heard us coming and stepped into the trees," said Collum Dyer.

They rode a little farther, until they could see a clear stretch of road before them. Even in the poor light it was quite clear no one was hurrying ahead of them. They turned and made their way back, riding slowly, peering into the thicket on either side of the road to see if their quarry was hiding there.

"A trick," Dyer said. "Do you think he was an enemy? A spy?"

"Perhaps, but . . ." Vansen suddenly pulled up in the middle of the road. His horse was restive, pawing at the ground impatiently. A little evening mist had begun to rise from the ground. "We've come back two bends of the road," he said. "Collum, where is the camp?"

Dyer looked startled, then scowled. "You'll frighten us both, Captain. A little farther ahead—we've just mistaken how far in this failing light."

Vansen allowed himself to be led, but after they had been riding for a while longer, Dyer suddenly reined up and began to call.

"Hallooo! *Hallooo!* Where are you all? It's Dyer—*halloooo!*"

No one answered.

"But we are still on the same road!" Collum Dyer said in panic and fury. "It's not even full dark!"

Ferras Vansen found he was trembling a little, although the evening was not particularly cold. Mist twined lazily between the trees. He made the sign of the Trigon and realized he had been silently murmuring prayers to the gods for some time. "No," he said slowly, "but somewhere, somehow, without even knowing it . . . we have crossed the Shadowline."

19

The God-King

DEEP HOLE:

The sound of a distant horn
The salt smell of a weeping child
The air is hard to breathe

—from *The Bonefall Oracles*

AS USUAL, THE HIGH PRIEST did not enter the dark room
until Qinnitan had already been led through an exhausting series
of prayers and the steaming golden cup had been set before her.
High Priest Panhyssir was another Favored, and was at least as large and
imposing as Luian, but seemed to have studied the ways of real men as
carefully as Luian had studied those of natural women. He also seemed to
have kept his stones until after he had reached manhood—his beard was
wispy but long, and he had a surprisingly deep voice, which he used to
great effect.

"Has she completed the day's obeisances?" he demanded. When the
acolyte nodded, the high priest crossed his arms on his chest. "Good. And
the mirror-prayers—has she said them all?"

Qinnitan swallowed her irritation. She didn't like being talked about as
if she were only a child who couldn't understand, and considering that the
hours-long prayer rituals in this small, mirror-lined chamber in the temple
never changed, and that she had never been allowed to skip even one of the
dozens of intricate chants (those many-named invocations of the different

characters of Nushash spoken into the largest of the sacred mirrors, prais-
ing the god in his incarnations as the Red Horse, the Glowing Orb of
Dawn, the Slayer of Night's Demons, the Golden River, the Protector of
Sleep, the Juggler of the Stars, and all the others) Qinnitan thought it was
a bit much for the priest to act as if during his absence she might have been
doing something else instead.

"Yes, Great One, O treasured of Nushash." The subordinate priest, also
one of the Favored, had the voice and smooth skin of a young boy, although he was clearly full grown. He was vain, too: he liked to observe
himself in the sacred mirrors when he didn't think Qinnitan was looking.
"She is prepared."

Qinnitan accepted the cup—a splendid thing of gems and hammered
gold in the shape of the winged bull that drew Nushash's great wagon
across the sky, worth more than the entire neighborhood in which she had
grown up—and did her best to look solemn and grateful. High Priest Panhyssir, after all, was one of the most powerful men in the world and probably held her life in his hands. Still, she could not help wrinkling up her
face a little as she took the first swallow.

It was lucky that the young priest always said his invocation so loudly—
it made it easier for her to drink slowly, and not to worry about the noises
she made as she forced the dreadful stuff down. The elixir, the Sun's Blood
as they called it, did taste a little bit like actual blood, salty and with a smoky
hint of musk, which was one of the reasons Qinnitan had to force herself
not to gag on it. There were other flavors as well, none of them particularly
nice, and although it wasn't spicy, it made her entire mouth tingle as though
she had eaten too many of the little yellow Marash peppers.

"Now close your eyes, child," Panhyssir told her in his deep, important
voice as she finished draining the cup. "Let the god find you and touch you.
It is a great, great honor."

The honor came more quickly than usual, and it was no mere brush this
time, no dreamy caress as in past days, but more like being grabbed and
shaken by something huge. It started as a feeling of heat at the back of her
stomach and then spread swiftly up and down her spine, both directions at
the same moment like a crackle of fire through dry grass, flaring at last behind her eyes and between her legs so that she would have fallen off the
chair if the younger priest had not grabbed her. She felt his hands as though
they were far, far away, as though they touched a statue of her rather than
the real Qinnitan. The rush of noise and darkness into her head was so

powerful that for long moments she was certain she would die, that her skull would burst like a pine knot in a cook fire.

"Help me!" she screamed—or tried to, but the words only existed in her own thoughts. What came out of her mouth instead were animal grunts.

"Lay her down," Panhyssir commanded. His voice seemed to come from another room. "It has well and truly taken her this time."

"Is there anything . . . ?" Qinnitan could not see the young priest—she was in a night-dark fog—but he sounded frightened. "Will she . . . ?"

"She is feeling the touch of the god. She is being prepared. Lay her back on the cushions so she does not harm herself. The great god is speaking to her . . ."

But he's not, Qinnitan thought as Panhyssir's voice grew fainter and fainter, leaving her alone at last in blackness. *No one's speaking to me. I'm all alone. I'm all alone!*

It grew thick around her, then—although she didn't know, couldn't even guess, what "it" was. She was having enough difficulty just holding what she was and who she was in her heart: the darkness threatened to suck it all away, all of what made her Qinnitan, just as winter nights of her childhood had yanked the warmth from her face when she ran outside in a sweat after jumping and playing with her cousins.

Now the darkness began to change. She still could not see anything, but the emptiness around her began to harden like crystal, and every new thought that passed through her mind seemed to make it ring, a deep, slow tolling like a monstrous bell of ice. She was heavy, heavier and older than any mere living thing. Qinnitan could understand what it was to be a stone, to lie in the earth without moving, measuring out thoughts as deliberate as mountains rising, how it felt to live not just flitting moments but millennia, each dream an aeon long.

And then she could feel something outside herself, but close—frighteningly close, as though she were a fly walking all unknowing on the belly of a sleeping man.

Sleeping? Perhaps not. For now she could sense the true size of the thoughts that surrounded and penetrated her, thoughts that she had for a moment imagined were her own, although she realized now that she could no more make sense of these vast ideas than she could speak the language of an earth tremor's rumble.

Nushash? Could it be the great god himself?

Qinnitan did not want to be locked in this diamond-hard, resonant darkness anymore. The horrid shudder of the god's slow pondering was too much for her frail thoughts, so far from her and so, so much greater than she or any mere man or woman could ever be, big as a mountain—no, big as Xand itself, bigger, something that could lie across the whole night sky and fill it like a grave.

And then whatever it was finally noticed her.

Qinnitan came up thrashing, her heart battering at her ribs as though trying to leap from her breast. As she woke to the burning brightness of the lanterns in the small temple room, she was weeping so hard she thought her bones would break, with a taste in the back of her mouth like corpse flesh. The younger Favored priest held her head as she vomited.

At last, an hour later, when the female servants had cleaned up after her and bathed her and robed her, she was taken back to Panhyssir. The paramount priest held her face in his hard hand and stared into her eyes, not in sympathy, but like a jewel merchant evaluating facets.

"Good," he said. "The Golden One will be pleased. You are progressing well."

She tried to speak but couldn't, as weary and sore as if she had been beaten.

"Autarch Sulepis has called for you, girl. Tonight you will be prepared. Tomorrow you will be taken to him."

With that he left her.

The preparations were so exhausting and kept her up so late that even as she was being hustled down the hallways of the Orchard Palace to her morning meeting with the autarch, and having got out of bed only an hour before, Qinnitan was stumbling with fatigue. She was also still suffering the effects of the potion the high priest had given her the previous day, feeling it much more strongly than she ever had before. Even in these shadowed halls the light seemed too painfully bright, the echoes too persistent—it made her want to run back to bed and pull something over her face.

At the golden doors of the autarch's reclining chamber, she and her small retinue had to step back and wait as the great litter she had seen once before was maneuvered somewhat awkwardly out into the passage. The crippled Scotarch Prusas pulled a curtain aside with his cramped fingers to watch the proceedings, then he caught sight of Qinnitan and his head twisted toward her, mouth hanging open as though in shock, although she thought that was more the slackness of his jaw than any real surprise at seeing a minor bride-to-be waiting for an audience with the autarch. He looked her up and down, his head trembling on his thin neck, and if the look he gave her was not contempt or even hatred, she was certain it was something close, a chilly examination made more disturbing still by his twitches and little gasps of breath.

Why would the most powerful man in the world pick such a frail, mad creature as this for his scotarch? Qinnitan could not even guess. The scotarchy was an old tradition of the Falcon Throne, meant to make sure an heir was always in place until an autarch's own son was old enough to take power; it was designed to forestall crippling warfare that had often broken out between factions when the autarch died without an heir ready. The strongest and oldest part of the ritualistic tradition, however, was that if the scotarch died it meant that the autarch had lost favor with heaven and thus he had to give up his throne as well. This had been meant to stave off treachery from sons and relatives not likely to be named as heir, and because of this ancient Xixian constraint on even their god-kings, scotarchs were chosen not so much for their actual worthiness to rule but for health and likely endurance, prized like racehorses for brightness of eye and strength of heart. Until a few generations back, they had always been chosen during ceremonial games in which all contestants but the winner might die. This had been deemed fitting, since the path to the Falcon Throne for aspiring autarchs also tended to work the same way, except that the deaths were not generally so public.

As Qinnitan watched the trembling figure of Prusas withdraw into the cushioned depths of his litter with a stammering cry that his bearers should hurry on, she could only wonder how anyone, especially someone like Sulepis with no suitable male heirs even born, let alone ready to rule, could have chosen such a pathetic creature as Prusas for his scotarch, a cripple who looked to be tottering on the lip of the grave. (Qinnitan was not alone, of course: *nobody* in the Seclusion seemed to know the answer to that question, although it was much guessed-at throughout the entire Orchard Palace. Some brave ones whispered that it proved that Autarch Sulepis was either the maddest of his unstable family or, putting a more pleasant face on it, touched by the gods.)

The tall doors had barely swung shut behind the scotarch's litter before they swung open again for Qinnitan and her pair of attendant maids and complementary pair of Favored guards.

The Reclining Chamber with its slender purple-and-gold columns was only slightly smaller than the great throne room, although there were many fewer people in it, only a dozen soldiers mostly ranged at the back of the dais and another two dozen servants and priests. In any other circumstances it would have felt strange to be the object of so many male stares after so long in the Seclusion, but even with Jeddin one of those watching her, the Leopard captain's eyes rapt but his thoughts hidden as though behind a curtain, Qinnitan's gaze was drawn to the man on the white stone bench as though by a lodestone. It was not just the autarch's obvious power that seized her attention, the way the others in the room stayed as close to him as they could while still obviously fearing him, like freezing peasants around a huge bonfire, or even the fierce madness of his eyes, pitiless as a hunting bird's, whose force she could feel even from a dozen paces away. This time, there was another reason for her fascination: except for the golden circlet in his hair and the golden stalls on his fingertips, the autarch was completely naked.

Qinnitan realized that her cheeks were growing hot, as though the god-king really did burn with some kind of flame. She didn't quite know where to look. Nakedness itself did not bother her, even that of a grown man—she had often seen her father and brothers bathe themselves, and the people of Great Xis did not wear much even when they were walking in the crowded, sun-blasted streets—and the autarch's golden-brown limbs although long and thin were by no means ugly. Still, there was a disturbing heedlessness to Sulepis that made his unclothed form seem somehow more like that of an animal that did not know it was naked than a man who knew and reveled in it. There was a shiny film of sweat on all his skin. His member lay against his thighs, limp and long as the snout of some blind thing.

"Ah," the autarch said in a bored tone that didn't match the expression in his eyes, "here she is, the young bride-to-be. Am I not right, Panhyssir? Is this not her?"

"You are right, as always, Golden One." The priest stepped out from behind the slaves with the fans and waited behind the couch.

"And her name was . . . was . . ."

"Qinnitan, Golden One—daughter of Cheshret of the Third Temple."

"Such an unusual name you have, child." The autarch lifted his hand, crooked a long, shining finger at her. "Come closer."

Never in her life had she wanted more fervently to turn and run away as fast as she could, a beast-panic that struck her as shockingly as if a jar of cold water had been dashed against her skin. For a moment she could feel again the endless depths that had suddenly opened before her after drinking the Sun's Blood elixir: it seemed that if she did not do something, she would fall into blackness and never stop falling. Qinnitan stood, desperate to escape although she couldn't quite say why, but in any case unable to do so and fighting for breath.

"Step forward!" Panhyssir said harshly. "The Golden One has spoken to you, girl."

His eyes held hers now and she found herself taking one small step forward, then another. The gold-tipped finger curled and she moved still closer, until she stood beside the couch with the god-king's long face only a handsbreadth or two below her own. She had never seen such eyes, she knew now; she could not imagine such bright, mad depths attached to anything that walked on two legs. Beneath the attar of roses and other perfumes lurked something base and disturbing, a salty tang like blood or even hot metal—the autarch's breath.

"Her parentage shows, I think." The mightiest man on earth reached up his hand to touch her. She flinched, then held steady as his fingertip in its little basket of warm gold mesh drew a line down her cheek that in her imagination rasped her skin and left behind a bloody path. She closed her eyes, feeling as though at any moment some terrible joke would be revealed and someone would step forward, throw her down, and hack off her head. It almost seemed it might come as a relief.

"Open your eyes, girl. Am I so frightening? The Seclusion is full of women who have felt my touch with joy, and many others still praying I will come to them soon."

She looked at him. It was very difficult. There seemed nothing else in the great room—no columns, no guards, nothing but herself and those eyes the color of old linen.

"Do not fear," he said quietly. "Rather, rejoice. You will be the mother of my immortality, little bride-to-be. An honor like no other."

She could not speak, could not even nod until she swallowed down the lump in her throat.

"Good. Do what the old priest bids you and you will have a wedding night that lifts you in glory above all others." He let his hand slide from her face to her breast and she felt her nipples harden as if with fever-chill beneath the thin robe. "Remember, all this belongs to your god." His hand slipped down over her belly, the finger-stalls hard and cruel as a vulture's talons as he carelessly cupped her groin. She could not suppress a little grunt of shock. "Prepare and rejoice."

He let her go and turned away, lifted his hand. A cupbearer sprang forward to give him something to drink.

The autarch was clearly finished with her. Panhyssir clapped and the guards led her toward the door. Qinnitan was trembling so badly as she left the Reclining Chamber that she almost fell and had to be steadied. Beneath her robe she thought she could still feel every instant of his touch, as though his fingers had left a burning stain.

20
Lost in the Moon's Land

MIDDLE OF THE FOREST:

Name the guardian trees—
White Heart, Stone Arm, Hidden Eye, Seed of Stars
Now bow and they bow also, laughing

—from *The Bonefall Oracles*

BARRICK WAS FURIOUS, to be summoned across the huge residence to Avin Brone's chamber in the middle of the night as though he were a mere courtier. He growled at the small boy who opened the lord constable's door when the child did not get out of the way fast enough, but he was disturbed as well by the urgent words of Brone's messenger.

"The lord constable begs you to come to his rooms, Highness," the page had told him. *"He respectfully asks that you come quickly."*

Barrick's sleep had been plagued again, as so often, by evil dreams; as the door opened a sickly fearful part of him wondered if the big man planned some treachery. Barrick almost flinched when the lord constable came across the small sitting room toward him, dressed in a monstrous night-gown, his buckled shoes pulled directly onto his bare feet. When Brone did nothing more suspicious than to bow slightly and hold the door open, another fear occurred to Barrick.

"Where is my sister? Is she well?"

"To the best of my knowledge. I imagine she will arrive any moment."

Brone gestured to a chair, one of two placed side by side. "Please, Highness, sit down. I will explain all." His beard, uncombed and unribboned, strayed all over his face and chest like a wild shrub: apparently whatever had caused this unlikely summons had come after the Lord of Landsend was in bed.

When Barrick had seated himself, Brone lowered his own large frame onto a stool, leaving the other chair empty. "I have sent the boy for some wine. Forgive the meagerness of my hospitality."

Barrick shrugged. "I will take some mulled."

"Good choice. There is an ugly chill in the corridors."

"There certainly is," Briony announced from the doorway. "I'm sure you have good reason for getting me out of my warm bed, Lord Brone."

Briony's huge, hooded velvet mantle did not entirely disguise the fact that she, too, was in her nightdress. Of the three, only Barrick wore day-clothes. He did not like preparing himself for bed, these days, and preferred falling asleep in a chair while still dressed. Somehow it seemed as though that might make it harder for the bad dreams to find him.

"Thank you, Highness." Brone rose again and made a bow before leading Briony to the other chair. He winced a little as he moved. Barrick was at first merely interested—the lord constable had always seemed, like Shaso, a man made of something sterner than mere flesh—but a moment later he felt a pang of worry. What if Brone died? He was not a young man, after all. With their father and the master of arms both prisoners, and Kendrick dead, there were few people left that the Eddons could trust who knew all the political business of Southmarch. Barrick suddenly felt more than ever like a child sent out to do a grown man's chore.

The lord constable must have seen something of this thought in Barrick's face. His smile was grim. "These cold nights are a trial to my old joints, Highness, but nothing I cannot weather. Still, I am glad that you have many, many years ahead of you before you must worry about such things."

Briony seemed more interested in her brother than in the lord constable's infirmities. "Have you not been to bed, Barrick?"

He didn't like being asked in front of Avin Brone, as though she were his older sister, or even his mother, instead of his twin. "I was reading. Does that meet with your approval, Your Highness?"

She flushed a little. "I only wondered . . ."

"I have been meaning to ask you, Princess," the lord constable asked, "whether my niece Rose Trelling was giving you good service." He did not meet her eye. Brone's look was distracted, almost confused, as though they had woken him up rather than the other way around. "We were very grateful for your kindness to her. She is a good girl, if a little silly sometimes."

"I am very happy with Rose." Briony stared at him. "But I cannot believe you woke us after the midnight bell to ask whether my ladies-in-waiting are serving me well."

"Forgive me, Highness, but I am waiting our true business until . . ." The lord constable fell silent, nodding significantly as the page returned with three flagons of wine. The boy knelt by the fire and heated them one by one with a poker, then served Briony first. It was clear Avin Brone wouldn't speak until the boy had left, so they all sat and watched the seemingly endless process, the room silent but for the quiet rumble and crackle of the fire.

When the boy was gone, Brone leaned forward. "Again, I apologize for calling you both here, out of your beds. The fact is, it is easier for me to empty my rooms of listening ears and less conspicuous to do so. If I had come to you and asked for all your pages and maids and guards to be sent away, it would be the talk of the castle tomorrow."

"And you do not think anybody will know or discuss the fact that Barrick and I came across the castle to your rooms?"

"It will not occasion as much speculation. And there is another reason to meet here, which you will see."

"But why this alarm?" Barrick couldn't lose the twist of fear in his guts. Was this what being a king was always like? Fearful midnight summonses? Distrust and doubt all the time? Who would want such a thing? He had a sudden horror—he prayed it was only a horror and not some kind of premonition—of Briony lost or dead and himself left alone to rule. "What is so urgent?" he almost shouted. "What cannot wait for morning and needs to be held secret?"

"Two things, two pieces of information, both of which reached me this evening," said Brone. "One of them will require you to get up, so I will begin with the other while you finish your wine." He took a long swallow from his own flagon. "Thank Erilo for the blessed grape," he said fervently. "If I could not have a cup or two of warm wine at night so I can bend my old legs, I would have to sleep standing up like a horse."

"Talk," said Barrick through clenched teeth.

"Your pardon, Highness." Brone tugged at his gray-shot beard. "Here are the first tidings, whatever they may mean. Gailon Tolly seems to have disappeared."

"What?" Barrick and Briony spoke at the same time. "The Duke of Summerfield?" he asked, unbelieving. *"That* Gailon Tolly?"

Avin Brone nodded. "Yes, my prince. He never reached Summerfield Court."

"But he left here with a dozen armed men," Briony said. "Surely, so many knights can't simply vanish. And we would have heard something from his mother, wouldn't we?"

"That's right," said Barrick. "If anything had happened to Gailon that old cow would be at our gate by now, screaming murder."

The lord constable raised his broad hands in a gesture of helplessness. "They have only just begun to realize at Summerfield Court that he is missing. He sent word by a fast courier when he left here, and they expected him back a week ago, but no one was surprised he hadn't arrived— I imagine they thought he had stopped for some hunting, or to visit one of his . . . his cousins." He looked at Briony, then quickly away. "It was only the day before yesterday that people began to grow alarmed. A horse that belonged to his friend, Evon Kinnay, son of the Baron of Longhowe—you remember young Kinnay, of course . . . ?"

"A weasel," snapped Barrick. "Always going on about how he wanted to become a priest, and touching up the servant girls."

". . . Kinnay's horse, still with saddle and saddle blanket, was found wandering a few miles from the grounds of Summerfield Court. Gailon had mentioned in his letter to his mother that Kinnay was one of the men coming back with him. The Tollys have now searched the area all around the forest. No trace."

Briony put down her wine cup. She looked now like Barrick had felt since he first received Brone's summons. "May the gods preserve us from evil. Do you think it is something like what happened with that merchant caravan? Could it be . . . the Twilight People?"

"But Summerfield Court is miles and miles south of the Shadowline," Barrick hurriedly pointed out. He didn't like the thought of dark things slipping past that barrier and roaming the lands of men. He hadn't had even a single good night since the news of the caravan. "We are much closer than they are."

"Nothing is impossible," admitted Avin Brone. "I want you also to consider the possibility of something closer to home. Gailon Tolly left Southmarch a very angry man—a very powerful man, too, especially now that your brother Kendrick is dead. I do not have to tell you that there are many people of influence in the land who think you two are too young to rule. Some even say that you are my puppets."

"Perhaps you should consider that the next time you make us walk across the castle to your chamber in the middle of the night, Brone." Anger helped Barrick feel a little better—it was like dipping the hot poker into the wine, sharing the heat.

"What does it matter what people think?" his sister demanded. "We did nothing to Gailon! I was glad to see the back of him."

"But think on this," said the lord constable. "Imagine that Gailon appears again some days from now. Imagine that the Tollys cry that you sent soldiers after him to kill him, that you feared his claim on the throne . . ."

"What nonsense! Claim? Gailon has a claim only if our father and all of his family are dead!" Barrick's anger returned, so strong that he had to get up and pace. "That means Briony and I would have to be dead, too. And our stepmother's child as well . . ."

Brone held up a hand, requesting quiet. Barrick stopped talking but could not make himself sit down again. "I only ask you to imagine a possibility, Highnesses. Imagine if Gailon were to reappear in a few weeks and say you tried to murder him—perhaps claim that the two of you were going to avoid paying your father's ransom so you could continue to rule and that he had objected, or something like that."

"That would be treachery—revolution!" Barrick slumped down in his chair again, feeling suddenly weak and miserable. "But how could we prove it wasn't so?"

"That is the problem with rumors," said Avin Brone. "It is very hard to prove that things are *not* true—much more difficult than proving they are."

"But why do you propose such an unlikely possibility?" asked Briony. "I don't much like Gailon, but, surely, even if the Tollys had designs on the throne, he would wait until there is some problem—a bad crop, or a plague of fevers much worse than the one that Barrick and others have had—wait until people are truly frightened before trying to turn them against us? They hardly know my brother and me. We have reigned only scarcely a season."

"Which is exactly why they might believe lies spread about you," said Brone.

Briony frowned. "But even so, aren't you stretching for an answer? If Gailon is truly lost and not just hunting, as people thought, there are a dozen explanations more likely than him preparing to accuse us of trying to harm him."

"Perhaps." The big man stood slowly, putting his hand on the seat of the stool to steady himself. He picked up an oil lamp and the room's shadows writhed. "But now we come to the next part of my concern. Will you come with me?"

They followed him out of the sitting room and down a narrow, unornamented hallway. Brone paused outside a door. "This is why I am not in my own bed tonight, Highnesses." He pushed the door open.

The room was lit by many lamps and candles—far more than would seem normal in a bedchamber. At first, even with all this light, Barrick had trouble making sense of the knot of shapes at the center of the bed: only after a few moments had passed could he see that it was one man kneeling atop the bed next to another, the kneeling one with his head pressed against the other's chest in a pose almost like a lover's embrace. The one on top held a finger against his lips, asking for silence. His lined face was familiar to Barrick, something he thought he had seen in one of the nightmares, and he had to suppress a gasp of fear.

"I think you two must both know Brother Okros of the Eastmarch Academy of scholars," Brone said. "He came to help you when you were ill, Barrick. Now he is caring for . . . for one of my servants."

There was blood on the bed, on the sheets; Brother Okros' hands were wet with it. The monk gave them a quick, distracted smile. "You will forgive me, Highnesses. This man is not yet beyond danger and I am very occupied."

The man on the red-smeared sheets had a dark, untrimmed beard, and his skin, hair, his clothes were all very dirty, but even groomed and clean he would not have made anyone look twice. His eyes were open, staring at the ceiling, his teeth clenched as if to hold in his straining, rasping breath. His shirt had been pulled open and Brother Okros had his fingers deep in a ghastly hole in the man's chest just below the shoulder.

"Just a moment," said the physician-priest, and finally Barrick recalled the voice if not the face, remembered hearing it float through one of his fever dreams, talking about correct alignments and improved balances. "There is a broken arrowhead still lodged here. I . . . ah! There it is." Brother Okros sat up, a pair of bloodied tongs clutched in his fingertips with a small piece of what looked like metal between the tines. "There. At least this will not now make its way to his lungs or his heart." He rolled his patient over, gently but firmly—a deep groan came up from the wounded man, only partially muffled in the bed linens—and began to wipe at another bloody hole above the man's shoulder blade. "This is where it went in—do you see? I will need to pack the wound with comfrey and a willow bark poultice . . ."

Briony's face was pale, as Barrick felt sure his own was, but his sister swallowed and spoke calmly. "Why is this man lying bloodied in your rooms, Lord Brone? And why is Brother . . . Brother Okros . . . tending him? Why not our castle doctor? Chaven has been back several days."

"I will explain everything in a moment, but I wanted you to hear this from the man's own lips. Turn him back over, Okros, I beg of you. Then we will leave you alone to bind his wounds and give him whatever other physick he needs."

Together Brone and the little priest got the bearded man onto his back again. Okros held pieces of cloth tightly against the wounds on both sides.

"Rule," said the lord constable. "It's me, Brone. Do you recognize me?"

The man's eyes flickered across him. "Yes, Master," he grunted.

"Tell me again what you saw at Summerfield Court, Rule. Tell me what sent you riding back here in such a hurry, and probably earned you an arrow in the back." Brone looked at the twins. "This man should have died on the road. Clearly someone thought he would."

Rule groaned again. "Autarch's men," he said at last. "In Summerfield." He fought to moisten his lips, swallowed hard. "The cursed Xixy bastards were . . . honored guests of the old duchess."

"The Autarch's men . . . ? With the Tollys?" Barrick couldn't help looking around as though at any moment the shroud-faced men of his nightmares might appear from the shadows.

"Aye." Brone was grim. "Now come and I will tell you the rest of the tale."

Paying the cold night its due, Brone had wrapped a blanket around his massive shoulders. Half his beard was covered. He looked like a giant from an old story, Barrick thought, like something that gnawed bones and toppled stone walls with his hands.

How much do we really know about him? Barrick was struggling to keep his mind straight. He felt light-headed, as though fever were plucking at him again with fingers both hot and cold. *Our father trusted him, but is that enough? Someone has killed Kendrick. Now Brone tells us that Gailon Tolly has disappeared, and also that Gailon's family makes alliance with the Autarch. What if the criminal is our lord constable himself? I might not like Tolly—in fact, I never liked him or his bloody father, with his red nose and his shouting voice—but is it enough just to take Brone's word or the word of his spy that he's some kind of traitor?*

As if she shared his thoughts, his sister said, "We are certainly grateful for your efforts on behalf of the crown, Count Avin, but this is a bit much to swallow in one mouthful. Who *is* that man on the bed? Why didn't you summon the royal physician?"

"More to the point, where's Gailon?" Barrick asked. "It's convenient that he's not around to defend himself and his family."

What Barrick felt sure was an angry light glinted for a moment in the lord constable's eye. Brone paused to drink more wine; when he spoke, his voice was even. "I cannot blame you for being surprised, Highnesses, or for being mistrustful. And for the last question I have no answers. I wish I did." He scowled. "This has gone cold—the wine, I mean." He stumped to the fireplace and began heating the poker. "As to the other matters, I will tell you and then you must make up your own minds." He grunted, flashed a sour smile. "As you always do.

"The man Rule is, as you've guessed, a spy. He is a rough fellow, not the sort I would prefer to use in a place like Summerfield Court, but I have had to make shift. Do you remember that musician fellow, Robben Hulligan? Red hair?"

"Yes," said Briony. "He was a friend of old Puzzle's. He died, didn't he? Killed by robbers on the South Road last year."

"By robbers . . . perhaps. He died on his way back from Summerfield, within a few weeks after we heard that your father was a prisoner, although even I did not think much of it at the time, except the inconvenience to me. It may or may not surprise you to learn that much of what I knew about the Tollys and Summerfield came from Hulligan. He was close with many in the court there and the old duchess loved him. He was allowed to roam where he pleased, like a pet dog."

"You think . . . you think he was killed? Because he was your spy?"

Brone grimaced. "I do not want to jump at every shadow. The only certain thing is that since Robben's death I have known little about what happens in Summerfield, and it has bothered me enough that I sent Rule. He has many skills and usually has little trouble finding work in a great house—tinkering, fletching, acting the groom."

"These spies," Barrick said slowly. "Do you have them in all the great houses of the March Kingdoms?"

"Of course. And to save you a question, Highness—yes, I have spies in this household as well. I hope you do not think I could do without them. We have already lost one member of the royal family."

"Which your spies did nothing to prevent!"

Brone looked at him coolly. "No, Highness, they did not, and I have lost many nights' sleep thinking about just that, wondering what I might have done more carefully. But that does not change what is before us. Rule is a careful man. If he says there are agents of the Autarch at Summerfield Court, I believe him, and I suggest very strongly you do not dismiss what he has to say."

"Before we go on," Briony said, "I still wish to know why that priest was seeing to him, not Chaven."

Brone nodded. "Fair enough. Here is the answer. Brother Okros was not in the castle when your brother was killed. Chaven was."

"What?" Briony sat up straight. "Do you suspect Chaven of my brother's murder? A brutal stabbing? He is the family physician! Surely if he wanted Kendrick dead, he could poison him, make it appear an illness . . ." She broke off, looking suddenly at her twin. It took him a moment to understand her thoughts.

"But I'm alive," Barrick said. "If someone tried to kill me, they failed." All the same, he did not feel well. Barrick shook his head, wishing he had never come to the lord constable's rooms, that he had stayed in bed, struggling against nightmares that were at least arguably imaginary. "Brone, are you saying that Chaven might have murdered Kendrick, or been in league with whoever did?"

The old man slid the poker into his flagon, then blew the steam away so he could watch the wine bubble. "No. I am saying no such thing, Prince Barrick. But I am saying that I trust almost no one, and until we know who *did* kill your brother, everyone who could come near to him is suspect."

"Including me?" Barrick almost laughed, but he was furious again. "Including my sister?"

"If I had not had you watched, yes." Avin Brone's smile was a grim twitch deep in his beard. "The next in succession are always the likeliest murderers. Take no offense, my lord and lady. It is my duty."

Barrick sat back, overwhelmed. "So we can trust no one except you?"

"Me least of all, Highness—I have been here too long, know too many secrets. And I have killed men in my day." He looked hard at them both, almost challenging them. "If you have no other sources of information than

me, Prince Barrick, Princess Briony, then you are not being careful enough."
He stumped back to his stool. "But whatever else you may learn
tonight, this news of the Autarch's men in Summerfield is very grave,
and of that there is no question. I cannot but fear that Gailon Tolly's disappearance may have something to do with it. And certainly someone
took enough of a dislike to Rule to put an arrow in his back as he rode
up the Three Brothers Road, heading back here. If he were not a tough
old soldier and made mostly of sticks and leather, we would not have this
information."

Briony drank her wine. She was pale, miserable. "This is too much. What
are we to think?"

"Think whatever you like, as long as you do think." Brone grunted in
discomfort as he tried to find a more comfortable position. "Please understand, I have no serious reason to doubt Chaven's loyalty, but it is an unfortunate fact that he is one of the very few people in the castle who knows
much about the Autarch. Did you know his brother was in the Autarch's
service?"

Barrick leaned forward. "Chaven's brother? Is this true?"

"Chaven is Ulosian—you knew that, I'm sure. But you did not know
that his family was one of the first to welcome the Autarch into Ulos, the
first conquest of Xis in our lands of Eion. The story is that Chaven fell out
with his brother and father over just that matter and fled to Hierosol, and
that is why your father King Olin brought him here—because he knows
many things more than just how to physick the ill, not least the gossip that
his own family brought back from the Xixian court. He has never shown
himself to be anything other than loyal, but as I said, from my point of view
it is unfortunate that he is one of the few who knows much of the Autarch.
One of the few others with any direct knowledge is locked in the stronghold even as we speak."

"Shaso," said Briony heavily.

"The same. He fought the Autarch and lost—well, in truth he fought
against this Autarch's father. Then, later, he fought your own father and lost.
Even if Shaso were not in all likelihood your brother's murderer, I do not
know how much use his advice would be—almost anyone can advise on
how to lose battles."

"That is not fair," Briony responded. "No one has beaten Xis—not yet.
So no one can give any better advice, can they?"

"True enough. And that is why we are speaking now, just you two and

I. I fear the threat from the south more than I do any fairies on our doorstep." Brone reached into his pocket and pulled out a pile of creased papers. "You should read this. It is your father's letter to your brother. He mentions the Autarch's growing power."

Briony stared at him. "*You* have the letter!"

"I have only just discovered it." Brone handed her the papers. "There is a page missing. What is gone seems of little import—talk about maintaining the castle and its defenses—but I cannot be sure. Perhaps you will notice something I did not."

"You had no right to read that!" Barrick cried. "No right! That was a private letter from our father!"

The lord constable shrugged. "These days, we cannot afford privacy. I needed to see if there was anything in it that might speak of immediate danger—it has been missing for some time, after all."

"No right," Barrick said bitterly. Was it his imagination, or was Brone looking at him oddly? Had there been something in it that had made the Count of Landsend suspect Barrick's secret?

Briony looked up from the letter. "You said you found it. Where? And how do you know there is a page missing?"

"The letter was in a pile of documents Nynor left for me in my workroom, but he says he knew nothing of it and I think I believe him. I believe someone crept in and slipped it among the other papers on my table, perhaps because they wanted to make it look as though Nynor or myself had taken it in the first place—perhaps even implicate us in . . ." He frowned. "I also read it because I wondered if it had something to do with your brother's death, of course."

"The missing page . . . ?"

He leaned over and shuffled through the pages with his thick forefinger. "There."

"This page ends with Father talking about the fortifications of the inner keep . . ." Briony squinted, turning between the two pages of the letter. "And the next page he is finishing up, asking us to have all those things done. You are right, there is something missing. 'Tell Brone to remember the drains.' What does that mean?"

"Waterways. Some of the gates on the lagoons are old. He was worried that they might be vulnerable in a siege."

"He was worrying about a siege?" Briony said. "Why?"

"Your father is a man who always wishes to be prepared. For anything."

"For some reason, I don't believe you, Lord Brone. About that, anyway."

"You wrong me, Highness, I assure you." The lord constable seemed almost uninterested, too tired to fight.

Barrick, his worst alarm past, was also beginning to feel lethargic. What good all this posturing and imagining? What difference in what their imprisoned father might have written, or what it might have meant? Whoever killed Kendrick had ended the prince regent's life in the midst of all the power of Southmarch, such as it was. *If it was the Autarch, who has already conquered an entire continent and now begins to gulp at this one as well, bite by bite, how can a tiny kingdom like ours hope to save itself?* Only distance had protected them so far, and that would not be a bulwark forever. "So one way or other, there is a traitor in our midst," said Barrick.

"The person who had the letter may have no connection to Prince Kendrick's death, Highness."

"There is another question," Briony said. "Why return it at all? With a page missing, it is as much as proclaiming that someone else has read a letter from the king to the prince regent. Why make that known?"

Avin Brone nodded. "Just so, my lady. Now, if you will pardon me, I will ask you to take the letter with you. You may think of some suitable punishment for my reading it as well, if you choose. I am old and tired and I still must find someplace to sleep tonight—I doubt Brother Okros will let me move Rule out of my bed. If you wish to talk to me about what it says, send for me in the morning and I will come at once." Brone swayed a little; with his great size, he looked like a mountain about to topple and Barrick could not help taking a step backward. "We are come on grave times, Highnesses. I am not the only one relying on you two, for all your youth. Please remember that, Prince Barrick and Princess Briony, and be careful of what you say and to whom."

Courtesy was the victim of exhaustion. He let them find their own way out.

It was not proving easy to make a fire. The forest was damp and there was little deadfall. Ferras Vansen eyed the small pile of gathered wood in the center of their ring of stones and could not help a longing look at the great branches stretching overhead. They had no ax, but surely an hour's sweaty work with their swords and he and Collum Dyer might have all the wood they wanted. But the trees seemed almost to be watching, waiting for some such desecration: he could hear whispers that seemed more than the wind. *We will make do,* he decided, *with deadfall.*

Collum was working hard at the pyramid of sticks with his flint. The noise of the steel striking echoed out through the clearing like the sound of hammers deep in the earth. Vansen couldn't help but think of all the stories of his youth, of the Others who lurked in the shadowy woods and in caves and burrowed in the cold ground.

"Done it." Dyer leaned forward to blow on the smoldering curls of red, puffing until pale flames grew. The mists had cleared a little around them, revealing sky beyond the distant crowns of the trees, a sprinkling of stars in a deep velvety darkness. There was no sign of the moon.

"What time of the clock is it, do you think?" Dyer asked as he sat up. The fire was burning by itself now, but it remained small and sickly, shot through with odd colors, greens and blues. "We have been here for hours and it is still evening."

"No, it's a bit darker." Vansen raised his hands before the fire; it gave off only a little heat.

"I can't wait for bloody daylight." Dyer chewed on a piece of dried meat. "I can't wait."

"You may not get it." Vansen sighed and sat back. A wind he couldn't feel made the tops of the trees wave overhead. The campfire, weak as it was, seemed a kind of a wound in the misty, twilit clearing. He couldn't help feeling the forest wished to heal that breach, to grow back over it, swallowing the flames and the two men, scabbing the injury over with moss and damp and quiet darkness. "I do not think it is ever full daylight here."

"The sky is above us," said Dyer firmly, but there was a brittle sound to his voice. "That means the sun will be there when day comes, even if we can't see it. Not all the mists in the world can change that."

Vansen said nothing to this. Collum Dyer, veteran of many campaigns, dealer and risker of death, was as frightened as a child. Vansen, an elder brother in his own family, knew you did not argue with a frightened child about small matters until the danger had passed.

Small matters. Like never seeing the sun again.

"I will take first watch tonight," he said aloud.

"We must keep calling for the others." Dyer rose and walked to the edge of the clearing, cupping his hands. *"Halloooo! Adcock! Southstead! Halloooo!"*

Ferras Vansen couldn't help flinching at the noise, which was quickly swallowed by the trees. His every instinct told him to stay quiet, to move slowly, not to attract attention. *Like a mouse on a tabletop,* he thought, and was bitterly amused. *Don't want to wake anyone.* "I think by now the others must have made camp," he said. "And if shouting were enough, they would have found us hours ago."

Dyer came back and sat by the fire. "They will find us. They are looking for us. Even Southstead, although you might doubt it, Captain. The royal guard won't walk away while two of their number are lost."

Vansen nodded, but he was thinking something quite different. He suspected that somewhere the rest of the guards and poor Raemon Beck and the mad girl were just as lost and frightened as he and Dyer. He hoped they had the sense to stay put and not to wander. He was beginning to understand a little of what happened to the girl, and even to the madman in his own childhood village who had come back from beyond the Shadowline.

"Try to sleep, Collum. I'll take first watch."

At first he thought it merely a continuation of the strange dreams that had seeped into his increasingly desperate attempts to stay awake. It was not full night-dark—he sensed it would never be fully dark because the mists were shot through with the glow of the moon, which had at last appeared in the sky above the trees, round and pale as the top of a polished skull—but it was definitely the dog-end of night. He should have woken Dyer hours ago. He had fallen asleep, a dangerous thing to do in such a strange place, leaving the camp unguarded. Or was he asleep still? It seemed so, because even the wind seemed to be quietly singing, a wordless chant, rising and falling.

Something was moving in the trees along the edge of the clearing.

His breath caught. Vansen fumbled for his sword, reached out with his other hand to wake Collum Dyer, but his companion was gone from the spot where he had lain sleeping only a short while earlier. Vansen had only a few heartbeats to absorb the terror of that discovery, then the movement at the clearing's rim became a white-shrouded, hooded figure, as strangely translucent as a distillation of mists. It seemed to be a woman, or at least it had a woman's shape, and for a moment he was filled with the unlikely hope that the girl Willow had gone sleep-wandering from the guards' camp, that the rest of the company were somewhere nearby after all and Dyer had been right. But the hairs rising on the back of his neck proved it was a lie even before he saw that the figure's feet did not touch the earth below her faintly shimmering gown.

"Mortal man." The voice was in his head, behind his eyes, not in his ears. He could not say whether it was old or young or even male or female. *"You do not belong here."* He tried to speak but couldn't. He could see little more of her face than pallid light and faint shadows, as though it were hidden behind many veils of glimmering fabric. All that was truly visible were her eyes, huge and black and not at all human. *"The old laws are ended,"* the specter told him. The world seemed to have collapsed into a single dark tunnel with the luminous, vague face at the other end. *"There are no riddles left to solve. There are no tasks by which favors can be won. All is moving toward an ending. The shadow-voices that once cried against it have gone silent in the House of the People."*

The figure moved nearer. Vansen could feel his heart thundering in his breast, beating so hard that it seemed it must shake him to pieces, but yet he could not by choice move a single muscle. A gauzy hand reached out, touched his hair, almost seemed to pass through him, cool and yet prickly along his cheek like sparks from a campfire settling on damp skin.

"I knew one like you once." Some tone was in the voice that he almost recognized, but in the end the emotion was too strange to grasp. *"Long he stayed with me until his own sun had worn away. In the end he could not remain."* As the face loomed closer it seemed charged with moonlight. Vansen wanted to close his eyes but could not. For a brief instant he thought he could see her clearly, although what or who he was seeing he couldn't entirely understand—a beauty like the edge of a knife, black eyes that were somehow full of light like the night sky full of stars, an infinitely sad smile—yet during that moment it also felt as though a chilly hand had tightened on his heart, squeezing it into an awkward shape from which it would never completely recover. He was gripped as though by death itself . . . but death was fair, so very fair. Ferras Vansen's soul leaped toward the dark eyes, toward the stars of her gaze, like a salmon climbing a mountain rill, not caring whether death was at the end of it.

"Do not look for the sun, mortal." He thought there was something like pity in the words and he was dashed. He didn't want pity—he wanted to be loved. He wanted only to die being loved by this creature of vapor and moonlight. *"The sun will not come to you here. Neither can the shadows be trusted to tell you anything but lies. Look instead to the moss on the trees. The roots of the trees are in the earth, and they know where the sun is, always, even in this land where his brother is the only lord."*

And then she was gone and the clearing was empty except for the quiet hiss of wind in the leaves. Vansen sat up gasping, heart still stuttering. Had it been a dream? If so, part of it had proved true, anyway—there was no sign of Dyer. Vansen looked around, dazed at first, but with increasing fear. The fire was all but out, little glowing worms of red writhing in the blackness inside the stone circle.

Something crackled behind him and he leaped up, fumbling at the hilt of his sword. A figure staggered into the clearing.

"Dyer!" Vansen lowered his blade.

Collum Dyer shook his head. "Gone." The soldier's voice was mournful. "I could not catch up to . . ." Now he seemed to see Vansen truly for the first time and his face twisted into a mask of secrecy. For an instant Ferras Vansen thought he could read the other man's clear thoughts, see him decide not to share his own vision.

"Are you well?" Vansen demanded. "Where were you?"

Dyer made his way slowly back to the fire. He would not meet his captain's eye. "Well enough. Had . . . a dream, I suppose. Woke up wandering." He eased himself down and covered himself with his cloak and wouldn't talk anymore.

Vansen lay down, too. One of them should keep watch, he knew, but he felt as though he had been touched by something wild and strong, and was somehow certain that touch would keep other things of this place at bay . . . for this night anyway.

He was as tired as if he had run for miles. He fell asleep quickly beneath the trees and the strange stars.

Ferras Vansen woke to the same dim gray light—a little more milky, perhaps, but nothing like morning. The wind was still talking wordlessly. Collum Dyer had slept like a dead man, but he awakened like a sick child, full of moans and sullen looks.

The words of the midnight visitant, whether ghost or dream, were still in Vansen's head. He allowed Dyer time only to empty his bladder, waiting impatiently in the saddle while the soldier did up the strings of his breeches.

"Can't we even light a fire?" Dyer asked. "Just to warm my hands. It's so bloody cold."

"No. By time we make one, we will be tired again, and then we will sleep. We will never get away. We will stay here while this forest swirls around us like an ocean and drowns us." He did not know exactly what he meant, but he felt it unquestionably to be true. "We must ride while we can, before the place sucks away all our resolve."

Dyer looked at him strangely. "You sound as though you know a great deal about this country."

"As much as I need to." He didn't like the accusing tone in the man's voice, but didn't want to be pulled into an argument. "Enough to know I do not wish to end up like that girl-child Willow, wandering mad in the woods."

"And how will we find our way out again? We searched for hours. We're lost."

"I was raised on the edge of these woods, or at least something like them." He suddenly wondered whether they were even in the world he knew, or wandering in a place more distant than the land of the gods. It was a harrowing thought. What had the phantom said? *" . . . Even in this land where his brother is the only lord."* Whose brother? The sun's? But the moon was a goddess, surely—white-breasted Mesiya, great Perin's sister . . .

It was too much to think about. Vansen forced himself back to what was before them now, the hope of escape. It was hard to think, though—the voice of the wind was ever-present and insinuating, urging sleep and surrender. "The moss will grow thickest on the southern side of the trees," he said. "If we continue south long enough, surely we will find our way back into wholesome lands again."

"Leaving this place behind," Dyer said quietly, thoughtfully. It was strange, but to Vansen he sounded almost unwilling, a notion that sent a pulse of fear chasing up the guard captain's backbone.

The morning, or at least the stretch of hours after waking, slid by quickly. There was moss everywhere, on almost every tree, deep woolly green patches. If it grew more thickly on one side than another, it was a minute difference; after a while, Vansen began to doubt his own ability to distinguish. Still, he had no other plan and he was growing increasingly frightened. They had lost the road in a thicket of black-leaved trees too thick to pass and they had not found it again. He had not seen a single thing that looked familiar. It was hard not to feel that the forest was continuing to grow around him, that its borders were stretching outward faster than he and Dyer could ride, and that not only wouldn't they find their way out again, the shadow-forest would soon cover everything he had ever known, like wine from an upended jug spreading across a tabletop.

Dyer's mood also worryed him. The bearded guardsman had grown increasingly more distant, even as their horses strode shoulder to shoulder; he hardly spoke to his captain, but talked much to himself and sang snatches of old songs that Vansen felt he should recognize but didn't. Also, the man kept looking at him oddly, as though Dyer were harboring doubts of his own—as if he no longer quite recognized someone who had been his daily companion for years.

There is something in the air here, Vansen thought desperately. *Something in the shadows of these trees. This place is eating us.* It was a terrible idea, but once it lodged in his mind, he could not shift it. He had a dreamlike vision of himself and Dyer lying beside the lost road, dead and decaying like the woman he had once found in her cottage, yet it was not insects that would devour them but the forest itself—tendrils of green growing into their mouths and noses and ears, seeds sprouting out damp, dark vegetation from their bellies and skulls, filling the vaults of their rib cages.

Maybe it is a true vision, he thought suddenly. *Perhaps we are already dead, or nearly so. Perhaps our bodies are already disappearing under the moss and we only dream we are riding on through this dark land beneath the endless, gods-cursed trees . . .*

"I feel the fires," Dyer said abruptly.

"What fires?" The horses had stopped; they stood weirdly still and silent. A forested valley leaned close above the two guardsmen on either side, as though they were in the mouth of some huge thing that in a moment would close its jaws and shut them away from the light forever.

"The forge fires," the bearded guardsman replied in a distant voice. "The ones that burn under Silent Hill. They make weapons of war, Bright Fingers, Chant-Arrows, Wasps, Cruel Stones. The People are awake. They are awake."

As he struggled to make sense of Dyer's bizarre statement, Vansen felt a sharp but noiseless wind come hurrying down the canyon. The mists swirled upward, rising and parting, and for a brief instant he thought he could see an entire city at the top of the valley, a city that was also part of the forest, a mass of dark trees and darker walls, the two almost indistinguishable, with lights burning in a thousand windows. His horse reared and turned away from the vision, dashing back down the path they had followed. He heard Dyer's horse's hoofbeats close behind him, and another sound, too.

His companion was singing quietly but exuberantly in a language Vansen had never heard.

★   ★   ★

Dyer was still behind him, but silent now: he wouldn't answer any of his captain's questions, and Vansen had given up asking, simply grateful not to be alone. The twilight had grown thicker. The guard captain could no longer distinguish any difference in the thickness of the moss on the trees—could barely tell the trees from the darkness. The voices in the wind had crawled deep inside his head now, cajoling, whispering, weaving fragments of melody through his thoughts that tangled his ideas just as the thickening brambles tugged at their horses' hooves, making them walk slower and slower.

"They are coming," Dyer abruptly announced in the voice of a frightened dreamer. "They are marching."

Ferras Vansen did not need to ask him what he meant: he could feel it, too, the tightening of the air around them, the deepening of the twilight gloom. He could hear the triumph in the wordless wind-voices, although he still couldn't hear the voices themselves except where they echoed deep in the cavern of his skull.

His horse abruptly reared, whinnying. Caught by surprise, Vansen tumbled out of the saddle and crashed to the ground. The horse vanished into the forest, kicking and bounding through the undergrowth, grunting in terror. For a moment Vansen was too stunned to rise, but a hand clutched him and dragged him to his feet. It was Collum Dyer, his horse gone now, too. The guardsman's face was alight with something that might have been joy, but also looked a little like the terror that Vansen himself was feeling, a pall of dread that made him want to throw himself back down on the ground and bury his head in the spongy grass.

"Now," Dyer said. *"Now."*

And suddenly Ferras Vansen could see the road again, the road they had sought for hours without success. It was only a short distance away, winding through the trees—but he barely noticed it. The road was full of rolling mist, and in that mist he could see shapes. Some of the figures, unless the mist distorted them, were treetop-tall, and others impossibly wide, squat, and powerful. There were shadow-shapes that corresponded to no sane reality, and things less frightening but still astonishing, like human riders dimly seen but achingly beautiful, sitting high and straight on horses that stamped and blew and made the air steam. Many of the riders bore lances that glittered like ice. Pennants of silver and marshy green-gold waved at their tips.

An army was passing, hundreds and perhaps thousands of shapes riding, walking—some even flying, or so it seemed: teeming shadows fluttered and soared above the great host, catching the moonglow on their wings like a handful of fish scales flung glittering into the air. But although Vansen could feel the tread of all those hooves and feet and paws and claws in his very bones, the host made no sound as it marched. Only the voices on the wind rose in acclaim as the great troop passed.

How long was a sleep? How long was death? Vansen did not know how much time passed as he stood in amazement, too moonstruck even to hide, and watched the host pass. When it had gone, the road lay all but naked, clothed only in a few tatters of mist.

"We must . . . follow them," Vansen said at last. It was hard, painfully hard, to find words and speak them. "They are going south. To the lands of men. We will follow them to the sun."

"The lands of men will vanish."

Vansen turned to see that Collum Dyer's eyes were tightly closed, as though he had some memory locked behind his eyelids that he wished to save forever. The soldier was trembling in every limb and looked like a man cast down from the mountain of the gods, shattered but exultant.

"The sun will not return," Dyer whispered. "The shadow is marching."

21
The Potboy's Dolphin

THE PATH OF THE BLUE PIG:

Down, down, feathers to scales
Scales to stone, stone to mist
Rain is the handmaiden of the nameless

—from *The Bonefall Oracles*

THERE WAS A TOWER in Qul-na-Qar whose name meant something like "Spirits of the Clouds" or "The Spirits in the Clouds," or perhaps even "What the Clouds Think"—it was never easy to make mortal words do the dance of Qar thought—and it was there the blind king Ynnir went when he sought true quiet. It was a tall tower, although not the tallest in Qul-na-Qar: one other loomed above all the great castle like an upheld spear, a slender spike that was simply called "The High Place," but its history was dark since the Screaming Years and even the Qar did not visit it much, or even look up at it through the fogs that usually surrounded their greatest house.

Ynnir din'at sen-Qin, Lord of Winds and Thought, sat in a simple chair before the window of one of Cloud-Spirit Tower's two highest rooms. His tattered garments fluttered a little in the winds but he was otherwise motionless. It was a clear day, at least by the standards of Qul-na-Qar: although as always there was no sun visible in the gray sky, the afternoon's sharp winds had chased away the mists: the slender figure who waited patiently in the chamber's doorway for Ynnir to speak could see all the rooftops of the vast castle spread out below in a muted rainbow of different shades of black and deep gray, glittering darkly from the morning's rains.

The one who waited was patient indeed: nearly an hour passed before the blind king at last stirred and turned his head. "Harsar? You should have spoken, old friend."

"It is peaceful to look out the window."

"It is." Ynnir made a gesture, a complex movement of fingers that signified gratitude for small things. "All morning I listened to the anger of the Gathering, all that arguing about the Pact of the Glass, and thought about the time when I would come here, away from it all, and feel the breeze from M'aarenol on my face." He lifted his fingers and touched them to his eyes once, twice, then a third time, all with the precision of ritual. "I still see what was outside it on the day I lost my sight."

"It has not changed, Lord."

"Everything has changed. But, come, you have waited for me patiently, Harsar-so. I do not believe the view alone has brought you here."

Harsar inclined his hairless head ever so slightly. He was of the Stone Circle People, a small, nimble folk, but was tall for his kind: when Ynnir rose and Harsar stepped forward to help him, his head reached almost to the king's shoulder. "I have good news, Lord."

"Tell me."

"Yasammez and her host have crossed the frontier."

"So quickly?"

"She is very strong, that one. She has been waiting long years for this, preparing."

"Yes, she has." The king nodded slowly. "And the mantle?"

"She carries it with her, at least for now, but the scholars in the Deep Library think it will not sustain itself if stretched too far. But everywhere she has raided the mantle has spread, reclaiming that which is ours, and even when it will spread no farther, she will go on with fire and talon and blade." Even patient Harsar could not keep his voice altogether even; a hint of exultation writhed in his words. "And everywhere she goes, the sunlanders will wail behind her, searching for their dead."

"Yes." Ynnir stood silent for a long time. "Yes. I thank you for these tidings, Harsar-so."

"You do not seem as pleased as I would have thought, Lord." The councillor was startled by his own words and lowered his head. "Ah, ah. Please forgive my discourtesy, Son of the First Stone. I am a fool."

The king lifted a long-fingered hand, made a gesture that signaled "acceptable confusion." "You have nothing to apologize for, friend. I simply have much to consider. Yasammez is a mighty weapon. Now that she has been loosed, all the world will change." He turned his head toward the window once more. "Do me the favor of excusing me, Harsar-so. It was good of you to come so far to give me this news." His long face was grave and still; a hovering mote of light like a pale lavender firefly had begun to flicker above his head. "I must think. I must . . . sleep."

"Forgive me for imposing myself, great Ynnir. Will you permit one more unforgivable imposition? May I offer my company on your journey down to your chambers? The stairs are still damp."

A tiny smile came to the blind king's face. "You are kind, but I will sleep here."

"Here?" There was only one couch in the Cloud-Spirit Tower and it was a place of power, of shaped and directed dreams. A moment later, the man of the Stone Circle People brought his hand to his mouth. "Forgive me, Lord! I do not mean to question you again. I am a fool today, a fool."

This time Ynnir's response was a degree or two closer to frost. "Do not distress yourself, Councillor. I will be well."

Harsar bowed and bowed again, backing out of the room so quickly that an observer might have feared the councillor himself was in greater danger of tumbling down the long, steep stairwell than the blind king, but he spun neatly on his heel at the edge of the steps before starting his descent. Many of the towers of Qul-na-Qar had stairs that yielded quiet music, and of course the infamous steps of the High Place moaned softly, like children in troubled sleep, but the stairway of Cloud-Spirit Tower surrendered no noise except that of a visitor's tread. Ynnir listened to his councillor's velvet-soft footfalls grow fainter and fainter until he could no longer hear them above the skirling wind.

Ynnir din'at sen-Qin moved through a door in the wall that separated this highest place in the tower into two rooms. That other chamber, that twinned space, had its own window, facing not across the expanse of the castle and its countless rooftops glinting wet as beach stones but away into the misty south—toward the Shadowline and the great host of Lady Yasammez and the lands of mortals. Like the other room, it was sparsely furnished. That room had a chair: this one had a low bed. The king lay down on it, lavender light glittering above his brow, then folded his arms across his breast and began to dream.

Chert had barely slept at all. The long watches of the night had passed like guests who sensed they were unwelcome and were all the slower to leave because of it.

We're caught up in bad things. It was in his every thought. For the first time he understood what the big folk must mean when they asked him how he could stand to live in a cave under the ground. But it was not the stone of Funderling Town that oppressed him any more than a fish was oppressed by water; it was the feeling that he and his small family were surrounded and enwebbed by a faceless, invisible *something,* and it was precisely because he did not know what it was that he felt so miserable, so helpless. *We're caught up in bad things and they're getting worse.*

"What in the name of the Mysteries are you up to?" Opal's voice was muzzy with sleep. "You've been twitching all night."

He was tempted to tell her it was nothing, but despite their occasional squabbling, Chert was not one of those fellows who felt more comfortable in the company of other men than with his own wife. They had come far together and he knew he needed not only her comfort, but her good wits, too. "I can't sleep, Opal. I'm worried."

"What about?" She sat up and pushed at the strands of hair escaping from her nightcap. "And don't talk so loud—you'll wake the boy."

"The boy is part of what worries me." He got up, padded to the table, and picked up the jar of wine. Funderlings seldom used lamps in their own homes, making do with the dim, dim glow spilling in from the street lanterns, and found it amusing that the big folk couldn't seem to blunder around aboveground without a blaze of light. He took a cup from the mantel shelf. "Do you want some wine?" he asked his wife.

"Why would I want wine at this hour?" But her voice was definitely as worried as his, now. "Chert, what's wrong?"

"I'm not sure. Everything, really. The boy, those Rooftoppers, what Chaven said about the Shadowline." He brought his cup of wine back to bed and slid his feet under the heavy quilt. "It wasn't simply an accident that child appeared, Opal. That he was brought out of that place and dumped here on the very same day I find that the Shadowline has moved for the first time in years."

"It's not the boy's fault!" she said, her voice rising despite her own injunction to quiet. "He's done nothing wrong. Next you're going to say he's some kind of . . . spy, or demon, or . . . or a wizard in disguise!"

"I don't know what he is. But I know that I'm not going to go another night wondering what's in that bag around his neck."

"Chert, you can't. We have no right . . . !"

"That's nonsense, woman, and you know it. This is our house. What if he brought home a poisonous snake—a fireworm or somesuch? Would we have to let him keep it?"

"That's just silly . . ."

"Well, it's at least as silly when there are dangers all around, when the Twilight People may walk right out of the old stories and come knocking at our very doors, to pretend as though this was an ordinary time and ordinary circumstances. We found him, Opal, we didn't birth him. We don't know anything about who he is—or even *what* he is—except that he came from behind the Shadowline. You didn't see the way those Rooftoppers treated him—like he was an old friend, an honored ally . . ."

"He helped one of them. You said so!"

"And he's carrying something we haven't looked at that might tell us about his past."

"You don't know that."

"No, and you don't know that it doesn't. Why are you fighting me, Opal? Are you so afraid we might lose him?"

There were tears in her eyes—he needed no light to know that: he could hear it in her voice. "Yes! Yes, I'm afraid we might lose him. And mostly because you wouldn't care if we did!"

"What?"

"You heard me. You treat him well enough because you're a kind man, but you don't . . . you don't . . . you don't love him." She was fighting to be able to speak now. "Not like I do."

For a moment anger and astonishment ran together in him. She turned onto her side. Her sobs shook the mattress and something in the broken-hearted sound of it pushed everything else away. This was his Opal, weeping, terrified. He curled his arms around her.

"I'm sorry, my old darling. I'm sorry." He heard himself saying it, regretted it even as the words left his mouth. "Don't worry, I . . . I won't let anyone take him from you."

★   ★   ★

"Isn't there any other way?" she asked. They had lit one of the smallest lamps; her face was red and her eyes swollen. "It seems a terrible thing to do—it seems wrong."

"We are parents now," Chert said. "I suspect we must get used to feeling terrible about some things we must do. I suspect it is the tunnel-toll for having a child."

"That's just like you," she whispered, half angry, half not. "Anything you take up, you decide you know all about it. Just like with those racing moles."

The sleeping boy, who as usual had kicked his blanket off, was lying belly-down, face turned to the side like a swimmer taking a breath, pale hair white as frost. Chert stared with a mixture of fondness and fear. He knew he had just signed a treaty of sorts, that in return for getting a look at the contents of the sack he had as good as promised that whatever they might be, he would abide by Opal's judgment. And he knew in his heart that unless they found evidence that the child had actually committed murder—and not just any old murder, but something important and recent— she would not consider it grounds to send the boy away.

How did that happen so quickly? Chert wondered. *Are all women like that— ready to love a child, any child, just as a hand is ready to grasp or an eye ready to see? Why don't I feel the same way?* Because although he knew he truly did care for the child, there was nothing in him like the fierce possessiveness that his wife felt, the almost helpless need. *Does she burn too hot? Or is my heart too cold?*

Still, watching as the boy moaned a little and shifted, looking at the help-less, smoothly vulnerable neck, the open mouth, he found himself hoping that they discovered nothing damning.

Someone is using this child. Chert suddenly felt certain of this, but did not know why he thought so or what it meant. *For good or for ill, there is another will behind him. But what is he? A weapon? A messenger? An observer?*

Confused by these thoughts, Chert got down on his knees and carefully slid one hand under the shirt the boy used as a cushion. His fingers touched something solid, but Flint's head rested firmly on top of it; he would rouse the boy if he tried to pull it free. He put a hand under the child's shoulder and gently pushed.

"You'll wake him up . . . !" Opal whispered.

Would that be so bad? Chert wondered. There was no reason they needed to hide what they were doing, surely. In fact, he would have gladly waited until morning, except that he knew he would not sleep if he did. Still, as the boy yawned and rolled onto his side, allowing Chert to pull the sack and its cord out from under the rolled shirt, he did feel more than a little like a thief.

At least he hasn't hidden it, Chert thought. *That's a good sign, isn't it? If he knew it was something bad, he would hide it, wouldn't he . . . ?*

Chert carried it out of their bedchamber to the table, Opal as close behind him as if it were not simply a possession of Flint's but an actual piece of the boy. Chert had been distracted last time by the discovery of the strange stone, the one that he had passed to Chaven. Now he examined the bag all over again. It was the size of a hen's egg but almost flat, only as thick as a finger. The needlework was exquisite and complex, in many colors of thread, but the design was a pattern, not a picture, and told him very little. "Have you ever seen work like that?"

Opal shook her head. "Some eyestitch from Connord I saw in the market once, but that was much simpler."

Chert took it gently in his hands, prodded at it with his finger. It gave beneath his touch with a faint, springy crunch, but there was something hard at the middle of it, hard like bone. "Where's my knife?"

"That clumsy thing?" Opal was already walking across the room toward her sewing box. "If you're going to steal the boy's possessions and cut them open, you don't have to do it like some butcher's prentice." She returned and lifted out a tiny blade with a handle of polished maker's-pearl. "Use this. No, I've changed my mind. Give it back. I'll be the one who has to sew the thing up again after you've finished poking around in it."

Assuming it's something that can be put back in a sack as though nothing has happened, Chert thought but didn't say. The boy himself certainly hadn't been like that, so why should this be different?

Opal carefully sliced away a few of the threads down one side, where the ornamental stitchery was minimal. Chert had to admit that he wouldn't have thought of that, that he would have opened the top and spoiled much more of the embroidery.

"What if . . . what if the stitchery itself is some kind of shadow-magic?" he said suddenly. "What if we've spoiled it by cutting it, and whatever's inside won't be held in there anymore?" He didn't know exactly what he was he trying to say but in these deep hours of the night it was hard not to feel they were trespassing on unfamiliar and perhaps hostile ground.

Opal gave him a sour look. "That's just like you to think of that *after* I've started." But she paused, and suddenly her face was worried. "Do you think there's something alive in here? Something that . . . that bites?"

"Give it to me, then," Chert said, trying to make a joke of it. "If someone has to lose a finger, it shouldn't be the one who's going to sew the thing up again."

He squeezed it a little to force the snipped seam open, held it up to the light. All he could see was something that looked like bits of dried flowers and leaves. He leaned forward and sniffed it cautiously. The scent was exotic and unrecognizable, a mix of spicy odors. He probed inside with his finger, trying to be gentle, but he was crushing the dried plant material and the smell was getting stronger. At last he touched something hard and flat. He tried to pull it out, but it was almost the same size as the sack.

"You'll have to cut more threads," he said, handing it back to Opal.

She sniffed the open side. "Moly and bleeding-heart. But that's not all. I don't recognize the rest." When she had widened the gap all the way down to the bottom and even a little beyond, Chert took it back.

He pulled, gently. Dried petals fell to the table. He pulled again and at last the object slid out. It was an oval of polished white—a quick glance told him it was made not of stone but something more recently and aggressively animated—which had been carved in a decorative manner that, like the embroidery, was not meant to represent anything obvious. For a moment he could only stare at it in surprise—why would anyone spend so much care carving and polishing a simple round of ivory or bone like this?—but Opal took it for a moment, nodded, then put it back on his palm, this time with the other side facing up.

"It's a mirror, you old fool." There was relief in her voice. "A hand mirror like a highborn lady might have. I daresay your Princess Briony owns a few of these."

"*My* Princess Briony?" He fell into their old rhythms because it was the easiest thing to do; he, too, was relieved, although not as completely as his wife. "She'll be very entertained to hear that, I'm sure." He stared at the mirror, lifted it up, turned it until it caught the reflection of the lamp. It did seem quite ordinary. "But why does the boy have a mirror?"

"Oh, can't you see?" Opal shook her head at his obtuseness. "It is as clear as skyglass. This must have belonged to his . . . his true mother." She did not like saying the words, but she continued bravely. "She likely gave it to him as . . . a sort of reminder. Perhaps she was in danger and they had only a few moments before she had to send him away. She wanted whoever found him to know that he came of a good family, that his mother had loved him."

"It seems strange," Chert said, unable to hide his disbelief completely, "that a woman would keep her mirror sewed up so tightly in a bag."

"She wouldn't! She sewed it up so that he wouldn't lose it."

"So you're saying that a noblewoman with only moments left to spend with her little son—perhaps with her castle under siege and on fire, like in one of those big-folk ballads that you like to listen to when we go to the market upground—took the time to sew this bag shut with these careful little stitches?"

"You're just trying to make trouble about it." Opal sounded amused, not irritated. She could afford to be magnanimous, since she had obviously won the day. It was only a mirror, not a ring with a family crest or a letter detailing Flint's heritage or confessing a dreadful crime. Just to make sure, Chert pulled the rest of the dried leaves and flowers out onto the tabletop while Opal made little tutting sounds, but there was nothing else in the sack.

"If you are quite finished making a mess, give all that to me." The glow of triumph was unmistakable now. "I have a lot of work to do to make that right again before the boy wakes up. You might as well go back to bed, old man."

And he did. But he still did not sleep, although it was not the quiet sounds Opal made as she plied her needle that kept Chert awake. What was in the sack had not turned out to be something terrible. Nothing would change, at least not for the moment. But that was part of the problem.

I will tell Chaven about it when next I get the chance. He was tired, so tired, and desperate for sleep. He was even more desperate to believe that Opal was right, that there was nothing to worry about, but something still nagged at him. *Yes, Chaven, if he'll see me. He didn't seem very pleased with my company the last time. But there is no one else to ask. Yes, Chaven is versed in such things. Perhaps he can tell me what it might signify—whether a mirror could be anything more than simply a mirror . . .*

Briony had been carrying it for hours, looking at the familiar handwriting again and again, as though it were her father's actual face and not merely words he had written. She had not realized how much she missed him until she had read it, and in reading it she had heard his dear voice speaking to her as though he were in the room with her instead of hundreds of miles away and half a year gone. Could such a homely, intimate thing have possibly been the cause of Kendrick's murder?

But for an object so freighted with family sorrow, its meaning was somewhat opaque. It did speak of the Autarch, as Brone had said, and of King Olin's concerns about the southern conqueror.

"Here we come to the meat of your father's concern, Kendrick, my son,"

she read for the sixth or seventh time,

"which is that all the talk of the Autarch's spreading empire that has come north to us is not exaggerated. All the continent of Xand above the great White Desert has fallen under the sway of Xis, and while his father and grandfather were content merely to conquer and exact tribute, this newest Autarch is not a gentle ruler to these subjects. It is said that he considers himself not just king but god, and that all these subject lands must worship him as the true child of the sun itself—yes, the sun that shines in the sky! He has not yet pressed such harsh demands on our cities and states of Eion that have fallen to his influence, but I cannot doubt he will want the same from them when his grip has become adequately tight.

"Do not think, however, that because he is mad he is also foolish. This Autarch was forged of hot metal indeed. He was born Sulepis, third youngest of twenty-six brothers in the royal family of Xis—a nest of vipers that became legendary even in troubled Xis, which has never had any shortage of savagery and murder among its ruling clans. The stories say that only one of his brothers, the youngest of the family, was still alive when Sulepis finally ascended to the throne a year after their father's death. After this younger brother set the crown on Sulepis' head at the coronation, the poor wretch was taken away and dipped into molten bronze. After the tortured figure cooled, the Autarch had it set in front of the royal palace. A traveler told me that the Autarch likes to tell horrified visitors this ornament is meant to represent The Importance of Family.

"His grip on Xand is nearly complete, but although he has made conquests in Eion, they are all small states with poor harbors or no harbor at all. He knows that none of them will provide him a suitable base for an invasion, and that without a secure foothold his conscripted army, no matter how large, will not defeat determined men fighting for their own lands, especially if Syan and Jellon and the March Kingdoms stand together . . ."

* * *

Briony put the letter down, as angry as the first time she read it. Jellon— that swamp of treachery! How like her father, to continue to believe even as he languished in prison because of Jellon's greed, that he could convince that pig King Hesper to do the right thing, to make common cause against a greater enemy.

And he probably will convince him, given enough time, Briony thought. *Then what will I do? What if we do make common cause and they send that oily Count Angelos back here, and I must treat him as an ally instead of sticking my sword in his heart as I would rather?* She promised herself she would go to the armory this afternoon and practice with the blade for a while. If Barrick still felt too ill to trade blows, she could always spend an hour pretending that the sawdust-stuffed dummy was Angelos or his master Hesper. It would be good to hit something.

As for the letter's missing section, she couldn't guess what might have drawn someone to steal it. From what she could make of the beginning and the end, it seemed only to have been a general and workaday conversation about maintaining the castle walls and gates. Could some spy of the Autarch's, or some nearer enemy, have taken it because they thought Olin might mention some weakness in Southmarch's defenses? How could they think her father would be foolish enough to trust information that might endanger his family and home to the hands of Ludis Drakava's envoy? They didn't know him. As Brone had said, Olin Eddon was a man who took nothing for granted.

She skipped down to the bottom of the letter, although she knew it would make her cry again to read his farewell.

"And give my best love to Briony, too, tell her that I am sorry I am detained and cannot be there for the birthday she and Barrick share. There is a cat here in this rather drafty old castle who has taken to sleeping at the foot of my bed, and by the way she has grown stout, I suspect soon she will become a mother. Tell Briony that not only will I come back to my family presently, I will bring with me a small surprise, and that she may spoil it all she likes, because unlike dogs or most children, a cat cannot be ruined by too much affection."

She was pleased with herself. She didn't cry. Or at least, only a few drops, and they were easily wiped away before Rose or Moina returned.

★ ★ ★

Despite his useless arm, Barrick's greater strength ordinarily made him more than her equal at swordplay, but her brother was still feeling the effects of his illness: his face quickly grew flushed, and before very long he was breathing harshly. Slower than usual, he took several blows to the body from Briony's padded sword and managed to touch her only once in return. After a much shorter span than Briony would have liked, he stepped away and threw his falchion down with a muffled clatter.

"It's not fair," he said. "You know I'm not well enough yet."

"All the more reason to build up your strength again. Come on, gloomy, let's try just once more. You can use a shield this time if you want."

"No. You're as bad as Shaso. Now that he's not here to plague me, do you think I'm going to let you take his place?"

There was something more than ordinary anger in his tone, and Briony fought down her own resentment. She was restless, full of fury and unhappiness like storm clouds. All she wanted after days of sitting and listening to people talk at her was to move her limbs, to swing the sword, to be something other than a princess, but she knew trying to force Barrick to do anything was useless. "Very well. Perhaps we should talk instead. I read Father's letter again."

"I don't *want* to talk. Perin's Hammer, Briony, I've done enough talking lately! Plots and intrigues. It makes me weary. I'm going to go have a nap."

"But we've hardly spoken about all the things Brone told us—about Gailon Tolly, and the letter, and the Autarch . . ."

He waved his hand dismissively. "Brone is a troublemaker. If there is no intrigue, no mysterious plots to protect us from, he has no influence." Barrick scarcely untied his chest padding before yanking it off, peevish as a child sent away from the supper table.

"Are you saying we have nothing to worry about? When our brother was murdered under our own roof . . . ?"

"No, that's not what I'm saying! Don't twist my words! I said that I don't trust Avin Brone to tell us any truth that doesn't do himself benefit. Don't forget, he's the one who convinced our father to marry Anissa. Nynor and Aunt Merolanna argued against it, but Brone would not let go until he convinced Father to do it."

She frowned. "We were so young—I scarcely remember it."

"I do. I remember it all. It's his fault we're saddled with that madwoman."

"Madwoman?" Briony didn't like the look on her twin's face—an edge of savagery she was not used to seeing. "Barrick, I don't like her either, but that is a cruel thing to say and it's not true."

"Really? Selia says she is acting very strangely. That she allows no one to visit her except women from the countryside. Selia says that she has heard several of them have the name of witches in the city . . ."

"Selia? I didn't know you had seen her again."

His high color, which had begun to subside, suddenly came flooding back. "What if I have? It is any business of yours?"

"No, Barrick, it isn't. But aren't there other girls more worthy of your interest? We know nothing about her."

He snorted. "You sound just like Auntie Merolanna."

"Rose and Moina both admire you."

"That's a lie. Rose calls me Prince Never-Happy, says that I always complain. You told me." He scowled.

She kept her face sober, although for the first time since the conversation began she was tempted to smile. "That was a year ago, silly. She doesn't say it anymore. In fact, she was very worried about you when you were ill. And Moina . . . well, I think she fancies you."

For a moment something like honest wonder came over his face, coupled with a look of yearning so powerful Briony was almost shocked. But an instant later it was gone, and he had put on the mask she knew far too well.

"Oh, no, it's not enough for you that you're the princess regent. You act like you wish you were the queen—like I wasn't even around to interfere with things. Now you want to tell me who I can and can't talk to, and maybe even set one of your ladies on me to pretend she likes me so that she can keep an eye on me. But you can't, Briony." He turned, dropping the rest of his practice gear, and walked out of the armory. Two of the guards who had been standing discreetly along the back wall followed him out.

"That's not true!" she called. "Oh, Barrick, that's not true . . . !" But he was already gone.

She didn't really know why she had come. She felt as though she were walking through a high wind and trying to hold together some fantastically complex and delicate thing, like one of Chaven's scientific instruments but a hundred times larger and more fragile. There were moments when it seemed to her that the entire family was under a curse.

The heavyset guard would not open the door to the cell. She argued, but even though she was the princess regent and could do what she liked, it was clear that if she insisted on her sovereignty the guard would go straight to Avin Brone and she didn't want the lord constable to know she had come. She didn't really understand this herself, and couldn't imagine trying to explain to the dour and practical Brone.

In the end she stood at the cell door's barred window and called him. At first there was no reply. She called again and heard a stirring, a dull clink of iron chains.

"Briony?" His voice had only a shadow of its old strength. She leaned forward, trying to see him in the shadows of the far wall. "What do you want?"

"To talk." The stink of the place was terrible. "To . . . ask you a question."

Shaso rose, the darkness moving upon itself as though the shadows had by magic taken human form. He walked forward slowly, dragging behind him the chain that bound his ankles, and stopped a little way from the door. There was no light in his stronghold cell: only the torch that burned on the wall behind her illumined his face, but it was enough for her to see how thin he had become, the shoulders still wide but the long neck almost fragile now. When he twisted his head so that he could better see her—she must be only a silhouette in front of the torch, she realized—she could make out the shape of his skull beneath the skin. "Merciful Zoria," she murmured.

"What do you want?"

"Why won't you tell me what happened?" She fought to keep her voice even. It was bad enough to weep in the privacy of her chamber. She would not cry in front of this stern old man or the guard who stood only a few yards away, pretending not to listen. "That night? I want to believe you."

"You must find it lonely."

"I am not the only one. Dawet does not believe you would kill Kendrick."

For long moments he did not answer. "You spoke to him? About me?"

Briony couldn't tell if he was stunned or enraged. "He was the envoy of our father's kidnapper. He was also someone who might have been the murderer. We spoke many times."

"You say 'was.'"

"He's gone. Back to Hierosol, back to his master, Drakava. But he told me that he thought you were too honorable to have broken your oath to the Eddon family, no matter what the appearance."

"He is a liar and a murderer, of course." The words came cold and heavy. "You can trust nothing he says."

She was fighting a losing battle to keep anger out of her own voice. "Even when he proclaims a belief in your innocence?"

"If my innocence hinges on that man's word, then I deserve to go to the headsman."

She struck the door so hard with the flat of her hand that the guard jumped in surprise and took a few hurried steps toward her. She angrily waved him away. "Curse you, Shaso dan-Heza, and curse your stiff neck! Do you *enjoy* this? Do you sit here in the dark and rejoice that now we have finally shown how little we truly appreciated you, gloat over how poorly we have repaid all your services over the years?" She leaned forward, almost hissed the words through the barred window. "I still find it hard to believe that you would kill my brother, but I begin to think that you would allow yourself to be killed—that you would murder yourself, as it were—out of pure spite."

Again Shaso fell silent, his great head sagging to his chest. He did not speak for so long that Briony began to wonder if, worn down by the rigors of confinement, he had somehow fallen asleep standing up, or had even died on his feet as the poems claimed the great knight Silas of Perikal did, refusing to fall even with a dozen arrows in his body.

"I can tell you nothing about that night except that I did not kill Kendrick," Shaso said at last. His voice was weirdly ragged, as though he fought back tears, but Briony knew there was nothing in the world more unlikely. "So I must die. If you truly do wish me any kindness, Princess—Briony—then you will not come to see me again. It is too painful."

"Shaso, what . . . ?"

"Please. If you indeed are the single lonely creature in this land who thinks I have not betrayed my oath, then I will tell you three more things. Do not trust Avin Brone—he is a meddler and there is no cause as dear to him as his own. And do not trust Chaven, the court physician. He has many secrets and not all of them are harmless."

"Chaven . . . ? But why him—what has he . . . ?"

"Please." Shaso lifted his head. His eyes were fierce. "Just listen. I can give you no proof of any of these things, but . . . but I would not see you harmed, Briony. Nor your brother, for all he has tried my patience. And I would not see your father's kingdom stolen from him."

She was more than a little stunned. "You said . . . three things."

"Do not trust your cousin, Gailon Tolly." He groaned. It was a sudden, weird, and terrible sound. "No. That is all I can say."

"Gailon." She hesitated—almost she wanted to tell him the news of Gailon's disappearance, and more important, of Brone's assertion that the Tollys had hosted agents of the Autarch, but she was suddenly confused. Shaso said that neither Brone nor Gailon were to be trusted, so then which one was the betrayer, the Duke of Summerfield or the lord constable? Or was it both?

Tell him? Am I going mad? The thought was like a splash of icy water, sudden and shocking. *This man may have killed my brother, whatever I wish to believe. He could be the arch-traitor himself, or in the employ of someone even more dangerous like the Autarch of Xis. It's bad enough I have come down here by myself, without Barrick—should I treat him as though he were still a trusted family counselor?*

"Briony?" Shaso's voice was faint, but he sounded concerned.

"I must go." She turned and walked away, tried to nod to the guard as though nothing out of the ordinary had happened, but by the time she reached the steps up out of the stronghold she was practically running, wanting only to get out of that deep, dark place.

Matty Tinwright woke in his little room beneath the roof of the Quiller's Mint with a head that felt as though it were full of filthy bilgewater. Notwithstanding his two years' residence above the tavern (and thus his presumed familiarity with the room's confines) he managed to strike his head on a beam as he stood—lightly, only lightly, praise to Zosim, godling of both drunkards and poets (a useful coupling since one was so often the other)—and fell back on the bed, groaning.

"Brigid!" he shouted. "Damned woman, come here! My pate is broken!"

But of course she had gone. His only solace was that she must be back in the inn tonight, since she was employed downstairs, and he could tax her then with her cruelty for deserting him. Perhaps it would result in a row or a show of sympathy. Either was acceptable. Poets needed excitement, the rush of feeling.

It was increasingly clear that no one was going to bring him anything. Tinwright sat up, rubbing his head and making self-pitying sounds. He emptied his bladder into the chamber pot, then staggered to the window.

If it had been earlier or later in the day, he would have dispensed with the pot as an unnecessary intermediate stage, but Fitters Row was crowded. It was caution rather than courtesy that led him to empty the pot carefully in a place where no one was walking: only last month a burly sailor had objected to being pissed on from a high window and Tinwright had barely escaped with his life.

He made his way down what seemed like an endless succession of stairs to the common room. The bench where Finn Teodoros and Hewney had kept him up past midnight with their cruel drinking game was empty now, although there were silent men sitting on a half dozen of the other benches, laborers from Tin Street drinking an early lunch. Matty Tinwright couldn't understand how the poet-clerk and the playwright could both be twenty years his senior and yet hold so much drink, forcing him to match them to preserve honor and thus giving him this head like a broken pot in a bag. It was dreadful the way they carried on, and terrible the way they led a young man like Tinwright into bad habits.

There was no sign of Conary, the proprietor. The potboy, Gil—boy in name only, since he looked to be at least a decade older than Tinwright—sat on a stool behind the plank, guarding the barrels. He had an odd, distracted look on his face at the moment, but he was no bright spark at the best of times. He had already been at the Quiller's Mint when Tinwright had first arrived, and in all that time had never said anything remotely interesting.

"Ale," the poet demanded. "I must have ale quickly. My stomach is like a storm at sea—only the sunshine that is pent in the brewer's hop can quiet this tempest." He leaned on the counter, belched sourly. "Do you hear? Thunder!"

Gil did not smile, although he was usually polite enough about Tinwright's jokes in his quiet way. After a little more fumbling than usual, he slid a tankard across the plank. The potboy was blinking like an owl in daylight and seemed even more befuddled than usual; Tinwright was delighted to notice that he did not demand payment. Conary no longer gave his lodger even a sniff without coin in hand, and was threatening to evict him from the tiny closet-room at one edge of the top floor as well. Unwilling to risk losing this windfall, Tinwright was preparing to retreat with the tankard to his room before the potboy realized what he had done, and was heartbroken to hear Gil say, "You are a poet . . . ?"

It was too far to the stairs to pretend he had not heard. He turned, an excuse ready on his lips.

"I mean, you can write, can't you?" the thin-faced man asked him. "You have a good hand?"

Tinwright scowled. "Like an angel using his own quill to dip ink. A great lady once told me that my ode to her would be just as beautiful and useful were the words to be assembled in a completely different order."

"I wish you to help me write a letter. Will you do that?" Gil saw Tinwright's hesitation. "I will pay you money. Would this be enough?" He extended his hand. Nestled in the palm like a droplet of raw sunshine was a gold dolphin. Tinwright gaped and almost dropped his tankard. He had always imagined Gil to be a little simpleminded, with his staring and his silences, but this was idiocy like a gift from the gods. Zosim had heard a simple poet's prayers, it seemed, and they had reached the god on a generous morning.

"Of course," he said briskly. "I would be happy to help you. I will take that ..." he plucked the coin out of the potboy's hand, "and you will come up to my room when Conary has come back." He drained the tankard in a long, greedy swallow and handed it to Gil. "Here—I will save you having to carry it down later."

Gil nodded, his face still as expressionless as a fish lying in a dockside stall. Tinwright hurried up the stairs, half certain that when he reached his room beneath the sloping ceiling the dolphin would be gone, vanished like a fairy-gift, but when he opened his fist it was still there. For the first time a suspicion flared within him and he bit at the coin, but it had the soft solidity of the true stuff. Not that Tinwright had found many chances to bite on gold during his twenty years of life.

Gil stood just inside the door with his arms at his sides.

He truly is more strange than usual, Tinwright thought, *but it's brought me nothing but good.* He couldn't help wondering if Gil had any other little tasks that might need Matty Tinwright's help—mending his shirt, perhaps, or helping him off with his boots. *If he has more dolphins, I'll be proud to call him employer, be he ever so stupid.* A thought came to him for the first time. *But where would a potboy come by gold like this? Killed someone? Well, let us just hope it was somebody who won't be missed. . . .*

At last, Gil spoke. "I want to send a letter. Write the words I say. Make them proper if they need changing."

"Of course, my good fellow." Tinwright took up his writing board, one of the few things left he had not been forced to pawn, and sharpened the quill with an old knife stolen from Conary's kitchen. *With this gold,* he realized, *I will be able to get my bone-handled penknife back. Hah! I will be able to buy one with an ivory handle!*

"I do not know greetings such as would go on a letter. You write them."

"Splendid. And who is the letter for?"

"Prince Barrick and Princess Briony."

Tinwright dropped his quill. "What? The prince and princess?"

"Yes." Gil looked at him with his head tilted to one side, more the expression of a dog or a bird than a person. "Can you not write this?"

"Of course," Matty Tinwright said hurriedly. "Without doubt. As long as it is nothing treasonous." But he was worried. Perhaps he had been too quick to give thanks to Zosim, who after all was a very capricious sort of godling.

"Good. You are kind, Tinwright. I write to tell them important matters. Write this, the things I will say." He took a breath. His eyes were almost closed, as though he were remembering rather than inventing. "Tell the prince and princess of Southmarch that I must speak to them. That I can tell them important things that are true."

Tinwright breathed a sigh of relief as he began an elaborate greeting, since it was clear the letter would be nothing but the self-important ramblings of an unlettered peasant that the royal twins would doubtless never even see—*"To the noble and most honorable Barrick and Briony,"* he wrote, *"Prince and Princess Regent of Southmarch, from their humble servant . . ."* But what is your name? Your full name?"

"Gil."

"Have you no other name? As mine is not just Matthias, but Matthias Tinwright?"

The potboy looked at the poet with such incomprehension that Tinwright could only shrug. " . . . *From their humble servant, Gil,*" he wrote. *"Potboy at the inn known as . . ."*

"Tell them that the threats they face are worse than they know. That war threatens. And to show them I know the things I speak of, I will tell them what happened to the Prince of Settland's daughter and her blue dowerstone, and why the merchant's nephew was spared. You must use just the words I will tell you."

Tinwright nodded, writing happily as Gil stuttered out his message. He had earned a magnificent wage for the simplest of tasks. No one would take this dream-born nonsense seriously, least of all the royal family.

When he had finished he gave the potboy the letter and bade him good-bye—Gil was going to take it himself to the great keep and give it to the prince and princess, he said, although Tinwright knew the poor fool would get no farther than an amused or irritated guardsman at the Raven's Gate. As the potboy's descending footfalls sounded on the stairs, Tinwright lay back on his bed to think of all the ways he would spend his money. His head no longer ached. Life had suddenly become very good.

Gil did not return to the Quiller's Mint that afternoon. Tinwright was arrested by the royal guard an hour before sunset, with ink stains on his fingers and his gold still unspent.

22
A Royal Appointment

WITHOUT NAMES:

Hard as stone beneath the ground
Buzzing like wasps
Twining like roots, like serpents

—from *The Bonefall Oracles*

T LEAST, MATTY TINWRIGHT reflected, they hadn't put him in chains, but nothing else about the experience had been very pleasant at all. He had almost pissed himself when the guards arrived at the Mint to arrest him. Then, seeing the castle's stronghold for the first time, smelling the dank, ancient stones and the various scents of miserable, confined humanity, he had nearly done it again. It was one thing to write couplets about the sufferings of Perikal's Silas in the fortress of the cruel Yellow Knight, but the actuality of a dungeon was far more unsettling than he had imagined.

He let out a sigh, then worried that it might sound like a complaint. He didn't want these very large guards with their big, callused hands and scowling faces to be angry with him. Two of them were sitting on a low bench talking while a third stood only a few yards away on his other side, pike in hand. This was the one who was making him most uncomfortable; he kept looking at Tinwright as though he was hoping the prisoner would make an attempt to escape so he could spit him like broiled hare on a sharpened stick.

But the poet wasn't going to move. His mind was fixed on passivity like a compass needle pointing north. *If the bloody castle suddenly fell down, I'd still sit right here on the floor. That evil-eyed whoreson's getting no excuse from Matty Tinwright.*

From where he sat he could see the potboy Gil slouching on the floor on the far side of the guards' table. Tinwright hoped it was a good sign that there were three guards between Gil and the door and only one for him, that it meant they thought Gil was the true miscreant. Not that the potboy looked any more likely than the poet to attempt escape. His thin face was blank and he stared at an empty spot on the opposite wall as though he were someone's befuddled grandfather left at the market by accident.

The guard who had been giving Tinwright unpleasant looks took a few steps toward him, mail clinking, until he stood just over him. The man carefully—but not *too* carefully—lodged the point of his pike in the cracks of the stone floor only inches from Tinwright's groin. If this had been an important occasion, or at least the nicer sort of important occasion, it would unquestionably have been crimping Matty's codpiece.

"I saw you in the Badger's Boots," the guard said. Painfully conscious of the pike planted between his thighs like a conqueror's flag, Tinwright was momentarily bewildered, thinking that he had been accused of stealing the footwear of some guard-troop mascot. "Did you hear me, little man?"

Suddenly, his wits began to work again. The man was talking about a tavern by the Basilisk Gate that Tinwright had visited a few times, usually in the bibulous company of the playwright Nevin Hewney. "No, sir, you mistake me," he said with all the honesty he could feign. "I have never passed the door. I am a partisan of the Quiller's Mint in Squeakstep Alley. A fellow like yourself would not know the Mint, of course—it is a low, low place."

The guard smirked. He was young, but already with a sizable belly on him and a doughy, unpleasant face. "You took my woman away from me. Told her she would enjoy being with a clever fox like you more than the pig who was squiring her."

"I'm sure you're wrong, good sir."

"You said she had breasts like fine white cake and an arse like a pomegranate."

"No, a peach, surely," said Tinwright, remembering how drunk he had been that night and horrified to think he might have employed a simile as clumsily unlovely as "pomegranate." A moment later he clapped a hand over his mouth in horror, but it was too late. His unruly tongue had betrayed him again.

The guard favored him with a gap-toothed grin that the poet felt sure did not have much to do with concern for his well-being or appreciation for an adept bit of flirtation. The guard leaned close and reached out with his thick fingers, then took Tinwright's nose and twisted it, hanging on until the poet let out a terrified squeak of pain. The guard bent until his cheese-stinking maw was only a finger's breadth away, which meant there was one small benefit of Tinwright's nose being at this moment so agonizingly crimped shut. "If the lord constable doesn't want your head off—and if he does, I'll be first in line for the chore—then I'll be over to see you at Quiller's Mint, and soon. I'll cut some bits off you,"—he gave the nose another twist for emphasis, "—and then we'll see how the ladies like you."

The door to the stronghold rattled open. The guard let go of Tinwright's snout and straightened up, but not before giving it a last cruel tweak. Tinwright was left with tears welling in his eyes and a feeling like someone had set fire to the center of his face.

"Perin's smallclothes, is the swindler crying?" a voice boomed from just above him. "Are there no true men left in this kingdom who are not soldiers? Are all the rest just pimps and coney-catchers and womanish weepers like this one?" The vast shape of Lord Constable Avin Brone loomed over him, his beard a gray-black thundercloud. "Are you grizzling because of your crimes against the crown, man? That may help you with the Trigonate priests, but not with me."

Tinwright blinked away the tears. "No, my lord, sire, I am guilty of nothing."

"Then why are you blubbing?"

Somehow Tinwright did not think it would be a good idea to mention what the guard had done. That might turn the beating the man intended to give him into something more likely to prove fatal. "I . . . I have a catarrh, sire. It strikes me like this, sometime. This damp air . . ." He waved his hand to indicate the surroundings, but then had another moment of panic. "Not that I have any complaint against the place, sire. I have been excellently well treated." He was babbling now. Tinwright had never seen Brone from closer than a stone's throw: the fellow looked as though he could crush a poet's skull with one meaty hand. "The walls are very sturdy, my lord, the floor well-made."

"I suspect someone struck you," said the lord constable. "If you don't shut your mouth now, I will probably do it again myself." He turned to one of the royal guards who had risen from the bench. "I'm taking both prisoners." He waved to one of the pair of soldiers whom he had left waiting by the stronghold door; both wore the livery of Landsend, Brone's own fiefdom. "Fetch this pair along," he told his man. "Beat them if you have to."

The stronghold guard looked a little surprised. "Do . . . are the prince and princess . . . ?"

"Of course they know," Brone growled. "Who do you think has bid me bring them out?"

"Ah. Yes. Very good, my lord."

Tinwright scrambled to his feet. He was determined to go without trouble. He did not want to be hurt anymore, and he certainly did not want the huge and frightening lord constable to get any angrier.

Despite his terror, Tinwright couldn't help but be surprised when Brone and the two soldiers took them a long, winding way through the back of the great hall and at last into a small but beautifully appointed chapel. One look at the paintings on the wall told him that it must be the Erivor Chapel itself, dedicated to the Eddons' patron sea god, one of the most famous rooms in all of Southmarch. The decor seemed appropriate in a way, because Gil the potboy had walked all the way there as slowly and distractedly as if he were in water over his head. Tinwright was puzzled to be in such a place, but felt a little better: surely they would not just kill him outright, if for no other reason than fear of getting blood on the celebrated wall frescoes.

Unless they strangle me. Didn't they used to strangle traitors? His heart raced. *Traitors! But this is mad—I am no traitor! I only wrote the letter because that criminal Gil blinded me, a poor poet, with his ill-gotten gold!*

By the time Avin Brone was seated on a long bench that had been set near the altar, Tinwright was almost crying again.

"Quiet," Brone said.

"My lord, I . . . I . . ."

"Shut your mouth, fool. Do not think that because I have sat down I will not get up and hit you. The pleasure will be worth the exertion."

Tinwright subsided immediately. The fists sticking out of the man's lace cuffs were the size of festival loaves. The poet stole a look at Gil, who not only did not seem frightened, but actually seemed mostly unaware of what was going on around him. *Curse you and your gold!* Matty Tinwright wanted to scream at him. *You are like some poison-elf out of a story, bringing bad luck to everyone.*

Figuring the best way to keep himself out of trouble would be to squeeze shut his eyes and mouth and pray to the god of poets and drunkards (even though the answer to his last prayer seemed to have led him to the doorstep of a traitor's cell), he was not aware for a moment that newcomers had entered the room. It was the girl's voice that startled his eyes open.

"These two?"

"Yes, Highness." Brone pointed at Gil. "This is the one who made the claims. The other says he only wrote it for him, although I have my doubts—you can see which one looks more likely to have put the other up to mischief."

Tinwright had a strong desire to shriek out his innocence, but he was slowly learning how to behave in a situation where he had no power. A half dozen new people had entered the chapel. Four of them were royal guards, who had established themselves near the door and were exchanging mildly contemptuous glances with the lord constable's red-and-gold-clad Landsenders; the other two, he was astonished to recognize, were King Olin's surviving children, Princess Briony and Prince Barrick.

"Why here?" the fair-haired princess asked. Tinwright had to look twice to make sure she was the one speaking. She was pretty enough in a tall, bony sort of way—Matty Tinwright liked his women soft, pale, and round-edged as a summer cloud—but her hair was loose and she was dressed very strangely in a riding skirt and hose and a long blue jacket like a man's. Her wan, red-ringleted brother was all in black. Tinwright had heard of the prince's perpetual mourning attire, but it was quite astounding to see Barrick Eddon so close, as though he were just another drinker in the Mint—to see both of the young regents here in front of him, as close and as real as could be, as though Tinwright himself were a court favorite they had come to visit. A fantasy about it warmed him for a flickering instant. Ah, what bliss that would be, to have royal patrons . . . !

"We are here because it is private," Brone said.

"But you said they were only trying to trick us into giving them money for false information."

Tinwright suddenly lost interest in patronage and how the prince and princess were dressed. In fact, he was having great difficulty swallowing: it felt as though a hedgehog had crawled into his throat. If they decided that he was guilty of trying to defraud the royal family, they might very well have his head; at the least, he would be banished to one of the smaller islands or sent to work the fields until he was old, until even a tinker's skinny wife would not slip him a copper for his charming speech (and more physical attentions). Trying to swindle the royal family! He pressed his legs tightly together so as not to piss himself in front of the Eddon twins.

"I said that's what I suspected," Brone replied, patiently ignoring the prince's quarrelsome tone. "But if either or both of them actually *do* know something, I thought it would be better we found out here instead of in front of the entire court."

Briony, who had been looking at Tinwright in a way that did not seem entirely unkind—although it did not appear particularly sympathetic either—suddenly turned to lantern-jawed Gil. "You. They say you are a potboy at an alehouse in the outer keep. How could you know anything other than tavern gossip about what happened to that Settland caravan?"

Gil stirred, but he seemed to have trouble fixing his eyes on her. "I . . . I do not know. I only know that I had dreams, and that those dreams . . . showed me things."

"Say, 'Your Highness,' scum," Brone snarled.

Briony waved her hand. "He is . . . I don't know, simpleminded, I think. Why are we troubling with him at all? With either of these two lackwits?"

Tinwright wished he had the courage to bristle, to protest. It was disappointing that the princess seemed to be unaware of his small but growing reputation, but surely it must be obvious from looking at him that he was not of the same mettle as poor Gil.

"She's right," said Prince Barrick. He spoke more slowly and haltingly than reports of his mercurial nature would have suggested. "That merchant fellow probably told everyone in Southmarch what happened to him. And spread it over half the countryside before he even got here, as well."

"If you look at the letter these two sent us," Brone told them patiently, "it says, *'I can tell you of the Prince of Settland's daughter and why she was taken, with her guards and her blue dower-stone.'* That's why we're bothering with these lackwits."

"I don't understand," said the princess.

"Because the merchant Beck didn't *know* about the great sapphire the girl was bringing to Earl Rorick as part of her dowry. Nobody in the caravan knew, not even the guards, because her father was afraid of theft. I only know myself because I received a letter out of Settland a few days ago, carried to me by a monk. The prince wrote to ask after his daughter and her safety, since he had heard disturbing rumors, and he specifically mentioned the sapphire she was carrying—in fact, it seemed almost as important to him as his child, so it is either a very expensive stone or he is a less than doting father. In any case, how . . . ?"

"How can a mere potboy know about the stone?" Briony finished for him. She turned to Gil. "And you claim this came to you in dreams? What else can you tell us?"

He shook his head slowly. "I have forgotten some of what I meant to say, some of the things I heard and saw when I was sleeping. I was going to have Tinwright put it all down in writings for me, but the guards came and took me away from the Quiller's Mint."

"So even if he did somehow know something," said Barrick, his words ripe with disgust, "he doesn't know it now."

"I know you saw the ones in black," Gil told the prince.

"What?"

"The ones in black. The walls aflame. And the man with the beard, running, calling you. I know you saw it . . ."

He did not finish because Barrick leaped forward and wrapped his hands around the potboy's neck. Although Gil was a grown man, he offered no resistance. Barrick shoved the scrawny figure down to the floor and climbed onto his chest, shouting, "What does that mean? How could you know about my dreams?"

"Barrick!" Briony rushed forward and grabbed at his arms. The potboy was not struggling, but his face was turning a terrible, hectic red. "Let go— you'll kill him!"

"How could you know? Who sent you? *How could you know?*"

As Tinwright watched in astonishment, the lord constable—moving with surprising swiftness for all his bulk—yanked the boy off the gasping but still unresisting Gil. "I beg your your pardon, Highness, but have you lost your wits?" he demanded.

The prince squirmed free of the big man's clutch. Barrick was breathing harshly, as though he had been the one strangled instead of the other way around. "Don't say that! Don't you dare say that!" he shouted at Brone. "Nobody can speak to me like that!" He seemed about to cry or to scream again, but instead his face suddenly went stony as a statue. He turned and walked out the chapel door, although it was a walk that was only one headlong step away from becoming a run. Two of the guards exchanged a weary look, then peeled off and followed him.

The potboy was sitting up now, wheezing quietly.

"How could you know about my brother's dreams?" Briony Eddon demanded.

Gil took a moment to answer. "I only tell what I saw. What I heard."

She turned to Brone. "Merciful Zoria preserve me, I think sometimes I'm going mad—I must be, because otherwise I can make no sense of the things that happen in this place. Do you understand any of this?"

The lord constable did not answer immediately. "I . . . for the most part, I am as puzzled as you, my lady. I have a few ideas, but I think it unwise to share them in front of these two." He jabbed his bearded chin toward Tinwright and the potboy.

"Well, we must do something about them, that's sure." Briony frowned. Tinwright still did not find her particularly fetching, but something about the princess definitely drew his attention, and it was not just her fame and power. She was very . . . forceful. *Like one of the warrior goddesses,* he thought.

"Clearly we must at least keep the potboy until we find the secret of his knowledge," Brone said, giving the poet a spark of hope. Perhaps they would let him go! "Not to mention discovering how he got his hands on that gold dolphin he gave to this so-called poet. I suppose I can find a place for the potboy in the guard room—he'll be under many eyes there. But I am not sure we want this other one gossiping in the taverns about what he's seen." Brone frowned. "I imagine you won't simply let me kill him." Suddenly breathless, Tinwright could only hope it was meant as a joke. He was relieved when the princess shook her head. "Too bad," Brone told her, "because there is little need for his shiftless sort, and Southmarch already has armies of them."

"I don't care what you do with the one who wrote the letter." Briony was staring fixedly at Gil; Tinwright had an inexplicable twinge of jealousy. "I doubt he has anything to do with this matter—the potboy cannot write and needed someone to do it. Send the poet back home and tell him we'll cut his head off if he whispers a word. I need to think."

Tinwright had suffered a series of glum realizations. If he went back to the Quiller's Mint, he would soon be getting that promised visit from the guard whose woman he apparently stole; not only would he be brutally beaten, but it would be for something he couldn't even remember—drinking with Hewney nearly always ended in oblivion. He could only hope the wench had been pretty although, looking at the guard, he rather doubted it. But since the lord constable had confiscated his gold dolphin, he couldn't afford to move elsewhere. There was no well-heeled lady in his life at the moment to take him in, only Brigid who lived at the Mint. And the cold weather had come. It would be a bad time to live in the streets.

Tinwright was now feeling extremely sorry for himself. For a moment he considered concocting a story of his own to make himself more useful and important, pretending that he shared some of the potboy's strange knowledge, but one look at the massive Brone convinced him of the folly of that. For some reason, Gil actually did know things he shouldn't, but Tinwright could summon no such weaponry, even in bluff. He contemplated the distracted princess and an idea struck him so abruptly that he couldn't help wondering if Zosim was trying to make up for the fickle cruelty of his other gift. He dropped to his knees on the floor.

"My lady," he said in his most sincere voice, the one that had kept him in food and drink since he first ran away from home, "Highness, may I beg a favor? It is far too much and I am far too lowly, but I beg you at least to hear me . . ."

She looked at him. That was a first step, at least. "What?"

"I am a poet, Princess—a humble one, one whose gifts have not always been rewarded, but those who know me will tell you of my quality." She was losing interest so he hurried ahead. "I came here in fear and trepidation. My attempt to do a kindness for my simple friend the potboy has caused you and your brother pain. I am devastated . . ."

She smiled sourly. "If you tell anyone about this, you certainly will be devastated."

"Please, only hear me, Highness. Only hear your humble servant. Your attention to the cares of the land have doubtless prevented you from knowing of the panegyric I am writing about you." That, and the fact that he had been writing no such thing before this moment.

"Panegyric?"

"A tribute to your astonishing beauty." He saw her expression and quickly added, "And most importantly, to your wisdom and kindness. Your mercy." She smiled again, although it still had a nasty little curl to it. "In fact, as I sit here, fortunate enough finally to be within the radiant glow of your presence instead of worshiping you like the distant moon, I see that my central conceit was even more accurate than I had hoped—that you are indeed . . . *indeed* . . ."

She got tired of waiting. "I am indeed what?"

"The very embodiment of Zoria, warrior goddess and mistress of wisdom." There. He could only hope that he had guessed correctly, that her odd way of dressing and her solicitation of the goddess' mercy were not chance occurrences. "When I was young, I often dreamed of Perin's courageous daughter, but in my dreams I was blinded by her glow—I could never truly imagine the heavenly countenance. Now I know the true face of the goddess. Now I see her born again in Southmarch's virgin princess." He suddenly worried he had gone a bit too far: she didn't look as flattered as he had hoped she would, although she didn't look angry either. He held his breath.

"Shall I have him beaten before I take him back to that brothel?" Brone asked her.

"To tell the truth," Briony said, "he . . . amuses me. I have not laughed in days, and just now I almost did. That is a rare gift in these times." She looked Tinwright up and down. "You wish to be my poet, do you? To tell the world of my virtues?"

He was not sure what was happening, but this was not a moment to be wasted on truth of any sort. "Yes, my lady, my princess, it has always been my greatest dream. Indeed, Highness, your patronage would make me the happiest man on earth, the luckiest poet upon Eion."

"Patronage?" She raised an eyebrow. "Meaning what? Money?"

"Oh, never, my lady!" *In due time,* he thought. "No, it would be a boon beyond price if you simply allowed me to observe you—at a distance, of course!—so that I could better construct my poem. It has already been years in the making, Highness, the chief labor of my life, but it has been difficult, composed around a few brief glimpses of you at public festivals. If you favor me with the chance to witness you even from across a crowded room as you bring your wise rule to the fortunate people of Southmarch, that would be a kindness that proves you are truly Zoria reborn."

"In other words, you want a place to stay." For the first time there was something like genuine amusement in her smile. "Brone, see if Puzzle can find a place for him. They can share a room—keep each other company."

"Princess Briony . . . !" Brone was annoyed.

"Now I must talk to my brother. You and I will meet again before sunset, Lord Constable." She started toward the door, then stopped, looked Tinwright up and down. "Farewell, poet. I'll be expecting to hear that ode very soon. I'm looking forward to it."

As he watched her go, Matty Tinwright was not quite sure whether this had been the best day of his life or the worst. He thought it must be the best, but there was a small, sick feeling in his stomach that surely should not be part of the day he had become an appointed poet to the royal court.

At first, it seemed that Collum Dyer would be able to follow the fairy host like a blind man tracking the sun: despite the confusion of the fogbound forest and the serpentine inconstancy of the road, the guard set off in a way that Vansen would have called confident, except that the rest of the man's demeanor spoke of nothing so humble and human as confidence. In fact, Dyer might have been a sleepwalker, stumbling and murmuring to himself like one of the crazed penitents that had followed the effigies of the god Kernios from town to town during the days of the Great Death.

Quickly, though, it became clear that if Dyer was a blind man following the sun, that sun was setting. Within what seemed no more than an hour they were staggering in circles. So maddening was the forest-maze that Vansen would not even have known *that* for certain except that Dyer stepped on his own sword belt, which he had lost far back in the day's march.

Exhausted, devastated, Vansen sank to the ground and crouched with his face in his hands, half expecting that Dyer would go on without him and mostly not caring. Instead, to his surprise, he felt a hand on his shoulder.

"Where are they, Ferras? They were so beautiful." Despite the dark beard, Collum Dyer looked like nothing so much as a child, his eyes wide, his mouth quivering.

"Gone on," Vansen said. "Gone on to kill our friends and families."

"No." But what he had said troubled Dyer. "No, they bring something, but not death. Didn't you hear them? They only take back what was already theirs. That is all they want."

"But there are people *living* on what was already theirs. People like us." Vansen only wanted to lie down, to sleep. He felt as though he had been endlessly, endlessly swimming in this ocean of trees with no glimpse of shore. "Do you think the farmers and smallholders will simply get up and move so your Twilight People can have their old lands back? Perhaps we can pull down Southmarch Castle as well, build it again in Jellon or Perikal where it won't interfere with them."

"Oh, no," said Dyer very seriously. "They want the castle back. That's theirs, too. Didn't you hear them?"

Vansen closed his eyes but it only made him dizzy. He was lost behind the Shadowline with a madman. "I heard nothing."

"They were singing! Their voices were so fair . . . !" Now it was Dyer who squeezed his eyes shut. "They sang . . . they sang . . ." The child-face sagged again as though he might burst into tears. "I can't remember! I can't remember what they sang."

That was the first good thing Vansen had heard in hours. Perhaps Dyer's wits were returning. *But why am I not mad, too?* he wondered.

Then again, how do I know I'm not?

"Come," said the guardsman, pulling at his arm. "They are going away from us."

"We can't catch them. We're lost again." Vansen pushed down his anger. Whatever the reason that Collum Dyer's wits were clouded and his own were not, or at least not as badly, it was not Dyer's fault. "We do have to get out of here, but not to follow the Twilight People off to war." A few tattered scraps of duty seemed to be all that held him together. He clutched them tight. "We have to tell the princess about this . . . and the prince. We have to tell Avin Brone."

"Yes." Collum nodded. "They will be happy."

Vansen groaned quietly and set about looking for enough damp sticks to try to make a fire. "Somehow I don't think so."

After a succession of terrible dreams in which he was pursued by faceless men through endless mist-cloaked gardens and unlit halls, Ferras Vansen gave up on sleep. He warmed his hands beside the fire and fretted over their dismal circumstances, but he was exhausted and without useful ideas: all he could do was stare out at the endless trees and try to keep from screaming in despair. A child of the countryside, he had never imagined he could grow to hate something as familiar as a forest, as common as mere trees, but of course nothing here was mere anything. Outwardly familiar—he had seen oak and beech, rowan and birch and alder, and in the high places many kinds of evergreen—the dripping trees of this damp shadow-forest seemed to have a brooding life to them, a silence both purposeful and powerful. If he half-closed his eyes, he could almost imagine he was surrounded by ancient priests and priestesses robed in gray and green, tall and stately and not very kindly disposed toward his intrusion into their sacred precincts.

When Collum Dyer finally woke, he also seemed to have awakened from the evil fancy that had gripped his mind. He looked around him, blinking slowly, and then moaned. "By Perin's Hammer, when will day come in this cursed place?"

"This is as much day as you'll see until we are in our own lands again," Vansen told him. "You should know that by now."

"How long have we been here?" Dyer looked down at his hands as though they should belong to someone else. "I feel ill. Where are the others?"

"Don't you remember?" He told the guardsman all that had happened, what they had seen. Dyer looked at him mistrustfully.

"I remember none of that. Why would I say such things?"

"I don't know. Because this place sends people mad. Come—if you're feeling like yourself again, let's get moving."

They walked, but even the small idea that Vansen had of which direction might lead them back across the Shadowline toward mortal lands quickly failed. As the day wore away, with Dyer cursing fate and Vansen biting back his own anger at his companion—*he* hadn't had the luxury of being mad for two days, and had suffered this endless, defeating landscape the whole time Collum Dyer had been babbling about the glories of the Twilight folk—it began to seem that not only would they have to sleep in the forest again, they might never find their way out. They were hopelessly lost and almost out of food and drink. Vansen did not trust the water in this land's quiet streams, but it seemed they soon must drink it or die.

Somewhere in the timeless and arbitrary middle of their day, Vansen spotted a group of figures traveling away from them, struggling along a ridgetop at what looked like half a mile's distance. He and Dyer were down in a small canyon, hidden by trees, and at first his strong impulse was to hide until these creatures were gone. But something about the stockiest of the climbing shapes snagged his attention; after a moment, attention turned to incredulous delight.

"By all the gods, I swear that must be Mickael Southstead! I would know his walk anywhere, like he had a barrel between his legs."

Dyer squinted. "You're right. Bless him—who would ever have thought I'd be happy to see that old whoreson!"

Energies renewed by hope, they ran until they no longer had the breath for it, then continued the climb up the steep hillside at a slower pace. Dyer wanted to shout—he was terrified that they would lose their comrades again—but Vansen did not want to make any more noise than was necessary: it already seemed as though the very land was disapprovingly aware of them.

They reached the top of the ridge at last, staggering up onto the crest and stopping to gasp for breath. When they straightened up, they could see the others just a few hundred yards ahead along the ridgetop, still laboring forward, unaware of Vansen and Dyer. This joyful sight was undercut slightly by the view from the crest. The forest stretched as far as they could see on all sides with no landmark more recognizable than a few hilltops like the one on which they stood, jutting up at irregular intervals from the mists that blanketed the shadow-country like islands in the Vuttish archipelago surrounded by the cold northern sea.

Vansen was still winded, but Dyer sprinted ahead. Now that they were so close, Vansen could see that there were only four other survivors, and that one of them was the girl Willow. His heart lifted—the idea that he had brought the poor, tortured creature back to the place that had affected her so badly the first time had been troubling him in his more lucid moments—but only a little. Far more troubling was the rest of his missing guardsmen. Until now he had been able to convince himself that the rest of the troop was together and looking for them. Now he had to admit the problem was not simply that Vansen and Dyer had got themselves lost, but rather that Ferras Vansen, a captain of the royal guard, had lost most of his men.

The princess was right, he thought bitterly as he started after Dyer. *I am not to be trusted with the safety of her family. And I should not have been trusted with the lives of these men, either.*

Dyer had caught them and embraced Mikael Southstead though he had never liked him much. As Dyer threw his arms around the other two soldiers—Balk and Dawley, it appeared—Southstead turned to Ferras Vansen with a self-satisfied grin. "There you are, Captain. We knew we'd find you."

Vansen was vastly relieved to see even this small portion of his men alive, but was not quite certain he agreed with Southstead's idea of who had found whom. "I am pleased to see you well," he told Southstead, then clapped the man on the shoulder. It was a little awkward, but he wanted no embraces.

"Father?" the girl said to him. She looked more ragged than the others, her dress torn and muddy, and her face had lost the cheer it had possessed even in madness. He had a terrible notion of what might have happened in his absence, but also knew that there was nothing he could do about it, nothing. He beckoned her toward him.

"I am not your father, Willow," he told her gently. "But I am happy to see you. I am Ferras Vansen, the captain of these men."

"They wouldn't let me go home, Father," she said. "I wanted to, but they wouldn't let me."

Vansen couldn't help shuddering, but when he turned back to the others all he said was, "We will make camp, but not here. Let us move down into the valley where we're not so easy to see."

Between them, Vansen and the remains of his troop scraped together enough biscuit and dried meat for a meager meal, but that was the last of their provisions gone and their waterskins were also nearly empty. Soon they would have to drink from the shadow-streams and perhaps eat shadow-food as well. He had already had difficulty restraining Dyer from eating berries and fruit while they traveled, some of which looked quite familiar and wholesome, so how much more difficult would it be now that he had five of them to watch?

It quickly became apparent that Southstead and the others had experienced some of the same things as Vansen and Dyer, but not all; the Shadowline had crept over them while they slept, and the rest of the men and the merchant Beck apparently went mad much as Dyer had done, disappearing with the horses and leaving Southstead, Dawley, Balk, and the girl Willow stranded on foot. But Southstead and his company had not seen the host of the Twilight People on the march, and with the return of his wits Collum Dyer did not truly remember it either, leaving Vansen as the lone witness. He fancied that the others looked at him strangely when he spoke of it, as though he might have invented it all.

"What would they be doing, Captain?" young Dawley asked. "I mean, going to war? With whom?"

"With us," Vansen said, trying to keep his temper. "With our kind. Which is why we must hope we can get back to Southmarch with the news before that army of unnatural things gets there."

It also quickly became clear that despite his claim of finding Vansen, Southstead and the other two guardsmen had been completely lost, wandering hopelessly, although Southstead claimed he would have found his way out of the woods, "given a proper chance." The fact that these three guardsmen, none of whom Vansen thought of as very clever, had not been

driven mad by the magic of the shadow-forest made him a little more uncertain about his own resistance. There seemed to be no reason for who was
completely overcome and who was only buffeted by the strangeness of the
place. More disturbing, resistance did not seem to give them the ability to
find their way out again, but Dyer in his former madness had seemed certain he knew which way to go.

As the men argued about who would stand watch, Vansen suddenly had
an idea: although he still feared his men had mistreated the girl Willow, perhaps even raped her, he realized he might in his anger have misunderstood
something she was trying to tell him.

She was sitting close to him, not speaking, but clearly more comfortable
near the man she sometimes imagined was her father. "You said they would
not let you go home," he said to her quietly. "What do you mean?"

She shook her head, wide-eyed. "Oh, I can see the road! I tried to tell
them, but they wouldn't listen. The one who looks like our old bull pup
said he knew where to go and that I should keep my mouth shut." She slid
closer to him. "But you will let me go home. I know you will."

Vansen almost laughed at the girl's description—the jowly Southstead
did indeed look more than a little like a bulldog—but what she had said
was important. *She found her way out of shadow once,* he thought, *before we
found her.* He patted her on the head, carefully disengaged his hand from
hers—she had a good, tight grip on it—and stood up. "I'll take first watch,"
he announced. "The rest of you play drop-stones or whatever you wish to
settle your turns. Tomorrow you follow a new leader."

Southstead did not look happy, but he grinned anyway. "As you wish,
Captain, o' course. But you and Dyer did no better than us."

"I'm not going to be leading," he said. "She will."

Despite the grumbling of the men, after the little troop had been up and
following Willow through the gray forest for a few hours Vansen actually
saw the moon for the first time since they had fallen into shadow. It was
only a glimpse when some unfelt wind in the heights scattered the mists
for a moment, and he was a little disturbed to think it might be the middle of the night when his body had been telling him it was day, but he still
regarded it as a good sign. The girl seemed certain of where she was going,
walking on ahead of them in her tattered white dress like a ghost leading
travelers to the place of its murder.

Perhaps it was hunger—the younger the man, Vansen had learned during his time as a guard captain, the more they thought about food—but somewhere during what everyone except Mesiya's pale orb believed was the afternoon, Dawley suddenly stopped in his tracks.

"There's something in that thicket," he whispered to Vansen, who was closest to him. He took his bow off his shoulder and pulled out one of the two arrows he had saved from the collapse of their mission and the disappearance of the horses and packs. "If it's a deer, Captain, I'm going to shoot it. I don't care if it's the King of Elfland in disguise, I'll eat it anyway."

Vansen laid a hand on the young soldier's arm as he nocked the arrow, squeezed the arm hard. "But what if it's Adcock or one of the other guards wandering lost, maybe wounded?" Dawley slowly lowered the bow. "Good. Take Dyer and Balk and see if you can move in quietly."

While Vansen and Southstead and the young woman watched in silence, the men closed in on the thicket. Dawley abruptly dove into the deepest part of the undergrowth and Balk clambered in after him. The leaves were rattling, and both Dawley and Balk were shouting to each other.

"*There!* It's running there!"

"It's a cat!"

"No, it's a bloody ape! But it's *fast!*"

Dyer waded in last and the three converged. The branches thrashed furiously, then Dyer straightened up with something the size of a small child struggling in his arms. Vansen and the others hurried forward.

"Perin's Balls!" swore Vansen. "Don't get scratched, Collum. What is it?"

The whining, scratchy cries of the thing as it fought helplessly against the much larger Dyer were disturbing enough, but hearing it suddenly speak the Common Tongue was terrifying. "*Let go me!*" it shrilled.

Startled, Dyer almost did let it go, but then he squeezed until it subsided. The guardsman was breathing hard, his eyes wide with fear, but he was holding the thing tightly now. Vansen could understand why the others mistook it for an ape or a cat. It was vaguely man-shaped, but long of arm and short of leg, and was furred all over in shades of gray and brown and black. The face was like a demon-mask that children wore on holidays, although this demon seemed to be as frightened as they were.

"What are you?" Vansen asked.

"Something cursed," said Southstead, his voice cracking.

The thing stared at the guardsman with what looked like contempt, then turned its gaze on Vansen. The bright yellow eyes had no white and only thin black sideways slits for pupils, like a goat's. "Goblin, am I," it rasped. "Under-Three-Waters tribe. You dead men, all."

"Dead men?" Vansen repressed a superstitious shiver.

"She bring white fire. She burn all you houses until only black stones." It made a strange hissing, spitting sound. "Wasted, my leg, old and bent. Fell behind. Never I see the beauty of her when she ends you."

"Kill it!" Southstead demanded through clenched teeth.

Vansen held out a hand to still him. "It was following the army of the Twilight People. Perhaps it is one of them—it's certainly their subject. It can tell us things." He looked around, trying to think of what they could use to bind the creature, which was struggling again in Dyer's grasp.

"Never," the thing said, the words raw and strangely-shaped. "Never help sunlanders!" A moment later it squirmed abruptly and violently, contorting itself in such a way that it seemed to have no backbone, and sank its teeth into Collum Dyer's arm. He screamed in pain and surprise and dropped the thing to the ground. It scrambled away from them, but one of its legs was clearly lame and dragged behind it. Before Vansen could even open his mouth to shout, young Dawley took two steps and caught up to it, then smashed it to the ground with his bow. A moment later Dyer was there as well, holding his bloody arm against his body as he began to kick the writhing shape. Southstead caught up to them with his sword out and his mouth full of angry curses. The other two stepped back as he began hacking and hacking. All three men were making sounds like dogs baying, howls of terror and rage.

By the time Vansen reached them the goblin was long dead, a bloody tangle of meat and fur on the mossy forest floor, its lantern eyes already going dull.

Barrick still refused to see her, but Briony was determined. Her brother's outbursts and anger had been bad enough before, but now he was truly frightening her. He had always been prickly and private, but this strangeness about the potboy was something else again.

She leaned down close to the wide-eyed page, who had his back against the prince's chamber door as though he meant to defend it with his ten-year-old life. "Tell my brother that I will be back to speak with him after the evening meal. Tell him we *will* speak."

As she walked away, she heard the page hurriedly open the door and then almost slam it closed behind him, as though he had just escaped from the cage of a lioness.

Are there people here who fear me as much as they fear Brone? As they fear Barrick's moods? It was an odd thought. She had never conceived of herself as frightening, although she knew she was not always patient with what she deemed foolishness or dithering.

Zoria, virgin warrior, Zoria of the cunning hands, give me the strength to be gentle. The prayer reminded her of that fool of a poet, and her sudden whim. Why had she decided to keep such a creature around? Just to annoy Barrick and the lord constable? Or because she truly did enjoy even such ridiculous flattery?

Her mind muddled with these thoughts, she walked down the long hall beneath the portraits of her ancestors living and dead, her father and her grandfather Ustin and her great-grandfather, the third Anglin, without really seeing them. Even the picture of Queen Lily, scourge of the Gray Companies and the most famous woman in the history of the March Kingdoms, could not hold her attention today, although there were other times when she would stand for hours looking at the handsome, dark-haired woman who had held the realm together in one of its bleakest hours, wondering what it would be like to make such a mark on the world. But today, although the familiar sight of her other clansmen and clanswomen had not moved her, the picture of Sanasu, Kellick Eddon's queen, caught her eye.

It was unusual for Briony to give the portrait more than a glance. What little she knew of Queen Sanasu was dreary, of her painfully long years of mourning after the great King Kellick died, an obsessively silent, solitary widowhood that had made her a phantom to her own court. So detached had Sanasu become in the last half of her life, family stories related, that the business of the kingdom had fallen entirely to her son years before he became king in fact, something that made the responsible Briony loathe the woman without knowing anything more about her. But today, even as absorbed in worries as she was, Briony could not help staring at something in the likeness she had never really noticed before: Sanasu looked very much like Barrick—or rather Barrick, her many-times-great grandson, looked much like Sanasu, which was accentuated by the black mourning garb they both favored. And these days, with his pallor and striking, haunted eyes accentuated by his bout with the fever, Barrick looked more like the long-dead queen than ever.

Briony stood on her toes for a better look, wishing the light in the ancient hall were better. The artist who had made the portrait had no doubt prettified his queen, but even so, the Sanasu in the picture had the almost transparent look of someone very ill, which only made her red hair even more shocking, like a bloody wound. She also seemed astonishingly young for someone who had lost her husband in middle age. Her face was odd in other ways, too, although it was hard to say exactly why.

I can see Father's eyes in her, too, and his coloring. Briony suddenly wished she knew more about great Kellick's widow. The portrait made Sanasu look mysterious and foreign. Briony couldn't recall being told anything about where the melancholy queen had come from before marrying Kellick, but whatever distant land might have spawned her, it had now been part of the family heritage for centuries. Briony was suddenly struck by how the blood of the Eddons, her own blood, was like a great river, with things appearing and disappearing and then appearing again. *And not just looks, but moods and habits and ruling passions, too,* she thought: Queen Sanasu had famously stopped talking to those around her and exiled herself to Wolfstooth Spire, so that she was seen by only a few servants and became all but invisible for the two or three decades before her death. Was that what was in store for her moody, beloved Barrick?

That ghastly thought, and the continuing fascination of Sanasu's white, otherworldly face, had grasped Briony's interest so firmly that she nearly screamed when the ancient jester Puzzle stepped out of the shadows nearby.

"By the gods, fellow," she demanded when her heart had slowed again, "what are you *doing?* You startled me out of my wits, creeping up like that."

"I am sorry, Princess, very sorry. I just . . . I was waiting for you . . ." He seemed to be considering whether he should get down onto one extremely creaky knee.

Briony reminded herself of her own prayer for Zorian patience. "Don't apologize, I will live. What is it, Puzzle?"

"I . . . it is just . . ." He looked as anxious as Barrick's page. "I am told that someone will share my room."

She took a breath. *Patience. Kindness.* "Is that too much trouble? It was a sudden thought. I'm sure we can find somewhere else to put this newcomer. I thought he might be company for you."

"A poet?" Puzzle couldn't seem to grasp the connection. "Well, we will see, Highness. It is possible we will get on. Certainly I do not speak to many people since . . . since your father has gone. And since my friend Robben died. It might be nice to have . . ." He blinked his rheumy eyes. It was possible that her father Olin was the only person on the continent of Eion who had ever found Puzzle amusing, or at least amusing in the way the jester tried to be. What must it be like, she wondered, to be supremely unfitted for your life's work? Even if she was impatient with him now, Briony couldn't help regretting the way she and Barrick had teased the bony old fellow all these years.

"If it turns out not to your liking, tell Nynor and he will find the poet some other place. Thinwight, or whatever his name is, is young and should be agreeable. Bad poets *need* to be agreeable." She nodded. "Now I have much to do . . ."

"My lady," the old man said, still having trouble meeting her eyes, "it was not that which I wished to speak about—well, not as much."

"What else?"

"I have a very great worry, my lady. Something that I have remembered, and that I fear I should have told earlier." He stopped to swallow. It did not look easy for him. "I think you know I visited your brother on the night of his death. That he called for me after supper and I came to his chamber to entertain him."

"Brone told me, yes." She was alert now.

"And that I left before Lord Shaso came."

"Yes? So? By the gods, Puzzle, don't make me work it out of you word by word!"

He winced. "It is just . . . your brother, may the gods grant his soul peace, sent me away that night. He was . . . not kind. He said that I was not diverting, that I never was—that my tricks and jests only made him feel . . . made him feel even more that life was wretched."

Kendrick had only told the truth, but she knew he must have been distressed indeed to be rude to old Puzzle. Her older brother had always been the most mannerly of the family. "He was unhappy," she told him. "It was an unhappy night. I am sure those were not his true thoughts. He was worried about me, remember, about the ransom for the king and whether he should send me away."

The jester shook his head in confusion and defeat. He was bareheaded, but the gesture was so familiar she could almost hear the tinkle of his belled cap. "That is not what I wanted to tell you, Highness. When Lord Brone asked me about that night, I told him what I remembered, but I forgot something. I think it is because I was so disturbed by what Prince Kendrick had said—a hard blow for someone who has devoted his life to the pleasure of the Eddons, you must admit . . ."

"Whatever the reason, what did you forget?" *Gods defend me! He certainly does test a person's patience.*

"As I left the residence, I saw Duke Gailon walking toward me. I was in the main hall, so it did not occur to me he might be going to see your older brother and I did not mention it to the lord constable after . . . that terrible event. But I have been thinking and thinking—sometimes I lay awake at night, worrying—and I think now that he was walking the wrong direction to be going to his own chambers. I think he might have been going to see Prince Kendrick." He bowed his head. "I have been a fool."

Briony didn't bother to reassure him. "Let me understand this. You are saying that you saw Gailon Tolly heading toward the residence as you were leaving. And you saw nothing of Shaso?"

"Not that night, but I went straight to my bed from there. Are you very angry, Highness? I am an old man, and sometimes I fear I am becoming a witling . . ."

"Enough. I will have to think about this. Have you told anyone else?"

"Only you. I . . . I believed you would . . ." He shook his head again, unable to say what he believed. "Shall I go to tell the lord constable?"

"No." She had said it too forcefully. "No, I think for now you should tell no one else. This will be our secret."

"You will not put me in the stronghold?"

"I suspect that sharing a room with that poet fellow will be punishment enough. You may go, Puzzle."

Long after the old man had tottered away she remained, standing beneath the pictures of her forebears, thinking.

23
The Summer Tower

SLEEPERS:

Feet of stone, legs of stone
Heart of aromatic cedar, head of ice
Face turned away

—from The Bonefall Oracles

HE PRACTICALLY HAD TO fight his way through the women to get to her. The physician could feel their resentment, as though he were some long-absent lover who had put this baby in her and then left her shamed and alone. *But the king is the father here, not me, and Olin is not absent by choice.*

Queen Anissa had grown so round in the belly that it made the rest of her slight frame seem even smaller. Seeing her in the center of the bed, surrounded by gauzy curtains like trailing cobwebs, he had a momentary image of her as a she-spider, gravid and still. It was unfair, of course, but it set him thinking.

"Is that Chaven?" To make room for him, she pushed away one of her small dogs, which had been sleeping against the curving side of her stomach like a rat dreaming of stealing a hippogriff's egg. The dog blinked, growled, then stumbled down to join its companion who snored near her feet. "Come here, quickly. I think I will give birth at any moment."

From the look of her, she might have been right. He was surprised by the dark circles under her eyes. In this room of draped windows, the only light an unsteady glow from the candle-studded altar, she looked as though she had been beaten.

"You need more air in this bedchamber." He took her hand and gave it a quick, formal kiss. The skin was dry and warm—a little too much of both. "And you look like you aren't getting enough sleep, my queen."

"Sleep? Who could sleep in such a time? Poor Kendrick murdered in our own house by a trusted servant, and then plague all through the town? Do you wonder I keep the windows covered to keep out bad airs?"

Calling Shaso a trusted servant seemed an interesting way of characterizing him, and the fact that she had not counted her husband's absence in her list of worries might also have been thought strange, but Chaven did not respond to her words. Instead, he busied himself examining the queen's heartbeat and the color of her eyes and gums, then leaned in to smell her breath, which at the moment was a little sour. "The plague is all but spent, Highness, and I imagine you were in far greater danger from your own maid when she had it than from it floating in from the town."

"And I sent her away until she was better, you can be sure. Didn't I, Selia? Where has she gone? Has she gone for seeing why I have no breakfast yet? Aah! Must you poke me so, Chaven?"

"Just wishing to be certain that you are well, that the baby is well." He let his hands move across the drum-taut arc of her stomach. The old midwife was still staring at him in a way that was a little less than friendly. "What do you think, Mistress Hisolda? The queen seems well enough to me, but you have more experience with such things."

The old woman showed a crooked smile, perhaps recognizing his gambit. "She is stronger than she looks, though the baby is a big one."

Anissa sat up. "That is just what I am feared of! He *is* big, I can tell—how he kicks! One of my sisters died birthing such a child—they saved the baby, but my sister died all . . . washed in blood!" She made a southern sign against evil happenstance. She was afraid, of course, Chaven could see that, but there was also a hint of falsity to her words, as though she played up her fear in hopes of sympathy. But why shouldn't she? It was a frightening business, childbirth, especially the first time. Anissa was already well past twenty winters, he reminded himself, not yet in the time of danger for first mothers but certainly past her prime according to all the learned men who had written about it.

This was also the first time Chaven had heard her refer to the baby as "he." The royal physician did not doubt that the midwife and her coven of helpers had been at work, perhaps dangling a pendulum over Anissa's stomach or reading splatters of candle wax. "If I order you a medicinal draught, will you promise to drink it every night?" He turned to Hisolda. "You will have no trouble finding the constituents, I'm sure."

The old woman raised her eyebrow. "If you say so, Doctor."

"But what is it, Chaven? Is it another one of your binding potions that will turn my bowels to stone?"

"No, just something to help you sleep. The baby will be strong and hearty, I am sure, and so will you be if you do not sit up nights frightening yourself." He stepped over to the midwife and listed the ingredients and their proportions—mostly wild lettuce and chamomile, nothing too strong. "Every night at sundown," he told the old woman. He was beginning to doubt that flattery worked on her, so he tried another tack, the truth. "I am a little frightened to see her so restless," he whispered.

"What are you saying?" Anissa moved herself heavily toward the edge of the bed, disturbing the dogs and setting them growling. "Is something wrong with the child?"

"No, no." He came back to her side, took her hand. "As I said, Highness, you are frightening yourself without need. You are well and the child is well. The plague seems to have passed us by, praise to Kupilas, Madi Surazem, and all the gods and goddesses who watch over us."

She let go of his hand, touched her face. "I have not been out of this place so long—I must look a dreadful monster."

"You look nothing of the sort, Highness."

"My husband's children think I am. A monster."

Chaven was surprised. "That is not true, my queen. Why would you say such a thing?"

"Because they do not come to see me. Days go by, weeks, and I do not see them." When she was excited her accent grew thicker. "I do not think they will love me like a mother, but they treat me like a serving maid."

"I don't believe Princess Briony and Prince Barrick feel that way at all, but they are much occupied," he said gently. "They are regents now, and many things are happening . . ."

"Like that handsome young Summerfield. I heard. Something bad has happened to him. Didn't I say that, Hisolda? When I heard he left the castle, I said 'Something is not right there,' didn't I?"

"Yes, Queen Anissa."

Chaven patted her hand. "I know nothing for certain of Gailon Tolly except that there are many rumors. But rumors are not to be trusted, are they? Not in a household already so upset by death and your husband's absence."

She grabbed his hand again. "Tell them," she said. "Tell them to come to me."

"You mean the prince and princess?"

She nodded. "Tell them that I cannot sleep because they shun me—that I do not know what I have done so they are angry with me!"

Chaven resolved to pass the message along in a slightly less heated form. It might be useful to convince the twins to come and visit their stepmother before the child arrived, for any number of reasons.

He removed his hand, disguising the escape as another kiss across her knuckles, then bowed and bade her farewell. He suddenly found that he wanted to be alone to think.

The little page had been roused from his pallet on the floor and sent to make his bed anew in the outer chamber. They were finally alone.

"What's troubling you so?" Briony sat down on the edge of the bed. "Talk to me."

Her brother pulled the fur lap robe up across his chest and huddled deeper into the blankets. It was not a warm night, not with true winter on the doorstep and Orphan's Day less than a month away, but Briony did not find the room particularly cold. *Is he still suffering with that fever?* It had been at least a tennight but she knew some fevers did not loose their grip for a long time, or came back again and again.

"Why did you say that idiot poet could stay in the household?"

"He amused me." Was she going to have to discuss it with everyone? "In truth, I thought he might amuse you, too. He tried to convince me he was writing an epic poem about me—a 'pangegyric,' whatever that is. Comparing me to Zoria herself. The gods alone know what he'll compare *you* to. Perin, probably . . . no, Erivor in his seahorse chariot." She tried to smile. "After all, Puzzle isn't as diverting as he used to be—I think I'm beginning to feel too sorry for him. I thought it would do the two of us good to have someone new to make fun of. Which reminds me, Puzzle came to me when I was leaving your room earlier today. Told me that on the night Kendrick was killed, he saw Gailon in the hallway."

Barrick frowned. He seemed not just sleepy but a little dazed. "Kendrick saw Gailon . . . ?"

"No, *Puzzle* saw Gailon." She quickly repeated what the old jester had told her.

"He has heard that Gailon has disappeared," Barrick said dismissively. "That is all. He wishes to be remembered as denouncing him if it turns out that Gailon is a traitor."

"I don't know. Puzzle never bothered with politicking before."

"Because Father was here to protect him." Barrick's expression suddenly changed into something vague, distant. "Do you like him?"

"Who?"

"The poet. He is handsome. He speaks well."

"Handsome? I suppose, in a prettified sort of way. He has an absurd beard. But that is certainly not why I said he could . . ." She realized she had been led astray again. "Barrick, I don't want to waste any more breath on that callow fool. If you dislike the poet so much, give him some money and send him away, I don't care. I'm convinced he's nothing to do with the greater matter. Which is what we're going to talk about."

"I don't want to." He spoke with all the dolefulness that he had made his art. Briony wondered if other siblings felt this way, sometimes loving and hating at the exact same moment. Or was it only twins, so close that it often seemed she had to wait for Barrick to breathe before she could get air into her own lungs?

"You *will* talk. You almost killed that potboy. Why, Barrick?" When he didn't reply, she leaned across the bed and clutched his arm. "Zoria preserve us, this is me! *Me!* Briony! Kendrick is dead, Father is gone—we only have each other."

He looked at her from beneath his lashes like a frightened child. "You don't really want to know. You just want me to behave well. You just hate it that I embarrassed you in front of Brone and . . . and that poet."

She blew out breath in exasperation. "That's not true. You are my brother. You're . . . you're nearly the other half of me." She found his eye and held it, but it was like trying to keep a skittish animal from bolting. "Look at me, Barrick. You know that's not what happened. The potboy said something about . . . about dreams. About your dreams. Then you tried to throttle him."

"He had no right to talk about me that way."

"*What* way, Barrick?"

He pulled the blankets even tighter, still deciding. "You said you read the letter from Father again," he said at last. "Did you notice anything interesting?"

"About the Autarch? I already told you . . ."

"No, not about the Autarch. Did you notice anything interesting in it *about me?*"

She stopped, confused. "Anything . . . no. No. He sent you his love. He said to tell you his health had been good."

He shook his head. His face was grim, as though he were stepping out onto some narrow prominence, trying not to look down at a great distance opening before him. "You don't understand."

"How can I? Talk to me! Tell me what has you so upset. You tried to kill an innocent man . . . !"

"Innocent? That potboy's no man, he's a demon. He saw into my dreams, Briony. He spoke about them in front of you and Brone and that mongrel quill-carver!" Despite the chill, Barrick had a thin sheen of sweat on his forehead. "He is probably talking about them still to anyone who'll listen. He knows. He knows!" He turned and rammed his face against the cushion. His shoulders heaved.

"Knows what?" She grabbed at his arm with both hands and shook him. "Barrick, what have you done?"

He turned, eyes damp, red-rimmed. "Done? Nothing. Not yet."

"I can't make any sense of this at all." She combed a tangle of damp red hair back off his brow with her fingers. "Just talk. Whatever is wrong, you're still my brother. I'll still love you."

He let out a snort of disbelief but the storm had passed. He let his head fall back on the cushion and stared up at the timbered ceiling. "I'll tell you what Father's letter said. *'Tell Barrick that he should be glad for me. Although I am a captive, my health has actually been much better this last half year. I almost think it has done me good to get away from the damp northern airs.'* That's what he wrote."

Briony shook her head. "What, do you think he means that he is happier being away from us—from you? He is jesting, Barrick. Trying to make light of a terrible situation . . ."

"No. No, he's not. Because you don't know what he's talking about and I do." The fire in him had died down. He closed his eyes. "Do you remember the nights when Father couldn't sleep? When he would go to the Tower of Summer and sit up all night with his books?" She nodded. The first few times Olin's ability to slip away had been the cause of much alarm around the residence, until his family and the guards had learned to look for him in his library in the tower. The king had returned each time from these midnight excursions with an embarrassed air, as if he had been found in drunken sleep on the throne-room floor. Briony had always believed that it was thoughts of his dead wife that tormented him so badly on those nights that he could not sleep: he always spoke of their mother Meriel as though he had loved her very much, even though the marriage had originally been arranged by his father, King Ustin, when Olin and Meriel, the daughter of a powerful Brennish duke, were both very young. Everyone in the household knew that her death had been a hard, hard blow for him.

"And you remember that he would always bar the door?"

"Of course." Locked out, the guards had only been able to rouse the king by banging on the door until he came to open it, blinking like an owl and wiping at sleepy eyes. "I . . . I think he cried. He didn't want anyone to see him weeping. Over our mother."

Barrick showed a strange, tight-lipped smile. "Weeping? Maybe. But not over our mother."

"What . . . what do you mean?"

He glanced up at the ceiling and took a few deep breaths, as though he were not merely standing on some high, lonely place but preparing to jump. "I . . . I went there one night. I had a nightmare. I think I must even have been walking in my sleep—it might have been the first time—because I woke up outside his chamber and I was very frightened and I wanted him to . . . to tell me things would be all right. I went in and he wasn't there, even though his servants were all there, sleeping. I knew he must be in his library. So I went out of the residence by that back chapel door so the guards wouldn't stop me. It was near Midsummer, I think—I only remember it was warm and it felt so strange being out in the courtyard in my nightshirt and bare feet. I felt like I could go anywhere—just walk where I wanted to, even walk to another country, as though the moon would stay up and bright as long as the journey would take, and that when I woke up there, I would be a different person." He shook his head. "It was a full moon, very big. I remember that, too."

"How long ago was this?"

"The year that part of the roof fell off Wolfstooth. And the cook with the skinny arms died and we weren't allowed to go in the kitchen all spring."

"Ten years ago. You mean the year . . . the year you hurt your arm."

He nodded slowly. She could sense that he was balancing something, trying to decide. She tried to sit quietly, but her heart was beating fast and she was unexpectedly frightened.

"The downstairs door was locked, but the key was still in the other side and he hadn't turned the lock all the way. It popped open when I wiggled the latch, then I went up the steps all the way to the library. There were no guards at the tower, no one there at all. I didn't think it was strange while it was happening—the whole night seemed like a dream, not just that—but I should have wondered why he'd sent them away, or slipped away from them, just to be by himself. But I wouldn't have wondered long. When I reached the door, I could . . . hear him."

"Was he crying?"

Barrick took a moment to answer. "Crying, yes. Making all kinds of noises, although I could barely hear them through the door. Laughing, it almost sounded like. Talking. At first I thought he was having an argument with someone, then I thought perhaps he was asleep and having a nightmare, just like the one that had woken me up. So I knocked on the door. Quietly at first, but the noises on the other side just went on. So I banged on it with my fists and shouted, 'Father, wake up!' Then he opened the door." For a moment it seemed Barrick would continue, but instead his shoulders heaved and he took in a ragged gasp of air. He was sobbing.

"Barrick, what is it? What happened?" She climbed up onto the bed and wrapped her arms around him. His muscles were as tight as the cording on a knife hilt and he trembled as though in the full grip of fever again. "Are you ill?"

"Don't . . . ! Don't talk. I want . . ." He sucked in another rough breath. "He opened the door. Father opened the door. He . . . he didn't recognize me. I don't think he did, anyway. His eyes . . . ! Briony, his eyes were wild, wild like an animal's eyes! And his shirt was off and he had scratches on his belly—bleeding. He was bleeding. He took one look at me and then grabbed me, pulled me into the library. He was talking nonsense—I couldn't understand a word—and he was pulling at me, growling at me. Like an animal! I thought he was going to kill me. I still think it."

"Merciful Zoria!" She didn't know what to believe. The world was upside down. She felt like she had been thrown from Snow's saddle and all the air had been knocked out of her chest. "Are you . . . could you have dreamed it . . . ?"

His face was twisted with pain and rage. "Dreamed it? That was the night my arm was crippled. Do you think I dreamed that?"

"What do you mean? Oh, by all the gods, that was when it happened?"

"I broke away from him. He chased me. I was trying to get to the door but I kept tripping over books, knocking over piles of them. He had every book in the library on the floor, stacked up like towers, with candlesticks on top of each one. I must have knocked over half a dozen trying to get away—I still don't know why that wretched tower didn't burn down that night. I wish it had. I wish it had!" He was breathing hard now, like someone near the end of a race. "I got to the door at last. He kept chasing me, growling and cursing and talking nonsense. He grabbed me at the top of the stairs and tried to pull me back to the library again. I . . . I bit him on the hand and he let go. I fell down the stairs.

"When I woke up, it was the next day and Chaven was setting the bones of my arm—or trying to. I could barely think from the pain, and from the way my skull had been rattled when I fell. Chaven said that Father had found me at the foot of the steps in the Tower of Summer, which was probably true, that he had carried me to Chaven himself, crying over my injuries, begging him to heal me. That was probably true, too. But Chaven says that Father brought me to him at dawn, which means that I had been left lying there the rest of the night. The story told was that I had come looking for him and had fallen down the stairs in the dark."

Briony could barely think. Like Barrick on that night, she was in a waking nightmare. "But . . . Father? Why would he do such a thing to you? Had he . . . was he drunk?" It was hard to imagine her abstemious father drinking himself into that kind of roaring, black mood, but nothing else made sense.

Barrick was still shaking, but only a little now. He tried to slide out of her arms, but she held on. "No, Briony. He was not drunk. You haven't heard the rest, although I'm sure you won't want to believe me."

She didn't want to hear any more, but she was afraid to let Barrick go, afraid that if she did he would somehow fly away like that half-tamed pigeonhawk she had lost when its creance snapped and it had gone spiraling out from her, never to return. She tightened her grip so that for a moment they were almost wrestling, rucking the covers around Barrick's legs until he gave up trying to escape her. "I have always had nightmares," he said at last, quietly. "Dreamed that there were men watching me, men made of smoke and blood, following me all through the castle, waiting to catch me alone so they could steal me away, or somehow make me one of them. At least, I always believed they were dreams. Now, I'm not so certain. But after that night, I began to have one that's worse than the others. Always him—his face, but it isn't his face. It's a stranger's face. When he came after me, he looked . . . like a beast."

"Oh, my poor Barrick . . ."

"You may want to be more careful with your sympathies." His voice was partially muffled by the cushion. He seemed to have grown smaller in her arms, curled into himself. "You remember I was in bed for weeks. Kendrick came to bring me things, you came and played with me every day, or tried to . . ."

"You were so quiet and pale. It frightened me."

"It frightened me, too. And Father came, but he never stayed more than a few moments. Do you know, I might even have believed it had all been a nightmare—that I really had just been sleepwalking and then fell down the steps—except for the way he could not be around me without fidgeting and avoiding my eyes. Then, one day, when I was finally up and limping around the household instead of confined to that cursed bed, he called me into his chambers. 'You remember, don't you?' was the first thing he said. I nodded. I was almost as frightened then as the night it happened. I thought I was the one who had done something terribly wrong, although I wasn't sure what it was. I half thought he might try to murder me again or have me thrown in the stronghold to rot in a cell. Instead he burst into tears—I swear it's true. He wrapped his arms around me and pulled me to him and kissed my head, all the time crying so hard that he got my hair wet. He was hurting my arm badly, which was tied up in a sling. Once I stopped being frightened, I hated him. If I could have killed him at that moment, I would have."

"Barrick!"

"You wanted the truth, Briony. This is what it looks like." He finally wriggled himself free of her. "He told me that he had done a terrible thing and begged my forgiveness. I took him to mean that chasing me so that I fell down the stairs and shattered my arm, crippling myself so that I could never play or ride or draw a bow like the other boys was the terrible thing, but as he clutched me and talked I began to understand that the terrible thing he had done was to sire me in the first place."

"What?"

"Be quiet and listen!" he said fiercely. "It is a madness that Father has. It came on him when he was a young man—first as terrible dreams, later as a restless, monstrously angry spirit that, on the nights when it takes him, grows so strong it cannot be resisted. He has it and one of his uncles had it. It is a family curse. He told me that it had grown so strong in him that although months might go by and it remained absent, on the nights he felt it coming back he could only lock himself away to rage by himself. That was how I had found him."

"A family curse . . . ?"

He showed her a bitter smile. "Fear not. You don't have it and neither did Kendrick. You are the lucky ones—the yellow-haired ones. Father told me that he had studied the Eddon family histories, and that he had never found any trace of the curse in any of the fair-haired children. Only the gods know why. You are the golden ones, in more ways than one."

"But you have . . ." She suddenly understood. Again, it was like being struck a hard blow. "Oh, Barrick, you are afraid you might have this, too?"

"Might have it? No, Sister, I already do. The dreams started even earlier for me than they did for Father."

"You had a fever . . . !"

"Long before the fever." He let out a shaky breath. "Although, since then, they have been worse. I wake up in the night cold with sweat, thinking only of killing, of blood. And since the fevers, I . . . I see things, too. Waking, sleeping, it almost makes no difference. I am watched. The house is full of shadows."

She was stunned, helpless. She had never felt so distant from him, and for Briony that was a shocking, raw feeling, as though a part of her own body had been torn away. "I hardly know what to say—this is all so strange! But . . . but even if Father has some . . . madness, he still has managed to be a good man, a loving father. Perhaps you are worrying too . . ."

Again he interrupted her. "A loving father who threw me down the stairs. A loving father who told me he should never have sired me." His face was stony. "You have not been listening very carefully. It started early in me. My madness won't be mild, like Father's—a few days a year when he must shut himself away from the rest of mankind. That is what he meant in the letter, do you see now? That he has not suffered badly from the madness since he has been captive. It is nothing to do with making jokes, he was talking to me about something ugly we both share—our tainted blood. But his will seem mild next to mine. Mine will grow and grow until you have no choice but to lock me away in a cage like a beast—or to kill me."

"Barrick!"

"Go away, Briony." He was weeping again, but without much movement this time and with his eyes half shut: the tears came out of some deep, hard place, like water through a cracked stone. "You know what you came to learn. I don't want to talk anymore."

"But I . . . I want to help you."

"Then leave me alone."

The mists had grown so thick that they all had to travel like blind pilgrims, each one clinging to the one before him and being clung to in turn. Only the girl Willow who led them was not hung between two fellows front and back. She walked more slowly now in the smothering whiteness, but still with purpose, always forward.

Dab Dawley had hold of Vansen's cloak. Sound was confused in the mist and it was sometimes hard to hear even words spoken in a loud voice by a man a few yards away, but Vansen thought the young guardsman might be whimpering.

They had slept two times and walked for most of the waking hours between those sleeps, yet still had found no end to the terrible forest. Ferras Vansen did not have the sense they were walking in circles in the aimless way he and Collum Dyer did before, but he was still disheartened that two days' march had not taken them back to the fields of men.

It could be that even if we're not going in circles, we've turned the wrong direction. Perhaps I've trusted in the girl too much. The moon, after an initial appearance when they were setting out, had been as scarce as the sun. *But perhaps we are going in the right direction, only the Shadowline has continued to spread.* It was a hard, chill thought. *Perhaps all the lands everywhere are now truly under shadow.*

"Are you sure you know where home is?" he whispered to the girl when they were all standing together on a shelf of rock above what sounded like either a quiet stream just beneath them or a very noisy one far below. Whatever the distance stretching beneath them, they were taking no chances; they leaned back against the cliff face side by side as they rested.

She smiled at him. Her thin, dirty face was weary, but some of the early expression of almost religious ecstasy had worn away, along with some of the fear and confusion. "I will find it. They have just dragged it far away."

"Dragged what?"

Willow shook her head. "Trust in the gods. They see through all the darkness. They see your good works."

And my bad ones, Vansen couldn't help thinking. The two days or however long it had been, struggling step by slow step through the murk, had left him much time to brood on his failures of command. Now that the worst shock of losing most of his company had worn down to a persistent, painful ache, he felt almost as wretched about losing the merchant's nephew, Raemon Beck. He couldn't help seeing Beck's miserable face in his mind's eye. *The poor fellow was certain something like this would happen— that we would drag him back into shadow, that he would meet his doom here. And it seems he was right.* But perhaps Raemon Beck and the other guardsmen were alive, merely lost as he and Dyer had been lost. Perhaps he might even discover them before leaving the shadowlands. It was something to cling to, a hope to make the bleak hours a little less haunting.

"What's that?" Dawley said in a sharp whisper, yanking Vansen's thoughts back to the damp, mist-shrouded hillside where the company was resting.

"I heard nothing. What was it?"

"A tapping sound—there it is again! It sounds like . . . like claws clicking on stone."

A thought that would make no one any happier, Vansen knew. He himself could not hear it, but Dawley had by far the sharpest ears of any of them. "Let's move on, then," Vansen said, doing his best to keep his voice calm. "Willow? We need you to lead us again, girl."

"Lead us where, I'm asking?" said Southstead. "Right into the nest of some great cave bear or something like."

"None of that," Dyer told him sharply. They had found something a little like military discipline again, but it was fragile.

They moved carefully along the narrow trail. Vansen held onto the girl's tattered shift only lightly, wanting to be able to move his arms quickly if he stumbled and lost his balance. The unknown distance to the side of them began to feel even more frightening as they hurried along. In his imagination, Vansen could almost feel the invisible bottom of the ravine grow deeper, dropping away from them like water running out of a leaky bucket.

"There's something there!" shouted Balk, the last in line; his voice seemed to come to them down a long tunnel. "Up there! Behind us!"

Vansen tightened his grip on the girl's smock and turned to look back. For a moment he could see it coming along the top of the cliff face behind them, a grotesque, drawn-out shape like a scarecrow going on four legs, but more tattered and less comprehensible, then it reared up to an unbelievable height, stiltlike legs pawing, before the mist folded around it again.

Terror set his heart rattling in his chest. "Perin save us! Faster, girl!"

She did her best, but the trail was narrow and untrustworthy. The men behind him were cursing and even sobbing. Gravel slid from beneath Vansen's feet.

Now he could hear the thing just above them, clicking and scratching like the armored claws of a crab dragging across the wet rock between tide-pools. The mists had grown thicker. He could barely see the girl moving before him as she climbed a short rise, even though he was still clinging to her hem. A shower of stones fell between them and he looked up to see a dark and indistinct shape loom out of the curtaining fogs only half a dozen yards above. If that was the thing's head, it was misshapen as the stump of a twisted tree. For a moment he could hear it breathe, a deep, scratchy wheeze, as a scrabbling leg probed down the rock face. Vansen let go of Willow's garment so he could draw his sword, but the ragged limb stopped short. The thing was still too far above them. It drew back into the mists.

"Go—quick as you can to open ground!" he told the girl, then turned to shout back to the others. "Let go and draw your swords, but don't get separated! Dawley, do you have arrows still?" He heard the young guardsman grunt something he could not quite make out. "Try to get a shot if you can see it well enough."

Vansen scrambled up the path behind the girl, doing his best to lean in toward the hillface despite every screaming sense telling him to lean back, away from the reaching arms of the thing that stalked just up the slope. Behind him the men had become a disorganized rout, but he did not know what else to do; to make them try to continue walking while holding onto each other and their weapons would be to invite disaster. They needed to find their way to some open space where Dawley's bow and their swords might save them.

He staggered and put his foot down on loose soil, then windmilled his arms to keep from tipping out into the misty invisibility behind him. As he regained his footing, another scrabbling noise came from behind him, then a strange wooden creaking and a sudden screech from one of the men—a sound of such naked animal terror that he could not even tell who was making it. He turned, blade held high, to see the huge thing had lunged downward out of the fogs like a spider gliding down a web. The men around it were screaming and hacking away. In the instant it was among them, it still had no semblance or shape of anything he could understand—spindly arms long as tree branches, hanging rags of skin or fur almost like singed parchment. It was a madness, an obscenity. For an instant only he saw in the chaos what seemed to be a sagging hole of a mouth and a single empty black eye, then the huge thing went scuttling backward up the cliff face with a kicking, shrieking bundle clutched in its folding limbs. Beside him, Dawley cursed and wept as he loosed a single arrow at the shape, then it disappeared into the mists again.

It had taken Collum Dyer.

They staggered now in silence, Vansen choked with despair. The thing had caught what it wanted and they did not see it again, but it was as though it had reached down and plucked their hearts away with their comrade. Vansen had known Collum Dyer since he first came to Southmarch. He found his thoughts turning helplessly again and again to that moment, to Dyer's screams. Once he had to stop and be sick, but there was little in his stomach to vomit out.

When they finally reached the edge of the cliff path they stopped, gasping for breath as though they had been running at uttermost speed, although they had spent most of the hour since the attack barely at walking pace. Mickael Southstead and Balk were gray with fear; they knelt on the ground, praying, although to what gods Vansen couldn't guess. The girl Willow was clearly frightened, too, but sat on a stone as patiently as a child being punished.

Young Dawley stood with his bow still in his hand and his last arrow on the string, tears in his eyes.

"What was it?" he asked his captain at last.

Ferras Vansen could only shake his head. "Did you hit it?"

It took Dawley a moment to reply, as though he had to wait for Vansen's voice to blow down a long canyon. "Hit it?"

"You shot at it. I want to know what happened, in case it comes back. Did you hit it?"

"I wasn't trying to hit it, Captain." Dawley wiped at his face with the back of his hand. "I was . . . was trying to kill Collum . . . before it took him away. But I couldn't see if . . . if I . . ."

Vansen closed his eyes for a moment, fighting back tears of his own. He put his hand on the young guardsman's quivering shoulder. "The gods grant you made a good shot, Dab."

★　　★　　★

So bleak and quiet was the company, so defeated, that when Vansen saw the moon again he didn't speak of it, not wanting to raise hopes that had been so often dashed. But after an hour more trudging silently behind the girl he could not ignore the fact that the mists were clearing. The moon was not alone—there were stars, too, speckled across the sky as cold and bright as ice crystals.

They walked on through the high grass of wet hillside meadows and through thinning stands of trees, still alert to any sound, but after a while Vansen was certain that something truly had changed. The moon was far down in the sky now, a sky that had always before been blurry with fog and cloud.

They were all staggeringly tired, and for a few moments he considered stopping to build a fire so they could dry out wet clothes and snatch a little sleep, but he was afraid that if he closed his eyes he would open them again to find everything submerged in silvery nothingness again. Also, the girl was striding determinedly forward despite her weariness, like a horse on the path back to the barn at the end of a long day, and he didn't want to disturb her. Now that the mists had thinned, he let go of her ragged smock and dropped back to walk for a little while with each of the men in turn, Southstead, Dawley, Balk, saying nothing unless they spoke to him, trying to turn his savaged company back into something whole again, or at least into something human. He couldn't pretend that he was not overseeing a disaster, but he could make the best out of what he had.

They trooped on through shadowy glens and over moonlit hills. The sky began to change color, warming from black to a purple-tinted gray, and for the first time in days Vansen began to believe they might actually find their way out again.

But where? Into the middle of that fairy army? Or will we find that we have been wandering for a hundred years, like one of the old tales, and that all the world and the folk we knew are gone?

Still, even with these heavy thoughts in his head, he couldn't help smiling when he saw the first gleam of sunrise on the horizon. His eyes welled up, so that for a moment the patch of bright sky smeared. There would be some kind of day after all. There would be east and west and north and south again.

The sun didn't burn through the mist until it was high into the sky, but it was the real sun and the real sky, beyond doubt. No one wanted to stop now.

Most astonishingly of all, before the sun was halfway up the morning sky, they struck the Settland Road.

"Praise all the gods!" shouted Balk. He ran forward, did a clumsy dance on the rutted dirt that covered the ancient stones and timbers. "Praise them each and every one!"

As the other men tumbled down into the grass by the roadside, laughing and clapping each other on the back in joy, Vansen looked up and down the road, not completely ready to trust. It was the same road, but what arrested him was what part of the road it was.

"Perin Cloudwalker!" he murmured, half to himself. "She's brought us back to the place where we met her. That's miles from where we crossed over. And miles closer to Southmarch, thank the gods!" He staggered on aching legs to where the girl stood, smiling a little, staring around her in calm confusion. He grabbed her and kissed her cheek, lifted her up and put her down again. He had a sudden thought then and hurried eastward down the road with the men shouting questions after him. Sure enough, at the next long straight stretch he found a height where he could climb up and see that mists had enveloped the road not a mile away to the east. *She's brought us back to our side of the Shadowline, but also we're now between the shadow-army and the city, bless her! But how could that be?* He tried to understand what had happened but could only guess that the substance of the lands behind the Shadowline was different than that of other lands, and not just because of mists and monsters. Somehow the girl had managed to find her way across a fold of shadow and bring them back to the place where she herself first crossed over, long before they even found her.

He hurried back to the others. "We will rest for a short while," he said, "but then we have to find horses and ride as fast as we can. Southmarch is ahead of us and the enemy is behind us, but who knows how long until they catch up? The girl has given us a precious gift—we must not waste it, or waste the lives of our comrades either." He turned to Willow. "I may wind up in chains for my part in all this, but if Southmarch survives, I'll see you dressed in silks and laden with gold first. You may have saved us all!"

24
Leopards and Gazelles

GROWING JOY:

The hives are full
The leaves fall and drift slowly
Death is agreeable now

—from *The Bonefall Oracles*

Q INNITAN GROANED. "Why do I feel so ill?"

"Get up, you!" Favored Luian slapped at one of her Tuani servants, who ducked with a practiced shrug so that the blow only grazed the girl's black-haired head. "What are you doing, you lazy lizard?" Luian shrieked. "That cloth is dry as dust." She reached out and gave the girl's arm a cruel pinch. "Go and get Mistress Qinnitan some more water!"

The slave got up and refilled the bowl from the fountain splashing quietly in the corner of the room, then returned with it and resumed cooling Qinnitan's forehead.

"I don't know, my darling," Luian said as if the outburst had not happened. "A touch of fever, perhaps. Nothing dreadful, I'm sure. You must say your prayers and drink dishflower tea." She seemed distracted by something more than Qinnitan's miseries, her eyes flicking from side to side as though she expected to be interrupted at any moment.

"It's that potion they give me every day, I'm sure." Qinnitan tried to sit straight, groaned, and gave up. It was not worth the expenditure of strength.

"Oh, Luian, I hate it. It makes me feel so wretched. Do you think they're poisoning me?"

"Poisoning you?" For a moment Luian actually looked at her. Her laugh was harsh and a bit shrill. "My small sweet one, if the Golden One wished you dead, it would not be poison that killed you, it would be something much . . ." She paled a little, caught herself. "What a thing to say! As if our beloved autarch, praises to his name, would want you dead, in any case. You have done nothing to displease him. You have been a very good girl."

Qinnitan sighed and tried to tell herself Luian must be right. It didn't quite feel like being poisoned, anyway, or at least not how she imagined such a thing would feel. Nothing hurt, and she wasn't exactly ill—in fact, generally her appetite was extremely good and she slept well, too, if a little too long and deeply sometimes—but something definitely felt strange. "You're right, of course. You're always right, Luian." She yawned. "In fact, I think I feel a little better now. I should go back to my room and have a nap instead of lolling around here and being in your way."

"Oh, no, no!" Luian looked startled at the suggestion. "No, you . . . you should come for a walk with me. Yes, let us take a walk in the Scented Garden. That would do you more good than anything. Just the thing to brush away those cobwebs."

Qinnitan had been living in the Seclusion too long not to see that something was troubling Luian, and it was strange for her to suggest the Scented Garden, which was on the opposite side of the Seclusion, when it would have been much easier to stroll in the Garden of Queen Sodan. "I suppose I can bear a walk, yes. Are you certain? You must have things to do . . ."

"I can think of nothing more important than helping you feel better, my little dear one. Come."

The Scented Garden was warmer than the halls of the Seclusion, but the canopies atop its high walls kept it cool enough to be bearable and its airs were very sweet and pleasant, suffused with myrtle and forest roses and snakeleaf: after a short while Qinnitan began to feel a little stronger. As they walked, Luian spouted a litany of petty complaints and irritations in a breathless voice that made her seem far younger than she was. She was more sharp-tongued with her servants than usual, too, so savage in her scolding of one of the Tuanis when the girl bumped her elbow that several other people in the garden, wives and servants, looked up, and the usually expressionless slave girl curled her lip above her teeth, as though she were about to snarl or even bite.

"Oh, I've just remembered," Luian said suddenly. "I left my nicest shawl in that little retiring room here yesterday—there, in the corner." She pointed to a shadowed doorway far back between two rows of boxwood hedges. "But I'm so hot, I think I'll just sit down on this bench. Will you be a dear and get it for me, Qinnitan? It's rose-colored. You can't miss it."

Qinnitan hesitated. There was something strange about Luian's face. She suddenly felt frightened. "Your shawl . . . ?"

"Yes. Go get it, please. In there." She pointed again.

"You left it . . . ?" Luian almost never came to this garden, and it was famously warm. Why bring a shawl here?

Luian leaned close and said, in a strangled whisper, "Just go and get it, you silly little bitch!"

Qinnitan jumped up, startled and more fearful than ever. "Of course."

As she approached the dark doorway, she could not help slowing her footsteps, listening for the breath of a hidden assassin behind the hedges. But why would Luian resort to something so crude? Unless it was the autarch himself who had decided it had all been a mistake, that Qinnitan was not the one he wanted. Perhaps the mute giant Mokor, his infamous chief strangler, was waiting for her inside the doorway. Or perhaps she wasn't important enough and her death would be effected instead by someone like the so-called gardener, Tanyssa. Qinnitan looked back, but Luian was looking in another direction entirely, talking rapidly and a little too loudly with her slaves.

Her nerves now stretched tight as lute strings, Qinnitan let out a muffled shriek when the man stepped from the shadows.

"Quiet! I believe you are looking for this," he said, holding out a shawl woven of fine silk. "Do not forget it when you go out again."

"Jeddin!" She threw her hand over her mouth. "What are you doing here?" A whole man in the Seclusion—what would happen to him if they were caught? What would happen to her?

The Leopard captain quickly and easily moved between her and the door, cutting off her escape. She looked frantically around the small, dark room. There was nothing much in it but a low table and some cushions, and no other way out.

"I wished to see you. I wished to . . . speak with you." Jeddin stepped up and caught her hand in his wide fingers, pulled her deeper into the room. Her heart was beating so quickly she could scarcely take a breath, but she could not entirely ignore the strength of his grip or the way it made her feel. If he wished, he could throw her over one of his broad shoulders and carry her away and there would be nothing she could do.

Except scream, of course, but who could guess what she would earn for herself if she did?

"Come, I will not keep you long," he said. "I have put my life in your hands by coming here, Mistress. Surely you will not begrudge me a few moments."

He was looking at her so searchingly, so intently, that she found she could not meet his eye. She felt hot and feverish again. Could this all be some mad dream? Could the priest's elixir have driven her mad? Still, Jeddin looked disturbingly solid, huge and handsome as a temple carving. "What do you want with me?"

"What I cannot have, I know." He let go of her hand, made his own into a fist. "I . . . I cannot stop thinking of you, Qinnitan. My heart will not rest. You haunt my dreams, even. I drop things, I forget things . . ."

She shook her head, really frightened now. "No. No, that is . . ." She took a step toward him and then thought better of it—his arms had risen as if to pull her toward him, and she knew that more than his strength would make it hard to break away again. "This is all madness, Jeddin . . . Captain. Even if . . . if we forget why I am here in the Seclusion, who has brought me here . . ." She froze at a noise from outside, but it was just two of the younger wives shrieking with laughter as they played some game. "Even if we forget that, you scarcely know me. You have seen me twice . . . !"

"No, Mistress, no. I saw you every day that I was a child and you were a child. When we were children together. You were the only one who was kind to me." The look on his face was so serious that it would have been comical if she had not been in terror for her life. "I know it is wrong, but I cannot bear to think that you will . . . that you are for . . . for *him*."

She shook her head at this blasphemy, wanting only to be far away. There was something about the young Leopard chieftain that made her heart ache, made her want to comfort him, and there was no question she felt something for him that went beyond that, but she could not push away her growing fright. Each moment that passed she felt more like the quarry of some ruthless hunting pack. "All that will happen is that we will both be killed. Whatever you think, Jeddin, you scarcely know me."

"Call me Jin, as you once did."

"No! We were just children. You followed my brothers. They were cruel to you, perhaps, but I was no better. I was a girl, a shy girl. I said nothing to any of my brother's friends to stop them."

"You were kind. You liked me."

She let out a murmured groan of frustration and anguish. "Jeddin! You must go away and never do this again!"

"Do you love him?"

"Who? You mean the . . . ?" She moved closer, so close she could feel his breath on her face. She put a hand on his broad chest to keep him from trying to embrace her. "Of course I don't," she said quietly. "I am nothing to our master, less than nothing—a chair, a rug, a bowl in which to clean his hands. But I would not steal a washing bowl from him, and neither would you. If you try to steal me, we'll both be killed." She took a breath. "I do care for you, Jeddin, at least a little."

The anxious lines on his forehead disappeared. "Then there is hope. There is reason to live."

"Quiet! You did not hear me out. I care for you, and in another life perhaps it could be more, but I don't wish to die for any man. Do you understand? Go away. Never even think of me again." She tried to pull away, but he caught her now in a grip she could not have broken in a thousand years. "Let go!" she whispered, looking in panic toward the doorway. "They will be wondering where I've gone."

"Luian will distract them a while longer." He leaned forward until she almost whimpered from the size and closeness of him. "You do not love him."

"Let me go!"

"Ssshh. I am not long for this place. My enemies want to throw me down."

"Enemies?"

"I am a peasant who became chieftain of the autarch's own guards. The paramount minister Vash hates me. I amuse the Golden One—he calls me his rough watchdog and laughs when I use the wrong words—but Pinimmon Vash and the others wish to see my head on a spike. I could kill any one of them with my bare hands, but in this palace it is the gazelles that rule, not the leopards."

"Then why are you giving them this chance to destroy you? This is beyond foolishness—you'll murder us both."

"No. I will think of something. We will be together." His eyes went distant and Qinnitan's speeding heart bumped and seemed to miss a beat. In that moment he looked nearly as mad as the autarch. "We will be together," he said again.

She took advantage of his distraction and yanked her wrist out of his grasp, then backed hurriedly toward the doorway. "Go away, Jeddin! Don't be a fool!"

His eyes were suddenly shiny with tears. "Stop," he said. "Don't forget." He threw her the rose-colored shawl. "I will come to you one night."

Qinnitan almost choked. "You will do *no such thing!*" She turned and hurried out the door, back into the heavy air of the Scented Garden.

"Are you mad, too?" she whispered to Luian as she handed her the shawl. A few of the other wives were watching her, but with what she prayed was no more than a bored interest in the comings and goings of a fellow prisoner. "We will all be executed! Tortured!"

Luian did not look at her, but her face was mottled with red underneath the heavy face paint. "You do not understand."

"Understand? What is there to understand? You are . . ."

"I am only one of the Favored. He is the chief of the autarch's Leopards. He could have me arrested and killed on almost any pretext he chose—who would believe the word of a fat castrate in women's clothes over the master of the Golden One's muskets?"

"Jeddin wouldn't do such a thing."

"He would indeed—he said so. He told me he would."

Qinnitan was shocked. "He thinks he is in love," she said at last. "People do mad things when they feel that way."

"Yes." Luian faced her now, and there were tears in the Favored's long-lashed eyes. One had made a track down the powder of her cheek. "Yes, you silly little girl, they do."

25
Mirrors, Missing and Found

THE WEEPING OF ANCIENT WOMEN:

Gray as the egrets of the Hither Shore
Lost as a wind from the old, dark land
Frightened yet fierce

—from *The Bonefall Oracles*

CHERT HAD ALREADY SAT DOWN on the bench to rest his tired legs when he realized Opal had not followed him in, but was still standing in the doorway, peering out into Wedge Road. "What is it, my dear?"

"Flint. He's not with you?"

He frowned. "Why would he be with me? I left him home with you because he's such a distraction where we're working right now—won't stay with me because he doesn't like it there, but won't stay where I tell him aboveground either . . ." He felt a clutch in his chest. "You mean he's gone?"

"I don't know! Yes! He went with me to Lower Ore Street. Then, when I came back, he was playing beside the road, piling up stones and making those walls and tunnels and whatnot he likes so much—the dust that comes in on that boy!" Tears filled her eyes. "Oh, and I don't know—I went out to call him in to eat, hours ago, and he was gone. I've been up and down the roads, down to the guildhall—I even went to the Salt Pool and asked little Boulder if he'd been there. Nobody's seen him at all!"

He got himself up despite his aching legs and hurried to put his arms around her. "There, my old darling, there. I'm sure he's just up to some pranks—he is a boy, after all, and a very independent lad at that, the Earth Elders know. He'll be back before our evening meal is over, you'll see."

"Evening meal!" she almost shrieked. "You old fool, do you think I've had time to prepare an evening meal? I've been hurrying all around town the length of the afternoon with my heart aching, trying to find that boy. There is no evening meal!" Sobbing out loud now, she turned and stumbled back toward their bed and wrapped herself in a blanket so all that could be seen was a shuddering lump.

Chert was troubled, too, but he couldn't help feeling that Opal was getting a bit ahead of things. Flint would not be the first boy in Funderling Town—or the last—to wander off on some childish quest and lose track of time. It had only been a short while ago he had disappeared during the prince regent's funeral. If he wasn't back by bedtime, they could start fretting in earnest. In the meantime, though, Chert had put in a long day and his stomach felt shrunken and empty as a dried leather sack.

He halfheartedly examined the larder. "Ah, look, we have greatroots in!" he said loud enough for Opal to hear. "A bit of cooking and those would go down a treat." She didn't answer. He picked through the other roots and various tubers. Some were looking a bit whiskery. "Perhaps I'll just have a bit of bread and some cheese."

"There isn't any bread." The lump under the blanket shifted. It did not sound like a happy lump. "I was going to go back out and get the afternoon's baking, but . . . but . . ."

"Ah, yes, of course," Chert said hurriedly. "Never fear. Still, it's a shame about the greatroots. A bit of cooking . . ."

"If you want them cooked, cook them yourself. If you know how."

Chert was sadly chewing a piece of raw greatroot—he had not realized how much more bitter they tasted if they had not been boiled in beet sugar—and beginning to admit to himself that the boy was not coming back for his evening meal. Not that a raw root and a piece of hard cheese was particularly worth coming back for, but Chert couldn't deny that the pang of disquiet was growing inside him; although his mug of ale had helped to wash down the fibrous root and remove a little of the worst of the throbbing of his legs and back, it had not gone very far toward soothing his mind. He had been out into Wedge Road several times. The dimmer stonelights were lit for evening and the streets were nearly empty as families finished their suppers and prepared for the night. The children must all be in bed now. The other children.

He decided to take a lamp and go out looking.

Could the boy have gone into one of the unfinished tunnels, he wondered, been caught by a slide in one of the side corridors where the bracing was less than adequate? But what would he be doing in such a place? Chert let his mind run across other possibilities, some happier and others much more frightening. Could he have gone home with another child? Flint was so unworldly in some ways that Chert could easily imagine he would forget to send word of where he was, let alone ask permission, but he had never really made friends with any of the Funderling children, even those in nearby houses who were of his own age. Where else? Down in the excavations where Chert had been working, near the Eddon family tomb? Certainly there were treacherous spots there, but Flint had made it clear he hated the place, and in any case how could Chert have missed him?

The Rooftoppers—the little people. Perhaps the boy had gone to see them and either stayed or not been able to get back before dark. Unbidden, a horrid vision came to him, of the boy fallen from a roof and lying helpless in some shadowy, unvisited courtyard. He put the greatroot down, sickened.

But where else could he be?

"Chert!" Opal shouted from the bedchamber. "Chert, come here!"

He wished she did not sound frightened. Suddenly, he didn't want to walk through the door and see what she had found. But he did.

Opal had not found anything—in fact, rather the reverse. "It's gone!" she said, pointing at the boy's pallet, at the blanket and shirt lying across it in twisted coils like weary ghosts. "His bag. With that . . . that little mirror in it. It's gone." Opal turned to him, eyes big with fear. "He never puts it on anymore, never wears it—it's always here! Why isn't it here now?" Her face suddenly grew slack, as though she had aged five years in a matter of moments. "He's gone away, hasn't he? He's gone away for good and so he took it with him."

Chert could think of nothing to say—or, in any case, nothing that would make either of them feel better.

"By the gods, Toby, are you falling asleep again? You've jogged the glass!"

The young man stood up quickly, raising his hands in the air to show that he couldn't possibly have done such a thing; his look of wounded honor suggested that he was always awake and at his best in the midnight hours and that Chaven was being needlessly cruel to suggest otherwise. "But, Master Chaven . . ."

"Never mind. I expect you to be a man of science and I suppose that is asking too much."

"But I want to be! I listen! I do everything you say!"

The physician sighed. It was not really the lad's fault. Chaven had put too much stock in the recommendation of his friend, Euan Dogsend, who was the most learned man in Blueshore but perhaps not its best judge of character. The young man worked hard . . . for his age . . . but he was distracted and touchy at the best of times, and worst of all, although he was by no means stupid, he seemed to have an unquestioning pattern of mind.

It is like trying to make my dear mistress Kloe pursue friendship with the mice and rats.

Still, the young man was standing right there with his face screwed up in a look of furious attention, so Chaven tried again. "See, the perspective glass must not move once we have found the spot we seek. Leotrodos down in Perikal says that the new star is in Kossope. Once we have set the eye of our glass on Kossope, we must tighten the housing so that it does not move—thus, we can make measurements, not just tonight, but other nights. And we most certainly must not lean on the perspective glass while we are making those measurements!"

"But the sky is full of stars," said Toby. "Why is it so important to measure this one?"

Chaven closed his eyes for a moment. "Because Leotrodos says he has found a *new* star. A new star has not been seen in hundreds of years—perhaps even thousands, since the methods of the ancients are sometimes obscure and thus open to question. More importantly, it raises many doubts about the shape of the heavens." The boy's puzzled look told him all he needed to know. "Because if the heavens are fixed, as the astrologers of the Trigonate so loudly tell us, yet there is a new star in the sky, *where did it come from?*"

"But, Master, that doesn't make sense," Toby said, yawning but a little more awake now. "If the gods made all the spheres, couldn't the gods just make a new star?"

Chaven had to smile. "You are doing better. That is a proper question, but a more important question is, why haven't they done it before now?"

For a moment, just a moment, he saw something ignite in the young man's eyes. Then caution or weariness or simply the habit of a lifetime dulled the expression again. "It seems like a lot of thinking about a star."

"Yes, it is. And one day that thinking may teach us exactly how the gods have made our world. And on that day, will we not be nearly gods ourselves?"

Toby made the pass-evil. "What a thing to say! Sometimes you frighten me, Master Chaven."

He shook his head. "Just help me get the perspective glass fixed on Kossope again, then you can take yourself to bed."

It was just as well he was now alone, Chaven thought as he wrote down the last of the notations. Even Toby might have noticed the way his hands had begun shaking as the hour he was waiting for came nearer. It was powerfully strange, this feeling. He had always coveted knowledge, but this was more like a hunger, and it did not seem to be a healthful one. Each time he used the Great Mirror, he felt more reluctant to cover it up again. Was it simply lust for the wisdom that he gained or some glamour of the spirit which gave that wisdom to him? Or was it something else entirely? Whatever might have caused the craving, he could barely force himself to take the time to drape his long box full of rare and costly lenses with its heavy covering, and only the sharp chill of the night air persuaded him to add even more delay so that he could crank shut the door in the observatory roof, shutting out those intrusive, maddening stars.

His need was especially sharp because it had been so long—days and days!—since the mirror had gifted him with anything but shadows and silence. How frustrating it had been all of tonight, trying to concentrate on Kossope when it was the three red stars called the Horns of Zmeos, also called the Old Serpent, that had his deepest attention: when they appeared behind the shoulder of Perin's great planet, as they would do tonight, he could consult the mirror again.

When the observatory room and the perspective glass were both secured, he went in search of Kloe. Tonight, if the gods smiled, her work and his offering would not lie ignored again.

Chaven's need had grown so strong that he didn't notice how roughly he was handling Kloe until she gave him a swift but meaningful bite on the web of his thumb and forefinger as he put her out. He dropped her, cursing and sucking at the wound as she scampered away down the passage, but although his anger was swiftly replaced by shame for his carelessness toward his faithful mistress, even that shame was devoured by the need that was roaring up inside him.

He sat before the mirror in a dark room that already seemed to be growing darker still, and began to sing. It was an old song in a language so dead that no one living could be certain they were pronouncing it correctly, but Chaven sang the words as his onetime master, Kaspar Dyelos, had taught them to him. Dyelos, sometimes called the Warlock of Krace, had never owned a Great Mirror, although he had possessed broken shards of more than one and had been able to do wonderful things with those shards. But mirror-lore as a discipline was as much about remembering and passing that memory along for the generations to come as it was about the practical manipulation of the cosmos—Chaven often wondered how many wonderful, astounding things had been lost in the plague years—and so Dyelos had taught all that he had learned to his apprentice, Chaven. Thus, on that day when Chaven had found this particular mirror, this astounding artifact, he had already known how to use it, even if he had not precisely understood every single step of the process.

Now Chaven rubbed his head, troubled by an errant thought. His brow was starting to ache from staring into the mirror-shadows and wondering if something else was looking at the shadow-mouse that lay on the shadow-floor, and whether that something would finally come. Was he doomed to failure again tonight? He was distracted, that was the problem . . . but he could not help being puzzled by the fact that he suddenly couldn't remember where he had acquired the mirror that was before him now, leaning against the wall of his secret storeroom. At least it *seemed* sudden, this emptiness in his memory. He could recall without trouble where and when he had obtained each of the other draped glasses on the shelves, and their particular provenances as well, but for some reason he could not just at this moment remember how he had obtained the jewel in his collection, this Great Mirror.

The incongruity was beginning to feel like an itch that would not be scratched and it was growing worse. Even the powerful hunger he felt began to weaken a little as the puzzle took hold of him. *Where did it come from, this powerful thing? I have had it . . . how long?*

Just then something flared in the center of the looking glass, a great outwash of white light as though a hole had been torn through the night sky to release the radiance of the gods that lay behind everything. Chaven threw his hands up, dazzled; the light faded a little as the owl settled, folded its bright wings, and looked back at him with orange eyes, Kloe's sacrificial mouse in its great talons.

All his other thoughts flew away, then, as though the wings had enfolded him as well, or perhaps as though he had become the tiny thing clutched in that snowy claw, in the grip of a power so much greater than his own that it could seem a kind of honor to give up his life to it.

He came up out of the long emptiness at last and into the greater light. Music beyond explaining—a kind of endless drone that was nevertheless full of complicated voices and melodies—still filled his ears but was beginning to grow less. His nostrils also seemed still to breathe that ineffable scent, as powerful and heady-sweet as attar of roses (although such roses never grew on bushes rooted in ordinary earth, in soil steeped in death and corruption), but it was no longer the only thing he could think about.

It might have only been with him a moment, that deepest bliss, or he might have been basking in those sensations for centuries, when the voice-that-was-no-voice spoke to him at last, a single thought that might have been *"I am here,"* or simply, *"I am."* Male, female, it was neither, it was both—the distinction was of no importance. He expressed his gratefulness that his offering had been received again, at last. What came back to him was a kind of *knowing,* the powerful calm of something that expected nothing less than to be adored and feared.

But even in the midst of his joy at being allowed within the circle of this great light again, something tugged again at his thoughts, a small but troubling something, just as shadows in his room of mirrors sometimes seemed to take odd shapes at the corner of his eye but never at the center of his vision.

Questions, he remembered, and for an instant he was almost himself. *I have questions to ask. The Rooftoppers,* he announced, *those small, old ones who live in hiding. They speak of someone they call the Lord of the Peaks who comes to them and gives them wisdom. Is that you?*

What came back to him was something almost like amusement. There was also a sensation of dismissal, of negation.

So they do not speak of you? he persisted. *It is not you who visits them with dire warnings?*

The shining thing—it looked nothing like an owl now, and although at this moment its shape was perfectly plain to him, he knew he would not afterward be able to explain it in words, nor even quite remember it—took a long time to answer. He felt the absence in that silence almost as a death, so that when it did speak again, he was so grateful that he missed part of what it told him.

Things had been awakened that would otherwise be sleeping, was all the sense that he could make of its wordless, fragmented thought. The shining thing told him that its works were subtle, and not meant for him to understand.

He sensed he was being chided now; there was more than a hint of discord in the all-surrounding music. He was devastated and begged forgiveness, reminded the shining thing that he only wanted to serve it faithfully, but in the one piece of his secret self which remained to him, the small sour note had allowed him to think a little more clearly. Was that truly his only wish—to serve this thing, this being, this force? When he had first touched it, or it had touched him, had they not almost seemed to have been equals, exchanging information?

But what did it want to learn from me? What could I possibly have given to this . . . power? He couldn't remember now, any more than he could remember how the mirror, the portal to this painful bliss, had first come into his hands.

The radiant presence made it clear that it would forgive him for his unseemly questioning, but in return he must perform a task. It was an important task, it seemed to say, perhaps even a sacred one.

For a moment, but only a moment, he hesitated. A little of himself still hung back, as though the mirror were a fine sieve and not all that had been Chaven could pass through it into this singing fire. That tiny remainder stood and watched, helpless as though in a nightmare, but it was not strong enough to change anything yet.

What must I do? he asked.

It told him, or rather it put the knowledge into him, and just as it had chided, now it praised; that kindness was like honey and silvery music and the endless, awesome light of the heavens.

You are my good and faithful servant, it told him. *And in the end, you will have your reward—the thing you truly seek.*

The white light began to fade, retreating like a wave that had crested and now ran backward down the sand to rejoin the sea. Within moments he was alone in a deep, secret room lit only by the guttering flame of a black candle.

★   ★   ★

Pounding on the kitchen door brought Mistress Jennikin out in her nightdress and nightcap. She held the candle before her as though it were a magic talisman. Her gray hair, unbound for the night and thinning with age, hung in an untidy fringe over her shoulders.

"It is only me. I am sorry to rouse you at such an hour, but my need is great."

"Doctor . . . ? What is wrong? Is someone ill?" Her eyes widened. "Oh, Zoria watch over us, there hasn't been another murder . . . !"

"No, no. Rest easy. I must go on a journey, that is all, and I must leave immediately—before dawn."

She held the candle a little closer to his face—scanning for signs of madness or fever, perhaps. "But Doctor, it's . . ."

"Yes, the middle of the night. To be more precise, it is two hours before dawn by my chain-clock. I know that as well as anyone and better than most. And I know at least as well as anyone else what I must do, don't you think?"

"Of course, sir! But what do you want . . . I mean . . ."

"Get me bread and a little meat so that I can eat without stopping. But before you do that, rouse Harry and tell him I need my horse readied for a journey. No one else, though. I do not want everyone in the household watching me leave."

"But . . . but where are you going, sir?"

"That is nothing you need to know, my good woman. I am going now to pack up what I need. I will also write a letter for you to take to Lord Nynor, the castellan. I hope to be gone only a day or two, but it might be more. If any of the royal family needs the services of a physician, I will tell Nynor how to find Brother Okros at the Academy—you may send anyone else who comes in search of me and cannot wait to Okros as well." He rubbed his head, thinking. "I will also need my heavy travel cloak—the weather will be wet and there may even be snow."

"But . . . but, Doctor, what about the queen and her baby?"

"Curses, woman," he shouted, "do you think I do not know my own calling?" She cowered back against the doorframe and Chaven was immediately sorry. "I apologize, good Mistress Jennikin, but I have given thought to all these things already and will put what is needed in the letter to Nynor. Do not worry for the queen. She is fit, and there is a midwife with her day and night." He took a deep breath. "Oh, please, take that candle back a little—you look like you intend setting me on fire."

"Sorry, sir."

"Now go and rouse Harry—he's slow as treacle in winter and I must have that horse." She clearly wanted to ask him something else but didn't dare. Chaven sighed. "What is it?"

"Will you be back for Orphan's Day? The butcher has promised me a fine pig."

For a moment he almost shouted again, but this was the matter of her world, after all. This was what was important to her—and in ordinary times would have been to Chaven as well, who dearly loved roast pork. So what if these were not ordinary times? Perhaps there would be no more Orphan's Day feasts after this one—a shame to ruin it. "I am as certain I will be back before Orphan's Day—and in fact, before Wildsong Night—as anyone can be who knows the gods sometimes have ideas of their own. Do not fear for your pig, Mistress Jennikin. I am sure he will be splendid and I will enjoy him greatly."

She looked a little less frightened as he turned—as though despite the hour, life no longer seemed quite so dangerously topsy-turvy. He was glad that was true for one of them, anyway.

The physician's manservant did his best to turn Chert away. The old man seemed distracted, guilty, as though he had been called away from the commission of some small but important crime and was in a hurry to get back to it.

Taking a nap, Chert guessed, although it seemed early in the morning for such things. *A late lie-in, then.* He would not be chased off so easily. "I don't care if he isn't seeing anyone. I have important business with him. Will you tell him that Chert of Funderling Town is here." If the physician was just busy and not at home to visitors, Chert thought, perhaps he could go around through the secret underground passage—surely Chaven would not dare to ignore a summons to *that* door—but it would take him a very long time to manage going and then making his way back, and he bitterly resented the idea of losing so much of the day. Each hour last night spent in fruitless search for the boy had been more galling than the last and was even more infuriating now, as though Flint were on some kind of wagon or ship that sped further away with each passing moment.

The manservant, despite Chert's protests, was about to shut the door in his face when an old woman stuck her head under the tall old man's arm and peered out at the Funderling. He had seen her before, just as he had seen the old man, although mostly from a distance as Chaven led him through the Observatory. He couldn't remember either of their names.

"What do you want?" she asked, eyes narrowed.

"I want to see your master. I know it is inconvenient—he may even have given orders not to be disturbed. But he knows me, and I'm . . . I'm in great need." She was still looking at him with distrust. Like the old man, she had faint blue shadows under her eyes and a fidgety, distracted air. *No one has had much sleep in this house either,* Chert thought. After his own night stumping up and down Funderling Town and even through Southmarch aboveground, he felt like an itching skin stretched over a stale emptiness. Only fear for the lost boy was keeping him upright.

"It can't be done," she said. "If you need physick, you must go to Brother Okros at the academy, or perhaps one of the barbers down in the town."

"But . . ." He took a breath, pushed down the urge to shout at this obstinate pair. "My . . . my son is missing. Chaven knows him—gave me some advice about him. He is a . . . a special boy. I thought Chaven might have some idea . . ."

The woman's face softened. "Oh, the poor wee thing! Missing, is he? And you, you poor man, you must be heartsick."

"I am, Mistress."

The manservant rolled his eyes and vanished back down the hallway. The woman stepped out into the courtyard, drying her hands on her apron, then looked around as though to make sure they were safe from prying eyes. "I shouldn't tell you, but my master's not here. He's had to go on a sudden journey. He left this morning, before dawn."

A sudden suspicion, fueled only by coincidence, made him ask, "Alone? Did he go alone?"

She gave him a puzzled look, but it began to shade into resentment as she answered. "Yes, of course alone. We saw him off. You surely don't think . . ."

"No, Mistress, or at least nothing ill. It's just that the lad knows your master and likes him, I think. He might have tagged along with him, as boys sometimes do."

She shook her head. "There was no one about. He left an hour before the sun was up, but I had a lamp and I would have seen. He was in a terrible hurry, too, the doctor, although I shouldn't speak of his business to anyone. No offense to you."

"None taken." But his heart was even heavier now. He had hoped at the very least that Chaven's keen wit might strike on some new idea. "I'm sure you have a great deal to do, Mistress. I'll leave you. When he comes back, could you tell him that Chert of Funderling Town wanted urgently to speak with him?"

"I will." Now she seemed to wish there was more she could do. "The gods send you good luck—I hope you find your little lad. I'm sure you will."

"Thank you. You're very kind."

In his weariness he almost slipped twice going up the wall. When he reached the top, he had to sit and gasp for some time until he had air enough to speak. "Halloo! It is Chert of Funderling Town!" He dared not shout too loud for fear of attracting attention below—it was the middle of the morning and even this less-traveled section of the castle near the graveyard was not entirely empty. "Her Majesty Queen Upsteeplebat very kindly came to meet me and my boy, Flint," he called. "Do you remember me? Halloo!"

There was no reply, no stir of movement, although he called again and again. At last, so tired he was beginning to be concerned about the climb down, he rose to a crouch. Out of his pocket he took the small bundle wrapped in moleskin. He opened it and lifted the crystal up until it caught a flick of morning light and sparkled like a tiny star. "This is a present for the queen. It is an Edri's Egg—very fine, the best I have. I am looking for the boy Flint and I would like your help. If you can hear me and will meet with me, I'll be back here tomorrow at the same time." He tried to think of some suitable closing salutation but could summon nothing. He made a nest of the moleskin and set the crystal in it. *What a beautiful, shining monster might hatch out of such a thing,* he thought absently, but couldn't take even the smallest pleasure in the fancy.

He picked his way with aching caution back down the wall, so heavy with despair that he was almost surprised that he did not sink deep into the ground when his feet finally touched it.

It was only a day like many others, but as she awakened in the early hours to hear the bell in the Erivor Chapel tolling as the mantis and his acolytes began the morning's worship, Briony was almost as gloomy and disturbed as if it were the day of an execution.

Rose and Moina and her maids came into the room, exaggeratedly quiet as though the princess regent were a bear that they feared waking, but still managing to make as much noise as a pentecount of soldiers in Market Square. She groaned and sat up, then allowed them to surround her and pull off her nightclothes.

"Will you wear the blue dress today?" Moina asked with only the smallest hint of pleading in her voice.

"The brown," suggested Rose. "With the slashed sleeves. You look so splendid in that . . ."

"What I wore yesterday," she said. "But clean. A tunic—the one with the gold braid. A riding skirt. Tights."

The maids and the two ladies did their best not to look upset, but they were very poor mummers. Rose and Moina in particular seemed to feel that Briony's boyish costumes were a personal affront, but on this morning the tender feelings of her ladies were of little interest to her. Briony was tired of dressing for other people, tired of the forced prettiness that she thought gave others the unspoken right to ignore what she said. Not that anyone dared completely ignore the princess regent, but she knew that when they were in private, the courtiers wished for Olin back, and not simply because he was the true king. She felt it in their glances: they did not trust her because she was a woman—worse, a mere girl. It made her almost mad with resentment.

Is there a one of them, male or female, who did not issue from a woman in the first place? The gods have given our sex charge of the greatest gift of all, the one most important to the survival of our kind, but because we cannot piddle high against a wall, we do not deserve any other responsibility?

"I don't care if you're angry with me," she snapped at Rose, "but don't pull my hair like that."

Rose dropped the brush and took a step backward, real upset on her face. "But, my lady, I didn't mean . . ."

"I know. Forgive me, Rosie. I'm in a foul mood this morning."

While the women braided her hair, Briony took a little fruit and some sugared wine, which Chaven had told her was good for healthful digestion. When her ladies had succeeded in piling her tresses into a tight but intricate arrangement on top of her head, she let them pin the hat into place, although she was already anxious to be moving.

Underneath it all, threatening to pull her down like the sucking black undertow in Brenn's Bay that sometimes formed beneath a deceptively placid surface, lay the horror of what Barrick had told her. She was frightened for her brother, of course, and she ached for him, too; he had taken to his rooms in the days since, making the excuse of a recurrence of his fever, but she felt certain that what was really going on was that he was ashamed to face her. As if she could love him any the less! Still, it was a shadow between them that made all their other differences seem small.

But even worse, in a way, was what he had told her about her father. Briony had never been the kind of foolish girl who thought her father could do no wrong—she had felt Olin's sharp tongue enough times not to feel overly coddled, and he had always been a man of dark moods—but Barrick's story was astounding, devastating. To think that all through her childhood her father had carried that burden, and had kept it secret . . . She didn't know which was the stronger feeling, her pain at his suffering or her fury that he had hidden it from those who loved him best.

Whatever the case, it felt as though a hole had been torn through the walls of a familiar room to reveal not the equally familiar room presumed to be on the other side but a portal into some unimaginable place.

How could it be? How could all this be? Why did no one tell me? Why didn't Father tell me? Is he like Barrick—does he think I'd hate him?

Briony had always been the practical child, at least compared to her twin—no brooding, no flickering changes of mood—but this went beyond anything she had experienced. In some ways it was worse than Kendrick's death, because it turned upside down all that she had thought she knew.

She was in mourning again, not for the death of a person this time, but for her peace of mind.

I'm tired. I'm so tired. It was only ten of the morning. She couldn't help being angry at Barrick. Whatever dreadful thing he was suffering, he was letting all of the duties of ruling Southmarch fall onto her.

The throne room was jostlingly full of people with claims on her time, and some of those claims were inarguable. Just now the Lord Chancellor Gallibert Perkin and three gentlemen of his chambers were going into painful detail about the need either to find more money for the government of Southmarch or to use some of the ransom money collected for King Olin on expenses. The merchants were worried about the coming year, the bankers were being careful with their funds, and the crown had in any case already borrowed more than it should have, which made dipping into the ransom an attractive alternative. It was ultimately a problem without solution, although a solution would have to be found—to spend the ransom would be to betray not only her father but the people who had given, not always happily, to free him. But the household of Southmarch ate money like some gold-devouring ogre out of a folktale. Briony had never understood how much work there was in simply keeping an orderly house—especially when that house was the biggest in the north of Eion and the center of the lives of some fifty thousand souls—let alone an entire orderly country. The crown would have to come up with some other way of making money. As always, Lord Chancellor Perkin recommended levying more taxes on the people who had already given hugely toward ransoming her father.

The parade continued. Two Trigonate mantises spoke on behalf of Hierarch Sisel's ecclesiastical court, which believed it had jurisdiction over the town court in a particular case. This, too, was about money, since the crime was a major one—a local landowner accused of the death of a tenant by negligence—and whichever court supplied the judge would keep any levies or fines. Briony had hoped that being the princess regent would mean she would get to solve problems, punish the guilty, reward the innocent. Instead she had discovered that what she mostly did was decide who else got to hear suits of law, the town magistrate, the hierarch's justices, or—and this very occasionally, usually just in cases of nobility accused—the throne of Southmarch.

Midday came and went. The pageant of people and their problems dragged on and on like some official celebration of boredom and pettiness. Briony wished she could stop and have a rest but the line of supplicants seemed to stretch out to the ends of the earth and whatever remained undone today would need doing tomorrow, when she was supposed to have a lesson with Sister Utta. She had learned to be fierce in protecting her few moments of private time so, instead of resting, she called for some cold meat and bread and shifted back and forth in her seat to ease her aching fundament. It was strange but true that even two or three pillows could not make spending an entire day in a chair comfortable.

It was Lord Nynor the castellan who leaned in toward her now, wrapping his beard around his finger in a distracted way, waiting for her attention to return.

"I'm sorry," she said. "What did you say? Something about Chaven?"

"He has sent me a rather odd letter," the old man explained. Briony had been horrified and fascinated to learn that overseeing this wretched parade of demanders and complainers was the sort of thing Nynor had been doing every day of his long career, or at least through the several decades since he had become one of her grandfather Ustin's chief courtiers. He didn't look mad, but who would choose such a life? "The physician has had to leave on an unexpected journey," Nynor said. "He suggests I summon Okros of Eastmarch to the castle in his absence, which he says may be a few days or perhaps even more."

"He often goes to consult with other learned men," said Briony. "Surely that is not so surprising."

"But without telling us where to find him? And with the queen so close to giving birth? In any case, the letter itself struck me as strange." Nynor's eyes were red-rimmed and watery, so that even at the happiest of times he looked as though he had been crying, but he was sharp-witted, and his long years of service to the Eddon family had proved him worth listening to.

"He says nothing that is directly alarming? Then give it to me and I will examine it later." She took the folded parchment from the castellan and slipped it into the hartskin envelope in which she carried her seals and signet ring and other important odds and ends. "Is there anything else?"

"I need your permission to summon Brother Okros."

"Given."

"And the poet fellow . . . ?"

"Tinlight? Tin . . . ?"

"Tinwright. Is it true you wish him added to the household?"

"Yes, but not in any grand way. Give him an allowance of clothing, and of course he is to be fed . . ."

There was a murmur in the crowd as someone pushed his way forward, a drawing back as though an animal, harmless but of doubtful cleanliness, had been set loose in the room. Matty Tinwright burst out of the front row of courtiers and cast himself down on the stones at the foot of the dais. "Ah, fair princess, you remembered your promise! Your kindness is even greater than is spoken, and it is spoken of in the same proverbial way as the warmth of the sun or the wetness of rain."

"Gah. Perin hammer us all dead," rumbled Avin Brone, who had been lurking beside the throne all day like a trained bear, growling at those he deemed were wasting the monarchy's time.

The poet *was* amusing, but just now Briony wasn't in the mood. "Yes, well, go with Lord Nynor and he will see you served, Tinwright."

"Do you not wish to hear my latest verse? Inspired this very day in this very room?"

She tried to tell him no, that she did not wish to hear it, but Tinwright was not the type to wait long enough for rejection—a trick he had needed to learn early, judging by his verse.

" 'Dressed all in mannish black she stands, like the thunderheads of Oktamene's dour wrath in the summer sky. Yet beneath those sable billows there is virgin snow, white and pure, that will make the land in cool sweetness to lie . . .' "

She couldn't help sympathising with the lord constable's groans, but she wished Brone might be a little more discreet—the young man was doing his best, and it had been her idea to encourage him: she didn't want him humiliated. "Yes, very nice," she said. "But at the moment I am in the middle of state business. Perhaps you could write it down for me and send it so that I can . . . appreciate its true worth without distraction."

"My lady is too kind." Smiling at the other courtiers, having established himself as one of their number—or at least believing so—Tinwright rose, made a leg, and melted into the crowd. There were a few titters.

"My lady is too kind by half," Brone said quietly.

Steffans Nynor still lingered, a slightly nervous look on his face. "Yes, my lord?" Briony asked him.

"May I come near the throne, Princess?"

She beckoned him forward. Brone also moved a bit closer, as though the scrawny, ancient Nynor might be some kind of threat—or perhaps simply to hear better.

"There is one other thing," the castellan said quietly. "What are we to do with the Tollys?"

"The Tollys?"

"You have not heard? They arrived two hours ago—I am shamed that I did not inform you, but I felt sure someone else would." He gave Brone a squint-eyed look. The two were political rivals and not the best of friends. "A company from Summerfield Court is here, led by Hendon Tolly. The young man seems much aggrieved—he was talking openly about the disappearance of his brother, Duke Gailon."

"Merciful Zoria," she said heavily. "That is dire news. Hendon Tolly? Here?"

"The middle brother, Caradon, is doubtless too pleased to find himself next in line for the dukedom to want to come stir up trouble himself," Brone said quietly. "But I doubt he tried very hard to stop his little brother—not that it would have done him much good. Hendon is a wild one, Highness. He must be closely watched." As the lord constable finished this little speech, one of the royal guard appeared at his shoulder and Brone turned to have words with him.

"Wild" was not the word Briony would have chosen. "Almost mad" would have been closer—the youngest Tolly was as dangerous and unpredictable as fire on a windy day. Her sigh was the only voice she gave to a heartfelt wish to be out of this, to turn back the calendar to the days when there had been nothing harder to think on than how she and Barrick would avoid their lessons.

And curse Barrick for leaving this all to me! A moment later she felt a pang of sorrow and even fear about her unkind thought: her brother needed no more curses.

"Treat the Tollys with respect," she said. "Give them Gailon's rooms." She remembered what Brone had said about the Summerfield folk and the agents of the Autarch. "No, do not, in case there has been some communication left behind in a secret place. Put them in the Tower of Winter so they are not underfoot and will find it harder to move around unmarked. Lord Brone, you will arrange to keep them watched, I assume? Lord Brone?"

She turned, irritated that he was not paying attention. The guardsman who had spoken to him was gone, but Brone himself had not moved and there was a look on his face Briony had never seen before—confusion and disbelief. "Lord Constable, what is wrong?"

He looked at her, then at Nynor. He leaned forward. "You must send these people away. Now."

"But what have you heard?"

He shook his great, bearded head, still as slow-moving and bewildered as a man in a dream. "Vansen has returned, Highness—Ferras Vansen, the captain of the guard."

"He has? And what has he discovered? Has he found the caravan?"

"He hasn't, and he has lost most of his company beside—more than a dozen good men. But, stay, Lady—that is not what is most important! Call for him. If what I hear is true, we will need to speak to him immediately."

"If what you hear is . . . But *what* do you hear, Brone? Tell me."

"That we are at war, Princess, or shortly will be."

"But . . . war? With whom?"

"The armies of all fairyland, it seems."

26
The Considerations of Queens

THE DISTANT MOUNTAINS:

We see them
But we will never walk them
Nevertheless, we see them

—from *The Bonefall Oracles*

SHE ARRIVED WITH SURPRISINGLY little ceremony, not mounted on a dove this time but on a fat white rat with a fine spread of whisker. She was accompanied only by a pair of guards on foot—their tiny faces pale and drawn because of this great responsibility—and by the scout Beetledown. Chert had been sitting longer than he would have liked and was glad he was not expected to rise; he was not certain his legs would bend that well without a little limbering first. But neither could he imagine greeting a royal personage without making some show of respect, especially when he hoped to beg a favor, so he bent his head.

"Her Exquisite and Unforgotten Majesty, Queen Upsteeplebat, extends her greetings to Chert of Blue Quartz," announced Beetledown in his small, high voice.

Chert looked up. She was watching him in an intent but friendly way. "I thank you, Majesty."

"We heard your request and we are here," she said, as birdlike in pitch as her herald. "Also, we enjoyed your generous gift and it has joined the Great

Golden Piece and the Silver Thing in our collection of crown jewels. We are sad to hear that the boy is missing. What can we do?"

"I don't know, to tell you the truth, Majesty. I was hoping you might be able to suggest something. I have searched all the places that I know—all of Funderling Town knows he is gone—but I have found no sign of him. He likes to climb and explore and I know little of the rooftops and other high places of the castle and city. I thought you might have an idea of where he might have gone, or even have seen him."

The queen turned. "Have any of our folk seen the boy, faithful Beetledown?"

"Not hair nor hide, Majesty," the little man said solemnly. "Asked in many holes and away down all the Hidden Hall last night, did I, without a sniff of un to be found."

The queen spread her hands. "It seems that we can tell you nothing," she told Chert sadly. "We, too, feel the loss, because we believe the Hand of the Sky is on that boy and thus he is important to our people, the *Sni'sni'snik-soonah*, as well."

Chert sagged. He had not truly thought that the Rooftoppers could solve the mystery, but it had been the only hope left to him. Now there was nothing he could do but wait, and the waiting would be terrible. "Thank you, anyway, Your Majesty. I am grateful that you came. It was very kind."

She watched as he began to climb to his feet. "Hold a moment. Have you smelled for him?"

"Have I what?"

"Have you smelled for his track?" When she saw Chert's expression, she raised an eyebrow more slender than a strand of spiderweb. "Do your people know nothing of this?"

"Yes, we do, I suppose. There are animals used for hunting game and certain other things we eat. But I would not know how to try to find the boy that way."

"Bide with us here a while longer." She folded her tiny hands together. "It is a pity, but the Grand and Worthy Nose is not well—a sort of ague. This often happens when the sun shines for the first time after the winter rains begin. Most pathetic he becomes, eyes red and his wonderful nose red, too. Otherwise I would send him with you. Perhaps in a few days, when the indisposition has passed . . ."

Chert was not exactly heartened to think that his hope of finding the boy might rest on the fat and fussy Nose, but it was something, at least, something. He tried to look grateful.

"Your Majesty, if a humble Gutter-Scout can speak . . ." said Beetledown.

The queen was amused. "Humble? I do not think that word describes you well, my good servant."

Chert imagined that the little man was blushing, but the face was too small and too distant to be certain. "I wish only to serve 'ee, Majesty, and that's skin to sky. Sometimes, it is true, I find it hard to keep quiet when I must listen to the boasting of tumblers and other pillocks who are not fit to serve you. And perhaps tha wilst deem me boastful again when I say that after the Nose, some do reckon that Beetledown the Bowman has the finest nostrils in all Southmarch Above."

"I have heard that said, yes," said the queen, smiling. Beetledown seemed hard-pressed not to leap in the air and cheer for himself at her admission. "Does that mean you are offering your services to Chert of Blue Quartz?"

"Fair is what it seems, Majesty. The boy bested me and then gave me quarter, fairly as tha might please. I reckon that un has my debt, as 'twere. Perhaps Beetledown can help bring him back safe in un's skin."

"Very well. You are so commissioned. Go with Chert of Blue Quartz and carry out your duties. Farewell, good Funderling." She tapped with her stick at the white rat's ribs; the animal chittered, then turned and began to move back up the roof. Her guards hurried after her.

"Thank you, Queen Upsteeplebat!" Chert called, although he was not really sure how much help he was going to get from a man the size of a peapod. Her hand went up as the rat disappeared over the roofcrest, but even small queens did not wave good-bye, so he imagined it must have been an acknowledgment of his gratitude. He turned to Beetledown, with whom he was now alone on the rooftop. "So . . . what should we do?"

"Take me to something of the boy's," suggested the little man. "Let me get my fill of un's scent."

"We've got his other shirt and his bed, so I suppose I should take you home. Do you want to ride down on my shoulder?"

Beetledown gave him an unfathomable look. "Seen 'ee climb, I have. Beetledown will make un's own way and meet up at bottom."

Not surprisingly, the Gutter-Scout was already waiting on the ground by the time Chert set his feet on the cobbles once more. The morning sun was high behind the clouds—perhaps an hour remained until noon. Chert was tired and hungry and not very happy. "Do you want to walk?" he asked, trying to be considerate of the Rooftopper's feelings.

"Oh, aye, if we had three days for wandering," Beetledown replied a bit snappishly. "Said tha hast shoulder for riding. Ride, I will."

Chert put his hand down and let the little man climb into it. It was an oddly ticklish feeling. As he put Beetledown on his shoulder, he imagined for the first time what a vast expanse even this small cobbled courtyard must seem to a man of such small size. "Have you been on the ground much?"

"Proper bottom ground? Aye, oncet or twice or more," Beetledown said. "Not one of your stay-at-homes am I. Not afraid of rat or hawk or nowt but cats is Beetledown the Bowman, if I have my good bow to hand." He brandished the small, slender curve of wood, but when he spoke again, he sounded a little less confident. "Be there cats in your house?"

"Scarcely a one in all Funderling Town. The dragons eat them."

"Having sport, th'art," said the little man with dignity. Chert suddenly felt ashamed. The tiny fellow might be a bit boastful, he might not think much of Chert's climbing, but he was offering his help out of a sense of obligation, entering a world of monstrous giants. Chert tried to imagine what that would feel like and decided that Beetledown was entitled to a little swagger.

"I apologize. There are cats in Funderling Town but none in my house. My wife doesn't like them much."

"Walk on, then," said the Rooftopper. "It has been a century or more since any Gutter-Scout has been to the deep places and today Beetledown the Bowman will go where no other dares."

"No other Rooftopper, you mean," said Chert as he started across the temple-yard toward the gate. "After all, we Funderlings go there rather often."

"Where is your brother? Prince Barrick should be here." Avin Brone could not sound more disapproving if Briony had informed him that she planned to hand over governance of the March Kingdoms to an assembly of landless yokels.

"He is ill, Lord Brone. He would be here if he could."

"But he is the co-regent . . ."

"He is *ill*. Do you doubt me?"

The lord constable had learned that despite the differences in their size, age, and sex, he could not outstare her. He tangled his fingers in his beard and muttered something. She was sensible enough not to inquire what he had said.

"Hendon Tolly is causing trouble already," said Tyne Aldritch of Blueshore, one of the few nobles she had asked to join her to hear the news from the west. Aldritch was terse, especially with her, often to the point of near-rudeness, but she believed it was a symptom of basic honesty. Evidence over the years supported this conclusion, although she knew she might still be wrong—none of the people of the innermost circles around the throne were as guileless or straightforward as they seemed. Briony had learned that at a young age. Who could afford to be? Briony had ancestors in the Portrait Hall who had killed more of their own nobles than they had slain enemies on the battlefield.

"And what is my charming cousin Hendon up to?" She nodded as another, only slightly more beloved relative joined the council, Rorick Longarren. The apparent invasion seemed to be on the borders of his Daler's Troth fiefdom, one of the few things that could lure him away from dicing and drinking. He took his place at the table and yawned behind his hand.

"Tolly showed up with his little court of complainers just as you left the throne room," Tyne Aldritch told her, "and was talking loudly about how sometimes people try to avoid those they have wronged."

Briony took a deep breath. "I thank you, Earl Tyne. I would be surprised if he was *not* talking against me—against us, I mean, Prince Barrick and myself. The Tollys are admirable allies in time of war but cursedly difficult in peacetime."

"But is this still peacetime?" the Earl of Blueshore asked with heavy significance.

She sighed. "That is what we hope to find out. Lord Brone, where is your guard captain?"

"He insisted on bathing before being brought to you."

Briony snorted. "I had doubts about his competence, but I didn't take him for a fop. Is a bath more important than news of an attack on Southmarch?"

"To be fair, Highness," said Brone, "they rode almost without stopping for three days to get here and he has already written everything down while he waited for me to come to him from the throne room." Brone lifted a handful of parchment. "He felt it would be discourteous to appear before you in torn and dirty clothes."

Briony stared at the parchment covered with neat letters. "He can write?"

"Yes, Highness."

"I was told he was born in the country—a crofter's son or something like. So where did he learn to write?" For some reason this did not fit the picture in her head of Vansen the guard captain, the man who had stood close-mouthed and emotionless while her brother lay dead in his own blood a few yards away, the fellow who had let her strike at him as though he were a statue of unfeeling stone. "Can he read, too?"

"I imagine so, Highness," Brone said. "But here he comes. You may ask him yourself."

His hair was still wet and he had put on not a dress tunic and armor but simple clothes that she suspected by their fit were not even his own, but she was still irritated. "Captain Vansen. Your news must be terrible indeed that you would make the princess regent wait for it."

He looked surprised, even shocked. "I am sorry, Highness. I was told that you would be in the throne room until after midday and could not see me until then. I gave my news to Lord Brone's man and then . . ." He seemed suddenly to realize he was perilously close to arguing with his monarch; he dropped to one knee. "I beg your pardon, Highness. Clearly the mistake is mine. Please do not let your anger at me cloud your feelings toward my men, who have suffered much and done so bravely to bring this news back to Southmarch."

He is too honorable by half, she thought. He had a good chin, she had to admit—a proud chin. Perhaps he was one of those men like the famous King Brenn, so in love with honor that it ate him up with pride. She didn't like the suggestion that she needed permission to be angry at someone, even permission given by the someone in question. She decided she would teach this crafty—and no doubt ambitious—young soldier a lesson by not being angry at all.

Besides, she thought, *if what Brone says is true, we do have more important things to talk about.* "We will speak of this some other time, Captain Vansen," she said. "Tell us your news."

★　　★　　★

By the time he had finished, Briony felt as if she had stepped into one of the stories the maids used to tell when she was a child.

"You *saw* this . . . this fairy army?"

Vansen nodded. "Yes, Highness. Not very well, as I've said. It was . . ." He hesitated. "It was strange there."

"By the gods!" cried Rorick, who had just divined the reason for his own presence, "they are coming down onto my land! They must be invading Daler's Troth even as we speak—someone must stop them!"

Briony had not particularly wanted him present, but since it was near his fiefdom, and his bride-to-be had been kidnapped with the convoy, she could not think of a reason to keep him out of the council. Still, she found it telling that he had not mentioned the Settish prince's daughter once. "Yes, it sounds that way, Cousin Rorick," she said. "You will, no doubt, want to ride out as soon as you can to muster and lead your people." She kept her tone equable, but to her surprise she saw a small reaction from Vansen, not a smile—the matters at hand were too serious—but a recognition by him that she didn't think Rorick was likely to follow this selfless course.

Ah, but Vansen is a dalesman, isn't he? And not as dull as I supposed him, either.

She turned her attention back to her cousin Rorick, who was not even trying to hide his fear. "Ride there?" he stammered. "Into the gods alone know what kind of terrors?"

"Longarren is right about one thing—he can do nothing alone," said Tyne of Blueshore. "We must strike them quickly, though, whatever we do. We must throw them back. If the Twilight People are truly come across the Shadowline, we must remind them of why they retreated there in the past—make them see they will pay with blood for every yard of trespass . . ."

"Still, these *are* your lands we are talking about, Rorick," Briony pointed out, "and your people. They do not see much of you as it is. Will you not lead them?"

"But lead them to what, Highness?" Surprisingly, it was Brone who spoke up: as a general rule, he did not think much of her cousin Rorick. "We know nothing so far. We have sent out a small party and only a few of them have come back—I think it would be a mistake for Lord Longarren or anyone else to ride off to battle without due care. What if we make a stand against these invaders and the same thing happens—the madness, the confusion—but this time to an entire army? Fear will run riot and the Twilight People will be here in these halls before spring. That conquest will not be anything like the Syannese Empire either, I suspect. These creatures will want more than tribute. What did Vansen say that his little monstrosity told him? That she—whoever *that* might be—will burn all our houses down to black stones."

The enormity of it struck her now; her contemptuous prodding of Rorick suddenly seemed petty. Unless Vansen was completely mad, they were soon to be at war, and not with any human foe. As if the threat of the Autarch, Kendrick's death, and their father's imprisonment had not been enough! Briony looked at the guard captain and, much as she might wish it, could not believe he was telling anything other than the truth. What she had been taking for dullness or priggish honor might instead be a kind of unvarnished simplicity, something she had difficulty recognizing because of where she sat. It could be that here was a man who did not know how to scheme, who would suffocate in the daily intriguing of the castle's inner chambers like an oak trying to grow beneath the strangling vines of the Xandian jungles.

I doubt he can even keep a secret. "Vansen," she said suddenly. "Where are those you brought back?"

"The guardsmen are waiting to return to their families. There is the girl, too . . ."

"They are not to go home, any of them, or to mix with others. Open talk of this must not be permitted or we will be struggling with our own fearful people long before we ever cross swords with this fairy army." She turned to the lord constable, who was already dispatching one of the guards to relay her order. "Who else needs to know?"

Brone looked around the chapel. "The defense of the castle and city is my task, and I thank Perin Skyfather that he put it in my head to do the repairs on the curtain wall and the water-gate last summer. We need Nynor, of course, and all his factors—we cannot put an army on foot without him. And Count Gallibert, the chancellor, because we will need gold as well as steel to protect this place. But, Highness, we cannot put an army on foot at all without everyone learning of it . . ."

"No, but we can do as much as we can before we must make it general knowledge." She looked at Ferras Vansen, who seemed uncomfortable. "You have a thought, Captain?"

"If you will pardon me, Highness, my men have suffered a great deal and they will be unhappy to be confined to the keep . . ."

"Are you questioning my decision?"

"No, Highness. But I would prefer to explain it to them myself."

"Ah." She considered. "Not yet. I haven't finished with you."

He looked as though he might say more, but didn't. Briony was briefly grateful for the power of the regency, for the prestige of being an Eddon; she didn't want to waste time explaining her every thought just now. In fact, she was feeling a certain pleasure, even in the midst of her great distress at what was happening and what must happen in the days ahead, to know that *she* was the one who must make decisions, that the nobles must listen to her no matter what they would prefer.

Pray Zoria I make the right decisions. "Bring Nynor and the chancellor and any other nobles that must know. This evening, here. It will be a war council—but do not call it so within the hearing of anyone who will not be joining us."

"And those bloody-minded Tollys?" asked Tyne. "Hendon will still be the brother of a powerful duke whether Gailon is alive or dead, and the Tollys cannot be ignored in this."

"No, of course not, but for the moment they will be." However, she knew she must not be foolish. "But perhaps you could tell Hendon Tolly that I will see him later—that we will talk privately before the evening meal. That courtesy I can give him."

Rorick excused himself—to down a cup of wine as quickly as possible, Briony guessed. As Avin Brone and Tyne Aldritch fell into a discussion of which of the other nobles must be present at so important a council, Briony rose to stretch her legs. Vansen, thinking she was leaving the room, went down on one knee.

"No, Captain, I am not done with you yet, as I said." It was a strange, almost giddy feeling, the power that was in her now. For a moment she thought of Barrick and was stabbed by pity and sadness, but also impatience. *I must give him the chance to be present for this,* she reminded herself. *It is his due.* But she wondered at her own thoughts, because it was indeed his due she was thinking of, not her own needs: she was not certain she actually wanted him to be involved, and she was disturbed by that realization. "You will wait outside until I have finished with the others, Vansen."

He bowed his head, then rose and walked out. Brone looked at him, then at Briony, one eyebrow raised inquiringly.

"Before you go, good Aldritch . . ." she said to Tyne, ignoring the lord constable.

He turned toward her, not sure what was coming. "Yes, Highness?"

Briony examined the earl's familiar face, the squint of suspicion, the scar beneath his eye. There was another jagged white line on his forehead only partly hidden beneath his graying hair—a fall while hunting. He was a good man but a rigid one, a man who saw almost all change as trouble. She sensed she was about to make the first of a long series of not entirely happy choices. "With Shaso imprisoned, you and Lord Brone have taken up most of his duties between you, my lord Aldritch."

"I have done my best, Highness," he said, a little angry color coming to his cheeks. "But this attack from behind the Shadowline, if it is true, could not have been foreseen . . ."

"I know. And I know . . . that is, my brother and I know . . . that you have done what you could in a difficult time. Now it seems the times will become more difficult still." She was aware that she was changing, that she had begun to speak less like Briony and more like a queen, or at least a princess regent. *Is this what happens? Is true royalty like some wasting illness that makes you grow farther and farther from everyone even while you remain in their midst?* "I wish you to continue, and in fact to become the castle's master of arms." She looked quickly to Brone, not for his approval, but to see how he reacted. He, in turn, was looking at Tyne; if he disagreed or agreed with her decision he gave no sign.

Earl Tyne's cheeks were still flushed, but he seemed relieved. "I thank you, Highness. I will do my best to fulfill your trust."

"I'm sure you will. So here is your first duty. We must assume this danger is real. We have a few hundred guards in the castle—not enough for anything except perhaps to resist a siege, and if it comes to that, it will mean we have abandoned the outer city. How quickly can we muster a proper army?"

Aldritch frowned. "We can have my Blueshoremen and Brone's Landsenders here in days, perhaps a week. With fast riders on the Westmarch Road we might be able to draw a few companies from Daler's Troth soon after, if we can get around this fairy army. Any levies from Marrinswalk and Helmingsea and the outliers like Silverside and Kertewall will take longer—at the very least two tennights, more likely we won't see them for a month." His frown became a scowl—Tyne had never been one to mask his thoughts. "A cursed shame, this whole bloody business with Gailon Tolly and his brothers, because our largest and best-trained muster always comes from Summerfield."

"I will treat with that," Briony said. "What seems important to me is that we meet this shadow-army, if it is truly moving on Southmarch as the guard captain fears, at least once outside the city walls."

"With unready troops?" Tyne protested. "Most of what we will turn up here under such haste will be local musters, especially after all these years without war—perhaps only one real fighting man for every dozen who have never swung anything sharper than a hoe."

"We must test their strength—and ours," Briony said firmly. "We know nothing of such an enemy. And if they draw a siege around us, we will have trouble getting any more help at all from the farther marches. We will have to rely on ships to bring men as well as supplies, which will make for an even longer wait for the landbound musters." She turned to Avin Brone. "What do you think?"

He nodded, pulling gently and meditatively on his beard. "I agree we cannot simply wait until this enemy arrives. But we do not know for certain that is what they plan. Perhaps they will harry the outlying marches first. Perhaps they seek only to expand a distance across the Shadowline, then sit on what they have won."

"It doesn't seem anything to count on," said Briony. "If they have brought an entire army across the Shadowline, it seems unlikely they did it merely to burn a few fields and barns." She almost couldn't believe she was talking about this so calmly. People were going to die. The country had been largely at peace for her entire lifetime and the Twilight People had not stirred out of their shadows for generations. How had this fallen to her?

Brone sighed. "I agree that we must begin the muster immediately, Highness. The rest we can discuss with the other nobles later today."

"Go, then, Tyne, and begin it," she said. "I may be asking an impossibility, but let your messengers go out with as much secrecy as they can and take their messages straight to the local lords and mayors without stopping to discuss it in the taverns. Tell them that if anyone hears of their errand before the one to whom they are sent, they will spend the next year chained in the stronghold next to Shaso."

"That will not keep everyone quiet," Tyne argued. "Some will risk shackles to warn their own families."

"No, but it will help. And we will not give the messengers any information that they do not need." She summoned a young page from outside the chapel door. He came in as hesitantly as a cat walking on a wet floor. "Call

Nynor," she told him, and when he was gone she said, "I will send out letters under my seal."

"Very good," said the Earl of Blueshore. "Then they will not be able to argue they did not understand the importance or that the messenger did not tell them straightly what was needed."

"You two go and see to it, please, and the arrangements for this evening's council as well. Send in Vansen as you go."

Brone gave her the raised eyebrow once more. "Do not be too hard on him, Highness, please. He is a good man."

"I will deal with him as he deserves," she promised.

Chert had managed by a certain stealthiness to make his way home through the back streets of Funderling Town without having to explain why a finger-sized man was riding on his shoulder. He could not, of course, avoid giving an explanation to everyone . . .

"Have you found him?" Opal demanded, then her reddened eyes opened wide as she saw Beetledown. "Earth Elders! What . . . what is that?"

"He's a 'who,' really," her husband told her. "As for Flint, no luck. Not yet."

The little man stood up on Chert's shoulder and doffed his ratskin hat before making a small bow. "Beetledown the Bowman, I hight, tallsome lady. Chief one of the Gutter-Scouts, directed by Her Sinuous Majesty, Queen Upsteeplebat, to help find your lost boy."

"He's here to help." Chert was tired and didn't have much hope left—in fact, the whole thing struck him as a bit ridiculous. Opal, however, was seeing a Rooftopper for the first time and for a moment seemed almost able to forget the terrible errand that had brought this newcomer to their home.

"Look at him! He's perfect!" She reached out a hand, as if he were a toy to be played with, but remembered her manners. "Oh! My name is Opal and you are welcome in our house. Would you like something to drink or eat? I'm afraid I don't know much about . . . about Rooftoppers."

"Nay, Mistress, not this moment, but I thank 'ee." He pulled at Chert's earlobe. "It seems best tha put me down. Smell is a tricksy thing. Fades like stars at sunrise."

"He's going to sniff Flint's shirt," Chert explained. It seemed to need some additional clarification, but he couldn't summon any.

Opal, however, seemed to find it all perfectly straightforward. "Let me carry you. I haven't swept the floors today and I'm ashamed." She reached out a hand and Beetledown climbed onto it. "Did your queen really send you? What is she like? Is she old or young? Is she beautiful?"

"Brave as a daw and fearful handsome," said Beetledown with real feeling. "Hair soft as the velvet pelt of a weanling mouse." He coughed to cover his embarrassment. "We are her special legion, we Gutter-Scouts. The queen's eyes and ears. A great honor it gives to us."

"Then we're honored she wishes to help us," said Opal as she carried the tiny man toward Flint's bed. Chert was bemused to see how much better his wife did this sort of thing than he did. "Do you need anything?"

"Is yon great tent of faircloth un's garment? Put me down, please 'ee, Mistress, and I will scent what I can." He scrambled across the folds, then dropped to his hands and knees and pressed his face against the sleeve. He worked his way up to the shoulder, sniffing as he went like a dog. At last he climbed to his feet and closed his eyes, stood silent for a moment. "I think I have it," he said. "Easier it gives itself to me because I have scented the boy upon the rooftop and un has un's own peculiar tang." He opened his eyes, looked at Opal and Chert, then shuffled his feet a little on the sleeve. "No wish am I having to shame 'ee, but to me un smells nothing like tha twain."

Chert almost laughed. "There is no shame. He is not our blood-child. We found him and took him in."

Beetledown nodded wisely. "Found him in some strange place, thinks I. True?"

"Yes," said Opal a little worriedly. "How did you know?"

"Un smells of Farther Rooftops." Beetledown turned to Chert. "Is it tha who will carry me now?"

"Carry . . . ?"

"On the track. Too much of un's scent there is here. Go where there is moving air, we must—even in these danksome caves there must be such a place, methinks."

Carefully, Chert lifted the little man back up onto his shoulder. He was tired in heart and body, but certainly it was better to be doing something than simply waiting. "Are you coming?" he asked his wife.

"Then who would be here if he comes home?" said Opal indignantly, as though the boy had merely gone to race sowbugs with the neighbor children and would be back any time. "You go, Chert Blue Quartz, and you let this fellow do all the sniffing he has to do. You find that boy." She turned to look at Beetledown and performed a strange, stiff courtesy, holding her apron up at the hem. She even smiled at him, although she clearly didn't find it easy, which reminded Chert that he was not the only one who was bone-weary with sleeplessness and dread. "We thank you and your queen," she said.

He gave Opal a kiss before leaving, wondering how many days it had been since he had remembered to do that. He couldn't help glancing back as he opened the door, but he wished he hadn't. In the middle of the room, his wife was rubbing her hands together and looking at the walls as though searching for something. Now that there was no longer a guest in the house, her face had gone slack with grief—it was a stranger's face, and an old stranger at that. For the first time he could remember, Chert could no longer quite make out the lovely young girl he had courted.

Captain Ferras Vansen came back into the chapel like a condemned prisoner walking bravely to the gallows. His expression, Briony thought, was a little like the idealized face of Perin in the fresco above the door which showed the mighty god giving to his brother Erivor the dominion over the rivers and seas. On the sky god the face was frozen in a mask of hard masculine beauty; Vansen, although not an unhandsome man, simply looked frozen.

He kneeled before her, head down. His hair was now almost dry, curling at the ends. She felt something almost like tenderness toward him, touched by the vulnerability of his bent neck. He looked up and she felt caught in some indiscretion, had to fight down a surge of warm anger.

"May I speak, Highness?"

"You may."

"Whatever you think of me, Princess Briony, I ask you again not to bear ill will toward the men who traveled with me. They are good soldiers tested by things that none of us have seen and felt before. Punish me as you will, but not them, I beg of you."

"You truly are a bit arrogant, aren't you, Captain Vansen?"

His eyes widened. "Highness?"

"You assume that you have done some great wrong for which you must be punished. You seem to think that, like Kupilas the Lifegiver, your crime is so great that you must be staked on the hillside as an example, to be picked at by the ravens for eternity. Yet, as far as I can see, you have only proved to be a soldier who has muddled a commission."

"But your brother's death . . ."

"It's true, I haven't forgiven you for your failures that night. But neither am I so foolish as to think someone else would have prevented it." She paused, gave him a hard stare. "Do *you* think I'm foolish, Captain Vansen?"

"No, Highness . . . !"

"Good. Then we have a starting point. I don't think I'm foolish either. Now let us move to more important matters. Are you mad, Captain Vansen?"

He was startled and she almost felt ashamed of herself, but these were times when she could not bend, could not be too kind and thus seem weak. There could be no whispering among the castle's defenders that they would fail because a woman ruled them. "Am I . . . ?"

"I asked if you are mad, Captain Vansen. Are your wits damaged? It seems a simple enough question."

"No, Princess. No, Highness, I do not think so."

"Then unless you are a liar or a traitor—fear not, I won't ask you to deny those possibilities as well, we don't have the time—what you have seen is real. Our danger is real. So let us talk about why your arrogant wish to be important enough to be punished will not be satisfied."

"My lady . . . ?"

"Silence. I didn't ask you a question. Captain Vansen, from what you've told me, it seems that not everyone is the same when it comes to this fairy-magic. You said that some of the men were bewildered, even bewitched, and that others were not. You were one of those who were not. True?"

"Or at least very little, Highness, as far as I could tell." He was looking at her with something like surprised respect. She liked the respect. She did not like the surprise.

"Then I would be a fool to throw a soldier who seemed armored against such charms and snares into chains at a time when we may need that talent far more than strong arms or even stout hearts . . . would I not?"

"I . . . I take your point, Highness."

"Here is another question. Did you see any reason, any differences in those affected, that might explain why some of you were overwhelmed by the Shadowline magic and some were not?"

"No, Highness. One of my most trusted and sensible men, Collum Dyer, was swept away into a dream very quickly, but a man who is for all purposes his opposite was not touched and, in fact, made it home with me."

"So we have no way to know who has the weakness until it is revealed." She frowned, biting her lip. Vansen watched her, clearly masking deeper feelings, but this time more effectively. She wondered briefly what he was hiding from her. Irritation? Fear? "Despite what you think of him, this fellow you mentioned who was not overcome by the fairy-magic must be given a role in preparing to fight this strange enemy. He and all the others who were not poisoned by this strange dreaming. He and your other survivors must all be made captains."

"Mickael Southstead a captain?" Vansen was chagrined.

"Unless he is the lowest, vilest criminal ever born, his clear head will be worth more to us than if Anglin the Great himself were to come back from the heavens to lead us, then fall into a bewildered nightmare. As we have agreed, Vansen, I am no fool, and I don't think you are one either. Can you not see this?"

He bowed his head again briefly. "I can, Highness. You are right."

"Very kind of you to say so, Captain. We do not know where we will be fighting. It could be we will meet them in the hills of Daler's Troth in an attempt to keep them away from the cities. It could just as easily happen that we cannot stop them until they reach the walls of Southmarch itself. You are the only ones who have seen the enemy and returned to tell of it. You must help us prepare for them in any way you can imagine. I am not happy about it, Vansen, but I need you just as much as I need Brone and Nynor and Tyne Aldritch. The matter of my brother's murder and your failure is not closed, but until better times I will push it from my mind, and so will you. It could be that if you serve me well . . . if you serve Southmarch well . . . then what is in the ledger of that night can be scraped away, or at least inked over."

"I will do all that you ask, Highness." This new expression was hard to unriddle, both elevated and miserable, so that for a moment he appeared to have stepped down from a different fresco altogether.

You are a strange man, Ferras Vansen, she thought. *Maybe I was wrong to think you are the sort that has no secrets.* "Go, then. Gather those who came back with you. See that they are fed and rested, but in no circumstance let them leave. I will speak to them myself tomorrow morning."

"Yes, Highness." He rose, but hesitated. "Princess Briony . . . ?"

"Speak."

"There is a young woman, too—I believe I told you."

A cold irritation crept over her. "What about her? We cannot let her go either, even if she is mad and suffering. I regret it. Make her comfortable." She narrowed her eyes. "Do you have some feelings for her?"

"No!" He flushed: she was certain she had touched a nerve. That made her grow even more chill, although she did not know why. "No, Highness. Responsibility, perhaps—she is like a child and she trusts me. But although she seemed just as lost in the Shadowline dream as Dyer and the others, she also found a way out again for us. She seems to be in some middle ground between the two . . ."

"We have no time or patience to try to make sense out of some unfortunate young woman. If the magic took her and confused her, she is no use to us. Make her comfortable. Bring me the others tomorrow at ten of the clock."

Vansen bowed and went out, looking not exactly like one reprieved, but perhaps like one who had found out the gallows makers were all ill with a bad fever.

She sat for a long time after he was gone, her thoughts an unsettled swirl. She had only an hour or so before she had to meet with the nobles and make a plan of war. She would have liked to go to Utta—she missed the Zorian sister's wisdom and calm—but she knew there was a more important visit she had to make. Whatever complicated feelings she might have and whatever terrors might be punishing him, she did not wish to go to this evening's council without her twin.

The Scourge of the Shivering Plain stood on a hillside at the edge of the line of trees, looking down on the valley and the town that bestrode the river at its bottom. The sun had vanished behind the top of the hills and lamps were already being lit all along the dark valley, even though evening was still an hour away.

Yasammez turned and reached out with her thoughts, feeling back toward the Shadowline. The mantle of shadow, the web of careful, ancient enchantments that had trailed behind her for days like a cape of mists, the vast, mortal-bewildering essence of the Qar heartland that had hidden and protected her marching army, had now stretched to its limits and was begin-ning to thin. She knew that it would reach no farther into these fields, that where she went from now on she must do beneath the bright sun or the unclouded stars. That was why she waited for night.

The Seal of War glowed on her chest like a coal. Its weight was both comforting and terrifying. For year upon long year she had waited for this hour to come. Whatever befell would have much to do with her decisions in the days ahead, and she would have had it no other way. Still, many would die, and many of them would be her own kind. Like almost all war-riors, no matter how fierce, it was not easy for her to see her own killed, whatever the need.

She turned and walked back up the hillside. Although her armor was covered in long spines and the trees grew close together here, she made no sound.

In the woods along the hilltop her army had gathered. With the man-tle's weakening their bright eyes glittered in the gathering dark like a sky full of stars as they watched her pass. No fires had been lit. Later, when she had a better idea of what she faced, had learned something of the mettle of her sunlander enemies, Lady Porcupine might find it useful to let them see her army's fires burning on the hills and plains, let them count the blazes with chilling blood—but not tonight. Tonight the People would come down on their foes like lightning from a cloudless sky.

Her tent was a thing woven of silence and thickened shadow. Several of her captains awaited her inside its surprisingly large expanse, seated around the dim amethyst glow of her empty helmet in a circle like the Whisper-ing Mothers who nursed the Great Egg.

Yasammez wished she could send them all away—there was always that still moment before the noise and the blood and she preferred to spend it by herself—but first there were things she had to do and even a few hated formalities she must observe.

Morning-in-Eye of the Changing People was waiting, her naked chest heaving. She had just run a long way. *"What do you bring me?"* Yasammez asked her.

"They are no more than they seem, or else they have grown a thousand times more skilled in trickery than they once were. A small garrison lives inside the town gates. There are other small forces of armed folk in the larger houses, and an armory that suggests they can muster more when need be."

"But the armory is full?"

Morning-in-Eye nodded her sleek head. *"Pikes and helmets, bows, arrows—none have been given out. They do not suspect."*

Yasammez showed nothing, but she was pleased. An easy victory would bring its own problems, but it was more important that her army's first blooding not be too perilous. Even with all those she had mustered, the People were still vastly outnumbered by the mortals who now filled the lands that once had belonged to her folk. She relied on surprise and terror to increase the size of her host tenfold.

"Hammerfoot of Firstdeep?"

"Yes, Lady."

"It is long since we have come against mortal men or their works. When the village is afire, take some of your women and men and pull down the walls. See to the way of their building. It is only a town, but perhaps we will see something of what we must defeat when we come against the Old Place."

"Yes, Lady."

She turned to Gyir, the most trusted of her captains, and for a moment their thoughts commingled. Compared to her or even many of the others present he was merely a stripling, but his ferocity and cunning were second only to hers. She tasted his cold resolve and was pleased, then spoke so that the others might hear. *"When we are putting the town to fire and the people to slaughter, it is my wish that a large number be allowed to escape, or at least to believe that they are escaping."* She paused for a moment, considered unflinchingly the horror that would come. *"Let them be mostly females and their young."*

Stone of the Unwilling stirred, flickered. *"But why, Lady? Why show them mercy? They never showed us any—when they found my people's hive in the last great battles they burned it and clubbed our children to death as they came out, screaming and weeping."*

"It is not mercy. You should know that I of all the People have no such failing when it comes to the sunlanders. I wish the news of what happened here to spread—it will fill their land with terror. And the females and young we allow to escape will not take up arms as their males might, but in the cities we besiege they will need to be fed and watered, taking resources from those who do stand against us." She slipped Whitefire from its sheath and laid it beside her helmet. There was no fire in her pavilion of shadow; the sword's lunar glow gave all the light. *"We have not spilled the blood of mortals since we retreated behind the Shadowline. Now that is ended. Let the Book of Regret re-*

member this hour even beyond the world's end." She raised her hand. *"Sing with me, for the sake of all the People. We must now praise the blind king and the sleeping queen and swear our fealty to the Pact of the Glass—yes, we will all swear to it together, think what we might—then we will take flame and fear to our enemies."*

PART THREE
FIRE

. . . And Perin went among them and heard their cries, and when they told him, not knowing who he was, of the terrible beast that beset them, he smiled and patted his great hammer and instructed them not to be afraid . . .

—from *A Compendium of Things That are Known*
The Book of the Trigon

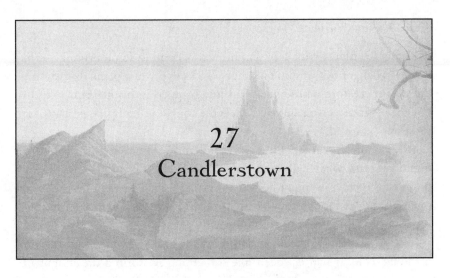

27
Candlerstown

THE TALE OF YEARS:

Each page turned is a page of fire
The tortoise licks his burned feet
And stares into darkness

—from *The Bonefall Oracles*

E KNEW HE HAD TO PAY attention. Barrick knew that what was happening was terribly important, if hard to believe. He also knew that his sister was expecting him to shoulder some of the burden. He just didn't know whether he could do it or not.

It was the dreams, his harrowing dreams, wearing him away just as the powerful ocean waves broke down the causeway between Southmarch's castle and town, so that men had to labor constantly to build it back up again. Sometimes he found it difficult to remember what it felt like simply to be Barrick. There were nights when he woke scratching like a beast at the inside of his chamber door, locked each night by his servants to prevent him from walking in his sleep. Other midnights he came gasping up from nightmares, half certain that he had changed into something else entirely, and could only sit in the dark feeling at first his hands and arms and then, reluctantly, his face, terrified that he might find some dreadful transfiguration had taken place to match those dreams of violence. In many of the dreams he was surrounded by faceless shapes that wanted to imprison him, perhaps even kill him, unless he destroyed them first. Always he woke sweating, breathless with fear that he was becoming some brute beast like a shape-changer out of some old nurse's tale, and worst of all, that this time the dream creature whose neck had just snapped in his hands would turn out to be a real person he had attacked—someone he knew, perhaps even someone he loved.

In fact, there seemed little separation now between the madness of nightmare and what had been the sanctuary of wakefulness. In the dim hours of the previous night he had awakened with a voice in his ear, someone speaking as though they sat right next to him, although the room was silent but for the breath of his slumbering page.

"We do not need the mantle any longer," it had said—a woman's voice, commanding, cold. It had *not* been like something heard in a dream, but had seemed to resound inside the very bones of his skull. He had whimpered at the sound, the nearness of it. *"We will sweep down on them like fire. They will fear us in light as well as darkness . . ."*

". . . Prince Barrick?" said a gruff voice.

Someone was trying to get his attention—a real voice, not a midnight dream. He shook his head, trying to make sense.

"Prince Barrick, we know it is an effort for you to be here and we are all grateful for that. Shall I have someone bring you wine?" It was Avin Brone speaking, clumsily trying to let him know he was not paying attention.

"Are you ill again?" Briony asked quietly.

"I am well enough. It is . . . the fever, still. I do not sleep well." He took a breath to clear his head, struggling to remember what the others had been saying. He wanted to show that he was worthy to sit beside his sister. "But why should these fairy-beasts come here and attack us? Why now?"

"We do not know anything for certain, Highness." That was the quiet one, Vansen, the guard captain. Barrick wasn't certain what he thought about the man. Briony's anger with him had been reasonable—letting a reigning prince be killed in his own bedroom was obviously a dereliction of duty, and under old King Ustin the captain's head would probably have been on a spike above the Basilisk Gate weeks ago—so he was not quite certain why she now seemed to be treating the young soldier like an important adviser. He dimly remembered Briony saying something about it as they made their way to this council, but his head had been pounding from the effort of getting up and getting dressed. "All I can say is that the creature we caught said something about someone leading an army, coming to burn our houses," Vansen went on. "Strangely, it was a *she* the goblin said was going to do it. 'She brings white fire,' that's what it told us. 'Burn all your houses to black stones.' But perhaps the monster did not speak our tongue well enough . . ."

Barrick felt a chill trace down his back. Vansen's words were much like his dream, the cold, female voice out of the empty night. He almost said something, but the stony, doubting faces all around made him hold his tongue. *The prince is imagining things,* they would whisper to each other. *His wits are going.* He should never have confessed his secrets to Briony. Thank the gods he had not given up all caution and had kept the strangest of them to himself.

"Is there some reason this enemy *couldn't* be a woman?" Briony demanded. Barrick could not help noticing changes in his sister: it was as though she had grown bigger, harder, while he grew smaller and more helpless daily. "Didn't Anglin's granddaughter Lily lead her people against the Gray Companies? If the Twilight People are somehow led by a woman, does that mean we have no need to be wary of them?"

"No, Highness, of course not." Vansen flushed easily. Barrick wondered if the man was trying to hide a great anger.

"But the princess raises an important question," said old Steffans Nynor with surprising matter-of-factness. The castellan seemed to have put aside his fluttery servility in this time of need. *Eyes of Heaven,* Barrick thought, *have I been asleep for a hundred years? Is everyone turning into something else?* For a moment the walls of the chapel seemed to drop away and he was turning, falling. He recovered himself by biting his tongue; as the pain jumped into the back of his mouth he heard Nynor say, ". . . after all. Perhaps they merely wish to test their strength—a raid or two, then back across the Shadowline."

"Wishful thinking," declared Tyne of Blueshore. "Unless Vansen is utterly mistaken, that is no raiding party. They are bringing a large army, the kind that will stay in the field until it has accomplished its task."

"But why me?" said Earl Rorick. "First they steal my bride and her splendid dowry, now they will attack my lands. I have done nothing to offend these creatures!"

"Opportunity, my lord—that seems most likely," said Vansen. He looked at Rorick with such a calm, measured gaze that Barrick could almost see him weighing the man and finding him to be a short measure. *But Vansen is a dalesman, isn't he? So Rorick is his lord.* The idea that a liege lord would not receive the unquestioning respect of all his liegemen was a slightly new one to Barrick, who had spent his childhood so taken with his own cynicism that it had not occurred to him others might also find the ancient order of things to be less than perfect.

"Opportunity?" asked Briony.

"When I was in . . . when I was behind the Shadowline, Highness," the captain said, "it was like falling into a fast river, even though I was less troubled than many of my men. But time and even . . . even the *substance* of things seemed different from place to place there, in the way . . . in the way that someone swept down a river might for a moment be pulled down and then be lifted to the surface again, or be caught for a moment in an eddy, then pushed helplessly into the rocks."

"What are you talking about?" Avin Brone demanded. "You said 'opportunity.' "

Vansen suddenly realized they were all looking at him. He colored again, lowered his head. "Forgive me, I am but a soldier . . ."

"Speak." There was something in his sister's voice that Barrick had never heard before; again he felt adrift, as though Vansen's river had whirled him far away from his own, familiar life. "You are here precisely because you have seen things the rest of us haven't, Captain Vansen. Speak."

"I meant only that . . . that I wonder why, if they have gathered such an army, they should choose to enter the March Kingdoms at Daler's Troth. I was born there, so I know it well. There are a few large towns, Dale House and Candlerstown and Hawkshill, but mostly it is hill crofts, a few larger farms, scattered villages. If they mean to come against us, and I believe they do, why should they start so far away? Even if they do not know that my men and I spied them and so they still believe they will surprise us, why should they take the chance that others will flee east with news of their coming and allow us to prepare? If they had come across the Shadowline in the Eastmarch hills, they would have been upon us already and I fear we would not be having this council, unless it was to meet our conquerors."

"That is treason!" said Rorick. "Who is this lowborn soldier to tell us such things? Are you saying we cannot defeat them?"

"No, my lord." Vansen's jaw was set. He would not look at Rorick, but didn't seem cowed. "No, but I saw them with these eyes—they have a great force. Had they come down on Southmarch in the night, this city would have been in terror and disarray."

"What exactly *are* you trying to tell us, Captain Vansen?" Briony asked.

"That perhaps the Twilight Lands have their own ebb and flow." He looked at her, almost imploring her to understand. "Perhaps they came through in the only place they could. It is hard to say what I mean—there are no words for it . . ."

"Perhaps the captain is right," said Earl Gowan, whose fiefdom in Helmingsea included a small but excellent personal navy. Gowan usually had the air of someone who joined a discussion, no matter how serious, chiefly for amusement. "But perhaps they have no interest in Southmarch. Perhaps the hobgoblins are only a raiding party after all and you are mistaken, or perhaps their goal is farther south, in Syan. Wasn't it King Karal of Syan who led the armies of Eion against them once upon a time? Perhaps they want revenge."

Barrick could feel an easing of tension around the table. Some of the other nobles nodded their heads, agreeing. "No," he said. He had been silent a long time: the others seemed surprised even to hear the prince speak. "They want this place—Southmarch. They lived here once."

"That is an old tale," Brone said slowly. "I am not certain it is true, Highness . . ."

But Barrick knew it was true, as certainly as if he had wakened on a cold, damp day and knew it was going to rain; he was not, however, able to explain why he was so sure. "Not just a tale," was all he could muster. "They lived here once."

Old Nynor cleared his throat. "It is true that . . . that there are stones beneath the castle and in the deep places that are part of some older stronghold."

"Men have lived here a long while, even before Anglin's folk," said Tyne dismissively. "And the Funderlings were here when men arrived, everyone knows."

"This is all beside the point," said Briony. "Much as some of you might wish it, we cannot hope the Twilight People are going to Syan to revenge themselves on Karal's heirs and leave it at that. They are in our lands. Every farm in Daler's Troth is a part of the March Kingdoms. Just as Rorick is their lord and must protect those people and those lands, it is up to the crown of Southmarch to help him."

Earl Rorick brushed a curl back from his forehead. He had made a concession to the fact of a war council—his outfit, though beautifully tailored, was considerably short of his usual extravagance, but he still looked no more ready for combat than would a peacock. "What . . . what do you plan,

Highness?" He looked around at the other nobles, unhappily aware of how glad they all were that his lands, not theirs, would bear the brunt of what was coming.

"We will fight them, of course." Briony suddenly seemed to remember her brother; she turned to Barrick with the tiniest flicker of the shamefaced smile that he alone knew well enough to recognize. "If you agree."

"Of course." A thought had come to him—a simple thing compared to all the dreadful visons that had been plaguing him, simple and satisfying. "We will fight."

"Then we must finish our preparations," she said. "Lord Brone, Lord Aldritch, you will proceed as we discussed earlier. We must put an army into the field now—if nothing else, to see how strong they are."

Avin Brone and Tyne slowly nodded their heads, weighty men with weighty concerns.

"And I will lead it," Barrick announced.

"What?" Briony recoiled as though he had slapped her. He was almost pleased to see her look so startled. A small, resentful part of him knew that she had grown accustomed to making decisions without him. Now that would end. "But, Barrick, you have been ill . . . !"

Avin Brone thumped his big hands down on the table, then crossed his arms, hiding those hands in his jacket as though he feared they would get into mischief. "You cannot take such a risk, Highness," he began, but Barrick did not let him finish.

"I am not a fool, Lord Brone. I do not imagine I am going to single-handedly drive off the Twilight People. I know you think I'm only a crippled child, and a headstrong one at that. But I will go and I will lead our army, at least in name. The Silver Wolf of Anglin must be on the field—anything else is unthinkable." The glorious idea that had seemed so clear and so obvious a moment ago now seemed a bit muddled, but he pushed ahead. "Someone said earlier that Rorick must go, to show that the nobles of these lands will fight for what is theirs. Everyone knows that the people of Southmarch are frightened by the terrible things that have happened—our father a captive, Kendrick dead. If Vansen is right, even darker days are coming to us—a war against things we hardly understand. The people *must* see that the Eddons will fight for them. There are two regents, after all, which is an uncommon luxury. One of us must go into the field."

His twin was so angry she could barely speak. It only made Barrick feel more coldly comfortable with his decision. "And what if you're killed?"

"I told you, Sister, I'm not a fool. When King Lander put on his father's crown at Coldgray Moor and fought the Twilight People, was he in the vanguard, trading blows? But he was remembered for a great victory and his people treasure his name." He realized too late he had said something foolish—they would misunderstand.

And they did. "This will be no place for a young man trying to make a name for himself," Tyne Aldritch declared angrily. "I beg Your Highness' pardon, but I will not stand silently and see men and land put at risk so you can earn a reputation."

Now Barrick was angry, too, but mostly at himself. What he couldn't explain, what he could barely acknowledge himself, was that the lure of his idea wasn't glory but resolution—that he would thrive in the simplicity of the battlefield, that he would not need to fear his own anger or even the madness growing inside him, and that if he died it would be a relief from the dreams and the great fear. "I know what kind of place it will be, Blueshore," he told the new master of arms. "Or at least I can guess. And I certainly know my own failings. Would you rub my nose in them?"

Tyne's mouth snapped shut but his eyes spoke for him.

"Prince Barrick and I must talk about this." Briony had pushed down her own anger now, hidden it behind a mask of determined calm. *She's turning into Father,* Barrick thought, *but not the way that I am.* It wasn't a happy realization. *She has inherited his grace. I have his curse.*

"We will talk all you wish," Barrick told his twin. "But I *am* going." And he knew it was true. He was one of the reigning Eddons, after all, and at this moment there was a hard, cold thing inside him that none of them could match. He would have his way.

"Hoy, Chert, have you found that boy?" shouted a woman he only vaguely recognized. He thought she might be one of the Sandstones; the woman with whom she was gossiping on the front porch certainly seemed to have the huge Sedimentary Clan's telltale chin.

"Not yet," he called.

"Must tha boom like the wind in the chimneys?" complained Beetledown from his perch on Chert's shoulder. "Fair collapsed my headbones, that did."

"Sorry." Chert was glad that he was far enough away from the women that they couldn't see the little fellow. Better to have them think he was talking to his own shoulder than to have every child in Funderling Town, and half the grown ones, chasing him down Gypsum Way in hopes of seeing a live Rooftopper. "Are you sure you can't ride in the pocket of my tunic where no one can see you?"

"And where I can't smell nothing, neither?"

"Ah. True enough."

Beetledown stirred and sniffed loud enough for even Chert to hear. "Turn . . . turn . . . *chi'm'ook!*" He drummed his tiny heels in frustration. "Where is the sun? Where is sunwise? How can I say the turning?"

"Left and right will have to do, because I don't think you know where the Stonecutter's Door or the Silk Door are. You do know left and right, don't you?"

" 'Course. But we call uns, 'leef' and 'reck' when we speak thy tongue. So go leef, left, what tha will. But there, turn."

Chert couldn't understand why the Rooftoppers would use different words than everyone else did in a language that wasn't even their own, but it had long been clear that Beetledown had his own odd way of talking; of all that small people, only the queen could speak to Chert in a clear, civilized fashion. He wondered again why she spoke the language of the larger world better than her subjects did, but he didn't waste much thought on it.

As they made a few more turns, Beetledown holding a lock of Chert's hair so he could stand up without tumbling as he sniffed the air, the odd pair began to move farther and farther from the center of Funderling Town; in fact, it soon became clear that Beetledown's nose was leading them toward the outermost reaches. If it was a true scent, the boy seemed to have gone by a rather circuitous route, but the overall direction was definitely outward and down. Thus, when they swung close enough to the Salt Pool, Chert turned and carried the little man into the great cavern.

"Going wrong way, th'art."

"We'll turn back, but we need something. We'll be beyond the streetlights soon and, whatever you may have heard about us Funderlings, we can't see in complete dark. Hoy, Boulder!"

The small Funderling came bounding toward them across the uneven stones, eyes widening at what was no doubt the first adult person smaller than himself he had ever seen. He grinned in surprise and delight. "What is this, Chert?"

"It's not a this, it's a who—Beetledown's his name. He's a Rooftopper.

Yes, a real Rooftopper. You heard about Flint? Well, this fellow's helping me look for him. I'll explain it next time I come, but I'd appreciate if you'd keep quiet about it for now. Meantime, I'm going down Silk Door way and I'll need light soon."

"Just brought up a basketful for the second shift," Boulder said as he spilled out a selection of glowing coral. "Take your pick, and for free. I'm sure the story will be worth it."

"Many thanks. And you've just reminded me of something. Is Rocksalt here today with his basket?"

"Just over there." Boulder pointed to a group of Funderling men and women and even a few children who were sitting at the edge of the cavern near the great door, waiting for the afternoon shift leader to come for them. As he walked toward them, Chert finally convinced Beetledown to get into his pocket and hide.

He fished out a few copper chips from his pocket and bought bread and soft white cheese from Rocksalt, as well as a waterskin, which cost him a few more chips even though he would be bringing it back to the peddler again afterward. Chert didn't like the expense, but it was becoming clear to him that he would not be back for the evening meal. This reminded him of something else.

"Jasper, is your boy staying with you or going home?" he asked a man he knew, one of the fellows waiting to start an afternoon shift.

"Home, of course. Earth Elders! He'd drive me mad in a hundred drips if he came along with me."

"Good." Chert turned to the boy. "Here . . . little Clay, isn't it? Pay attention. I'm giving your father this shiny chip, and if you take a message to my wife, he'll give that chip to you when he gets back from the pit tonight. Do you know my wife, Opal Blue Quartz? On Wedge Road?" The boy, eyes very big at all the attention, nodded solemnly. "Good. Tell her I said that I may be gone a while, searching, and not to hold supper for me. Not to worry if I'm not back by bedtime, even. Can you remember that? Say it back."

His memory tested and approved, young Clay was dispatched and Chert gave the boy's father the copper chip to hold in trust. "You've earned me a trip up to that fracturing big-folk market, you know," Jasper said. "He'll want to spend it up there."

"Do you good to get some fresh air," Chert said as he headed off across the uneven, rocky floor.

"Are you mad?" Jasper called after him. "Too much of that wind will suck the life out of a person's innards!" This was not an uncommon feeling among the inhabitants of Funderling Town and although it might not completely explain why Chert was the first Funderling in centuries to meet a Rooftopper, he reflected, it did explain why there hadn't been many other opportunities for such a thing to happen.

They went out through the Silk Door, Funderling Town's back gate, a huge arch carved into a sandstone wall whose natural streaking of pink, ocher, purple, and orange made it look like exquisitely dyed fabric. Once through, they passed in a fairly short time from the careful delving and carving of the town into an area where no digging had been necessary because the underside of the mount was already hollowed out by the ocean and the drip of water from above into the limestone caverns, although the Funderlings had enlarged many of them and created a network of tunnel-roads to connect them all. What was not remembered, at least by anyone of Chert's acquaintance, was whether the strangely regular caverns below Funderling Town that spiraled deep down into the bedrock of the mount, down below the bottom of the bay itself, had always existed, or had been created by even earlier hands. All that was known for certain by living Funderlings was that the Mysteries were there, hundreds of feet below the heart of the castle's inner keep, and that the less the big folk knew about those secret depths, the better.

Chert stood now far on the outskirts of Funderling Town, at the entrance to those very same Mysteries, looking down at a long, creamy slope gated by two rock walls. At the bottom was a scalloped fringe of pale-pink-and-amber stone that glowed like a translucent curtain in the light of the torches that burned before and behind it. "This way? Are you certain?" Chert asked the Rooftopper. Why would the boy have come so far into the earth, to a place he made it very clear he didn't like? The Eddon family tombs were two levels up from here, but that was really only a few yards overhead.

"What my nose tells me be true," Beetledown said. "Stronger here than anywhere past thy home roofs and rookeries."

It took Chert a moment to realize that this very little man meant that he had not smelled Flint so strongly since they had left Chert's own neighborhood back on Wedge Road. "Well, lead on, then." He made his way down the stairs that crisscrossed the pale slope and led ultimately into the first antechamber of the caverns.

"Go leef," announced Beetledown. "No, loft, that is what I mean."

"Left."

"Aye, that be un."

They stepped out of the antechamber and beneath a low archway into the first of what Chert had known since childhood as the Festival Halls, a massive set of linked caverns full of columns and flowstone canopies that had begun as natural formations but then been carved and decorated over the centuries until almost every piece had been extensively shaped. Only one extended section of grottoes had been left untouched. Its name was a consonantal grumble in the old Funderling language that roughly translated as "The Lord of the Hot Wet Stone's Garden of Earth Shapes." The carvings in the rest of the Festival Halls were as meticulous as anything in the wonderful roof of Funderling Town, but where the town's famous roof portrayed a riot of natural greenery, of leaves and branches and fruit, and also birds and small treetop animals, to a people who hadn't lived among such things in time out of memory, the Festival Halls were something altogether different, a collection of mysterious, endlessly repetitive shapes that made a person's eyes blur if he or she looked at any one spot too long. These had been done so long ago that nobody remembered whether earlier Funderlings had carved them or why, and it was easy to see almost anything in the odd shapes—animals, demons, portraits of the gods themselves.

"I do not understand this place," said Beetledown in a voice so quiet and nervous that Chert could barely hear him, despite the immense silence of the caverns.

"We are approaching some of the most sacred spots of the Funderling People," Chert said. "Very few others ever see them. It is one reason I wanted to hide you from others at the Salt Pool, to avoid someone making a stink if they found out where we were going."

"Ah, yes." Beetledown's voice sounded a little strained. "Laws against it, then? Forbidden, eh? Like us with the Great Gable or the Holy Wainscoting. 'Course with the Holy Wainscoting, none but the rats be small enough to follow us in."

Chert couldn't help smiling. "I can see that would work in your favor. Hmm, I suppose most of the big folk would have trouble making their way through some of the tight places down here, too. But you won't." He began walking again. "And it's not really forbidden for you to be in these places, but it's certainly unusual."

"Just don't leave me here," Beetledown begged him, and Chert suddenly recognized that the undertone he had been hearing in the Rooftopper's voice was pure fear. For the first time he considered what it must feel like for his minuscule companion to come so far beneath the ground, away from the open roofs and sky. "Not even Beetledown the brave bowman can live long by himself in such a place," the tiny man said, "—not with the air so tight and close and even un's breathing's so unnatural loud."

"I won't leave you here."

They crossed down through the Festival Halls and toward the cavern called the Curtainfall, which was a side doorway to the great honeycomb of caves known as the Temple. But when first seen, it didn't look like the doorway to anything: at one end of the small cave a broad sheet of water drizzled from a lip of jutting rock, down into a pool. The waterfall shimmered blackly in the weak light of the cavern's single bracketed torch although, as Chert moved closer to the curtain of water, he could also see the pale reflection of his coral lamp move like a firefly across its surface.

"Who comes down here so far to light torches?" Beetledown asked, distractedly sniffing.

"You'll see." Chert stepped out into the pool on a bridge of submerged stones near the edge of the cataract and headed straight for the falling water.

"Tha'll drown us!" Beetledown chirped in alarm.

"Don't fear. There is space between the water and the stone—and look!" There was more than space between water and wall—there was a hole in the great slab of stone, a hole that from most angles was hidden behind the waterfall. Chert stepped through, taking more care than he normally would to avoid the edge of the waterfall so that Beetledown would not accidentally be washed off his shoulder. On the far side of the water they entered a single chamber the size of an entire Funderling Town neighborhood, whose walls were lined with bracketed torches and whose high ceiling was covered with the same kind of strange carvings that filled the Garden of Earth Shapes. At the far side of this massive chamber stood the pillared front of the Temple of the Metamorphic Elders, cut directly into the living rock.

"By the Peak!" the little man said in wonder. "Un goes on and on! Have tha Funderling folk truly dug all the way down in the dark earth and out through the bottom?"

"Not quite," Chert told him, looking at the intricately worked stone facade—only the unevenness of some of the shapes showed that it had been natural cavern once. "But we have found many of the deep places of the earth that water dug, then carved them even more to make them our own."

Beetledown made a face, sniffed. "But for the first time I do not scent the boy strongly. Un's track runs weaker here, behind the water-wall."

Chert sighed. "I will ask the temple brothers, anyway," he said. "But I'm afraid you'll have to wait here."

"Art coming back for me?"

"I won't go out of your sight. Just sit here on this stone." He placed Beetledown atop a relatively flat bit of carved wall, high off the cavern floor. He was glad he didn't have to go far: he felt a responsibility for the little man he had not expected. He remembered the tiny fellow's worry about cats and the joke he had made about it and was again struck by shame. *It's true there aren't too many cats down here,* he thought, *but I don't think I remembered to tell him that many here keep snakes against rats and voles and other vermin. I doubt Beetledown likes snakes any better than cats.*

He hurried across the wide floor of the temple chamber. It was here that the people of Funderling Town made pilgrimage, gathering on the nights when the Mysteries themselves were celebrated and for other important holiday observances. Chert was relieved to see a dark-robed acolyte standing just inside the doorway of the temple proper, so that he didn't have to break his word to stay within Beetledown's sight. "Your pardon, Brother."

The acolyte came out into the full glow of the torches. The Metamorphic Brothers did not use stonelights, considering them to be dangerously modern, even though the glowing lamps had been used in the streets of Funderling Town for at least two centuries. "What do you seek, Child of the Elders?" he asked. He was dressed in the temple's costume of archaic, loose-fitting clothes and was younger than Chert would have expected. He looked like he might be from one of the Bismuth families.

"I am Chert Blue Quartz. My foster son is lost." He took a breath. Here was where the trouble might really begin. "He is one of the big folk. Has he come past here?"

The acolyte raised an eyebrow but only shook his head. "Do not go away just yet, though. One of the brothers came back from the market and said he saw a *Gha'jaz* child." Chert was not surprised to hear the man use the old Funderling word—he had spoken the Common Tongue of big folk and Funderlings awkwardly, as though he didn't use it very often. The Temple had always disliked change. "I will bring him out."

Chert waited impatiently. When the other acolyte at last emerged, he confirmed that he had seen a boy much like Flint hours earlier, fair-haired and small but clearly not a Funderling, in one of the outer Festival Halls, but heading away from the Temple rather than toward it. Just as Chert was absorbing the implications, he heard a clamor from behind him. Three more acolytes, apparently returning from some errand, had stopped and clustered around the bit of wall where he'd left Beetledown.

"Nickel!" one of them shouted to the first acolyte. "Look, it is a real, living *Gha'sun'nk!*"

Chert cursed under his breath.

Several more of the Metamorphic Brothers spilled out of the temple, some bare-chested and sweaty as though they had just come from forges, kilns, or ovens; within moments a dozen or so had surrounded the Roof-topper. They seemed even more curious than he would have expected. Chert waded through them and lifted the little man up onto his shoulder; Beetledown was looking a bit panicky.

"Is he really *Gha'sun'nk?*" asked an acolyte, again using the old Funderling name for the Rooftoppers—*the little, little people.*

"Yes. He is helping me hunt for my foster son."

As the other acolytes whispered to each other, Nickel approached, a strange gleam in his eyes. "Ah! This is a terrible day," he said and laid both fists on his chest in a gesture of surrender to the Earth Elders.

"What do you mean?" Chert asked, startled.

"We had hoped that Grandfather Sulphur's dreams spoke of a time still to come," said the acolyte. "He is the oldest among us, our master, and the Elders speak to him. Lately he has dreamed that the hour is coming when Old Night will reach out and claim all the *di-G'zeh-nah'nk,*"—he used an old word that meant something like "left-behinds"—"and that our days of freedom are over."

The acolytes began to argue among themselves. Chert had left Beetledown on the wall simply to avoid having to explain him and acknowledge the breach of tradition, but the Metamorphic Brothers' unhappy confusion was real and honest.

"Will they kill me?" Beetledown fluted in his ear.

"No, no. They're just upset because the times are strange—like your queen and her Lord of the High Place or whatever it was, the one that she said warned you that some kind of storm was coming."

"The Lord of the Peak," said Beetledown. "And he is real. The storm is real, too, mark tha—'twill blow the very tiles of our roofs out into darkness."

Chert did not reply, but stood suddenly rigid in the midst of the tumult like a traveler lost without light on one of the wild roads on the outskirts of Funderling Town. He had just realized where Flint must be going, and it was a fearful thought indeed.

The snores of Finneth's husband seem loud as the roar of his forge fires.

The clanging all day, she thought, *then lying sleepless in the dark with him snoring like a bull all night. The gods give us what they think fit, but what have I done that this is my lot?* Not that she had only complaints. Her man, called Onsin Oak-arms, was not the worst husband a woman could have. He worked hard in his little smithy and did not spend too much time at the tavern at the end of the drove road. He was not one of the wasters lolling on the bench beneath the eaves, shouting at the passersby. If he was not the most affectionate of men, he was at least a responsible father to their son and daughter, teaching them to love the gods and to honor their parents while hardly ever resorting to any punishment more painful than a cuff on the top of the head or the snap of his thick fingers against a child's backside. *A good thing, too,* Finneth thought. *He is strong enough to kill a grown man with those big hands.* Thinking of his broad back and how the dark curly hair grew tight on his thick neck, the way he held up a bar that would be an ox shoe to show their son the color it should be when it was ready for shaping, she felt a little tickle of desire for him, snoring or no snoring. She rolled against his back and pressed her cheek against him. His sleep-rumble changed—there was a note almost of question in it—but then subsided again. Their daughter Agnes stirred in her cot. To her mother's immense terror, both children had caught the fever that had lately passed through Candlerstown and all the dales, but although little Agnes had taken it the worse, her breathing had been almost normal again for a week. Zoria the Queen of Mercy, it seemed, had heard Finneth's prayers.

She was floating toward sleep, thinking of the damp straw on the floor that would have to be replaced with dry now that wet weather had come, and of how she must also press Onsin to plaster up the cracks around the window of their little house, when she heard the first faint sounds—

someone shouting. When she realized it was not the watchman calling out the hour, suddenly all her sleepiness was gone.

At first she thought it must be a fire. It was different living in a town than the village where Finneth had grown up. Here a fire could start so far away that you had never even seen the people whose houses it took first, but still come rushing down your own narrow street like an army of angry demons, jumping from roof to roof at horrifying speed. Was it a fire? Somewhere a bell was ringing, ringing, and more people were shouting. Someone was running through the streets calling for the reeves. It had to be a fire.

She was already shaking Onsin awake when she heard a voice louder than the others, perhaps at the bottom of their own road, screaming, *"We are attacked! They are climbing the walls!"* Finneth's heart lurched. Attacked? Climbing the walls? Who? She was heaving at Onsin's bulk now, but he was like a great tree, too much for her to move. At last he rolled over and sat up, shaking his head.

"War!" she said, tugging his beard until he knocked her hands away. "The reeves are out—everyone's crying war!"

"What?" He slapped and pinched at his face as though it were not his own, then heaved himself up off their pallet. Agnes was awake and making questioning sounds, crying a little. Finneth pulled the child's blanket around her and kissed her, but it didn't soothe her, and Finneth had to see to Fergil as well. The boy was waking but still half in a dream, twitching and looking around as though he had never seen his own house before; for a moment the sight of her confused children brought tears to Finneth's eyes.

Onsin had pulled on his heavy breeches and, strangely, his best boots, but had not bothered with a shirt. He had his hammer in one hand, the hammer that no one else in the drove road could even lift, and an ax he was straightening for Tully Joiner in the other. Even in this wild moment Finneth thought her husband looked like something out of an old story, a kindly giant, a bearded demigod like Hiliometes. He was listening to the shouting, which had moved down to the end of the street. Now Finneth heard another sound, a rising wail like the wind, and she was filled with a helpless, sickening terror unlike any she had known.

"I will be back," Onsin said as he hurried out the door. He did not kiss his children or wait for her blessing, which only added to Finneth's growing despair.

Attacked? Who could it be? We have been at peace with Settland since before Grandmother's time. Bandits? Why would bandits attack a town?

"Mama. Where did Papa go?" asked little Fergil, and as she squatted to comfort him, she realized she was shivering, wearing nothing but the blanket she had wrapped around her. "Papa went out to help some other men," she told the children, then began to pull on her clothes.

She couldn't believe that it could still be the same night—that only just the other side of the midnight bell she had been lying in her bed thinking about Onsin's snoring, worrying about the sound Agnes was making when she breathed. It was as though Perin himself had lifted a hammer large as a mountain and brought it down on all their lives, smashing everything into powder.

Candlerstown was aflame, but fire was the least of her worries now. The streets were full of shrieking figures, some bleeding, others only running aimlessly mad, eyes staring wide and dark out of pale faces, mouths open holes. It was as though the earth had vomited out all the unhappy dead. Finneth couldn't think, didn't want to think—such terror was too large to fit into one head, one heart, especially when she had to cling to a pair of frightened, weeping children and try to find a place where the flames were not burning, where people were not screaming. But there was no such place anywhere.

Worst of all were the glimpses of the invaders, impossible nightmare shapes clambering over walls and dashing across rooftops—some in animal shapes, others bent and twisted as no living thing that could wear armor and carry a weapon should be. As she dragged the children past a public square she saw a tall figure on a rearing horse in the midst of a crowd of Candlerstown men, and that figure looked so much like a man that for an instant she was heartened—here was some noble lord, perhaps even Earl Rorick himself, a person Finneth had never seen despite his importance in her life. Yes, Rorick must have come down from his castle at Dale House to rally the frightened townfolk and lead them against these monstrous invaders. But then she saw that this shaggy-haired lord was taller than any man, that he had too many fingers on his long white hands, and that his eyes, like those of his rearing horse, were as flame-yellow as a cat's. As for the men around him, the ones she had thought he might be rallying, they were crawling and moaning beneath his horse's hooves as he pricked at them with his long spear, driving them like a flock of sheep to slavery or death.

Agnes stumbled and fell and Fergil began to shriek. She caught them both up in her arms and limped away from the square. She was in a part of the town she hardly seemed to know at all, but everything had become something else on this ghastly night: it might be her own street for all she could be certain, her own house that she staggered past as barking, whistling shapes came pouring out of the windows like beetles from a split log. Overhead, the stars had vanished. Finneth couldn't understand that either. Why were there no stars, and why had the sky turned that dull, dark red? Was it blood—was the whole town bleeding up into the sky? Then she knew. It was the smoke of burning Candlerstown itself, hiding what was happening even from Heaven.

She found herself in a crowd of people, although it was more river than crowd, a heedless wash of screams and waving arms that flooded down the Marsh Road, past the Trigonate temple. The outer walls and roof of the temple were crawling with something that looked like moss but which glowed like sullen lightning. The priests had nearly all been slaughtered, although some of them were still crawling despite terrible, obviously mortal wounds. In their haste to flee, the shrieking crowd was trampling the survivors, which might have been a mercy. Even Finneth stepped on a motionless human figure and did not care—it was all she could do to keep upright. She could not stop, could not turn, certainly could not waste pity on the dead and soon-dead. She was hemmed in on either side and all she could think of was holding Agnes and Fergil tight against her, so tightly that even the gods could not pull them from her.

All who fell now were crushed underfoot. The crowd moved like a single living thing, rushing to the open Eastside Gate and the darkness beyond, toward the blessed cold fields where no fires burned.

Finneth ran until she couldn't run any farther, then shoved her way to the outskirts of the torrent of people, which was beginning to slow and scatter.

They were outside the walls, knee-deep in the stubble of a harvested field, when she fell to the ground at last, exhausted and helpless. She wondered if she, too, might be dying; she was not wounded, but it seemed impossible anyone could experience such a night and live. She clutched her son and daughter and wept, every sob clawing painfully at her smoke-scorched throat.

Gone, all gone—Onsin, her house, her few possessions. Only these two small, precious, panting creatures kept her from running back to throw herself into the flames of Candlerstown. Most dreadful of all, as she lay with her shivering children on the cold ground just outside the murdered town, she could hear the destroyers of everything she had, and they were singing. Their voices were painfully lovely.

Darkness claimed her then, but only for a while.

28

Evening Star

WHITE SANDS:

See the moon scatter diamonds
His work is bone and light and dry dust
In the garden where no one strays

—from *The Bonefall Oracles*

S HE HAD LOST TRACK of how many different Favored had taken her up as though she were an ill-wrapped package, walked her to the next way station, and then turned her over to another functionary, but at last she was led into the receiving room of the paramount wife. Arimone looked up from her cushions and smiled indulgently as Qinnitan abased herself. "Oh, do get up, child," she said, although she looked not much more than a girl herself. "Are we not all sisters here?"

If we were all sisters, Qinnitan could not help thinking, *I wouldn't have gone down on my knees in the first place.* The invitation had arrived that morning and Qinnitan had spent hours under the expert ministration of a half dozen slaves, a mix of Favored and born-females, until her appearance had been polished to a blinding brilliance like a gemstone; after some consideration, she was then deconstructed and redressed in slightly less formal splendor.

"After all, we don't want the Evening Star to think we aspire to become the Light of the Morning, do we?" a Favored named Rusha had said with mocking severity. "We shall be beautiful—but not *too* beautiful."

Luian, who had been a bit absent of late, as if ashamed of her part in

bringing Qinnitan to meet Jeddin, had not been involved in the preparations for the audience, but she had sent one of her Tuani women to help
Qinnitan arrange her hair, which was now piled atop her head and held in
place with jeweled pins. Qinnitan had been quite taken with her own
image in the glass when it was done, but that seemed like pure foolishness
now: Arimone, who was perhaps ten years older than Qinnitan, was unquestionably the most beautiful woman she had ever seen or even imagined, like a temple image of Surigal herself, her hair jet black and so long
that even in a braid it coiled like a sleeping snake all over the cushions on
which she sat. Qinnitan could only wonder what such an amazing cascade
of hair would look like untethered and brushed out; she also felt certain
everyone else who met Arimone, most assuredly including any whole men,
were meant to wonder about that as well.

The autarch's paramount wife had an arresting figure, small-waisted and
wide-hipped, both features accented by her clinging robe, and she also had
a perfect, heart-shaped face, but it was her eyes—huge, thick-lashed, and almost as black as her hair—that made her look as though she belonged with
the other goddesses in Heaven rather than languishing among mere mortals
in the Seclusion. Qinnitan, who was already frightened and felt a bit of an
impostor in her fine clothes, suddenly felt not like one of the all-powerful
autarch's chosen brides, but like the dirtiest street urchin imaginable.

"Come, come, sit with me," Arimone said in a voice so light and musical it
suggested years of exhausting practice. "Will you take some tea? I like to drink
it cool on days like this, with plenty of mint and sugar. It's very refreshing."

Qinnitan did her best to seat herself without tripping over any of the
striped cushions mounded at the center of the room. In one corner a young
girl played the lute with surprising skill. Several other servant girls, when they
were not waiting on the paramount wife, sat talking quietly in the corners of
the room. Two youths with the dewy, beardless faces of the Favored stood behind the cushions waving fans of peacock feathers. The decoration of the receiving room seemed designed to remind visitors of one thing and one thing
only—a bedchamber, which was after all the root of Arimone's power. She
had not yet given the autarch an heir, but he had spent much of his first reg-
nal year traveling through all his lands, so none of the other wives dared even
whisper rumors of unhappiness in the royal bed. Should another year pass
without sign of a male heir, of course, they would do almost nothing else.

"Forgive me for waiting so long before having you to visit," said the
paramount wife. "You have been here, what, half a year?"

"More or less, Highness."

"You must call me Arimone—as I said, we are all sisters here. I have heard much about you, and you are just as charming as I imagined." She raised an eyebrow that had been plucked into a line as delicate as a spider's leg. "I hear you are great friends with Favored Luian. The two of you are cousins, are you not?"

"Oh, no, High . . . Arimone. We are merely from the same neighborhood."

The first wife frowned prettily. "Am I so foolish, then? Why did I think she and you . . . ?"

"Perhaps because Luian is a cousin of Jeddin, the chief of the Leopards." Arimone was watching her closely; Qinnitan suddenly wished she had kept her mouth shut. She was even more disturbed to realize that she was still babbling about it. "Luian talks of him much, of course. She is . . . she is very proud of him."

"Ah, yes, Jeddin. I know him. He's a handsome fellow, isn't he?" The Evening Star was still looking at Qinnitan in a way that made her very, very uncomfortable. "A fine, firm piece of manflesh. Don't you think so?"

Qinnitan did not know what she was supposed to say. The women of the Secluded talked very frankly about men, in a way that virginal Qinnitan often found embarrassingly informative, but this seemed somehow different, as though she were being tested in some way. A chill ran over her. Had the paramount wife heard rumors? "I have scarcely seen him, Arimone, at least since we were all children together. Certainly he could not be as handsome as our lord the autarch, all praise to his name, could he?"

Her hostess smiled as if at a well-played gambit. Qinnitan thought she heard a few of the slave girls giggle behind her. "Oh, that is different, little sister. Sulepis is a god on earth, and thus not to be judged as other men. Still, he is very taken by you, it seems."

The footing was again unsteady. "Taken by me? You mean the autarch?"

"Of course, dear. Has he not had you given special instruction? I hear that you are with that wheezing priest Panhyssir almost every day. That there are prayers and . . . rituals of preparation. Arcane practices."

Qinnitan was confused again. Hadn't this happened with all the wives? "I did not know that was unusual, Mistress."

"Arimone, remember? Ah, I suppose it is not surprising that the autarch has become interested in something new. He knows more than the priests, has read more of the ancient texts than they have themselves. He knows everything, my oh-so-clever husband—what the gods whisper to each other in dreams and why they live forever, the old, forgotten places and cities, the secret history of all of Xand and beyond. When he speaks to me, I can scarcely understand him sometimes. But his interests are so widespread that they do not last for long, of course. Like a great golden bee, he moves from flower to flower as his mighty heart leads him. I am sure whatever has taken his interest this time will be . . . short-lived."

Qinnitan flinched, but she was puzzled and determined to find out why the other wives seemed to think of her as different. "How . . . how were you prepared, Arimone? For marriage, I mean. If you will forgive an impertinent question. This is all very new to me."

"I imagine it is. You may not know, but of course I was married before." *My current husband murdered my only child, then killed my first husband, too, and made his death last for weeks,* she did not say, nor did she have to—Qinnitan already knew it, as did everyone else in the Seclusion. "So my circumstances were a bit different. I came to our lord and master's bed already a woman." She smiled again. "We are quite intrigued by you, many of us here in the Seclusion. Did you know that?"

"You . . . you are?"

"Ah, yes, of course. A very young girl—a child, really—" Arimone's smile was a bit cold, "from, let us be frank, an undistinguished family. None of us can quite imagine what it was that lifted you to the Golden One's eye." She spread her hands, which glittered with rings. The nails were half the length of her long, slender fingers. "Other than the beauty of your innocence, little sister, which is of course charming and formidable."

Never in her life, even standing before Autarch Sulepis, had Qinnitan felt less significant.

"Come, will you have a little more tea? I have prepared a surprise for you. I hope it will be a pleasant one. Will you promise not to tell on me if I do something that is a little naughty?"

Qinnitan could only nod.

"Good. That is how it should be between sisters. So you will not be too shocked if I tell you that I have brought a man into my house today—a true man, not one of the Favored. You are not afraid to meet a true man, are you? You have not been so long away from the streets of your childhood that you view them all as monsters and rapists, do you?"

Qinnitan shook her head, confused and frightened. Did the first wife know about Jeddin? Why else all this taunting?

"Good, good. In truth, he is very harmless, this man. So old that I do not think he could mount a mouse." She laughed between her teeth and her serving girls echoed her. "He is a storyteller. Shall I summon him?" The question was not meant to be answered: Arimone lifted her hands and clapped. A moment later a bent figure in colorful clothes stepped through one of the curtained doors and into the receiving room.

"Hasuris," she said, "I apologize for keeping you waiting."

"I would rather wait for you in a dark alcove than be served honeyed figs by any other woman, Mistress." The old man bowed low to Arimone, then gave Qinnitan a look so saucy and self-satisfied that he might as well have winked at her. "And this must be the young wife you told me of. Greetings, little Mistress."

"You are a shameless flirt, Hasuris," said Arimone, laughing. "None of your nonsense or the Golden One's guards will come and you will join the Favored."

"My stones and I adventure together only in memory, Great Queen," he said, "so it makes little difference. But I suppose their departure could be painful, so I will stay silent and behave well."

"No, to behave well you must not stay silent at all. Instead you must tell us a story. Why else would I have brought you here?"

"To admire the turn of my calf?"

"Wretched old fool. Tell us a tale. Perhaps . . ." Pondering, or pretending to, the paramount wife put a finger to her red, red lips. Even Qinnitan could not help staring at her like a lovesick boy. "Perhaps the story of the Foolish Hen."

"Very well, Great Queen." The old man bowed. Now that he was closer, Qinnitan could see that his white whiskers were stained yellow around his mouth. "Here is the tale, although it is a rather simple one, without any good jokes but the last one:

"Once there was a very foolish hen, who preened and preened herself, cer-tain that she was the most beautiful of her kind in all creation,"

he began.

"The other hens grew weary of her posturing and began to talk behind her back, but the foolish hen paid no attention at all. 'Jealous, that is all they are,' she told herself. 'Who cares what they think? They are of no importance com-pared to the man who feeds us. That is someone whose opinion matters, and

who will recognize my quality.' So she set out to gain the attention of the man who came every day to spread corn on the ground.

"Every time he arrived, she would push her way out from the midst of the other hens and strut back and forth before the man, head held high, breast shoved forward. When he looked away, she would call to him—'Ga-gaw! Ga-gaw!'—until he looked her way again. But still he treated her no differently from any of the others. The foolish hen became very angry and resolved to do whatever it took to be noticed."

Qinnitan was feeling a chill again. Was there a point to this story? Was Arimone suggesting that the younger wife had gone out of her way somehow to attract attention? The autarch's? Or someone else's? It was all too difficult to understand, but the penalties would be no less mortal because the crimes weren't altogether clear. She suddenly wanted nothing more than to be back in the Temple of the Hive, surrounded by the sweet hum of the sacred bees.

"The foolish hen could not sleep for trying to imagine a way to get the man's attention. Her lovely voice had not moved him. Perhaps he needed to see that she valued him more than the others did, but how could she do that? She resolved to eat more of the corn he dropped than anyone else, and so she followed him from the first moment he arrived until he went away again, pecking at the other hens to drive them away and eating as much corn as she could manage. The other hens despised her as she grew fatter and sleeker, but still the man did not speak to her, did not single her out in any way. She decided she would fly to him and show him that she alone was worthy of his attention. It was not easy, because by now she was quite plump, but by practicing every day she at last managed to stay aloft long enough to flutter a good distance.

"One day, after the man finished spreading the corn and began to walk back to the house, the hen flew after him. It was harder than she thought it would be and she did not catch up to him until he had already gone through the door. She hurried after and flew inside, but it was dark and she could not see, so she began to call out—'Ga-gaw! Ga-gaw!'—to let him know she had arrived.

"The man came to her and picked her up. Her heart was full of joy.

" 'I have tried to ignore you, you fat thing,' he said, 'because I was going to save you for the Feast of the Rising at the end of the rainy season, but here you are in my kitchen, shouting at the top of your lungs. Clearly it is the great

god's will that I eat you now.' And so speaking, he wrung her neck and set a fire in the oven . . ."

Qinnitan stood suddenly and the old man Hasuris fell silent. He looked a little shamefaced, as if he had somehow guessed the story might upset her, which didn't seem possible. "I . . . I don't feel very well," she said. She was dizzy and sick to her stomach.

Arimone looked at her with wide eyes. "My poor little sister! Can I get you something?"

"No, I . . . I think I had better go home. I'm v–very s–s–sorry." She put her hand over her mouth—she had a sudden, powerful urge to vomit all over the first wife's beautiful striped cushions.

"Oh, no, must you really? Perhaps it would be better for you to have a little more mint tea. Surely that would settle your stomach." Arimone picked up Qinnitan's cup and held it out to her, gaze doe-innocent. "Go ahead, little sister. Drink some more. It is made to my special recipe and it cures nearly all ills."

Filled with horror, Qinnitan shook her head and stumbled out without even bowing. She heard the slaves laughing and whispering behind her.

29

The Shining Man

FIVE WHITE WALLS:

Here is the shape with its tail
In its mouth
Here is the inside turned outside, the outside in

—from *The Bonefall Oracles*

"**L**ISTEN CAREFULLY," CHERT SAID when he had put some distance between himself and the temple of the Metamorphic Brothers. He raised his hand to his shoulder to let Beetledown climb onto his palm, then held him so that he could see the man's tiny face. "If your nose is telling you the truth and this is the way Flint went, I think I know where he's going."

"If my nose . . . ?" The Rooftopper's features screwed up in indignation. "Wasn't bred for it like the Grand and Worthy, me, but leaving un out, there be not a better sniffiter in all of the Southmarch heights . . ."

"I believe you." Chert took a deep, shaky breath. "It's just that . . . where he's headed . . ." His knees felt weak and he had to sit down, which he did carefully: the Rooftopper was still standing on his hand. For the first time that Chert Blue Quartz could remember, he wished he were outside, under the sky, instead of beneath the unimaginable weight of stone that had been the top of his world almost all his life, and had always held that place in his thoughts. "Where he's headed is a very . . . strange place. A sacred place. Sometimes it can be a dangerous place."

"Cats? Snakes?" The Rooftopper's eyes were wide. Despite his growing fear, Chert almost smiled.

"No, nothing like that. Well, there might be animals down there, but that's the least of my worries."

"Because th'art a giant."

Now Chert did smile: being called a giant was something that would probably never happen to him again. "Fair enough. But what I need to tell you is that I have a decision to make. It's not an easy one."

The little man looked at him now with keen interest, just like Cinnabar or one of the other Guild leaders being presented with a tricky but possibly lucrative bargain. The Rooftoppers were not just like people, they *were* people, Chert knew that now; they were just as complicated and lively as the Funderlings or anyone else. So why were they so small? Where did they come from? Had they been punished by the gods, or was there something even stranger in their origins?

Thoughts of the gods and their fabled propensity for vengeance were, at this moment, more compelling than usual.

"Here is my problem," he told Beetledown. "I told you before that places like the temple . . . that some of my people might frown on you being there. We are uncomfortable with outsiders seeing the things that are most important to us."

"Understood," said the little man.

"Well, I think Flint has gone deeper still into . . . into what we call the Mysteries. And I *know* that many of my people will be upset if I bring an outsider there. It was one reason I haven't even taken Flint anywhere near the place, even though he is my foundling son."

"Then time has come for me to go back to my own home." Beetledown sounded quite cheerful about it, and Chert wasn't surprised: the little man had become less comfortable the longer and deeper their journey became. In fact, he seemed positively to glow with satisfaction at the thought that his travels below ground were about to end, which made Chert's already wretched position even more so.

"But I'm afraid to lose so much time—if the boy's down there, it's been hours already. It's a dangerous place, Beetledown. Strange, too. I . . . I'm very frightened for him."

"So?" The Rooftopper frowned in puzzlement, then gradually his tiny brows unkinked, although the understanding obviously brought him no happiness. "Tha wants to take me down with."

"I can't think of anything else to do, any other way to track him—there are many paths, many ways. I'm sorry. But I won't take you against your will."

"Th'art much the bigger of us twain."

"That doesn't matter. I won't take you against your will."

Beetledown's frown returned. "Tha said 'twas a sacred place—banned to outliers."

"That's why I said I had a difficult decision. But I've decided I'd rather break the law and take you into the Mysteries than leave my boy alone down there any longer than I have to—if you'll go. Besides, the boy himself is no Funderling, so the law's already fair cracked and riven, as we say."

The little man sighed, a minuscule noise like the squeak of a worried mouse. "My queen bade me give 'ee help with nose and otherwise. Can Beetledown the Bowman do less than un's mistress bids un?"

"The Earth Elders bring you and all your people good luck," said Chert, relieved. "You are as brave as you keep saying you are."

"That be the solemn truth."

Their paths intersected at the doorway of the armory. Vansen had his arms full of polishing cloths, which he was borrowing, since they had run out in the guards' hall, and he almost did not see her—in fact, almost knocked her over. Astonishingly, she seemed to be alone. She was dressed in a simple long shirt and breeches like a man's, and Ferras Vansen was so surprised to see the face that had been in his mind's eye all day that for a long moment he simply couldn't believe it was true.

"M—My lady," he said at last. "Highness. Here—you must not do that. It is not fitting."

Princess Briony had been picking up his dropped cloths, her face wearing a pleasantly distracted expression that was almost insulting—it was obvious that she did not recognize him outside of the formal setting of an audience or council chamber. Her features abruptly changed and tightened, eyebrows lifting in a formal gesture of polite surprise. "Captain Vansen," she said coolly. He had a brief glimpse of her guards—two of his own men—hurrying toward them across the armory courtyard, as if their own captain might be a threat to the princess.

"Your pardon, please, Highness." He did his best to get out of her way, a gesture made difficult not only by the fact that she was holding the handle of the door, but because he was full-laden and she was not. He only managed it by clumsily dropping a few of the cloths again as he backed into the armory. He hid his terrible embarrassment by bending to pick them up.

Gods save me! Even when we meet almost as equals, alone in the armory doorway, I immediately turn myself into a bumbling peasant.

A second, equally unpleasant thought suggested that maybe this was just as well. *After all, the sooner you get over this stupidity the better,* a more sensible part of himself pointed out. *If shame alone will do that, then shame is a good thing.*

He glanced up at her face, saw the mixture of amusement and annoyance moving there. He had managed to block her way again. *But I will never get over it,* he thought, and in that painful, radiant instant he couldn't imagine knowing anything with more certainty, not his love of his family, not his duty to the guards or to the all-seeing gods themselves.

Princess Briony suddenly seemed to realize she was smiling at his discomfiture; the transition of her features back to bland watchfulness was astonishingly swift and more than a little saddening. *Such a lively face,* he thought. But over the past weeks she had been slowly, purposefully turning it into something else—the marble mask of a portrait bust, something that might stand for decades in one of the castle's dusty halls. "Do you need any help, Captain Vansen?" She nodded to her two hurrying protectors. "One of these guards could help you carry those things."

She would lend him one of his own guardsmen to help him carry a few pieces of cloth. Was it real malice, or just girlish snippishness? "No, Highness, I can manage. Thank you." He bent a knee and bowed a little, careful not to drop his burden again. She took the hint and moved from the doorway so that he could escape, although he had to glare her two panting guards back out of the way first. He was so relieved to escape her overwhelming presence that it was all he could do, after a final turn and bow, to walk rather than run away.

"Captain Vansen?"

He winced, then wheeled to face her again. "Yes, Highness?"

"I do not approve of my brother appointing himself head of this . . . expedition. You know that."

"It seemed clear, Highness."

"But he is my brother, and I love him. I have already . . ." Oddly, she smiled, but it was clear she was also fighting tears. "I have already lost one brother. Barrick is the only one I have left to me."

He swallowed. "Highness, your brother's death was . . ."

She raised her hand; at another time he might have thought she was being imperious. "Enough. I do not say it to . . . to blame you again. I just . . ." She turned away for a moment so she could dab at her eyes with the long sleeve of her man's shirt as though the tears were little enemies that had to be swiftly and brutally eradicated. "I am asking you, Captain Vansen, to remember that Barrick Eddon is not just a prince, not just a member of the ruling family. He is my brother, my . . . my twin. I am terrified that something might happen to him."

Ferras was moved. Even the guardsmen, a pair of young louts who Vansen knew well and did not think could muster the finer feelings of a shoat between them, were nervous now, unsettled by the openness of the princess regent's grief. "I will do my best, Highness," he told her. "Please believe that. I will . . . I will treat him as though he were my own brother."

Immediately upon saying it he realized that he had been foolish again—had insinuated that under ordinary circumstances he would give more care to his own family than to his lord and master, the prince regent. This seemed a particularly dangerous thing to say considering that one prince regent had already died while he, Vansen, was the officer of record.

I am truly an idiot, he thought. *Blinded by my feelings. I have spoken to the mistress of the kingdom as though she were a crofter's daughter from the next farm over.*

To his surprise, though, there were tears in Briony's eyes again. "Thank you, Captain Vansen," was all she said.

She had looked forward all morning to stealing a little time for practice, been desperate for the release of swinging the heavy wooden sword, but now that the time had finally come, it only made her feel clumsy and tired.

It is that man Vansen. He always unsettled her, made her angry and disturbed—just seeing him reminded her of Kendrick, of that terrible night. And now it seemed he might be standing by to watch another of her brothers die, for none of her arguments could make Barrick change his mind. But was it Vansen's fault, or was it only some terrible joke of the gods', that he should be attached to so much of her misery?

Nothing made sense. She let the sword drop into the sawdust of the practice ring. One of the guards moved forward to pick it up but she waved him off. Nothing made sense. She was miserable.

Sister Utta. She had scarcely had time for her tutor lately, and Briony suddenly realized how much she missed the older woman's calming presence. She snatched up a cloth to wipe her hands, then stamped her feet to shake off the sawdust before setting out for Utta's apartments, guards scuttling after her like chickens behind a grain-scattering farmwife. She had crossed the courtyard and was just walking into the long, narrow Lesser Hall when for the second time in an hour she nearly knocked over a young man. It was not Vansen this time, but the young poet—*well, the so-called poet,* she could not help thinking—Matty Tinwright. He reacted with elaborately pleased surprise, but by the care he had put into his hair and clothes, his swift breathing, and his position just inside the doorway, she rather thought he had been watching her come across the courtyard from one of the windows and then had hurried down the hall to manufacture this "accidental" meeting.

"Highness, Princess Briony, lovely and serene and wise, it is a pleasure beyond words to see you. And look, you are robed for battle, as is fitting for a warrior queen." He leaned in close for a conspiratorial whisper. "I have heard that our land is threatened, glorious princess—that the army is being mustered. Would that I were one who could meetly raise a sword as your champion, but my own war must be fought with stirring songs and odes, inducers of brave deeds which I will construct for the good of crown and country!"

He was not at all bad to look at—he was in fact quite handsome, which was likely one of the reasons Barrick disliked him—but she was far too impatient for even this harmless nonsense today. "Do you want to go with the army so you can write poems about the battlefield, Master Tinwright? You have my permission. Now, if you will excuse me . . ."

He seemed to be swallowing something the size of a shuttlecock. "Go with . . . ?"

"The army, yes. You may. Now if that was all . . ."

"But I . . ." He seemed dazed, as though the possibility that he might be directed to join the army of Southmarch had never occurred to him. In truth, Briony was mostly being spiteful—she did not actually wish to saddle any commander with both her brother *and* this idiot poetaster. "But I did not come to ask . . ." Tinwright swallowed again. It was not getting easier for him. "In truth I came to you, Highness, because Gil wishes an audience with you."

"Gil?"

"The potboy, Mistress. Surely you have not forgotten already, since it was his errand that first brought me to your attention."

She remembered now, the thin man with the strange, calmly mad eyes. "The one who has dreams—he wishes to speak to me?"

Tinwright nodded eagerly. "Yes, Highness. I was visiting him in the stronghold—the poor man scarcely sees anyone, he is almost a prisoner—and he asked me specially to speak to you. He says that he has something important to tell you of what he called 'the upcoming struggle.' " For a moment Tinwright's forehead wrinkled. "I was surprised to hear him use such a term, to be honest, Mistresss, since he is not at all educated."

Briony shook her head as if to clear it, a bit overwhelmed by the poet's swift and highly inflected speech. He was a popinjay in more than just his cheapstreet finery. "Gil the potboy wants to talk to me about the upcoming struggle? He must have heard about it from the guards in the stronghold." The stronghold held another prisoner, she could not help remembering. A moment of dislocation washed over her, something approaching real panic. Shaso dan-Heza was the one who should be commanding both this war party and the defense of the castle that might come later. Had someone anticipated just that? Had he been made to look guilty of Kendrick's murder for just that reason?

"Yes, Highness," Tinwright confirmed. "Doubtless that was where he heard of it. In any case, that is the message I was asked to give you. Now, about this riding off with the soldiers . . ."

"I already gave you my permission," she said, then turned and headed off at a fast walk toward Sister Utta's room. Behind her she could hear her guards snarling as they struggled to push past Matty Tinwright, who seemed to be following her.

"But, Highness . . . !"

She turned. "The potboy—he gave you a gold dolphin to write that letter, did he not?"

"Y—yes . . ."

"So where did a potboy get a thick, shiny gold piece?" She saw that Tinwright obviously had no answer to that and turned away again.

"I don't know. But, Highness, about what you said . . . the army . . . !"

Her mind was too full. She scarcely even heard him.

"We do not often go deeper than the temple," Chert explained to his small passenger as they made their way down the twisting slope known as the Cascade Stair. The curve of the wide spiral, at its uppermost reaches wider in circumference than Funderling Town itself, was beginning to tighten, and the air was noticeably warmer. A seam of white quartz in the limestone directly above them seemed to undulate back and forth above their heads like a snake as Chert descended. They had left the last of the Funderling wall lamps behind; Chert was glad he had brought coral from the Salt Pool. "I think the acolytes come down this way to make offerings, especially on festival days, and of course all of us come here for the ceremonies when we reach manhood or womanhood." Even with all his worries he couldn't help wondering how many young ones the acolytes would take down into the depths this year. Chert would know them all, of course—Funderling Town was a small, clannish community and there were never more than a couple of dozen who had reached the proper age on the night the Mysteries were formally celebrated. As he walked, he told Beetledown some memories from his own initiation into adulthood, so many years ago now—the giddiness brought on by fasting, the strange shadows and voices, and most frightening and exhilarating of all, that brief glimpse of the Shining Man that the young Chert had not been entirely certain was real. In fact, much of the experience now seemed like a dream.

"Shining Man?" asked Beetledown.

Chert shook his head. "Forget I said it. The others will already think it bad enough I bring you to these sacred places."

As they stepped down from the Cascade Stair and into a natural cavern full of tall, hourglass-shaped columns, Chert walked forward until they stood in front of the one unnatural thing in the chamber. It was a wall even larger than the Silk Door, with five big arched doorways in it, each one a black hole into which the coral-light could not reach.

"Five?" said Beetledown. "Have thy people naught better to do than dig tunnels side by side?"

Chert was still keeping his voice low, although the unlit lamps in these chambers suggested that if the acolytes had been down today they had already left. "That is more to do with the weight of stone and less to do with the number of tunnels. If you cut one tunnel it makes an arch in the fabric of the living stone above it—I cannot think of the words to explain it, since we use an old Funderling word, *dh'yok,* to describe such a thing. That one arch will be a small one, and eventually the stone above it will crush the tunnel closed again."

"Wind from the Peak!" swore Beetledown, scrambling in from the point of Chert's shoulder to the presumably greater protection next to the Funderling's head, making Chert's neck itch and tickle in the process. "The stone crushes un?"

"Even that doesn't happen right away, never fear. But when you make several tunnels beside each other, the *dh'yok,* the . . . arch in the stone is much bigger and stronger, and even when the weight of the stone above starts to collapse it at last, it takes the outer tunnels first, giving us plenty of warning to shore up the inside tunnels and eventually to stop using them altogether."

"You mean, someday mountain will just crush all down? All thy building? All thy digging?" He sounded almost more outraged on the Funderlings' behalf than fearful of the danger.

Chert laughed a soft laugh. "Someday. But that's a long time—that's stone time, as we call it. Unless the gods take it into their minds to send an earthshaking—a far stronger one than we've ever had before—even these outside tunnels will still be standing when the grandchildren of the men and women joining the Guilds today are brought down to see . . . brought down for their coming-of-age."

His explanation didn't seem to mollify Beetledown all that much, although the little man was reassured when Chert chose the middle tunnel, presumably the safest, to continue their journey, and Chert didn't share the less inspiring truth with him—that nobody ever used any of the other tunnels anyway, since they existed purely to support the passage through which he and the Rooftopper were descending to the next level.

"But why build tunnels here at all?" Beetledown asked suddenly, perhaps to break the silence in the close-quartered passage, whose abstract carvings seemed just as weirdly unsettling to Chert now as they had on that long-ago night of his initiation, and which must seem even more so to a stranger like the tiny man. "All else down here in deeps be touched by no hand."

Again he was struck by the sharpness of the little man's wits and his keen eye for details in an unfamiliar place. "A good question, that." But Chert was beginning to feel the power of the place, the importance and the strangeness of it, and did not feel much like talking. His people didn't enter the Mysteries lightly, and even though he would walk into the smoking heart of J'ezh'kral Pit itself to find the boy and save his Opal from feeling so miserable, he could not be happy about his responsibility for this comparative parade of outsiders, first Flint and now Beetledown, both of whom were in the ceremonied depths because of Chert Blue Quartz and no other.

"I don't want to tell the whole story now. Perhaps it will be enough to say that our ancestors came to realize that there was another set of caverns they could not reach, and that they cut these tunnels to reach down from the caverns we knew—those in which we have been traveling until now—into these deeper and more unfamiliar spaces."

It was not enough, of course—it barely explained anything, let alone the profound revelations at the heart of the Mysteries, but there was only so much that could be put into words. Or that should even be put into words at all.

The idea of needing to talk to the potboy had upset her, but not because of the potboy himself. Even if the fellow was some kind of dream-scryer, even if he could do to her what he did to Barrick, calling up and naming the things that haunted her sleep, what Briony feared was no secret from anyone who had any wits at all. She feared that she would lose her brother and father, what remained of her family. She feared that she would fail Southmarch and the March Kingdoms, that in this time of growing danger, with Olin imprisoned and her brother strange and often ill, she would be the last of the Eddons to wield power.

No. I will not let that happen, she swore to herself as she strode along the Lesser Hall toward the residence. *I will be ruthless if it is needed. I will burn down all the forests that lie beyond the Shadowline, throw every Tolly into chains. And if Shaso truly is a murderer, I will drag him to the headsman's block myself to save our kingdom.*

This was what had upset her, of course, the thought of her father's trusted adviser still locked up in the stronghold during such times. If she went to see the potboy Gil in his makeshift accommodations there, could she avoid speaking to Shaso? She didn't even want to see him: she was not certain of his guilt and never had been, despite all the signs, but much of the autumn had passed with no change in the circumstances and she and Barrick couldn't avoid passing judgment on him forever. If he had murdered the reigning prince, he must himself be put to death. Still, Briony knew she didn't really understand what had happened that fatal night, and the idea of executing one of her father's closest advisers—a man who also, for all his sour temper and rigidity had been almost another parent to her—was very disturbing. No, it was terrifying.

Her guards had caught up to her again as she reached the high-walled Rose Garden, where the Lesser Hall became a covered walkway that ran the garden's length. It was sometimes called the Traitor's Garden, because an angry noble had lain in wait there to murder one of Briony's royal ancestors, Kellick the Second. The assassin had failed and his head had wound up on the Basilisk Gate, the tattered remains of his quartered body shared out over the entrances of the cardinal towers. Something of this legend had stuck to the garden, and it was not her favorite place, even in spring. Now the roses were long gone, their thorny branches so thick on the walls that it looked as though they were holding up the ancient bricks rather than the other way around.

Caught up in her thoughts, Briony barely noticed her guards until one of them sneezed and mumbled a quiet prayer. She suddenly thought, *What am I doing? Why should I go down to the stronghold? I am the queen, almost—the princess regent. I will have the potboy brought to one of the council chambers and speak to him there. There is no need for me to go down there at all.* The relief that washed over her brought a little shame with it; this would be another day she did not need to think too much about Shaso dan-Heza. . . .

She was startled by a pressure on either side as the two guards suddenly stepped in close to her like a pair of dogs heading a straying sheep. She was about to snap at them—Briony Eddon would not be anyone's lamb—when she saw a man and a woman rise from a bench in the late-autumn sun and walk toward her. It took her a moment to recognize the first of the pair before they joined her in the shade of the walkway: she had not seen Hendon Tolly for almost a year.

"Your Highness," he said, sketching a not very convincing bow. The youngest Tolly brother was still thin as a racing dog, all length and tendon. His dark hair had been cut high above his ears in the current Syannese style and he even wore a little tuft of beard on his chin; with his short gown in golden satin and his parti-colored hose and velvet trim he looked every inch a prince of one of the more fashion-conscious southern courts. Briony thought it was strange that he could look both so much like his brother Gailon in the face and so little like him in all else—dark for fair, slim for well-muscled, foppish for stolid, as though this were

Gailon himself dressed up for some outrageous, impossible Midsummer Festival mummery.

"Ah, I see by your attire we have caught you at a bad time, Princess Briony," Hendon said with an edge of superiority in his voice that was meant to make her bristle, and did. "You have apparently been engaged in something . . . strenuous."

She barely resisted the temptation to look down at what she had worn to practice at the armory. For the first time in longer than she could remember she wished she were dressed properly, in the full panoply of her position.

"Oh, but there are no bad times for relatives," was what she said, as sweetly as she could, "and family is, of course permitted a certain informality of both dress *and* speech. But even among family, one can go too far." She smiled, with teeth showing. "You will, of course, forgive me for meeting you while dressed this way, dear cousin."

"Oh, Highness, the fault is all ours. My sister-in-law was so anxious to meet you that I took a chance we might find you out and about. This is Elan M'Cory, the sister of my brother Caradon's wife."

The girl made an elaborate courtesy. "Your Highness."

"We were introduced at your sister's wedding, I think." Briony was furious that she should be forced to stand here in her sweaty clothes, but Hendon Tolly was playing a deliberate game and she would not let him see her irritation. She concentrated instead on the young woman, who was roughly her own age and pretty in a translucent, long-boned way. Unlike her brother-in-law, Elan kept her eyes cast down and offered little in the way of reply to Briony's equally perfunctory questions.

"I really must go," Briony announced at last. "There is much to do. Lord Tolly, you and I must speak on important matters. Will this evening suit you? And of course you will join us for supper, I hope. We missed your company last night."

"Tired from the journey," he said. "And with worry for my missing brother, of course. Doubtless, fears for Duke Gailon have made things difficult for you, too, Highness."

"It seems there is a conspiracy to make things difficult for me, Lord Tolly, and your brother's sudden absence is certainly one of them. You might also have heard that my brother Kendrick died."

He raised an eyebrow at this broad stroke. "But of course, Highness, of course! I was devastated when I heard the news, but I was traveling in northern Syan at the time, and since Gailon was actually here to represent the family at the funeral . . ."

"Yes, certainly." She suddenly wondered what had really brought Hendon here now, of all times. The two-or-three-day ride from Summerfield Court seemed a bit of a long distance to come simply to cause trouble. Briony couldn't forget Brone's spy and his warnings that the Autarch had been in touch with the Tollys, although she couldn't quite make sense of it. She did not put treachery beyond them, but it seemed a large step—and a large risk—for a family that was already living a fat and comfortable life. Still, as her father had always said, the prospect of a throne could make people do some very strange things indeed. "Now, as I said, I have much to do. I suspect that you will be busy as well. For one thing, you will want to send a message home to your family as soon as you have heard my news."

He was clearly caught by surprise. "News? Have you heard something of Gailon?"

"I fear not. But I have news, nonetheless."

"You have the advantage of me, Highness. What is afoot? Will you make me wait until tonight to find out?"

"I'm surprised you haven't heard already. We are at war."

For a moment Hendon Tolly actually blanched—seeing that was worth the humiliation of standing for a quarter of an hour in sweaty clothes. "We . . . we . . . ?"

"Oh, no, not Southmarch and Summerfield Court, Lord Hendon." She laughed and did not try to make it nice. "No, we are family, of course, your folk and mine. In fact, you will no doubt be joining us—all the March Kingdoms will be going to war together."

"But . . . but against whom?" he asked. Even the girl was looking up now, staring.

"Why, against the fairies, of course. Now you must excuse me, there really is a great deal to be done. Our army rides out at dawn tomorrow."

She had the immense satisfaction of leaving Hendon Tolly and his companion speechless, but the cut and thrust with him had driven whatever else she was thinking about straight out of her head, and already a dozen other matters were clamoring for attention. She hoped it had been nothing important.

Neither Chert nor Beetledown spoke much now. The food was long gone, the waterskin was less than half full, and it had become very warm in these very close spaces.

Once through the tunnels bored by the Funderlings and into the caverns on the far side, they had passed down a bewildering variety of passages, all perfectly natural as far as Chert could tell, although it was strange to find natural passages so long and clear. Even though they were not difficult going—in most places he didn't even have to bend his head—they were complex and confusing: if he had been forced to rely on his memories of his own pilgrimage so many years ago they would have gone far astray. Only Beetledown's near-silent communication of directions—pokes and prods and the occasional whispered word when his nose detected a stronger scent in one direction—gave Chert any hope of finding Flint and getting out again.

They were decidedly odd places, these tunnels, and not simply because it was difficult to know whether they were entirely natural. The air might be hot and thick, but there was also a strange sweetness to it that made everyone who breathed it light-headed, adding immeasurably to the awesomeness of the ceremonies that took place in the depths.

They were walking along a thin path now, scarcely more than a ledge above a deep emptiness, and Chert was moving very carefully, not least because the light from the first piece of coral was dying. He realized that by any sensible measure they should turn back soon. He hadn't guessed they would be descending so far, and in fact had thought himself quite clever to have brought a second chunk, but now as he fitted the new lump into his headpiece of polished horn, and the touch of salt water brought it to light, he realized he was one bad choice by little Boulder from being lost in darkness. Chert was a Funderling and did not panic in the dark or deep places, and his sense of touch and knowledge of the deeps were both well-developed, but he still might wander for days before finding his way out—which might be entirely too late for young Flint.

"What *does* be down here?" rasped Beetledown suddenly. The thick, perfumed air seemed to be affecting his voice. "Thy boy, why should un be here at all?"

"I don't know." Chert didn't have much breath for talking either. He wiped sweat from his forehead, then had a moment of fright when he almost brushed his strapped lantern off his head and down into the pit. "It's . . . it's a powerful place. The boy has always been strange. I don't know."

As they continued down the narrow path, Chert soon began to wonder whether the fetid air was beginning to choke him or whether something stranger was going on. There were times when he thought he heard voices—just the faintest sighing words, as though one of the Guild work gangs were a few hundred steps away down a side passage. At other moments little flashes of light moved through the greater darkness around him, swift as the flecks that gleamed behind closed eyelids. Such things could be a sign of poison air, and in any other place Chert would have turned and retreated, but the air in the deepest part of the Mysteries, although never fresh, was also, as far as he knew, never fatal. Beetledown was having real trouble breathing, however; the Funderling reminded himself that the little man was used to the clean air of the rooftops. In fact, even Chert was beginning to slip in and out of waking dreams about that cold, clean air, so much so that at one point he realized he had wandered only a step from the edge of the path. It was a long way down into blackness, although how long he could only guess.

The murmuring continued all around him. It might have been air currents pushed through the tunnels from the halls above by the tide changing—they were far below the sea now—but Chert thought he could hear snatches of words, sobbing, even distant shouts that raised the hackles on his neck. The temple brothers came down here, he reminded himself, and they survived it, but the thought did little to ease his fears. Who knew what preparations they made, what secret sacrifices they gave to the lords of these deep places? He considered the holy mystery of the Earth Elders and the Quiet Blind Voice and struggled against growing terror.

What *was* indisputable was that light was growing all around him: Chert could begin to see the shape of the chamber through which they were passing. For the first time in hours he felt something like hope. They were reaching an area he recognized, a part of the pilgrimage route. A few moments later, as he escaped the treacherous ledge-path at last, following it through an arch as it burrowed deep into the stone, the milky, blue-white light rose all around them.

"Moonstone Hall," Chert announced with relief, if not much breath. The coolness of the glowing walls studded with great fractured chunks of palely translucent gemstone was in strange contrast to the swampy air. "You see, these places down here make their own light. We are near to the center of the Mysteries."

Beetledown said nothing, only nodded, presumably overcome by the grandeur of the cavern, its walls glowing like smoky blue ice.

Chert continued down through the Chamber of Cloud Crystal and into Emberstone Reach, the light like a living thing all around him. His head swimming and eyes dazzled after so long in darkness, he could not help wondering how these great caves could each be so different: it was like no natural place he had seen anywhere else in Southmarch or in his journeys around Eion in his younger days.

But it isn't a natural place, he reminded himself. *These are the Mysteries.* A shiver of superstitious dread climbed his spine. What *was* he doing here? Caught up in the search for Flint, he hadn't performed even the simplest rituals before descending, said none of the litanies, made not a single offering. The Earth Elders would be furious.

It was in Emberstone Reach that he suddenly realized there was a reason for Beetledown's long silence when the little man swayed and tumbled off his shoulder. Chert caught him and crouched, holding him up to look at him in the light from the orange-gold ember crystals. The Gutter-Scout was alive but clearly in great discomfort.

"Too hot," he said weakly. "Can't . . . get air."

Chert fought a powerful dread. He was so close now! They were only a short distance from the end of the tunnels, at least the end of those parts he and the rest of the Funderlings knew, and thus only a short distance from Flint, but he didn't want to kill the tiny Rooftopper in the act of saving the boy. He forced himself to think as carefully as he could with head and limbs so weary, then untied the shirt he had tied around his waist when the air got too hot and made a nest for the little man. He put Beetledown in it and set him on a knob of stone high off the ground. Chert knew that poison air, even the milder varieties, was heavy and tended to stay low. He also left the little man his coral lantern for company.

"I'll be back soon," he said. "I promise. I'm just going down a little farther." He gave the tiny bowman his kerchief moistened in water to fight thirst.

"Cats . . . ?" asked Beetledown weakly.

"No cats down here," Chert assured him. "I already promised you that."

"Just in case," the little man said, and sat up—it took much of his strength—then pulled his bow and quiver off and set them down within easy reach before slumping back into the makeshift bed.

Chert hurried on. He had all the more reason for haste now—not just his worries about the boy and about Opal and the dying light of the coral, but also about whether he would repay the kindness of the Rooftopper queen and of brave Beetledown himself with the emissary's death.

Emberstone Reach ended and the Maze began. He cursed the luck that had brought him into the befuddling labyrinth without the Rooftopper and his keen nose, but there was nothing to be done. Chert remembered something he had been told as a child, at an age when whispering about the initiation was more important than whispering about girls. *Always turn left,* his friends had said with the confidence of those who had not been tested. *When you hit a dead end, turn and backtrack, then do the same thing again with the next tunnel.* At their intiation they had not needed to solve the Maze after all—they had been led in by the acolytes, abandoned for a while, and then led out. Now he had no choice but to try the ancient advice, since this time there were no temple brothers around to help him.

Here between the Reach and the Sea in the Depths there were also no natural lights, and Chert had to make his way through the Maze in darkness, with only the sound of his own ragged, weary breathing and the thump of his heart for company. After what seemed like an hour tracing and retracing what to the touch were indistinguishable passages, he finally grew certain he was lost; he was just about to sit down and weep with despair when he felt moving air on his face. Heart pounding now for joy and relief, he followed the breeze a few more turnings until he stepped out of the Maze and into the blue-lit vastness of the Sea Hall, but his happiness lasted only moments. He was on the balcony on the outside of the Maze with a long fatal drop below him, a barrier so effective that even the pilgrims who completed the Mysteries never saw more of the monsterous Sea Hall cavern than this. There was no way down to the cavern floor, and no sign of Flint on the great raw stone balcony.

There was nowhere else the boy could be.

Now Chert did weep a little, exhausted and despondent. He got down on his knees and crawled close to the edge, half certain that he would see the boy's mangled body on the jagged, rocky shore beneath him, illuminated by the weird blue crystals of the cavern's roof. Instead, the reach of broken, piled stone was empty all the way to the silvery Sea in the Depths and the unreachable island at its center where the vast rocky form stood that figured in so many Funderling nightmares and revelations. The man-shaped formation was shrouded in shadow, but the roof-stones shed their light almost everywhere else. There was no sign of Flint, either living or dead.

Chert was plunged back into the misery of uncertainty. Had he and Beetledown walked right past Flint at some other turning, not knowing that the boy lay senseless or even dead nearby? The Mysteries and the tunnels and caves above them were unimaginably complex. How could he even guess where to start a new search if the Rooftopper's nose was not to be trusted?

Then, as if it had sensed Chert's distant presence, the huge and mysterious stone figure known as the Shining Man began to flicker alight on its island at the center of the Sea in the Depths, and Chert's heart sped until he thought it might burst. He had seen the statue only one other time, at his initiation, in the company of other young Funderlings, under the guidance of the Metamorphic Brothers. This time, he was alone and full of an interloper's guilt. As the massive crystalline shape suddenly blazed with blue and purple and golden light, it threw strange reflections on the sea itself, which was not water but an immense pool of something like quicksilver, so that all the cavern was full of leaping colors and the Shining Man almost appeared to move, as if awakening from a long slumber. Chert flung himself down, his belly against the stone. He begged the Earth Elders' forgiveness and prayed to be spared.

The gods did not see fit to strike him dead, and after a few moments the light dimmed a little, enough that he dared to raise his head, but when he did so, Chert's superstitious terror was suddenly made worse. In the new light he could see a small shape on the island—a moving figure that advanced, crawling slowly upward from the edge of the shining metal sea toward the feet of the glowing giant, the Shining Man. Even from this distance, with the figure small as an insect, Chert knew who it was.

"Flint!" he shouted, and his voice echoed out across the quicksilver sea, but the small shadow did not stop or even look back.

30

Awakening

RED LEAVES:

The child in its bed
A bear on a hilltop
Two pearls taken from the hand of an old one

—from *The Bonefall Oracles*

THE CEILING OF THE MAIN trigonate temple was so high that even with the great doors closed it had its own subtle winds— the thousands of candles on altars and in alcoves were all fluttering. At this hour of the morning it was also very cold. Barrick's arm ached.

The prince regent was surrounded by the men who would accompany him into the west, his unloved cousin Rorick Longarren and more proven warriors like Tyne of Blueshore and Tyne's old friend, the extravagantly mustached Droy Nikomede of Eastlake, along with many others Barrick knew mostly by reputation. In fact, much of the flower of the March Kingdoms' nobility had gathered for this blessing—doughty Mayne Calough from far Kertewall, Sivney Fiddicks who some called the Piecemeal Knight because his armor and battle array were all prizes he had won in various tilts, Earl Gowan M'Ardall of Helmingsea, and several dozen other high lords dressed in white robes, plus five or six times that number of humbler stature who yet possessed their own horses and armor and at least a cottage or field somewhere so they could call themselves "landed."

Like all the others, Barrick Eddon was down on one knee, facing the altar where Sisel told the blessing, the ancient Hierosoline phrases rolling from the hierarch's tongue like the meaningless babble of a fast-running stream. Barrick knew he would soon be riding to war, perhaps even to death. Not only that, the enemy they all faced were the wild creatures from the shadowlands, the old terror, the stuff of nightmares—yet he felt oddly flat, empty and unconcerned.

He raised his eyes to the vast tripartite statue behind the altar, the three gods of the Trigon standing atop an artfully carved stone plinth that became clouds around the sky god's feet, stones and waves respectively for the gods of earth and sea. The three towering deities stared outward, with Perin in the center in his rightful place as the highest of the high, fish-scaled Erivor on his right, glowering Kernios on his left. They were half brothers, all children of old Sveros, the night sky, from different mothers. Barrick wondered if any one of the Trigon would be willing to die for his brothers as he would give his life for Briony—as he almost certainly was going to give his life for her. But since they were gods and thus immortal and invulnerable, how would such a thing happen? How could gods be brave?

Hierarch Sisel was still droning. The old man had insisted on leading the ceremony himself because of the importance of the occasion—and because, Barrick suspected, like so many others he wished to do something to help, to feel himself a contributor. Word had passed swiftly through castle and city: there was not one person in a hundred now who did not know that war was coming, and that it was apparently going to be a strange and frightening sort of war as well.

How Barrick himself felt about it all was even stranger, he had to admit—like reaching for something on a high shelf that was just out of reach no matter how one jumped or strained. He simply couldn't make himself feel much of anything.

When the hierarch's part of the ceremony was over, Sisel took Barrick aside as the other nobles were having their robes perfumed with sacred smoke by the blue-clad temple mantises. The hierarch had a half-humble, half-irritated expression that Barrick knew very well: it was a look his elders often wore when they wanted to scold him but couldn't help remembering that one or two of Barrick's ancestors had imprisoned people—or even killed them, if certain popular rumors were true—for giving unwelcome advice.

"It is a brave thing you are doing, my prince," Sisel said.

He means to say "stupid," Barrick decided, but of course that was a word even a hierarch of the Trigonate would not use to an enthroned prince. "I have my reasons, Eminence. Some of them are good ones."

Sisel raised his hand. It was meant to signify *no more needs to be said,* but to Barrick it was irritatingly close to Shaso's raised hand, which throughout his childhood usually meant: *Shut up, boy.* "Of course, Highness. Of course. And the Three Powerful Ones grant that you and the others come home safely. Tyne is to lead, of course?" His forehead wrinkled as he realized what he had said. "In support of you, of course, Prince Barrick."

He almost smiled. "Of course. But let us be honest. I'm to be a sort of . . . what do they have on the front of a ship? A masthead?"

"Figurehead?"

"Yes. I don't expect the soldiers to listen to me, Hierarch—I have no experience of war yet. In fact, I hope to learn something from Tyne and the others. If the Three grant I come back safely, that is."

Sisel gave him a strange look—he had perhaps detected something a little false in Barrick's pious manner—but he was also relieved and clearly didn't want to think about it much. "You show great wisdom, my prince. You are unquestionably your father's son."

"Yes, I think that's true."

Sisel was still puzzled by whatever lurked beneath Barrick's words. "These are not natural creatures we face, my prince. We should not be troubled at what we do."

We? "What do you mean?"

"These . . . things. The Twilight People, as they are superstitiously named, the Old Ones. They are unnatural—the enemies of men. They would take what is ours. They must be destroyed like rats or locusts, without compunction."

Barrick could only nod. *Rats. Locusts.* He let himself be censed. The perfumes in the smoke reminded him of the spice stalls of Market Square, made him wish badly to be there again with Briony, as when they were children and had escaped for a delicious, giggling moment or two with half the household in ragged pursuit.

After he had removed the ceremonial robe, Barrick followed the knights and nobles out of the temple. Tyne Aldritch and the others looked rested and refreshed, as though they had just come from a bath and a nap, and Barrick couldn't help being jealous that the trip to the temple had given them this comfort—a comfort he himself did not feel.

Earl Tyne saw Barrick's troubled face and slowed until they were walking side by side. "The gods will protect us, never fear, Prince Barrick. The creatures are uncanny things, but they are real—they are made of flesh. When we cut them, their blood will flow."

How can you be sure of that? he wanted to ask. After all, the only person in all of Southmarch with any experience of their enemy was that soldier Vansen, who had actually been present for the killing of one of the Shadowline creatures, although admittedly a small and not very dangerous one, and who had also been attacked by a much larger thing that half a dozen soldiers had not managed to harm at all, even as it took one of their company like a child snatching a sweetmeat from an unguarded plate.

Barrick did not share any of these thoughts either.

"The monsters will be frightening, no doubt," said Tyne quietly. They paused as the temple acolytes pushed open the heavy bronze doors and let the bay air spill in, ruffling hair and clothing and making the candle flames sputter. "Remember, Highness, it is important that we show the men a courageous face."

"The gods will give us what courage we need, no doubt."

"Yes," said Tyne, nodding vigorously. "They did for me when I was a youth."

Barrick suddenly realized that although Tyne Aldritch was more than twice Barrick's own age, he was still a great deal younger than the twins' father, King Olin. He was a man still young enough to have ambitions—perhaps he hoped that Barrick would remember him as a loyal friend and mentor if they all survived, that his fortune would rise even higher if Barrick Eddon became king someday. Tyne's daughter was nearly of marriageable age, after all. Perhaps he dreamed of a royal connection.

Up until this moment it had been hard for Barrick to think of most of his elders as anything other than an undifferentiated mass, at least those who were not yet dodderingly old. Now for the first time he examined the battle-scarred Earl of Blueshore and wondered what Tyne himself saw when he gazed out at the world, what he thought and hoped and feared. Barrick looked around at Sivney Fiddicks and Ivar of Silverside and the other lords, faces held up, jaws set in expressions meant to be brave and inspiring as the pale sunshine spilled in through the open doors, and realized that every one of these men lived inside his own head just as Barrick lived in his, and that all of the hundreds of people waiting anxiously on the stairs outside the temple for a glimpse of the nobility of Southmarch lived within their own thoughts as well, as completely and separately as Barrick himself did.

It's as if we live on a thousand, thousand different islands in the middle of an ocean, he thought, *but with no boats. We can see each other. We can shout to each other. But we can none of us leave our own island and travel to another.*

This idea hit him with a far stronger force than any of the ritual he had just experienced inside the temple, and so he did not realize for a moment that the crowd of people on the steps was pushing the ring of guards back toward the temple doors, that in their fear over the rumors of war and even more terrifying things, the throng of common folk was only moments away from trampling the very people they expected to defend them. Some of the priests began to shut the great doors again. The guards were shoving back with the long handles of their pikes and a few of the crowd were knocked down and bruised. A woman screamed. Some men began trying to pull the pikes away from the guards. A few clods of dirt thudded down on the steps; one hit a Marrinswalk baron on the leg and he stared dumbfounded at the stain on his clean hose as though it were blood. Rorick shouted in alarm, perhaps as much at the threat to his own cleanliness as the danger to his person. Then, as if it happened in a dream—he was still caught up in the idea of people as islands—Barrick watched Tyne draw his sword, heard the rattle and hiss of a dozen blades leaving their scabbards as other nobles followed Blueshore's lead. The smell of the crowd so close around them was an animal reek, alien and frightening.

Tyne and the others—they're going to kill people, he realized. It scarcely seemed possible it was happening so swiftly. *Or the people may kill us. But why?* He looked at the faces around him, saw a growing realization reflected between the nobles and commons that things were falling to pieces and that none of them knew how to stop it.

But I can, he realized. It was a heady feeling, although oddly cheerless. He raised his good hand and walked down a few steps. Tyne snatched at him but Barrick ducked away.

"Stop!" he cried, but no one could hear his words above the shouting of frightened people: most of the faces staring up at the temple portico couldn't even see him. He turned and bounded back up the steps to where the massive bronze doors still stood halfway open—one of the cleverer priests, perhaps Sisel himself, had realized it would not be a good idea to lock out the prince regent and the other nobles while they were surrounded by a furious mob—then he yanked a pike away from one of the nearest guardsmen, who surrendered it with a look of complete confusion and misery, as though he suspected that for some inscrutable princely reason Barrick was about to strike him with his own weapon. Instead, Barrick used the heavy pike head to pound against the bronze door until the raw echoes flew across the yard. Heads turned and the shouting slowly began to diminish.

Barrick was breathing very hard: it was difficult to wield the pike with only one hand, bracing it under his arm to hammer at the door, but it had worked. Most of the crowd stared openmouthed at their young prince in front of the temple doorway.

"What do you want?" he cried. "Do you *want* to crush us? We are going out to fight for the city—for our land. In the holy name of the Three, what do you think you're doing, pressing in on us like this?"

Some of those caught up with the guards stepped back, shamefaced, but others were more entangled; the process of undoing the near-riot was as complicated as unpicking delicate stitchery. A guardsman still grappling with a sullen onlooker overbalanced and fell with a clang of armor and several of his fellow guards moved forward angrily. Barrick raised his voice again. "Stop. Let the people tell me. What do you want?"

"If you and the other lords go, Prince Barrick, who will protect the city?" a man shouted.

"The fairy folk will come and take our children!" cried someone else, a woman.

Barrick made a show of his confident smile. It was strange how easily this kind of thing came to him, this useful duplicity. "Who will protect the city? The city is protected by Brenn's Bay, which is worth more than any knights, even these fine nobles. Look around you! If you were a warlord, even the warlord of a fairy army, would you want to come up that causeway and against these high walls? And don't forget, my sister Briony will still be here, an Eddon on the throne—believe me, even the Twilight People don't want to get *her* angry."

A few of the people laughed, but others were still calling out anxious questions. Tyne made a show of sheathing his sword.

"Please!" Barrick said to the crowd. "Let us get on with this day's work—we are to ride soon. Avin Brone the lord constable will come back here and speak at midday, to tell you of how we will defend the castle and the city, what each of you can do to help."

"The Three bless you, Prince Barrick!" a woman called, and the pained hope in her voice was real enough to touch him, even to frighten him. "Come home safe to us!"

Other blessings and good wishes rained down; a moment before it had been clumps of dirt and even a few stones. The crowd didn't disperse, but they opened a path so that Barrick and the rest of the knights could head back toward the Raven Gate and the inner keep.

"You handled that well, Highness." Tyne sounded a little surprised. "The gods told you the right words to say."

"I am an Eddon. They know my family. They know we do not lie to them." But he couldn't help wondering. *Did I truly do that? Or did the gods indeed work through me? I felt no god, that's all I know.* In truth he was not certain how he felt at all—proud that he had quelled an anxious mob and given them hope, or distressed by how easily they could be swayed from one extreme to another?

And we are not even truly at war. Not yet. He had a sudden chill of presentiment. *What will it be like when things begin to go bad?*

And where will the gods be then?

The noise of hammers was almost deafening, as though a flock of monstrous woodpeckers had descended on Southmarch Castle. Men clambered on every wall and tower, it seemed, putting up wooden boardings against the possibility of a siege. After the torpor that had gripped the castle in the past months, it was almost a relief to see so much activity, but Briony knew this was no mere attack from a neighboring kingdom against which they must defend themselves. The March Kingdoms were at war with a completely unknown and perhaps unknowable enemy. When the men on the walls and towers looked out toward the still innocent western horizon, and they looked often, the fear on their faces was plain even from the ground.

Not only the workers found their attention compromised: the princess regent was so busy watching the work that she stumbled into a low boxwood hedge. Rose and Moina hurried forward to help her, but she shook them off, murmuring angrily.

"These cursed hedges! How can a person even walk?"

Sister Utta appeared in one of the gallery archways. Despite the cool gray skies she wore only a light wrap over her plain gown. A wimple of the same color covered her hair, so that her handsome face seemed almost to hang in the air like a mask on a wall. "It would be hard to make a knot garden without hedges," the Zorian sister said gently. "I hope you haven't hurt yourself, Highness."

"I'm well, I suppose." Briony rubbed at her lower leg. She had discovered one of the disadvantages of wearing hose like a man—there was nothing to protect your shins from pokes and bumps.

Utta seemed to know what the princess regent was thinking; in any case, she smiled. "It was kind of you to visit me."

"Not kind. I'm miserable. I have no one to talk to." She looked up in time to catch the hurt glance that jumped from Moina to Rose. "No one but these two," she said hastily, "and I have complained to them so much that they are surely tired of hearing my voice."

"Never, Highness!" Rose said it in such a clattering hurry to make her feel better that Briony almost laughed. Now she *knew* that they were tired of listening to her.

"We worry for you, Briony, that's all," Moina agreed, and by forgetting to use her mistress' title she proved that she was speaking the truth.

They are good and kind, these girls, she thought, and for a moment felt herself old enough to be their grown sister, even their mother, although small, yellow-haired Rose was her own age and dark Moina almost a full year her elder.

"How is your great-aunt?" asked Utta.

"Merolanna? Feeling better. With these musters of soldiers marching in and all these guests in the castle, she is in her element—like a sea captain in a storm. She's been looking in on my stepmother, too, since Anissa's time is close and Chaven has seen fit to disappear." It was hard for Briony to keep her anger at the physician to a polite growl. Finished brushing the bits of boxwood off her hose and the bottom of her tunic, she straightened up. The smell of hyssop and especially lavender were strong here despite the cold breeze off the bay, but they were not soothing. She wondered if anything would soothe her. "And you, Sister—are you well?"

"My joints are sore—it always happens when the wind freshens. If you wish to go in out of the garden, I will not complain."

"I can barely hear you with all this clattering, anyway, and it won't be better anywhere else out of doors. Where shall we go?"

"I was about to go to the shrine and make an offering for the safety of your brother and the rest. It is quiet there. What do you think?"

"I think that would be lovely," Briony told her. "Rose, Moina—stop making eyes at those men on the wall and come along."

The castle's Zorian shrine had none of the ostentation of the Erivor Chapel, let alone the huge and grand Trigonate temple. Little more than a single large room, it stood in a corner of the keep near the residence, just below the Tower of Summer. The altar was simple and only one small stained-glass window brought in the daylight, a rendition crafted in the previous century of Zoria with her arms outstretched and seabirds landing on her hands and flying about her head. It was a strangely beautiful picture, Briony had always thought, and even in today's poor sunlight the colors glowed. The shrine was empty, although Briony knew that an older Zorian priestess and at least two or three young novices lived in the apartment beside the chapel. They were Utta's friends—her family, really, since her true kin were far away in the Vuttish Isles and far in the past as well.

"When did you last see any of your family?" she asked her tutor. "Your blood family."

Utta appeared startled by the question. "My brother visited me here once some years ago. Before that—oh, my, Princess Briony, I have not seen any of them since I joined the Sisters."

Which must have been thirty years or more, Briony guessed. "Don't you miss them?"

"I miss the time when I was young. I miss the sense of being in that house, on that island, and feeling that it was the center of the whole world. I miss how I felt about my mother then, although later I came to feel differently." She bowed her head for a moment. "Yes, I do, I suppose."

Briony thought it strange to have to consider whether or not you missed your family. She hid her puzzlement in the act of choosing and lighting a candle and setting it on the altar before the statue of Zoria. This version of the goddess was much more staid than the one in the colorful window; her arms hung at her side and her eyes were cast down as though she looked at her own feet, but there was a faint smile on her lips that Briony had always liked, the smile of a woman who kept her own counsel. Moina and Rose came forward and lit candles also, although they both seemed a little confused and made the three-fingered sign of the Trigon over their breasts as they set the candles down. They were doing their best, Briony reminded herself, fighting annoyance: they were both girls from country families and had barely been exposed to Zoria's worship or sisterhood at all until coming to live in Southmarch castle.

Merciful Zoria, robed in wisdom, bring my brother Barrick home safe, Briony prayed. *Bring them all back safe, even Guard Captain Vansen. He is not such a bad man. And help me do what is best for Southmarch and her people.* She looked up, hoping to see something in Zoria's face that would tell her the goddess had heard her and would honor her request (she *was* the princess regent, after all—didn't that count for something?) but the serene features of Perin's virgin daughter were unchanged.

She suddenly remembered. *And bring Father home safe again from Hierosol.* She had prayed for that thing every day, but today she had almost forgotten. A quick chill moved over her. Did it mean anything? Was a god whispering to her, trying to tell her something had happened to him? Could it be her fault—had she shown too much pride in her own abilities as ruler of Southmarch?

"I hoped this place would bring you some peace, Princess," said her tutor. "But you look troubled."

"Oh, Utta, how could I look otherwise?"

Brother and sister were silent as they rode down the causeway across Brenn's Bay toward the great field where the mustered soldiers had been quartered, a swath of harvested land an hour's ride distant, at the southernmost edge of Avin Brone's fiefdom of Landsend. The day was cold and clear but the wind was rising. It wrapped the new cloak Merolanna had embroidered for him around Barrick's neck in a strangler's grip. He grunted as he used his crippled arm to free himself, but still did not speak. He knew Briony wanted him to, but he did not want to hear what she would say in turn. He had heard it enough times already.

From the center of the causeway they could see that the low-tide shallows and mud flats at the base of the castle mount were full of workers—almost another army, it seemed, swarming above the mud on makeshift platforms. They had demolished the ramshackle market town before the gate, and now were pulling apart the stones of the causeway itself beneath the castle walls, preparing to replace it with a wooden bridge that could be torn down in moments, thus completely cutting the castle off from the land and forcing any invader to ride over sucking mud with water up to the horses' necks, or else find a way to get boats across the bay's tricky currents under fire from the walls when the tide came back in. Little wonder, Barrick reflected, that Erivor of the Dark Seas had always been held the special patron of the Eddons. Who else but the sea god had given them this almost unconquerable vantage?

Briony and the others will be safe here no matter what, he thought.

His twin didn't seem to be sharing his thought, but gnawed at her lower lip in the way she did when she was worrying about something, a habit carried over from childhood so completely it almost seemed a cherished memento. He followed the line of her sight. The captain of the guard, Vansen, was riding a short distance to the side of them. Barrick felt a touch of jealousy, although he knew it was absurd.

She still hates that one, he thought. *Loathes him to the point of unfairness, as if it were all his fault Kendrick died.*

They rode in silence for a long time, so that Barrick was almost drowsing in his saddle when his sister finally spoke, and at first he could make no sense of her words.

"He won't defend the city."

"Who? What city?"

"Avin Brone," she said, as if the name tasted bad. "The rest of Southmarch, of course, the mainland. He said that the walls are too long and too low on the inland side, and it's too hard to defend."

"He's right. How would we do it?" Barrick pointed to the thicket of gabled roofs stretching away down the coastline and outward as far as the base of the hills. He was grateful to be distracted from his own heavy thoughts, but it seemed odd to be talking with his sister about such things—as though they were playing at being adults.

"I don't know," she said. "But we can't possibly get all those people inside the keep . . ."

"The gods save us, no, we bloody well can't, Briony! You couldn't get a quarter of them into the castle and have room for them to sit down, let alone feed them all."

"So we should just abandon them if there's a siege?"

"We have to hope there won't be a siege. Because if there is, we'll have to do more than leave those people to fend for themselves. We'll have to burn that part of the city down."

"What? Just to keep the besiegers from getting their hands on the stores there?"

"And the wood, and everything else that we don't destroy. As it is, you . . . we . . . will probably have to stand by while the catapults throw the stones of our own city onto us."

"You don't know that, and neither does Avin Brone." Her anger seemed mostly sadness. "Nobody knows anything! There haven't been any sieges of proper cities in the Marchlands for half a hundred years—I heard Father talk about it once. Some people say there won't ever be again because of cannons and bombards and . . . and all those other things that blow stones and metal balls through the air. There's no point."

It annoyed Barrick to be told things about war by his sister. It annoyed him even more that she had clearly been paying more attention than he had. "No point? So what should we do, just surrender?"

"That's not what I meant and you know it."

The hour wore on as they rode in silence up the coast road into the lower reaches of Landsend. The chill air carried little except the clean tang of the pines and the ever-present smell of the sea.

Briony finally said, "We can't be certain it *will* be a siege, Barrick. We don't even know what these twilight creatures plan—they're not men, they're something else. Only the gods can guess what they'll do."

"We'll have an idea soon enough. If they've marched into Daler's Troth, we'll meet people who know something about them and how they fight. We'll send you back word as soon as we hear anything."

She turned abruptly to face him. "Oh, Barrick, you will be careful, won't you? I'm so angry with you, I don't want you to go."

He felt himself stiffen. "I'm old enough to decide for myself."

"But that doesn't mean it's right." She stared, shook her head. "I'm frightened for you. Don't let's argue anymore. Just . . . just don't do anything foolish, please. No matter what . . . what dreams you have, what you fear."

The cold heaviness that had cast a shadow over him all day was abruptly pierced by a shaft of regret and love. He looked at his sister, her so-familiar face—his own face, but seen in a bright mirror, open where he was pinched and hidden, golden and pink where he was angry, bloody-red, and corpse-pale—and wished that things had turned out a different way. For just as he had been struck earlier that day by the powerful certainty that some unstoppable downward slide had begun, so also he couldn't help feeling deeply, wordlessly, that he and his beloved twin, his best and perhaps only friend, would never again be together in this way.

The certainty hit him now like a blow in the stomach: a gulf would open between them, something wide and deep. Was it death whose cold breath he could almost feel, or something stranger still? Whatever it was, he began to shudder and it quickly became so strong that he could barely stay upright in his saddle. Suddenly he pitched forward, falling down some dark tunnel, flailing away into a nothingness where a cold, knowing presence awaited him. . . .

"*Barrick!*" He heard her terrified voice as if from the other side of a crowded, noisy room. "Barrick, what's wrong?"

The roaring in his ears eased a bit. The gray day returned and pushed back the darkness. He was leaning low over his saddle, his head almost on his horse Kettle's neck. "I'm well enough. Leave me alone."

A measure of Briony's fright was that she had seized his crippled arm. He snatched it back and straightened up. No one around them seemed to be staring, but he could tell by the studied way in which they all looking at anything *except* the prince and his sister that they had only just averted their eyes.

"The gods make a mockery of us," he said quietly.

His attention distracted by his near-swoon, he had failed to notice that they had arrived at the field. The mustered men were waiting below them in ragged array among the shorn stalks of grain, a thousand or more of the earliest arrivals who had been chivvied into lines by their sergeants, but still did not look much like an army. More men streamed in every day from the provinces, but instead of joining this westbound company most of the newcomers would bolster the defenses of Southmarch itself.

"Don't say such things about the gods," Briony pleaded. "Not when you are about to go away. I can't bear it."

He looked at her and despite his shame and misery, felt a thump of love for her in his chest. After all, what else did he have in this world? What else did he fear to lose? Nothing. He reached out and patted her hands where they clutched the reins of her horse Snow. "You're right, strawhead. I'm sorry. And I don't mean it. I don't believe the gods are mocking us."

And he was telling the truth. For in this open place, beneath this low gray sky, Barrick had suddenly decided that he did not believe in the gods at all.

After clambering all the way down the treacherous paths hidden below the balcony at the end of the Maze—who could have guessed there even were such things as paths going down to the Sea in the Depths? Who used them, the temple brothers?—Chert had finally reached the shore to stand on the rounded stones in a madness of shimmering colors, but he couldn't find any evidence of how the boy had crossed the silvery sea. He couldn't help wondering whether he was being punished by the Earth Elders for bringing an outsider down to the sacred Mysteries, for approaching their deep haunts without the proper ceremony. He felt impious just being so close to the Shining Man, which loomed like a mountain at the center of its island. Even here on the shore he could still make little sense of it except for its roughly manlike shape. It wasn't easy even to see that much: the Shining Man's uneven glow lit the ceiling and reflected from the Sea in the Depths as well, so that all the walls of the huge cavern were painted with smears of wobbly, many-hued light.

But why would the Elders punish me and yet allow the boy to cross? Chert felt a moment of doubt. Perhaps he had not seen Flint at all—perhaps he had been fooled by a bat's shadow, by his own fatigue, or more likely by the heady, disturbing air of the deepest Mysteries.

Then he saw a movement again on the island, a shadowy silhouette against the glow of the Shining Man that pushed all uncertainty from his mind. "Flint!" he shouted, cupping his hands around his mouth, jumping up and down on the rocky shore. "Flint! It's me, Chert!"

He fancied that the shadow froze for a moment, but there was no reply to his call and an instant later it vanished in the confusion of pulsing light.

Cursing, he hurried up and down the shore again, but still could find no trace of how the boy had crossed the metallic underground sea. As he stood, muttering in exhausted frustration, he suddenly remembered another small person in his charge, one he had almost completely forgotten in the excitement of seeing what he felt sure was the boy.

"Beetledown! Fissure and fracture, I've left him up there alone for an hour or more!" And sick, too, having trouble getting a full breath. Chert was stabbed with the sharp point of his own helplessness—so many things gone wrong and no way to fix any of them. The boy—everything in life had gone wrong since the moment he and Opal saw that sack dropped beside the Shadowline.

We should have left him there, he thought, and even with the aching in his heart, the love he had to admit he felt for the pale-haired child, it was hard to argue with that thought.

He scrambled back up the path, which was really little more than a goat track—but whoever heard of goats living a thousand feet below the ground? That thought had scarcely passed through his head when he saw something gleaming farther up the cliffside, something pale that stood between himself and the balcony at the end of the Maze. He stared in amazement at what he could only believe in these hot, flickering depths must be a sort of fever-vision.

Even on the surface in the waking world—at least this side of the Shadowline—there was no such thing as a deer with skin white to the point of translucence, a ghostly stag with weirdly slender legs and antlers like a tangle of sprouting roots, not to mention those huge, milky-blue eyes that glowed bright as candleflame. But that was what seemed to be staring down at him, at least for one astonishing moment. A heartbeat later it was gone.

Chert paused, clinging to a jutting outcrop, suddenly light-headed and fearful he might fall. Could it have been real? Or had he breathed too deeply of the Mysteries?

Oh, Lord of the Hot Wet Stone, help me—was that what I saw on the island, too? One of those things and not Flint at all? But unless the light and shadow had distorted the island-shape beyond anything he could credit, surely what he had seen there walked on two legs, had a round head—had been, in fact, a person.

When he reached the spot where the glassy-white deer had stood, he found no sign of anything living.

Chert was feeling quite sickened with terror of the gods and their sacred places by the time he reached the spot where he had left Beetledown: it took him a few stupefied moments to be quite certain he was standing before the same knob of stone where he had left the Rooftopper, even though his own coral lantern was sitting where he had placed it, still gleaming.

The little man, however, was nowhere to be seen.

His stomach now roiling so that he feared he might be sick—he had lost everyone in his charge, all those who needed him most!—Chert got down on his hands and knees, holding the lantern close to the ground as he searched desperately around the base of the limestone knob for some sign of his companion. He could only pray to the very gods he had impinged upon that when he found him, Beetledown would still be alive.

It was an undignified position to be in, but he did not care at all until he heard a small voice, a yard or so from his ear, say, "Didst tha drop somewhat?"

"Beetledown! Where are you?"

"Just here, hinden this clutter of stone whatnots, but mind tha come quiet. Don't scare un away."

"Scare *who* away?" The Funderling crept forward, his gloom lightening a little for the first time since he realized he could not reach the Shining Man's island. Against all reason, he felt a small swell of hope. "Is it Flint? Did you find my boy?"

"Not unless thy boy wears whiskers and long tail."

Chert stopped. The bowman was crouching a bit unsteadily in the fork of a two-part stalagmite, a formation that did not reach Chert's waist but was a hilltop for the little man. Beetledown had his bow trained on something Chert couldn't see until he crawled closer and marked the shiny black eye and twitching nose in the shadows. Startled by his appearance, the rat flinched and began to skitter along the stone wall, but one of Beetledown's tiny arrows smacked against the wall just in front of its head and it froze again, only its nose moving.

"How long have you been trying to kill it?" Chert asked, amused as well as relieved. He would never have taken the Rooftopper for such a poor shot, but he supposed the heady, close airs of the caves had taken a toll. "Are you really that hungry?"

"Hungry? Th'art a huge, daft thing. No idea to eat it, I foremeant to ride it."

"Ride it?"

"Too far for me to walk back to the good air," explained Beetledown. "But now here tha stand with thy huge, daft shoulder." The tiny man smiled weakly. "So will tha carry me back home again?"

"You were going to ride this rat?" Chert was coming to his understanding slowly, but he had the beginnings of an idea. "All the way back up?"

"A Gutter-Scout am I," Beetledown said a little indignantly. "Well-used am I to breaking a wild ratling to the saddle." He shook his head. "And I'll tell 'ee true—I cannot take this heavy, choking air much longer."

"Then let's catch that rat. He might make us both happy."

Beetledown was putting the last touches on a makeshift saddle—more of a harness, really—constructed from one strap of the coral lantern knotted with threads and fraying cloth from Chert's shirt. The saddle's eventual recipient was currently a prisoner in the bottom of Chert's bag, happily scavenging up the crumbs left there from the meal Chert had purchased at the Salt Pool. And after he ate, Chert hoped, the beast might stop trying to bite.

"But why will tha stay?"

"Because there has to be a way onto that island—the boy's there, after all. And I'm going to find it."

"P'raps a boat there is, that un's found and crossed with."

Chert's heart sank. He hadn't thought of that. "Well, even so," he said at last, "if he comes back across, I'll be here to make certain he doesn't get away again. And what if he needs help? How do you cross quicksilver with a boat, anyway? What if it . . . overturns or comes apart. They come apart sometimes, don't they?"

"Never tha hast been on a boat, true?" said Beetledown with a little smile.

"True," Chert admitted.

"And I'm to ride away, then send 'ee help. From where, good Master Funderling?"

"My wife Opal, if you can find her again. Otherwise, ask any of my folk to take you to her."

Beetledown nodded. He pulled a knot tight on his rat-bridle, squinting at it with a sharp, experienced eye. "Un'll do." He stood. "Perchance 'twould be better were I to send some of yon temple fellows—what did tha call uns? The Metal Marching Brothers, somewhat?"

"The Metamorphic . . . Oh, fissure and—I never thought of that! And they've already met you—they'll know who you are. Of course." He was angry with himself for not coming up with such an obvious idea, but events had overwhelmed him.

He helped Beetledown fasten the harness. The rat was calmer now but still not precisely docile and it took no little time. The Rooftopper was patient and skillful, however, and at last Chert was gingerly holding the rat in place while Beetledown climbed onto the creature's back. As soon as Chert took his hand away, the rat tried to bolt, but the Rooftopper gave the creature a stinging slap on the muzzle with his bow; the rat squealed and tried to take off in another direction and was again punished. When all the cardinal points had proved equally dangerous, the rat crouched low and motionless except for huffing sides and anxiously blinking eyes.

"Un's learning," said Beetledown with satisfaction.

"Take a little of the coral light," Chert told him, breaking off one of the brightest bits; the Rooftopper fastened it under one of the straps of the rat's harness. "It'll make it easier to see in some of the dark places. Good journey, Beetledown. And thank you for your help and kindness." He wanted to say something more—he had a sense that this exceptionally small man had become more than an odd acquaintance, that a friendship, however unlikely, had sprung up between them, but Chert was not a man comfortable with sentiment. In any case, he was tired and very frightened. "The Earth Elders protect you."

"And the Lord of the Peaks watch over 'ee in thy turn, Chert of Blue Quartz." The Rooftopper kicked his booted heels against the rat's sides, but the animal didn't move. Beetledown smacked his bowstaff against the creature's flank and it scuttled forward. He was still flicking its hindquarters with the bow, this time trying to get it to turn, as rider and mount vanished into the shadows of the path leading away uphill; all Chert could see of them in the last moments was a moving point of light, the piece of coral strapped to the rat's back.

"That is, if un can find 'ee again 'neath all this mucky stone!" Beetledown called back to Chert, his small voice already sounding as though it came from miles away.

The straggling end of the army had finally disappeared around a bend in the coastal highway, heading toward the Settland Road and the hills, leaving behind only a few hundred watchers and a muddy, trampled field. It wasn't right, Briony knew—this army should have marched out with trumpets, with a parade through the streets, but there hadn't been time to arrange such a thing—nor, to be honest, would she have had the heart for it. But the people would be frightened because of this near-secrecy, a thousand men simply gone. In the past, wars had almost always begun with a brave show.

Perhaps the day is coming for a different kind of war, she considered, although she had no idea what such a thing might be. *The world is changing swiftly, after all, and not entirely for the worse. Besides, the times are too grim for parades and trumpets.*

But then again, she thought, *perhaps that is when we need such things most.*

She couldn't eat her food and couldn't stop weeping. *Barrick went away like a man to the gallows,* was all she could think. His jests, the cheerful farewell when he kissed her the last time, had not fooled her. Rose and Moina were desperate to get her to lie down, but sleep was the last thing Briony could do, and in any case it was only late afternoon.

Oh, Barrick! she thought. *You should have stayed with me. You should have stayed.* She sniffled angrily, ignored a maid's offer of a kerchief and wiped her nose with her sleeve instead, getting a tiny bit of pleasure out of hearing her ladies-in-waiting moan their disapproval.

"I will go and talk to Lord Brone," she announced to them. "He said there were things he needed to speak to me about—siege preparations, no doubt. And I will have to talk to Lord Nynor about feeding the new muster that just came in from Helmingsea."

"But . . . but shouldn't they come to you?" Rose asked.

"I will walk. I like to walk." She immediately felt better. Having something to do was so much better than sitting helplessly, thinking about Barrick and the others riding off into . . . what?

Halfway across the inner keep, her ladies scuttling after her like baby quail, the women followed by a contingent of anxious guardsmen, Briony suddenly remembered what she had forgotten from yesterday—or had it been the day before that? That idiot poet's message, the mysterious potboy asking to see her. She slowed and was almost knocked down by Rose and Moina in their blind hurry to keep up.

"Have the potboy brought to me," she told one of the guards. "I will see him in the Erivor Chapel."

"Just him, Highness?"

She thought of the potboy's erstwhile companion, the poet Tinwright. The last thing she wanted just now was to have to endure his boobish flattery. "Bring him and nobody else."

She almost forgot the potboy again, but after she left the lord constable, the smell of incense wafting out of the shrine to Erilo in Farmers' Hall reminded her and she made her way to the chapel.

The strange man named Gil seemed to be waiting extremely patiently, his long, sleepwalker's face almost empty of expression, but the guards around him looked a little itchy, and Briony realized with some dismay that she'd kept them all waiting for a good piece of the day.

Well, I am the princess regent, am I not?

Yes, she reminded herself, but this was also a castle readying for siege. Perhaps there were other things these men should have been doing. Still, it nettled her a bit.

"Your fellows look tired," she said to the sergeant. "Did you have a hard time getting him here?"

"Not him, Highness. We had a hard time keeping the girl from coming along."

"Girl?" Briony was completely confused. "What girl?"

"The one Captain Vansen brought back, Highness. What's her name—Willow? The girl from the dales."

"But why should she want to come along?"

The sergeant shrugged, then realized it was not what one did in front of princesses. He lowered his head. "I don't know, Highness, but the men in the stronghold say she is there every day, watching this one like a cat beside a mousehole, sitting with him when she can. They don't say nothing, either of them, but she watches him and he doesn't watch her." He colored a little. "That's what I'm told, Ma'am."

Briony narrowed her eyes, turned to the apparently fascinating potboy. "Did you hear that? Is it true about the girl?"

His cool, clear eyes were almost as empty as the stare of a fish. "There are people," he said slowly. "I seldom look. I am listening."

"To what?"

"Voices." He smiled, but there was something wrong with it, as though he had never completely learned the trick. "They try to speak to *you,* some of them. They bid me to tell you about your brother—the one who has the dreams."

"What voices?" It was hard not to be angry with someone who looked at you as though you were a chair or a stone. "And what do they tell you about Prince Barrick—your liege lord?"

"I am not certain. The voices speak in my head, in sleep and sometimes even when I am awake." The blank eyes closed, opened, slow as the flutter of a dead leaf. "And they say he is not to leave the castle—he is not to go into the west."

"He's not . . . ? But he already has left! Why . . . ?" She was about to rage over being told this only now, but she knew it was her own fault. The flash of anger turned into something quite different, something icy in her chest. "Why shouldn't he go?"

Gil slowly shook his head. She suddenly realized that she knew nothing about him at all—that Brone had told her only that he worked in a low inn near Skimmer's Lagoon. "If he goes into the west," the potboy said, "he must beware of the porcupine's eye."

"What does that mean?" The sense of having made a terrible mistake was on her, but what was she to do about it? Even if she believed it utterly, was she to send a fast messenger just to pass Barrick this . . . this prophecy? He had already been infuriated once by the man's soothsaying. No, she decided, she would put it in a letter to go with the first regular courier. She would phrase it as though to amuse him—perhaps it would stick in his head, and if there turned out to be any truth to it, that would help him. She offered a prayer to the gods that her foolishness and laxity would not have some terrible cost.

"What does it mean?" The potboy shook his head. "I do not know—the voices do not tell me, they only speak so that I can hear them, like people on the other side of a wall." He took a maddeningly long breath. "It is happening more often now, because the world is changing."

"Changing?"

"Oh, yes. Because the gods are awakening again." He said it very simply, as if it were a truth available to all. "Right under our feet."

31
A Night Visitor

A STORY:

The tale is being told
In the corridors, in the courtyards
It is only the sighing of a dove's wings

—from *The Bonefall Oracles*

THE DAY'S PRAYERS AND RITUALS had been particularly grueling. Qinnitan found herself ill now almost every time Panhyssir gave her one of the potions, but also sometimes full of a useless, undirected vigor, and that was the case now, hours after she had heard the song of midnight prayers. She couldn't sleep and wasn't sure she wanted to, but neither did she want to lie in bed and listen to her own breathing.

That morning, when she had drunk the priest's elixir, she could almost feel it scouring away her insides, as though she were being cleaned like a gourd filled with pebbles and boiling water. The weird sense of being untethered also seemed to last longer each time, as though she were becoming a guest in her own body, and not a particularly welcome one either. Worst of all, and something she could not bear thinking about too much, was that when she drank the Sun's Blood and dropped into that momentary but still terrifying darkness, that living death, she felt like a cricket stuck flexing on a fishhook, as though she were living bait dangled above ultimate depths while something huge moved beneath her, sniffing, deciding . . .

And what could that something be, a thing with thoughts as slow and shuddering as the movements of the earth itself? Could there even be such a thing, or was the elixir disordering her mind? Just a few months back one of the young queens had lost her wits and had not been able to stop laughing and weeping. The girl had claimed that the Favored spied on her even in her dreams. She had torn her clothes and walked up and down the passageways singing children's songs until at last she disappeared from the Seclusion altogether.

What do these people want from me? Qinnitan wondered hopelessly. *Do they truly wish to drive me mad? Or are they simply murdering me slowly, for some strange reasons of their own?*

She was becoming obsessed with the idea of being poisoned, and not just because of the high priest's foul elixir. Each time someone handed her a cup, any time she accepted food that was not spooned out of a communal pot, she felt as though she was about to step off a cliff. It was not merely the open and obvious malice of Paramount Wife Arimone—many of the other women had begun to look at her strangely, too, regarding her sessions with Panhyssir and the other priests of Nushash as a sign of some kind of unwarranted favor, as though that daily misery was some prize Qinnitan had secured for herself! Even Luian, who had been her staunchest ally, had grown a little distant from her. Their conversations had become awkward, like two women meeting in a marketplace who both knew that one had slandered the other recently. It was Jeddin and his ridiculous, unreasonable passion for her—it stood between them now like a closed door.

So now Qinnitan lay sleepless in her narrow bed in the deep watches of the night, thoughts scurrying like busy ants, the occasional snoring of her maids outside her door poking at her like a cruel child every time it seemed she might be drifting toward slumber. The days in the Hive seemed impossibly far away. Everything that was happy and simple seemed beyond reach. And because she lay wakeful, thinking such feverish, miserable thoughts, Qinnitan heard the quiet noise of someone moving at the far side of her chamber as plainly as if they spoke to her, and knew that she was not alone.

Her heart lurched, sped. She slowly sat up, squinting into the near-darkness beside the door. All she could see by the glow of the shuttered lamp was a shape, but it was a shape that had not been there when she had crawled into her bed.

Tanyssa. The First Wife has sent her for me. She could see the Favored gardener's square face in her mind's eye, the eyes empty but for the guarded sullenness of a whipped dog. *Even if I scream, she'll kill me before help can come.*

And if the gardener was on Arimone's business, Qinnitan knew she might scream herself hoarse without bringing any help at all.

She slid out of the bed and onto the floor as quietly as she could, letting out a small whimper like a disturbed sleeper in the hope of covering the sound of her own movements and perhaps even making the assassin stop moving for fear of waking her up. Desperate, her heart still hammering painfully fast, she struggled to think of what she might use for a weapon. The scissors that the slaves used to cut and shape her hair! But they were at the bottom of the basket under her bedside table, inside the ivory sewing kit—she could never get them out in time.

As her hand passed over the small table, she touched something cold and hard and her fingers closed on it. It was a dressing pin Luian had given her, a handspan long and ornamented with a gold-and-enamel nightingale. She curled the nightingale into her fist, raised the pin like a dagger. Tanyssa would not murder her without bleeding for it, Qinnitan decided. Her mouth was dry, her throat as tight as if the strangling cord were already twisting tight.

The shape by the doorway began to move again, slowly, silently, feeling its way with outstretched hands. With much of the dim light behind it now, it seemed scarcely even human, too thin of limb to be Tanyssa, let alone any of the other stranglers Arimone or the autarch might send. For a moment Qinnitan's already racing heart threatened to stop entirely. Was it a ghost? A shadow-demon from out of Argal's night kingdom?

The thing was almost upon her. She saw a shadowed face loom up and her superstitious terror turned her arm to stone when she should have struck with the pin, should have buried it in the dark spots of the intruder's eyes; instead she felt the thing bump against her and recoil. The feeling of cool, human flesh was so startling that the sinews of her arm finally caught life and she slashed at it. Her attacker fell back with a strange, breathy whimper but no words, no shout of pain or surprise, and Qinnitan's heart stuttered again with superstitious fear.

"Leave me alone!" she cried, but it came out a choked murmur. The thing scrambled away from her, still making the strange, animal noise, and cowered on the floor. Qinnitan leaped past it and ran toward the door, ready to scream for the huge Favored guards waiting only a few dozen paces away from the sleeping chambers, but then she stopped in the doorway. The thing was weeping, she realized, a bizarre, rasping sound.

She reached up and burned her fingers pulling the lamp from behind its slotted screen, but when she had the handle and lifted it up, flooding the room with yellow light, she saw that the fearsome thing crouched on her floor was only a small, dark-haired boy.

"Queen of the Hive!" Caution and fear still kept her oath of surprise quiet. She moved closer. The boy looked up at her with wide, frightened eyes. A long scratch down his chest dripped blood, showing where she had caught him with her nightingale pin. "Who are you?" she whispered.

The child stared at her, tears in his eyes and on his cheeks. He opened his mouth but what came out was only a low grunt. She flinched and he threw his arm in front of his face to protect himself.

One of the Silent Favored! He was a mute slave taken in one of the wars of Xis, an infant at his capture, perhaps. The autarchs of the Orchard Palace and their highest servants had always liked to surround themselves with such boys, who could neither spill secrets nor cry out, no matter what kind of cruelties were visited on them. "You poor thing," Qinnitan said, half to herself— it did not immediately occur to her that one who could not speak might yet be able to hear and understand. She put out a cautious hand and he shrank away again. "I won't hurt you," she said, hoping that at least the tone of her voice would convince him. She was talking too loud, she realized—she might wake up her maids, and although moments earlier she would have welcomed it, suddenly she did not want anyone intruding. When she spoke again, only the wounded child could hear her. "Let me help you. I am sorry. Do you understand? I thought you were . . . You frightened me."

The boy whimpered again but let her examine his wound. It was long but shallow. Still, blood was already soaking the waist of his white linen breeches. She hunted for a moment until she found one of the clean cloths waiting for her next moonblood and pressed it against the cut, then found an old scarf and tied it around his waist to hold the bandage in place.

"It is not a bad wound," she whispered. "Can you understand me?"

He touched the cloth gingerly. He still looked as though he might bolt at any moment, but at last he nodded his head.

"Good. I am sorry I hurt you. What are you doing here?"

Even in the lamplight she could see his face pale so quickly that she feared she had given him a mortal wound after all. She tried to restrain him, but he clambered grunting to his feet and reached into the blood-soaked waistband of his breeches, making soft hooting noises like a dove. He pulled out a bag that had been tucked away there between his body and the clothing. It was red with the blood of his body and wet, and for a moment she was reluctant to take it, but his expression was so anguished she realized that he was afraid something within had been ruined. She took it from him and saw that the drawstring was sealed with silver thread and wax. She held the lamp close, but did not immediately recognize the seal printed on it. Qinnitan took a breath, suddenly reluctant again, but the boy made a little whimpering sound like a dog waiting to be let out of doors and so she broke the wax away from the string and shook out into her hand a curl of parchment and a gold ring.

The signature at the bottom of the parchment said "Jeddin." She cursed again, but silently this time.

"I have it," she said. "It is safe—the blood has not soaked through. Was it the captain who sent this? The Leopard captain?"

The boy shook his head, puzzled. Qinnitan was puzzled, too, then she had another thought. "Luian? Favored Luian? Did she send this?"

Now he smiled, although it was a pained and sickly one, and nodded his head.

"Very well. You have done what was asked. Now you must go out again, as silently as you came, so as not to wake the ones sleeping outside. I truly am sorry. Have someone dress that wound properly. Tell them . . . tell them you fell on a stone in the garden."

The boy looked doubtful, but he rose and patted his bandage to make sure it was still in place. He bowed to her, and the courtly display was so strange in the middle of the night, with the lamplight and the smears of blood on the floor, that she almost laughed with shock to see it. A moment later he slipped out through the curtains and was gone.

Qinnitan waited, listening to the silence, then bent to the task of cleaning the blood from the floor, blotting it up with another of her own rags. The thought of reading what Jeddin had to say filled her with a sour dismay. Was it some foolish love poem that had almost cost a child his life? Or was it something newer and more dangerous, him ordering her to meet him somewhere, with the same sort of threats he had used to cow Luian into cooperation?

Finished, with the room exactly as it had been before the midnight visitor's arrival, she set the lamp on her bedside table and sat cross-legged on the bed, leaning close so she could read.

Beloved,

it began. She stared at Jeddin's precise and surprisingly delicate script. *At least he's left my name off it,* she thought, but a moment later the power of that single word reached out and struck her as powerfully as a blow. How had things come to this? It was like something out of an old story, that this powerful man should risk both their lives to prove his love, and that another even more powerful man—the mightiest on earth—should have already claimed her as his own.

Me! Me, Qinnitan. It was impossible to compass.

I was a fool to take the risk of meeting you. You were right to tell me so. There is talk. One of my enemies suspects. It must be Vash the chief minister but he can prove nothing.

Dread seized her, so powerful it almost stopped her breath. She did not want to read any more. But she did.

However the day may come when he can act against me despite the favor the autarch all praise to His name has shown me. No it is because of the favor that the Golden One has shown me. He hates me. Vash I mean. As do others here.

I must prepare for a day when things might change. I have my own followers loyal to me but my own safety would mean nothing to me without you. If such a day should come I will send a messenger to you who will speak the sacred name Habbili. And just as the son of the great god went down from the mountains and his enemies and onto the boat that brought him wounded to Xis so we will sail to freedom. In the harbor in a slip near to the Habbili temple there is a small fast ship named Morning Star of Kirous. *I did not name it after you my beautiful star I have had it since I was first lifted to my place over the autarch's Leopards but when I learned that some in the Seclusion called you by that name it only proved to me that the fates have meant this for us from the first. When you go there show the captain this ring. He will know it and show you all courtesy and when I join you you will see how sweetly that morning star sails.*

I hope it will not come to this beloved. I may yet defeat Pinimmon Vash and my other enemies and perhaps find some way that our love can grow under the Golden One's sunshine. But as the saying goes there is no rest in a viper's den—not even for vipers.

He had signed his name with a flourish.

Fool, she thought. *Oh, Jeddin, you fool!* Had the boy woken up the guards or even her servants, had this fallen into anyone's hand, she and Jeddin and probably Luian would all be kneeling before the executioner this very moment. The captain of the Leopards was infected with a particularly dangerous sort of madness, Qinnitan thought, one in which he could praise the autarch even as he schemed to rob the ruler of the earth of his chosen bride.

She did not love Jeddin, she knew that, but something in his madness touched her. Beneath that powerful body beat the heart of a child—a sad child, running after the rest but forever too slow. And as a grown man he was handsome in a way she could not ignore, that was also true. Qinnitan caught her breath. Could there be something to it after all? Did she dare to have feelings for him? Was there a way he actually could save her from this horrid place?

She thought about it for only a very short time, then burned the parchment in the lamp's flame until it was powdery, black ash. But she saved the ring.

32

In This Circle of the World

TEARS:

*Laugh and be joyous
Says the wolf
Howl at the sky*

—from *The Bonefall Oracles*

THE COLD RAIN WAS SLAPPING down and Fitters Row was a river of mud. Matty Tinwright stepped gingerly from board to board—some of which, like foundering boats, had sunk into the ooze until only the tip of one end protruded—in a determined effort to keep his shoes clean. His new clothing allowance had not run to wooden clogs, or at least the choice between clogs and the largest, most ostentatious ruff for his collar had been no choice at all as far as he was concerned. More than ever, he was determined to make a good appearance.

One of the boards in mid-street had now disappeared entirely and old Puzzle stood like an allegorical statue of his own name, marooned and peering shortsightedly at the gap in front of him, two full yards of mud as sticky as overboiled marrow. An oxcart was rumbling downhill toward him, filling the road, its drovers making a great clamor as they guided it through the most treacherous spots. Others coming into Fitters Row from Squeak-step Alley—several tradesmen, some soaked apprentices, and more than a few soldiers mustered out of the provinces—now stopped in the shelter beneath the overhanging buildings to watch the unfolding events. The oxcart would not arrive in a hurry, but neither did the ancient jester seem to see it coming.

Tinwright sighed in irritation. He absolutely did not want to go back into the muddy street to drag the man out of danger, but Puzzle was the closest thing to a friend he had these days and he was reluctant to see the old fellow crushed by a wagon.

"Puzzle! The gods damn your shoes, man, come on! That beast will be standing on you in another moment!"

The jester looked up, blinking. Puzzle was dressed in what Tinwright thought of as his civilian attire, funereal dark hose and hooded cloak and a hat whose giant, bedraggled brim made it hard for him to see beyond his own muddy feet. It was a far more comic outfit than his motley could ever be; Tinwright thought the old man should wear it to entertain the nobility.

"Hoy!" shouted Tinwright. The jester seemed to see him at last, then looked around at the approaching oxcart, the irritated animal and its team of cursing drovers so intent on skidding down the muddy street that Puzzle might as well be invisible. He blinked and swallowed, finally understanding his peril. One storklike leg went out, his muck-covered slipper reaching unreasonably for the distant board, then he stepped off and directly into the mud and with a few squeaks and thrashes sank in up to his skinny thighs.

It was fortúnate for Puzzle that the oxcart and its drovers were more attentive than they had seemed. He suffered nothing worse than a further splattering as the cart slewed to a stop a yard or two away. The ox lowered its head and stared at the blinking, mud-slathered jester as though it had never seen such a strange creature.

It was not the entrance that Tinwright had planned, so it was just as well that his old haunt the Quiller's Mint was dark and crowded and scarcely anyone even glanced up to see them come in. A trio of outland soldiers laughed at the brown shell hardening on Puzzle's lower extremities, but made a little room for the shivering old man as Tinwright deposited him beside the fire. He snagged the potboy as he ran past—a child of nine or ten had replaced Gil, he noticed, doubtless one of Conary's multitude of relatives, but young enough not to have become work-shy yet—and bade the boy bring a brush and some rags to get off the worst of the mud. This done, Tinwright sauntered up to the serving table where Conary was breaching a cask. It was a real table now, not just a trestle-board; the poet couldn't help being impressed and a little irritated. The coming siege had brought some good to someone, as the crowd of unfamiliar drinkers gathered in the Quiller's Mint proved, but it did take a bit of the luster off Tinwright's own advancement in the world.

Conary's look was sour, but it took in the huge ruff and the new jacket. "Tinwright, you whoreson, you stole my potboy."

"Stole him? Not I. Rather, it was him that nearly got me banged up in the stronghold under the keep. But good has come of it, so I do not begrudge him. I am the princess regent's poet now." He examined a stool, then wiped it with a kerchief before sitting down.

"The princess gone deaf, then, has she? Poor girl, as if she didn't have troubles enough." Conary put his hands on his hips. "And if you're riz so high in the world, you can bloody well pay me them three starfish you owe, or I'll have the town watch in to pitch you into the street again."

Tinwright had forgotten about that and couldn't help making a face, but he had come flush today thanks to money he had borrowed from Puzzle, and he did his best to move the coins ungrudgingly from his purse to the tabletop. "Of course. I was detained at the pleasure of the regent, you see, or else I would have been back to·pay you long ago."

Conary looked at the coppers as though for the first time—new ruff and quilted jacket notwithstanding—he might consider believing in Tinwright's exalted new position. "Are you drinking, then?"

"Aye. And my companion is the king's own royal jester, so you would do well to bring a jug of your best ale over to the fire. None of that rubbish you give everyone else." He waved his hand grandly.

"Another starfish, then," said Conary. "Because them three are mine, remember?"

Tinwright grunted—was he not clearly now worthy of credit?—but disdainfully dropped another coin on the tabletop.

Puzzle appeared to have thawed out a bit, although he had abandoned the scraping of his soiled hose and slippers with quite a bit of mud still on them and was staring into the fire as though trying to imagine what such a fascinatingly hot and shiny thing might be called.

"Now, is this not better than trying to find a place to drink in the castle kitchens?" Tinwright asked him loudly, "with the soldiers elbowing and shoving like geese fighting for grain?"

Puzzle looked up. "I . . . I think I have been in this place before, long ago. It burned down, didn't it?"

Tinwright waved his hand. "Aye, many years back, or so I'm told. It is a low place, but it has its charms. A poet must drink with the common folk or else he will lose himself from too much contemplation of high things, so I sometimes came here before I was raised up." He looked around to see if anyone had noted his remarks, but the outlanders by the fire were playing at dice and paying no attention.

"Well, well." A jug of ale and two tankards clanked down onto the hearth at their feet and Puzzle's eyes bulged at the expanse of bosom revealed by the woman bending over. She straightened up. "Matty Tinwright. I thought you were dead or gone back to West Wharfside."

He gave Brigid his most amiable nod. "No, I have had other duties that have kept me away."

She pinched at his jacket, let a finger trail across his starched ruff. "It seems you've come high in the world, Matty."

This was more like it. He smiled and turned to Puzzle. "You see, they remember me here." The old man didn't appear to be listening very closely. His weak eyes were following the quiver of flesh above Brigid's bodice like a starving man eyeing a dripping roast. Tinwright turned back to the girl. "Yes, Zosim has smiled on me. I am now poet to the princess regent herself."

The wench frowned a little, but then her own smile came back. "Still, you must get a bit lonely up at the castle, even with all those fine ladies. You must miss your old friends—your old bed . . . ?"

Now it had become a bit much, and even though the old man was still goggling at the girl's breasts, happily oblivious, Tinwright himself didn't really want to be reminded of his previous situation. "Ah, yes," he said, and though he spoke airily he gave her a stern look. "I suppose a few nights Hewney and Theodoros and I did sleep here after having a few scoops too many. Riotous times." He turned for a moment to Puzzle. "We poets have a weakness for strong drink because it sets the fancy free to roam." He patted Brigid on the bum, as much to get her attention as anything else, and tried to slip her a ha'fish. "Now, my girl, if you don't mind, my companion and I have important business to discuss." She stared at him and his proffered coin. "Be a good lass, Brigid—that is your name, if I remember correctly, yes . . . ?"

Afterward he was glad she had not been holding a mug or a tray, but even the bare-handed slap on the back of the skull was enough to bring tears to his eyes and pitch his new hat into the ashes at the front of the hearth.

"You dog!" she said, so loud that half the crowded tavern turned to watch. "A few days past the walls of the inner keep and you think your pizzle has turned to solid silver? At least when Nevin Hewney falls asleep on top of a girl, drooling and farting and limp as custard, he doesn't pretend he's done her a favor."

He could hear laughter from the other patrons as she flounced away, but his ears were ringing from the blow and their gibes were no louder in his throbbing head than the noise of a distant river.

With a few tankards of ale in his belly, even the watery piss that Conary sold at the Mint, Puzzle had become positively animated. "But I thought you said the other day that you were commanded to go with the soldiers," the old man asked, wiping a thin line of froth from his lips. "To be a war-poet or somesuch."

Much of the good cheer had gone out of him now, but Tinwright did his best. "Oh, that. I spoke of it to the castellan—Lord Naynor, his name is?"

"Nynor." Puzzle frowned a little. "Not a mirthful fellow. Never been able to make him laugh. Thinks too much, I suppose."

"Yes, well. I was eager to go, of course, but Nynor felt I would be of more use if I stayed here—to lift up the spirit of the princess, with her brother away and all." In actuality, it had been Nynor who had come to him to make arrangements—he had heard of Princess Briony's offhand commission through some source Tinwright could not even guess—and Tinwright had gone down on his knees, even wept a little, swearing that it was all a mistake, that someone had misunderstood one of Briony's offhand remarks. Nynor had said he would have to speak with her himself, but that had been days ago and the prince regent and the army had ridden out since then, so Tinwright felt he was now fairly safe. Still, even thinking about it, he could barely restrain a shudder. Matty Tinwright going to war! Against monsters and giants and the gods alone knew what else! It didn't even bear thinking about. No, his smooth skin and handsome face were suited only for battles of the more intimate kind, the sort that took place in beds and secluded hallways, and from which both combatants walked away unharmed.

"I asked to go," Puzzle suddenly proclaimed. "They've no use for me here, those two. Not like their father. There was a good man. He understood my jokes and tricks." In a moment he had gone from chucklingly cheerful to teary-eyed. "They say he is still alive, King Olin, but I fear he will never come back. Ah, that good man. And now this war and all." He looked up, blinking. "Who are we fighting? Fairies? I understand none of it."

"Nobody does," Tinwright said, and here he was again on firm ground. "The rumormongers are running mad even in the castle, so who knows what they are saying out in the city?" He pointed to a group of men standing over a table, smoking long pipes and sharing a broadsheet. "Do you know what that scurrilous pamphlet claims? That the princess regent and her brother have murdered Gailon Tolly, the Duke of Summerfield." He shook his head, genuinely angry. To think that someone could speak such calumnies of the lovely young woman who had recognized Tinwright's quality and raised him up from the undeserved muck of places like this to the heights for which he was meant . . . He shook his head and downed the remains of his fourth or fifth tankard. He would have liked another, but Brigid was still serving and he dared not call her over again.

Puzzle was looking around, too. "She's very pretty, that girl."

"Brigid? Yes, pretty enough, but her heels are as round as the full moon." He scowled into the lees at the bottom of his mug. "Be grateful you are past the age of such things, my good fellow. Women like that are the bane of man's existence. A night's innocent tumble and they feel they can tie a string to your freedom and drag it around behind them like a child's toy."

"Past the age . . . ?" Puzzle said, a little doubtfully perhaps, or merely wistfully, then fell silent. He was quiet for such a long time that Tinwright finally looked up, thinking that the old man had fallen asleep, but instead Puzzle's eyes were wide. Tinwright stared around, wondering if perhaps Brigid's dress had come entirely unfastened, but the old fellow was staring at the tavern door as it swung closed, shutting out the rainy afternoon.

"Curfew tonight," Conary shouted from behind his table on the far side of the room. "Closing time is sunset bell. The jack-o'-lanterns will be here soon, so drink up, drink up!"

"But I thought . . ." Puzzle said slowly.

"What?" Matty Tinwright set down his tankard, considered another drink, then tried to decide whether he would prefer a trip to the Mint's unspeakable privy or to stand in the pouring rain emptying his bladder against a wall on the way back. "What is it?"

"I . . . I just saw someone I know. Chaven the physician—the royal physician. He was talking to that man in the hood over there." Puzzle stirred. "No, the one in the hood's gone too. Maybe they went out together."

"What is so strange in that? A physician of all people must know the good that ale will do—the best physick of all."

"But he is gone . . . or rather he is not gone, obviously." Puzzle shook his head. "He has left the castle, gone on a sudden journey. Everyone was surprised. Ah, well, I suppose he has come back."

"Clearly, he has been somewhere dire indeed, if this is the first place he visits on his return." Tinwright heaved himself up onto his feet. He was beginning to think that maybe he had drunk a bit more than he had thought, lost count somewhere. "Come, let us go back ourselves. They are a poor lot here at the Mint, despite the occasional doctor or royal poet." He helped Puzzle up. "Or king's jester, of course," he added kindly. "No, they do not understand quality here."

Briony had always liked Barrick's rooms better than her own in some ways. She had the view down to the Privy Garden from her sitting room, and that was pretty enough, especially on sunny days, and on rainy days the doves all perched on the windowsill, murmuring, and it felt as cozy as pulling a blanket over her knees. But from her window the stony bulk of Wolfstooth Spire took up most of the horizon, so her view was foreshortened, limited to the local and domestic. Barrick, though, could see out across the rooftops from the small window in his dressing chamber, past the forest of chimneys and all the way to the sea. As Briony stared out of her brother's window now, the Tower of Autumn was glinting white and brick red, and beyond it lay the open ocean, blue-black and moody. The little storm that had just passed had left the sky sullen, but it was still heartening somehow to look out across all this space and open sky, across the roofs of the castle like mountainous small countries, and to think about how big the world was.

Did they give him these rooms on purpose, because he was the son and I was the daughter? For me the gardens, the quiet places, the old walls, to let me grow used to the idea of a life confined, but for him this view of the world that is part of his birthright—the sky, life, and adventure stretching out in all directions . . . ?

And of course now her brother was riding out into that world and she was terrified for him, but also envious. *It is two separate betrayals, not only to leave me behind at all, but to leave me with the throne and all those people clamoring, begging, arguing* . . . Still, it didn't diminish her love for him, but changed the powerful connection into something like an overfond child who wouldn't stop pestering but could not be safely put down.

Oh, and Barrick is in danger, if what that strange potboy said is true. But there was nothing she could do—nothing she could do about anything except to wait and prepare for the worst. *And the gods awakening, the strange man said, wouldn't explain it. What did that mean? What does any of this mean? When precisely did the whole world begin to run mad?*

A cloud slid past. A single ray of sunlight angled down, dazzled for a moment on the Tower of Summer, then was swallowed up in gray again. Briony sighed and turned to her ladies. "I must dress."

"But, Highness," said Moina, startled. "These clothes are . . . they . . . you . . ."

"I have told you what I will do and why. We are at war, and soon that will be more than words. My brother is gone off with the army. I am the last of the Eddons in this castle."

"There is your stepmother," Rose offered timidly. "The child . . ."

"Until that baby is born, I am the last of the Eddons in Southmarch." Briony heard the iron in her own voice and was amused and appalled. *What am I becoming?* "I told you, I cannot merely be myself any longer," she said. "I am my brother, too. I am my whole family." She saw the looks on her ladies' faces and made a noise of exasperation. "No, I am not going mad. I know what I'm doing."

But do I, truly? A person can fall into a rage of grief or despair and do themselves and others harm. Other madnesses could creep into the sufferer's heart so stealthily that they did not even realize they had gone mad. Was this really just fury against the scorn of men and a desire to hold her brother close in the only way now left to her? Or was this rage against ordinary courtly dress a kind of fever that had taken her, that had gradually grown to un-woman her entirely? *Oh, gods and goddesses, I ache so! They are all gone! Every day I want to weep. Or curse.*

She spoke none of this, or let any of it show on her face except perhaps by a certain angry stiffness that silenced Rose and Moina completely. "I must dress," she said again, and stood as straight as she could, as proudly upright as any queen or empress, while they began to clothe her in her brother's clothes.

At the very last the ladies pretended they could not do it, that they did not understand the working of the thing, although it was much more simple than any lady's garment, so she put on the heavy sword belt herself and buckled it tight across her hips before sliding the long blade into the sheath.

If it was a weather change, it was a strange one. Vansen stood on the hillside behind the scouts and looked out across the expanse of valley, at the Settland Road winding along at its bottom, and tried to make sense of what he felt. The air was close, but not from the nearness of any storm, although a heavy rain had swept through at midday and the road had been hard going for the rest of the afternoon. Neither was it a smell, although the air had a certain sour tang that reminded him of the burning season in autumn, of bonfires now two months past. Even the light seemed inexplicably strange, but for no reason he could name: the sky was darkening quickly now, the sun setting behind a slate-colored blanket of clouds, and the hillsides seemed unusually green against the dark pall, but it was nothing he had not seen hundreds of times.

It's because you're afraid, he told himself. *Because you crossed that line once and you're afraid you might find yourself behind it again. Because you've seen what's coming and you're afraid to meet it.*

All morning and afternoon they had encountered people fleeing the rape of Candlerstown, most merely hurrying ahead of rumors of its end, but some—almost all women and children lucky enough to have escaped in wagons—who had actually survived its destruction. The stories of these last were particularly terrifying and Tyne Aldritch and Vansen and the others had spent much of the afternoon trying to understand what it meant for them, vainly trying to concoct a strategy that could counter such nightmarish madness. The first few refugees' tales had so unsettled the soldiers who heard them, themselves conscripted farmers little different from the husbands and fathers these families had so recently lost to such ghastly enemies, that with Earl Tyne's permission Vansen had ridden ahead with a company of scouts to glean what information he could from the oncoming victims and then give them what aid he might before turning them aside to where outliers of the army could give them food and water, hoping to prevent the dreadful stories washing repeatedly across the main body of troops like waves of freezing water. Ferras Vansen already knew this second night out from Southmarch would be a grim, anxious camp; no sense in turning it into anything worse.

It was pointless, of course: those who couldn't stand even to hear about the terrible Twilight People would probably have scant chance of surviving a battle with them, but Vansen hoped that the fact of real combat would give men back their hearts no matter how frightened they were. Any enemy who could be touched, fought, killed, was better than the one you could only imagine.

He turned to Dab Dawley, one of the survivors of his own ill-fated expedition across the Shadowline. It was only with great reluctance and at the express order of Princess Briony that he had increased the responsibility of Mickael Southstead, whom he didn't trust very much at all—the night he was named a captain he had caused two bad fights back in Southmarch with his bragging—but young Dawley was a different story, cautious and thoughtful despite his years, and much more so since their shared adventure. Had it not been for his own desire to see what was ahead of them, Vansen would happily have let Dawley lead this scouting party himself, despite his lack of experience.

"I think we stay here tonight, Dab, or at least that is what I will suggest to Earl Tyne. Will you take the men down and start looking for water? It seems to me there should be a stream there, beyond that hillock."

Dawley nodded. The other scouts, wilderness veterans almost to a man, had heard the captain—there was no need for the formality of orders. They clicked softly to their mounts and started down the road.

A few hundred such as these and I might not fear even the Twilight folk, Vansen told himself, but he knew it was not true. Even standing in the midst of a thousand of the stoutest men in the world would not thaw a freezing, terrified heart.

The valley was full of fires. This close to home, they were still eating fresh meat and bread that could be broken without having to saw at it with a knife, which was a rare pleasure on march. Some of the guardsmen from Kertewall were playing pipes and singing. Despite the mournful Kertish tunes it was a pleasingly ordinary sound; Vansen was glad of it and certain that others felt the same.

He was wandering back toward the fire when he saw a figure standing at the crest of one of the low hills, inside the ring of sentries but not near any of them. He puzzled for a moment before he recognized it as Prince Barrick. Vansen was a little surprised, thinking that the prince would have preferred to be in the midst of Lord Aldritch and the other nobles, drinking and being waited upon, but Vansen knew from his experience with the royal family that the boy had always been odd and solitary.

But he's a boy no longer, I suppose. In fact, Barrick was the same sort of age Vansen himself had been when he first left home to seek his fortune in the city—an age when he had been certain that he was a man, despite no confirming proof. Watching Barrick, he could not help remembering Princess Briony's fear for her brother. Certainly the lad should be safe enough—he was scarcely two dozen yards from the nearest campfire—and Ferras Vansen had a respect for solitude that many others did not, but he couldn't help being anxious. *After all, Collum Dyer was within my arm's reach when he was taken.* It would be horror enough to have to tell that lovely, sad young woman that her brother had died honorably in battle—he couldn't imagine telling her the prince had been stolen by fairies right out of camp.

As he strode up the hill, the wet grass slapping at his legs, Vansen suddenly wondered what the Twilight People wanted. Although there had been few true wars during his lifetime, he had ample experience of violence and knew that there were some men who could only be stopped from taking what they wanted by strength, and some who feared that others meant to take what was theirs even when it was not true, that greed and fear lay at the bottom of most fights. But that army he had seen beyond the Shadowline, that array of the sublime and terrible, that ghastly, glorious host—what could *they* want? Why had they left the safety of their misty lands after two centuries or more, a time in which their original enemies had long since disappeared and new mortals unnumbered had been born, lived, and died again, all without knowing the shadow folk as anything but the stuff of old stories and evil dreams?

He fought a shudder. They were not men, not even animals, but demons, as he knew better than anyone, so how could a mere man hope to understand their reasons?

Young Barrick turned at his approach and watched for a moment before turning back to what he had been gazing at so intently—nothing, so far as Vansen could tell. "Prince Barrick, your pardon. Are you well?"

"Captain Vansen." The young man continued staring out at the night sky. The wind had herded the clouds away and the stars had come out. Ferras Vansen couldn't help remembering how, as a small child, he had once thought they were the cook fires of people like himself—sky shepherds, perhaps, living on the other side of the great bowl of the heavens, who called the fires of the Vansen family and their neighbors stars in turn.

"It is getting cold, Highness. Perhaps you would be more comfortable back with the others."

The prince didn't answer immediately. "What was it like?" he finally asked.

"What was it like . . . ?"

"Behind the Shadowline. Did it feel different? Smell different?"

"It was frightening, Highness, as I told you and your sister. Misty and dark. Confusing."

"Yes, but what was it *like?*" His bad arm was hidden in his cloak, but the other hand pointed at the sky. "Did you see the same stars—Demia's Ladder, the Horns?"

Vansen shook his head. "I can't quite remember now. It—it was all very much like a dream. Stars? I'm not sure."

Barrick nodded. "I have dreams about . . . about the other side. I know that now. I've had them all my life. I didn't really know what they were, but hearing what you said about . . ." He turned to fix Vansen with a surprisingly sharp glance. "You say you were frightened. Why? Were you afraid you'd die? Or was it something else?"

Vansen had to stop and think for a moment. "Afraid to die? Of course. The gods give us the fear of death so that we won't squander their gifts too lightly—so that we will use what is given us to the fullest. But that isn't what I felt there—that's not the whole of it, anyway."

Barrick smiled, although there was something incomplete in it. "*So we will use what is given us to the fullest.* You are a bit of a poet, Captain Vansen, aren't you?"

"No, Highness. I just . . . that is what the village priest taught me." He stiffened a little. "But I think it's true. Who knows what will happen to us in Kernios' cold hands?"

"Yes, who indeed?"

Now the memories of his days in the shadowland were seeping back, as though the lid he had put on them had been kicked loose. "I was afraid because the world there was strange to me. Because I could not trust my own senses. Because it made me feel like a madman."

"And there is nothing more frightening than that." Barrick was darkly pleased by something. "No, that is true, Captain Vansen." He peered at him again. "Do you have a first name?"

"Ferras, Highness. It is a common enough name in the dales."

"But Vansen isn't."

"My father was from the Vuttish Isles."

Barrick had turned back to the stars again. "But he made his home in Daler's Troth. Was he happy? Is he still alive?"

"He died, Highness, years ago now. He was happy enough. He always said he would trade all the wide ocean for a crofter's patch and good weather."

"Perhaps he was born out of his place," said Prince Barrick. "That happens, I think. Some of us live our whole lives as if we were dreaming, because we haven't found where we're meant to be—stumbling through shadows, terrified, strangers just as you were in the Twilight Lands." He suddenly tucked his other hand under his cloak. "You're right, Captain Vansen—it's getting cold. I think I will have some wine and try to sleep."

The prince turned and walked down the hill.

He is still a boy, really, for all his philosophy, Vansen decided as he followed several paces behind, alert for any threat, even here among the campfires. *A child—clever, angry, and fearful. The gods grant that he lives long enough for some of that knowing to turn into wisdom.*

The murmur of disapproving conversation, which at times threatened to become a roar, had begun the moment Briony walked into the room and had not stopped since she took her place at the head of the table. Meals in the Great Hall were seldom quiet or restful, and on any other day she would have taken something quietly in her chambers, but she had decided on a brave show and she would take what came.

Hierarch Sisel sat on her right. Brone, although a few others at the table outranked him, took the place on her left because he was the lord constable and the castle was at war—or soon to be so. The hierarch, after an initial widening of the eyes and pursing of the lips when he saw her, had made polite conversation just as though she were wearing proper womanly clothing; she was not certain whether she admired this or disliked it. Brone was disgusted, of course, but she had come to know him well enough to feel certain that his annoyance had more to do with her making what he considered an unnecessary spectacle of herself at a delicate time than any particular disapproval of this provocative unsexing. The lord constable had other things on his mind he deemed more important, and he clearly meant to use the stir over the arrival of the main courses to speak to her.

As the chicken carcasses were carried away, and the huge half-bullock sweating in its own juices was carted in, surrounded by what to Briony's taste was an overly festive array of peacocks roasted and then dressed again in their own feathers, the dogs barked excitedly and snuffled in the rushes for dropped bones. She reached down and scratched a furry head, glad somebody here was deservedly happy, anyway.

"The work on the fortifications is largely done," Brone told her quietly. "But the strongest walls will not hold if the hearts inside are weak. The nobles are restive. Several have gone already, preferring to take their chances in their own homes, or even to take to the sea lanes if things seem to go badly."

"I know." She had granted enough spurious requests in the last days, thin excuses that she felt certain she could pull to tatters in an instant if she chose. "Let them go, Lord Brone. Those are not the folk we'll want at our sides if things do grow worse rather than merely *seem* bad, as they do now." She glanced at Hendon Tolly and his sister-in-law Elan, halfway down the table but in a different world, surrounded by admirers like Durstin Crowel, the Baron of Graylock, all but the girl laughing broadly at one of Tolly's jokes. "In truth, it's too bad they do not all leave. Southmarch might be harder to defend, but the waiting would be more pleasant."

"But that is just the thing . . ." Brone leaned back and waited for one of the squires to drop a slice of beef onto his trencher. "For every fainthearted noble that rides off south or sets sail to the east," he said when the youth had moved on, "a retinue of men-at-arms goes with him, and we can scarcely afford to lose a one of them."

Briony waved her hand: what could she do? One could not compel love, she had decided, especially not for the child when it was the father who had earned it. All the faces that had come before her, mouthing reasons why they were urgently needed on the family lands or promising to return with a fresh muster of troops had begun to look as distant and dead as the likenesses in the portrait hall. But she would remember them, if one day the sun shone on Southmarch again. She would recall who left and she would most certainly recall who stayed, and she would punish and reward them accordingly. She owed that to her father and Kendrick, now that they were helpless to protect this place both had loved so much.

She was startled to realize that she had been thinking about her father again as though he were dead. She made the sign of pass-evil, something she had scarcely done since childhood when she learned it from one of her nursemaids. *He is well,* she told herself. *I will write him another letter tonight, send it out with a courier on a ship going south.* She felt a wash of shame. *I have told him nothing of this coming war, if that is what it is, and only the barest details of Kendrick's death.* But was this the sort of news to send to a man imprisoned, that his kingdom stood threatened, and so strangely? Even prisoned in Hierosol, he would have heard about Kendrick, and of Shaso's imprisonment, whether or not he had received her last letter—was that not heartache enough? She suddenly missed her father so badly she found it hard to breathe. Barrick, too. She wished her twin were beside her now, that they could escape together later to discuss all these yawning, greasy-mouthed courtiers, Lady Comfrey M'Neel with her hair already half-undone after drinking too much wine, fat Lord Bratchard who saw himself against all evidence as a wit and a ladies' man, who used to paw Briony's hair and face when she was small and tell her what a pretty young woman she was growing to be.

I hope that if this castle falls, the Twilight People take the lot of them and march them off to Vansen's foggy shadowlands with chains around their necks.

It was a stunningly uncharitable thought, and ignored the many kind and good hearts around her, but at this moment the shout of conversation and clanking of cups and knives seemed little better than the clamor of the barnyard, and these people, for all their finery, little better than pigs shoving to reach the trough.

Hierarch Sisel was trying to say something to her, but at that moment a loud bray of laughter from handsome, stupid Durstin Crowel pricked at her like a needle and she flinched. The Baron of Graylock was roaring at something that Hendon Tolly had said, laughing so hard that he choked on his wine and sprayed some on his ruff and down his front, occasioning fresh laughter from the others around him. The author of the remark met her eye, his lips drawn in a satisfied smile. She knew, or felt certain she did, who was the butt of Hendon Tolly's jest.

"Lord Tolly," she called, "like Erilo putting a blessing on the grape harvest, it seems you are bringing much-needed mirth to our table tonight, when otherwise people might be sitting quiet and thoughtful, wondering what the gods have in store for us."

Beside her Brone cleared his throat and on the other side the hierarch tried his remark again, some innocuous comment about how all the fortification work had made him think about some additions to the temple, but she was paying neither of them any attention. She and Hendon Tolly had locked eyes. She was waiting for his reply, and now others were, too: a few dogs beneath the table were growling and playing tug-o-war with a bone, but otherwise the room had grown remarkably still.

"It is a credit to your hospitality, Princess Briony, that you provide us many diversions. You have given us so many interesting things to think about that I had almost forgotten that I am mourning the loss of my brother, Duke Gailon."

"Yes, we have all been saddened by Gailon's disappearance," she said, ignoring another warning cough from Avin Brone. "It was especially a blow because his departure from this house followed so soon after the death of my own brother."

A palpable unease had fallen over the table. Even Crowel, who had been ready to laugh, sat with his mouth open, surprised.

"We are all unhappy," Avin Brone said loudly. "To have lost two such noble men so close together . . . well, we can only pray that Lord Tolly's brother comes back to us safe."

Tolly raised an eyebrow and smiled a little, content to wait and see which way she would take this—whether she would acknowledge Brone's offered flag of truce. His self-confidence was itself an insult: Briony found it maddening that he should feel so secure as to bandy words with the reigning princess in her own hall, at her own table, and then leave it to her to grasp for peace if she wished.

She did not wish. Not tonight.

"Yes, certainly many people hope that Gailon Tolly appears again after such a mysterious disappearance. My brother Kendrick, though, will not be coming back, not in this circle of the world."

The Tolly eyebrow climbed yet higher. It was a strangeness she could not get used to, that he was both so much like and unlike his brother. She had never liked Gailon Tolly, had found him dour and self-righteous and even a little dim, but his younger brother had a smell of sulfur about him, a dark glint of something deep and more than a little mad. "Is Her Highness suggesting that my brother—my brother the duke, the head of a family that has served Southmarch for centuries—might have had something to do with the death of the prince regent?"

"Here now!" said Hierarch Sisel, and though it trembled, his voice was surprisingly strong. He had spoken even before Brone, a demonstration of his dismay. "This is a terrible thing to suggest or even to think, and may the gods forgive us all for such talk when our soldiers are riding into danger."

"Well said," growled Avin Brone. There were a few nods around the table as the nobles of better—or at least fainter—heart reacted with relief to the puncturing of the growing tension. "No one here suspects Duke Gailon of anything and we all pray for his safe return. The guilty man is chained in the stronghold even as we speak, and we have found not the slightest suggestion that he had any confederates."

But Briony was suddenly remembering old Puzzle's strange report of Gailon's visit to Kendrick's chamber, as well as Brone's own revelation that his spy had seen agents he thought were the Autarch's at Summerfield Court. She kept her mouth shut, but she did not move her eyes from Hendon Tolly's stony stare.

Let it go, Briony, she told herself. *This is pointless. No, worse than pointless.*

His lips quirked. He was enjoying the moment.

"Of course Lord Brone is right," she said aloud. It was like swallowing a bitter remedy. "The Summerfields are always welcome here—we are family, after all, heirs of Anglin himself and Kellick Eddon. After the cares of the day, I was merely curious to hear the joke that those around you found so cheering."

Hendon Tolly's smile did not falter, but it definitely grew smaller and his eyes narrowed a little as he considered. "It was nothing, Princess," he said at last. "A bit of drollery. I do not even remember it now."

Lord Brone was murmuring at her ear again, trying to get her attention. Briony was weary. It was time to let it go—let it all go. There were problems enough, the gods knew, without allowing this man under her skin. She nodded, letting him have a more or less graceful retreat, but now Durstin Crowel tugged drunkenly at Tolly's arm.

"You remember it, Hendon," he said. "It was very droll indeed. About . . ." he affected a whisper the entire table could hear, ". . . *Prince Barrick.*"

Something grabbed at Briony's heart. A low groan escaped from the lord constable. "Ah," she said. "Was it? Then I really think you should share it."

Tolly gave the Baron of Graylock a look of contempt, then turned back

to her. He took a swallow of wine; when he was finished, his face was composed again, but she could still see that strange light dancing in his eye—
not drunkenness, but something more permanent. "Very well," he said.
"Since both my friend and my princess insist. I was much taken with your
raiment, Briony—your clothes."

She felt herself grow stiff and cold-masked as a statue. He had deliberately left out her title, as though they were both children again and he was
taunting her, the mere girl who wanted to play with her betters. "Yes? I am
glad it impresses you, Hendon. These are warlike times so I thought that a
more warlike garb might be in order."

"Yes, of course." He inclined his head a little. "Of course. Well, all I was
wondering is, if you are wearing *that* . . ." he made a disdainful gesture,
"does it mean that Prince Barrick is riding to battle in a dress?"

The shocked murmur and the few startled gasps of laughter had scarcely
begun when Briony found herself standing, her chair tumbled over behind
her. Brone grabbed for her arm—she almost struck him for trying—but he
could not stop her. Her sword hissed from the scabbard.

"If you think my clothes amusing," she said through teeth clenched so
hard her jaw would ache later, "perhaps you will find my blade amusing, too."

"Princess!" hissed Sisel, shocked, but he was not such a fool as to grab at
someone with a naked blade quivering in her hand, woman or no.

Hendon Tolly stood up slowly, pleased and not doing much about hiding it. His hand dropped to his own hilt and caressed it briefly, his eyes all
the time fixed on hers. "Amusing indeed," he said, "but of course I could
not raise my hand against the princess regent, even for such diverting sport.
Perhaps we could have a test with children's weapons sometime, so that no
one takes harm."

Her heart was thundering now. She was tempted to charge him, to force
him to unsheathe, no matter the result, if only to wipe that mocking satisfaction from his lean face. She did not even care that he was a well-known
swordsman and she was simply the pupil of another famous blade, a pupil
who had scarcely practiced since the summer and could not hope to equal
Tolly even on her very best day. It would almost be worth it to force him
to kill her in self-defense. Nobody would be laughing then, and all her cares
would be over.

But I'd never see Barrick again, or Father. Her arm was shaking badly. She
lowered the blade until the tip clicked against the table leg. *And one of the
bloody Tollys would wind up as regent until Anissa's child is born—if they let it live.*

"Get out of my sight," she said to Hendon Tolly, then turned her eye on the rest of the table, the rows of pale, gaping faces, some still with lumps of gravied meat congealing in their fingers, arrested halfway from plate to mouth. "All of you. *All of you!*"

But it was Briony herself who slammed the sword back into its sheath and then turned and stalked out of the Great Hall, scattering servants as she went. She managed to wait until the door fell shut behind her before letting the flood of angry tears overwhelm her.

33

The Pale Things

STAR ON THE SHIELD:

All the ancestors are singing
The stones are piled one on another in wet grass
Two newborn calves wait trembling

—from *The Bonefall Oracles*

IT WAS A GRIM THING TO STAND at the Northmarch cross-road where he had stood only the month before and see the hills now smothered by dark vines and nodding, bruise-colored flowers. The soldiers whispered among themselves and scuffed their feet like restless cattle, but it was a far more disturbing sight for Ferras Vansen. He had seen such vegetation before, but forty miles or more to the west. It had spread far in a short time.

"Where are those scouts?" asked Earl Tyne for the fifth or sixth time in an hour. He slapped his gloved hands together as though the day were bitterly cold, though the sun had not set and the wind was mild for Ondekamene. The war leader had dumped his helmet on the ground like an empty bucket and pushed back his arming cap; his coarse, gray-shot hair stood up in tufts. He stared out at the strange sheen of the meadows and the black blossoms moving in the breeze like the heads of children watching them silently from the deep grass. "They should have been back by now."

"Doiney and the others are good men, my lord." Vansen looked across at the resting soldiers. At any other time after such a long halt they would have gone straying off into the grass like untended sheep, but instead they stood uncomfortably where they had stopped, as if prisoned by the edges of the road. These sons of farmers and shopkeepers wanted no part of the thorny vines or the unnatural, oily-looking flowers.

"You said you've seen this before, Vansen."

"Yes, Lord Aldritch. With my troop, in the north of Silverside. Just a little while before . . . before things began to go wrong."

"Well, blood of the gods, keep your mouth shut about that, will you?" Tyne scowled. "This lot are all about ready to turn tail and run all the way back to Southmarch." He glared at a shaven-headed mantis making an elaborate show of wafting a bowl of incense around in the middle of the crossroad, moaning and singing as he went about his task of banishing evil spirits. Many of the men watched this spectacle with obvious unease. "I'm going to have that priest's head off," the Earl of Blueshore growled, almost to himself.

"I think this lot will be all right when the time comes, my lord. Many of them have fought on the Brenland borders or against the Kertish hill bandits. It's the waiting that's hard on them."

Tyne took a drink from his saddle-cup and looked at the guard captain for a long, considering moment. "It's hard on all of us—that's the cursed thing. Bad enough waiting for the enemy to show themselves when you know you're fighting mortal men. What are they supposed to make of all this . . . ?" He waved his hand at the poisoned hills.

Ferras Vansen was glad the earl didn't really expect an answer.

"Ah," the older man said suddenly, with real relief in his voice. "There they are." He squinted. "It is them, isn't it?"

"Yes, lord." Vansen also felt the tightness in his chest loosen a bit. The sentries had been expected back at noon and the sun was on the hilltops now. "They are riding fast."

"They look as though they have something to say, don't they?" Tyne turned and stared back at the line of soldiers on the road. It had been a full day or more since they had encountered the last refugees from Candlerstown, and although the tales were terrible, almost unbelievable, their presence had at least proved that men could cross these hills in safety. But since they had passed the last of those stragglers, the army of Southmarch had traveled through empty, near-silent lands, and now a stir was moving through the ranks at the sight of the distant scouts. Behind the soldiers the first row of drovers, anticipating that the train would soon move out again, began whipping back the oxen who had strayed a little distance from the road to graze. "Ride out to them, bring them straight through to me," commanded Tyne. "I think under that tree, there, just a short way up the hill. That will let us talk away from sharp ears."

"Perhaps we should set the men to making camp, lord," Vansen suggested. "It is getting late to ride much farther and it will occupy them."

"A good idea, but let's hear what the scouts say first." The earl turned to his squire. "Tell Rorick and Mayne and Sivney Fiddicks to join me on the hill there. The young prince, too, of course—wouldn't do to leave him out. Oh, and Brenhall—he's probably under a tree somewhere, sleeping off his noon meal."

Vansen barely heard the last of this as the earl's other squire helped him into the saddle, then he spurred away to meet the scouts.

"But how many *are* they, curse it?" Tyne tugged at his mustache and looked as though he would like to slap Gar Doiney. "How many times must I ask?"

"I'm sorry, your lordship." The scout's voice was dry and cracked, as if he didn't use it much. "I've heard you, sire, it's just hard to answer, like. With mist and such we can only just tell they're camped on the hilltop and in the trees. We rode around the long way for a better look—that's why we're so long back." He shook his head. The scar between Doiney's eye and mouth that pulled up his lip and made him seem to smirk had gotten him into trouble before now, and Vansen guessed it might have had something to do with the man's choice of a usually solitary profession—but Vansen felt sure that even in his anger Tyne couldn't fail to mark the skittish look on the scout's weathered, bony face. Even a hardened, taciturn campaigner like Doiney was disturbed by this unknown, unnatural enemy. "Come back with us, sire—there must be an hour still of light. You'll see. It's hard to make out anything. But there are hundreds there, thousands perhaps."

Tyne waved his hand. "It's only that it is dangerous to have to guess. At least we know *where* they are."

"And you are certain there are no more of them anywhere else?" young Prince Barrick asked. He had joined the circle on the hillside, the nobles standing close together to provide each other some protection from the stiffening wind. The prince looked interested—almost too interested, Vansen thought, as if he had forgotten that the men unrolling their bedrolls would soon have to cross swords with this interesting phenomenon, that some of them would almost certainly die. It was hard for Vansen not to feel a little resentment on behalf of Dab Dawley and all the other soldiers not much older than the prince who would not be surrounded and protected as Barrick would be, to make certain their experience of battle didn't become too dangerous.

But who is it asked me to take care of the lad, to protect him? Was it the prince himself? No, it was his sister. Perhaps I do him a disservice. Vansen was unsure again: sometimes Barrick Eddon seemed a mere boy, younger even than his years, petulant and anxious; at other moments he seemed a hundred years old, far beyond anything so mundane as fear of death.

"If Your Highness means perhaps it is a token force to draw us, with the rest in ambush," said Doiney, awkward and uncomfortable at speaking to royalty, "then I say anything is possible, your good Highness, but if they have another force squirreled away, they are either so small they are hiding under the clovers or they are floating on a cloud in the sky, like, or whatever it is they say fairy folk do. Because of the morning mist we did not mark the ones on the hill until our way back, and we rode far across these lands on both sides of the Settland Road and up the far reaches of the old Northmarch way as well, across all kinds of ground." He stopped, clearly trying to think it all through, to make sure that he had said what he meant to say. Vansen had never heard so many words out of the man in all the years he had known him. "Meaning to say, Highness, by your pardon, there are none others we can see for miles beyond except for those as are nearly on top of us."

"What do they look like?" asked Rorick, his voice a little too gruffly ordinary to be quite believable.

"Hard to tell," Doiney told him. "Apologies, your lordship, but it's that cursed mist and those trees. But we could see some of them in what looked like good, plain armor, not much different than you or me, and there were horses and tents and . . . and all you'd expect. But there were other shapes too, in the trees . . ." He trailed off, made the pass-evil. "Shapes that didn't seem right at all, what we saw of them."

Tyne stepped backward until the tree was almost against his spine. He peered out into the distance, although the wooded high place the Twilight People seemed to have chosen as their camp was blocked from view by the intervening hills. "First things first, then," he said. "Vansen, we need a string of pickets across the hills behind them and some miles down both roads, changed often enough that they won't start to see shapes in the night that aren't there, but do see the ones that truly are. They must keep ears open, too. If there is some other force coming—if it *is* a trap—we must know about it before they arrive. And let's have the rest start making camp." Tyne's sergeant ran down the hill to give the orders.

Vansen leaned over and had a few quick words with Gar Doiney as the nobles talked quietly among themselves. ". . . But the others that Muchmore took out have been back since noontime," Vansen finished, "so tell him it's them I want out, and you get your fellows something to drink and eat."

Doiney nodded, then bowed to the nobles and made a clumsy, unaccustomed leg for the prince before he swung himself back onto his horse again. He cantered back toward his little troop of horsemen, visibly relieved to escape the councils of the great.

Vansen stared at the blossoming campfires. They were a reassuring sight against the descending twilight and he decided that Earl Tyne was a thoughtful commander: it was doubtful the enemy was ignorant of their arrival, and the fires would give the men much-needed heart's ease through a long, worrisome night.

"So what do we do, then, Lord Aldritch?" asked the prince. "Do you think they will they stand and fight?"

"If they won't, then we have learned something useful," Tyne told him. "But do not doubt that I fear a trap as much as you do, Highness, although I suspect we may be overthinking. Still, if they break and run we should not follow them, in case they mean to lead us into the place we have heard about, beyond the Shadowline where everyone runs mad."

"Almost everyone. Not our Captain Vansen." It was hard to tell how Prince Barrick meant it, as compliment or gibe.

Vansen broke the short silence. "If my experience is to be of use, then I must remind everyone that my men and I had no idea we were crossing over into . . . into those lands . . . so I think Earl Tyne speaks wisely. If we best them, even if we seem to break them, still we should go slowly and carefully."

Barrick Eddon stared at him for a moment, gave a sober nod, then looked around at the others and realized they were all watching him. "What, do you wait for me? I'm not a general, not even a soldier yet. I've said that and I mean it. Aldritch, you and the others must decide."

The Earl of Blueshore cleared his throat. "Well, Highness, then I say we must be alert and on guard all this evening, and double the usual sentries— and that is not counting your pickets, Vansen. If these shadow folk do not stir, then in the morning when the light comes back, we will go up and test their strength. I do not think any of us much wants to go against them in these unfamiliar fields when the sun is setting."

There were nods and a few grunts of agreement, but otherwise nobody said anything. There was no need.

Chert had been up and down the shore of the quicksilver sea a hundred times, it seemed, calling and calling until he was quite dizzy, with no reply except echoes. He had discovered no hint of a way across the liquid metal, no bridge, no mooring post, and—as best he could tell in the inconstant, flickering light—no boat on the shore at the far side. He had discovered one thing, though: somewhere in the blue-and-rose-shot darkness above his head some sort of cleft must open to the distant surface, a rock chimney of sorts where the fumes could disperse into the air above Brenn's Bay. Chert knew enough about quicksilver to know that if this were the true stuff, unaired, he likely would be not just light-headed but dead or dying.

He wondered if that could be the answer to the puzzle—could the boy have somehow come down onto the island from above? But what had Beetledown been following if it hadn't been Flint's scent? And how could the boy have gotten down from such a height? The rock face on the side of the silver sea—the side Chert couldn't reach—was distant from the island, at least as far from it as the side where he stood. He had a momentary, fanciful vision of the child somehow drifting down like a mote of dust or a bit of mushroom spore, but that was ridiculous. Flint might have come from behind the Shadowline, he might be a good climber, but he had given no sign whatsoever of being able to fly.

Still, Chert walked back to the slope below the jut of stone balcony where he himself had entered and stared up the jagged face, scouting with his eye up the deer track—*the ghost-deer track* as he now had to think of it—wondering if there was some other way across from near the Maze itself, some high path made invisible by a trick of the light. Sighing—a sigh that the thick, hot air quickly turned into a wheeze and then a cough—he clambered back up the slope.

He paused on the balcony of the Maze, peering out at the weird glow of the Shining Man that filled the great cavern without fully illuminating it, then took out his remaining chunk of lantern-coral to make his way back through the Maze. He was glad he had reclaimed it and did not have to traverse the labyrinth in darkness again—it had been too much like his age-ceremony, too much like that sense of helplessness when he had been forced to march without touching any of his peers, following the voice of an acolyte he could not see, a voice made strange and inhuman by the dark and the echoes. But this time he would have light. . . .

How did Flint get through the Maze, then? It was a question he should have asked before, and Chert was again angry with himself. Did Flint go to the Salt Pool first for a piece of Boulder's wares? Somehow Chert didn't believe it—the little man would have said something. But how could the child have made his way through the Maze in utter blackness otherwise?

For that matter, how did he find his way around down here at all? It was a mystery to rival the strangest parts of the tale of Kernios and his fabulous battles.

Chert paused for a short rest, wondering what time of day it was now, since even his Funderling sense of how time passed in the skyless depths had been compromised by this place, then slowly made his way back through the twisting Maze. He emerged into the soft, warm light of Emberstone Reach without having discovered a single hint of how the boy might have made his way across the Sea in the Depths, or even any sign of Flint's passage at all. Chert turned and began to make his weary way through the Maze again, more and more certain he would never know what had happened to the boy, but this time, in his exhaustion, he took a wrong turning and found himself in a section of the labyrinth he had not entered before. He could tell because it felt different beneath his feet, and he realized for the first time that the route between the Reach and the feature called the Balcony had been worn low in the middle over the centuries by the shuffling passage of innumerable feet. He also abruptly understood at least one of the ways that the acolytes made their way through the Maze in darkness. Now he found himself in a part of it where the floor stones were smoothly level, as if no one had ever walked on them before.

He fought down a moment of panic. Even if he was lost, surely he would be no worse off here than wandering the shore of the quicksilver sea. The temple brothers, if they came, were the guardians of the Maze. They should know its every corner.

Still, he could not forget his own proverbial bad luck. *They should, yes. But perhaps they don't.*

Chert did his best to retrace his steps, but he had been distracted when he chose the wrong path and couldn't remember how long he had walked or how many times he had turned before realizing his mistake. Chert held his glowing chunk of coral up to the slate walls, seeking some sort of clue, but although they were covered with the same indecipherable carvings as the Maze's more familiar reaches—vast, wall-wide figures with huge eyes and contorted limbs, as well as curls and dots of what looked like writing but in no script he had seen anywhere else—it was all too much the same from wall to wall and room to room to help him find his way.

Still, I've seen what not many other than the Metamorphic Brothers can have seen, he thought, recalling his journey through blackness in his coming-of-age ceremony. *What does it all mean? Can the brothers read it?*

The face and words of Brother Nickel came back to him suddenly—the odd look in the man's eyes as he told of their elder, Grandfather Sulphur, and his dreams that *". . . An hour is coming when Old Night will reach out . . . that our days of freedom are over."* Chert shivered despite the thick heat of the place. Here in the depths, wandering beneath the eyes of these supernatural beings, it was easy to feel the breath of Old Night on the back of his neck.

He turned sharply, suddenly convinced that something was following him, but the corridor behind him was empty. *I am making it worse,* he thought. *I should stop and wait until the temple brothers come.*

And if the light from his coral finally died while he waited? Darkness had never frightened Chert before, but now it was a dreadful thought.

He turned another corner and found himself in a dead-end facing three stone walls. Vast faces carved on those walls stared down at him so that he felt like a child surrounded by angry parents. He let out a little gasp of surprise and heard it echo and fade, but before he stopped walking he could hear something else as well, a hollowness in his footfalls, an echo that had not been there before. It confused him—for a moment he thought someone else was in the Maze with him—but then he crouched down and held the gleaming coral close. He stared at the scratches on the stone flags, then rapped on them with his knuckle. The sound was unquestionably different.

Chert pried at the edge of one of the stones and to his astonishment it rose a little in his hands, shuddering as it slid out of its collar of ancient mortar. Then, as he strained and heaved, it was not just one that rose, but four stones together. He got the fingers of both hands under it and, growling and moaning with the strain, lifted the whole mass like the cover of a cistern and slid it rasping to one side. The conjoined stones made a rough square less than a big-one's yard across and were no thicker than the width of Chert's closed fist. Beneath the spot where they had lain was darkness.

A little heat and a stronger smell of the quicksilver sea floated up from the opening. Chert leaned over and poked the coral light into it. Stairs, steep stairs, wound down and away before vanishing in the depths. He sat up, rubbing his head. Was this what the boy had found? Or was it merely some other part of the Mysteries, a path that would lead him to a worse fate even than being stranded in darkness in the Maze?

It's not like I've anything better to do, he told himself. *And if the Elders are angry with me . . . well, surely this won't make it any worse.*

He had heard better arguments, but he carefully let himself down through the opening, then squatted on one of the lower steps to look as far down the crude little stairwell as he could, just in case the whole thing might come to a sudden end a few yards deeper and fall away beneath his feet, pitching him down into some abyss. Although the tunnel looked far less carefully finished in its construction than the rest of the Maze, it still seemed solid Funderling work and there were no sudden drops in view. As he cautiously inched down a few more steps, he looked up and saw that a slot had been cut into the bottom of one of the four stones that covered the hole, a handhold to drag the cover back into place from below.

Not very likely I'll be doing that, he thought, but he wondered how Flint could have managed to do it if he had descended these stairs. The boy was wiry, but was he that strong?

All this thinking gave Chert another idea and he crawled back out of the hole. He untied the shirt he had been wearing around his waist since he had got it back from Beetledown—it was far too hot down here for him to have felt any need of it—and tossed it out to the mouth of the dead-end so that someone in the passage would be able to see it without turning the corner.

With the stone cover off the opening, I couldn't give the temple brothers a better idea of where I've gone if I wrote them a letter.

Feeling a little heartened despite his worries over what might be waiting in this narrow place, Chert Blue Quartz began to make his way down the stairs.

Either the quicksilver vapors were truly much stronger here or something else about the downward passage was . . . *strange* . . . because Chert was finding it hard to keep his mind on the very important task of not falling down the narrow steps.

The stairwell was largely featureless: every few dozen steps he passed a string of symbols that might have been a single, enlarged word, rendered in the same stylized writing he had seen above, but there were no faces on these walls, no figures. Still, he couldn't escape the idea that things were moving around him, and that the failing light of his coral was being reflected back at him somehow from the bare walls as though it bounced off something less opaque than mere stone, as though the stairwell burrowed down not through the castle's well-known limestone, but some huge, murky crystal. The dimensions of the place seemed to change, too, swelling and contracting even as he continued his trudge downward. For a time he couldn't make sense anymore of how he had found his way here, and he became gripped by the dreadful certainty that he was descending the living stone throat of the Shining Man, being swallowed down into the heart of the Mysteries. Then the sensation passed, replaced by flickers of light all around him like the sparks that danced on the inside of closed eyelids. Wordless whispers swam up the stairwell, a dull and distant rush like waves crashing on a shore, and superstitious terror gripped him again.

This is not my place. Only the temple brothers should be here, and perhaps even they do not know about this tunnel . . . !

Flint, he reminded himself, trying to fight off the panic that had him huddling on a step, hugging himself in exhausted terror. *Remember the boy.* That small, fiercely solemn face, the arms thin as Opal's broom handle, the white-gold hair that would never lie flat, and stood up like iron-flower crystals despite Opal's best work with the brush. And Opal herself, of course—if Chert couldn't bring the boy back to her, she would be crushed. Something inside her would die.

He forced himself to his feet and began descending again. *One step. It all starts with one step, then another. Then another . . .*

No, the Shadowline, he thought blearily, *it all started that day beside the Shadowline . . .* But even as the memory came into his head with a sudden bizarre clarity—the forested hillside, the noise of hooves, the smell of the damp soil under his nose—as if a door had been opened and the past had crashed in, like a noisy guest into a quiet room, he put his foot down onto the next step and discovered something was very wrong. Chert stumbled, flailed, and shrieked; then, with his heart pounding so hard it seemed it might cannon through the cage of his ribs, he realized that the wrong thing was not a deadly chasm beneath his feet but the opposite, a floor—not too much distance but too little. He had reached an end to what had seemed an endless downward spiral of steps.

He raised the chunk of coral and peered around, but if the world had suddenly gone from vertical to horizontal, it had not changed in many other ways: before him lay more corridor hewed through the same featureless stone. He was having trouble seeing clearly, but the passage extended as far as the light reached and probably much farther than that.

Beneath even the Sea in the Depths? If so, there might be an end to the journey at some point—he had half feared that he might simply continue down into the earth for days and weeks, perhaps at last to arrive at the black tourmaline doors of Kernios' own subterranean palace, doors that were famously guarded by Immon the Gatekeeper. It was a place Chert definitely did not wish to see while still alive, even if much of the original tale had been distorted by the big folk. The Funderling version was even more frightening. He tried to remember the distance across the quicksilver sea but the unstable light had confused him. Never having been any closer, he could only guess now in the most formless kind of way. He shrugged and took a deep breath. The hot, sour air did not seem to clear his thoughts. He staggered down the corridor.

"The deeps are no more like the town than the sky is like the ground, lad."

It was his father's voice in his head now, strangely. Big Nodule (unlike his firstborn son, Chert's brother, who was the current magister, his father would never have let himself be called anything so pretentious as "Nodule the Elder") had been lamed by a rockfall in the early part of Olin's reign, and had spent the last years of his life moving between his bed and his chair before the fire, but during Chert's boyhood he had still been vigorous. Of all his sons, Chert had been the one most like him—*"the boy loves stone for stone's sake,"* Big Nodule had often proclaimed to his cronies at the guildhall—and he had taken Chert for long walks through the unfinished works outside Funderling Town, and even a few times to some of the hills aboveground or along the edge of Brenn's Bay, pointing out the way limestone came to light where the rainwater washed away the earth, or the trapped centuries that were pressed in a sandstone bank above the waves like dried flowers in a noble lady's book.

"A man who knows stone and its ways is as good as any man, big 'un or Funderling, prince or kern, and he'll never lack for things to do and think about." That had been another of the old fellow's favorite sayings.

Chert was astonished to find that he was walking blind, not because his coral lamp had finally died, but because he was weeping.

Hold on, you, he told himself. *That man strapped you raw with his tie-rope for stealing a few sugarcap mushrooms out of Widow Rocksalt's garden. When he finally died, your mother didn't last even a year after, not because she missed him so much but because he'd worked her so in those last years that she was just bone-tired and couldn't go on any longer.*

Still, the tears wouldn't stop. He found it hard to walk. His mother's face was before him now, too, the heavy-lidded eyes that could seem either beautifully dignified or painfully distant, the mouth that turned down at any hint of what she deemed an unnecessary fuss. He remembered Lapis Blue Quartz's nimble, work-gnarled hands as she made a yarn doll for one of her grandchildren, her fingers always busy, always doing something. He couldn't think of a time when she had been awake and those hands were not occupied.

"And what is this now?" He could hear her as clearly as if she stood beside him, her voice sour but not without humor. *"What noise is this? Fissure and fracture, it sounds like someone's skinning a live mole in here!"*

Chert had to stop for a while to get his breath, and when he started again, it was hard just to keep walking. The walls, unbroken now even by the occasional glyph, featureless as a rabbit scrape, squeezed in on him as though they meant to catch him and hold him until the world changed. He could again imagine himself in the belly of the Shining Man, being digested and changed, becoming something hard like crystal, immobile and eternal, but with his thoughts still alive in the center of it, battering hopelessly to get out like a fly beneath an overturned cup.

And now, as though the deep places that contained him suddenly went through some sort of paroxysm, he could feel the sensation of power, the presence that he thought was the Shining Man, shift and grow less diffuse, more localized: it was something he sensed as powerfully as he could know *down* from *up* with his eyes closed—the presence was no longer smotheringly all around him, but instead had taken on a very definite location, up and ahead of him. Instead of giving him a goal, the power of it became something that pushed against him like a strong, constant wind, as though he and it were two chunks of lodestone repelling each other. Chert put his head down, eyes still prismed with weeping, and forced himself to take step after agonizing step.

What is this place? What does it all mean? He tried to remember the words of the temple brothers at his coming-of-age ceremony, the ritual tale of the Lord of the Hot Wet Stone, but it came back only as a jumble of sonorous words that buzzed in his head almost without meaning, in pictures that were smeared like wet paint. *The earth was a broken thing,* the voices murmured and roared, *a new thing, the lights in the sky so bright and the face of the world yet so dark, the battle to take this place away from older, crueler gods a thing not of days or weeks but of aeons, throwing mountains up where no mountains had stood, tearing the face of creation so that the water rushed in and made great, steaming seas.*

"*In the Days when there were no Days,*" the oldest of the temple brothers had chanted, beginning the initiation ceremony, and Chert and the other celebrants had only moaned, their heads full of waking dreams that painted the dark around them, their stomachs sour from the *k'hamao* they had been given to drink after fasting and purifying themselves for two days before the being taken down into the Mysteries. *In the Days when there were no Days.*

But what now? What was this? The tunnel had somehow been yanked upright like a length of string. It rose above him into the shadowy distance. Somehow Chert found himself on stairs again, but this time he was climbing, not descending, his head chaotic with ideas, with visions that were not quite visible, with the endless roar of The Lord of the Hot Wet Stone battling his foes, a roar that made the very roots of the world quiver. Chert felt that roar in his bones now, felt it beginning to rattle him to pieces, to crumble him like the sandstone cliffs his father had shown him, falling to the relentless waves. Soon there would be no more Chert, only fragments, crumbled smaller and smaller until they became dust, then the dust would scatter and waft away and spread into all the dark places even the stars had never reached. . . .

When his thoughts at last came back to him, when the dreams finally began to shred and disperse like wind-tormented clouds, Chert couldn't make sense of what he saw; in fact, he wondered if he hadn't merely passed into some different and only slightly less hectic realm of madness. He was standing at the foot of a mountain, a great jut of dark stone, a massive shadow in the thin, dim light that seemed to come from all directions and none—but how could there be such a thing, a mountain inside a mountain? Nevertheless, there it was, a monstrous black lump rising a hundred times his own height or more; he stood at its foot like an ant gazing up at a man.

Oh, Elders save me, it's the gate, the black gate. I have climbed all the way down to Kernios . . . and Immon—Noszh-la himself—is going to find me wanting and chew me in those terrible, stony teeth . . . !

Something flickered like lightning inside the vast black shape that loomed above him. A moment later a mad radiance began to leak out from every part of it, but strongest in the center, where it formed the rough shape of a man. A shining man.

Chert stared in horrified fascination, but also with a growing sense of relief. He was standing right at its feet. He had crossed under the Sea in the Depths.

Still, he had never imagined what it would be like to stand before it. The rock seemed half translucent, half solid black basalt, and the light that streamed out bent as it came and broke into more colors than surely could be contained in a rainbow—so many colors and all moving so strangely! He had to narrow his eyes until they were almost shut and still it made him dizzy, made his head waver and his stomach lurch. He collapsed to his knees on the stony shore of the island. The heart of the blazing, coruscating brilliance did indeed have the shape of a person, although the stone—semi-translucent as volcanic glass, and the very inconstancy of the lights made it hard to discern. Still, it almost seemed to move, to writhe within the rock as though racked with nightmares, or as though it sought escape.

At last Chert could not look at it even through squinting eyes and so he lowered his face. He crouched on all fours like a dog, feeling as though he would be sick, and it was then, as the glare faded, that he saw the boy lying stretched out on the gravel slope a few yards above him.

"*Flint!*" His voice flew out—he could almost see the echoes spreading and chasing each other, growing smaller like ripples. He scrambled up the loose stones. The boy was curled on his side but almost facedown, one arm reaching upslope as though offering a gift to the gleaming giant. Chert saw something flat and shiny in the boy's hand as he turned him over, noted distractedly that it was the mirror that he and Opal had discovered in the boy's cherished bag, the child's one possession, but then the sight of Flint's face, pale as bone beneath the dark dust, eyes half open but sightless, drove all other thoughts from his mind.

He would not wake, no matter how Chert shook him. At last the Funderling dragged the boy up and pulled him to his chest, then pressed the cold cheek tight against his neck and shouted for help as though there were people around to hear him—as though Chert Blue Quartz were not the last living creature in the whole of the cosmos.

The sky had lightened a shade, but still no birds were singing. Barrick's heart hurried, fast as a dragonfly's wings, until he found it hard to get his breath. The quiet sounds of the camp rising were all around him. He wondered if any of the others had managed to sleep.

He tested the saddle straps once more, loosened and then retightened one even though it did not need tightening. His black horse, Kettle— named to irritate Kendrick as much as anything else, who had believed in noble names for noble steeds—whickered in irritation.

Barrick watched Ferras Vansen, the guard captain, going from one smol- dering fire to another, talking to the men, and found himself irritated by the man's calm attention to duty. *Slept like an innocent child, no doubt.* He didn't really know what to think about Vansen, but didn't much want to trust him. No one could truly be quite that honest and forthright—years in the South- march court had taught Barrick that. The guard captain was playing some deeper game—perhaps the innocent one of craving advancement, perhaps something more subtle. Why else would he be watching Barrick so closely? Because he was, there was no doubt of that; Vansen's eyes were on him every time Barrick turned around. Whatever the case, the man bore watching. Briony might have forgiven him his derelictions, but his sister's angers were always quicker to cool. Barrick Eddon was not so easily mollified.

A hand touched his shoulder and he jumped, which made Kettle prance in place, snorting nervously.

"Sorry, lad," said Tyne Aldritch. "I mean, your pardon, Highness. I didn't mean to startle you."

"You didn't . . . I mean . . ."

The Earl of Blueshore stepped back. His breath smelled of wine, al- though he showed no signs of having drunk more than he should. Barrick remembered the stream winding down through the thorny black vines and couldn't really blame the man for not wanting to drink from it. "Of course," Tyne said. "It's only that I was remembering the night before my first battle. Did you sleep?"

"Yes," Barrick lied. What he really needed to do now, he realized, was piss. Tyne had almost frightened the water out of him.

"I was reminded of when I went as my uncle's squire to Olway Coomb. Dimakos Heavyhand was one of the last chieftains of the Gray Companies, and he and his men had come into Marrinswalk, burning and looting. Your father was down in Hierosol with most of the hardened Southmarch fighters, but those remaining made common cause with the Marrinswalk men and such others as we could gather, then met the raiders in the valley. Dimakos had come there first and had the high ground, although we were the larger force." Tyne smiled a hard smile. "My uncle Laylin saw that I was fearful about the battle to come and brought me to the questioning of a prisoner, a scout from Heavyhand's company we had captured. The man would say nothing of use no matter the persuasion, I will give him that, and when it became certain we would get nothing more from him, my uncle slit the man's throat and rubbed the hot blood on my face. 'There,' he told me. 'Well-blooded is well-begun.' Nor would he let me wash it off until we rode. It itched so that that I scarcely thought of anything else until I struck my first blow in anger." Tyne laughed quietly. "Harsh, but my uncle was one of the old men, the hard men, and that was their way. Be glad we do not live in such times . . . although perhaps we will miss his like before long, if the gods are unkind." He made the sign of the Three, then clapped Barrick on the back so that the prince almost lost control of his bladder once more. "Fear not, lad. You will do your father proud. We will send these Twilight folk back to their boggart hills with something to think about."

Was that supposed to make me feel better? Barrick wondered as Tyne walked away, but he couldn't worry about it long, as he was already fumbling with the laces of his smallclothes.

Expecting little in the way of siege play, they had brought only a small contingent of Funderling miners, but these were also serving as gunnery men. Barrick tried to sit still in the saddle as the tiny shapes in leather hoods and cloaks, their eyes insectlike behind thick spectacles of smoked crystal, aimed the bombards up the hillside. Although he was armored, Barrick was not going in the first waves of mounted men, not least because he could only carry a light sword instead of a lance; he should have been angry at the coddling but found he was grateful. Dawn was just touching the edge of the eastern sky. The clumps of shadow were becoming bushes and trees again, and although the forest at the top of the hill was still shrouded in mist, beneath the lightening sky it did not look quite so fearsome and mysterious. In fact, everything was equally strange to Barrick's eye just now, befogged forest and mortal army; even though he was in the midst of it, he felt as though he looked down on the scene from some high window, perhaps from Wolfstooth Spire.

Still, he held his breath as fire was touched to the train and the guns began to speak, barking like bronze dogs and spewing stone balls toward the trees on the hilltop. The first shots fell short, bouncing up the slope and vanishing into the leafy cover, but the Funderlings raised the bombards and let fly again; this time the round stones crashed into the center of the hillcrest, tearing away branches and knocking down trees. When the roaring stopped, there was only silence for a moment as Barrick and the others peered through the drifting smoke. A wailing cry went up from the hilltop, and at first he felt a fierce, relieved joy—they had killed most of them, they must have! Then he heard the note of defiant triumph in the inhuman voices. It sounded like there were hundreds of them, perhaps thousands.

Tyne had waited impatiently for the barrage to finish. He had already made it clear that he believed cannons were for siegework, nothing else, but he had bent to the wishes of Ivar Brenhill and the other more progressive war barons. Now he lowered the visor on his helmet and waved his arm. The first row of archers let fly, then crouched as the second row filled the air with their own arrows. Tyne waved again and with a shout that was almost as daunting as the cry from the hilltop, the first wave of pikemen dashed up the slope, pike shafts waving and clacking like a denuded version of the forest above, the wielders sped by the knowledge that the mounted men behind them would ride down any stragglers. A flight of arrows whistled toward them from the heights, strangely few but terribly accurate. A dozen men were down already, at least one of them a knight: his horse was dying beside him, legs thrashing as the other mounted men surged past.

Long, confused moments of noise and smoke passed before Barrick and the men around him spurred their own horses up the hill, time enough for the first wave of foot soldiers to reach the top and plunge into the trees. He heard shouts, excited cries, even a few screams, but over everything he heard the unnatural voices of the enemy—keening noises like seabirds, like the howls of wolves and the barks of foxes, but with words buried in them to make the strange sounds even more terrible.

"*Briony . . .*" he murmured, but even he could not hear the name.

Some of the first wave of soldiers came reeling back, bloodied and shrieking. The fairies had built a wall of thorns. The mounted men behind them pushed on, some wielding axes, hacking their way in and killing many of the wall's defenders. Arrows were snapping out of the trees at them, but still strangely few, and Barrick could almost feel the mounting concern of Tyne and the other war leaders—was it an ambush, after all? But the hillsides and meadows all around were still empty: for this moment, the forested crest seemed the angry heart of the world, an island of noise and struggle surrounded by stillness.

"They break out!" someone called in a throttled, high-pitched voice— Barrick thought it might be his cousin Rorick. On the hilltop a knot of men had been forced backward out of the trees, fighting hand-to-hand with a group of howling, white-haired warriors. At the center of the defenders a hugely tall figure stood in his stirrups, slashing with what even from a great distance seemed a bizarre, misshapen blade. The defender was tall, with snowy hair flowing free in the wind like a woman's, and Barrick thought for a moment he must be an old man, but a glimpse of his face showed youthful features, and skin stretched tight over bones sharp enough to cut leather. The Twilight man struck down one of Tyne's soldiers, then another, spinning the blade in the second man's guts like a peasant churning butter. One of the mounted nobles spurred toward him, lance lowered, and the white-haired fairy or elf or whatever kind of creature he was knocked the weapon aside before closing with his attacker. Barrick lost sight of them behind a clump of trees as he neared the crest, then the forest was all around him and the men with whom he rode, mist puffing up from their horses' hooves.

"Forward!" someone else shouted. "But *stay together!*" Barrick was surprised to realize it was Vansen, that the man had found his way to them through the trees and the mayhem, but he did not have long to contemplate it. A figure suddenly sprang up from the undergrowth—no, two figures, three!—and Barrick had to strike away a hand clawing at his bridle. The sound of many voices echoed through the trees, as many unnatural as natural, and in the cloudy, slanting light a thousand weird shapes loomed between the trunks—shadows and tricks of the light, perhaps, but there were enough real bodies and enough pale, hating faces that he had no time to consider anything except staying alive.

Half a dozen men of Barrick's party were left of the original dozen, although some of the others had merely become lost among the trees. Vansen was one of those remaining and he leaned close to Barrick and asked quietly, "Are you well, Highness?"

Barrick could only nod. He was gasping for breath and there were cuts and scratches on his hands and no doubt elsewhere, but he thought he had killed at least one of the fairy folk—a face that came toward him down a shadowy tree branch, and which he had split with a startled swing of his blade—and he did not seem to have any major wounds. The forest was mostly empty here, although the fearful sounds of the Twilight folk were still loud, and unnatural shapes still flitted between the distant trees.

"I think I hear Tyne this way," Vansen said, then spurred across the clearing. Barrick and the others followed him, all struggling for breath, their necks prickling, not certain when the next attack would come. Barrick felt as though he was peering down one of Chaven's optical tubes, that everything around him had been bent except for that at which he stared. All his blood seemed to be rushing through his head while his body was coldly numb, hard and unfeeling as iron. It was a strange, terrifying, exhilarating feeling.

Ferras Vansen suddenly reined up beside a patch of deep brush and struck downward with his sword, then swung out of the saddle and began hacking away at something unseen. He was shouting, and although the guard captain's words couldn't be heard over the shrilling of fairy voices, there was a wild look of disgust and fear on his face that cut through Barrick's numbness, clutched at the pit of his stomach. He spurred forward with the others just as a great number of the keening fairies all went silent at the same moment. Unearthly voices still sounded, but only from the other side of the hilltop.

Vansen stood upright, his killing finished, his blade dripping with blood and something else translucent as tree sap. His face was a mask of horror. Barrick dismounted awkwardly and made his way to the captain's side.

He was standing in the midst of what might almost have been a huge nest hidden in the undergrowth, trampled and exposed now, with bodies and body parts piled at his feet, glistening with blood and other fluids. The things lying there, Barrick could see after a moment of confusion at the unusual forms, were naked and mostly manlike, pale as maggots. Those whose heads he could see had huge swollen throat pouches, like frogs. Their dead eyes were solid black, rapidly losing luster.

"What are they?" someone asked.

"*Horrible,*" someone else said, and it was true.

"The things that made the noises," Vansen told them. "Listen." And for a moment they all heeded the silence.

"What . . . what does it mean?" Barrick asked. "Why?"

"Because we have been tricked," said Vansen. Beneath the spatters of blood, his face was almost as pale as the grotesque shapes at his feet. "Only a few waited for us on this hilltop—a few soldiers to cross blades with us, a few deceiving shapes, a few of these making the noise of hundreds."

"Gods! An ambush, after all?" Barrick looked around, expecting to see dozens more of the strange faces appear in the branches over their heads, grinning savagely.

"Worse," said Vansen. "Worse. Because they have held us here and stolen a day from us with a very few while the rest of their army rode on around us."

"Rode on . . . ?"

"Yes. Toward Southmarch."

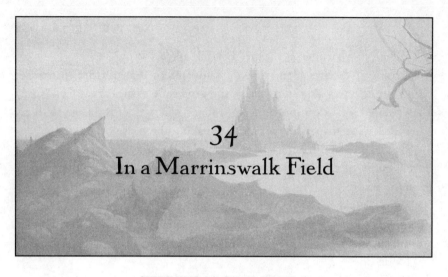

34

In a Marrinswalk Field

IT HAD BEEN A BAD NIGHT, a night of little sleep. Briony had been up since an hour before dawn with such anger running through her that she could scarcely sit still—anger at Hendon Tolly, of course, but also at herself for her foolish loss of control, at Barrick for not being with her, at everything.

And I stood there, waving a sword at him in front of everyone, and they all knew he could not lift a finger against me—his ruler, and a woman at that. A . . . girl. And they all knew he didn't need to, either, because he'd already won. What a fool I must have looked!

For a long moment it was all she could do to stay seated at the writing desk—she was itching with embarrassment despite being the only person awake in the room. She wanted to run, to lose herself somewhere in the great castle until everyone forgot what happened. But of course, nobody would forget and she couldn't run away. She was an Eddon. She was the princess regent. They would be talking about last night's dinner for years.

There was nothing to do but go on. Nothing. Briony picked up her pen, dipped it into the inkwell, and continued her letter to her father.

"I have not heard from you since Kendrick's death, and as I said, I can only pray that you received my letter telling you of that terrible day, that this which I write now is not the first you have heard of it. I miss him, dear Father, I miss my big brother very much. Because he was the oldest, he was always certain he was right, and of course that was vexing at times, but I honestly think he tried every day to do right. He wanted to be you, of course, that is why. Even before he became the regent, he held himself like a man who will rule one day, who concerns himself with the needs of the least of his subjects as well as the demands of his most powerful allies.

"But, of course, that is what everyone else will remember about him. What I will always remember about our dear Kendrick was the way he would fume and scowl when Barrick and I teased him, but at last would give in and laugh as hard as any of us. Why is it that you and Kendrick could both do that, that you could see your own foolishness and admit it, even laugh about it, but Barrick and I cannot?

"There is more, certainly, that . . ."

She stopped. A memory of Kendrick pretending to be angry at her while struggling to hide a smile had suddenly come back with such power that for a moment she could only sit and weep silently. Rose Trelling stirred in her bed on the opposite side of the room, murmured something, then fell back to sleep. Anazoria, Briony's youngest maid, scarcely ten years old, was snoring like an ancient dog on her little pallet on the floor. It was strange to be awake in the midst of all these sleepers—like being a ghost.

She went back and scratched out part of the last sentence, changed it to read, *". . . that Kendrick could do that and you can do it, too,"* because she realized she had put the king, her father, into the past again as though he were dead instead of only imprisoned. *The gods willing, it is nothing but a false fear!* Still, the whole thing seemed a hopeless exercise. How could she tell him what truly was happening without making him frantic with worry? How could she describe any of it, the terrifying Twilight People, the Tollys' flirtation with the Autarch, the seemingly unending stream of dreadful tidings? How could she tell her father how frightened she was for Barrick without breaking Olin's heart?

She put the pen back down and read over what she had written. The greatest problem, of course, was that she couldn't speak about what was troubling her most—her twin's terrible story. Since Barrick had told her, it had stayed in the middle of her like a swallowed stone, a great, indigestible lump. Some days the heaviness of it made it hard for her to walk, to talk, even to think. She hoped that by hearing it she had lightened her brother's load, because he had certainly burdened her. How could such a thing be true? But if it was not true, how was it possible that Barrick, her twin, could be such a liar? And if it *was* true, how could she possibly write to her father as though nothing had changed, as though she was the same loving daughter in the same, unchanged world?

Either Barrick is the world's greatest liar . . . or Father is . . .

It was pointless. She had thought she could write to him, but she couldn't.

Briony was holding the last of the burning parchment to the candle when someone knocked at the door. She immediately dropped the ashes and stub of paper into the candleholder, as though she had been caught doing something wicked. "Who is there?"

"It's Lord Brone, Your Highness," said one of her guards through the door. "He wishes . . ."

"Oh, Perin's bloody red beard, I can tell her myself," growled the lord constable. "Let me come in, please, Princess. I have urgent business."

Even this early, with the sky outside still quite dark, Avin Brone was dressed for the daylight hours, although he looked to have accomplished it in a hasty manner. He stared around the room as though searching for enemies but saw only slumbering women.

"We must speak in private," he told her.

"They are all deep sleepers, but if you fear for their modesty, we can step into the hallway . . ."

"No. This is not to be discussed in front of the guards. Not yet." He looked around the bedchamber once more. "Ah, well," he said at last. "We must speak quietly, then."

She gestured for him to sit down at the writing desk, but she herself remained standing. Something in his manner had alarmed her; she felt an almost animal urge toward flight. Although Brone seemed his ordinary dour, distracted self, she could sense something deeper was wrong, and she began to wonder how long it would take the guards to respond if she called out for them. Almost without thinking about it, she took a step back from the lord constable, then another; then, a little ashamed, she turned the movement into a search for a thicker wrap. She was conscious for the first time in an hour that her slippers were thin and her feet were cold.

"Gailon Tolly has been found."

"Where?"

"In a Marrinswalk field. In a ditch, to be more precise, covered over with branches."

"What?" For a moment she had a mad vision of Gailon in a kind of hiding-hole, playing a child's game. Then she understood. "Oh, merciful Zoria, in a ditch? Is he . . . ?"

"Dead, yes. Oh, most assuredly dead—along with the men who rode beside him. Half a dozen in all, thrown together into a hasty grave, if you can even call it such."

She was stunned. "But . . . how . . . ?" Briony forced herself to think more carefully. "What happened? Who found him?"

"One of the last musters out of south Marrinswalk, four or five pentecounts, I don't recall. They came in late last night, an hour or so after the last bell, hurrying to bring in their news. They had been coming up the Silverside Road outside Oscastle and saw a great number of ravens and other birds swarming in a field. When their leader took them closer they saw something shining. It was a buckle."

Briony's knees suddenly felt weak; she had to take a step to steady herself. Brone came up out of the chair quickly and guided her to it in his stead. "But . . . how?" she asked. "Who did this? Bandits? Surely the fairy folk have not moved so far south?" Gailon Tolly, dead. Handsome, selfsatsified Gailon. She hadn't liked him, but she had never wanted . . . never imagined . . .

"I can't say, Princess. Bandits seem the most likely explanation—almost all their money and jewelry had been taken. Horses, too. There are more than a few such bands who range the border between Silverside and Marrinswalk and call the Whitewood their home. The thieves missed a brooch, though, and one of the Marrinswalk men brought it in. That is our only advantage—the discoverers do not know yet whose bodies they found, which has given me enough time to tell you first, before it spreads all through the castle." He extended his broad fist and uncurled the fingers. A round brooch with a thick pin covered much of his palm, the kind worn at the neck of a riding cloak. The silver was still streaked with mud, but the humped shoulders and horned head of the bull were impossible to mistake.

Briony forced herself to swallow. She felt as though she would be ill. "That's his. I've seen him wear it."

"Or at least it's one of the Tolly family brooches. But I think we must assume one of the corpses is Gailon."

"Where are they?" she asked at last, staring at the muddied silver circle as though it were an actual piece of bone. "The bodies?"

"They have been taken to a temple in Oscastle. Until they got there, the soldiers who found them thought the dead were local men, but no one in Oscastle had any idea who they could be. The mantis in that town thought he recognized one corpse as being Gailon Tolly, however, and being a wise man, he put his fears in a letter and entrusted it to the captain of the Marrinswalk pentecounts for secrecy. Still, the rest of the muster are already telling their story to anyone here who will listen. It is only hours at the most until Hendon Tolly hears of it, and he will have no trouble deciding who these mysterious dead really are."

"Merciful Zoria! As it was, he all but accused us of murdering Gailon— he will trumpet it from the walls now!"

"Yes, and you did not help things with your foolishness at dinner. Go ahead and throw me in the stronghold, but it must be said."

She waved her hand. The sour taste in her mouth had worsened. "Yes, yes, and I agree, and now you've said it. But what do we *do?* What do we do when Hendon starts up again, claiming I've had his brother killed?"

"Perhaps he won't."

"What do you mean?"

"Perhaps he won't. Perhaps it wasn't bandits, or even these Twilight folk. Maybe it was the Tollys' southern friends."

It took her a moment. "The Autarch? Are you suggesting the Autarch would reach all the way into the March Kingdoms to murder one of his allies—one of his only allies, as far as we know?"

"Perhaps they didn't become allies. Perhaps the Tollys turned him down."

If what Brone told me in the first place was even true, she reminded herself. Briony put her hands to her head. Now that Barrick was gone, she could fully trust no one. "What a dreadful tangle! I can't make sense of it—I have to think. Perhaps you're right, but that still doesn't help us any. Unless Hendon Tolly also suspects the Autarch's hand and decides he can't afford to make too much of a fuss . . ." She took a long, shuddering breath, trying to calm stomach and spirit. "I only know that it will make matters worse at a time when I believed such a thing wasn't possible." As Briony spoke, she picked up the inkwell and moved it back into the drawer, carefully put away the blotter, then the sealing wax.

"What are you doing?" asked Brone. For the first time she noticed the dark circles under his eyes, the weariness on his pouchy face. He had probably not slept more than an hour or two.

"Just clearing things away. I was going to write a letter to someone, but it's become clear that there's not much point to it." She paused. "Dead— Zoria preserve us! Poor Gailon. I never thought I'd say that . . ."

For a moment she thought Avin Brone was shaking her chair for some reason—that he was angry and had been hiding it—but then she realized he was several steps away and swaying unsteadily too. In fact, it seemed the whole world was shaking. A bench hopped on the floor like a skittish horse. One of her jewelry chests jittered off a table and smashed on the flagstones. Across the room, Moina sat up and stared around blearily. By the time the trembling stopped little Anazoria was awake too, frightened and crying loudly. Even heavy-sleeping Rose seemed to have been shaken almost to wakefulness.

"Just a tremor of the earth," the lord constable said, frowning at his sluggard niece, who had only yawned and turned over, but his leathery face had gone pale. "I felt one like it when I was a boy. It is over now."

Briony's heart was beating very fast. "Is it, Lord Brone? Or is it that the world is approaching its end?"

"I must say that I have never known it so discomforted in my lifetime," he admitted.

The Lord of the Hot Wet Stone had no face, or at least no face that Chert could see, only a murky, red-shot blackness between his gigantic shoulders and his shining crown. Big as a mountain, he looked down from his throne but said nothing. The only sound in his immense throne room was the low groan of great stones shifting, the roots of the world still alive and unsettled even all these aeons after the Days of Cooling.

At last Chert could take no more. "Please, Grandfather, do not punish me!"

The groaning continued, but the mighty figure said nothing.

"I meant no harm. I trespassed, but I meant no harm!"

The murk regarded him. A hand as vast as a wall slowly lifted and spread above him—a benediction? A curse? Or did his god simply mean to crush him like a fly? The groaning stopped for a moment, then began again, and for the first time Chert began to hear something like words in it, a dim, gnashing cadence.

He is speaking to me, *Chert realized.* But it is too slow, too deep, for me to hear!

Too slow . . . too deep . . . The light was flickering now, the massive shape hard to see. Too deep . . . He couldn't understand the words. His god was speaking to him, but he couldn't make sense of what was being said.

"Tell me!" he shouted as the darkness closed in. "Tell me so that I can understand . . . !"

But his god had no comprehensible tale to tell.

He woke up shivering from the oppressive dream—if dream it had truly been. For a moment he couldn't remember what place he was in, but the boy's body pressed against him brought it back. Shivering, Chert was shivering—no, shaking all over.

So cold . . . he thought, but realized a moment later that the air was actually hot, hot enough to suck the sweat off his skin. Nevertheless an unpleasant chill was on him, an icy, bone-deep discomfort, nor could he stop shaking. Also, and far more frightening, the voice of the god still rumbled in his ears.

No, it was the earth itself growling—one of the tremors his people called a Wakeful Elder, unusual but not exceptional. Chert himself was not trembling—the ground beneath him was moving. He darted a fearful glance up at the Shining Man, in size and threatening juxtaposition so much like the god in his dream, but where earlier it had flashed and smoldered it had now gone strangely dark at its center, only a few glimmers moving beneath the surface of the crystalline stone like silvery fish in a pool.

The ground shuddered again, then the groaning died and the greater movement stopped. For another heartbeat or two he could hear the hiss of the beach stones around him as they continued to slide, to find new arrangements, then everything was silent once more.

Flint whimpered. Chert, who had been certain he held a dead child, almost dropped him in surprise, then his heart leaped with unexpected joy and a new terror. "Lad! Talk to me! It's me, Chert!"

But the boy was still again, his skin still clammy-cold beneath the dirt and dust.

The tunnel. I must carry him back.

He tried to stand, but it was too much effort—he couldn't even rise to his knees while holding the boy. He set Flint down as gently as he could and then clambered up to stand unsteadily over him. The boy was his own height, weighed almost as much as Chert did: there was only one way to carry him, and that was to get the boy's entire weight up onto his shoulders, as it was said that Silas of Perikal—or was it one of the other heroes of the big folk's tales?—had carried a young bullock every day, so that as the bullock grew into its maturity, Silas also grew more and more powerful, eventually to become the mightiest knight of his age.

Or was that Hiliometes the Kracian? Chert wondered blearily as he squatted beside the senseless child. Absently, he pulled the mirror out of the child's grasp—the boy's grip was fierce, even in near-death—and put it in his own pouch. It felt like nothing special, no heavier or lighter than it did before, no warmer, no cooler. *Yes, it was the Kracian. No, wait, Hiliometes was a demigod—he needed no training to lift great weights.* Chert could never keep all the stories of the big-folk heroes straight. So many of them, killing monsters and saving maidens, and they all seemed more or less the same . . .

He hauled the top of Flint's body up onto his shoulder, then grabbed him around the thighs and lifted until the side of the boy's belly was against his neck. Grunting, cursing under his breath, yet all the time able to watch his own ludicrous travails as though he were two people at the same time, Chert slowly rose to his feet with the boy's legs dangling in front and his head dangling down behind. For a moment he was full of the glory of having accomplished the near-impossible; then he took a step and felt his legs already trembling with the exertion, his back knotting at the weight it must bear. Worse, he remembered that he did not know where he had come up out of the tunnel and onto the island. Chert knew he should put the boy down and search instead of trying to carry his weight any farther than necessary, but he also knew that if he did that, he would never manage to lift him again.

It was hard to be certain in the dim light which were footprints and which only shadowed valleys in the piles of smooth stones, but he turned his back to the darkened Shining Man and did the best he could. At the beginning each step was very hard; by the time he had staggered fifty yards and still had not found the tunnel mouth, each step was a sweating, wheezing agony.

Lie down and wait for help, a voice in his head instructed him.

Lie down and die, suggested another as he missed his footing and almost tumbled, almost dropped the helpless child.

The gods help those who help themselves, he thought, and then: *I hate the gods. Why should the Elders torture me in this way? Why should they use the boy to hurt me and to hurt Opal?*

Another step. Gasping, he almost fell. One more step. *But what can you know about what the gods want? Who are you, little man?*

I am Chert of the Blue Quartz clan. I know stone. I do my work. I take care . . . I take care of my . . . my own . . .

But then he did stumble, and fell, and lay panting on the stones with the boy on top of him. When he tried to make himself move again he could not because something dark was covering him, closing his eyes, stealing his wits.

He came up out of exhausted sleep to find himself face to face with horror.

Something was touching his chin and his cheek: a small but ghastly, malformed mask stared down on him from only a short distance away, flarenostriled, fang-toothed, with leathery black skin. Chert squeaked—he had the breath for nothing more—and tried to beat away the looming, blurry monstrosity, but he was lying on his belly and something was pinning his arms.

"Demon!" he moaned, struggling. The thing retreated, or its horrid face did, but he could still feel something scratching at his neck.

"Not pretty, mayhap," a voice said, "but un's carried me well. Seems sour t'name un so."

Chert stopped fighting, astonished, wondering if he had lost his wits again or was wandering in the tunnels of dream. "Beetledown?"

"Aye." A moment later the little man clambered down Chert's shoulder and into his view.

"Why can't I move? And what was that thing?"

"For movin', well, it's thy boy lying athwart 'ee hampering thy arms. That thing, as tha says, well . . . a flittermouse, I calls it. Rode it back here, did I."

"A flit . . . A bat?"

"Aye, likely." Something dark leaped past Chert's face. "There un goes," said Beetledown a little sadly. "Gone now, afeared because tha would try to roll over un." He shook his head. "Testing and fidgeting, thy flittermouse may be, but a treat to ride once going along proper."

"You rode a bat?"

"How else to get over yon evil-smelling silver water?"

Chert slid out from under Flint, letting the boy down onto the stony beach as gently as he could.

"How fares thy boy?" asked Beetledown.

"Alive, but I don't know anything more. I have to get him away, but I can't carry him." He wanted to laugh and cry. "Good as it is to see you, you won't be much help there. And now you've lost your bat, so you're stuck here, too." It seemed impossibly sad. Chert sat on the loose stones, staring out across the Sea in the Depths.

"Mayhap if tha tell how *tha* came here, yon temple fellows who followed me can come across and help carry thy boy."

"Temple fellows . . . ?" He looked up. There were shapes on the far side of the quicksilver sea, small dark forms moving atop the great balcony of stone. Chert's heart sped. "Oh, Beetledown, you brought them! The Elders bless you, you brought them!" He cupped his hands around his mouth, tried to shout, coughed, then tried again. "Hoy! Nickel! Is that you?"

The temple brother's voice came down to him, faint but echoing with urgency. "In the name of the Elders, *how did you get across?*"

Chert started to reply, then stopped. When he did speak, he couldn't keep the astonishment out of his voice, for surely it was the Metamorphic Brothers' own tunnel he had used. "Do you mean—do you mean to say you don't know . . . ?"

There were more surprises—Chert even managed to surprise himself. Despite being grateful to his rescuers, not to mention having been raised in the lifetime habit of trained respect toward their order, when he finally stumbled back into the temple, he answered all the brothers' questions about his journey and the Shining Man as truthfully as he could but volunteered nothing about the mirror or Flint's unusual origins.

If I tell them anything about where the boy comes from, they won't let him leave. He felt certain of that, although he was not sure why. The brothers were concerned, of course, and even a little angry about the boy's incursion into the Mysteries, but not inordinately so. He knew that his reticence was selfish, perhaps even foolishly dangerous, but Opal was waiting for him back on Wedge Road, and she must be frightened now not just for the boy but for her husband as well. He couldn't bear to think of going back to her only to tell her the boy was being held prisoner in the temple.

For their own part, the brothers brought him no farther into the temple than the outer chamber, the great room of natural stone that the people of Funderling Town were allowed to see on a few of the highest holy days. Even Chert's carefully shaped version of the tale was enough to make them examine the boy very carefully while they made a fruitless attempt at waking him. Flint had no visible wounds, no lumps or bruises anywhere on his pale skin, but nothing they did could raise him from his deep sleep. Even wrinkled, wild-eyed old Grandfather Sulfur, whose prophetic dreams had apparently contained Rooftoppers and a disturbance at the Sea in the Depths, came in on the arms of two acolytes to examine Flint, which made Chert as nervous as walking on a slope of loose tailings, but the ancient fellow went away again shaking his hairless head, saying that he saw and felt nothing special about the boy.

At last Brother Nickel told Chert, "We can do nothing more for him. Take him home."

Chert finished his cup of water. He had drunk a bucket's worth in the last hours, he felt sure, every drop a splendor. "I cannot carry him myself."

"We will send a brother who can help you take him in a litter."

"Methinks I will ride on that, friend Chert," said Beetledown in his tiny, high-pitched voice. "Better than thy pocket, being less whiffsome, beg thy pardon, and better than yon old flittermouse, which tended to the bony."

Nickel stared at the Rooftopper with superstitious distrust, as though he were a talking animal, but went off to make arrangements.

Chert let a young acolyte named Antimony, moonfaced and broad-shouldered, take the front of the litter while he took the back. A silent crowd of temple brothers watched them go. Tired as he was, Chert was quite content to let someone else find the way and pick the best spots. He looked down at Flint, pale and motionless but oddly peaceful, and even through his fear for the boy he felt a new rush of gratitude to Beetledown and to the Metamorphic Brothers: at least he was bringing a living child, however ill, back to Opal.

"You really rode a bat?" he asked Beetledown who, to lessen the chance of being accidentally crushed, was riding on the top edge of the litter near Flint's head.

"A Gutter-Scout am I. All animals we master to perform our duty." The tiny man coughed, then grinned. "And yon rat fellow was so piddling slow I could have outrun him my ownself."

"All I can say is thank you."

"Uns be useful words, so no need to apologize on them."

"You've been very kind to us."

"All for honor of queen and Rooftops." He made a little salute. "And I have found thy stone world not so dull as I thought. Could tha only bring a little more wind, rain, and sunlight down into these holes, I would come again to make a visit."

Chert smiled wearily. "I'll mention that to the Guild."

The shaking of the earth had frightened almost everyone in the castle, but there was not too much damage. Some crockery had fallen and shattered in the keep's huge kitchen and a serving maid had been terrified into apoplexy when an ancient suit of royal armor in the Privy Gallery shook off its stand and collapsed to the floor in front of her, but otherwise the toll had been light. Still, even without the news from Marrinswalk and the tremor, it would have been a hectic morning. Briony was kept busy until after the noon bell, mostly working with Nynor and Brone to sort the movement and housing of the incoming troops as well as many of the folk from the city outside the castle walls. The keep seemed crowded to bursting with people and animals and the time had almost come when no more could be accommodated.

She stole a part of an hour to eat a meal with her great-aunt, but it was not much relief. The dowager duchess was consumed with fear for Barrick just as Briony was, and had also been waiting to question the princess regent—and in several cases, argue with her—about the disposition of various nobles and their families within the inner keep. When their voices rose, Merolanna's little maid Eilis watched with wide, frightened eyes, as if at any moment something horrible could happen in this unexpected and unsteady new world.

Almost staggeringly tired, and with a long afternoon still stretching in front of her, Briony walked back to the throne room from Merolanna's chambers through the Portrait Hall; for once her guards didn't have to hurry to keep pace. Although she had seen the pictures of her ancestors in their finery many times, so often that she scarcely glanced at them most days, today it was easy to imagine that they were looking down on her with disapproval, that Queen Lily's kind eyes were full of disappointment, that even the portrait of mournful Queen Sanasu looked more desolate than usual.

It had only been a matter of a few months since Kendrick had been murdered, Briony told herself, and far less than a year since her father himself had last sat on the throne, yet what had happened? The kingdom was tottering, and that was more than just a fancy, as had been proved today most emphatically. It was difficult not to believe the trembling earth was the anger of the gods made manifest, a warning from heaven. Briony knew she could not escape a heavy share of blame: she and Barrick hated to be called children, but what else had they been? They had let what was given to them to protect fall from their fingers, left it out to rot like a discarded toy. Like the body of a murdered man in a field . . .

So grim were her thoughts that when the black-clad figure stepped out of a side corridor her first unsurprised assumption was that one of her dead ancestors, perhaps Sanasu herself, restless and discontented, had come to point a finger of shame at her. It was unsurprising, though, that in such times her guards' first thoughts were more practical: they clattered to a stop around her and leveled their pikes at the veiled woman.

"Is that you, Princess?" the figure whispered as she pulled back her veil.

The superstitious prickle on Briony's skin subsided, but only a little, as she recognized the face. "Elan? Elan M'Cory?"

The Tolly sister-in-law nodded. Her young face wore the mark of a terrible grief—a grief that Briony recognized, as powerful as that which had seized her after her brother's death. "Gailon is dead," the girl said.

Briony waved the guards back. For a moment she thought about saying the politic thing: it was early yet to be certain, after all. Nobody had seen the body who had known Gailon well. But the look of misery in the girl's gray eyes—eyes that were nevertheless bone-dry—touched her in that place of understanding, of shared sorrows. "Yes. Or at least it seems so."

Elan smiled, a strange, grim little tug at the corners of her mouth, as though she had been confirmed in something larger and longer-lived than just a fear for Gailon Tolly's life—reassured in some bleak view of all existence, perhaps. "I knew it. I have known it for days." The eyes fixed Briony again. "I loved him, of course. But he had no interest in me."

"I'm sorry . . ."

"Perhaps it is better this way. Now I can mourn him for the right reasons. I have one more question. You must tell me the truth."

Briony blinked. Who was this girl? "I must answer only to my father, the king, Lady Elan. And to the gods, of course. But go to—ask your question."

"Did you kill him, Briony Eddon? Did you have it done?"

It was shocking to be asked so directly. She realized, in the split-instant between hearing and answering, that she had become used to deference—more used to it than she had known. "No, of course I didn't. The gods know that Gailon and I did not agree on everything, but I would never . . ." She stopped to catch her breath, to consider what she was saying and doing. Standing a couple of yards away against the wall, the guards were trying to hide their fascination. After a moment she decided it was too late for anything in this particular case except the truth. "In fact, and you may hold this against me as you wish, Elan M'Cory, Gailon wanted to marry me—but I didn't want to marry him."

"I know that." But she sounded coldly satisfied. "For his ambition."

"I do not doubt you are right. But that was not enough to endear him to me. The gods may bear witness that I'll have no husband who thinks he can tell me where to go, what to say, how to . . ." She stopped herself again. What was it about this girl that had made her say so much more than she intended? "Enough. I did not kill him, if he is truly dead. We do not know who did."

Elan nodded. She pulled her veil back over her face. "Neither you nor any other woman will have him now." For the first time there was a muffled noise that might be a sob. "I wish you heaven's mercy," she said quietly, then turned and walked away without a courtesy or farewell.

It was indeed a very long afternoon, and as the news of the murdered men found in Marrinswalk began to circulate, along with speculation about their identities, the day threatened to stretch without end. The news impinged directly on Briony only slightly in her royal duties—questions and quiet asides from Brone, a perfunctory meeting with the hedge-baron in command of the Marrinswalk muster who was enjoying his moment of fame and attention, and an expanded set of concerns from Nynor, who had to decide whether to house these particular Marrinswalk troops with all the others brought in to garrison the castle or try to keep them separate—but she also saw speculation in the faces of almost everyone who passed through the throne room. As if things had not been bad enough after her outburst at Hendon Tolly! It was so grueling that the appearance of Queen Anissa's maid was almost a relief.

"Selia, isn't it?" With Barrick gone it was hard to hold onto her resentment toward the young woman. "Tell me, how is my stepmother?"

"Well enough, Highness, with the baby so close, but she has concern not to see you."

Briony's head hurt and she had trouble making sense out of the girl's foreign diction. "She wants me to stay away?"

Selia colored very prettily. Like all else she did, it seemed an affront to any woman who wanted to do something other than make men sigh—or at least so it felt to Briony, whose dislike of the maid was already returning. "No, no," the young woman said. "I do not speak so well. She wishes very much to have talk with you before the baby comes."

"I am quite busy, as my stepmother knows . . ."

The young woman leaned forward and spoke quietly; Brone and Nynor worked harder to pretend they were not listening. "She fears you are angry with her. This is bad for the baby, for the birth, she thinks. She was too ill for talking with you before, and now your brother has gone, the poor Barrick." Selia looked genuinely sad, which only made Briony less sympathetic.

That's my brother you've set your cap on, girl. Aloud, she said, "I will do my best."

"She asks that you come and take a cup of wine with her on Winter's Eve."

Sweet Zoria, that's only a few days away, Briony realized. *Where has the year gone?* "I will do my best to come to her soon. Tell her I wish her only well."

"I will, Princess." The young woman dropped a graceful courtesy and withdrew. Briony caught Brone and Nynor watching the maid as she walked away and was disgusted that even old men should still be such lechers. She tried to keep it off her face as they all returned to work, but not as hard as she might have.

The day's business dragged on, as what seemed like almost every living soul in the castle came before her with a complaint or a worry or a request, with problems ranging from the crucial to the ridiculous. What she didn't see was Hendon Tolly, nor—after her meeting in the Portrait Hall with his sister-in-law—any sign whatsoever of the Tollys or their faction.

"They are doubtless trying to decide what this discovery means," Brone told her in a quiet aside. "I am told they were out and about as usual this morning, but when they heard the news, they beat a retreat back into their rooms."

"I suppose it makes sense. But why did we put the Tollys and Durstin Crowel and the other troublemakers all so close together?"

"Because Crowel requested it some time back, Highness," said Nynor. "At the end of the summer he told me he would be hosting an entertainment with the Tollys during the Orphan's Day celebrations. I thought at the time he simply meant Duke Gailon and his entourage."

Briony frowned. "Does that mean they were planning something even then?"

Avin Brone grunted. "I don't trust the Tollys, but let us not pretend they're the worst of our problems."

Old Nynor shook his head. "It is possible they had some scheme, Highness, but it is also possible that all they were planning was a banquet. And, speaking of which, Princess, we must make some arrangements about the feasting."

For a moment she didn't understand what he was talking about. "Feasting? Do you mean for Orphan's Day? Are you mad? We are at war!"

"All the more reason." Steffans Nynor could be stubborn, and had not been castellan so many years without developing ideas of his own. Briony was irritated and tempted simply to say no and dismiss him, but thought of what her father would say—something like, *If you are going to give men tasks to do, then once they have proved themselves, you should let them get on without you standing over them. There is no point giving responsibility without trust.*

"Why, then, do you think we should do this?"

"Because these are holy days in which we praise the gods and demigods, and we need their help now more than ever. That is one reason."

"Yes, but we can perform the sacrifices and the rituals without the feasting and merrymaking."

"Why else do people *need* merrymaking, Highness, if not to take some of the thorns out of life?" The old man rapidly blinked his watery eyes, but his gaze was sharp and demanding. "Forgive me if I speak out of turn, Princess Briony, but it seems that what a city under siege most needs is courage. Also to be reminded what it is fighting to protect. A little happiness, a little ordinary life, is a powerful aid to both those things."

She saw the wisdom in what he said, but a part of her couldn't help feeling it would be a sham, that falsity was worse than misery.

Avin Brone seemed able to hear those thoughts as if they had been spoken. "People will not forget the true dangers, Highness. I think Nynor is right. A muted festivity perhaps—we do not want to seem to be celebrating too grandly in the shadow of war, and most especially in the shadow of Gailon's murder—and your brother's death, too, of course—but neither do we want to make this winter any more dreary than necessity dictates."

"Very well, a quiet celebration it will be."

Nynor nodded, then bowed and withdrew. He looked pleased, almost grateful, and for an unpleasant moment Briony wondered if the castellan had some other agenda, if he had manipulated her for some secret, selfish purpose.

And so it goes, she thought. *I cannot do even the simplest thing without doubt anymore, without fear, without suspicion. How could Father live this way all those years? It must have been a little better in more peaceful days, but still . . .*

Curse these times.

Before they reached the populous areas, Beetledown announced that he was taking his leave. He dismissed Chert's worried questions. "I'll find my way, sure. Naught else, these caves seem full of slow, stupid rat-folk. I'll go home mounted proud, tha will see."

He was too tired to do more than thank the Rooftopper again. After all they had shared, it was a hasty and strangely muted parting, but Chert didn't have long to consider it.

In the midst of such strange times their little procession was not the oddest thing the people of Funderling Town had heard of, but it was certainly one of the odder things they had actually seen: by the time Chert reached his house with Flint and the acolyte he was surrounded by a ragtag parade of children and more than a few adults. He did his best to ignore their questions and fondly mocking comments. He had no idea what time it was, or even what day. The young temple brother Antimony at the front end of the litter told him it was Skyday, fourth chime. Chert was astonished to realize that he had been almost three days in the lower depths.

Poor Opal! She must be cracked with worry.

The news had run ahead on child feet; a crowd of neighbors waited at the mouth of Wedge Road to join the throng. The tale had reached his own house as well: Opal ran out before he had even reached the dooryard, her face a confusion of joy and terror.

He tried not to be upset that the first thing she did was throw her arms around the senseless boy, even though it nearly upset the litter. He was even wearier than he had realized, and could only struggle to hold his end up and shake his head in silent dismissal of his neighbors' questions. Burly Antimony helped clear a path to the door.

"He isn't dead," Opal said, kneeling beside the boy. "Tell me that he isn't dead."

"He's alive, just . . . sleeping."

"Praise the Elders—but he's so cold!"

"He needs your nursing, dear wife." Chert slumped onto a bench.

She paused, then suddenly rushed to him and put her arms around his neck, kissed his cheeks. "Oh, I'm so glad you're not dead either, you old fool. Disappearing for days! I've been fretting over you, too, you know."

"I've been fretting over me as well, my girl. Go on, now. I'll tell you all this strange story later."

Antimony helped Opal move the boy to his bed, then turned down her distracted offer of food or drink and went out instead to placate the waiting crowd with some unspecific answers. Chert suspected the acolyte didn't find this too dreadful a chore. From what he knew, the temple brothers, especially the younger ones, didn't get much chance to come up to Funderling Town: the market trips and other such opportunities for distraction and temptation were reserved for the older, more trustworthy brothers.

He could hear Opal in the bedroom, crooning over the boy as she took off his dirty rags, cleaning him and checking for injuries just as the Metamorphic Brothers had done. Chert didn't think fresh smallclothes would be the thing that woke the boy, but he knew very well his wife needed to do something.

Chert looked up at a rustling noise, aware for the first time that he was not alone in the room. A very young woman, one of the big folk, sat on their long bench in the shadows against the wall, staring back at him with an air of patient detachment. Her dark hair was gathered untidily and she wore a dress that did not quite fit her thin frame. Chert had never seen her before, could think of no reason on or under the earth why someone like her should be in his house, even on a day of such bizarre branchings and cross-tunnels.

"Who are you?"

Opal came out of the back room with a look close to embarrassment on her face. "I forgot to tell you, what with the boy and all. She came about the second chime or so and she's been waiting ever since. Said she must speak to you, only to you. I . . . I thought it might be something to do with Flint . . ."

The young woman stirred on the bench. She seemed almost half-asleep. "You are Chert of the Blue Quartz?"

"Yes. Who are you?"

"My name is Willow, but I am nothing." She stood up; her head almost touched the ceiling. She extended a hand. "Come. I have been sent to bring you to my master."

35

The Silken Cord

THE CRABS:

All are dancing
The moon is crouching low for fear
He will see the naked Mother of All

—from *The Bonefall Oracles*

A S THE GREAT HAND CLOSED *around her, she felt it ringing like a crystal, a deep, shuddering vibration that had nothing to do with her, but which ran through that monstrous hand like a blood pulse, as if she were bound to a temple bell big as a mountain. The impossibly vast shape lifted her and although she could not see its face—it stood in the center of some kind of fog, light-shot but still deeply shadowed, as if a lightning storm raged inside the earth— she could see the greater darkness that was its mouth as it brought her nearer, nearer . . .*

She shrieked, or tried to, but there was only silence in that damp, empty place, silence and mist and the dark maw that grew ever larger, spreading above her like a rolling thundercloud. The titanic thing was going to swallow her, she knew, and she was frightened almost to death . . . but it was also somehow exciting too, like the shrieking, terrified childhood joy of being whirled in the air by her father or wrestling with her brothers until she was pinned and helpless . . .

Qinnitan awakened wet with perspiration, heart galloping. Her wits were utterly jangled and her skin twitched as though she lay in the middle of one of the great hives in the temple covered in a slow-buzzing blanket of sacred bees. She felt used by something—by her dream, perhaps—even defiled, and yet as her heart slowed a languid warmth began to spread through her limbs, a feeling almost of pleasure, or at least of release.

Qinnitan slumped back in her bed, breathing shallowly, overwhelmed. Her hand strayed down to her breasts and she discovered the tips had grown achingly hard beneath the fabric of her nightdress. She sat up again, shocked and disturbed. The idea of that dark, all-swallowing mouth still hung over her thoughts as it had hung over her dream. She leaped to her feet and went to the washing tub. The water had been sitting since the previous night and was quite cold, but instead of calling for the servants to bring her hot water, she squatted in it gladly and pulled her nightdress up to her neck, then splashed herself all over until she began to shiver. She sank down into the shallow bath, still trembling, and put her chin on her knees, letting the water wick up the linen nightdress until it clung to her like a clammy second skin.

The rest of the day was quieter and more mundane, although the torments of the endlessly droning prayers and the drinking of the Sun's Blood were as bad as ever. If Panhyssir or the autarch were trying to kill her with that potion, they were taking a ridiculously long time about it, she had to admit, but whatever they intended, they were certainly making her miserable.

Just after Qinnitan's evening meal the hairdressing servant came to dye her red streak—her witch streak, as her childhood friends had named it—which was beginning to show at the roots again: Luian and the other Favored had decreed within days of her arrival that such a mongrel mark had no place on one of the autarch's queens. The hairdresser also dried her hair and arranged it into a pleasing style, on the one-in-a-thousand chance the autarch should finally call for her that very evening. Qinnitan tried to sit quietly; this hairdresser had a way of poking you with a hairpin—and then apologizing profusely, of course—when you moved too much.

I doubt she pulls that trick with Arimone.

But Qinnitan didn't like thinking about the Paramount Wife. Since the day Qinnitan had gone to her palace, there had been no further invitations and no outward sign of hostility, but it was not hard to see the way those wives and wives-to-be who considered themselves friends of the Evening Star watched Qinnitan and made clear their dislike of her. Well, they might think themselves friends of the great woman, but she doubted Arimone looked on them the same way; Qinnitan felt sure there was little room for friends or equals of any kind in the world of the Paramount Wife.

The hairdresser was finishing up just as the soldiers on the walls outside began to call out the old ritual words for the sunset change of the guard— *"Hawks return! To the glove! To the glove!"* Qinnitan, reasonably certain that the autarch was not going to break his nearly year-long habit and summon her tonight, was looking forward to an hour or two of time to herself before sleep and whatever unsettling dreams might come with it. She thought she might say her evening orisons, then read. One of the other brides, youngest daughter of the king of some tiny desert land on the southern edge of Xis, had loaned her a beautifully illustrated book of poetry by the famous Baz'u Jev. Qinnitan had read some of it and enjoyed it very much—his descriptions of sheepherders in the arid mountains who lived so close to the sky they called themselves "Cloud People" spoke of a freedom and simplicity that seemed achingly attractive to her. The young desert princess seemed quite nice, really, and Qinnitan entertained a hope that one day they might become friends, since they were two of the youngest in the Seclusion. This did not mean she had abandoned all sense, of course. She never touched the book without wearing gloves. The tale of a Paramount Wife from a century or so before who had dispatched a rival by having poison painted on the edges of a book's pages was one of the first cautionary stories Qinnitan had heard upon coming to her new home.

That tale spoke much of the Seclusion, not just the murderousness of the place, but the fact that the older wife had been willing to wait weeks or even months for the autarch's new favorite to cut her finger in such a way that the poison could enter when she turned the pages. Whatever men might say about women and their reputed fickleness, the Seclusion was a place of immense patience and subtlety, especially when the stakes were high. And what stakes could be higher than to be certain it was your own child who would one day sit on the throne of the most powerful empire in the world between the seas?

Gloves or no, Qinnitan was looking forward to a little time with the epic simplicity of Baz'u Jev, so it was disappointing—and, as always in the Seclusion, a little frightening—when a messenger came just as the hairdresser was leaving.

She was startled to recognize the mute boy who had come into her room not a fortnight before. He was wearing a loose tunic tonight, so she could not see how his wound had healed, although he seemed perfectly well. He would hardly meet her eyes as he handed her the roll of parchment, but although that saddened her, it was not as though she was surprised that he didn't want to be her friend; she had almost stabbed him to death with a dressing pin, after all.

Strangely, the message was not tied or sealed in any way, although she could tell from the strong violet perfume that the paper was Luian's. She waited until the hairdresser had gone out into the passageway before unrolling it.

The letters had been made in a great hurry. It read:

Come now.

There was nothing else.

Qinnitan did her best to be calm. Perhaps this was just an example of Luian in a bad mood. They had spoken only occasionally in the last weeks, and had taken tea together in their old way just once, an awkward occasion in which the subject of Jeddin was in the air the entire time but never acknowledged. The two of them had labored through a conversation of what should have been interesting gossip, but which had instead seemed like wearying labor. Yes, it was unusual for Luian to write in this hurried, informal way, but it might be evidence of some great swing of feeling—after all, Favored Luian was prone to moments of heightened emotion that might have come out of a folktale, or even from a book of love poetry. Perhaps she planned to shame Qinnitan for being a bad friend. Perhaps she planned a weeping renunciation of her own rights to Jeddin—if even Luian could be that self-deceiving. Or perhaps she just wished them to be on good terms again.

All the same, Qinnitan found herself following the mute boy across the Seclusion with a heavy, untrusting heart.

Qinnitan was shocked to find a huge, ugly man weeping in Luian's bed. Several heartbeats passed before she realized it was Luian herself she was seeing, a Luian without face paint or wig or elaborate dress, wearing only a simple white nightgown damp with tears and sweat.

"Qinnitan, Qinnitan! Praise to the gods, you're here." Luian threw her arms wide. Qinnitan could not help staring. It really had been Dudon under that paint, after all—the lumpy, self-absorbed boy who had walked up and down the streets muttering the Nushash prayers. Qinnitan had known it, of course, but until now she had not really seen it. "Why do you shy away from me?" Luian's face was red and mottled, wet with tears. "Do you hate me?"

"No!" But she could not bring herself to enter that embrace, not from fastidiousness so much as the sudden fear of swimming too close to someone who might be drowning and dangerous. "No, I don't hate you, Luian, of course not. You've been very kind to me. What's wrong?"

It was a wail that just avoided turning into a scream. "Jeddin has been arrested!"

Qinnitan, for the second time that day, felt as though her body was no longer her own. This time it seemed to have become a statue of cold stone in which her thoughts were trapped. She could not speak.

"It is all so unfair!" Luian snuffled and tried to cover her face with her sleeve.

"What . . . what are you talking about?" she finally managed.

"He has been arrested! It is the talk of the Seclusion, as you would know if you came out to eat the evening meal instead of sitting in your ch—chambers like a h—hermit." She wept a little more, as though at Qinnitan's unsocial behavior.

"Just tell me what happened."

"I don't know. He's b—been arrested. His lieutenant has been made chief of the Leopards, at least for now. It's Vash's doing, that horrid old man. He's always hated our Jin . . ."

"For the love of the gods, Luian, what are we to do?" Qinnitan's mind was already racing, but in a weary, defeated way, as if she were a runner at the end of a long chase instead of just at the beginning.

Luian sobered a little, wiping her eyes with the back of her hand. "We must not lose our heads. Of course, we must not lose our heads. We must stay calm." She took a deep breath. "It is possible he has done something that has nothing to do with us . . . but even if they suspect the worst, he will never tell. Not Jeddin! That is why I called you here, to make you swear to say nothing, not even if they tell you he has confessed. Don't speak a word—they will be lying! Our Jin will never say a word to Pinimmon Vash, not even . . . not even if they . . ." She burst out weeping again.

"They would torture him? Kill him? For sneaking into the Seclusion?"

"Oh, yes, perhaps." Luian flapped her hands in agitation. "But that is not the worst of it." She suddenly realized the mute boy was still standing in the doorway, waiting for further orders and she waved him away with angry gestures.

"*What* is not the worst of it? Are you saying he has done worse things than proclaiming his love for one of the autarch's wives? Than smuggling himself into the Seclusion where whole-bodied men are killed on sight? By the Bees, what other crimes did he have time to accomplish?"

Luian stared at her for a moment, or rather this familiar yet unfamiliar man who talked like Luian stared, and then burst into tears again. "He wished to . . . to . . . to depose the Golden One. The autarch!"

In the first lurch, Qinnitan thought her heart might never beat again. She could speak only in a strangled whisper, which was perhaps just as well. "He . . . was going to kill *the autarch?*"

"No, no!" Luian looked aghast. "No, he would never raise his hand against the Golden One. He has sworn an oath!" She shook her head at Qinnitan's foolishness. "No, he was going to kill the scotarch, Prusas the Cripple. Then the autarch would fall and . . . and somehow, Jeddin thought, he would be able to take you for his own."

Qinnitan could only back away, waving her arms in front of her as though to keep away some approaching beast. "The fool! The fool!"

"But he will never tell—he will never speak a word of it!" Luian was up on her knees now, arms spread again, begging Qinnitan to come back and be enfolded. "He is so brave, our Jin, so brave . . . !"

"Why did you help him? Why did you let him put your life and . . . and *my* life at risk?" Qinnitan was shaking, full of rage and terror. She wanted to run at Luian and beat that doughy, wet face with her fists. "How could you do that?"

"Because I loved him." Luian fell back against the cushions. "My Jin. I would even help him to have you. I would do anything he asked." She looked up, her eyes red-rimmed, but she was smiling. "You understand about love. You are a woman. You were *born* a woman. You understand."

Qinnitan turned and ran out the doorway.

Luian called after her, "Say nothing! He will never say a word, our Jin will never . . ."

Qinnitan reached the corridor, her thoughts tumbling like pearls from a broken necklace. Was Luian right? Would Jeddin's warrior code keep him silent even under torture?

But it's not fair! I didn't do anything! I sent him away!

She heard footsteps then—not the sandaled thump of the Seclusion's guards, men big as oxen, but not the whispering slide of barefooted women either. She hesitated, but decided she did not want to be seen so close to

Luian's rooms. It would make it seem as though they had something to hide, meeting in the very hour of Jeddin's arrest. If Luian was right, that Jeddin could hold his secrets even under torture, the best hope was that all should seem normal, blameless.

Qinnitan stepped back into a shadowy cross-passage just before the approaching figure turned the corner into the main hallway; she silently thanked all the gods there was no lamp in the wall niche. She looked for somewhere to hide, but could only draw back close against a tapestry that hung on the wall. If whoever was passing gave anything more than the quickest glance, they would see her.

She flattened herself and turned her head away, knowing that the magic of eyes invariably drew the attention of others, especially unwanted attention. Whoever it was stalked by without slowing. Qinnitan let out a silent sigh of relief. She crept to the edge of the cross-passage and saw a short, stocky shape turn into Luian's chambers. It took her a moment to realize who had just passed.

From the room, Luian let out a shriek of startled fright. Qinnitan could not help taking a few instinctive steps toward one who had been her friend and was now in danger, then her better judgment stopped her.

Tanyssa's voice was hoarse, as though the gardener herself was a bit frightened, too, but there was also a note of triumph in it. *"Favored Luian of the Royal Seclusion, I am here as the hand of God. You have betrayed your sacred trust. You have betrayed the Master of the Great Tent."*

"Wh-what are you talking about?"

"There is no argument," said the gardener. *"The Golden One has put his seal on it."*

Luian's squeal of alarm suddenly turned into a loud grunting, a noise so horrid that for the first moments Qinnitan couldn't even imagine it coming from a person.

"You . . . are for . . . the worms." Tanyssa, breathing hard, spoke in almost ordinary tones now—Qinnitan could barely hear her, although she stood trembling only a pace or two from Luian's doorway—but there was clear hatred in the voice. *"You fat, meddling bitch."* The grunting turned to a choking hiss, then Qinnitan heard only the drumlike thumping of flesh on the stone, heels or hands beating helplessly until they too fell silent.

Her bones turned to leaden bars by terror, Qinnitan could scarcely move. She stumbled to the shadowed cross-corridor and looked back to see the hangings on Luian's door billow outward. Her head was pounding. She pushed her face against the wall, burrowed into the space where the tapestry hung a little away from the cool stone, and prayed. The footsteps went past more slowly this time, so slowly that it was all Qinnitan could do to keep her face turned into the wall, to stand unmoving. Whether because of the darkness of the passageway or because her mind was taken up with what she had just done, the gardener who was also an executioner did not pause or even slow but walked on down the corridor. Qinnitan listened until she could no longer hear the footfalls.

She wanted to weep, but she felt as though some terrible cold fire had swept through her and evaporated every tear. Even her mouth was parched. Where could she go? What could she do?

She stood in the passageway only a few moments, stepping from foot to foot in an agony of indecision. Was Luian only the first of Tanyssa's tasks? Was she even now on her way to Qinnitan's chamber?

I can't go back there. But where can I go? Where can I hide? She thought for a moment of the little room off the Scented Garden that Jeddin had used for their assignation, then realized with a lurch of fear that such a place must now be infamous to the autarch's lieutenants. In fact, there was nowhere she could hide, nowhere at all. *They will turn the whole palace over like a jewelry box to shake me out.*

The only faint hope she had was to get out of the Seclusion. But how? How in the name of the Hive could she hope to get out past guards who would undoubtedly be looking for her?

Jeddin's seal ring! She reached into her sleeve and found it and its chain, still in the secret pocket she had sewn there. A premonition—that, and the knowledge that there was no privacy for anyone within the Seclusion—had kept her from leaving it hidden in her chamber. *But what good will it do me? Even if by some tiny chance they are not looking to execute me, too, even if my name has been kept from them, trying to pass the gate with a forged message from Jeddin would catch their attention for sure.*

Now the tears finally came, hot tears of helplessness that burned against her cheeks. Could she believe that Jeddin had given up Luian but had kept silent about Qinnitan herself? No. The chance was so small as to be invisible.

You can't stand here weeping! she told herself. *Stupid girl! Get out of the hallway! Hide!* But where could she go? She was in the middle of the autarch's own palace and now she was his enemy. The most powerful man in the world wanted her dead, and that death was not likely to be either quick or painless.

Poison, the terror of the Seclusion, suddenly seemed a blessing. If she had possessed any, Qinnitan would have drunk it then.

36

At the Giant's Feet

BLACK SPEAR:

He is smeared with blood and fat
He is fire in the air
He is called "One Rib" and "Flower of the Sun"

—from *The Bonefall Oracles*

"I AM IMPRESSED," TINWRIGHT said as he looked down from their high perch and across the choppy water. The narrow reach of Brenn's Bay between the castle and the mainland city teemed with small watercraft, strange in such unsettled weather but not surprising in such an unsettled time: now that the causeway had been dismantled all those who would travel between city and keep had to do so by boat, braving the high, whitecapped waves. "I did not think anyone but the royal household were allowed into the Towers of the Seasons."

"I *am* part of the royal household." Puzzle drew himself up to his full height, but couldn't stay unbent very long; after a moment he rounded his shoulders and let his head nod forward again. "I am the king's jester, you know. And when Olin comes back, I will be in good odor once more."

If such a day ever comes. Matty Tinwright couldn't help feeling sorry for the old fellow who had lost favor, but he knew he would be no different. When the royal family reached out to touch you, it was like air to a drowning man—anyone with a bit of ambition would tread water forever in hopes of continuing to breathe that air, scorning any other.

And look at me, he thought then. *Look how far I have come since I tasted that air—how high!* It was far more than poetic metaphor. He stood on a balcony of the Tower of Winter with nearly all of Southmarch below him, only the black stones of Wolfstooth Spire looming at his back like a stern parent. *A month ago I was in the mire.* He watched the overloaded boats being pushed back from the Winterside water gate by soldiers, heard the faint sound of people pleading, children crying. *I would have been begging for sanctuary like the rest of them. Instead, I am assured my place. I am fed and housed by the Eddons—by the word of Princess Briony herself. Ah, the gods, and most especially Zosim, Patron of Poets, have smiled on me.*

Still, he couldn't help wishing the gods would do something about the war that had brought so many frightened souls into the castle that Tinwright now found himself sharing his bed in shifts again, just as in his days at the Quiller's Mint. For a moment he felt a twinge of real fear.

It could not be that the gods have some plan to trick me, could it? That they have brought me to this high estate only to let me die at the hands of warlocks and fairies . . . ? He shook his head. The gloomy day had put foul thoughts in his mind. *Briony Eddon herself elevated me, defends me. She recognizes my art and has brought me under her mantle. And everyone knows this castle will never be taken by siege—the ocean will defend it just as the princess regent protects me.*

Dark thoughts banished, Tinwright took a long swallow of the wine and then passed the heavy jug to Puzzle, who had to hold it with both hands, trembling with the effort as he lifted it to his lips. The thin jester swayed a little, like a sapling.

"It's a good thing you're holding that," Tinwright told him. "The wind is growing fierce."

"Good, that." The old man wiped his lips. "Wine, I mean. Warms a man up. Now, sir, I did not call you up here merely to admire the view, although it is very fine. I need your help."

Tinwright raised an eyebrow. "My help?"

"You are a poet, sir, are you not? Winter's Eve is almost upon us. There will be a feast, of course. I must entertain the princess regent and the others. The good old duchess will be there." He smiled for a moment, lost in some memory. "She likes my jests. And the other great and good—all will be gathered together. I must have something special for them."

Tinwright was watching the bay again. A small boat had capsized; a family was in the choppy water. It all seemed very distant, but still Tinwright was glad to see that a number of other boats, mostly Skimmer crafts, were moving toward the place. A Skimmer man, one long arm still holding the tiller of his tiny sailboat, reached out and pulled what looked like a small child out of the gray-green water. "Sorry," Tinwright said. "I don't understand."

"A song, man, a song!" The intensity in the jester's voice was such that Matty Tinwright turned away from the rescue. Puzzle's lined face seemed lit from within, full of glee. "You must write something clever!"

How much wine has the old fellow drunk? "You want me to write a song for you?"

Puzzle shook his head. "I will write the tune. I was much known for it in my younger days. For my voice, too." His face sagged. "Never grow old. Do you hear me? Never grow old."

In truth, Tinwright could not quite imagine such a thing, although he knew it lay in the distance somewhere, just as he had been told there was another continent far to the south, a place he had never seen and thought of not at all except to borrow the occasional metaphor set there—"dusky and sweet as a Xandian grape"—that he had heard used by other poets. Old age was like that to him as well. "What kind of song do you wish to sing?"

"Nothing to make people laugh. These are not the times for levity." The old man nodded, as if being unfunny was for him a careful decision instead of the helpless tragedy of his life's work. "Something heroic and light-hearted. Some tale of Silas or one of the other Lander's Hall knights might do. Perhaps *The Ever-Wounded Maid*—that takes place at a Winter's Eve feast, after all."

Tinwright considered it. There was no obvious value in the favor: Puzzle, despite his reminiscences, was no closer to the heart of power in Southmarch these days than Tinwright himself. Then again, what if the king did return? Odder things had happened.

Also—and it took Tinwright a moment to understand this, so unusual was the impulse—he liked the old man and would enjoy doing him a favor. After all, the gods knew that Puzzle had not been blessed with the natural gifts of art, as Matt Tinwright had in his own calling.

"Very well," he said. "But you have not given me much time."

Puzzle beamed. "You are a stout fellow, Tinwright. Truly, you are a friend. It need not be overlong—the attention of the court tends to wander by the time the meal is over and they have been well into the wine. Ah, thank you. This calls for another drink." He heaved up the jug for a healthy swallow, then passed it to Tinwright, who almost dropped it, his attention again on the water.

"The Skimmers have saved that family," he noted. "May the gods bite other gods, look at them! Half-naked in this cold! I will never understand Skimmers. They must have blubberous hide like a seal."

"It *is* cold," said Puzzle. "We should go down." He squinted into the distance. "Look, you cannot even see Landsend for the fog. And it has come down out of the hills, too, and all across the downs. It will cover the city soon." He wrapped his thin arms around himself. "Shadow-weather, we used to call it." He turned suddenly to Tinwright. "You do not think it has anything to do with the Twilight People, do you?"

Tinwright looked at the thick mists crawling down from the tops of the nearby hills, combs of white that mirrored the wind-slapped waves of the bay. "This is a spit of land between the bay and the ocean. There are always fogs here."

"Perhaps." Puzzle nodded. "Yes, of course, you are right. We older folk, when the cold gets into our bones, it makes us think of . . ." He wiped his eyes: the wind had made them water. "Let us go down. There will be a fire in the kitchen and we can finish the jug and talk about my Winter's Eve song."

"Who *is* your master?" Chert asked.

The girl Willow suddenly looked shy, the first thing she had done that seemed in keeping with her age and appearance. "I do not know his name . . . but I know his voice."

He shook his head. "Look, child, I don't know you or what brings you here. It could be that at some other time I would go with you, if only to find out what sort of strangeness this is, but I have just returned from a journey beneath the earth that would make the Lord of . . . that would make Kernios himself fall down and nap for a week. Our boy is in the other room, sick, perhaps dying. My wife has been terrified for us both. I cannot go with you to see your master, especially when you cannot even name him."

For a long moment she faced him, narrow face solemn, as though the words he had spoken had not yet reached her ears. Her heavy-lidded eyes fell shut. When she opened them, she said, "Do you have the mirror?"

"The *what?*"

"The mirror. My master says that if you cannot come yourself, you must send the mirror with me." She reached out her hand, guileless and direct as a girl half her age demanding a sweet. Even in his startlement, Chert couldn't help wondering about her. She was tall even for one of the big folk, and pretty enough, but even though she was washed and her frock was clean, if plain, there was something offhand and bedraggled about her, as though she had dressed herself in the dark.

"Your master . . . wants the mirror?" Without thought Chert put his hand into the pocket of his tattered, sweat-stained shirt, closed it on the smooth, cool thing. Too late he realized he had given away that he had it, but the girl was not even looking at him. She stood, palm still extended, staring into the middle distance as though looking right through the wall of the house.

"He says that each moment that goes by brings Old Night closer," she said.

Chert was startled to hear Chaven's words, Chaven's terrible warning, coming from the mouth of this moonstruck child. He groaned.

"I must tell my wife," he said at last.

Few folk were still on the streets of Funderling Town now that the lamps had been lowered for evening, but those who were out watched Chert with surprise. Most had already heard about the bizarre little parade that had signaled his return from the depths, but even that could not have prepared them for this sight: Chert Blue Quartz, only just finished one set of wild adventures, glumly following one of the big folk back out of town as though walking to his own execution. And in truth, his thoughts were nearly that heavy.

Opal didn't even shout, he thought as he followed the girl toward the town gates. *I could have borne it if she had shouted at me, called me names. I can scarcely believe I am going out again myself. But to see her turn her back on me, with nothing more than, "You do what you must." Is it the child? Has she found something she cares for more than me?*

Or perhaps she's just like you, old fool, a part of him suggested. *Perhaps with the boy so still and deathly she's got enough under her pick that she doesn't have time for something she doesn't understand. Not that you understand it either.*

Music drifted out of the guildhall as he passed, the voices of men and boys lifted in song. The men's choir was practicing for year's end, the timeless songs of their people shared between them like a meal. Schist the chorister would be pacing back and forth, listening, frowning, absently wagging one hand to show the rhythm. For the singers all was ordinary tonight, even the threat of war and tales of Chert's weird adventures largely a diversion. The Funderlings outlasted wars, or at least they always had: builders, diggers, miners, they were too valuable to kill and too hard to catch in their serpentine retreats even if someone wished to kill them. *We stone folk stay close to the ground,* his father used to say. *The view is not so proud, but we're harder to knock down.*

Would they outlast Old Night, too, if it came?

Why has my life been broken into pieces? Chert wondered. *Why have I been singled out?*

To his growing amazement, the girl led him into the very heart of the castle. A crush of people surrounded the Raven's Gate, guards arguing with a variety of petitioners, but one of them recognized her and let her through, although he cast a mistrustful eye over Chert before allowing the Funderling to follow her into the inner keep. Willow did not speak to anyone, but led him through open spaces, gardens, and covered walkways until even his fine sense of direction was confused. The sun had set and the air was bitingly cold. Chert was glad that he had brought his warm coat, although it had been hard to believe he would need it when he left, so much was he still remembering the heat of the depths. It made him a little sad that Opal had not reminded him to take it as she usually did, but he told himself that even his all-seeing, all-knowing wife couldn't remember everything, especially in the midst of such a strange day.

As he finally pulled on the coat, Willow led him through a gate and into an arbored garden lit by a few torches in stands. Chert did not know what garden it was, and he certainly didn't recognize the man waiting on a low bench. He had half-suspected he would find Chaven on the other side of this mysterious summons and it was hard to fight a feeling of disappointment bordering on real fear to discover this stranger instead.

The man turned his face toward them as they approached; his eyes seemed as disturbingly incurious as the girl's. He was almost Chaven's opposite, younger than the physician and much thinner, with hair close-cropped in an awkward way that looked as if he had done it himself with a knife, and without looking.

Perhaps that's why he needs the mirror, Chert thought, but he was not amusing anyone today, least of all himself. "You sent for me," he said aloud, as firmly as he could manage. "As though you were my master and not just the girl's. But you are not, so tell me your business."

"Did you bring the mirror?" The man's voice was slow and quiet.

"You will answer my questions first. Who are you and what do you want?"

"Who am I?" The stranger said it slowly, as though it were an unexpected question. "Here, in this place, I am called Gil. I think I have another name . . . but I cannot remember it."

Chert felt a quiver of panic move down his backbone. The man had the detachment of the mad, as calm as Chert's old grandfather had been in his last years, sitting beside the fire in his house like a lizard in the sun, barely moving at all from unseen dawn to day's end.

"I don't know what that nonsense means, but I know you have called me out of my home at a time when my family has great need of me. I will ask you again—what do you want?"

"To prevent the destruction of two races. To put off the finality of the Great Defeat a little longer, even if it cannot forever be averted." The one named Gil nodded slowly, as if he only now understood his own words. For the first time, he smiled—a thin, ghostly thing. "Is that not enough?"

"I have no idea what you mean, what these things are you speak about." Chert wanted badly to turn around and walk, even run, until stone was above him once more. Clouds hung overhead, night clouds so thick that he couldn't see the moon or stars, but it was still nothing like being in his own place, among his own people and his own homely things.

"Neither do I," said Gil. "But I am given to understand a little, and that little is this—you must give me the mirror. Then your work is done."

Chert almost clutched at the mirror again, even though neither the strange man nor the girl looked like much of a threat to take it away from him. Still, they were twice his height . . . *Just let them try,* he thought. *Just let them try to get the thing my son almost died for* . . . And then he realized for the first time what he had been thinking in a wordless way for some time; the mirror was the answer. The mirror was what had taken Flint down into the depths of the Mysteries, and what had almost killed him. "No, I will not give you the mirror—if I even had such a thing."

"You have it," Gil said mildly. "I can feel it. And it is not yours to keep."

"It is my son's!"

Gil shook his head. "I think not, although that is somewhat dark to me. But it doesn't matter. You have it now. If you give it to me, you may go home and never think of it again."

"I will not give it to you."

"Then you must come with me," the strange man said. "The hour is almost upon us. The mirror must be carried to her. It will not prevent Old Night and the destruction of all, but it may gain a little time."

"What does this mean? What are you talking about? Carried to her? Who in the name of the Earth Elders is 'her'?"

"She is called Yasammez," the stranger told him. "She is one of the oldest. She is death, and she has been loosed on your kind at last."

The afternoon sun was beginning to settle behind the hills. From where they sat on a rocky hilltop prominence, looking southeast toward the castle, although it was still too far away to see, the grass was a damp, rich green and the sky was marbled with sunlight and cloud. In all ways it would have seemed a crisp, cool day at the turning of winter had it not been for the clot of fog rolling across the land below them, obscuring all but the highest slopes of the downs as it reached toward Southmarch.

"It must be them," said Tyne Aldritch, and spat. "You said that it came down from the Shadowline, Vansen, a fog like that. You said they traveled under it like a cloak."

The captain of the guard stirred. His face was pinched, worried. "That is what the merchant's nephew told us, the one whose caravan was attacked. When my men and I stumbled across the boundary, there was no fog. But, yes, I think it's likely our enemies are in that murk."

Barrick was finding it hard to do anything at this moment except stay upright in his saddle. They had driven the army far and fast already today, and even though he was mounted, he was astonishingly weary and his bad arm ached as though someone had pushed a dagger between the bones of his wrist. Not for the first time today he wished he had kept his mouth closed and stayed at home.

But if we don't stop them, it will only be a different sort of death for those who remained behind in Southmarch. All during the day today the memory of the pale faces of the shadow-things, the dead but still terrifying eyes, had troubled him. He had not eaten. He could not imagine putting anything in his stomach except water.

"Are our scouts fast enough to beat them to the city?" asked Lord Fiddicks. "If we can get Brone's garrison out, we can catch them as between hammer and anvil."

"Our scouts might, but I think we should not trust to them alone," said Earl Tyne. "Ah, but we have pigeons, don't we? We will send messages that way. A bird will go faster than any man, especially if that man is riding a tired horse."

Ferras Vansen cleared his throat. Oddly, he looked at Barrick for permission to speak. Despite his weariness and misery, Barrick was amused that the world of title and privilege should still exist after the morning's debacle, but he nodded.

"It is just . . ." Vansen began. "My lords, it seems to me that we cannot wait."

Tyne growled in irritation. "You would make the gods weep, man, you take so long to speak your mind. What do you mean?"

"If we go at this pace, we will not overtake them. They are mostly on foot, as are we, but their troops seem to move swiftly. If they can march at night, they will reach the mainland city by morning."

"Good," said Rorick. He had sustained only a few small cuts in the fighting—Barrick had noticed that he had not been one of the first into the thick of things—but wore his bandages with a prideful flair. "Then we will trap them against the bay. Fairies do not like water, everyone knows. When Brone comes out against them, we will tear them to pieces."

Vansen shook his head. "I beg your pardon, my lord, but I fear that idea. I think we must try to stop them on the downs, in the farmlands outside the city."

The other nobles made mocking noises—some even quietly called Vansen a fool, although he ignored their words. Even Tyne Aldritch seemed annoyed and turned to send his squire for wine. Barrick saw foot soldiers stealing the chance to sit or even lie down while the nobles argued on the hilltop; he realized that the men had been walking all day with armor and weapons, and were at least as aching and dispirited as he was, but perhaps twice as tired.

"Yes, tell us what you mean, Captain Vansen," Barrick said out loud. "Why shouldn't we wait and catch them between our two forces?"

Vansen nodded at him like a tutor pleased by his pupil, which made Barrick regret taking the man's side. "Because there are too many unknowns," the guard captain said. "What if we cannot get a message through to the lord constable?"

"Then he will come out when he sees the fighting," said Rorick. "Really, that is a foolish fear. This is a waste of time. What is this man doing here?"

"He is here because until today, he was the only one of us who had met the enemy," said Tyne; his irritation was obviously not confined to Vansen alone. "And while not all of us can say the same, he acquitted himself bravely this morning as well."

Rorick flushed, covering it by sending his own squire for wine.

"Just say what you are thinking, Captain." Barrick wondered how he had suddenly become Vansen's protector.

"First, as we have seen, strange things happen around the Twilight People. Can a pigeon find its way through or around that murk? Possibly. Will Brone be able to see what happens as the fog comes down and covers the coast and the city—will he know we are fighting for our lives just a half mile away? It seems obvious, but believe me, things in those shadows are not always what they seem, as I learned to my regret. You've seen a little of that now, too, all of you.

"More importantly, what happens when our enemy reaches the city along the shore? Will they stand and fight us on open ground? Or will they disappear instead into the streets and alleyways, into the sewers and cellars and deserted buildings? How will we fight them then? We will be muddled, confused—you all remember that wood on the hilltop, fighting against a tenth of the numbers of this force. Would you give them a thousand more places to hide? It will be as though their army had grown tenfold again."

"But the city is largely empty," said one of the other nobles, puzzled. "The people have been taken inside the castle walls or have fled south."

"What of it?" asked Vansen.

"If they move into the city," Rorick said scornfully, "then we will put fire to it. We will burn them out. What better way to deal with unnatural creatures?"

"Forgive me, my lord," said Vansen, although he didn't look as if he wanted or expected forgiveness, "but that is spoken as only a man who owns several castles can speak. Thousands of people make their homes there! And the city and its farms keeps Southmarch Castle alive."

"I have had enough of this peasant's insults," Rorick said, pawing at the hilt of his sword. "He must be punished."

"You have the right to challenge him, Longarren," Tyne pointed out, "but I will not punish a man for speaking as Vansen has spoken."

Rorick looked from Tyne Aldritch to Vansen. He appeared notably reluctant to pull his sword from its sheath. At last he tugged on his horse's reins and turned and rode down the hill. His squire, who had just returned with his saddle-cup, hurried after him.

"Continue, Captain," said Tyne.

"Thank you, my lords." Vansen turned to Barrick, his face grim. "Leaving aside what my liege lord Earl Rorick thinks, Highness, do not forget that they seem to be at least as many as we are. And even if we would sacrifice many men in close fighting and then put the torch to the greatest city in the March Kingdoms, what makes us think that we could burn that city without hindrance? Having met this enemy twice, I think it is madness to suppose them such children. They plan! They are patient! And we do not know the half yet of what they can do."

"So what would you suggest?" Barrick suddenly didn't want to hear it. It seemed obvious it would not be anything comfortable, with a fire and a meal at the end of it, and sleep to help ease his aching arm. "Go ahead, Vansen, tell. And may the gods curse us all for fools for having got ourselves in this situation in the first place!"

Several of the nobles were startled by this into making the sign against evil.

"Do not speak so, Highness," said the Earl of Blueshore, scowling. "Do not bring the anger of the gods down on us. I will tell that to even you. Take my head for it if you wish."

"No, Tyne, I was wrong. I apologize."

"It is not me who needs an apology, my prince."

"Don't worry, it's not you the gods will punish either." Barrick turned away from Tyne's surprised look. "Speak, Captain. Tell us your plan."

Vansen took a ragged breath; it was clear that he was as exhausted as everyone else. A cut on his jaw had reopened; a trickle of blood crawled down his neck like a tiny red snake. "We must ride, all of us. We must leave the men on foot to come as fast as they can. Otherwise, we will never catch the shadow folk. Who knows if even the water will stop them? Not me, and certainly not Earl Rorick, begging my lords' pardon. Who knows if even the walls of the keep will keep them out? We must catch the shadow folk and force them to turn and fight us, try to hold them until the rest of our force catches up—there'll be no shame in retreating once we first touch them and punish them, especially with full dark only a few hours ahead. But if we wait until tomorrow's daylight, they will have already reached Southmarch. We mounted men must nip at them like a pack of dogs then scamper away, then strike again so they can't ignore us. We must stop them and turn them until the men on foot arrive."

"But what about Brone and his troops?" asked Tyne. "This seems madness when we have a garrison that can come out to support us."

"Let them, then!" said Vansen. "Send our messengers, those with wings and those without. But I cannot say this strongly enough, my lords—if we let them reach the city before us, I fear that we'll regret it."

Tyne looked a question at Barrick, who felt more than a little queasy in his stomach. He had known he would not like hearing what Vansen had to say, but it was too late now: he had heard it and he had recognized the dire truth in it. It was all he could do to nod his head.

Kettle stumbled in a rabbit hole and Barrick almost flew out of the saddle at full gallop, but he wrapped his hand in the horse's mane and held on until he could get himself straightened up again. He was momentarily grateful that he was not carrying a lance as many of the other riders were, that his crippled arm didn't permit it, since he would surely have lost it or, worse, let it slip down point-first as the horse fought for balance, likely knocking himself out of the saddle. Then he remembered that a man without a lance couldn't keep an enemy any farther away than the tip of his falchion.

They would have let me stay behind. They all told me not to come. The words seemed to bounce in his head like loose stones in a bucket. The horses thundered down the slope, riders able to do nothing more at such speed than lean forward and hang on. The fog that only moments before had been sailing past in tendrils like individual flags was now growing thicker; great white billows of it flew up before Barrick, as if serving maids were shaking out the castle linens. He seemed to be moving through a world that was half green grass and dying winter sunlight, half gray emptiness where he was alone but for the distant sound of horses and armor and the occasional shout of his fellows, sun and fog turning the world alternately light and dark like a swinging door.

He reentered the world of light for a few brief moments, then plunged again into swirling mists. Men rode on either side of him, but he could not see their shields or crests well enough to recognize them. The one on his left suddenly stood in his stirrups. Something protruded from the joint of the rider's chest and right shoulder like a long-stemmed black flower, then the man fell backward, spinning heels over head, and his horse veered away into the mist—mist that did not clear but seemed to grow ever thicker.

Vansen was wrong, was all Barrick had time to think, *it is night already.*

He turned to shout to the man on his other side, but as he looked for him something snapped past his face, so close he could feel it brush his nose. The pale man riding on his right had tipped his visor back; his black eyes were huge and had no whites. Even as Barrick stared, the man . . . the creature . . . whatever he was, nocked another arrow. Barrick knew he couldn't outrun it or duck swiftly enough, so he yanked with his good hand on the reins and sent Kettle sideways into his attacker's mount. There was a thump of contact as the bowstaff slapped against Barrick's face. The arrow vanished harmlessly up into the air. Barrick still had not had a chance to draw his falchion, but he managed to pull Kettle away again just as his enemy lunged at him, leaving the manlike creature hanging, his hands wrapped around Barrick's saddle strap, his feet still locked in his own stirrups as his horse galloped alongside Kettle. Despite the pulling and bumping of the horses, Barrick's enemy was slapping at his leg for what looked like a knife sheathed there.

Shouting in disgust and fear, Barrick kicked at the unprotected face over and over. The helmet flew off, revealing streaming silvery hair. The creature, despite all this, continued to pull himself nearer until the two horses were only a yard apart. Barrick finally dragged his falchion out of its scabbard and shoved it artlessly at the man's face, then hacked at the clawing white hands wrapped around his saddle strap until suddenly their grip dissolved in blood and the face with its staring black eyes fell away—a flash of his armor as he tumbled into the grass, then nothing. The riderless horse continued on for a few dozen paces, then turned and vanished through the fog.

Barrick reined up and sat for a long moment, gasping for breath, fearing that his jittering heart might crack like a newborn chick bursting its shell. Men screeched hoarsely somewhere in the fog to his right, and though he was terrified, Barrick realized it was better to be moving than to sit waiting for something to come down on him out of the roil of mist.

They would have left me behind. I could have stayed behind.

He spurred toward the shouting.

Tyne of Blueshore and a dozen other knights and nobles had found each other, and Barrick had found them. The enemy was thick around them, but not endless. There were moments between one spate of fighting and the next, sometimes long enough for Barrick to catch his breath and even drink from his waterskin. He was holding his own despite being forced to fight with only one hand, and he found himself embarrassingly grateful for his old nemesis, Shaso, who had worked him so mercilessly all those years.

Once or twice the fog cleared so that he could see knots of combat all over the downs. Those instants when the mists rolled back and they could actually see something like a wholesome, natural twilight dragged a cheer from even the weariest of the fighters around Barrick, his own voice as loud as any. They had held their own against the first attack of the Twilight People. Barrick felt something almost like hope. If they could reach some of their fellows, they could begin to make an organized resistance, to make a real stand or, as Vansen had suggested—only hours ago, but it felt like years—then withdraw and try to lure the shadow folk after them.

The fairies didn't seem to be as many as they had feared, but they were terrible foes. Their strangeness even more than their ferocity made them so. Most were man-sized and man-shaped, armored and carrying weapons of odd shapes and hues, but a few were twice the size of any mortal, massive things with patches of mangy fur and thick, sagging tortoise skin, powerful but slow. Barrick had already seen one of these monstrosities brought down by three mounted men with lances, and he had shouted with joy as the giant fell and lay shuddering in its own slow-oozing black blood. The fairy army contained swarms of small creatures with ruddy hair and faces almost as narrow as foxes' muzzles, too, and others not much larger than apes who were covered all over with some dark, tangled fur so that they appeared faceless except for the staring gleam of their eyes. Some of the enemies seemed to carry their own blankets of mist, so that even in the moments of clear light they were dim and hard to see as a reflection in a muddy pond, and the thrusts of lances and swords never quite seemed to strike them straight. Wolves accompanied them, too, silently swift and horrible in their intelligence. They had already pulled down several of the horses by tearing at legs and unprotected bellies until the beasts stumbled and fell.

"That way!" Tyne shouted. The war leader's helmet was battered and his sword was bloodied and notched, but his voice was still strong. Men moved to him without hesitation as he spurred his horse toward one of the clumps of fighting, a fog-shrouded mass of bodies and flashing metal—Mayne Calough and a company of Silverside nobles, perhaps three or four dozen mounted men all together, hard-pressed by at least that many foes. Tyne clearly planned to bring the two groups together with an eye toward mounting a coordinated defense, and Barrick was only too happy to follow. He had spent most of the last hour floating in a kind of singing silence, hearing but not recognizing the sounds of combat, terror, and pain all around him, lost in red-shot mists, but now the mists were beginning to clear—at least those in his head, even if the fogs that blew across the hillside showed no sign of doing the same.

As something like ordinary thought returned, he realized that he wanted only to get out of this ghastly murk any way he could. He didn't want to kill anymore, not even monsters like these. He didn't want to make anyone proud of him. He didn't care what anyone thought.

War is a lie. The disjointed words did not quite form in his head, but they were there all the same, like broken pieces of an object whose original shape could still be recognized. *Because no one ever would. Terrible. If they knew, no one ever. Never.*

Tyne was at the front of their small company, and reached the cluster of men on the hillside just in time to rein up in surprise as something huge burst through the rank of knights, flinging aside heavy, armored men and horses like a drunkard batting away a cloud of bees. Tyne had only a moment to raise his sword in a gesture of helpless defiance before the leathery giant brought down its great cudgel of stone and wood on him with such force that Tyne's horse was smashed to the ground with its back broken and its legs fractured and splayed. Nothing was left of Tyne Aldritch, the Earl of Blueshore, but a headless jelly in a wreckage of crushed armor.

It was so sudden, so horrid, that Barrick could only gape as Kettle shied and stutter-stepped. The Silversiders scattered from the giant, mounted men running down those who had lost their horses, all of them leaping past the prince, a few shouting at him to turn, to ride for his life. The giant thing lumbered toward him, the massive club whistling back and forth as it came, dispatching those who couldn't force their way past their fellows to escape, knocking them to pieces. One of the fleeing knights lost control of his horse and the beast slammed into Kettle and forced Barrick's mount sideways. This time Barrick did not catch its mane before he fell. The wet ground drove the breath out of him so powerfully that for a moment he thought it was the giant's club that had struck him, but the fiery stab of pain in his arm told him otherwise: he was still alive and there was worse to come. He rolled over and scrabbled along the ground to stay out of the way as his black horse tried to right itself, but it only bought him a moment.

Better if Kettle had kicked my brains out . . . Better than this . . .

The monstrous thing stood over him now, pouched eyes squinting from a face as bristly and wrinkled as the hind end of a wild boar. It was so huge it seemed to block the light, but there was almost no light left anywhere now, it seemed, anywhere in the world. It prodded him with the cudgel, shoving him a yard across the ground, and seemed surprised and pleased to discover he was still alive. He could feel his rib crack as the giant poked him again, then it raised its club high. The great weapon hung above him like a quivering outcrop of mountain about to break loose and tumble down to earth.

Barrick closed his eyes.

Briony.

Father.

I wish . . .

37
The Dark City

Count the spears, then build fires
For those who have no spears
Sing together the old, old words

—from *The Bonefall Oracles*

EVEN WITHOUT THE shadow-mantle it had been dark on this battlefield hours before the true night that was now falling—the Mist Children had made sure of that. As Yasammez rode, she saw the murk they had created as a shade, a hue that only dimly stained her vision, but she guessed that to the sunlanders the Mist Children's work must seem like something else entirely. Like blindness. Like despair.

All around her the struggle continued, a chaos of blood and fog and the clash of metal on metal, but nothing was hidden from Lady Porcupine. It had been a near thing—the decision of the mortals to ride her down in the open had been a clever one and she guessed there must be at least a few real commanders among them—but the sunlanders had suffered by having to leave behind their foot soldiers, and although they had fought bravely and surprisingly well, the tide had now turned against them.

The first step, she thought—*but just barely. And the Year-Turning Day almost upon us. The king has lost. There can be no question but that it must be done my way from now on.*

She had blooded Whitefire today, but Yasammez did not lust after combat for its own sake—her anger was too refined, too pure, to need expressing in that fashion. She left the rest to Gyir and her other attendants and spurred her black horse up to a place where she could better see the sunlanders' city and especially the castle that crouched on its mound of stone across the water—the old hill, the sacred, terrible place, soon to belong to the People once more. She considered how her eremites would cause the Bridge of Thorns to grow above the water, how her troops would cross through its sheltering branches and come to the castle walls. Many would be lost in the assault, but she had been thrifty of her army so far and it would be the last great sacrifice in this part of the world. First, though, they would invest the castle's front garden, the deserted sunlander city on the mainland. Her troops and followers would rest and tend their wounded, then they would dance and sing their victories, the first over their enemy for centuries. Those parts of the city they did not need would burn, and the sight of those fires would steal the castle dwellers' sleep for their last nights of life, as though Yasammez herself had reached out and bent their dreams into nightmare shapes.

Her horse stepped nimbly over the corpses of mortals and Qar. Warriors of both armies still beat at each other in small knots across the damp downs. Screams filled the air, along with howls of many of the Changing tribe and the buzzing songs of the Elementals, which to the mortals no doubt sounded even more frightening than the other sounds. In the midst of this confusion her attention lit briefly on one of the giant servitors of Firstdeeps. The creature had killed several mortals despite his own streaming wounds, and was about to dispatch another who lay on the ground at his feet, a youth whom the giant was prodding with his club like a cat playing with a stunned mouse. She was about to turn away when something in the boy's features and dress arrested her. The giant lifted his dripping cudgel.

"Stop."

The servitor had never heard her voice, but he knew his mistress. He paused, the great weapon barely trembling, although it had to weigh as much as the trunk of a good-sized tree. The boy looked up as she rode toward him, his eyes bleary, face bloodlessly white. Yasammez was wearing her featureless helm and knew she must look as grotesque to his frightened eyes as the giant itself, her black armor bristling with spikes, Whitefire gleaming in her hand like one of the moon's rays turned to stone. She lifted her helmet, stared at the momentarily reprieved prisoner. The boy's eyes, which at first had been empty of anything but terror and a sort of resignation, opened even wider.

Yasammez looked at him. He looked back at her. His jaw worked, but he could not speak.

She extended her hand, spreading her fingers. His surprised, frightened eyes closed and he fell back on the wet grass, limp and senseless.

The Winter's Eve pageant and its attendant temple rituals had commenced early in the morning, and even though it was not yet noon, already Briony had begun mightily to regret letting Nynor talk her into holding these most unfestive festivities. Rather than such familiar events reassuring everyone as the castellan had suggested, bringing the entire court together merely allowed rumor to travel faster and farther than ever it would have. Rose and Moina had told her that although none would admit it in public, many of the nobles seemed half-inclined to believe the Tollys' assertion that Briony and Barrick had ordered Gailon killed. The fact that Hendon and the rest of the Tolly supporters had kept themselves away from the gathering only made it worse, made it seem that Briony was cruelly celebrating during their time of mourning.

Where are all those we have supported—where are those whose loyalty we've earned time and again? Do they forget what my father did for them, what Kendrick did, what Barrick and I have tried to do even in our short time? Staring at the people crowded into the great garden, which with its border of tents put up for the pageant had somewhat the look of a military camp, she couldn't help but believe that those she saw whispering were speaking against her. She knew she dared say nothing herself—to deny such gossip was to give it even more force—and it maddened her.

"I would like to see them all horsewhipped, every disloyal one of them," she muttered.

"What, Highness?" asked Nynor.

"Nothing. Even on this chilly day, I am stifling in this costume." She flicked at the confining dress of the Winter Queen that Anissa had worn the year before, the vast white hooped skirt and rock-hard stomacher, all covered with pearly beads like frozen dewdrops. On such short notice even half a dozen seamstresses had not been able to alter it enough to make it fit Briony's larger frame in a comfortable way. "Is it not time yet for me to finish this foolish pageant? I want to eat."

"The ceremony is almost over, Highness." Skilled courtier that he was,

Nynor tried to sound apologetic, but he clearly disapproved of her complaints. "In a moment you will . . . ah! There, now go and take what the boy offers. Do you know your speech?"

She rolled her eyes. "Such as it is." She swept across the yard and stood while little Idrin, Gowan of Helmingsea's youngest son, handed her a sprig of mistletoe and a posy of dried meadowsweet as he lisped his ceremonial lines about the returning of the sun and the days of bloom to come. He was an attractive child, but his nose was running in a most unflattering way; after she had already clutched it, Briony realized to her dismay that the mistletoe was sticky.

"Yes, good Orphan," she told the boy, struggling to hold the gifts as she surreptitiously wiped her fingers with her kerchief. "Because of your sacrifice, I will allow the Summer Queen to return and take her throne at the far end of the year. Go now to the gods and be rewarded."

Little Idrin lay down and died with a great deal of kicking and groaning, but this year the crowd—perhaps superstitious in these days of bad news—was not amused by such antics. They clapped politely, but continued to murmur after the applause had died and the smallest scion of Helmingsea arose from death and returned to his mother's side, his shepherd's costume now furred with wet grass.

Briony had just finished dismissing the court so that they might have a rest and a chance to change clothes before the feast began when she noticed Havemore, Avin Brone's factor, who was standing and waiting for her in a way meant to be both unobtrusive and compelling. She sighed. It was the functionaries of busy men who were usually the most insufferable in their self-esteem.

"What does your master want?" she asked him, letting a little more of her anger show than she had meant to. "He was supposed to be here. If *I* can stomach such things, he can certainly make an appearance."

"Begging your pardon, Highness," said Havemore without meeting her eyes, "but Lord Brone wishes to speak to you. Urgently, he says. He humbly requests you to come to the Winter Tower as quickly as your Highness' convenience will allow."

She was immediately suspicious. She didn't know Havemore all that well. He came from Brone's wealthy fiefdom in Landsend and was known to be ambitious. Could this be some trick to get her alone—some scheme of the Tollys for which they had enlisted the lord constable's servitor? But even they would not dare anything in the light of day. Briony decided she was letting mistrust get the better of her—she would have her guards with her, after all. It was not the first time Brone had summoned her rather than the other way around. Still, it was irritating and she wondered if the lord constable did not need a reminder about who was the regent and who was not.

"I will come," she said. "But tell him he must wait until I get this outlandish costume off and something more sensible on."

"What is your name?" she asked the young guard who had insisted on walking before her into the Tower of Winter. It had occurred to her that she knew less about these men who guarded her life than she knew about her horse or her dogs, despite the fact that she had been seeing some of the faces for years.

"Heryn, Princess Briony. Heryn Millward."

"And where do you come from?"

"Suttler's Wall, Highness. Just north of Blueshore lands, on the Sandy."

"And who is your lord?"

He flushed. "You, Highness. We Wall folk owe our fealty direct to Southmarch and the Eddons." He seemed unsure, perhaps feared he had spoken too much. Certainly the other three guards who had stepped into the antechamber were looking at him as though they were going to make him regret his volubility in the guardroom later. "Most of the royal guards are from Suttler's Wall or Redtree or one of the other Eddon holdings."

It only made sense. "But your captain, Vansen, he is not an Eddon vassal by birth."

"No, Highness. He's a dalesman, is Captain Vansen . . . but he's steadfast loyal, Ma'am."

The sergeant stepped forward. "Is he troubling you, Highness?"

"No, not at all. I asked him a question, he answered." She looked at the rawboned sergeant, who seemed nervous and irritated. *He does not like having a girl my age on the throne,* she realized. *He'd like to tell me to be quiet and hurry up—that I am keeping that wise old man Brone waiting, not to mention giving this guardsman thoughts above his station.* For once she was more wearily amused by this sort of thing than angered. There were bigger foes and fears just now, after all. "Let us go, then."

The summons was no Tolly trickery. Avin Brone was waiting for her in the wide room on the third floor, a public room once when the Tower of Winter was a residence, although it was now largely given over to storage. "Highness," he said, "thank you. Please come with me."

Masking her irritation, she directed her guards to wait and allowed him to lead her out to the chilly air of the balcony. She looked down and saw a handkerchief with a heel of bread and a few crumbs of cheese on it lying on the boards at her feet. At first she thought Brone himself had carelessly dropped it, but the bread was sodden and gray as though it had lain there a day or two.

"Have you brought me to see where some spy has snuck into the Tower of Winter and dropped his midday meal?"

Brone looked at her for a moment, uncomprehending, then glanced down at the bread on the kerchief and frowned. "That? I care not for that—some workman or guard shirking, nothing more. No, Highness, it is something more fearful I brought you here to see." He pointed out across the rooftops of the castle, out to the narrow sleeve of Brenn's Bay and the city beyond. The city was covered in mist, so that only the temple towers and the roofs of the tallest buildings were visible through the murk—a cloak of fog or low-lying cloud that extended out across the fields and downs beyond the city so that most of the land on this side of the hills was invisible. But as she stared at this gloomy though largely unsurprising sight, Briony saw a few bright spots deep in the fog, as though torches and even some bonfires burned there.

"What is it, Lord Brone? I confess I can't make out much."

"Do you see the fires, Highness?"

"Yes, I think so. What of it?"

"The city is empty, Highness, the people gone."

"Not completely, as seems apparent. A few brave or foolish souls have stayed behind." She should have been afraid for them, but she had come almost to the end of her ability to feel for others, the suffering of displaced and frightened people had now become so universal.

"I might guess the same," Brone said, "had not this message come this morning." He pulled a tiny curl of parchment from his purse, held it out to her.

Briony squinted at it for a moment. "It is from Tyne, it says, although I would never think him to write such a small and careful hand."

"Written by one of his servants, no doubt, but it is indeed from Tyne, Highness. Read it, please."

Before she had digested more than a few lines she felt the hair on the back of her neck rise. "Merciful Zoria!" It was scarcely a whisper, although she felt like screaming it. "What is he saying? That they have been tricked?

That the Twilight People have crept past them and are coming down on the castle even now?" She read on, felt a little relieved. "But he says they are going to catch them up—that we must be ready to ride out in support." She fought down a rising wash of terror. "Oh, my poor Barrick. It says nothing of him!"

"It says at the end to tell you he is safe—or was when this was written." Brone looked very grim, bristle-bearded and lowering like one of the hoary old gods thrown down by Perin, Thane of Lightnings.

"What do you mean—'when this was written'?"

"He sent it yester-morning, Highness. I have only just received it, although from what he says of the spot where they were deceived, it cannot be much more than a score of miles outside the city."

"Then how could they have not caught up to them yet . . . ?" But she was beginning to guess at the terrifying truth.

"The sentries heard noises last evening and into the night, noises they thought came from madmen left behind in the town—clashes of weapons, groans, screams, strange singing and shouting—but faint, as though from behind the city's closed doors . . . or from far away, in the fields on the city's far side."

"What does that mean? Do you think that Barrick and the others have already caught the Twilight People?"

"I think perhaps they have caught up with them, Highness. Briony. And I think perhaps they have failed."

"Failed . . . ?" She couldn't make sense of the word. It was a common one, but suddenly it had become cryptic, meaningless.

"Tyne writes of the fog of madness that surrounds the fairy folk. What is that covering the city below? Have you seen a mist like that before, even in winter, that was still forming at midday? And who is lighting fires there?"

Briony wanted to argue with him, to come up with reasons the old man must be wrong, answers that would explain all he had said and more, but for some reason she could not. A cold horror had stolen over her and she could only stare out at the mostly invisible city—separated from the place where she stood by nothing except less than half a mile of water—and the fires that burned in that gray mist like the eyes of animals watching a forest camp.

Barrick . . . ? she thought. *But he must be . . . he cannot be . . .*

"Highness?" said Brone. "We should go down now. If the siege is about to begin in earnest, we must . . ." He stopped when he saw the tears on her cheek. "Highness?"

She dabbed at her face with the back of her sleeve. The brocade was rough as lizard skin. "He will be well," she said as though Brone had asked her. "We will send out our men. We will cut the fairies down like rats. We will kill them all and bring our brave soldiers back."

"Highness . . ."

"Enough, Brone." She tried to pull on the mask of stone—*the queen's face,* as she thought of it, although she was only a princess still. *Perhaps that's why I can't do it properly yet,* she thought absently. *Perhaps that's why it hurts.* Struggling, she spoke more coldly to Lord Brone than she had intended to. "Enough talking. Do what you must to make sure the walls and gates are secure, and prepare troops for a sortie if you are wrong and we do see Tyne come and engage with the enemy. You and I will talk after the banquet."

"Banquet?"

"After all Nynor's trouble, the people must eat and be merry." Tears drying now, she did her best to smile, but it felt more like a snarl and she did not try too hard to amend it. "As he said, it may be the last joy for some time, so it would be a shame to waste all those puddings."

The first gleam of dawn should have come as a relief, but it did not. They had held their ground and they were still alive, but there was no one else in sight or earshot with whom they could join forces. They were lost like shipwrecked mariners.

Ferras Vansen and a few men—Gar Doiney and two other scouts, along with the knight Mayne Calough of Kertewall and his squire, had held this high place since middle-night, an outcrop of stone in the middle of the field, not much bigger than a small farmhouse—held it mostly, Vansen guessed, because it was on the fringes of the battle and of little strategic value. Not that strategic value meant much anymore. Vansen had known for hours with a certainty as straightforward as a mortal wound that the fight was over and they had lost.

He was angry with himself, although he still believed he had been right to insist they catch the fairy folk outside the city. It had proved almost impossible to overcome the Twilight People without the superiority of numbers—or even apparent superiority, since everything to do with the fairy folk was slippery and hard to calculate. Already Vansen was plotting in the lulls between fighting what to do next time, how to take the advantage of surprise and concealment away from the shadow-people and their weird magicks, but all the time he had been doing it he knew that there might be no next time, that more than this battle might have been lost. With Tyne Aldritch dead, all was in disarray, and Tyne's second-in-command, the stolid, unimaginative Droy of Eastlake would not have been able to salvage things even if he had lived. In fact, it had been Droy's pig-headedness that had made the loss so desperate. By the time he had arrived with the weary foot troops, their torches making a fiery snake along the downs as they hurried to support the mounted knights, Vansen had sent one of the scouts to him to tell him that it was useless now, that Tyne had fallen and the best thing Droy's foot soldiers could do was to try to flank the Twilight folk and beat them to the deserted city, or, failing that, to fall back into the hills so that his army might eventually be able to provide the other half of a pincer with Brone's defensive force. Instead, the Count of Eastlake had ignored Vansen's message as the cowardly advice of a commoner, a jumped-up sentry in Droy Nikomede's estimation, and had plunged his weary soldiers into battle. Within moments, half of them had become completely disoriented by the mists and the strange noises and shadows—Lord Nikomede and the others had learned nothing from the first fight, it seemed—and had been cut down by archers they could not even see. Their own arrows seemed to do as much damage to the survivors among Tyne's knights as to the enemy.

A disaster. Worse, a mockery. This is how we defended Southmarch—with battle plans out of some player's comedy, with bravery sacrificed by blockheaded generalship.

Doiney tugged at the hem of Vansen's surcoat, startling him out of his reverie. "Shadows, Captain. Over there. Coming near, I think."

Vansen squinted. It was a little easier to see now that the sun was coming back, but not much. The mists were thinner, little more than what would be expected on these meadows at this hour of the day, but they still made the world an eerie and untrustworthy place. Something was indeed moving up the small rise toward the pile of stone they defended, a moving clot of shadowy shapes.

An arrow snapped past. Vansen jumped down from the prominence on which he had been crouching. The horses, herded together into a crack at the base of the outcrop because for the moment they were useless, whinnied in fear. No more arrows came. That was one small solace.

"Up!" Vansen shouted as half a dozen strange figures came charging out of the mist, eyes bright and faces as pale as masks. One ran on all fours like a beast, although he seemed to have been arrested in the middle of some transformation, with stripes of bushy fur sprouting unevenly down his back and sides and his face misshapen, as though someone had pushed a human face out from within, making half a muzzle out of nose and mouth. Seven hours ago this sort of thing had sickened Ferras Vansen, made him feel lost, as though the world he knew had suddenly fallen away beneath his feet. Now it was only another reason to want to kill them, kill them all, these horrid, unnatural creatures that had themselves destroyed so many of his fellows.

"To me!" he shouted and helped Mayne Calough to his feet, the knight's armor grating against stone as he dragged his aching body erect. "To me! Keep your backs together!"

The bright-eyed things were almost on them now, teeth bared as though they would not waste such sweet work on their swords. As he had at least a dozen times already, Vansen let his deeper thoughts go away so he could concentrate on the business of staying alive a little while longer.

Lord Calough and his squire were dead, or at least the knight was dead and the squire was clearly dying, with a great streaming gash beneath the point of his jaw. The hands with which the youth tried to hold in his own blood were all red, but his face had gone parchment-pale beneath the dirt and the blood was pumping more slowly now. The squire stared off into the misty morning sky, his bubbling prayers slipping down into silence though his lips still moved. Vansen wished there was something he could do to help the boy. Perhaps, though, this was the most merciful way. Who knew what would happen to the rest of them when the shadow folk came again? Only Vansen knew even a little of the way a man's own thoughts could betray him under the dark magicks of faerie.

Calough lay on top of the milk-skinned warrior he had destroyed—a woman, although Vansen thought that meant no less honor, for the fairy women fought like demons, too—but the knight's own breastplate had been torn open like a bite taken from an apple and his guts were out. Three fairy corpses had rolled down the rock and lay tumbled together at its base in the meadow. The other attackers had retreated into the murk, but only to get reinforcements, Vansen felt sure. It had been hours since he had seen any other mortals. Something was going on to the east of their outcrop, where the mist still lay thick on the ground, but the discord of music and screams didn't sound like any kind of fighting he knew.

It sounded like the fairies were singing sweetly-sour temple harmonies as they killed the wounded, that was what it sounded like.

"Get down, Captain," Doiney whispered from his perch behind some rocks at the crown of the outcrop. "They still have arrows left and they're probably gathering up those they've already shot, too. You'll get a shaft in the eye."

Ferras Vansen was about to take this good advice when he saw something moving across the sloping meadow, not coming toward them but passing from left to right in front of them. It was a mounted man, or at least a mounted creature of some sort, a dark figure on a black horse. Vansen crouched, but despite the superstitious fear that surprised him into shivers—he had thought there was nothing left in him that was still alive enough to be frightened—he couldn't take his eyes off the apparition that sailed past them through the swirling ground fog. Fear turned to astonishment as the figure moved into a shaft of weak sunlight and he could see it clearly.

"By Perin Skyhammer, it is the prince himself! *Barrick! Prince Barrick, stop!*" Too late Vansen realized that he had just directed the attention of any ransomers to the greatest prize on the field, but the shadow folk had not seemed very interested in keeping any of their mortal enemies alive, no matter their station.

"Get down!" Doiney yanked at his leg, but Vansen paid no attention. The mysterious figure that looked so much like the prince sailed by on a black horse, passing scarcely a dozen yards from where Vansen watched, stunned. He shouted again, but Barrick Eddon or his supernatural double did not even turn to look at him. The familiar face was distant, distracted, eyes fixed firmly on the northwestern hills despite the intervening mists.

"By all the gods and their mothers," said Vansen, "he's riding in the wrong direction—straight toward the Shadowline." He remembered Briony and his promise to her, but Doiney was tugging at him again, reminding him that he had other duties as well. "It's the prince," he told the leader of the scouts. "He's riding away to the west. He must be confused—he's heading straight for the shadowlands. Come with me, we have to catch him."

"It's just a will-o'-the-wisp," said Doiney, mouth stretched in a panicky scowl. "A fairy trick. There are men here somewhere who need our help, and if there aren't, we need to go east, try to get back to the keep."

"I can't. I promised." Vansen scrambled down the rock to where his horse was hidden. "Come with me, Gar. I don't want to leave you here."

Doiney and one of the other scouts, who had poked his head up now to see what was happening, both shook their heads, wide-eyed. Doiney made the pass-evil. "No. You'll be killed or worse. We need your sword, Captain. Stay with us."

He could only bear to look at their weary, frightened faces for a moment. "I can't." But which vow was more important, the one he had made to the princess, or the one he had made to old Donal Murroy when he had sworn to make the royal guard his own family and himself those guardsmen's dutiful father? He had little hope that the scouts would find the other survivors, but at least they had a chance of making a run toward the east, although he knew their chances were considerably lessened without him: he was the best swordsman among them and the only one in full armor.

He hesitated once more, but Briony Eddon's face was in his thoughts, shaming him, haunting him like a ghost. "I can't," he said at last, and led his horse out onto the foggy grass. He swung up into the saddle then spurred away. Barrick, or the thing that looked like him, had disappeared, but the marks of the horse's hoofprints were still fresh.

"Don't leave us, Captain!" cried one of the scouts, but Vansen was headed northwest and couldn't turn back. He wished he could put his hands over his ears.

"But why?" Opal could barely hold back the tears, but her anger made it a little easier. "Have you lost your wits? First you go off with that girl, then this? Why should you go outside the castle gates with a stranger? And *now*, of all times?" She gestured at Flint. The child was silent on the bed, only the faintest motion of his narrow chest showing that he lived. "He's so ill!"

"I do not think he is ill, my dear one, I think he is exhausted. He will be well again, I promise you." But Chert didn't know whether he actually believed that. He was tired himself, very tired, having snatched only a few hours' sleep after returning from the keep above. "The boy is the reason I have to go—the boy and you. I wish you could see this Gil fellow. I don't want to believe him, dear Opal, but I do." He lifted the mirror and examined it again. Hard to believe so much madness could surround such a small, unexceptional object. "Terrible things hang in the balance, he says. I wish you could see him, then you would understand why I believe him."

"But why can't I see him? Why can't he come here?"

"I'm not sure," he had to admit. "He said he couldn't come too close to the Shining Man. That is why the boy went instead."

"But it's all mad!" Opal's anger seemed to have won. "Who is this person? How does he know Flint? Why would he send our son to do such a dangerous thing, and by what right? And what does one of the big folk know about the Mysteries, anyway?"

Chert flinched a little under the volley of questions. "I don't know, but he's more than just one of the big folk." Gil's calm, empty stare had remained in his thoughts. "There's something wrong with him, I think, but it's hard to explain. He's just . . ." Chert shook his head. That was his problem. He had spent much of the last days in places where words meant little or nothing, but Opal had not. It saddened him, felt like a breach between them. He hoped he would survive this strange time so that he could patch it up again. He missed his good wife even though she was standing right in front of him. "I must do this, Opal."

"So you say. Then what are you doing here at all, you cruel, stubborn old blindmole? Do you think you're doing me a kindness, coming back to tell me you're off to risk your life again after you've just returned? Worrying me to death with these mad stories?"

"Yes," he said. "Not a kindness, but I couldn't go away again without telling you why." He walked across the bedroom and picked up his pack. "And I wanted some tools, also. Just in case." He didn't tell her that what he really wanted was his chipping knife, sharp-honed and the closest thing to a weapon they had in the house other than Opal's cookware. He couldn't quite imagine asking her for her best carving knife—it seemed as though that might be the last blow on a quivery rockface.

Opal had stamped out to the front room, fighting tears again. Chert knelt beside the boy. He felt his cool forehead and looked again to make sure Flint's chest was still moving. He kissed him on the cheek and said quietly, "I love you, lad." It was the first time he had said it aloud, or even admitted it.

He kissed Opal, too, although she could barely force herself to hold still for it, and quickly turned her face away, but not before he tasted her tears on his lips.

"I'll come back, old girl."

"Yes," she said bitterly. "You probably will."

But as he went out the door, he heard her add quietly, "You'd better."

Chert made a few wrong turns on his way back, since this time he didn't have the girl Willow to guide him. The big folk dashing here and there around the castle seemed even more distracted than might seem warranted with siege preparations still going on, and at first he thought it a little strange that no one bothered to question a lone Funderling wandering through the grounds. Then he remembered that today was Winter's Eve, the day before Orphan's Day, one of the most important holidays on the big folks' calendar. Despite the fear of war they seemed to be preparing for a feast and other entertainments: Chert saw more than a few groups of courtiers in costumes even more elaborate than usual, and a trio of young girls that seemed to be dressed as geese or ducks.

The man named Gil was sitting as still as a statue in a patch of weak morning sunlight in the garden when Chert found the place at last. Chert couldn't help wondering if the stranger had waited on that bench all the night long, ignoring winter chill and the soaking dew.

Gil looked at him as if hours had not passed, as if they had only left off their conversation moments earlier. "Now we will go," he said, and stood, showing no stiffness. Indeed, he was weirdly graceful, displaying such economy of movement that what at first sight appeared slow and awkward soon began to seem more subtle, movement without wasted effort, so that even his most mundane acts might have been the carefully planned steps of an elaborate dance.

"Hold a moment." Chert glanced around, but the garden seemed to be one of the few spots in the castle empty of people preparing for either siege or feast. "We can't just walk out the Basilisk Gate, you know. The castle is at war. The guards won't let us. Not to mention that the causeway is down. You say we must reach the city on the other side—we would have to find a boat and the bay is dangerous today. Some say a storm is coming."

Gil regarded him. "What does this mean?"

Chert let out a snort of exasperation. "It means you haven't thought this part out very carefully, is what it means. We'll have to find some other way. You can't fly, can you? I didn't think so. Then you'll have to come back with me to Funderling Town. There are tunnels—old roads, secret roads— that lead under the bay. They're not used much anymore even by us. We can go that way, or at least it's worth a try."

Gil continued to look at him, then sat down. "I cannot go down into Funderling Town, as you call it. It is too close to the deep places—to the thing you call the Shining Man. I . . . I cannot go there."

"Then we have hit bedrock with no tools." Chert wished again that Chaven had not vanished. Cryptic strangers and magical mirrors! The Mysteries coming to life! The portly physician would have had something useful to say—he always did . . . "Ah," Chert said. "Ah. Wait a moment." He considered. "The girl told me you have been living in the castle stronghold. That is beneath the ground."

Gil nodded his head slowly. "That is not so deep, I think. I feel it only a little."

"I know a way that also does not go too deep, at least not at first. When we are far away from the Shining Man, if that is what you really fear, we can go deeper. Follow me."

As he led the stranger across the inner keep, certain now for the first time of where he was going, he tried to plan what he would say to Chaven's housekeeper or to the manservant—what was that suspicious old man's name? Harry? Could he convince them of some errand so they would allow him to go through the house unsupervised? He didn't think any of them knew about the tunnel and the door off the cellar hallway.

He was still scheming when they reached the stubby observatory-tower, but the tale he had cobbled together—an important sample of stone Chaven had been testing for him, but which Chert now urgently needed back—was to remain unused. Nobody answered to his knock. The door was bolted, although Chert jiggled it to make sure. A layer of dirt on the threshold had been damped by the mist and drizzle into a muddy film naked of footprints, as though nobody had gone in or out for several days. He shook the handle again but the door was latched tight. It seemed that in Chaven's long absence the servants had closed up the house.

With sinking heart he began to explain to Gil, but realized that the odd man saw nothing that needed explaining. Chert looked up to the second-floor window and its wooden balcony. Perhaps the shutters there were less securely guarded.

"Can you climb?" he asked. Gil gave him that now-familiar, annoyingly expressionless gaze. "Never mind. I'll do it. The Elders know I've been getting enough practice at it lately."

It took him a while after he reached the balcony to catch his breath—half a night's sleep had not been nearly enough and his muscles were quivering with the exertion—but he was pleased to discover that the end of his chipping knife could slide between the shutters and still give him enough leverage to lift the bar on the inside. He went through as quietly as he could, considering he was still wheezing, and paused for a moment in the cluttered room to listen. All around him were the signs of Chaven's interests and obsessions, books and containers on every surface, caskets and sacks spilling their contents, apothecary chests with the drawers left open as though the physician had made one last hurried search of his belongings before rushing out the door. Nothing was too dusty, though; Chert decided that the housekeeper must have given it a good cleaning before she left. Still, he stood silent for a long time, feeling like a thief, until he was certain that nothing was stirring anywhere around him. He wondered briefly about the chunk of stone that Flint had brought back—such a long time ago it seemed now!—but to find anything in this hodgepodge would be the work of hours if not days. He hurried down the winding stairs and let Gil in through the front door.

"Follow me," he told him: he couldn't assume anything was obvious to this strange, fish-eyed fellow. Chert led him down through several floors to the bottommost corridor and its featureless hallway, where he was startled almost into a scream by a furry shape that scuttled out of the shadows in front of his feet, but it was only a spotted black-and-gray cat who stopped and gave him a stare as arrogant as Gil's. It seemed healthy and well-fed. He wondered if it had found the larder and was making a home of the Observatory now that the house was empty.

"Well met," Gil said as they all stood poised on the stairway. It certainly seemed that he was talking to the cat. The creature did not appear impressed; she showed the two of them her tail as she trotted past them up the stairs.

In the featureless corridor at the bottom of the house Chert heard a noise from behind a small and otherwise unexceptional door that made him stop and snatch at his companion's arm to halt him as well. In other circumstances Chert would have said someone in that room was moaning, although the voice did not sound much like anything human, but in the deserted house of a man with many arcane interests he was less certain. In fact, he was only sure that he didn't want anything to do with it, even if it was only the sound of some odd mechanical device of Chaven's, some tangle of leather hoses and bellows and glass pipes. After a heart-stuttering moment he pulled Gil past the spot and down to the door at the end with the bell hanging beside it. It was a relief to close that door behind them, to be out of the empty house and into the clean but crude Funderling tunnels he knew so well.

"We should be no deeper than the stronghold here," he whispered to his companion. "Can you stand it?"

Gil nodded.

"Good. Follow on, then. We've got a long distance to walk."

Chert did not have either the time or inclination to visit Boulder for any of the glowing coral, so it was with a conventional and very smoky oil lamp throwing huge shadows on the pale, sweating walls of the limestone cavern that he led Gil through the deep places underneath Brenn's Bay. At other times, Chert thought, it would have been interesting to take this old route from a time when Funderlings had less trust of their larger brethren (for good reason) and wished an escape to be available at all times. The old Exodus Road was largely unused these days, untended in many crumbling places and navigable only with the help of a long rhyme Chert's father had taught him that marked off the turnings as it wound from the outer reaches of Funderling Town, through dripping caverns beneath the bay and at last to the mainland. The current circumstances robbed the trip of any pleasure for Chert, not to mention his recent memories of having made his way beneath the silvery Sea in the Depths, plagued by nightmare visions every step of the way. This journey was not nearly so difficult, though it was much longer. Only the behavior of his companion made the experience anywhere near as frightening.

Gil, in fact, seemed to be suffering as Chert himself had suffered deep in the Mysteries, beset by things invisible to the Funderling—muttering, even once or twice speaking in an unfamiliar language. It was only after the lean stranger experienced his third or fourth such seizure that Chert finally realized he had seen something like this before.

Flint, down in the Eddon family tomb. The crack in the earth there. Something suddenly occurred to him, something he should have thought of before. *Did Flint know—was that why he acted so crosswise in the tomb? Did he know he must one day go down there? Or did it frighten him because it called to him, and it was only a few days ago that the call finally became too strong to resist . . . ?*

As they reached the far side where the paths turned upward again, his odd companion went through yet another change, this time as though a layer of his strangeness had actually been scrubbed away. Gil began to ask questions about where they were and how long it would take them to get to the surface that seemed as though they could have come from the mouth of an ordinary man. Chert couldn't compass it and didn't try: far too much of what had happened in these last days he not only didn't understand, but felt sure he never would.

The underground way reached the surface at last on the mainland, in a bank of seaside cliffs half a mile or so north of where the causeway had stretched. As they made their way out into the daylight, or as much of it as there was on this bleak, misty afternoon, Chert saw the castle they had left behind looming just across the strait, like a toy decorously carved by a giant and set down in the water to wait his return. From this distance Chert couldn't even see the sentries on the wall. The keep looked deserted, its windows empty as the cliff holes above his head where the shorebirds nested in spring. It was hard to believe there were any living souls at all inside that castle or beneath it.

He tried to shrug off the bleak thought. "We're on the other side of the water. Where do we go now?"

"Into the city. Those tunnels—have I ever been in them before?"

"I don't know," said Chert, surprised. "I shouldn't think so."

"Very much they remind me of . . . something. Some place I once knew well." For the first time Chert could see actual emotion written on the man's features, in his troubled eyes. "But I cannot summon it to my thoughts."

Chert could only shrug and start down the beach. Soon the seawalls of the city were looming above them. Only the base of the causeway remained where Market Road reached the shoreline, and the sea was empty into the distance, but a few tethered boats still floated along the quay—their owners taking their chances in the keep, no doubt, hoping one day soon to reclaim them. Otherwise the docks and the waterfront taverns and warehouses were deserted. It was stunningly empty and Chert could not help staring; it looked as though some great wind had come and blown all the people away. Fear stabbed at him anew. It wasn't just his own life: all the world had turned topside-down.

It was Gil who now took the lead, the Funderling who followed with increasing reluctance. A mist had crept down out of the hills and covered the city so that they could see only a few dozen paces ahead of them even on wide Market Road; the empty buildings on either side seemed more like the silent wrecks of ships lying on the sea bottom than anything wholesome. The damp walls and guttered roofs dripped like the deepest limestone caverns, so that their footsteps seemed to echo away multifold on all sides in a thousand tiny pattering sounds.

Everything was so gloomy and unnatural that when a half dozen dark figures stepped out of the shadows before them it seemed so much like the inevitable ending to a terrible dream that Chert did little more than gasp and stop in his tracks, blood thumping. One of the lean figures stepped forward, leveling a long black spear. His armor was the color of lead, and nothing showed of his face but a bit of bone-white skin and the catlike yellow gleam of the eyes in the slot of his helmet. The point of the spear moved from Chert to Gil and settled there. The apparition said something in a voice full of harshly musical clicking and hissing.

To Chert's dull astonishment, Gil responded after a moment in a slower version of the same incomprehensible tongue. The gray-armored figure answered back and the exchange went on. Water dripped. The sentries moved up behind their leader, nothing much of them visible but tall shadows and a half circle of burning yellow eyes.

"It seems . . . we are to be killed," Gil said at last. He sounded a little sad about this—wistful, perhaps. "I told them we bear an important thing for their mistress, but they do not seem to care. They are victorious, they say. There are no bargains left to be made."

Chert fought against panic that threatened to clamp his throat, choke him. "What . . . what does that mean? You said they would want what we have! Why do they want to kill us?"

"You?" Gil actually smiled, a sad twitch at the corners of his mouth. "They say because you are a sunlander, you must die. As for me, it seems I am a deserter and thus also to be executed. She who has conquered—she was my mistress once." He shook his head slowly. "I did not know that. Given time, it might have helped me understand other things. But it seems that time is what we do not have." And indeed, as Gil spoke, the semicircle tightened around them. Spear points hovered in front of their bellies, an ample supply for both of them. The only choice was to die standing up or running away.

"Farewell, Chert of Blue Quartz," his companion said. "I am sorry I brought you here to die instead of leaving you in your tunnels to find your own time and place."

38
Silent

IN THE DARK GREEN:

Whisper, now see the blink
And flicker of something swift
It is alive, it is alive!

—from *The Bonefall Oracles*

QINNITAN STOOD IN the corridor outside Luian's chambers like someone blasted by a demon's spell, amazed and defeated, waiting for death to come and take her.

When a dozen or so heartbeats had passed, her hopeless terror ebbed, if only a little. She didn't want to give up, she realized. What if darkness was like sleep, and that huge, terrible . . . *something* was waiting for her there as well? Except in death there would be no waking, no escape from that black and gaping mouth . . .

She slowly shook her head, then slapped at her own cheeks, trying to make herself feel again. If she wanted to live, she would have to escape from the autarch's own palace, an impossible task under the eyes of all his guards—and not just the guards: soon every servant would be watching for her, too, and everyone else in the Seclusion, royal wives and gardeners and hairdressers and kitchen slaves . . .

A glimmer of an idea came to her.

She forced herself to move, lurching back down the corridor to step through the hanging into Luian's chamber. Even knowing what she would find, it was impossible to suppress a groan of horror when she saw the sprawled body in the center of the floor, although the purple face was turned away from her. The strangling cord was so deeply embedded in the Favored's wattled neck that most of it was invisible. Luian's murderer had found that thick throat hard going: a muddy bootprint stood out starkly on the middle of the back of Luian's white nightdress like a religious insignia on the robe of a penitent.

Qinnitan was fighting her roiling stomach when a huge, fresh wave of misery washed through her. "Oh, Luian . . . !" She had to turn away. If she looked any longer, she would start weeping again and never move until they came for her.

She was rummaging furiously through Luian's baskets and chests of belongings when she heard a sound behind her. Her hands flew up to protect her neck as she turned, certain she would confront the grinning, dead-eyed face of Tanyssa, but the rustling noise had been made by the mute slave boy, the Silent Favored who had brought her Luian's message, as he tried to hide himself deeper into the room's naked corner. She had walked right past him.

"Little idiot! You can't stay here!" She was about to chase him out the door, then realized she might be throwing away the one thing that could save her life. "Wait! I need some of your clothes. Can you do that? Some breeches like the ones you're wearing. I'll need a shirt, too. Do you understand?"

He looked at her with the wide eyes of a trapped animal and she realized he had been even closer to Luian's killing than she had. Still, she had no time to spare on sympathy.

"Do you understand? I need those clothes, now! Then you can go. Tell no one you were here!" Qinnitan almost laughed at her own fatal foolishness. "Of course you will tell no one—you can't talk. No matter. Go!"

He hesitated. She grabbed his thin arm and pulled him upright, then gave him a shove. He hurried out of the door, bent so low his hands almost trailed on the floor tiles, as though he were crossing a battlefield where arrows flew.

She turned back to her search and a few moments later found Luian's stitchery basket. She took out the jewel-handled scissors—a present from the Queen of the Favored, Cusy, and thus hardly ever used—and began to shear off her own long, black hair.

Even after she had taken the pile of clothes and thanked him, the boy would not go. She gave him another push, but this time he resisted her.

"You *must* leave! I know you're frightened but you can't let anyone find you here."

He shook his head, and although terror still filled his eyes, his refusal seemed more than just fear. He pointed at the other room—Qinnitan could see the naked feet through the doorway, as though Luian had merely decided to lie down on the floor for a nap—and then at himself, then at Qinnitan.

"I don't understand." She was getting frantic. She had to get out, and quickly. The chances were good that Tanyssa had already checked her room and was now looking for her all through the Seclusion, perhaps raising the alarm. "Just go! Go to Cusy or one of the other important Favored! Run!"

He shook his head again, sharply, and again his finger traveled from the corpse to himself to Luian. He looked at her with imploring eyes, then mimed what she realized after a moment was writing.

"Oh, the sacred Bees! You think they will kill you, too? Because of the letters?" She stared at him, cursing Luian even though it was beyond the laws of charity to besmirch the dead before they had received the judgment of Nushash. Luian had ensnared them all, she and that handsome, foolishly arrogant Jeddin. It was bad enough what the two of them had done to Qin-nitan, but to this poor, speechless boy . . . ! "Right," she said after a long moment. She remembered what Jeddin was probably going through at this very moment and her anger died like a snuffed candle. "You'll come with me, then. But first help me get these clothes on and clean away the hair I chopped off. We can't burn it, since anyone would know that smell, so we'll have to put it down the privy. And here's another important thing—we'll need Luian's writing box, too."

The boy immediately proved his worth by leading her out of Luian's rooms and down a back corridor Qinnitan hadn't even known existed, skirting the Garden of Queen Sodan entirely, which would be full of wives and servants after the evening meal, especially on a warm night like this one. They encountered only one other person, a Haketani wife or servant, carrying a lamp—it was hard to tell which because Haketani women all wore veiled masks and shunned ostentatious dress. The masked woman went past with no reaction whatsoever, not even a nodded greeting; even in the midst of a desperate escape Qinnitan felt a reflexive irritation until she realized that the woman saw only two slave boys, and no matter what the woman herself might be, they still were beneath her notice.

I should be thanking the Holy Hive instead of grumbling.

The closer they got to the Lily Gate of the Seclusion, the faster her heart beat. Loose hairs were working their way down the back of her neck, making the rough cloth of the boy's shirt feel even more maddeningly itchy, but that was the least of her problems. Many more people were in the corridors now, servants off to shop for their mistresses, slaves with bundles piled high on heads or on shoulders, some even pulling small carts, a female peddler with a wheeled cage full of parrots, a Favored doctor in an immense, nodding hat arguing with a Favored apothecary on their way to examine the herbs at a local market, and although the presence of each person added to her fretfulness, especially the two or three servants she thought she recognized, she also told herself that the crowding made others less likely to notice two Favored boys, and certainly a lot less likely to wonder whether one of those two boys might be a Bride of the Living God.

Still, it was all Qinnitan could do to stand in the crowd waiting at the alcove on the Seclusion side of the gate when every instinct told her to shove her way through and bolt to freedom—just let them try to catch her! She did her best to slow her breathing, tried to think of what she would do on the other side. Small fingers curled around her hand and she looked down at the boy. Despite his own wide, fearful eyes, he nodded his head and did his best to smile, as if to tell her that all would be well.

"I don't know your name," she whispered. "What is your name?"

His mouth twisted and she felt cruel—how could he tell her? Then he smiled again and lifted his hands. He laced his thumbs together with the fingers held out on either side, then let the fingers flap like . . . wings.

"Bird?"

He nodded happily.

"Your name is Bird?"

He frowned and shook his head, then pointed up to the ribbed ceiling. Here, so close to the gate, the remains of nests still stood in some of the shadowed angles. She could see no birds in any of them. "Nest?" He shook his head again. "A kind of bird? Yes? Sparrow? Thrush? Pigeon?"

He grabbed her hand again and squeezed, nodding vigorously.

"Pigeon? Your name is Pigeon. Thank you for helping me, Pigeon." She looked up and discovered they had almost reached the front of the line, which narrowed like a bottle's neck before a trio of large Favored guards. The Lily Gate was only a few paces away, glowing with the lantern lights of the outside world like something magical from a story. Two of the guards were busy looking through a peddler woman's cart before releasing her back into the city—dwarfed by them, the peddler wore an expression that was so obviously and carefully no expression that it was almost insolent in itself—but the third guard was all too ready to look over Qinnitan and her companion.

"Where are you going . . . ?" he began, but was interrupted by Pigeon making grunting noises. "Ah, one of the tongueless whelps. Whose business?"

Qinnitan's stomach lurched. She had worked so hard on her other forged letter that she had completely forgotten she would have to produce some kind of permission to leave the Seclusion as well—slaves, even the relatively select Silent Favored, could not simply wander in and out at will.

An instant before she would have broken and run, the boy reached into his pocket and pulled out a small silvery article the size of a finger and showed it to the guard. Qinnitan's heart climbed into her mouth. If it was Luian's seal-stick and the word had already gone out . . .

"Ah, for old Cusy, is it?" The guard waved his hand. "Don't want to make the Queen of the Seclusion grumpy, do we?" He stepped aside, glancing with idle but focused curiosity at Qinnitan as though he sensed that something about her was not quite right. She dropped her eyes and silently recited the words of the Bees' Hymn as Pigeon steered her past the huge guard and in behind the peddler woman, who was just being released, apparently innocent of contraband.

"They say they were lovers once," one of the guards who had been searching the cart said quietly as he stepped out of the peddler's way. Qinnitan was startled until she realized he was talking to the other guard.

"Him? And the Evening Star?" asked his companion, equally quiet. "You're joking."

"That's what they say." The guard's voice dropped even lower, to a whisper—Qinnitan only heard a little of what he said before the pair of guards had fallen too far behind her. "But even if she cared for him still, she couldn't do him any good now. Nothing between the seas can help him . . ."

Jeddin? Were they talking about Jeddin?

Qinnitan felt hollowed, scorched, as though all her feelings had been burned away. The world had seemed mad enough, but today it had spun into realms of lunacy she could not have dreamed existed.

It was a warm evening and the streets were crowded. Outside the Seclusion the thoroughfare was full of expensive shops and teahouses—proximity to the great palace was almost infinitely desirable, no matter what the trade—and Qinnitan felt such a sense of relief and joy to be free among the loud and cheerful throng that it almost overcame the horror that still gripped her, but the feeling did not last long. Not only had she seen someone close to her murdered, she had now flouted one of the autarch's gravest laws. Even if by some strange chance she might have been allowed to live despite Jeddin's and Luian's crimes and her connection to them, the moment she had passed that door she had sullied herself. The autarch would have no use whatsoever for a sullied bride of unimportant parents.

I might as well be dead, she thought. *A ghost on the desert wind.* It was a curious feeling, both empty and exhilarating.

As they wound their way down through the hanging lamps of the market district and closer to the dark waterfront, the crowds became less friendly, the criminal element less cautious, and the menace increasingly tangible. As they passed down an alleyway between two long buildings, the only light that leaked in from a shabby teahouse at one end with its shutters half raised, she realized fatal misfortune was almost as likely to take them here as in the very heart of the autarch's palace. She would never have come to such a place in her woman's clothes, but there were many unpleasant folk who would be just as happy with a pair of comely boys—especially those who presumably could not scream for help.

Little Pigeon also sensed the danger—it would have taken someone not just mute but blind and deaf to miss it—and he allowed Qinnitan to hurry him along toward the docks. As they stepped out of yet another narrow, dimly lit alley into Sailmakers' Row, a wide road whose other end touched the shipyards and the nearest part of the docks, they found a tall shape standing in the road as if waiting for them.

"Hello, wee ones." The stranger wore sailor's garb, the pants barely below his knee and a mariner's cloth wrapped around his head, but his clothes were ragged and his voice shook like a sick man's. "And what brings you wandering down here at this time of the night? Are you lost?" He took a step toward them. "Let a friendly hand help."

Qinnitan hesitated for only a moment—he stood between them and their destination, but the autarch's wrath was behind them and they could not turn back—then she grabbed Pigeon's hand and started toward the stranger at speed. The boy hesitated only enough to make a slight drag on her hand, then he leaped forward and ran beside her. The man stood, his arms spread but his dark-sunken eyes wide with surprise. When they hit him, he was knocked onto his back. He rolled there for a moment cursing before scrambling to his feet.

"You peasecods, you puppies, I'll have your innards out!" he shrieked. "I'll spike you and gut you!" He was up and after them now, and although he was at least a dozen steps behind, when Qinnitan looked back over her shoulder he seemed to be closing the distance rapidly.

"Where are we going?" she gasped, but Pigeon did not know any better than she did, and could only run beside her. The boy was faster than her, she realized, but he paced her, still holding her hand. *What did Jeddin's letter say—a temple, was it? The boat moored across from a temple? But what temple?*

They came down out of Sailmakers' Row and onto the quay, their pursuer's steps banging on the boards not far behind them. Qinnitan slowed and almost stopped, daunted by the horrible sight of hundreds upon hundreds of masts, of boats lined in their slips for what looked like a mile, all bobbing in turn as gentle waves from the mild night sea ran down the length of the quay. The footsteps grew louder and she began to sprint again.

"Little scallops!" the man panted. He seemed almost at their shoulders and Qinnitan reached for her last strength to stay ahead of him. "I *eat* little scallops!"

In desperation she began to shout as loud as she could, "Hoy, the *Morning Star! Morning Star!* Where are you?" until she ran out of breath. There was no reply, although she thought she saw movement on some of the dark ships.

Now they all ran in silence for a moment, the man behind them wheezing but not slowing. *"Morning Star!"* Qinnitan screamed. "Where are you?"

"Just up a few slips," someone shouted from one of the boats as they passed.

Qinnitan stumbled but Pigeon held her up. *"Morning Star!"* she shouted again, or tried, but her voice seemed quiet and strengthless, her legs soft as cushions. She could barely summon breath. *"Morning Star!"*

"Here!" a voice shouted from a short way ahead. "Who's there?"

Qinnitan yanked Pigeon up what she hoped was the correct gangplank. The man who had been chasing them stopped, hesitated for a moment, then turned away and took a few staggering steps into the shadows and was gone from sight. Qinnitan leaned on the ship's rail, gasping as the stars in the sky seemed to drift down and swirl around her like sparks. The masts and rigging were all around her, too, like some kind of forest draped in spiderwebs, but she was able to take in nothing else except burning air.

A rough hand grabbed her arm and straightened her up, thrusting a lantern into her face. "Who are you? You shout as if you want to wake the dead."

"Is . . . this . . . the *Morning Star of Kirous?*" she gasped.

"It is. Who or what are you?" She thought she could see squinting eyes and a dark beard behind the lantern, but it was hard to face the light.

"We come . . . from Jeddin." Then her knees unlocked and the world spun around, the masts whirling like merrymaking dancers as she fell into first gray, then black emptiness.

"We were told to expect you—although dressed as a woman, not as a boy slave," said Axamis Dorza, captain of the *Morning Star*. He had brought her to the small ship's tiny cabin. The boy named Pigeon crouched at Qinnitan's feet, silent and wide-eyed. "We were even told that we might need to take you with us on short notice." Now he waved the forged letter she'd written in Luian's chamber and closed with Jeddin's seal. "We were *not* told we would leave without Lord Jeddin himself on board. What do you know about this?"

She breathed a silent prayer of thanks to the Hive and the sacred protection of her beloved bees: apparently the sailors had not heard of Jeddin's arrest. Now it was time to use the skills of deceit she had been forced to learn in the Seclusion. "I don't know, Captain. I only know that Jeddin told me to disguise myself and bring this slave here, and to give you this message." It was important, she reminded herself, not to know what Jeddin's purported letter said. "I know nothing else, I'm afraid. I am only glad we found you before that man who was chasing us did whatever he planned to do." She did her best to sound like a queen, regal and sure of herself.

But I am a queen, aren't I, at least of a sort? Or I was. But it had never felt that way, not for a moment.

The captain waved away the unimportant detail of their pursuer. "The docks are full of unnatural scum like that, and others even worse, believe me. No, what I do not understand is why we should leave without Lord Jeddin. I ask you again, do you know anything of this?"

She shook her head. "Only that Lord Jeddin told me to come to you and go where you carried me, that you and your men would protect me from his enemies." She took a deep, shuddering breath, glad that she had every excuse for anxiousness. "Please, Captain, tell me what my lord says."

Axamis Dorza picked up the letter in his thick fingers and squinted. His eyes were so netted in wrinkles that from the nose up he looked to be a great-grandfather's age, but she guessed he was considerably younger. "It says only, 'Take Lady Qinnitan to Hierosol. All other plans must wait. Take her there tonight and I will meet you there.' But meet us where, my lady? Hierosol is only a little smaller than Great Xis! And why cross the ocean to Eion instead of merely shipping to another port down the coast and waiting for him there?"

"I do not know, Captain." She suddenly felt as if she might tumble to the floor again in exhaustion. "You must do as you see fit. I put myself and my servant in your hands, as my lord Jeddin wished."

The captain frowned and stared at the seal ring that he held in his other hand. "You have his seal as well as the letter. How can I doubt you? Still, it is strange and the men will be restless when they hear."

"The palace is an unsettled place just now," she said with as much quiet meaning as she could muster. "Perhaps your men will be happy to find themselves away from Great Xis for a little while."

Dorza gave her a hard stare. "Do you say there is trouble in the palace? Is our lord involved somehow?"

She had baited the hook; it would not do to pull at the line too hard. "I have no more to say, Captain. To the wise, a single word is as good as a poem."

He went out then. Qinnitan fell back on the narrow bed, unable even to find the strength to protest when Pigeon curled up on the hard floor as though he really were her slave. Out of the confusion in her own head, she suddenly heard the oracle Mudry's voice:

"Remember who you are. And when the cage is opened you must fly. It will not be opened twice."

Was this what the old woman had meant? Qinnitan couldn't think anymore. She was too weary. *I'm flying, Mother Mudry. At least, I'm trying to fly . . .*

Within a few breaths she was asleep.

She woke for just a few short moments. Above her head bare feet thumped on the planks and voices rose, shouting instructions and singing songs of the hard sea life as the sailors of the *Morning Star of Kirous* prepared to journey to Hierosol.

39
Winter's Eve

DANCING FOR WINTER:

Dust, dust, ice, ice
She wears the bones for eyes
She waits until the singing stops

—from *The Bonefall Oracles*

P UZZLE WAS IN SURPRISINGLY fine voice, a slight quaver
the only thing to betray the passage of so many years. Otherwise,
Briony might have thought time had turned tail, that she was again
a little girl sitting on her father's lap, the wind plucking in angry frustration at the roofs outside while they all sat safe and warm in the great dining hall.

But those days were gone, she reminded herself. Nothing would bring
them back. And if Tyne had really lost the battle, it could be that soon no
one alive would even remember those times.

Puzzle strummed his lute, continuing with the long, sad story of *Prince
Caylor and the Ever-Wounded Maid.*

". . . Then did he first glimpse her, the bleeding maid:"

The old jester crooned, telling of the knight's entrance into the Siege of
Always-Winter,

"He thought her sore hurt, e'en dead, and his noble heart
Did quail with woe to think that such a bloom must fade
Before e'er it had been tasted by kiss, or figured by art;
But then opened she her eyes, and, as she saw him there,
Smiled, though her beauteous face was wan and sad—
A pearl display'd upon the cushion of her golden hair—
And he thought no empress of the south could match the loveliness she had.
Then Caylor's heart flew like an unhooded hawk, straight to her breast,
Although the troubled knight did not know whether he were curst or blest."

She had to admit she was surprised, not so much to find that Puzzle could still sing, but by the grace of Matty Tinwright's words. The young poet sat at the end of one of the front tables, near Puzzle's stool, looking as though he knew he had actually done something worthwhile.

It was certainly a change from his dreadful, lugubrious paeans of praise to her, his comparisons of her to a virgin deity, full of aching stretches for rhymes—there were not many things that rhymed with "Zoria," "merciful," or "goddess," after all. She was impressed and even pleased. She had given Tinwright a commission as much to irritate Barrick and amuse herself as anything else, but perhaps he would eventually prove a true poet after all.

Unless, she suddenly thought, *he has stolen the whole thing from some obscure source.*

No, it was Winter's Eve. She would be charitable. She would even say something nice to him, although nothing so fulsome as to fetch him puppy-dogging after her all evening.

"Thus, instanter, Caylor pledged himself her slave,
Declared that by her token whole worlds would he throw down;
Yet she only shook her fair head and a reproachful look him gave,
And raised her hands, white arms reaching from bloody-sleeved gown.
Then said she, 'Good knight, worlds shall not woo me, nor words,
But only and you free me from this wound that steals my life
Shall I be yours. One year gone I spurned haughty Raven, Prince of Birds,
And he did my breast pierce with his terrible slow knife.
All of the physick of my father's court cannot staunch or even slow
The wound that dire blade to me gave, nor stop this crimson flow.' "

*   *   *

Briony even smiled at Puzzle, who barely noticed. He was enjoying this moment of attention so much that he seemed to forget it was the royal family to whom he owed his position, not the courtiers, who considered the old man a rather tiresome jest. Still, he was the center of all eyes, or should have been, and he clearly reveled in it.

The rest of the assembled nobility seemed strange to Briony. Conversation was awkward, many whispering, others speaking too loudly, even after an evening's indulgence. The Tollys and their allies had made it clear they considered the feast as an insult to Gailon's memory and had not appeared. Thus, there had been even more drinking than would be expected on Winter's Eve, mulled wine being sluiced down throats as though many of those present expected the worst and expected it soon—for gossip about the possible fate of Southmarch's army had sped through the castle all evening, tales of terror and defeat flying to every corner like little white moths rushing out of a long-closed wardrobe. Briony herself had needed to soothe Rose and Moina, both in tears, who were certain that they would be ravished by monsters.

Yes, and they were certain that Dawet and his Hierosol men would ravish them as well, Briony thought sourly. *On that night. And precious little help they were to me or anyone else . . .*

She shied away from any more thoughts of Kendrick's death, let her mind instead hold the memory of Dawet dan-Faar. Surrounded by red-flushed, drunken faces, she found herself longing for his company. Not in a romantic way—she looked around as though even the thought might have been obvious to those around her, but the nobles were busy licking suet pudding from their fingers and calling for more wine. No, it would have been a pleasure simply because of the quickness of his wit. There was no blurriness in Dawet, who seemed always sharp as a knife. She doubted he drank at all, and felt certain that even if he did, few had ever seen him the worse for it . . .

Oh, by all the gods, what will we do? How will we save ourselves? It had been gnawing at her since she received Brone's news and she couldn't keep it at bay any longer. She couldn't even bear to consider that anything might have happened to Barrick, but had to accept the possibility that Tyne Aldritch and his army had failed. What then? How could she and her nobles plan for a siege against such a mysterious force?

Thoughts turning round and round between those who were missing— she could not have imagined a Winter's Eve so friendless, so bereft of family—

and the malevolent creatures who seemed now to be separated from her beloved Southmarch Castle only by the narrow protection of the bay, Briony suddenly remembered that she had promised she would see her stepmother Anissa tonight. Her first inclination was to send a servant to make her apologies, but as she looked around the room, at the sickly, over-cheerful faces of those who were still upright, at the ruin of the meal scattered down the tables, bones and shreds of skin and puddles of red wine like the remnants of some dreadful battle, she decided that she could think of nothing better than to walk for a time in the night air, and that a visit to her bedbound stepmother, who was only days away from giving birth at most, would be the most acceptable excuse.

Although it took some doing, she even managed to create in herself a small amount of sympathy for Anissa. If Briony felt so helpless, with the reins of the kingdom in her hands, how much worse must it feel to her stepmother, big with child and forced to sift through the conflicting rumors that flittered into her tower?

A smattering of lazy applause and a few drunken cheers caught her attention: the song had ended. Briony was a little shamed to realize she had missed most of it.

"Very fine," she said out loud, and clapped her hands. "Well sung, good Puzzle. One of the best entertainments we have had for many a year."

The aged man beamed.

"Serve him," she directed one of the pages, "for such splendid singing must be thirsty work."

"I will not take all credit, Highness," Puzzle said as he held out his hand for the cup. "I was assisted . . ."

"By Master Tinwright, yes. You told us. And to him I also say, well done, sir. You have breathed new life into an old and beloved tale." She tried to remember how the story of the Ever-Wounded Maid ended, hoping that Tinwright had not adopted some modern approach to the finish that she hadn't heard, which would make it embarrassingly clear that her mind had wandered. "Like Caylor, you have found the song that heals the Raven Prince's dreadful deed."

She seemed to have got it right. Tinwright looked as though he wished he could throw himself before her and become her footstool.

Yes, but he won't be able to find a rhyme for that either, she thought. It was hard to break old habits.

She stood with a rustling of underskirts and said, "I must go now and take the tidings of the new season to my stepmother, Queen Anissa." Those who could still do so levered themselves upright as well. "Please, sit yourselves down. The feast is not ended. Servants, keep the wine flowing until I return, so our guests may celebrate the warmth that the Orphan brought back. Remember, there is no season so dark that it does not see the sun come again."

Gods protect me, she thought as she swished toward the door in her great hooped skirt, *I'm beginning to talk like one of Tinwright's characters.*

Heryn Millward, the young soldier from Suttler's Wall, was one of the two guards accompanying her tonight; the other was a slightly older fellow, dark-stubbled and taciturn. She remembered to wish them both good tidings for this night and tomorrow's holy day—the courtesy acted as a sort of hedge against being impatient at how slowly they walked, encumbered by armor and halberds.

She had just crossed the outer courtyard and had almost reached Anissa's residence in the Tower of Spring when a figure stepped out of the shadows in front of her. Her heart slithered up into her throat and she only recognized the apparition one thin moment before young Millward shoved the spiked head of his halberd into the intruder's guts.

"Stop, guard!" she cried. "*Chaven?* Merciful Zoria, what are you doing? You could have been killed! And where have you been?"

The physician looked startled and even shamefaced as he stared down at the sharp spike wavering in front of his belly. When he lifted his gaze to Briony's, she saw that he was pale and puffy, blue-circled beneath the eyes, and that he had not put a razor to his beard for days. "My apologies for frightening you, Princess," he said. "Although it would have been worse for me than for you, it seems."

As great a relief as it was to see him, she was not prepared to forget her anger. "Where have you been? Merciful Zoria, do you know how many times in these latest days I wanted desperately to talk to you? You have always been our adviser as well as our doctor. Where did you go?"

"That is a long story, Highness, and not one for a cold and windy courtyard, but I will tell you all the tale soon."

"We are at war, Chaven! The Twilight People are on our doorstep and you simply disappeared." She felt her eyes fill with tears and wiped angrily with her sleeve. "Barrick is gone, too, fighting those creatures. And there are worse things, things you do not know. May all the gods confound you, Chaven, *where have you been?*"

He shook his head slowly. "I deserve that curse, but largely because I have been foolish. I have been hard at work trying to solve a dire riddle—more than one, to be honest—and it all has taken longer than I guessed it would. Yes, I know about the Twilight People, and about Barrick. I was absent from the court, but not from gossip, which travels everywhere."

She threw her hands up in exasperation. "Riddles—there are already too many riddles! In any case, I am going now to see my stepmother. I must do that before we can talk."

"Yes, I know that, too. And I think I should accompany you."

"She is close to her time."

"And that is another reason I should come."

She waved at the guards to lower their weapons. "Come along, then. I will drink a posset with her, then we will go."

"It may not be so swift, Highness," Chaven suggested.

Briony did not have the patience on this long, woeful night to try to work out what he meant.

There seemed no proper way, Chert reflected, to prepare yourself to die, but it also seemed as though this was the second or third time in the last few days he had been forced to try. "I don't want to," he said quietly. The armored, yellow-eyed shapes looked down at him without a glimmer of emotion, their spear points a ring of dull gleams in the grayish light, but the strange man beside him stirred.

"Of course not," Gil said. "All that live cling to life. Even, I think, my people."

Chert bowed his head, thinking of Opal and the boy, how little all this meant, how foolish and unnatural it was compared to his life with them. There was a rising patter that for a moment he felt certain was his own racing heart. Then he recognized the sound and looked up, not in hope, but instead almost in annoyance that the horrible waiting would continue.

The man, if it was a man, rode one of the largest horses Chert had ever seen: the top of his own head would barely reach its knees. The rider was large, too, but not freakishly so, dressed in armor that looked a bit like polished tortoiseshell, gray and brown-blue. A sword dangled at the newcomer's side; under his arm he carried a helmet in the shape of an animal's skull, some unrecognizable creature with long fangs.

But it was his face that was the strangest part. For a moment Chert thought the tall rider was wearing a mask of ivory, for other than the ruby-red eyes beneath the pale brow the stranger had no face, only a slight vertical ridge where a nose might be and a smooth expanse of white down to the chin. It was only when he caught a glimpse of the white neck working beneath that chin as the stranger looked Gil up and down that Chert was convinced once and for all that the stranger was not wearing a mask but his own actual flesh.

"His name is Gyir the Storm Lantern," Gil announced suddenly. "He says we are to follow him."

Chert laughed, a broken sound even to his own ears. If he had not gone mad, then Gil had—or the world had. "Says? He has no mouth!"

"He speaks. Perhaps it is only that I feel his words inside me. Do you not hear him?"

"No." Chert was weary, as exhausted as if seeping minerals had soaked his bones and changed them to heavy rock. When the faceless rider turned back toward the city and the guards prodded Chert with their spears, he marched ahead of them, but despite the sharp pikes at his back he did not have the will or the strength to move swiftly.

The Square of Three Gods had been draped all around with dark-colored cloths, so that even in the light of many torches the buildings hid behind veils of shadow. She was waiting for them in a chair before the temple steps, a plain, high-backed chair out of some merchant's house that she invested with the terrible dignity of a throne.

She was as tall as Gyir but both more and less ordinary to look at; she was beautiful in a weird, drawn-out way, the planes of her brown face and her bright eyes just a bit beyond human from most angles, then—when she cocked her head to listen to some sound Chert could not hear, or to look over the square, surveying her legions who sat patiently on the ground— she abruptly seemed too extreme to pass for a person even at a distance, like something seen through deep water or thick clear crystal.

She was dressed as for war in a suit of black plate armor covered almost everywhere, but most heavily on the back and shoulders, with shockingly long spines, so that from a distance it was hard to make out her shape at all. Now that he was kneeling before her, it was clear to Chert that she had two arms and two legs and a slender, womanly figure, but even when he finally gathered the courage to look up at her, it was hard to look very long. There was something in her, some blunt, terrifying power, that pushed his eyes away after only a few moments.

Yasammez, Gil had called her as he made a sleepwalker's obeisance. His onetime mistress, he had said before. He had not spoken to her again since he knelt and saluted her, nor she to him.

The tall woman with the thickly coiling black hair now lifted a gauntleted hand and said something in the unfamiliar tongue, her voice deep as a man's but with its own slow music. Chert felt all the hairs on his neck rise at once. *This is all a nightmare,* a part of him shrilled, trying to explain what could not be, but that part was buried deep and he could barely hear it. *A nightmare. You will wake up soon.*

"She wants the mirror," Gil said, getting to his feet.

The idea of resisting never even occurred to him. Chert fumbled out the circle of bone and silvered crystal, held it out. The woman did not take it from him; instead, Gil plucked it from Chert's palm and passed it to her with another bow. She held it up to catch the torchlight and for a moment the Funderling thought he saw a look of anger or something much like it flick across her spare, stony face. She spoke again, a long disquisition of clicks and murmurs.

"She says she will honor her part of the Pact and send the glass to Qulna-Qar, and that for the moment there will be no more killing of mortals unless the People are forced to defend themselves." Gil listened as she spoke again, then he replied, more swiftly and ably now, in that same tongue.

"She speaks to me as though I am the king himself," Gil said quietly to Chert. "She says that by the success of this deed, I have won a short truce for the mortals. I told her that the king speaks through me, but only from a distance, that I am not him."

King? Distance? Chert had not the slightest idea what any of this signified. The oppressive strangeness was so thick it made him want to weep, but there was also some stubborn thing in him like the rock that was in his people's names and hearts, a residue of spirit that did not want to show fear before these beautiful, savage creatures.

The woman Yasammez extended her arm, the mirror in her long, long fingers. The faceless creature called Gyir the Storm Lantern strode forward and took it from her. No words were exchanged, at least none that Chert could hear. Gyir made a bow as he put it into the purse at his waist, then drew his fingers across his eyes in a ritual manner before mounting his great gray horse.

"She bids him take it swiftly and carefully to the blind one in Qul-na-Qar," Gil explained, as though he could understand silent commands as well as spoken ones. "She says if anything happens to the queen in the glass, then she, Yasammez, will make all the earth weep blood."

Chert only shook his head. He was having trouble paying attention to any of what was happening now. It was all too much.

Gyir swung up into the saddle and jabbed at the horse's flanks with his spurs. The beast's hooves dug into the earth of Temple Square and then rider and mount sped off, vanishing from sight so quickly that they might have been marionettes suddenly yanked from the stage.

After a long silence the woman or goddess or female monster Yasammez spoke aloud again, her voice buzzing like a hummingbird's wings just inches from Chert's ear. Gil listened silently. The woman looked from him to the Funderling—her eyes seemed to glow before Chert's reluctant gaze, like twin candle flames in a dark cave, and he had to look away before he was drawn into that empty cavern and lost forever—then Chert's companion finally spoke.

"I am to stay." Gil sounded neither happy nor sad, but there was something dead in his voice that had been fractionally more lively before. "You are to go, since there is truce."

"Truce?" Chert finally located his own voice. "What does that mean?"

"It does not matter." Gil shook his head. "You mortals did not cause the truce and you cannot change it. But the place called Southmarch will be unharmed." He paused as Yasammez said something stiff and harsh in her own tongue. "For a little while," Gil clarified.

And then almost before he knew it, Chert was snatched up by rough hands and set on the saddle of a horse and within moments Market Road and the city began to fly past him on either side. He never saw the armored rider behind him, only the arms stretching past him on either side that held the reins. Like the orphan in the big folk's most beloved story, he dared not even look back until he was dropped unceremoniously on the beach beside the caves.

Chert knew he should try to remember everything—he knew it was all important, somehow; after all, his son had given everything but his life for that mirror and whatever bargain it might signify—but at the moment all he could imagine doing was crawling down into the nearest tunnel to sleep a little while, so he would have the strength to stagger home to Funderling Town.

Briony led Chaven through the covered walk and out into the open flagstone courtyard in front of the Tower of Spring. The two guards leaning against the great outer door straightened up in wide-eyed surprise when they saw her. She was too annoyed by this errand and how it forced her to wait before learning Chaven's news to remember to wish this new pair of guards the tidings of the season, but she remembered on the stairs and promised herself she would make amends on the way out.

They mounted to the door of Anissa's residence and knocked. A long time passed before the door opened a little way. An eye and a sliver of face peered out. "Who is there?"

Briony made an impatient sound. "The princess regent. Am I allowed to come in?"

Anissa's maid Selia opened the door and stepped back. Briony strode into the residence; her two guards, after a quick survey of the room, took up stations outside the door. Selia looked at the princess from beneath her eyelashes, as though ashamed to have kept her out even for a moment, but when she saw Chaven, her eyes grew wide with surprise.

He was certainly a surprise to me, Briony thought. *I suppose it's been just as long since they've seen him here either.* "I've come as invited, to have a Winter's Eve drink with my stepmother," she told the young woman.

"She is over there." Selia's Devonisian accent was a little stronger than Briony remembered, as though being caught off-guard made it harder for the young woman to speak well. The room was dark except for low flames in the fireplace and a few candles, and none of the usual crowd of serving-women or even the midwife appeared to be present. Briony walked to the bed and pulled back the curtains. Her stepmother was sleeping with her mouth open and her hands curled protectively across her belly. Briony gently rubbed her shoulder.

"Anissa? It's me, Briony. I've come to have a drink with you and wish you a good Orphan's Day."

Anissa's eyes fluttered open, but for a moment they didn't seem to take in much of anything. Then they found her stepdaughter and widened the way Selia's had when she saw Chaven. "Briony? What are you doing here? Is Barrick with you?"

"No, Anissa," she said gently. "He has gone with the Earl of Blueshore and the others, don't you remember?"

The small woman tried to sit up, groaned, then got her elbows planted in the cushions and finally managed to lever herself upright. "Yes, of course, I am still sleepy. This child, it makes me sleep all the time!" She looked Briony up and down, frowned. "But what brings you here, dear girl?"

"You invited me. It's Winter's Eve. Don't you remember?"

"Did I?" She looked around the room. "Where are Hisolda and the others? Selia, why are they not here?"

"You sent them away, Mistress. You are still full of sleep, that is all, and you forget."

But now Anissa noticed Chaven and again she showed surprise. "Doctor? Ah, is it truly you? Why are you here? Is something wrong with the child?"

He joined Briony by the bedside. "No, I don't believe so," he said, but with little of his usual good humor.

Anissa detected this and her face tightened. "What? What is wrong? You must tell me."

"I shall," said Chaven. "If the princess regent will allow me a moment's indulgence. But first I think she should call in the guards."

"Guards?" Anissa struggled hard to get out of bed now, her skin pale, voice increasingly shrill. "Why guards? What is going on? Tell me! I am the king's wife!"

Briony was completely bewildered, but allowed Chaven to move to the door and invite in young Millward and his stubbled comrade, both of whom looked more nervous to be in the queen's bedroom than if they had faced an armed foe. Selia moved to where her mistress now sat on the edge of the bed, the queen's pale little feet dangling down without quite reaching the floor. The maid put a protective arm around Anissa's shoulders and looked defiantly back at Chaven.

"You are giving fright to me," the queen said, her accent thicker now, too. "Briony, what are you doing here? Why are you treating me so?"

Briony didn't answer her stepmother, but couldn't help wondering if she had been too quick to let Chaven have his way. Perhaps he had disappeared because he was deranged. She caught young Millward's eye and did her best to hold it for a moment, trying to let the guardsman know to watch her, not the physician, while waiting to be told what to do.

"If you are innocent, madam, I will beg your pardon most devoutly. And in no case will I harm you or your unborn child. I wish only to show you something." Chaven put his hand into his pocket and produced a grayish object about the length of a child's thumb. Now that he had moved into the light, Briony noticed for the first time that the physician's clothes were ragged and dirty. She felt another stab of doubt.

Chaven held out the stone and both Anissa and her maid Selia shrank back as though it were the head of some poisonous serpent. "What is it?" Anissa pleaded.

"That is indeed the question," said Chaven. "A question I have worked hard to answer. It has taken me to some strange places and to some strange folk in recent days, but I think I know. In the south it is called a *kulikos*. It is a kind of magical stone, most often found on the southern continent, but they occasionally make their way north to Eion—to the sorrow of many."

"Don't touch me with it!" Anissa shrieked, and although Briony was puzzled by what the physician was doing, she could not help feeling that her stepmother was reacting too strongly.

Chaven looked at Anissa sternly. "Ah, you know of such things, I see. But if you have done nothing wrong, madam, you have nothing to fear."

"You are trying to bring a curse for my baby! The king's child!"

"What is the point of this, Chaven?" Briony demanded. "She is about to give birth, after all. Why are you frightening her?"

He nodded. "I will tell you, Briony . . . Highness. One of the workers on your brother's tomb brought this stone to me because he thought it strange. I thought little of it at the time, I must sadly admit, but there have been many things on my mind since Kendrick's death. I know I am not the only one."

Briony glanced at the two women huddled on the edge of the bed. The chamber felt odd, as though a storm hung just above them, making the air prickle. "Go on, get to the point."

"Something about this thing troubled me, though, and I began to wonder if it might be one of a certain class of objects mentioned in some of my older books. I discovered that the place it had been found was in a direct line between the outside window of a room near Kendrick's chambers and the Tower of Spring—the tower in which we now find ourselves, a building almost completely given over to the residence of the king's wife and her household."

"He is talking in madness," Anissa moaned. "Make him stop, Briony. I am getting so frighted."

The physician looked to her, but Briony's heart was beating faster now and she wanted to hear the rest. "The windows of those chambers are all high above the ground," she reminded him. "Brone searched them all. There was no rope left behind."

"Yes." The room was warm. Chaven was perspiring, his forehead glinting with sweat in the candlelight. "Which makes it all the stranger that I should find the mark of something having landed in the loose soil at the edge of the garden beneath that window. The marks were deep, so that even though many days had passed, they had not disappeared."

Briony stared at him. "Wait a moment, Chaven. Are you suggesting that Anissa . . . a woman carrying a child, the king's child . . . *jumped out of the upstairs window?* All the way to the edge of the garden? That she somehow killed Kendrick and his guards, then jumped down and escaped?" She took a breath, held out a hand as she prepared to have the guards arrest him. "That is truly madness."

"Yes, make him go away," Anissa wailed. "Briony, save me!"

"He is frightening my mistress, the queen," cried Selia. "Why don't the guards stop him?"

"It is certainly much like madness to believe such a thing, Highness," Chaven agreed. He seemed very calm for a lunatic. "That is why I think you should hear all my tale before you try to understand. You see, I knew I could not make anyone believe a tale like that—I did not really believe it myself—but I was frightened and intrigued by what I had learned about *kulikos* stones. I decided I must know more. I went in search of knowledge, and eventually found it, although the price was high." He paused and wiped at his forehead with his tattered sleeve. "Very high. But what I learned is that in the south of Eion they believe a *kulikos* stone summons a terrible spirit. So powerful is this ancient dark sorcery, so dreadful, that in many places even possessing one of these stones will earn the bearer death on the instant."

Listening to such words by flickering candlelight, Briony felt as though she were in some story—not a tale of heroism and heavenly reward like the one Puzzle had just sung at the feast, but something far older and grimmer.

"Why do you say all this foolishness to my mistress when she is not well?" demanded Selia in a shrill voice. "Even if someone has done some bad thing and then run past the tower where she lives, what is that to us? Why do you say that to her?"

The guards standing by the door were murmuring to each other now, confused and a little fearful. Briony knew she couldn't let it all go on much longer. "State your case, Chaven," she ordered.

"Very well," he said. "I have learned that there is something interesting about the murderous *kulikos* spirit. It is female, always female. When it is summoned, it only will inhabit the bodies of women."

"Madness!" cried Anissa.

"And it is particularly a favorite weapon among the witches of Xand and of the southernmost lands of Eion. Lands like Devonis."

Anissa turned to her stepdaughter, holding out her hands. Briony couldn't help shrinking back just a little. "Why do you let him say this to me, Briony? Have I not always been kind to you? Because I am from Devonis, I am a witch?"

"It is easy enough to discover," Chaven said loudly. He thrust the small gray object closer to the king's wife. "Here is the stone. Look at it. It was tossed aside by the one who employed it to murder the prince regent after she had used it up, but doubtless a little of those dark magicks still remain. Touch it, my lady, and if you have anything to hide, the stone will show that." He extended his hand, bringing the stone close to her bare arm. Anissa tried to squirm away from it as though it were a hot coal, but couldn't disentangle herself from the protective embrace of her maid Selia.

"No!" Selia snatched the milky-gray stone out of Chaven's hand so quickly that as he closed his fingers on nothingness, the girl had already pulled it against her own breast. He stared in surprise. "There is no need for this," the maid declared, then snapped out something in a language Briony did not recognize—a short, sharp cry like a hawk falling on its prey.

Briony tried to say something, to curse the young woman for interfering, but a change in the air of the room suddenly made it hard to talk, a cold filling and tightening of her ears as though she had dunked her head into the water.

"There is no need for this, or for anything else." Selia's voice suddenly seemed to come from a great distance. *"I did not drop the stone away as a man drops away a maid when she is a maid no longer. I was weary and it fell from me, and when I was strong enough again to go back and search for it, it was gone."* The girl's voice rose, ending on a triumphant cry, harsh, but still muted by the strange squeezing of the air. *"No one lets to drop a* kulikos *stone, little man! Not by choice!"* Selia lifted her hand and put the stone in her mouth.

Her face abruptly blurred and changed, her torchlit skin seeming to shrink away even as something darker unfolded from inside. This devouring of light by darkness spread over her in the matter of a few heartbeats, as though someone had tossed a rock into a stream in which the girl was reflected, muddying the surface. The strangling air of the chamber finally began to move, but instead of bringing relief it sped faster and faster, a breeze that became a harsh wind, then a full gale, swirling so swiftly that Briony could feel needle-sharp bits of dust and flecks of stone stinging her skin. The guards shouted in surprise and terror but she could hear them only faintly.

The candles blew out. Now only the fire gave light, and even the flames were bending toward the dark shape growing before the bed, the shape that had been the pretty maid Selia. Anissa screamed, a thin, threadlike sound. Briony tried to call to Chaven, but something had knocked the little man to the floor where he lay limply motionless, perhaps even dead. The room was filling with the mingled smells of hot metal and mud and blood—but blood most of all, powerful, heavy, and sour.

Strangely, Briony could still see something of Anissa's maid in the horror, a thickness at its core that echoed her shape, a gleam of her features in the dark, crude mask, but mostly it was a blur of growth, an inconstant, shadowy thing armored like a crab or spider, but far more irregular and unnatural. Jagged-edged plates and lengthening spikes of powdered stone and other hard things grew and solidified even as Briony gaped in astonishment, as if it built itself out of the very dust whirled through the chamber by the rushing air.

A glint of eyes from deep in the dark instability of the face, then the thing lifted an impossibly long hand. Scythelike claws clacked and rasped against each other as it advanced on Briony. She stumbled back, almost boneless with fear, knowing now beyond doubt what had killed her brother Kendrick. She was weaponless, wearing an impossible, ridiculous dress. She was doomed.

Briony grabbed up a heavy candleholder and swung it, but one of the thing's clawed hands swept it from her grasp with a ringing clash. Something rushed past her; a long pole crashed into the thing's stomach and for a moment it was driven back.

"Run, Highness!" screamed the young guardsman Millward, trying to keep the thing pinioned on the end of his halberd like a boar. "Lew, help me!"

His fellow soldier was slow to come forward; by the time he did take a few timid steps into the blinding storm of grit, the thing had shattered Millward's halberd like a stick of sugar candy and was free again. It closed with the second guard and dodged his swinging pike. Instead of running, Briony stared, transfixed. Why didn't the guards draw their swords—who could be fool enough to fight with such long weapons in a small room? The apparition ripped at the second guard's midsection with a dull flash of talons and he fell back, clutching at his shredded armor, gouting blood black as tar.

The thing now slouched between Briony and the door. Her moment of indecision had left her trapped. She thought she saw something moving behind the monstrous shape—was it Chaven escaping? The young guard Millward had finally drawn his sword; he swiped at the thing but it gave no ground, only let out a rumbling hiss, a sound more like stone scraping on stone than the breath of a living animal, and sank back on itself; its shadowy form became darker and thicker. For a heartbeat Briony thought she could see the maid Selia's face in it, triumphant and deranged, lips curled back in a silent scream of joy.

The young guardsman leaped forward, shouting with terror even as he hacked at the shapeless thing. For a moment it seemed he might even be hurting it—the monstrosity had shrunk to almost human proportions and the claws spread like pleading hands, the dark face all moaning, toothless mouth. Then the talons darted out almost too quickly to be seen and Heryn Millward sagged and collapsed backward, blood bubbling from the hole of his eye socket, his face a red ruin.

Briony could barely breathe, her heart squeezed in her chest by terror until it was near to bursting. The *kulikos* demon moved toward her, edges shifting, nothing quite clear except the gleam of its eyes and the clicking of the long, curved claws as they opened and closed, opened and closed. She stumbled and slid to the floor, fumbling desperately for a stool, anything to keep those terrible knives at bay. Her hand closed on something, but it was only the butt of dead Millward's halberd, a length of splintered wood. She held it in front of her, knowing it would be no more use than a broomstraw against that strength and those terrible, hooked talons.

Then a blossom of flame rose in the air behind the thing, haloing it for a moment so that it seemed to have taken on a new aspect, no longer a dark, muddy nightmare but a fire demon from the pits of Kernios' deepest realm. The fire crashed onto its murky head and shoulders in a shower of sparks and tumbling ribbons of flame. The creature let out a rasping howl of surprise that made Briony's insides quiver as though they had been completely turned to liquid. It turned to lash out at Chaven, who jumped back, dropping the iron fire basket from his smoking, blackened hands, and somehow avoided being torn in half by the sweep of the talons. Flames leaped on the thing's body and crowned its shapeless head, burning higher and higher until they licked at the ceiling. Stumbling backward, it pulled the curtains from the bed, tangling itself like a bear in a net. The diaphanous cloth sparked and swirled and now the flames were bound to it. The shadow-shape writhed, flapping its clawed hands, and Selia's face came into view again, this time twisted in a grimace of alarm. It tore at the flaming curtains and they began to fall away; in a moment it would be free again. Cold fury sent Briony forward with both hands wrapped around the broken halberd staff, which she drove as hard as she could into the center of the terrible thing. It was like running into a stone column— Briony flew back from the impact, dizzied—but the ragged hole of the thing's mouth popped open and something flew out and clattered across the stone floor.

The *kulikos* beast howled again, this time in true pain and terror, but the air was suddenly full of sparks and flying dust. The wind that had swirled it into being now seemed to be pulling it apart.

Briony tried to get up, but the beast's grating screech, so loud that it threatened to shake loose the roof timbers, made her stumble and fall again, and so the retaliatory sweep of claws missed her and she lived. The thing that had been Selia threw itself to the floor, moaning as it scrabbled after the lost *kulikos* stone. The crawling shape was wreathed in flame, but at its core the human and demon essences were in confusion now, flickering and rippling in smoke. It lurched up, hissing triumphantly, but the thing clutched in its taloned hand was only a thimble—perhaps one that had belonged to the maid herself. The shape dropped the silvery thing and took a lurching step backward with a bellow of pain and despair, the Selia-face now a visible mask of agony. Briony's broken pikestaff shuddered in its chest, the wound a fiery hole. It stumbled back against the bed and the entire canopy finally pulled loose and fell atop it, a blanket of roaring fire. The shadow-shape roared and thrashed as the fire leaped upward, then, with a mewling noise that for the first time had something human in it, fell forward and lay stretched on the floor, twitching in the flames.

In the sudden stillness, Briony felt as though she had been carried away to the moon, to some country from which she could never return to the life she knew. She stared at the thing wrapped in burning curtains, and the fire now smoldering in the carpets. When she was certain it had stopped moving, she picked up a chamber pot and emptied it over the burning shape, dousing the worst of the fire and adding the stench of boiling urine to the dreadful odor of fire and blood. As she listlessly began to stamp out the rest of the flames Chaven crawled toward her, his hands blackened, his face stretched in a rictus of pain.

"Don't," he said hoarsely. "We shall have no light."

As absently as if someone else inhabited her body, Briony found a candle and lit it from a bit of flaming bed curtain, then finished the job of putting out the fires. She lit another candle. She was not crying, but she felt as though she should have been.

"*Why?*"

Chaven shook his head. "I was a fool. Because she was ill before Kendrick died, and ill afterward, I thought the maid truly had the fever that struck Barrick. I see now she was only preparing the ground before time for the weakness that would overcome her after using the *kulikos*. I thought the witch must be Anissa and I tried to bluff her. I did not guess the stone could work again without much preparation, some kind of intricate charm . . ."

"No, why did she kill Kendrick? Was she going to kill me as well?"

Chaven stared down at the sodden, scorched mass. He peeled back a corner of the curtain. Briony was startled to see Selia's ordinary dead face, eyes open, mouth gaping. Whatever spell had gripped the girl had now passed, leaving nothing behind to show what she had been except a smeared residue of grit, dust, and ash on her skin, clotted into a foul mud. "Yes, she would have killed you, perhaps by poison—and Barrick, too, if he'd been with you. Your stepmother did not invite you here, Selia herself did. That is why Anissa seemed so confused. Why did she do it? *For whom*, I think is the better question, and I have no answer." He examined his black, blistered hands and said ruefully, "I was so certain it could only be Anissa . . ."

He looked at Briony and she stared back, both struck with the same thought. "Anissa!" she said.

Briony's stepmother was curled on the floor on the far side of the bed in a puddle of water, seemingly oblivious to anything that had happened. The queen was half-delirious with pain, her hands clutching at her belly. "It is coming," she moaned. "The child. It hurts! Oh, Madi Surazem, save me!"

"Get help," Chaven told Briony. "I am nearly useless with these burns. Send for the midwife! Quickly!"

She hesitated for a moment. Anissa's wide-eyed look of terror made her feel ill. She remembered her stepmother's fear as Chaven had all but accused her of murdering her stepson and the feverish feeling grew worse. The Loud Mouse, she and Barrick had called their father's young wife, teasing, resentful. She would never call this woman names again.

Briony staggered out into the deserted tower with one of the candles, made her way down the stairs and somehow did not fall. At the bottom she forced open the door and found the two guards waiting there. They looked her up and down, amazed. She could only guess what she looked like, smeared in ash and blood and worse, but the guards certainly seemed terrified.

There was no time to coddle them or make up stories. "By all the gods, are you both *deaf*? Did you hear none of that happening inside? People are dead. The queen is about to give birth. One of you go upstairs and help Chaven, the other run to find the midwife Hisolda. I don't know where she's gone—Anissa's maid probably sent her away."

"Sh–she and the other w–w–omen went to the kitchen!" said one of the goggle-eyed guards.

"Then go, curse you, go quickly! Fetch her!"

He ran off. The other, still looking at her as though Briony was the most frightening sight of his short life, turned and dashed up the stairs into the tower.

I won't be the worst thing he's seen for very long. She stood, trembling beneath the naked stars, trying to catch her breath. The sound of people singing floated to her across the empty courtyard.

Winter's Eve, she remembered, but now it seemed unutterably strange. Everything before the Tower of Spring seemed to have happened in another century. *I just want to sleep,* she thought. *Sleep and forget.* Forget that moment when that dark thing had grown out of dust and air and vile magicks, when her old life of certainty, frail as it was, had vanished forever. Forget her stepmother, twitching in pain and fear. *We've betrayed them all by our foolishness,* she thought. *Father, Kendrick, Anissa, all of them.*

Shaso.

She felt a dreadful stab of shame. Shaso, chained and suffering. She hesitated for a moment—she was so tired, so very tired—but pushed herself away from the wall on which she had been leaning, away from the stones that to her exhausted muscles felt soft and inviting as a bed, and set out limping toward the stronghold. One wrong would be put right before the dawn of Orphan's Day, in any case.

Zoria, merciful Zoria, she begged, *if you ever loved me, give me a little more strength!*

As Briony left the courtyard and entered the colonnade, she thought she heard footsteps behind her, but when she turned there was no one there, the stone path empty in the moonlight. She hobbled on toward the stronghold and the shackled ghost of her own failure.

40
Zoria's Flight

HEART OF A QUEEN:

Nothing grows from quiet
A pile of cut turves, a wooden box
Carved with the shapes of birds

—from *The Bonefall Oracles*

THE MAZE GARDEN BEHIND the main hall was full of voices. The guests had left the table and bundled up against the cold to go outdoors—at least those seeking privacy they couldn't find inside the brightly-lit halls. But how much privacy could there be, especially in full moonlight? It sounded like at least a dozen people were wandering through the maze, laughing and talking, women shushing the men, at least one fellow singing a bawdy old song about Dawtrey Elf-Spelled—something that didn't seem quite appropriate with the Twilight folk almost standing outside the gates.

Winter was indeed crouching close this Winter's Eve, the air sharp and the wind picking up. Briony wasn't cold, but she knew she should be; in fact, she could hardly feel her body at all. She went past the outskirts of the garden as quietly as she could, staying close to the hedge of ancient yew trees, drifting toward the stronghold like a floating spirit in a cloud of her own exhaled breath. She wanted nothing to do with any of the courtiers. It had been all she could do simply to look at them across the dining hall tonight. Now, with the memory of the inhuman thing that had killed

Kendrick lodged in her mind like a jagged shard of ice, like the never-healing wound of the maiden in the song, she felt as though she would not be able to look at any of their empty faces again without screaming.

She found her way in through a back door of the hall, but instead of making her way by the usual passages, crossed through one of the small chambers behind the throne room, avoiding the clutch of servants trying to finish up their chores in time for a Winter's Eve celebration of their own. No guards waited at the top of the stairs down into the stronghold, and when she pushed open the unbarred door at the bottom, she found only one man and his pike sitting through a lonely watch. The guard was at least half asleep: he looked up slowly at the noise of the door, rubbing his eyes. She couldn't even imagine what she must look like in her tattered gown, her face no doubt as streaked with ash and blood as her hands.

"P–Princess!" He scrambled up onto his feet, fumbling for the handle of his weapon, which he managed to lift with the wrong end up. It would have been comic were it not all so miserable, the night so ghastly and full of blood and fire . . . and if his stupidly earnest face hadn't looked so much like Heryn Millward's, the young guard now lying dead in a puddle of his own blood in Anissa's chamber.

"Where are the keys?"

"Highness?"

"The keys! The keys to Shaso's cell! Give them to me."

"But . . ." His eyes were wide.

I truly must look like a demoness. "Don't make me shout at you, fellow. Just give me the keys, then go and find your captain. Who is in charge with Vansen gone?"

The man fumbled the heavy key on its ring down from a peg on the wall. "Tallow," he said after a moment's panicky thought. "It's Jem Tallow, Highness."

"Then go get him. If he's asleep, wake him up, although I can't imagine why he would be asleep on Winter's Eve." But could it truly still be the same night? It had to be, but the thought was unmanageably strange. "Tell him to bring soldiers and meet me here. Tell him the princess regent needs him now." Until she knew why the witch-maid Selia had done what she did, until she found whether the southern girl had allies in the murder of Kendrick, no one must sleep.

"But . . ."

"By all the gods, *now!*"

The man dropped the keys in his alarm. Briony cursed in a very un-ladylike way and bent and snatched them from the floor. The guard hesitated for only a moment, then threw open the door and scuttled up the stairs.

The lock on the cell was stiff and hard to turn, but with both hands she managed to twist the key and at last the door groaned open. The shape huddled on the floor at the back of the cell did not move, did not even look up.

He's dead! Her heart, already so weary, sped again and for a moment the darkness of the damp, cold room threatened to swallow her up. "Shaso! Shaso, it's me, Briony! The gods forgive us for what we've done!"

She ran to his side and tugged at him, relieved to hear the rasp of breath but horrified by how thin the old man had become. He began to stir. "Briony . . . ?"

"We were wrong. Forgive us—forgive me. Kendrick . . ." She helped him sit upright. He smelled dreadful and she couldn't help taking a step back. "I know who killed Kendrick."

He shook his head. It was dark in the cell, the single brazier outside not enough to illuminate even such a small space. She couldn't see his eyes. "Killed . . . ?"

"Shaso, I know you didn't do it! It was Selia, Anissa's maid. She's . . . she's some kind of witch, a shape-changer. She turned into . . . oh, merciful Zoria, some . . . some *thing!* I saw it!"

"Help me up." His voice was rough with disuse. "For the love of all the gods, girl, help me up."

She did her best, tugging on his arm as he struggled to get to his feet. She babbled out the night's story to him, not certain if he could even understand her in his sick and weary state. The chains clanked and he slumped back down, defeated by their weight. "Where are the keys for these?" she asked.

Shaso pointed. "On that board on the wall." It was taking him a long time to say each word. "I do not know which key fits these shackles. They have scarcely ever been taken off."

Briony's eyes filled with tears as she hurried to the board. She could see no difference between any of the dozen rings so she brought them all, weight that pulled her arms down straight at her sides as she hurried back to the cell. "Why didn't you tell me?" She began to fumble through the keys. She had to lean close as she tried each in the lock of his shackles. The old man's stench reminded her of the thing in Anissa's chamber, but at least it was a more natural odor. "You didn't do it, so why didn't you tell me? What happened between you and Kendrick?"

He was silent. First one, then the second of the shackles opened with a click of sprung iron. She could not help feeling the wet wounds they had made on his wrists as she helped him to stand. He was smeared up and down with blood—but then, so was she.

Shaso wavered, then managed to stand erect. He held out his hands, struggling for balance. "I did tell you . . . that I did not kill your brother. I cannot speak of any more than that," he said at last.

Briony loosed a small shriek of frustration. "What do you mean? I told you, I know who murdered Kendrick. Don't you understand? Now you must tell me why you let us imprison you when it wasn't your fault!"

He shook his head wearily. "My oath prevented me. It still prevents me."

"No," she said, "I will not allow your stubbornness to . . ."

The door of the stronghold creaked open and the guard she had dispatched appeared in the doorway. He wore a distracted expression and his hands were pressed against his stomach as though he cradled something small and precious. He took a step into the chamber then stumbled and fell onto his face. In her anger and confusion it took Briony a moment to realize that he was not getting up, another instant to notice the dark pool spreading beneath him.

"Your master of arms is still the perfect knight, isn't he?" Hendon Tolly stepped out of the stairwell and into the room. He was dressed as though for a funeral, but smiling like a child who had just been given a sweet. "A Xandian savage who would actually die to preserve his honor." Three more men filed into the room behind him, all wearing the Tollys' livery, all with drawn swords. "That is what makes my life easy, you know—all these fools willing to die for honor."

"I have found out who killed my brother," Briony said, startled and frightened. "I did not believe you had anything to do with it. Why have you killed this guard? And why do you come before me in this threatening way?" She drew herself up to her full height. "*Did* you have something to do with it?" She didn't believe she could make Hendon Tolly hesitate about harming the reigning princess, but she might at least cause his minions to have second thoughts.

"Yes, you really might have made a queen in time," Tolly said. "But you are green, girl-child, green. You have come here without guards. You have left a trail of confusion and bloody deeds behind you all across the castle tonight. The story I will tell will explain it all—but not to your credit."

"Traitor," rumbled Shaso. He slumped back against the wall, his strength apparently at an end. "It was . . . you and your brother who caused all this."

"Some of it, yes." Hendon Tolly laughed. "And you, old man, like a drunkard wandering in front of a heavy coach, did not get out of my way. And now you will become the official murderer of the princess as well as of Prince Kendrick."

"What are you babbling about?" Briony demanded, hoping that Tolly would speak long enough for her to think of something, or for someone to come and save her. "Have you lost your mind?" But no one would come, she knew that. It was why he had stabbed the guard and let him die in front of her, as an illustration of her helplessness. The youngest Tolly was a cat who liked to sport with cornered prey, and this was a quality of sport he had been waiting for his entire life.

"Briony, little Briony." He shook his head like a doting uncle. "So angry with my brother Gailon because he wanted to marry you and turn you into a respectable woman instead of the headstrong little trollop your father allowed you to be. Such a monster, you thought him. But in truth, he was the only thing that stood between my brother Caradon and I and our plans for Southmarch. Which is why he had to die."

"You . . . *you* killed Gailon?"

"Of course. He opposed our contacts with the Autarch from the first—he even came to argue with Kendrick about it on the night your brother died. Caradon and I had contacted Kendrick separately, you see, because Gailon would not do it, and we had promised him that the Autarch would help him free your father in return for a few small concessions about the sovereignty of certain southern nations. Kendrick had decided to take up our ally in Xis on his generous offer, you see."

"My brother would never do that!"

"Ah, but he did, or at least he agreed to do so. His murder ruined what would have been a very useful bargain, at least for Caradon and myself. And for the Autarch, too, I suppose." He shook his head. "It is still a puzzlement to me—I can make no sense out of this Devonisian servant girl and her place in things at all."

Briony was about to ask him another question, just to keep him talking—she was far too stunned and terrified at the moment to absorb much of what Hendon Tolly was saying—but he raised his hand to silence her, then nodded at his guards.

"Enough," he said. "Kill them quickly. We still have to find that miserable little doctor."

"You'll never get away with it!"

Tolly laughed with genuine pleasure. "Of course we will. You Eddons, you talk of your sacred bond and the love of the people, but the world does not spin that way, however much you would like to believe it so. Your faithful subjects will forget you within months if not days. You see, someone will have to protect Anissa's newborn child—the last heir. It is a boy, by the by. The midwife is with her even now. Poor Anissa is much confused by the night's events, but I will explain them to her anon." He smiled again, mockingly cheerful. "By then you will be dead at Shaso's hand, a tragic echo of your brother's fate, and Shaso will be dead by mine, or so everyone will hear. Then once we have found and killed that fat physician, there will be no other story except ours. The Tollys will reluctantly take the infant monarch under their protection. My brother will rule at Summerfield Court and I will rule here—although Caradon doesn't know that yet." He actually made a small bow, as though he had done her a service. "You see, that is the secret of history, little Briony—who tells the last story."

Praise the gods, Chaven has escaped them, she thought. *At least for the moment.* Her heart was beating so fast it seemed to drive the air out of her lungs. It was little enough to hope for—that sometime after her death, someone at least would know the truth, that the Tollys' story would not be the only tale of these days.

Hendon Tolly snapped his fingers. The three guards moved forward, pikes out, pushing her back toward Shaso. In this last moment she could only think blindly of meaningless things—Barrick frowning over some petty irritation, Sister Utta drawing a careful circle on a scrap of parchment, the radiant smile of Zoria in an old book—then a black shape flew past her shoulder and smashed into the face of the nearest guard, who pitched over backward, knocking down one of his fellows. A hand yanked Briony backward, then something bright as a broken sun flew across the room and bounced off the wall, spattering blazing light across the guards and Hendon Tolly, who shouted in pain and surprise as flames sprang up on his heavy black clothes.

Shaso was gasping like a dying man from the effort of throwing first his chain, then the brazier. As he pulled her toward the back of the stronghold,

Briony knew they had only postponed death. There was nowhere to go, and the surprise assault had not been enough: already Tolly and his two remaining guards were batting out the flames, although one of the soldiers was screeching in pain.

As she staggered backward, she looked in anguish at the empty rack where the pikes were usually kept, where on any other night but this odd combination of siege and festival some might have been found, then Shaso tugged her into the last cell and slammed the door behind them.

"Hold it closed," the old man wheezed. "Just for . . . a moment."

Their enemy was just outside the door, too cautious to force it open without knowing what Shaso might be planning. "I will be happy to roast you alive in there," Hendon Tolly shouted. He sounded breathless and no longer quite so cheerful. Briony hoped his burns were agonizing. "It will suit our little tale just as well."

Something creaked. "Help me!" Shaso whispered, voice ragged with pain.

Briony took a step, stumbled and fell to her knees. She found him by touch, found the heavy wooden thing in his bony hands.

"Lift!"

She did, grunting with the strain. A slowly widening triangle of light spilling across the straw-covered cell floor showed that Hendon Tolly and his guards had decided to risk the door and were cautiously opening it, but Briony and Shaso had managed to get the trapdoor in the bottom of the cell open as well. She was astounded to discover there was such a thing, but this was no time for questions. At Shaso's mute gesture she slid into the trap and found the ladder, then stopped to hold it open so Shaso could clamber down above her without losing his balance, but she was not much heartened: the pit seemed as hopeless a hiding place as the cell, however deep it might go. Shaso let the door fall down behind them, covering them in blackness. She heard something scrape and realized he was slamming shut a hidden bolt. A moment later Tolly and his men were pounding on the trapdoor in a rage, the sounds echoing like thunder in the narrow pit.

"Crawl," Shaso said when they reached the bottom of the shaft. "You will be able to stand soon."

"By the gods—what is this?"

He shoved her hard. "Go! This is the stronghold of the castle, girl. The place of last resort in a siege. Don't you think there would be some secret way out if the worst came to the worst?"

"It *has* come," she said, then decided to save her breath for crawling.

In only a few moments Shaso's promise was fulfilled: the narrow space widened until Briony couldn't feel the walls or ceiling. "Where does this go?"

"It lets out by the Spring Tower's water gate."

"We must find Avin Brone. We must alert the rest of the guards!"

"No!" He grabbed at her leg. In the darkness, it was as though she had been clutched by some root-fingered monster. Shaso's words came slowly as he fought for breath. "I do not trust Brone. In any case, we do not know where he is. If Tolly's men find us, they will kill you immediately. They can always explain later that I had taken you hostage, that your death was an accident."

"No one will believe that!"

"Perhaps not, in the light of tomorrow's day, but what good would that do you tonight? Or me, as I am hacked to death in front of an angry crowd? Curse it, Briony Eddon, there is no time for this! We must get out. We must . . ." He paused to gasp for breath. It was terrifying to hear him so weak. What if he died? What would she do then? "You can stand now," he said at last. "Take my hand. There is a place we can go."

"What is this tunnel? How did you know about it?"

"I am the master of arms." He groaned in pain as he stood. "It is my task to know of such things. Avin Brone knows, too. That is why he had me imprisoned in a different cell."

"Then why weren't Barrick and I told?"

Shaso sighed, a mixture of regret and clench-jawed pain. "You should have been. Take my hand."

The journey seemed to last the better part of an hour, through damp stone corridors and treacherous narrows that seemed little more than holes dug through hard dirt, before they reached a small stone room that smelled of tidal mud and bird droppings. It had a high, slit window that bled moonlight, and for the first time since they entered the trapdoor she could see Shaso dan-Heza's bony, weary face.

"We are in a storage room by the water gate," he said, panting. She had actually heard him whimpering as he crawled, a sound so bizarrely unexpected that it had frightened her nearly as much as anything else she had experienced on this mad and dreadful night. Shaso showing pain, almost weeping! She could only imagine how dire his circumstances must truly be. "The Summerfield folk will be combing the castle. Others may be looking for you, too, but we can trust no one."

"Surely . . ."

"Listen to me, girl! It is plain now how long and how carefully the Tollys have been preparing, waiting for a moment like this. Even if we reached Brone, even if he proves loyal, who can know whether his guards are the same? We must get you away from here."

"Where? If there is so much danger, where can we go?"

"First things first, Briony." He was shaking, trembling with the cold. "The only safe way to leave the castle is by water."

"But the Twilight People are in the city just on the other side!"

He shook his head. "Then we will go another way. Across the bay and then southward down the coast. There are places in Helmingsea . . . I have prepared . . ."

"You . . . you thought something like this might happen?"

For the first time the old man laughed. It was a hard sound to hear, and quickly became a racking cough that was no more pleasant. "It is my task, Briony," he said when he could speak again. "My sworn task. To think of anything that might happen—*anything*—and then prepare for it."

Even with his body crippled and his life hanging by a thread, she thought she could hear a proud stubbornness in his words. It made her angry despite everything. "Shaso, why didn't you tell me the truth about Kendrick?"

He shook his head. "Later. If we survive." He got slowly and awkwardly to his feet and held out a hand. She shook it off and levered herself upright, conscious for the first time of how weary she was too, how badly all of her ached.

"Silent, now," he said. "Stay in the shadows."

The alleyway outside the storage room was empty, although they could hear sentries talking on top of the wall and a fire burned in the guardhouse beside the water gate. There had never been a night like this! Winter festival being celebrated in the castle while terrible enemies were encamped just across the water, her stepmother's maid changing into a demon—it seemed that anything, absolutely any horrible, ghastly, impossible thing could happen tonight, and she wondered if she could entirely trust Shaso's judgment. He was always so stiff-backed, so certain of his own rightness, but who could judge properly on such a night? What if he was wrong? Should she give up her throne without a fight, run away just for fear of Hendon Tolly? If she called to the guards, wouldn't they come to her in a heartbeat, their princess regent—wouldn't they hunt down Tolly like the murdering dog that he was?

But what if, as Shaso feared, they did not? What if they were secretly Tolly's men, already suborned with lies or gold?

Briony tried to imagine what her father would do, how he would think. *Stay alive*, he would have told her, she knew that. *If you are alive, you make all that Tolly says a lie. But if someone puts an arrow in you, then the people have no choice but to believe him, because Summerfield Court is the most powerful part of the kingdom outside Southmarch, and they have blood ties to the throne.*

Shaso was leading her along the back rows near Skimmer's Lagoon, she suddenly realized. She had hardly ever been to this part of the castle, its narrow streets full of ramshackle Skimmer houses, the quays jostling with the strangely shaped boats that seemed to house at least as many of the water folk as did the more conventional dwellings that loomed beside the docks. It seemed oddly quiet for Winter's Eve, although she realized then that the hour must now be approaching midnight; the streets were almost deserted, some lights in high windows and a few snatches of faint music the only signs that people even lived here. She could hear the tied-up boats bumping against the piers and the occasional sleepily questioning call of a water bird.

"Where are we going?" she whispered as they waited in the shadows to cross one of the larger streets. The dwellings were crammed so close together and leaned so alarmingly overhead that it seemed more like a hornet's nest than any human place. Shaso looked up and down, then waved for her to follow.

"Here," he said. "This is the house of Turley, the headman."

"Turley?" she whispered. It took her a moment to remember why the name was familiar. "I met him!"

Shaso did not reply, but knocked on the oval door; it was a strange pattern of sounds he made, too studied to be accidental. A few moments later the door opened just a slice and two wide eyes peered out. "I need to speak to your father," Shaso said. "Now. Let us in."

The girl stared as though she recognized him but hadn't expected ever to see him at her door. "Cannot be done, Lord," she said at last. "It is shoalmoot tonight."

"I don't care if it's the end of the world, child," the old man growled. "In fact, it *is* the end of the bloody world. Tell your father that Shaso dan-Heza is here on deadly urgent business."

The door opened and the girl stepped out of the way. Briony realized she had seen this one before—the girl who, with her lover, saw the mysterious boat come into the lagoon the night before Kendricks' death. Now she thought she knew what that boat had been carrying, and to whom.

Selia's cursed witch-stone. If I had only paid more attention to what the Skimmers said . . . !

The Skimmer girl recognized Briony and made a movement that was a sort of unschooled courtesy. "Highness," she said, but although interested, she did not look overawed. Briony couldn't remember the girl's name, so she only nodded back.

The narrow passageway creaked like ships' timbers as they walked down it. It smelled strongly, almost overpoweringly, of fish and salt and other less identifiable scents. The girl went ahead of them to open the door at the end of the hall. The room beyond was small and cold and the fire was tiny, as though meant more for light than heat. A few candles burned in the room as well, but it still wasn't bright enough for Briony to be sure how many people sat crammed into the little space. She counted a dozen gleaming bald heads before giving up, but more shapes were crouched in the shadows against the walls. They all seemed to be men and they all turned to look at her with roundly shining, blinking eyes, like frogs on a lily pond.

"Headman Turley," said Shaso. "I need your help. I need a boatman. The life of the princess is in danger."

A room's worth of wide, wet stares grew even wider.

The one called Turley muttered to his fellows for a moment before standing. "Honored, Shaso-*na,*" he said at last in his slow, strangely-accented way, "we are honored, but we are all here sworn to a shoal-moot. We may none of us leave until the night ends or else it be blasphemy. Even were one of us to die, his body would here remain until the sun's rise."

"Is blasphemy worse than the death of the Princess of Southmarch, Olin's daughter? Do you forget what you owe him?"

Turley winced a little, but his smooth face quickly became impassive again. "Still, even so, great Shaso-*na.*"

Briony realized that the master of arms had encountered someone as stubborn as Shaso himself and wished the situation allowed her to enjoy the spectacle. "Can't we wait until dawn?" she asked.

"We dare not try to leave by boat in daylight. And Hendon Tolly will not wait, but will find out soon where the passage we used gives out, and from there it will be short work to think of searching along Skimmer's Lagoon. Brone, too, if he thinks he is acting to save you, will not hesitate to send men house-to-house."

"But we *want* Brone to find us!"

"Perhaps. But again, if only one man be disloyal, an accident could happen—an arrow let fly at me that hits you by mistake, let us say . . ." The old Tuani warrior shook his head. Briony thought he looked as though he was having trouble standing so long. "Headman, can you not send us to someone else—someone you trust? We need a boatman."

"I will be their boatman," announced the Skimmer girl. Briony had not noticed her waiting and listening in the doorway behind them; the voice made her jump. The gathered men seemed to have missed her as well and they muttered in distress and surprise.

"You, Ena?" said her father.

"Me. I am as able with the boat as most men. This is Olin's daughter, after all—we dare not send her away. Who would give her shelter, who would take her where she needs to go? Calkin? Sawney Wander-Eye? There is a reason they are not here at the shoal-moot. No, I will take her."

Her father hesitated, listening to the discontented murmurs of his fellows as he considered. His skin mottled and his throat-apple bulged as though he would puff out some monstrous sack and give a froggy belch of anger, but instead he swallowed again and shook his head in disgust. Briony knew that gesture, had seen her own father make it many times.

"Yes, Daughter. I see no other choice. You take them. But be you careful, ever so careful!"

"I will. She is Olin's daughter and Shaso-*na* is a shoal-friend."

"Yes, but also careful for your own sake, you nasty little pickerel." He opened his arms to her and she stepped to him and gave him a quick, practical hug. "Will you accept this, Shaso-*na*?" Turley asked.

"Of course," said the old man hoarsely.

Ena looked at Shaso carefully for the first time, up and down. "You need some healing, those cuts and burns seen to. But first a tub of good seawater, to take the stink off you." She turned her heavy-lidded gaze on Briony. The nakedness of her eyebrows made the girl's eyes seem mysterious and distant, like those of someone who had lived a long time in illness. "You, too, Mistress. Highness, I mean. You will never get that great ragged skirt in the boat, so we must find you something of mine to wear, begging your pardon. But we must be quick about it all. The moon is swimming, but soon she will dive."

Ferras Vansen caught up to his quarry in the lower reaches of the hills, or at least that was where he thought he was, but he could not be sure. Only a few months ago this had been the border of the Shadowline, an eerie but otherwise ordinary place, but now the hills were shrouded in mist and nearly invisible and all the land down to the bay had become alien.

"Prince Barrick!" The rider didn't turn but glided on through the streaming mist. For long moments Vansen thought he might be mistaken, that perhaps he was calling to some phantom thrown up by the Shadowline, but as he drew closer and eventually pulled abreast of the black horse he could see the boy's pale, distracted face. "Barrick! Prince Barrick, it's me, Vansen. Stop!"

The young prince didn't even look. Vansen nudged his horse closer still, until it was rubbing shoulders with Barrick's mount, then reached across and grabbed at the prince's arm, remembering only too late that it was the wounded one, the crippled one.

Crippled or whole, it seemed to make little difference. Barrick snatched his arm away but still did not turn to look at Vansen, although he did speak for the first time.

"Go away."

There was something odd in his voice, a sleepwalker's distance; the boy's refusal to turn his head began to seem more like madness than contempt. Vansen grabbed him again, harder now, and the prince jabbed at him with his elbow, trying to wriggle free. The horses bumped against each other and whinnied, uncertain whether this was war or something else. Vansen ducked a lashing fist, then wrapped his arms around the prince and pulled Barrick toward him. Barrick's feet caught in the stirrups and he fell, taking the guard captain with him. Vansen avoided being kicked by the horses, but the ground seemed to rise up and hit him like a huge fist. For long moments he could only lie on his back, wheezing.

The horses had trotted on a little way and stopped. When Vansen at last sat up, still not able to fill his lungs completely, he saw to his dismay that Barrick was already on his feet and limping toward his large black horse where it cropped at the meadow grass, half-hidden by mist although it stood only a few dozen yards away. The prince was holding his side as though it hurt him badly, but showed no sign of letting it stop him. Vansen struggled upright and ran after him, but he was weary and battered from the day's fighting and the fall; Prince Barrick had almost reached his horse by the time Vansen caught him.

"Your Highness, I cannot let you go there! Not into that land!"

In reply, Barrick pulled his dagger from his belt and took a clumsy swipe at Vansen without even looking at him. Vansen stumbled back in surprise, tripped, fell. The prince showed no urge to follow up on his advantage; he turned and caught his horse again, which had skipped away in nervousness at their struggle. Just as Barrick got his fingers under the belly strap to hold the horse and began to search for the stirrup with his foot, Vansen reached him again.

This time he was expecting the knife and was able to twist it out of the prince's fingers. The boy let out a small grunt of pain, but still seemed to care little about Ferras Vansen himself; he simply turned again to clamber up onto his saddle. Vansen grabbed him around the waist and pulled him backward so that they both crashed to the ground. This time he shoved his helmeted head against the boy's cloaked back and held on. Barrick gasped with pain and his struggles became increasingly desperate, his arms and legs thrashing as wildly as those of a drowning swimmer. As it became apparent that Vansen was the stronger, that the boy couldn't reach the older man's eyes or vitals with his hooking fingers, Barrick writhed more and more madly. The low moan he had been making as they rolled on the ground rose to a shriek, a horrible raw noise that dug into Vansen's ears like a sharp stick, and the prince began to fling his arms and legs about, kicking, thrashing. Vansen could only hold tight. He felt a little like a father, but of a child who was very ill. An insane child.

How will I ever get him back to Southmarch? he wondered. Barrick's shrieking grew increasingly ragged but did not stop or even slacken. Vansen started to crawl, trying to drag the boy along the ground toward his horse. *I will have to tie him up. But with what? And how will I sneak him past the shadow folk?*

Barrick's struggles became even wilder, something Vansen would not have thought possible. He could pull the prince no farther, and had to stop a few yards from the horses, holding the boy wrapped in his arms and legs as Barrick went on screeching as monotonously as a broken-hinged gate fanning in the wind.

At last it was too much. Vansen's own limbs were achingly weary, the boy's cries so heartrendingly terrible, he began to believe he was somehow crippling the young prince's mind. He let him go, watched as the boy stopped shrieking, got to his feet, swaying—it was a blessed relief to have the silence come rushing back—and staggered toward his horse, which waited with unnatural calm.

Vansen got to his feet and stumbled after him. "Where are you going, Highness? Don't you know you are traveling into the land of shadows?"

Barrick climbed into the saddle, slipping, struggling, clearly almost as weary as Vansen. He sat up, holding his side again. "I . . . I know." His tone was hollow, miserable.

"Then why, Highness?" When there was no reply, Vansen raised his voice. "Barrick! Listen to me! Why are you doing this? Why are you riding into the shadowlands?"

The boy hesitated, fumbling for the reins. The black horse, Vansen noticed for the first time, had strange, amber-yellow eyes. Vansen reached out, gently this time, and touched the prince's arm. Barrick actually looked toward him for a moment, although his eyes did not quite touch Ferras Vansen's. "I don't know why. *I don't know!*"

"Come back with me. That way there's nothing but danger." But Vansen knew there was danger behind them as well, madness and death. Hadn't he first thought Barrick was fleeing the horrors of the battle? "Come back with me to Southmarch. Your sister will be afraid for you. Princess Briony will be afraid."

For an instant it seemed that he might have touched something in the prince regent: Barrick sighed, sagged a little in his saddle. Then the instant passed. "No. I am . . . called."

"Called to what?"

The boy shook his head slowly, the gesture of a doomed, lost man. Vansen had seen such a face once before, eyes so empty and distraught. It had been a man of the dales, a distant relation of Ferras Vansen's mother, who had found himself caught up in a border dispute between two large clans and had seen his wife and children slaughtered before his eyes. That man had worn just such a look when he came to say his farewells before going out to find his family's killers, knowing that no one would either accompany or avenge him, that his own death was inevitable.

Vansen shivered.

Barrick abruptly spurred his horse northward. Vansen ran to his own mount and spurred to catch him until they were riding side by side.

"Please, Highness, I ask you one last time. Will you not turn back to your family, your kingdom? Your sister Briony?"

Barrick only shook his head, his eyes once more gazing into nothingness.

"Then you will force me to follow you into this terrible place that I barely escaped the first time. Is that what you want, Highness, for me to follow you into death? Because my oath will not allow me to let you go alone." Vansen could see her now in his mind's eye, her lovely face and poorly hidden fear, as well as the bravery that was all the more striking because of it. *Now I pay back for your older brother's life, Briony. Now I pay for dead Kendrick's with my own.* But of course, she would likely never know.

For a moment, just a moment, a little of the true Barrick seemed to rise to his eyes, as if someone trapped in a burning house came scrambling to the window to shout for help. "Into death?" he murmured. "Perhaps. But perhaps not." He let his eyes fall closed, then slowly opened them again. "There are stranger things than death, Captain Vansen—stranger and older. Did you know that?"

There was nothing to say. Exhausted in body and spirit, Vansen could only follow the mad young prince into the shadowy hills.

Briony had never thought of Southmarch Castle as something oppressive or frightening—it had been her home for all her life, after all—but as they moved quietly on foot along the edge of the lagoon, the keep with its tall towers and lighted windows seemed to loom over her like a crowned skull.

The whole night seemed a fantasy, a perverse one in which serving girls were transformed into monsters and princesses had to go disguised through their own domains in Skimmer clothes that stank of fish.

Ena led them through the dank, narrow streets to a dock on the southern lagoon where the keep's huge outer wall shadowed Fitters Row, but they did not get into a boat. Instead, she took them through a weathered door that opened right into the wide wall of stone which defended the castle from the bay. The rough-hewn passage inside led to a stairwell that wound upward into the cliff wall for some twenty or thirty paces, then down again for quite a few more steps, where Briony was astonished to discover herself beside another tiny lagoon, this one entirely surrounded by a rock cave that was lit by lanterns perched here and there along the shore. *This must be hidden inside the seawall,* she marveled. Two Skimmer men sat cross-legged on the stony shore guarding a dozen or so small boats, but they were on their feet before Briony and her companions ever left the stairs. They both carried nasty-looking hooked blades on long poles and did not lower the weapons until Ena had spoken to them in a guttural undertone.

Did the Skimmers truly have their own tongue, then? Briony had heard many say that couldn't be true. She realized that she had learned very little about these people who lived inside her own castle. And a hidden lagoon! "Did you know about this place?" she asked Shaso.

"I have never seen it," he said, which didn't quite answer the question. She didn't press him further, though; he was barely able to stand upright as it was.

Ena appeared to have successfully explained her mission to the Skimmer sentries. She directed Shaso and Briony into a long, slender rowboat, then climbed in after them and rowed them out onto the tiny lagoon toward a low, apparently natural opening in the far rock wall that must have been invisible under water for at least half of every day. The oars moved easily in the girl's strong, long-fingered hands. In only a short while the little boat slipped out onto the gentle swell of the bay, with the cloudy, vast sky overhead and the night winds blowing.

"Why have I never heard of that lagoon?" Briony was cramped on the seat, her feet perched on the sack Ena and her father had provided that contained mostly dried fish and skin bags full of water. She looked back. "What if someone should invade the castle through that hole in the seawall?"

"It is only there for a little part of the day." The Skimmer girl smiled an oddly shy, wide-mouthed smile. "When the tide begins to come back up, we must take the boats out of the water and leave the cavern. There are other guards, too—guards you did not see."

Briony could only shake her head. It was clear that there was much she had yet to learn about her own home.

After a stretch of quiet, the motion of the little boat and the quiet repetitive creaking as Ena plied the oars began to lull her. Sleep was very tempting, but she was not ready to surrender yet. "Shaso? Shaso."

He made a grunting sound.

"You told me you would explain what happened. Why you did not tell me the truth."

He groaned, but very quietly. "Is this my punishment, then?"

"If you want to think of it that way." She reached out and squeezed his arm, felt where the hard muscle had begun to devour itself during his dark, malnourished weeks in the stronghold cell. "I promise I will let you sleep soon. Just tell me what happened . . . that night."

Shaso spoke slowly, stopping often to get his breath. "He called me in, your brother Kendrick. He had just been visited by Gailon Tolly. If that jackal Hendon told the truth in this one thing, anyway, Gailon must have been arguing against the Autarch's offer, not for it. I thought he was the one who brought it, but it seems I was wrong. In any case, your brother told me what he intended to do—to abandon your father's belief that all the nations of Eion must be defended. Kendrick thought that he could convince the other monarchs to let the Autarch take Hierosol, and that in return the Autarch would release your father.

"Leaving aside whether or not it was honorable, I thought it a foolish gamble. We drank wine and we argued. We argued a long time, Kendrick and I, and bitterly. I told him that he was a fool to bargain with such a creature, especially a creature of such growing power—that I would sooner kill myself than let him do this to his kingdom. All my life I have watched the monarchs of Xis at work, Briony. I saw Tuan and a dozen other nations in Xand dragged in chains before the Falcon Throne, and it is said this Autarch is the worst of his whole mad line. But Kendrick was certain that the only way to withstand the Autarch in the long run was to have your father Olin lead a defensive coalition of northern nations—to give up Hierosol and the other decadent southern cities. A demon's bargain, I called it—the kind that only the demon can win. Eventually, in drunken anger and despair and what I must admit was disgust as well, I . . . I left him. I passed Anissa's maid in the hall—summoned by Kendrick, I assumed. She was pretty and had a saucy eye, so I thought little of it."

A thought caught at Briony. *Kendrick said, "Isss . . ." He could not remember the girl's name. He was calling her "Anissa's maid" or "servant" as he . . . as he died.* It was too dreadful to think on long, and she did not want to be distracted. "You say you simply left, Shaso. But when we found you, we were covered in blood!"

"As we disputed, as I raged against his foolishness, I . . . turned my knife on myself. I told him . . . Oh, Briony, girl, I hate that these were the last words . . . the last words I spoke with him." For a long moment it seemed that he wouldn't continue. When he did, the rasp in his voice was harsher than before. "I told your brother I would cut my own arms from my body, the arms that had so long served his father, before letting them serve such a treacherous son. That I would stab myself in the heart. I was drunk—very drunk by then, and very angry. I could not bear facing Dawet dan-Faar across the table that night without wine and I had already had several cups before I went to your brother's room. I have cursed myself for it in the darkness of that cell many times. Kendrick tried to wrestle the knife away from me. He was furious that I would argue with him, that I did not merely doubt his strategy but denounced it and him. We fought for the knife and I was cut again. Him, too, I think, but only a little. At last I came back to my right mind. He sent me away, making me swear on my debt to your father that I would not speak of what had happened no matter how much I disagreed with him.

"To tell you truth, even after you freed me, I would never have spoken of what he planned, poor Kendrick, the dishonor of bargaining with the bloody Autarch . . ." Again Shaso had to stop. Briony would have felt sorry for him but the newness of the betrayal was too much—Shaso's for keeping stubbornly silent and her brother's for thinking he knew more than their father, for thinking himself a king before he had gained the wisdom, for supposing he could manipulate a great and powerful enemy. "I . . . returned to my rooms," Shaso went on. "I drank a great deal more wine, trying to make it all go away. When you came for me, I thought that Kendrick was still angry with me for insulting him, perhaps even that I had been too drunk and had hurt him in our scuffling, that I would be locked up for insulting him—made a slave again, after all these years. It only became clear to me later what had happened."

"But, you fool, why didn't you tell us?"

"What could I say? I gave my oath to your brother before he died that I would not speak of what had happened in that room. I was ashamed for myself and for him. And at first, before I understood the truth, my honor was outraged that you should come for me like a criminal, simply because I had disagreed with the prince regent. But when I learned what had happened, I told you that I hadn't killed him, and that was the truth." He trembled a little under her hand, which still touched his arm. "What does a man have if he gives up the bond of his word? He is worse than dead. Had Hendon Tolly not told you what your brother planned, I would be silent still."

Briony sat back, looking up at the jutting shadow of the castle. She was shiveringly cold and weary, still terrified by the night's events. Somewhere in that darkened keep, she knew, armed men were searching for her and Shaso. "So where do we go?"

"South," he said after a while. He sounded like he had fallen asleep for a few moments.

"But after that? After we land? Do you have allies in mind?" *South,* she thought. *Where Father is being held prisoner.* "My brother," she said out loud. "I . . . I'm afraid for him, Shaso."

"Whatever happened, he did what he thought was best. His soul is at rest, Briony."

For a moment her heart was startled up into her throat. Barrick? Did Shaso know something about him that she did not? Then she understood. "I didn't mean Kendrick. Yes, he did his best, the gods bless him and keep him. No, I mean Barrick." It was hard to find the strength even to speak: the long day had finally caught up to her. Tears made the dark geometries of the keep even more blurry. "I miss him. I am afraid . . . I'm afraid something bad has happened."

Shaso had nothing to say, but patted her arm awkwardly.

The boat slipped on, the oars moving steadily beneath Ena's skillful hands. Briony felt like Zoria in the famous tale, fleeing her home in the middle of the night. What was it Tinwright had written about that— overwritten, to be honest? *"Clear-eyed, lion-hearted, her mind turned toward the day when her honor will again be proclaimed . . ."* But the goddess Zoria had been escaping from an enemy and fleeing back to her father's house. Briony was leaving her home behind, perhaps forever. And Zoria was an immortal.

Midlan's Mount with its walls and towers no longer loomed over them like a stern parent, but was beginning to recede, the bay widening between their little boat and the castle, the forested shore growing closer, a blackness along the southern horizon that blotted the starry sky. Only a few lights burned where she could see them in the castle's upper reaches, a few in the Tower of Spring, a few lanterns in the guardhouses along the wall and atop the harbor breakwaters. She was filled with an unexpected, aching love for her home. All the things she had taken for granted, even some she had despised, the chilly, ancient halls as complicated as long stories, the portraits of glowering ances- tors, the gray trees below her window in the Privy Garden that budded so bravely each cold spring—all had been stolen from her. She wanted it all back.

Shaso was asleep now, but Briony had missed her own chance at healing slumber. For this little while, anyway, she was queerly wakeful, exhausted but full of fretful thoughts. She could only sit and watch as the moon dove down through the sky and the waters of the bay grew wider between her and all of her life until this moment.

The streets of Funderling Town were lit but deserted, so that they had the feeling of unfinished scrapes instead of thoroughfares. Chert, walking like a man who had lately seen too many of the world's strangest corners, could hear his footsteps echo from the stone walls of his neighbors' houses as he trudged up Wedge Road and in through his own front door.

Opal heard him in the main room and rushed out from the back of the house, face full of misery and fear. He thought she would demand to know where he had been all these long, long hours, but instead she just grabbed his hand and dragged him toward the bedroom. She was moaning and he suddenly knew the worst had happened: the boy was dead.

To his shock, Flint was not dead but awake and watching. Chert turned to Opal, but she still had the look of someone who had discovered her most prized possession had been stolen.

"Boy?" he asked, kneeling beside him. "How do you feel?"

"Who are you?"

Chert stared at the familiar face, the shock of hair so pale as to be almost white, the huge, watchful eyes. Everything was the same and yet the child also seemed somehow slightly different. "What do you mean, who am I? I'm Chert, and this is Opal."

"I . . . I don't know you."

"You're Flint, we're . . . we've been taking care of you. Don't you remember?"

Slowly, weakly, the boy shook his head. "No, I don't remember you."

"Well . . . if you're not Flint, who are you?" He waited in a kind of airless terror for the answer. "What's your name?"

"I said I don't know!" the boy whined. There was something in him Chert had never seen before, a trapped and frightened animal behind the narrow face. "I don't know who I am!"

Opal stumbled out into the other room, clutching her throat as though she couldn't breathe. Chert followed her, but when he tried to put his arms around her, she flailed at him in her misery and he retreated. Since he could think of nothing else to do he came back to the bed and took the boy's hand; after a moment of trying to pull his fingers free, the boy who looked like Flint relaxed and let him hold it. Helpless and weary, all thought of what had just happened to him outside the city gates swept aside, at least for now, Chert sat this way for an hour, calming a terrified child while his wife cried and cried in the other room.

Appendix

PEOPLE

Adcock—one of the royal guard under Vansen's command

Agate—Funderling woman, a friend of Opal's

Agnes—daughter of Finneth and Onsin

Anazoria—Briony's youngest maid

Andros—a priest, proxy to Lord Nynor

Angelos—an envoy from Jellon to Southmarch

Anglin—Connordic chieftain, awarded March Kingdom after Coldgray
    Moor

Anglin III—King of Southmarch, great-grandfather of Briony and
    Barrick

Anissa—Queen of Southmarch, Olin's second wife

Antimony—a young Funderling temple brother

Argal the Dark One—Xixian god, enemy of Nushash

Autarch—Sulepis Bishakh am-Xis III, monarch of Xis, most powerful
    nation on the southern continent of Xand

Avin Brone—Count of Landsend, the castle's lord constable

Axamis Dorza—a Xixian ship's captain

Back-on-Sunset-Tide—Skimmer extended family

Barrick Eddon—a Prince of Southmarch

Barrow—a royal guard

Baz'u Jev—a Xandian poet

Beetledown—a Rooftopper

Big Nodule (Blue Quartz)—Chert's father

Blackglass—a Funderling family

Boulder—a Funderling
Brambinag Stoneboots—a mythical ogre
Bratchard, Lord—a nobleman
Brenhall, Lord—a nobleman
Brigid—a serving-woman at the Quiller's Mint
Briony Eddon—a Princess of Southmarch
Brother Okros—physician-priest from Eastmarch Academy
Caddick—soldier of the Southmarch royal guard, known as "Longlegs"
Calkin—a Skimmer
Caradon Tolly—Gailon's younger brother
Caylor—a legendary knight and prince
Chaven—physician and astrologer to the Eddon family
Chert (Blue Quartz)—a Funderling, Opal's husband
Cheshret—Qinnitan's father, a minor priest of Nushash
Child of the Emerald Fire—a Qar tribe
Chryssa—Chief Acolyte of the Hive Temple in Xis
Cinnabar—a Funderling magister
Clemon—famous Syannese historian, also called "Clemon of Anverrin"
Cloudwalker—another name for Perin, the sky god
Collum—Willow's younger brother
Collum Dyer—one of Vansen's soldiers
Comfrey M'Neel—a noblewoman
Conary—proprietor of the Quiller's Mint
Conoric, Sivonnic, and Iellic tribes—"primitive" tribes who lived on
    Eion before conquest by the southern continent of Xand
Cusy—chief of the Favored (eunuchs) of the Royal Seclusion in Xis
Daman Eddon—Merolanna's husband, King Ustin's brother
Dannet Beck—Raemon Beck's cousin
Dawet dan-Faar—envoy from Hierosol
Dab Dawley—a Southmarch guard
Dawtrey—a legendary knight, sometimes called "Elf-spelled"
Derla—wife of Raemon Beck
Dimakos Heavyhand—one of the last chieftains of the Gray Companies
Donal Murroy—onetime captain of the Southmarch royal guard
Droy Nikomede—a.k.a. "Droy of Eastlake," a Southmarch noble
Durstin Crowel—Baron of Graylock
Dunyaza—Qinnitan's friend, an acolyte of the Hive
Earth Elders—Funderling guardian spirits

Eats-the-Moon—a Qar of the Changing tribe
Eilis—Merolanna's maid
Elan M'Cory—sister-in-law of Caradon Tolly
Ena—a young Skimmer girl, Back-on-Sunset-Tide clan
Erilo—god of the harvest
Erivor—god of waters
Euan Dogsend—Chaven's friend, "the most learned man in Blueshore"
Evander—Syannese count, envoy to Southmarch
Ever-Wounded Maid—a character out of legend
Evon Kinnay—friend of Gailon Tolly, son of Baron of Longhowe
Ewan—Finnith's son
Falk—a Southmarch guard
Fergil—son of Finneth and Onsin
Ferras Vansen—Captain of the royal guard
Finton—Raemon Beck's younger son
Finn Teodoros—a writer
Finneth—a woman of Candlerstown
Funderlings—sometimes known as "delvers," small people who specialize
    in stonecraft
Gailon Tolly, Duke of Summerfield—an Eddon family cousin
Gar Doiney—a scout
Gil—a potboy at the Quiller's Mint
Gallibert Perkin—Count of Craneshill, Lord Chancellor of Southmarch
Gowan M'Ardall—an earl, his fiefdom is in Helmingsea
Grandfather Sulfur—a Funderling elder of the Metamorphic Brothers
Gray Companies—mercenaries and landless men turned bandits in the
    wake of the Great Death
Great Mother—goddess worshipped in Tuan
Greenjay—a Qar of the Trickster tribe
Gregor of Syan—a famous bard
Grenna—a lady's maid
Guard of Elementals—a tribe of the Qar
Gwatkin—soldier of the Southmarch royal guard
Gyir—a Qar, Yasammez's captain, a.k.a. "Gyir the Storm Lantern"
Gypsum—a Funderling family
Habbili—a god, the crippled son of Nushash
Haketani—people of the Haketan tribe in Xand
Hammerfoot—a Qar, of Firstdeep

Hand of the Sky—a Rooftopper deity
Hanede—Shaso's daughter
Harry—Chaven's manservant
Harsar—Ynnir's counselor
Hasuris—a Xixian storyteller
Havemore—Brone's factor
Hendon Tolly—youngest of the Tolly brothers
Heryn Millward—a Southmarch royal guard
Hesper—King of Jellon, betrayer of King Olin
Hiliometes—a legendary demigod and hero
Hisolda—Anissa's midwife
Hornblende—Funderling, Stonecutters Guild foreman
Hull-Scrapes-the-Sand—Skimmer extended family
Iaris—an oracle of Kernios, a semi-saint
Idrin—young son of Gowan of Helmingsea
Ivar Brenhill—a knight and nobleman of Silverside
Jeddin—chief of the autarch's Leopard guards, also known as "Jin"
Jem Tallow—a Southmarch guard officer
Karal—King of Syan killed by Qar at Coldgray Moor
Kaspar Dyelos—Chaven's mentor, a.k.a. "Warlock of Krace"
Kellick Eddon—great-grandnephew of Anglin, first of Eddon family
    March Kings
Kendrick Eddon—Prince Regent of Southmarch, eldest son of King Olin
Kernios—earth god
Kert hillmen—a wild tribe that lives northwest of Kertewall
King Nikolos—Syan monarch who moved the Trigonarchy out of
    Hierosol
Krisanthe—Queen Meriel's mother, the twins' grandmother
Kupilas—god of healing
Lander III—son of Karal, King of Syan, a.k.a. "Lander the Good," "Lan-
    der Elfbane"
Lapis—Chert's mother
Laylin—uncle of Tyne Aldritch
Laybrick—a Southmarch guard
Leotrodos—Perikalese scientist friend of Chaven
Lepthis—an Autarch of Xis
Lew—a Southmarch guard

Lindon Tolly—father of Gailon, former First Minister of March Kingdoms

Lily—Anglin's granddaughter, queen who led Southmarch in time of Gray Companies

Little Carbon—a Funderling craftsman

Little Raemon—Raemon Beck's oldest son

Lord of the Peak—a Rooftopper deity

Lorick Eddon—Olin's older brother, who died young

Ludis Drakava—Protector of Hierosol

Luian—an important Favored in the Seclusion, previously known as "Dudon"

Madi Surazem—goddess of childbirth

Matthias Tinwright—a poet, a.k.a. "Matty"

Mayne Calough—a nobleman and knight

Meriel—Olin's first wife, daughter of a powerful Brennish duke

Merolanna—the twin's great-aunt, originally of Fael, widow of Daman Eddon

Mesiya—moon goddess

Metamorphic Brothers—a Funderling religious order

Mica—Schist family member, Hornblende's nephew

Mickeal Southstead—a Southmarch guard

Mistress Jennikin—Chaven's housekeeper

Moina Hartsbrook—a young Helmingsea noblewoman, one of Briony's ladies-in-waiting

Mokori—one of the autarch's stranglers

Morning-in-Eye—a Qar of the Changing People

Muchmore—a Southmarch scout

Nevin Hewney—a playwright

Nodule—Chert's brother, a.k.a. "Magister Blue Quartz"

Nose, Grand and Worthy—a Rooftopper dignitary

Nushash—Xixian god of fire, patron god of the autarchs

Nynor—Steffans Nynor, Count of Redtree, Lord Castellan of Southmarch Castle

Old High Feldspar—a wise elder of the Funderlings, now deceased

Old Pyrite—a Funderling acquaintance of Chert and Opal

Olin—King of Southmarch and the March Kingdoms

Onsin—a Candlerstown blacksmith, called "Oak-arms"

Opal—a Funderling, Chert's wife

Panhyssir—Xixian high priest of Nushash

Parnad—father of current autarch, Sulepis, sometimes known as "the Unsleeping"

Pedar Vansen—Ferras Vansen's father

Perin—sky god, called "Thane of Lightnings"

Pinimmon Vash—Paramount Minister of Xis

Prusus—scotarch of Xis, sometimes called "Prusus the Cripple"

Pumice—a Funderling guildsman

Purifiers—fanatics who banded together to punish Qar and others for the Great Death

Puzzle—court jester to the Eddon family

Qar—race of non-humans who once occupied much of Eion

Quicksilver—important Funderling family

Quiet People—a name for the Qar

Qinnitan—an acolyte of the Hive in Xis

Raemon Beck—member of a Helmingsea trading family

Rafe—Ena's friend, Hull-Scraped-the-Sand clan

Raven, Prince of Birds—character from legend

Robben Hulligan—a musician, friend of Puzzle

Rocksalt—a Funderling peddler

Rooftoppers—little-known residents of Southmarch Castle

Rorick—Earl of Daler's Troth, an Eddon cousin of Brennish ancestry, related to Meriel

Rose Trelling—one of Briony's ladies-in-waiting, a niece of Avin Brone

Rugan—the High Priestess of the Hive

Rule—Avin Brone's informant

Rusha—a hairdresser in the Royal Seclusion

Sanasu—widow of Kellick Eddon, known as "Weeping Queen"

Sandstone—a Funderling family

Sawney Wander-Eye—a Skimmer

Schist—a Funderling family, one of them is chorister of Funderling Town

Sedimentary—a Funderling clan made up of several families

Selia—Anissa's maid, also from Devonis

Shaso dan-Heza—Southmarch master of arms

Silas of Perikal—semi-legendary knight

Sni'sni'snik-soonah—Rooftopper name for "Rooftoppers"

Sisel—Hierarch of Southmarch, chief religious figure in March Kingdoms

Siveda—goddess of night

Sivney Fiddicks—a nobleman and knight

Skimmers—a people who make their livings on and around water

Stone Circle People—a Qar tribe

Stone of the Unwilling—a Qar of the Guard of Elementals

Surigali—Xixian goddess

Sveros—old god of the night sky, father of Trigon gods

Talc—Schist family member, Hornblende's nephew

Tanyssa—a gardener and errand-runner in the Royal Seclusion

Three Highest—reference to the gods of the Trigon

Timoid, Father—Eddon family mantis (priest)

Toby—Chaven's assistant

Tricksters—a tribe of the Qar

Trigon—priesthoods of Perin, Erivor, and Kernios acting in concert

Trigonarch—Head of Trigon, chief religious figure in Eion

Tully Joiner—a man of Candlerstown

Turley Longfingers—a Skimmer fisherman, Back-on-Sunset-Tide clan

Twelve Families—governing body of old Hierosol

Twilight People—another name for the Qar

Tyne Aldritch—Earl of Blueshore, an ally of Southmarch

Uncle Flint—Chert's uncle

Upsteeplebat, Queen—monarch of the Rooftoppers

Ustin—King Olin's father

Utta—a.k.a. "Sister Utta," a priestess of Zoria and Briony's tutor

Whispering Mothers—Qar, known as "They who nurse the Great Egg"

Widow Rocksalt—a Funderling

Willow—a young woman

Yasammez—Qar noblewoman, sometimes known as "Lady Porcupine,"
    or "Scourge of the Shivering Plain"

Yellow Knight—nemesis of Silas of Perikal

Ynnir the Blind King—lord of the Qar, "Ynnir din'at sen-Qin, Lord of
    Winds and Thought," a.k.a. "Son of the First Stone"

Young Pyrite—a Funderling

Zoria—goddess of wisdom

Zmeos—a god, Perin's nemesis

Zosim—son of Erilo, god of playwrights and drunkards

PLACES

Akaris—an island between Xand and Eion
Badger's Boots—a Southmarch inn
Basilisk Gate—main gate of Southmarch Castle
Beetle Way—street in Funderling Town
Bird Snare Market—a marketplace in Xis
Brenland—small country south of the March Kingdoms
Brenn's Bay—named after a legendary hero
Candlerstown—Daler's Troth town
Cascade Stair—in the Funderling Depths
Cat's Eye Street—a street in Xis
Chapel of Erivor—Eddon family chapel
Chamber of Cloud-Crystal—in the Funderling Depths
Cloud-Spirit Tower—a tower in Qul-na-Qar
Coldgray Moor—legendary battleground, from a Qar word, "Qul Girah"
Creedy's Inn—tavern in Greater Stell
Dale House—Daler's Troth town, seat of Earl Rorick
Deep Library—a place in Qul-na-Qar
Eastmarch Academy—university, originally in old Eastmarch, relocated to Southmarch at the time of the last war with the Qar
Eastside Gate—one of the gates of Candlerstown
Eion—the northern continent
Emberstone Reach—in the Funderling Depths
Fael—a nation in the heartland of Eion
Faneshill—a large town south of the Settland Road
Farmers' Hall—an ornamental hall in the Throne Hall
Feather Cape Row—a street in Xis
Firstdeeps—a place in Qar lands
Fitter's Row—a street in Southmarch
Free Kingdoms—the kingdoms of Eion which have not fallen under the Autarch's rule
Funderling Town—underground city of Funderlings, in Southmarch
Garden of Queen Sodan—a garden in the Royal Seclusion of Xis
Great Gable—Rooftopper sacred spot
Greater Stell—Dalter's Troth town
Gypsum Way—a street in Funderling Town
Hangskin Row—a street near the Old Tannery Dock

Hawkshill—Daler's Troth town
Hidden Hall—part of the Rooftopper kingdom
Hive—a temple in Xis, home of the sacred bees of Nushash
Hierosol—once the reigning empire of the world, now much reduced;
　　its symbol is the golden snail shell
Holy Wainscoting—Rooftopper sacred spot
Jellon—kingdom, once part of Syannic Empire
J'ezh'kral Pit—a place out of Funderling myth
Krace—a collection of city-states, once part of Hierosoline Empire
Kertewall—one of the March Kingdoms
Landsend—part of Southmarch, Brone's fief; colors red and gold
Lily Gate—gate leading out of the Seclusion into the city of Xis
Little Stell—Daler's Troth town
Lower Ore Street—a main street in Funderling Town
Marash—a Xandian province where peppers are grown
March Kingdoms—originally Northmarch, Southmarch, Eastmarch, and
　　Westmarch, but after the war with the Qar constituted by South-
　　march and the Nine Nations (which include Summerfield and
　　Blueshore)
Market Road—one of Southmarch's main roads
Market Square—main public space in Southmarch
Marrinswalk—one of the March Kingdoms
Marsh Road—main road in Candlerstown
Maze—in the Funderling Depths
Moonstone Hall—in the Funderling Depths
Mount (the), a.k.a. Midlan's Mount—rock in Brenn's Bay upon which
　　Southmarch is built
Mount Xandos—mythical giant mountain that stood where Xand now
　　lies
Northmarch Road—the old road between Southmarch and the north
Oak Chamber—a council chamber
Observatory House—Chaven's residence
Old Tannery Dock—Skimmer name for dock near the Tower of Autumn
Olway Coomb—a battle-site in Marrinswalk
Ore Street—a main street in Funderling Town
Oscastle—a city in Marrinswalk
Quarry Square—a meeting place in Funderling Town
Qirush-a-Ghat—cavern towns of the Qar; name means "Firstdeeps"

Qul-na-Qar—ancient home of the Qar or Twilight People
Raven's Gate—entrance to Southmarch Castle's inner keep
Redtree—an Eddon holding
Reheq-s'lai—Wanderwind Mountains
Rose Garden—at the center of the Lesser Hall, sometimes called "Traitor's Garden"
Sailmaker's Row—a street near the docks in Great Xis
Salt Pool—underground sea pool in Funderling Town
Sania—a country in Xand
Scented Garden—a garden in the Seclusion of Xis
Seclusion—home of the wives of the autarch
Sessio—an island kingdom in the south of Eion
Settland—small, mountainous country southwest of the March Kingdoms; ally of Southmarch
Shadowline—line of demarcation between lands of Qar and human lands
Shehen—"Weeping," Qar name for Yasammez's house
Shivering Plain—site of a great Qar battle
Siege of Always-Winter—a mythical castle
Silent Hill—place behind the Shadowline
Silk Door—a place beneath Funderling Town
Skimmer's Lagoon—body of water inside Southmarch walls, connected to Brenn's Bay
Silverside Road—thoroughfare leading, among other places, between Southmarch and Summerfield
Southmarch—seat of the March Kings, sometimes called "Shadowmarch"
Square of Three Gods—town square in mainland Southmarch
Stonecutter's Door—an exit from Funderling Town
Squeakstep Alley—a street in Southmarch
Summerfield Court—ducal seat of Gailon and the Tolly family
Sunken Garden—a Southmarch castle garden, Erilo's shrine is there
Sun's Progress Square—a plaza in Great Xis
Suttler's Wall—a Southmarch town near the Blueshore border
Syan—once-dominant empire, still a powerful kingdom in center of Eion
Tessis—capitol city of Syan
Three Gods—a triangular plaza in Southmarch; a populous district around that plaza

Three Brothers Road—thoroughfare leading, among other places, between Southmarch and Summerfield
Tin Street—a street in Southmarch
Torvio—an island nation between Eion and Xand
Tower of Autumn—one of the four cardinal towers of Southmarch Castle
Tower of Spring—one of the four cardinal towers of Southmarch Castle; Anissa's residence
Tower of Summer—one of the cardinal towers of Southmarch Castle
Tower of Winter—one of the cardinal towers of Southmarch castle
Tribute Hall—hall outside Briony's bedroom passage
Tuan—native country of Shaso and Dawet
Wedge Road—Chert and Opal's street
Wharfside—a district of mainland Southmarch
White Desert—vast desert that covers much of the center of Xand
Whitewood—a forest on the border between Silverside and Marrinswalk
Wolfstooth Spire—tallest tower of Southmarch Castle
Xand—the southern continent
Xis—largest kingdom of Xand; its master is the autarch

THINGS and ANIMALS
Astion—a Funderling symbol of authority
Blueroot—favorite Funderling tea-herb
Book of Regret—a semi-mythical Qar artifact/text
Book of the Trigon—a late-era adaptation of original texts about all three gods
Cloudchip—a type of crystal
Dado—a dog, raised by Briony
"Dasmet and the Girl With No Shadow"—a Xandian folktale
Days of Cooling—legendary time in Funderling history and myth
Days of the Week—in the Eionic calendar, there are three ten-day periods in each month, called "tennights." Therefore, the twenty-first day of August in our calendar would be more or less the third Firstday of Oktamene. (See the explanation under "Months" for more information.)

Firstday
Sunday

Moonsday
Skyday
Windsday
Stonesday
Fireday
Watersday
Godsday
Lastday

Demia's Ladder—a constellation
Earth-ice—a type of crystal
Eddon Wolf—the symbol of the Eddon family (silver wolf and stars on
black field)
"Ever-Wounded Maid"—a famous story
Family of Stones and Metals—a Funderling scheme of classification
Feast of the Rising—Xixian festival at the end of the rainy season
Firegold—a mineral
Fireworm—a poisonous snake
Great Death—plague that killed a large part of Eion's population
Great Golden Piece—part of the Rooftopper's crown jewels
Harrier—a hunting hound
Hierosoline—the language of Hierosol, found in many religious services
and scientific books, etc.
History of Eion and Its Nations—book by the historian Clemon
Horns of Zmeos—a constellation, also called the Old Serpent
K'hamao—a drink, part of Funderling ritual
Kettle—Barrick's horse
Kloe—a cat
Kossope—a constellation
Kulikos or *kulikos* stone—a reputedly magical object
Lastday—Funderling day of rest
Lander's Hall—a near-mythical setting for stories of knightly adventure
"Lay of Kernios"—a famous story and song, part of the funeral service
Leaf, Singers, White Root, Honeycomb, Waterfall—Flint's names for
constellations
Lymer—a hunting hound
M'aarenol—a location, possibly a mountain, in Qar lands
Maker's-pearl—a stone used by Funderlings for decoration

Mantis—a priest, usually of the Trigon

Meadowsweet—a common wildflower

Months—each Eion month is thirty days long, divided into three ten-nights, with five intercalary days between the end of the year—Orphan's Day—and the first day of the new year, also known as Firstday or Year Day. Thusly month/month correspondents are liable to differ by a few days: the first day of Trimene in Southmarch is not the exact same day as March 1 on our calendar.

> Eimene—January
>
> Dimene—February
>
> Trimene—March
>
> Tetramene—April
>
> Pentamene—May
>
> Hexamene—June
>
> Heptamene—July
>
> Oktamene—August
>
> Ennamene—September
>
> Dekamene—October
>
> Endekamene—November
>
> Dodekamene—December

Mordiya—Tuani for "uncle," can be honorary or actual

Morning Star of Kirous—Jeddin's ship

Mossbrew—a strong Funderling drink

Neverfade—a small white wildflower

Pass-evil—hand sign made to avert bad luck

Pentecount—a troop, numbering fifty

"Perin's great planet"—Perinos Eio, largest planet in the skies

Perinsday—a spring holiday

Podensis—a Hierosoline ship

Procession of Penance—a holy festival

Puffkin—a cat

Quiller's Mint—a tavern

Rack—a dog, raised by Briony

S'a-Qar—language of the Qar

Sandy—a river on the Blueshore border

Seal of War—a Qar gem, object of great importance

Screaming Years—an era of Qar history
Shining Man—center of the Funderling Mysteries
Shivering Plain—a famous Qar battleground
Silver Thing—part of the Rooftopper's crown jewels
Skyglass—Funderling name for a type of crystal
Snow—Briony's horse
Sun's Blood—an elixir prepared by the priest of Nushash
Vuttish longboat—a raiding boat used by Vuttish islanders in the north-
    ern ocean
Whitefire—the sword of Yasammez
Wildsong Night—a holiday evening, in the days after Winter's Eve
Wolf's Chair—throne of Southmarch Castle